Down All the Days

A Novel By

Christopher M. Basso

Christopher M. Basso

All rights reserved. No part of this publication may be reproduced, distributed, or transmitted in any form or by any means, including photocopying, recording, or other electronic or mechanical methods, without the prior written permission of the publisher, except in the case of brief quotations embodied in critical reviews and certain other noncommercial uses permitted by copyright law.

Copyright by

Christopher Basso 2011

GONZO BOOKS LTD.

Down All the Days

Christopher M. Basso

And with a gentle hand, lay it where childhood's dream are twined. In memory's mystic band, like pilgrim's withered wreath of flowers, plucked in a far-off land.
  -Lewis Carroll

Buy the ticket, take the ride.
-Hunter Thompson

Christopher M. Basso

Chapter One

The Parting Glass

Sleepy, heavy-eyed, Liam O'Shea stood before the large wrought iron windows with a placid expression, and gazed over the red and yellow patchwork shades of autumn in Central Park. He waited alone in the large corner office for the return of James Quinn, Esq., executor for the estate of the former Mr. William Henry O'Shea. Though it was late in the day, a warm light still filled the windows, casting delicate trellis patterns along the floor; on the wall, an old clock hummed a lulling cadence. The young man's eyes briefly scanned the room before settling on the photo of woman in a gilded frame. Her eyes were cold, a pale measure of a timeless contemplation. A quick thought crossed his mind, but just as soon it was gone.

Six weeks earlier, the former Mr. O'Shea was shown across when his newly purchased Ranger Rover "Sport" skidded off a wet road near his Westchester County pied-à-terre. His car was found down a steep ravine wedged up rather peaceably in the crook of an old stone wall. The Bedford police spent the following two days tracking down the next of kin. In the end there was Liam, his only child and last remaining family.

Now, mind you, Liam never had much use for the family brand. He and the old man had spoken only sparingly, perhaps a handful of times since childhood, and always with the stilted, halting expression of men who would rather be testing experimental parachutes than caught in the idle maw of familial chitchat. Theirs was a pact of mutually assured disengagement, fashioned through repetition and hardened with time. However, father and son recently, and at mortality's kind urging, managed a weekend of coolly measured civility; just long enough to bury their ex-wife and mother.

In the gathering twilight shades of a world crossing over, Tara O'Shea enjoyed a final skyward glance at the two men of her life, standing shoulder to shoulder over the lip of her grave. Her expression, veiled and sad, met their wayward flickering shapes, descending in a regrettable finality. She was buried in the shade of two chestnut oaks, at Grace Zion Cemetery in Rhinebeck, NY; aged forty-nine years.

No one had called William Henry O'Shea by his God-given name in the nearly twenty years since his own mother's death. Instead, a pair of bright blue eyes, a slightly hawkish nose, and an otherwise rakish, aboveboard countenance, earned him the handle of "Handsome Henry." Those near and dear would eventually shorten it to the simple "Hank," in a rather inelegant nod to fairly inelegant man.

Nicknames can be dangerous things however. Invariably, the owner feels some sense of obligation to live up to the imagined excess of an alter ego, and in this case the old man proved no exception. "Handsome Henry" loved a spectacle, or more precisely, he loved to be the center of the spectacle. For fifty-nine years he courted the high drama in this life, running the gauntlet from failed marriages and estranged relatives, right down to a gleeful relish in his own ham-fisted sense of timing. For the finale he managed to roll with the same thunder, crashing the high-end sports car just days before his son commenced with his final year of law school.... This was a *fine* shot across the bow of an aspirant little legal career, noteworthy for its hardscrabble pivot through state school, work-study character builders, right on up the big rock candy mountain of massive grad school debt, where a stylish Ivy League cachet could dovetail nicely with a life of equally stylish abject penury out in the wilds of hipster Brooklyn. Six years of this bilious rubbish were now on the cusp of the great reveal when the old boy came a-knocking.

The phone call found Liam in the wee small hours of a weekend morning, and three quick sentences from a stranger could sober you up like a bath of ice. He hung up the phone, lit up, and stared at the wall for a bit.... We're all on our way to Heaven, the Jesuit Brothers had told him as a boy, act accordingly. This was scant comfort with not much more than a bare wall and cold stillness for the guideposts.

After a lifeless stab at the back to school meet and greets, Liam retreated to the friendly confines of his Bushwick dungeon for the mind-numbing comforts of an increasingly barley-based lifestyle, and the last of some Hindu Kush he kept squirreled away for the really special occasions. In the pale light of early morning, he watched the last of the L train Harajuku wannabes drift past his windows. Just an endless stream of wholesome trust fund scions back from a very active brand of nothing in particular. He heard tangles of conversation here and there, as those with the least to say seem to say it loudest; a cluttered white noise based on an all too real reality.... Shit, man, at least Camus gave Meursault a gun. This was too much. He stretched out on the couch, his headphones mainlining a heady dose of "Houses of the Holy" right into the cerebral cortex—for regenerative purposes—as he drifted off into the never-never. All in all, a measured response to the lunacy of the day and the guarantee it would assail him no further.

The next afternoon he climbed aboard his Yamaha V Star and dodged the weekend traffic all the way up to his father's rambling spread in the country. As he rounded the last bend in the drive he was greeted with a far more elaborate affair than had been advertised. An imposing Queen Anne Revival, cast in the darkest of stone with steep pitched gables and slate covered turrets, sat overlooking a broad expanse of delicate pastureland. Liam's eyes trailed along the contours of the wild flower and meadow grass as they slowly resolved to a dark impenetrable forest at the edge of the borderline. He glanced back across the broad façade, broken by a line of French windows, glowing now with the soft light of the afternoon sun.... Had he the right address? As he waited for the baying of the hounds sent to greet the interloper he checked the address on his phone...this was in fact *the place*.

He parked the bike under the long porte-cochère and passed through the front door into a house he'd never known, and the traces of a life rarely shared. He tiptoed rather gingerly about the place at first, as the old floorboards creaked and strained under his step. With everything in its right place, Chez Henri evoked little more than a quiet sense of unease, as though its owner might yet return for the curtain call. Though no ghosts would appear, and only the creaks and groans of an old house deemed fit to greet him.... Oh well, spectral musings weren't much his speed anyway, and once that bit of sheepishness passed, he was able to walk about the place with a bit more *authority*.

He studied the rather large collection of framed pictures along the walls and tables, and resting above the mantles. A half-hearted curiosity drifted through his mind as he passed from room to room looking for something familiar, the something that would let him into this world. When he reached the study, young Liam finally found what he was looking for, as the home fires of the old man's healthy ego were still burning there to greet him.

He lingered in the doorway, surveying the scene.... The massive Georgian pedestal desk and the intricate Bokhara rugs were well within the limits of a casual poseurdom, but the bookcase, lined with rich leather-bound volumes from Herodotus to Chaucer, was probably pushing it. They looked about as pristine as the day the boys from the Easton Press stacked 'em there. Liam's eyes drifted about... what else? Various golfing trophies lined the end tables, and a fine bamboo fly-fishing rig sat in the corner. And lastly, not one, not two, but a trinity of nickel-plated shotguns rested on ivory mounts behind a few panes of heavy glass. This was ego scale of the first order; Versailles aspirations on Pottery Barn means, shape-shifting the disrepair of a Woolworth's past. Well, perhaps that was playing to the gallery a bit...perhaps even an "A" for effort was in order? A touch of the Freudian sublimation had always been the old boy's calling card—nothing like a big room for a little fella.

Little in a strictly pejorative sense of course—Henry was actually a bear of a man, 6' 3" at least, with broad shoulders and a level gaze that towered over all things in his world. Standing there, with his father's unbridled sense of self so prominently on display, generally would have annoyed the boy, but in the awkwardness of the moment it was the familiar and reassuring constant he needed. Besides, once he could laugh about it, the

Down All the Days

formidable old house felt less like a museum, but no more like a home. Liam saw all the makings for a nice bonfire stacked near one of the bookcases. Within minutes he had a fine blaze roaring away.

By the ornamental gun case in the corner sat a nicely stocked liquor cabinet. He found a few bottles of the old boy's highly prized twenty-year old Johnnie Walker Blue, and poured himself a drink. He sank back in the leather chair behind the desk, had a sip, and soaked in the inherent queerness of this setup. All that was missing were the stuffed marlin over the fireplace and some grainy photos of Handsome, bagging lions out in the Kalahari scrub brush. Yeah, leave it to Shoddy von Assclown not to play fair with the wildlife.... Whoa there, boyo, he caught himself in mid-harangue, take it down a notch—we've got a job to do.

He closed his eyes and concentrated. For just a moment Liam could imagine the old man's wandering spirit passing from room to room in his own private Elsinore, wandering, before pausing to observe this visitation with a just a measure of curiosity. The son rested his heavy boots on the desk and wondered whether this post game drive-by would have touched, or, rather, infuriated the old boy. Would it matter anyway what he thought? He was a ghost now, like all the other ghosts in the frames lining the walls and the mantels; all abstractions in that first light of reduction. *Bastard spooks,* they couldn't harm anyone now.

Liam finished his first drink and quickly poured another. After rummaging through a few drawers, stuffed with old issues of *Outlaw Biker* and something rather frightening called *Der Blonde Esel,* he found an open box of Cohíbas. Bingo. He lit up, tossed the cap into the fire, and rocked back in the plush chair. He could almost picture the glee in his father's eyes, sitting here, drinking swankish top-shelf spirits, and smoking contraband Cubanos. Papa Ernesto, sportsman and adventurer—the ultimate in genteel suburban revelry.

Liam settled in, putting his tumbler of Scotch through the paces. This was a fine test, working those half-formed shapes down from the weeping tree and breathing life into faded memories of grainy black and white. He soldiered on with this sad little séance, but in the end nothing appeared. The reductions of time, the resolution of certainty, and the final ruin of righteous belief had all conspired against him. The only revelations so easily grasped were that even expensive cheroots still tasted like mildewed death, and really good Scotch packs quite the blowback.

This was going *nowhere.* At best, he mourned the old man with a half-hearted efficacy which never rose above a remote sincerity, despite a fifth of Johnnie Walker's best intentions priming the well. Even then, that small glimmer of fondness was marred by a nagging intrusion of truth; truth that the old man was more like a stranger and only deserving a stranger's modicum of grief. A swirling mix of hazy memories and half-formed visions marked the limits and boundaries of his sadness and, with it, a weary understanding that this little visitation had all the foul shades of commencement rather than conclusion.... Or maybe it was delusion? Who knew? Such half-baked epiphanies were never welcome bedfellows.

He paused and marveled how it had all been so much clearer with his mother. There had never been a distance, only the perpetual love one receives with the calm surety of a warm sun. That was, 'til a cruel reality and a crueler fate would educate him otherwise. For Tara O'Shea's fortune was not as gentle as a rain-slicked road and a quick reckoning; rather, she was treated to an endless-nameless of raised hopes and small retreats, snake oil charms, and charlatan fix-it cures. All the guff greasing the skids for the great ride, the final capitulation, as one's world retreats to smaller and smaller corners, 'til all that's left are the measure of moments; the sleepy dreams which nature can no longer touch with decay.... No, for her the grief was honest, and lingered on like the pale twilight of a shadow passing from owner to owner.

...*Though I'll never know.* His mind danced in the calm stillness of the empty room. And there, Bonaparte's mantel, full of frozen moments glossed over, mocking merriment betraying time. *Why not indeed?* One image lingers though, his cheerful all-knowing face. Peer in a bit—catch a kind of questioning in the eyes. Is that how you imagined it would all play out? Unheralded and alone? In the cool shades of a summer night? Quick and blindly ushered through, or drawn out, like light and shadow vying across a chasm, slowly leveling out before they diminish and disappear.... And over the span of your own estimation, a wild, sad, and profound look in those eyes—having already gained a vision of things we cannot see, and a voice for words we dare not speak. Laugh it up, Handsome, like the old necromancer once said–it's all a gamble when it's just a game.

With the old man's Scotch kicked, and the room spinning gently around, Liam O'Shea let himself down from the flimsiest of penitent crosses. He tipped his glass, borrowed from a borrowed benediction, and made the final anemic toast for another taken Irishman. Too late now, he chuckled, in every sense. But a young man should take care, lest he too ends up in the stones and briars at the bottom of the hill. He ambled over for a quick crash on the soft couch beneath the bay windows. His new latitude provisioned a rather fine view of the Heavens. The sky was a blanket of white points, laced with flashes of yellow, green, and rose. The stars shined with such brilliance, his city eyes were genuinely taken aback. The gray-blue strands of the Milky Way snaked lazily across the sky, dreamy and indifferent to all false penitents and ginned up prophets. He sank back deep into the fine grain leather. Nice couch, most comfortable, his eyes glazed over... lovely Pottery Barn indeed. The world cued to black, the rest was silence.

Well, the world wasn't going to stand still and wait for the boy to find the right melodies of grief when, after all, the busy work of death *is* the ironic coda of so long life. As such, there were things to be done—calls to be made, catering to be arranged, and a first class planting to plan. And though the boy rolled a wee bit light in the empathy department, he could at least appreciate the realities of the situation. He reigned in an increasingly ephemeral sense of obligation, and marshaled some of that proper mourning gusto which did the Irish proud. Hell, he even thought to wear a black armband for the services—seemed about right for propriety's sake.

True, Handsome Henry hadn't much left in the way of family, but he was rich with friends. They came in force, like a herd of dyspeptic wildebeest and packed the rafters of tiny St. Ann's Church in Albany. Every last seat in the congregation was filled, leaving some of the tardier pilgrims, mostly shady non-church-going sorts, to mill about the vestibule in the back. A sea of faces Liam had never known turned out to mourn the old man with the kindest and most reverent of venerations. He sat in the first pew, armband in place and dumbstruck on the balance, watching this procession of rubes sing their hosannas. A slight grin spread across his sun-starved face at the thought of tipping back the casket for a quick confirmation he'd made the right church.... But this grim bunch didn't much look like the black humor sort of crowd; they might have considered such a thing, well... bad form.

Finally, the aged priest slowly climbed the pulpit for the last benediction, the one benediction that matters. All right then padre, hit us with the good stuff—the homily for the anomaly....Instead the old priest's kind eyes shone with a genuine sincerity as he recalled fond memories of when young William was first brought around to be an altar boy in his church....Creeping Jesus, these people were starting to give Liam *The Fear*.

This rolling cavalcade of misfits and halfwits must have been cashing in on some cosmic chits, or perhaps seeking a little of that radial atonement for closets full of spectral peccadilloes and ever so casual perversions. Fortunately for them, the last whinging nerve of restraint for sullying the family name still ran strong. Young O'Shea thought enough to honor these misguided strangers with a kind show of appreciation. He managed to muster some sadness at the church, a note of kindness at the wake, and a quiet reverence beside the grave. The procession of sheep followed the casket of their shepherd over to Ringsend Road Cemetery, by the banks of the Hudson River. The big fella was laid to rest on a Sunday morning near Troy, NY, guarded in reliable perpetuity between the stark weatherworn graves of his mother and father; aged fifty-nine years.

Chapter Two
Tomorrow Never Knows

  Liam remained at the sunlit windows still waiting for his host; gazing out, holding onto the calm view below. In the six weeks since the funeral he'd managed to dodge this get together, but Quinn's persistence, and a strange twilight curiosity for the father he hardly knew, slowly brought him around. He tapped his fingers along the base of the windowpane…. *He was nice to animals, never lifted a finger to any of us, good taste in cars…better taste in Scotch.* O'Shea broke out a smile, only slightly aware of the spiritless attempt to eulogize a hollow man to an empty room. While this sad state of affairs rattled around his mind, Quinn slipped back into the office and closed the door.

  He took quick stock of the young man staring out the windows. He bore a striking resemblance to his father, though not quite as tall, with the same roughhewn, Black Irish good looks. This was going to be strange, to say the least, nothing like closing a day with the walking echo of a voice you'll never hear again. He cleared his throat and casually motioned the boy towards one of the chairs facing his desk.

  James Quinn, Esq., was something of a study in contradictions. A tall man with broad shoulders and a boxer's chin, who walked with the easy, confident gate of a fellow who might have been comfortable cracking heads down along the waterfront once upon an incarnation. But the dark crisp cut of his Brioni bespoke best, the sharp yellow tie, and the mane of well-coiffed salt and pepper hair were enjoying this lawyerly incarnation far too much to dwell on such crass possibilities. His looks conjured a sense of studied ease, but there was something ever so slightly off in the mix. Like perhaps a fine Porterhouse was waiting down Smith & Wollensky way, if only he could get through the unsavory facilitation of this ungrateful daddy's boy.... Maybe a few glasses of a nice Pétrus Bordeaux to mellow things out, perhaps a bit of the give and go with his waitress? Hell, who knew, maybe even a Bourbon-fueled grab or two, should the mood move him—his heart like a Rhino, the Cialis running strong.... O'Shea caught himself in the arc of another fanciful bit of mind drift. Perhaps he'd been just a *tad* harsh at that.

But Liam did consider the cut of this man, and didn't like the vibe one bit. Indeed, he seemed to have found one of those professional Burgher-asshole types he'd heretofore managed to avoid; the type of Hun who made the law profession only slightly less estimable than, say, Las Vegas brothel matron or Calcutta organ merchant.... *Good Lord*, he shook his head sadly as the shyster prattled on, that old ivy-ivory tower had left him a bit on the virginal side of things.

Perhaps the oddball shyster act was just Quinn's way of maintaining the *clarity* of the situation. High end legal stylists often fancy the pomp and trappings of a regal solemnity not seen this side of brain surgeons and priests. All things are serious to these cats. But nonetheless, Quinn's little Kinderspiel sat diametrically opposed to Liam's easygoing affability. This was Liam's lawyerly Achilles heel if ever, but before the law there was life, and an only child who learned the value of working a room. It was a lonely boy's talent for forging instant, if only transitory, connections.

...Which on some level was fairly sociopathic, but then again we each play the hand we're dealt. Besides, when not bad mouthing the recently deceased, or his judo-legalese Doberman, he was widely considered an affable and charming young man. Throwback manners, they might have called them.... Like some proper southern gentleman who'd never actually lived in the South.

But for now, that affability was failing him. He was feeling the weight of this room and the ghoulish parade of long dead feelings and memories swirling about his mind. He needed to break the ice with this man, this stranger, who seemed to be lording something out there in the distance. But where to start?

Quinn's desk seemed perhaps the proper inroad. It was an impressive antique looking thing of heavy rosewood, broad and deep, with crisp lines and a shine that must have required some regular tender loving care. Maritime-themed reliefs were carved along the forward face, whalers and merchant ships, long forgotten commerce and trade. It was decidedly *not* one of those things you found in the Pottery Barn catalog.

No, this was a trophy of some note, the kind of thing an elegant eye comes across in the salvage shops of Portsmouth or Salem, or some such Goddamn place. It was a symbol meant to convey the station of its owner; a sea captain's desk, where atavistic puritanical types signed the deeds sending mad men off to slay the white whales of this world. Liam imagined, rather disdainfully, that the likes of James Quinn got off epically rambling about the things they lorded over.

But Quinn met any compliments and inquires with just the slightest of interest. Indeed this old desk had a story, but not today. Liam wasn't the only one rather dreading this get together. Henry O'Shea was a close friend and a good client. Shutting this door was not something he did fondly, particularly with this boy, who might have shared the looks but seemingly none of the temperament or grit of the departed.

Rather, Quinn mumbled something vaguely gracious about his fine desk and went back to his papers. This cold office and the chilly demeanor of its owner were the legal versions of a home court advantage. Besides, his bit in this Sisyphean gig was pushing the paper, not divining the meaning of life for his clients or, in this case, finding closure for wayward prodigal sons.

Liam retreated back across said desk, his dislike for this man increasing with each passing moment.... But at least the bastard was upfront with his bastardness, which just about conferred something of an enlightenment in this trade. However, failed small talk and daydream projections aside, it was time to get his game face on. After a few more minutes of lawyerly jabberwocky, the trailer before the legal feature, it was time to lay bare the bones of Handsome Henry's last goodbye. Quinn leaned forward resting an elbow on the polished shine of the desk and began. In a slow clear voice he made his way down the page, rattling off each provision of the will.

...O'Shea the elder, had been generous with his boy—well, sod it, when you've taken on the task of shaking an entire absolute, resolute, and destitute world to its plates, then a word like *generous* was the only polite place to start. And should generous be far too cheeky a metric for the occasion, swap out the euphemistic for the proper-literal and call it *damn near everything*. The scarcely prodigal son had struck the mother lode of misbegotten generosity. Damn near everything included: titles to two homes—the estate in Bedford and a summer place up in Maine; a fractional share of a golfing retreat in Bermuda; a broad portfolio of stocks and bonds—Microsoft, Boeing, Oracle, managed ever so diligently by the last man standing over at Citigroup; one undamaged Mercedes Coupe; a vintage 1937 Brough Superior—*truly* a collector's bike; and not to mention all the incidentals—good Scotch, contraband smokes, nickel-plated shotguns, and bougie mail order furniture. Then came the final wisdom—Liam James O'Shea was sole beneficiary of one *very* large life insurance policy.

Quinn, in his kindly way, had gone ahead and converted the old man's time on Earth to the estimated whole dollar amount. Uncle Sam would take his tribute, and Handsome left something sizeable to charity—maybe hoping a tithe could buy him out of a reckoning. But even then, the boy was left sitting on an amount which could only be described as unexpectedly prodigious.

Given life's variable uncertainty, it had always been something of a comfort to fall back on the old man's reliable unreliability. It was the fixed star you could steer your ship by and, over the years, it became the unwavering constant in the equation of life. So now, it was with no small sense of dash that the vagabond playboy could laugh from beyond the grave, at the dawning reclamation of his soul spreading across the ashen face of his hardworking son.

In the span of a few moments all the concrete surety measuring a father's lifelong apathy was toppled and, in its place, succeeded by a rising sense of dread; a dread which Liam lacked both the age and wisdom to conceal. The words were just a bit hard to find. Rather, he rolled one of Quinn's silver pens through his fingers and impassively shifted his glance out the windows. Quinn reached the end of the page and replaced it alongside the others. He leaned back in his chair, gathering himself a moment before speaking.

"Well... that's it." he let it hang there for a moment. "I think it's fairly straightforward. He left his second and third wives out of the settlement entirely. Now there is a possibility his third wife might contest some of this—they *were* married for seven years, but I wouldn't worry about that for now." There was a knowing grin across his face. "Here, I need you to sign and initial these."

Liam reached across the desk and signed the last three pages before falling back in his chair. His mind had gone around the sun and back in the last two minutes. Quite a thing to find your entire fatalist certainty thrown under the ol' metaphysical bus—replaced with the stark, sucker-punched reality that everything you'd known was wrong. The mixings for a fine headache had aligned and he suddenly very much wanted out....But that would have been for softer sorts, and he'd rather wear a cocktail dress singing the Cole Porter songbook than be one of those chirpy lads who goes all wobbly when they couldn't hit life's hanging curves. He took a few deep breaths, found his happy place, and summoned the best fuck you aplomb he could muster from the psychic cupboard.

"*Jesus*... you're going to have to excuse me." The words came soft as he slowly rubbed his eyes. "This is, needless to say... *unexpected*. I'd heard rumors my father was doing well the last couple of years, *but this?*"

Quinn looked at Liam. Liam looked at Quinn. From across that desk, the shyster's eyes were a perfectly paired union of dead and still.... O'Shea didn't seem to be *reaching* this man. He continued with a bit more force.

"I mean... he dies and a week later I get a call from you to come on in and discuss the disposition of his estate—his *estate*?" He let out a cackle. "C'mon now—William Henry O'Shea having *an estate?* That's a little of the pearls before the swine, don't you think?"

But the still eyes only glimmered back, an appraiser's wheels still kicking the tires on his half-formed appraisal. Liam shifted in his chair before continuing, a slight recalibration might be necessary.

"Look, Mr. Quinn—"

"No, Liam, you can call me Jim."

"Ok, *Jim,*" he smiled weakly, not quite thinking before he spoke, "listen, here's the thing…I've never been a part of something *like this*." He shifted ever so slightly in his chair, "I mean, calls from out the ether from the people I've never met, to discuss the father I hardly knew, regarding the estate that now bears my name?" He shook his head in a gesture of the most contrite bewilderment, "To be honest, I was thinking you were something more along the lines of process server or disgruntled loan shark; luring me down here to work me over for the sins of the father.... I mean, jilted creditors and ancestral gambling debts were really more the old boy's speed." Liam shifted again, his eyes meeting Quinn's in the breach, "So you'll have to excuse me, because none of this makes any sense; that house up in Westchester; the garage full of cars, the Fifth Avenue lawyer….My father was a *contractor*," he let the accusation hang there for a moment, "a bit of a salesman I suppose, but with all due respect, kind of a bum."

The boy could feel the coils unwinding a bit, the words more or less finding themselves. His newfound lawyer however didn't seem to share in this karmic détente. O'Shea could sense he *still* wasn't reaching this man. It was time to muster his best Dickensian orphan bravado from the time fog.

"Tell you what—I haven't many memories of the old Bard of Bedford—*but here's one*. When I was a kid, maybe seven or eight, Chase Manhattan sent their collection arm out to pay us a visit late one night. Now mind you this was back when banks could still talk about things like personal accountability with a straight face; and they didn't quite see the freak flag humor in my old man skipping out on his obligations as some sort of well honed egalitarian statement…. So the decision was made that repossessing my mother's car would be the finest way to render unto Caesar. And so it goes, his agents show up late one night to collect, but they're just a bit clumsy in their trade and soon manage to wake the half the world that wasn't already sleeping."

"Now here's where the *fun* starts. In short order the old man is beating down the front door with my Louisville "junior slugger" in one hand and a hot fireplace poker in the other, screaming 'call the police! Some bastards just stole my car!' At this point old Henry launches the poker like some cranked up whiskey tango Olympian, misses the mark completely, and nearly kills my poor dog Buddy in the process…. Well by now we, and by that I mean the royal *neighborhood* we, are all out on the sidewalk in our unmentionables watching the lights of my mother's Sebring growing smaller and smaller down the road, as the *pater familias* stands there, inglorious in his predawn best, railing on the rotten sons of bitches who did him in."

He nodded his head at the thought of good times gone to dust.

"Yeah, that was more your typical repartee out at the ol' O'Shea homestead. Needless to say marital fallout was *severe*.…Five months later and he was gone. The memories become a little sporadic after that."

Liam pointed a finger across the polished desk.

"*That's* the man I knew. So when you lay this trip on me—houses, stocks, antique motorcycles and fucking… *negotiable bearer bonds,* it's not adding up. I mean, we're talking about the same O'Shea—right? Not Horatio O'Shea or Commodore O'Shea perhaps?"

He'd gone to the well again, fishing for a little of that shared humanity, but Quinn wasn't about to bite. He held fast a gaze that never wavered. No matter, he probably couldn't quite grasp the *chi sting* of piling on mountains of debt while your father dabbled in bearer bonds when he wasn't hacking out the Bermudian bluegrass at the Mid Ocean Club.

"Well, I realize this must be shocking, what with this great gift your father left you, and I'm sorry to have thrown everything at you at once…but you're a hard man to reach—I wasn't sure when or if I'd ever get you down here."

There were enough bells and whistles behind those words to get the boy on edge. He held his tongue and let this breathing machine for legal malfeasance continue.

"Listen, I know it'd been a while for you two, but things started to change in his life. Your father worked hard, had a successful business he started from the ground up, and made some wise decisions with the things he had. Give it enough time and you can see the results."

Quinn weaved this little spiel with the smug, telling air of a low key indictment. As though a son should know, damn well, the particulars of his father's life for the better part of the past decade. Who knows, maybe Quinn had his own wayward progeny meandering down the road to filial perdition, or maybe it was something else. The slight contempt in his voice had Liam reeling a bit, wondering how well Quinn and the old man had known each other. Was this reading of the will merely a formality, another box in the day planner, or was this the chance for a cold man with a grudge to air some grievances and lay the seeds of guilt? Either way, it must have annoyed him having to be the facilitator for all this. Maybe those still eyes needed to pass some judgment along with the blessings of The Golden Ticket. Though, like any good lawyer, Quinn dropped his innuendo, his own *J'accuse*, and retreated across the polished shine of his desk saying nothing more.

O'Shea felt a renewed unease for this whole mess. He sat up in his chair; his affability quickly sinking into an agitated preparation. The light was fading from the windows, slowly retreating along the floor, bleeding into smaller and smaller shadows. A cold grayness followed hard on its heels. With the need for such niceties gone, O'Shea dug in and switched tacks.

"Okay, Jim, where did all this good fortune come from—*illuminate me*."

What followed was a brief history of the rise of *Handsome Henry, Inc.*, an inspirational tale of how an occasionally pickled hustler type had fallen ass backwards into a fortune. The opening gambit came ten years ago with a lucrative divorce settlement from well-to-do wife number two. Poor woman, she came in with good intentions and a bit of cash, and she left a bit poorer on both counts. In the past the big fella probably would have shot that wad right back into the gaming and service sectors, and the bosses down in Atlantic City, or at The Belmont, would've seen a nice spike for a month or two.

But the old man took his seed money and threw it into something he vaguely understood: sales. Selling *himself* that is, his father was anything if not persuasive. That sly boots could sell a Torah to a jihadist and a Speedo to an Inuit. Henry put his charm and money into the construction business, specializing in the kind of municipal projects that get bid out for state and federal contracts. Plenty of purveyors of the public good lined up at the trough and Henry was there to work every one of them. Hell, he even put his vices to work, weekends with the movers and shakers at Mohegan Sun, Saturdays in August out at the stately track in Saratoga with the politicos from the New York State machine. He probably knew more than a few of them from the Albany of his youth. No matter, Handsome Henry could charm them to the last.

But Liam had never shaken the image of his old man as a wayfaring playboy. It was forever frozen in his mind; a hard estimation that made no allowance for change. But something had obviously changed. Maybe time finally caught up with him? Maybe, just maybe, twenty years of a mid-life crisis had been enough.

Either way, he must have felt a bit of that bright light shining down the other end of the tunnel. And while the old lout never got around to finding Jesus, he netted a pretty good stockbroker along the way. With his guidance, Handsome Henry flourished in that pre-crash bull market where a gambler's nerves, or even a drunk's, could pave the road in gold. Well, one frightful morning the sun rose in the west and a snowball sailed through the halls of Hell, as William Henry O'Shea found one of those lucky moments where paper tigers find their paper fortunes....Bastard hitched his wagon to a little star called Google. Liam's stomach churned a bit at the image of the old man gloating like some hellish Lilliputian Gordon Gecko, grinning away, suitably impressed with his shrewd dealings and virile, bare-chested financial acumen.

Fitzgerald said there were no second acts in American

lives, but Handsome Henry was chomping at the bit to get on with his third, fourth, and fifth; as this windfall was not enough to ease the nervous tremor of idle hands. After squaring away his love for the finer things, he jumped head first into a world of painless philanthropy.

With Quinn's help he set up the Colleen Margaret O'Shea Memorial Foundation. Ah, even Liam's grandmother might have been proud of this one, her black sheep finally making good. The Quinn-O'Shea brain trust hatched a variety of tax-friendly charity schemes, perhaps none more successful than "The O'Shea Overachievers." Poor little urchins with some smarts and the good grades to match; city kids mostly from Boston and New York getting to spend their summers rusticating on the shores of Lake Winnipesaukee at the camp his father built. For some of the luckier ones there were even scholarships waiting—full rides to the redemption of their choice. Quinn mentioned that the little overachievers were to be funded out of a trust for the next ten years... Liam saw no problem with that. Hell, he even encouraged Quinn to throw a little extra loot their way. Not everyone should have to wear their flare, busing tables at Chotchkie's and jockeying the Kinko's overnight to get an education—unlike the original O'Shea overachiever. Besides, he chuckled, sour grapes weren't worth the picking.

Liam took a deep breath. He had to hand it to his father on some level. After all those years wandering out in the desert he had, at last, arrived. He found the elusive confluence of the fates that stab right to the heart of our American dream. Even those blue blood bastards down at the Union Club would have him now—he had finally gained a certain measure of *respect*.

At that point Henry was nearing sixty, and it'd been a hard sixty. A dissipated lifestyle and three failed marriages must have finally roused the firm stirrings of mortality. He became thoroughly obsessed with his legacy, and the notion of leaving something which endured beyond his own failings. Estranged from his family, he could at best imagine a memory elevated by the admiration of strangers. He hoped the reputation of a respected, civic-minded businessman would be enough to secure such a thing. In the last years of his life he poured all his energy into these projects, possessed like a man who thought his efforts might still snatch a kind of immortality from the gathering blackness. But never, in his wildest dreams did he think an automobile would do him in.... Sinking battleship, charging lion, *maybe*, but not the neighbor's orange tomcat standing out in the road.... Shit, at least the cat made it home.

Sans feline, Quinn recounted this fairytale with something bordering on adulation. He rocked back in his chair with his best 'gather round the campfire' face, and piled on the hyperbole like these were open callbacks and Oprah would be doling out the free cars. Here we have a fallen man, beaten down by life, forsaken by most who knew him. He finds the strength to take control of his destiny and makes a fortune in a uniquely American way. But then, he is struck down in the prime of his life, at the apex of his moment, by that cruel hand of fate.

Liam smiled as he listened—the shyster was *on a roll*. Must have been a trial lawyer back in his stud days. *Amazing*. Henry's arc had steered from the thinnest of penny dreadfuls, to something out of Aeschylus or Euripides; like a modern day P. T. Barnum, Mark Twain, and Horatio Alger all rolled into one. Too bad Liam knew the principal, otherwise he might have been touched by this inspirational tale. Quinn ended his story with something of a maudlin nostalgia in his voice.

"It's a hell of a shame when a good man is taken before his time."

...Well, hells bells. A big hand was in order for the Poet Laureate of the Upper East Side. This certainly sealed the deal on the burning question of whether Handsome Henry was cozy with his lawyer. But now it was Liam's turn to lean back in his chair and play around with the same story. *Interesting legacy*. A house built on the ironies of favorable divorce laws, lucky half-assed timing, and the smoke and mirror charm of a man better suited to chasing impressionable doe-eyed skirts than grasping the nuances of hard work and high finance. This was a bad funeral flashback. Here was another coquettish little Sally in Handsome's own Memphis Mafia, singing the praises of a man who so casually abandoned his wife and child twenty years ago. Yep, just like it was for so many scoundrels, all rose petals falling right past the thorns—at least 'til history gets a hold of them.

Well, maybe time *was* the ultimate expiation for sin, and no matter how many sins you've committed you are bound to receive an absolution from time. If no one else, time had forgiven his father, and *that* might just have been enough. The brass works on the clock had frozen on his early, wayward ways, and he was able to carve a new life free from those echoes of his past. Quinn was just a small piece of that new life. The church up in Albany was filled with other such "pieces" collected by his father on that long march home.

However, such roads were not without peril. A tactical deceit—that's what this was. Not much more than an elevated piece of bribery.... A *very* elevated piece, but bribery all the same. As he watched Quinn shuffling through the papers he could feel a dull, gathering anger in the back of his mind. Quinn was the salesman of that legacy, a low-rent Atticus Finch offering up his father for high-end canonization. He felt a growing need to get up and smack this fool, smack him right across the chops, smack him across the fine burnish of his antique desk until he received the bright warmth of divination. He imagined Quinn would understand; no hard feelings, just a quick slash in the yarbles ought to get this sinner back into the light.... But Quinn sideswiped any pulse for a rather gleeful retribution.

A few strokes of a pen and it was done. The who, the where, and the how much now all official, and with it a fairly confusing resolution to things. He'd take his money—what else could he do? What else would he want to do? Rather, he would accept the vagaries of Handsome Henry for the *fait accompli* they'd always been, but for once, in spectacular neutron bomb fashion, the karmic ledger seemed to have landed in the black.

What was the etiquette then? Fall on the floor like some babbling wingnut, all false contrition and giddy abandon? Perhaps play that Camus card after all—father died today, or maybe it was yesterday.... No, the good money said find the thin sincerity on both ends of your foul genetic impulse and run with it. Well, either way it was nice to be back in the warm embrace of the familial fold. All in all, another fine airing of the O'Shea dirty laundry—at least some things hadn't changed. All Liam could do was accept his fortune with a puzzled face that revealed the incredulity of a man struck by lightning in the rainless desert, and the knowledge that his benefactor was gone before he could even acknowledge the gift; though Quinn remained. He lingered on like the after clap of thunder, waiting to hear the echoes.

Quinn gathered up the paperwork, placed it in the folders, and for the first time that afternoon actually seemed to mellow a bit—he even smiled. It was a weird grin, Cheshire-like, bright and full of teeth. He extended a mitt for one of those steroid-fueled power grasps, as they made their way towards the door. The room was in the half light, and the dark shades had finally arrived. But Quinn still had the look of a man waiting to have his ring kissed or, at the very least, *shined* a bit.

It was he, after all, who tracked down the runaway son with all due diligence and led him ass backwards, kicking and screaming, into a small fortune.... Well, there'd be none of that action. An honest sincerity was wasted on a calculating intention, and a calculating intention wouldn't quite know what to do with an honest sincerity. Basically these boys cancelled each other out. All that was left was a spot in the funny papers. James Quinn, life counselor, raconteur, and cubist legal scholar, would have to settle for that.

O'Shea took a few breaths and thought about the smoke waiting for him down on the sidewalk. His anger began to fade, like a stone splashing in the water, rippling in ever descending waves of energy, fading out as they fade away. Instead, frustration gave way to a sudden weary desire to fuck with this charmless fellow a bit.

"So, you knew my father well?"

"We went back a ways, about ten or twelve years. Yeah, old Hank was a hell of a guy." Quinn paused a second, letting his face gather a twill sort of silly look. "You know, he was pretty proud of you."

Uh-oh, what rough beast was this? O'Shea felt the second coming of a guilt trip.

"Really? Guess you had to know him to know.... Know what I mean?"

"Well, he was. Damn, I can remember when you got into Columbia, the smile you brought to that man's face.... 'My son, the lawyer. First one in this family who isn't going to make a living with his hands,' he said."

The boy could only nod and smile.

"He had high hopes for you. He always thought you were going to make everyone proud. We used to talk about it sometimes." They paused for a second in the half light of the foyer. "Ah, well it's a shame you two weren't closer."

Liam didn't care to think he was the topic of *any* conversation between his father and the charmless fellow.

"Well you know how things can go." The boy paused, lining up the crosshairs. "*Ten years*, huh? You know I can't remember, that day was such a fog, but did I forget to say hello to you at the funeral?"

"No, unfortunately, I wasn't able to make it."

"That's a shame. You missed a good one. We had a hell of send off—old world, grill to the hill blarney craic, and all that bullshit he loved."

"I'm sure he would have liked it."

They walked through the narrow darkened lobby towards the elevators. Quinn looked worn, but not quite beaten.

"So, any thoughts on what type of law you're going to focus on?" The words barely hanging as a question before he continued, "You should think about this—estate planning. Not too sexy I'll grant you that, but a good living to be made here, an *easy* living."

"...Well, I was thinking I might like a job in government."

He laughed, "Sweet Jesus, where—the DA's office? Manhattan? A *graveyard* for a promising young legal career, nothing but a bunch of misanthropes and recovering idealists burnt to their bitter ends." He smiled, "That is, unless of course, you're an *idealist?*"

Quinn enunciated idealist as if it were the hard-charging business end of a medical probe out to violate every one of his sacred orifices. All Liam could do was smile and let another of these odd comments drift. While the young man didn't like the insinuation towards naiveté, he didn't necessarily take offense with the idealist dig. He wasn't quite sure where he fell on that scale anyway. Idealists were usually rich men's sons, not hardworking types who were seventy thousand in the hole for their idealist educations.

They reached the outer doors of the office, their time together drawing to a close. Young O'Shea had nothing to lose.

"Yeah," Liam laughed, "you got me there—but they do tend to drill that ethics, good governance noise into your head pretty good. Guess they want to at least give the impression of nobility in purpose before unleashing the werewolf within."

"A nice plausible deniability, the hallmark of our profession I'm afraid."

"Maybe I should *rethink* this thing," O'Shea said. "Get myself into one of those twelve step recovery networks or something?"

Quinn's smile turned sour, obviously another smartass straight off the farm.

"No, young man. I'm just saying *we all* start out as crusaders, but... it's a road that meanders more than it leads. It's my job to warn you about these things. Those were your father's wishes."

"His wishes?"

"Yes, I think he wanted our relationship, this family relationship that is, to endure. You've a large responsibility to manage. I think he envisioned my acting as a kind of... advisor to you, sort of a mentor."

"Really? And what about all the idealism talk? Are we billing for that, or is it free of charge?"

Quinn didn't miss a beat, "Nothing's free of charge, that's the problem with idealism."

For the slimmest of seconds, Liam sort of liked the old boy.

"So what you're saying is it's better to stay removed from

the particulars. I'll be one of those happy sorts if I just keep the minutiae moving and don't get too wrapped up in the details?"

"...Yeah, I suppose so—keep it easy." He paused like the wise sage of jurisprudence. "The law is simple if you stay back a bit and keep yourself removed. You're just there to move the paper. Remember that, young man. Move the paper and then leave it at the door."

The elevator doors opened. Liam lingered in the entrance.

"Is that what you do?"

"Always."

"Never take things personally?"

"Nothing's personal."

"Good. Then go ahead and consider the O'Shea account closed. Dot your I's, cross your T's, and send me a bill for all this." He waved a dismissive hand back towards the office. "I'll call you next week, and, uh, I'm going to need a record of everything, plus I want confirmation when the money posts to my accounts."

He paused and turned.

"By the way—thanks for helping out with things."

Before he could open his mouth Liam reached over and gave Quinn a firm handshake, looked him in the eye, and flashed the best smile he could muster; bright and frightening, 'til all that remained was the grin. Idealists, it would seem, are big on the final word.

Chapter Three
The Rolling People

Liam O'Shea sipped a Bloody Mary 37,000 feet over the Atlantic Ocean. He straightened up, arching his back a bit, as a slight ache ran through his mind; an ache which melted towards a beautifully realized tension cascading down the length of his spine. He glanced at the small video screen tucked into the seat in front of him. A map with all the colors of North Atlantic, greens, whites, and azure blues spread out before him—and there in the middle, trapped in the great nothingness between Iceland and Western Europe, sat the flashing red image of an airplane. With fixed eyes he watched and waited, and waited and watched, pausing here and there before settling again on the small icon....Yes, he was quite sure it was mocking him; refusing to inch either way, frozen in a kind of cruel perpetuity. He'd been at this vicious game for some time now; sleepless, bored off his ass, as strange visions of thrombo-pulmonary embolisms danced through his head.

He rubbed his eyes, red-rimmed and glassy. Too much bad air, stale air, passing through the lungs of three hundred of your newest friends; foul and pestilent—an old boggish petri dish of humanity confined down the narrow aisles of a midnight run. Mindful of this, the boy would make the effort to blink every now and then, but his mind was drifting in other places. An otherworldly sense of space and time had kicked in. His sense of gravity, the ability to focus, all long since compromised by the pitch and roll of the plane, and the last six hours of fermented entropy he'd thrown his weight behind with mucho gusto.

It began innocently enough with a couple of gin martinis back in the departures lounge at Kennedy. Nifty little bastards, overpriced to be sure, but poured with a strong hand. They did the job nicely, ratcheting down the karmic angst a peg or two. Check-in had, after all, been a bit of a bitch—lots of rumbling, shouting, and bad vibes all around. These were some serious omens at the outset of such an adventure, so he repaired to the Gold Circle Club where he drank heavily, thought heavily, and tipped heavily—thank you kindly, Handsome. A short wobble down the jetway and he was soon deposited in his plush seat where, before he could announce he was on the job, another greetings and salutations glass of fermented something or other was in his hand courtesy of a pretty, ginger-haired girl. Feeling ever so fortified, he sank back in the roomy seat, on his game, and geared up for the twilight liftoff. A gulp of water and a fistful of Xanax were the perfect finé as the engines revved heavy and Jamaica Bay zipped by the windows at *unmentionable* speeds.

Ker-chunk—wheels up.... Ah, sweet Xanax. A fine drug, gentle and forgiving, surprisingly subtle on the uptake, but, like all good benzos, not meant to be chased with The Drink—a caveat he'd just as soon gloss over. For his part, the collective *They* should've thought a bit harder on the merits of some sort of alcohol-friendly sedative—because more likely than not you're just taking one to jump start the other, so why put all these walls in the way? He sighed, probably just another cruel snapshot of the age, of the towering morality-based rage that rears its ugly head wherever a little illicit "fun" might be had—and this sort of impromptu chemistry experiment would just about fit the bill.

The whirl and purr of multiple buzzes and synaptic rushes would be too much of an effrontery to the good old fashioned puritanical miasma holding sway.... But come on then—this wasn't some avionic *Drugstore Cowboy* redux, this wasn't lining up with the forces of excess, or some bacchanal of illicit delights. This was merely the mild respite for the casual user, who mixes his relaxants out of necessity, rather than any sort of sick pleasures to be gained from such things.

Philosophical musings aside, he'd most likely pay for tonight's little experimentations. At some point, that giddy armor-plated feeling would fade and gradually shift gears to something along the lines of a sleepy paranoia...but, oh well, sometimes you eat the bar and sometimes the bar eats you. Yes indeed, straight from the mouth of either some wise fellow in the know, or some deranged Bukowski acolyte in the throes of a terminal psychosis. Such was life in the annals of the quick and the dead.

The ginger-haired lovely was, somewhere along the line, relieved by an older, rather stern looking... dame. Liam studied her for a moment, a bit more wisdom and command in those eyes. Eyes with a kind of fierce steadfastness which precluded any funny business and with *just* the right malevolent twinkle that spoke of heavier things, like a jolt of mace if you got on the wrong side of right.

Dear Lord—were these women actually *armed*? No matter, he was probably safe here. She was, after all, handling the front of the plane, and the diplomatic straddling act of modern day Business Class. Just seven rows of good clean folks expecting something more than a free Coke with their pretzels, yet still trapped on the wrong side of the wizard's curtain. Most would keep on their best behavior—hoping, always hoping, to push to the front of the beast; just one more finger-wrangled upgrade or socioeconomic hurdle to get through, 'til all that's left was the sweet-ass sheen of the cockpit door.

Proletariat grumblings from 13A aside, he'd be lying if he didn't admit it was interesting being on this side of things for the first time. He'd spent his whole life back in the cattle pen, wondering what sort of Caligula-themed horrors were playing out beyond those curtains. Thunderdome power-hours, candy apple red ball gags, Frank Booth nitrous whippets? Who knew, perhaps even some communal gimp stowed in the forward galley behind a pane of glass which read, "Break in case of a terminal atavistic tendency". For a gentle pilgrim, the terrifying possibilities abounded.

Yes, on the balance it was probably far safer in the places he'd grown accustomed to, and even if it had a bit of the correctional facility vibe, at least he knew *where it was at* in Coach. But, oh, what these eyes might glimpse when freed at last from the shackles of convention. What secrets were betrayed once you were through the looking glass?

Christopher M. Basso

A quick glance around proved nothing short of a letdown; an empty finale to one of those tedious Russian nesting dolls. The final box revealed little more than a hefty swath of pleated pants and stern patrician glares…. This sad bunch looked like a Brooks Brothers had just exploded all over the back nine at Wingfoot—the elastic khaki acid test as far as the eye could see; Titleist paunches, rictus Boxtox grins, and a vague Kipling-Kurtz D-bag air of corrupt entitlement.... But that might just have been the nicotine withdrawal talking. Otherwise, this was just your standard "Boomer" crowd, out and about, riding the snake on a never-ending sensory jag.

Damn, they might have sailed a freak flag or two back in the day, but nothing doing tonight. Perhaps they'd learned it was a far far better thing to keep one's private gimps and personal peccadilloes safely under lock and key, away from prying eyes. Well, not young Liam, who wore the angst in his eyes like the drink on his shirt. Shit, why even try the hard man act at this point? After all, capitulation had always been the better part of valor—almost comforting in its reliability. Ah, he smiled, the small mercies indeed.

Continuing with his own variations on a theme—two small bottles of a very serviceable pinot noir accompanied a nice selection of artisan cheeses, followed by the Tournedos Rossini in Madeira sauce, of course. All served on clean linens, porcelain, and bone china. This was some otherworldly thing. He tucked into his meal like a man thoroughly committed to the idea and, provincial as he might have felt, he kept such things to himself. Flatware, silverware, hardware…free hooch—he could get used to this. He polished off his meal and downed the last of the wine, before settling back a bit and letting things mellow to a warm, fuzzy, mahogany haze.

Well enough, O'Shea was feeling more like a wine man these days anyway…well, he was drinking more of it at any rate. He'd made the choice to ditch those beer-swilling halcyon days of youth and gracefully accept whatever age might have in store. Felt like the right thing to do—too many vicious late night memories and foxhole mornings at the hands of beer. Get yourself a new drink and discover a whole new set of fragile experiences to somehow mangle and corrupt. Besides, keep with the barley-hop exclusive and you ran the risk of early onset American Manopause; a vicious sinkhole of video games, couch surfing the PGA circuit, and 42-inch plasma screens to deftly accentuate a 44-inch waistline.... Fucking hell, some scary ghosts of Christmas future if ever. No, for now a little jig into the world of day tripping viticulture seemed about the place to be.

Bit of Xanax and a bellyful of wine on a brittle night such as this and you were drifting into a cubist sort of abstract mellowness, like some Guernica kitty having his tummy scratched while the flaming knives and screaming horses sailed past. A bottle you say? No problem, might you have another? But not too much there Cochise, or you'll be bellying up next to Elvis at the bar. He drained another glass. Wouldn't want that sort of ignominious ending now would we? Just another doom struck ghost in the machine, some cautionary tale of aviation gimpdom.... Just strike the right balance and all would be well—just enough to glance down the rabbit hole, yes sir, just enough education to perform.

It was a nice ride, but it wasn't built to last. Moment by moment, small creeping signs of reality drifted in around the edges, hard truths and soused meanderings of the mind. *Who were all these strangers?* What the primrose fuck were we all doing out here, strapped into these seats barreling along into the great unknowable? The random bits of half-formed gibberish danced about his mind—feeling the pull of great speeds, calculating and computing the vast distances, pondering such unreal heights—all of it a mess, all of it starting to conflict with the instincts, the ones wired way back there, somewhere heavy in the DNA.

The bad vibes danced around like bits of negative wiring, or some malfunctioning synapse poisoning the communal well. Well, air travel...this shit just ain't natural—in fact it's wholly unnatural.... Dig into the armrests a bit, let your inner cat rear up as you brood over the sillier things. This sucker's too big—a cored-out aluminum tube with Goddamn shamrocks painted hither and yon.... *Shamrocks*; who the hell were they fooling? These things, these things go down—down in big bundled flaming masses, all existence rendered in some cable news sound byte. A cyclically recycled recitation—a *moving* benediction from some starched up prissy suit—Dr. Stoned Wolffe McStrangelove

Christopher M. Basso

in his haberdashery best, rambling on about *the horror* before cutting to Alison Fleur du Mal and all the latest celebrity balderdash from the Lifestyle section.

Was that it? Twenty-nine years of a delicate work in progress left stranded in the middle of some half-baked incarnation? Is that how this fine little experiment would be heralded into the Ever After? By a pompous Brahmin shitheel with porcelain veneers and a not so clever weave? There's your horror, Kurtzy boy.... All the nonsense it has taken to get here, the careful cultivations, the bits of random messiness, the slick victories and tender mercies—all of it just riding on *fate* at this point.... Fate, as loaded as those dice old Faulkner talked about, just before tipping back the Yoknapatawpha corn mash again. Some people, well most people, can suppress the flashes of burgeoning madness by bringing some reason and faith to bear. But for the well-tuned caveman throwback types, the ones always looking for the next heaviness around the corner, these things become just slightly more pronounced.

Modern fears are a zero sum game, full of shameful winners and noble losers. Built inside the genome of apish convictions, we're fatally slow to adapt—so what's it worth in the end but a well-trained liver and the comings and goings of all these little karmic foibles? But unlike your average cave bear, O'Shea now had money on the cuff and booze at the ready. A little extra cash bought him the necessary leg room and breathing space needed to ponder the fates, but what he really wanted, more than anything, was his reasoning filthily corrupted—just one more round, because the medicinal benefits of the altered state held great mystery and sway at this point. Either way, the medicine was running low. So where was she, that stern lady of the fates? Perhaps it was time to switch things over, enough of this wine. Nix the mind expanding libations, move on to the soul-numbing ones. Yes, straight vodka with just a bitter dash of lime, a fine drink for a lapsed Catholic indeed. He gave the call sign a ding. She appeared at once.

The head screw with the mace bomb eyes took a tender line with him. Without saying a word she seemed to grasp the deeper psychic implications of the situation. Best to treat the thing with kid gloves, nip it quick before any heavy petting became necessary. And why not? As long as they didn't attack the crew or relieve themselves on the cockpit door they could keep this little game afloat. Best to just give them what they want, but always keep a ready finger on that chickenswitch, just one good shot right between the eyes—would stop a bull in its tracks and make a pacifist out of Genghis Khan. Hopefully, it wouldn't flow down that road. After all, mace tends to drift in tight spaces, and the marketing people generally frown on gassing the miles upgrades.

She served up several discreet rounds for the ashen faced young man in 13A, at a clip of every half hour or so. Altogether he blew through three of the little reason corrupting demons—well maybe it was more like five—but discretion could also be the better part of valor, particularly when this strange boy kept slipping her folded bills and thanking her ever so kindly.

Each time she arrived with his drink Liam gave her the kind, grateful eyes of a proud man who realizes he's being handled with care. And while the steady stream of mash staunched the wounds of an already jittery psyche, it also managed to trap his thoughts in a rattling, paradoxical din. A trembling unease which meandered nervously at first before falling pleasantly into rhythm with the drone of the engines and the enveloping darkness of the cabin.... A very New Age and zennish kind of fear mongered interlude. Like going off the rails on back alley Blue Barrels, as the pan flute stylings of some world music ingénue played away in your own sixth circle of Hell. Terrifying bedbug bugaboos in any tongue, but all the same, producing nothing in the way of that quiet, reflective time. Yep, *too much*, he thought, sitting there, one biscuit short of a tin, red-eyed, pie-eyed, and worse for the wear.

What was air travel after all but a tedious continuum of boredom bookended by moments of sheer terror? The boredom was more than obvious—but tonight's terror was courtesy of some bad air they picked up back Newfoundland way. The pilot had come over the intercom and chimed something about slight bump and moderate chop.... *Slight bump, moderate chop*? Sounded like lame-ass jigs you did half in the bag at your cousin's wedding. Well, euphemistic flourishes aside, this was something he could do without. Just keep telling yourself this was the safest form of transport known to man. There was a kernel of sanity in that; he could almost hear himself chanting the words, caught somewhere between a mantra and a prayer. After all, they made perfect sense on the ground, nice, clinical, and thoroughly antiseptic. But that kind of cold rationality is the first casualty when you're 7-1/2 miles above the Earth, giddy-upping along at 500 knots, hunkered down in the belly of the beast. Although, this was nothing that should have felt out of the ordinary, at least not to any sane man, and least of all not to the karma-challenged descendant of the unlucky Irish in 13A, working up a fine case of Carpal tunnel with some misplaced rosaries.

Go slow, sip your vodka, and take it easy, he thought. Keep this up and you'll give yourself a Goddamn embolism. Debatable if they kept a crash cart stowed up front, even for their special guests. Equally terrifying was the prospect of the dame straddling him with some gerry-rigged defibrillator shouting, "Clear!" No, deep breaths, more vodka, get a *grip* man, work it through.... Dull sweats, cold chills, hard to feel comfortable crawling around in your skin—no solace around these parts, dark lights, deafening noise—all vessels trapped in our moment.

He thumbed through a copy of *SkyMall*, trying to ignore the unholy terror creeping outside the cabin, but no sooner had the seat belt light clicked off when another heavier jolt kicked in causing that great sickening *here we go* sensation. O'Shea grabbed either side of the armrests and dug in. While this private terror played itself out, the autopilot slowly banked to the right and descended a bit before leveling out. Across the aisle a portly banker-type grunted something through a drunken sleepy haze of OxyContin and used Guinness stank before rolling over.

After the worst subsided, he pried his fingers from the surety of the seat and reached into his pocket for another piece of Nicorette. He fumbled with the silver packaging while nipping a quick glance to see if anyone was witnessing this rather unmanly bit of abdication. Appearances were, after all, still important to young O'Shea. His eyes drifted slowly around the cabin. The coast was clear.

Hell, this sorry bunch was even further down the rabbit hole than he was.... But were they just drifting through a night of innocent sleep, he wondered, or were they like himself, low rent

Dr. Feelgoods lost in the throes of some deviously over medicated state? No matter, nothing was stirring, the boy was riding shotgun on his own midnight perils. The lie-flat seats afforded the chance to get comfy and many of his fellow pilgrims had availed of the opportunity to let it all hang out. One lady, not content with the seventeen extra feet of pitch which came with the ticket was lying sidelong out in the aisle. Liam shook his head—greedy.

.... Didn't John the Baptist bust some ecclesiastical craziness about a certain number of years you'll twist in Purgatory before receiving the eternal reward? Yes, Liam seemed to recall the Jesuit Brothers beating something like that into him once or twice. But did those defrocked hucksters ever consider that *this* might be the crowd he'd have to spend it with? This was a heavy bummer on an already weighty kind of night.

The cold ocean air gave the big Boeing mule another sharp kick and there was a low rumbling sound as they lurched quickly to the left. Like some hellish atmospheric prize fight unfolding on the astral plane, the autopilot fought back with an aggressive slide to the right—this was now nearing the saturation point—the critical mass. The moment where one seriously pondered the anatomical feasibility of crushing the chalky white gum into a fine powder, wetting it with some preciously rationed vodka, and mainlining the whole mix into your veins using the cap to your Sharpie and the swizzle stick from your drink.... However, on quick reflection, this could prove a bit excessive—maybe a bit too far from the realm of legality, ethics, and sanity. Surely they'd catch onto his babbling odd man act. They'd bring out the duct tape and plastic cuffs, tie him to the seat for the remainder of the flight, and take turns beating him in the kidneys with some Clementines rolled in a hot face towel.

Aspiring lawyerly types prize the cardinal virtue of legality and the notion of the rule of law. He was fairly sure any aberrant behavior would nix his chances for a fair shake if not subsequent upgrades. Besides he couldn't handle any heavy legal scenes in foreign lands—the man from the embassy would take one look at his wild-eyed, disheveled state, disavow him completely, and recommend throwing him under the nearest train at once. If he was lucky it'd only be a few months in some minimum security playpen, but judging by the disposition of the family brand it was more likely the lead role in some hellish Hibernian *Midnight Express*.

But that wasn't what stopped him in the end. He *needed* that vodka for other things. With that particular plan dashed he sank back in his seat, crestfallen and resigned to ride out the storm with his only waking friend—the bastard red icon of an airplane, frozen still, somewhere across the ocean—mocking him. A twenty-nine year old man drooling Nicorette, vodka, and tomato juice—the complete, erudite picture of an impressively wealthy Young Turk.

Chapter Four
The Flower Child

    He looked over at her stretched out in the window seat next to his. Her back was turned and he couldn't quite tell if she was sleeping, or maybe staring out into the mix of starry night and early morning. He studied the way her body would softly rise and fall with each breath, measured in a delicate peaceful rhythm. Peaceful in a way he could never be. He peered in a bit closer....Perhaps he should just let her be? It would be the gracious and magnanimous thing to do.... But, then again, she *was* an excellent source of distractions. Perhaps he should just give her a bit of a kick, a love tap really, subtle-like, more for style, less for points. Yet she looked so peaceful.

    In the end he thought it best to just shelve this plan at the margins. She'd already saved the day once. Thank her blessed stars for the Nicorette; she was always looking out for his ill-prepared ass. His stoic self had thought he could handle it otherwise, but she had the inside track on what lurked in the recesses of his anxiety closet. She insisted he load up on the stuff for just such an evening of brittle angst and harrowing self-reflection time.... Well, maybe more like she just thought him a bit cranky when he flew. That being said, he'd like to thank her, but all the same he'd just as soon keep the last few hours to himself, lest anyone suss just how low he'd plumbed the psychic depths.

Christopher M. Basso

But even a brief shelter in the storm couldn't quite make the nut, as he fidgeted around his seat like a nine-year old with the Ritalin DTs. The seatbelt light was on and he could still feel the sharp staccato chop of air moving along the plane, but this seemed as good a time as any to go for a bit of a stroll. He briefly mulled this over as he generally kept his movements about the cabin to a minimum, lest he potentially throw off the delicate pitch and yaw of the hundred ton jet.

Well, screw those grim odds; it was time to stretch his legs. Stretch his legs or run the risk of that nasty pulmonary embolism he'd been considering—a heavy sort of mishap way above the Earth, and one which would mean a damn sight more in punitive damages than any turbulence related miscues.... His brain still trafficked in those crackerjack-slick lawyerly rhythms from time to time, particularly in moments like these, when he actually imagined he was doing those rigid, rule-crazy Bolsheviks a favor. He checked one more time to see if she was awake—*no?* He undid the seatbelt, and passed through the curtain towards Coach, making his wobbly way to the lavatories at the rear of the plane.

He stepped in, slid the door closed, and waited for the lights to kick on. Lovely, garish shades of fluorescent death made him look about as trim and healthy as he felt. He took quick stock of the situation. Nope, no good—the deranged plan of two drinks ago to rip the smoke detectors out and light up would have never sailed. Just another invitation to be handcuffed and lead off the plane into the waiting arms of some ruffian Gaelic law league. His altogether drunk and cheeky state would've clearly necessitated an epic beat down of the misbehaving half-breed with the Irish name.

"Ain't that a bitch," he muttered. He could *feel* the eyes of others watching for any transgression. He spat out the cigarette gimping gum, his mouth tasting like some trespassed cottony ulcer. His mind raced along at a barely ordered breakneck clip.... Jesus, has anyone ever linked that stuff to a chronic raging paranoia? If not, perhaps he should be the case study.

He relieved the burdens of too much drink, washed his hands, and took a long look in the mirror.... Always interesting to study yourself in the middle of some ordeal, if just to see how you were holding up. All illusions of grace under pressure seem to fade under a withering stare—don't they? His reflection met him with a smile. This seemed a good a time as any to take the measure of the man. Besides, he felt a kind of strange relaxation standing alone back here. Some of that claustrophobic angst seemed to dial down a peg or two and, despite the tight confines, he felt rather lightheaded and suddenly at ease.

Twenty-nine? He looked about it—no younger, no older. Though his eyes still looked young, even through the red-rimmed burn of dry air and no sleep they looked young and alive—sharp with greenish, hazel points and a shape giving the impression of thoughtfulness. A thoughtfulness that wavered between expressions of benevolence and mischief. You had to wait till he spoke to figure out which. He had a good beak on him and was more attractive than he realized. Indeed, he'd been blessed with the old man's looks—dark black hair, fair skin, a hawkish nose, and the same watchful eyes. He rolled his head back and forth and fumbled with the St. Christopher medal around his neck....A long forgotten keepsake from a simpler time, and who knows, some fortuity—because hell, even the occasional heretic needs a friend.

He'd let his hair grow out from its usual close-cropped look, with a bit of curl now around the edges, maybe owing something to the Spanish who'd washed up along Galway Bay so long ago. He marveled with a rather perverse fascination at the recent flecks of gray around the temples. His face told the conflicting tale of the years. At once youthful, but in the same breath something not, as if bestriding those two worlds, and not sure to which it belonged. Either way it was a handsome face; boyish cuteness evolving or devolving into a distinguished manhood, a work in progress. He figured he could live with that.

Ponderings for another day perhaps, but at the moment all he felt was the pleasant spreading sense of relief. The worst was over and the rest was just the gliding in. Even the turbulence wasn't that bad, not when you could stand and just let your body shift and ride with the waves. All in all another jump across the vast emptiness of the ocean was safely under the belt. Apparently, it didn't want him today. All that was left was the debriefing—not so bad, not so good. Only a few minor moments; nothing that would spell any lasting damage or residual psychosis.

He focused on his watch, snugly refitting the clasp before catching himself again in the mirror. This time he leaned in a bit closer, suddenly pleased with himself for keeping it together. No, not this unmitigated disaster of a flight but, rather, keeping the greater *It* together for the last nine months. Yes indeed, lots of weird shit had gone down between the here and there—variations on the comically strange and sundry musings of an overactive mind you might say.... Or maybe it was just a *rearranging* of things, like those deck chairs on the Titanic. Either way, he'd held it together well enough.

Here he was, unshaven with three days of growth, and a few flecks of gray running through otherwise jet black hair. But it was his eyes again, something about the eyes, something he'd recognize from time to time, and always with the same passing sense of dread. Eyes warding something off, locked in fits, wavering by turns between a fierce struggle and the staid, placid look of fish on a bed of ice. Under different circumstances they might have even been sad eyes, unduly burdened with the weight of things, the finality of things.

He snapped back to it. The moment passed, or rather he passed it—never easy to tell which. He ran some cold water through his hair and rubbed his eyes. All right then, ten more minutes. *Man up.*

As he walked down the aisle the first rays of sunlight shined through the windows, layering in slanted, jagged patterns along the backs of the seats. All the sleeping faces were slowly coming back to life, awakening, or perhaps "recovering" in the local custom—*Cead Mile Failte*. A hundred thousand welcomes indeed. Well, no one could knock this airline for a lack of hospitality. Another slight spasm rattled through the cabin, nothing too intense, but the sad proof they would have to ride this nut to the bitter end.

He braved a quick look out the window, peering down as far as he could see into the blackness.... Something deeply chuckle worthy about all these middle class tourists flying high in style over the cold waters below, over the paths of the coffin ships that carried among others, the clan O'Shea to America once upon a time…. But there was something far *deeper* traced in the annals and currents of the sea, the same sea which carried the children of the greatest exodus since Pharaoh cracked the whip and Moses got on the good foot.

By and large everyone on this tragedy-waiting-to-happen was just some pasty, sun-challenged Alex Haley out there *feeling* their Celtic roots, and this airplane was, for six hours at least, the great Hibernian soul searching express…. Jesus, what hellish bit of Debbie Downer had he suddenly shaded over to? To piss warm and drink cold the earth ain't the easiest of gigs when you find yourself the fringe player on the Marginal Mystery Tour….But then again, maybe such grim renderings were just the sort of ballast his hopped up mind required.

And after all, it was a fairly safe assumption that most of this bunch were some variation of the *little people*—his people in a sense. They were either the pure homegrown strains of Irish-Irish, or the watered down mongrel variations of the American cousin—embodied by just the likes of one Liam James O'Shea.

So now lit by the faint hue of darkness and the calm churn of the engines they sat forever locked together, forty-nine aisles, of an indistinguishable pastiche of the Eight Faces of Erin. Arms and legs draped over seats in the throes of deep sleep, they looked rather communally comfortable in a strange Haight-Ashbury meets the peat bog kind of way.

The young mendicant had been making this little jump across the pond for most of his childhood, as Tara O'Shea's roots still ran deep in the country of her parent's birth. Most of her maiden *Delaney* lineage still called Dublin home and the shared bonds ran deep. Liam had been their guest for many summers, and his materfamilias had played the host for all the rest—lot's of cousins, aunts, uncles, and various odds and ends roving about the mix.

So, what number would this have made then; how many hops across the great nothing had he under the belt? Eleven? Twelve? And despite bitchings over present confinements, he couldn't say his particular surliness was from lack of familiarity. This was a cast which changed but a script that forever remained the same; just the same wheezy variations on a theme. He looked

39

Christopher M. Basso

around at all the sleeping faces.... The Irish-Irish were always the easier ones to spot, as they seemed to enjoy a sounder sleep; a sleep that ignored the lunging roll and pitch of the plane, and the various karmic foibles that laid low the weaker sorts.

It was a sleep that spoke to a millennium of spectacularly dreadful luck; after bloodthirsty Vikings, plundering Edwardians, King Billy and the Boyne, Cromwell roaming the countryside lopping off Catholic heads, so-called famines, foreign occupation, partition, and sectarian strife—well then, what was air travel really except a joy laden *piece of piss*.

No doubt a few of these *bog boyos* were returning from various undeclared extensions of those burdensome three-month visas prescribed by the State Department. No doubt they had found safe shelter up and down the east coast of the U.S. in the fraternal arms of some Masonic bartending order. A sort of Underground Railroad for the young Irish Wildgoose who simply can't stay put in his own country. This beast is noted for an overworked mojo, questionable fashion sense, and keen desire to rove and wander about. But even the basest of them could transform into some wizardly Henry Higgins master of the linguistic flourish if they thought it might get them laid. These were some of the people he was heading out to visit. These were some of the people he grew up with and loved best.

And as life back at Chez Henry wasn't quite making the nut why not try his second home? Maybe then the worm would turn, or some such kooky erudition that had sent better sorts to perdition.... An invitation to a cousin's wedding, one of the main Delaney brood, was the proverbial sign that seals the deal for intrepid men of means. He loaded up on bougie French luggage and found a caretaker to mind the store back in Bedford. All was well, all roads lead home, and to this moment, 7 ½ miles in the sky, clipping along at 500 knots, *raging stoned*, hunkered down in the belly of the beast.

He found the young lady in 13B much as he'd left her, peacefully unaware. Despite that slight bump and moderate chop, she barely moved.... Good lord, man, this one could sleep in a cement mixer rolling through a tidewater hurricane. A benevolent gift for a spotless mind if ever, but it was *time* for the wake-up call. Leaning over for a better look out the window, he gave her a good nudge with his knee.

"Wakey-wakey," he smiled.

".... Did you just *kick me?*"

"Don't flatter yourself there Morning Glory—that was the plane. We've been bouncing around for hours."

She looked around, her bright blue eyes readjusting to the world. "What time is it?"

"12:30 back New York way." He glanced down at his little GPS friend. "And, uh, 5:30 in the local."

She rubbed her eyes. "When do we land?"

"Oh, not much longer."

She stretched back in the big chair, shaking out the last bits of sleep, and gazed out the window.

"How long was I out?"

"Two, maybe three hours."

"Did you sleep?"

Liam smiled. "What do you think?"

She chuckled. "I think you've kept your seat in the full upright position and white-knuckled this ride for the last couple of hours.... Am I getting warm?"

He politely ignored this withering abuse.

"Was it the karma thing again, Liam?"

"Very perceptive, Ms. Moneypenny."

He rolled the ice in his empty glass and stared at the ceiling. "While *you* were in the throes of greedy sleep, I was awake, on watch, *on point* if you will."

"Whatever for?"

"Oh you know, making canonical promises and striking deals for our eventual salvation—the usual. All of which has ensured our safe transit. You should be thankful for such diligence." He smiled. "*.... Free of charge.*"

"Well, thank you." She leaned over kissing his cheek.

Christopher M. Basso

"Keeping us all safe, my dear Liam, the karma police."

"Yes, yes—*laugh*. I've never expected to be understood in my lifetime."

"But one day they'll make you statues and sing your songs."

With each passing moment she grew more alert, more in the world—just as Liam was fading, his body nearing the sinewy synaptic misfired end of a thirty-three hour day. A few rows back he could hear the reassuring sounds of a baby crying and all around him voices rising and falling. His Irish *drink link* rolled by with beverage cart. He wondered if they could start it up again with the Bloody Marys as this was, after all, technically a morning drink…. Nah, daylight was here and she no longer looked in the mood to nurse his oddball vampire act. The dame shot him the thin narrow eyes which spoke volumes, yet said not a word. One toke over the line might be all it took to get her going. No matter, on further review it wasn't the booze cart after all, but the tea and coffee service.

Why yes, more stimulants—bring them here at once! Her counterpart was a few rows ahead laying out the makings of a full Irish breakfast: fried eggs, sausage, bacon, stewed tomatoes, toast, and the nebulous black discs his forbearers called *pudding*. O'Shea had been holding out for some of the stomach-coating, cloven-hoofed delicacies of Celtic haute cuisine. They were the perfect sort of counterpoint to a late night spent righteously abusing yourself.

Unfortunately, his drooling thoughts were interrupted by another sage observation from the Peanut Gallery, "What you *should* have done was taken one of those Ambien."

He felt a bit put on, but otherwise the words came easy, ragged and loose, "Ambien is for old ladies. Besides, it would have just confused the amazing amounts of alcohol, opiates, and nicotine already careening through my system. Might have turned me into a Goddamn werewolf… bleeding out the eyes or something."

"What?"

Liam slumped low in his seat like a carnie who'd dodged

his last train.

"I already ate most of that useless gum anyway," he said sadly. "Did nothing but wire me up. Now I've got enough of that evil shit running through my veins to orbit half of Kentucky."

"You've got to take it easy with that stuff, my love. They're not tic tacs. Besides, Elvis, I said take *an* Ambien, not a fistful of Percocet."

He laughed. "Well, I always make it a point to *just say no* to drugs honey and, besides, sleeping pills would've just humbled my edge, or pushed me over it—and we couldn't go having that now, could we?"

She was, by now, thumbing through a copy of *Vanity Fair* and munching on a granola bar. "Well, it's good to see you're dealing with your fears like a sane, rational man."

"Whoa there, Sunshine…it's not fear."

She chuckled, "Oh really? What is it then—a lifestyle choice?"

"I'd call it, let's just say… logical practicality born out of immediate necessity."

He looked around at the sardine-tight conditions, the swaying of the cabin, and the deafening roar of the engines, "I mean, c'mon now, you've got to admit this is unnatural—we weren't meant for this."

She said nothing, now quite engrossed in her magazine, some heavy article on thirty as the new nineteen. He could sense he'd lost her. Adding insult to injury, the nimble, industrious crew was suddenly slow to get the coffee flowing.

It was a pause that drifted a bit too long.

"You know," he said, "I was just thinking about how I used to genuinely *enjoy* flying, back when I was younger."

"What happened?" She lowered her magazine, now slightly interested.

Liam let out a low breath, his face a mix of sadness and bewilderment, "…. *I don't know.*"

"…. Good talk, *Sunshine.*" She tried giving him the kind

eyes, "Well…it used to bother me too—quite a bit actually. But it really doesn't anymore."

O'Shea quickly turned the tables. "Why's that?"

Her gaze was something thoughtful, "There's no effort in any of this." She gestured out towards the wider world. "No driving through traffic, no dealing with stress…. You just close your eyes, go to sleep, and wake up a few hours later someplace entirely new."

She perked up, "Maybe *that's* the way you should be thinking about it. Where else can you show up, sit back, do nothing, have a drink, take a nap, and fourteen hours later be on the *other side of the world?*" She paused for effect. "Look at the *positives.*"

O'Shea recoiled as a slight shudder ran through him. The thought of fourteen hours in a plane made him weak in the knees. He could feel a few more black hairs jumping over to the whiter side of life. He'd already estimated his threshold for these aerial leaps of faith at nine or ten hours. Anything after that and his behavior would become erratic and scattershot—like a race car hard charged way past the model specs.

She could see his mind dancing around in circles. Sensing her soft sell wasn't working, she changed tacks. "Think about that ride to the airport Liam—the FDR to the BQE to the Van Wyck—rush hour through Queens—*that* was by far the most dangerous thing you've done today…. *This* is safe."

"Yeah, well, I suppose you're right."

The boy flashbacked to the purple IROC-Z with the pulsing neon baseboards—the unofficial Queens County pace car, the one which nearly clipped the Lincoln ferrying them out to Kennedy. Woven into that bit of nastiness were hazy flashes of yellow jacket cabs, flashing red and white points of light, weaving in and out of *Ronin*-style death matches with a samurai grit long forgotten on these shores. All harbingers of an imminent doom.

She propped up in her seat, now clearly enjoying things. "This is all very cute actually. My boyfriend, the hard charger, the pragmatic caballero, is *this* afraid of flying?"

"It's not the flying part I'm afraid of, dear," he shot back.

"It's more the crashing thing I take issue with.... Let's clarify things—you can call it an acute concern for any sudden and unannounced deceleration resulting in the premature reunion with the ground."

It was her turn to sigh. "I'd call it the fear of long shots.... Start worrying about airplanes crashing after you've won the lottery or something."

This was not the most comfortable of comparisons. "Well, maybe I'll just chalk it up to being an excessive control freak?"

"See, you're already making more sense."

He thought about it for a moment, still trying to win a convert to his slightly twisted, yet highly enlightened manner of thought. ".... I mean, *Jesus*, doesn't it bother you, for example, that you can't see out the front of this thing?" He pointed down the aisle. "And, for that matter, what about the two complete *strangers* up there with our fates in their completely anonymous hands?"

He had a sharp, wild-edged look in his eye; he might have made a *fine* trial lawyer once upon a time. "Am I right? Hell, they could be drug-snorting, wife-swapping, nitrous-sucking, Bolshevik-loving...*fucking*—cross dressers for all we know, but right now they're calling all the shots—they hold all the cards." A grim paranoia had quickly replaced the confidence in his eyes.

She listened thoughtfully, nodding until it was her turn for evangelizing. "Well, I don't think there's too many Bolsheviks left these days, and the wife swapping market is really more of a media myth than anything; but look at it this way—can you fly a plane?"

"No."

"Then why do you need to see out the front of one?"

".... Can't argue with that one. Next you'll be telling me there are no monsters under the bed."

"Oh no, they're there—trust me."

Her strange, dove-like logic would generally have provoked a wide range of whelping smart-ass invectives, but on

45

this fine morning they were just the right sort of salve. He felt a bit like a scorched man who'd been through the valley and was coming out the other side, "Thought so...anyway, thanks for being the even-keeled one, know what I mean?"

Her eyes twinkled a bit. "I try my best.... Look, Magellan, you keep the ship running straight here—I've got to pee." She started to stand. "Be a good boy and snag me some orange juice and one of those muffins when the lady comes back."

"Roger that, captain my captain."

He stood to let her pass. She pressed close by him, their faces near; she gave him a smile that made the forgetting easy. And if his eyes projected a cunning thoughtfulness, hers exuded something of a generous warmth and comfort. Feeling better he rocked back in his chaise lounge of a seat and closed his eyes.

She started down the aisles, still grinning that smartass grin, when her foot caught some trifling piece of poorly-stowed luggage and she took a head-over-end spill onto the armrests of two pleasantly surprised older gentlemen who probably weren't expecting a show with the meal.

She regained her balance, but scarcely her composure. The dame had swung open the curtains between the cabins, so probably a good twenty or thirty rows had been in on the commotion. Sleepy early morning faces peering around seats and peeping over the tops of newspapers. An ocular flutter set off like a row of dominoes pointing her way.

He would later remember it as a grand and rather elegant spill—all arms, long legs, and a half graceful pirouette that made all those pricey dance lesson growing up come to fruition. Weaker sorts would have withered and crawled under the floorboards to ride out the rest of the flight with the air freight and the luggage, but she was made of something tougher. Rather, she let out a loud infectious laugh bordering on a chortle, which carried through the cabin, while covering her ever-reddening crimson face, her eyes lit in smiling, laughing shades of pointillist blue—all fire and warmth.

She unabashedly turned to the cabin; to everyone south of about row twelve who'd witnessed this and curtsied. The Irish-Irish, a genial bunch to begin with, clapped and hooted for both the fall and the redemption. In five seconds, Sara Connelly had made herself the most memorable thing on the New York to Dublin overnight.

Liam looked up from his seat, gave a slight whistle through the teeth, and forgot about his odd man-ogre act for a moment.... She definitely had a touch of the *je ne sais quoi* about her, he'd grant her that—on a rusting, fear-festooned bucket of one man's inner perils, she sang the calmest of grace notes.

It was a star struck quality that was somewhat lost on the boy; as one woman's state of grace could also be another man's cause for a restraining order. It was the kind of grace you couldn't teach, the kind that radiates from its own innate wellspring...and if she knew these things she never let on.... Truly something to see for the likes of Liam, whose *chi* ran a slightly colder shade of warm. To see the qualities in another so lacking in yourself was the kind of eye opener which could lay you out every time—particularly if you dwelled so, well, *exactingly* on your own shortcomings.

O'Shea, with a fair amount of practice, had a fine sense of these—shortly after realizing he hadn't "broken" the plane, he might just have come up swinging at any foul-mouthed, chicken shit bog bastard who had the temerity to laugh. Well, he thought, manners were still important to some. Too bad, but after all, this world's a big tent and it takes all comers—misanthropes got to go on vacation too.

Sara was greeted with several, "Are you okay, dear?" and, "You're not hurt are you?" as she made her way down the aisle. Each inquiry was met the same effusive self-deprecation that won many converts to her sunny disposition. With her safely working the room, he laid back in his seat, trying to find that one restive spot of comfortable which had eluded him thus far. He could feel the engines revving down, their drone growing softer and softer as they began bleeding off altitude. A general buzz of commotion swirled all around him—others coming up as one went under. He laid his head to the side and leaned back. The rest came naturally.

Christopher M. Basso

Chapter Five
Parklife

The fierce slam of touchdown snapped him out of his sleep like a heart attack man in the mid-throes of an amyl rush. Jesus! *Never* fall asleep at the wheel. They thundered down the runway as the powerful roar of the engines melted to a whirling kittenish purr before coming to a gentle halt. And then there were the sounds of many people clapping and applauding.... Oh yes, he'd forgotten about this particular bit of *Orishness*. Giving thanks where thanks was due—even in his burnt sleepy state he managed to join in the growing chorus.

The majestic green and white mule with the shamrock on its ass slowly lumbered towards the gate. Out the window there was a fog thick as thieves. He squinted, just barely able to make out the ghostly form of another airplane across the apron.

"We've been circling for nearly an hour," she added over his shoulder. "The fog was too heavy to land, we were almost *diverted*. Can you believe that? Thought maybe it was better to just let you sleep."

He blinked the grog from his eyes. "…. No arguments here."

They reached the gate, the light popped off and 267 seatbelts went off nearly in unison—like some strange clicking choir. They gathered up what was remaining in seats 13A and B

Christopher M. Basso

with Aer Cladhaire flight 1946, June 10th, now safely in the books. O'Shea straightened out his clothes and stood in the aisle, reaching into the overhead. He'd gone day tripper casual for this flight—faded jeans, close fitting gray t-shirt, motorcycle boots, and a shiny new Raymond Weil chronograph.

His weather-worn clothes and three days of wispy scruff gave him the bearing of some far out interloper who generally should've been eyed with some level of interest, if not suspicion.... But the man had the ticket to ride, and up here beyond the wizard's curtain that sort of sketchiness found a new tolerance as a healthy brand of eccentricity that could be at the very least tolerated, if not encouraged.

He grabbed a dark summer coat from the bin and checked for his wallet and phone. The contents of his pockets revealed various mashed packets of Nicorette, cigarettes, and one wallet containing three credit cards, a NY driver's license, two expired MetroCards, and $21 in cash.

Sara opted for the standard granola hues of her West Coast forbearers—jeans, light blue sweater, a bit torn and frayed, no jewelry or make-up, and sandy blond hair falling loose across her shoulders—a nice unaffected beauty. Contents of her pockets: two credit cards, a CA driver's license, Sierra Club membership card, and a ticket stub for last April's Dar Williams show at Irving Plaza. A minimalist look about her, a subtle harmony in the rare kind of beauty that was built up the more it was stripped down.

They made their way towards the door for a farewell from the assembled crew.... There she was again, the stern-eyed dame who played such an intricate part in last night's mischief. O'Shea never realized there could be an aviation variation on the walk of shame, but there was no mistaking, this had to be it. Yes, The Fates had worked him over pretty soundly on all fronts, but no infamy in that—just remember—keep your head high....Don't slouch.

He gave her a slight grin and a bit of a wink and then set a suspicious, appraising scowl on the pilots standing by the doorway—a long hard stare at these two who'd been playing up the quasi-deity card for the last seven hours. Was there any obvious trace of an untoward depravity about them? Flecks of white powder around the nose, red-rimmed Visine eyes, any nervous uncontrollable grinding of the teeth? It didn't seem like it, but appearances can be deceiving. Behind every straight-laced flyboy in a pressed suit lurked some freakish beast, ever ready to take a stroll on the wild side—some primrose Bacchus garden where Bolshevism still sailed and a general sexual depravity was *de rigueur* for those in the know.... Yeah, that's right, chuckles, keep smiling at the rubes, but we knew better, and the good money said it was all fur-gripping bestiality and ritual sacrifice behind closed doors, just like it always was with the straight ones. But that was just one paranoid man's sleepy opinion.

"Right then, have a nice day, come again."

"Blow me, you chipper sodomites," was what he heard in his head, but the words sounded something closer to, "Thanks, you too."

And with that they deplaned.

Dublin Airport was fairly modern and fairly small. A short walk and they were in line for Passport Control. As they were the first international arrival of the morning things moved along at a good clip. Before long, O'Shea was presenting his *Irish* passport to the man for the all important judgment-appraisal and stamping process. If you were clever with paperwork, like one bleary aviophobe, dual citizenship was one of the strange serviceable quirks of having a grandmother born out in the bog lands of County Mayo.

The Immigration man barely raised an eye to him, even with Liam's utter lack of a brogue and slightly noticeable New York bray, but, shit, Ireland was really more of a state than some states anyway—but don't say that too loud. And just so long as you weren't jumping the EU fence from some rusting Soviet hulk in Eastern Europe into the warm filial embrace of the dying Celtic Tiger, they were just as soon inclined to stamp you on your way.

Another short walk brought them to the luggage carousels on the lower level where their bags quickly came down the chute—numbers three, seven, and nine; a karma reaffirming serendipity was in the air for sure. Liam bought some smokes and a couple of coffees from the newsstand, and they made for the shuttle out to the rental stands.

They hopped on the shuttle for the far side of the airport property. Off towards the horizon, a steady stream of jets were making the big turn lining up for their landing slots as the morning traffic kicked into high gear. Tiny cascading points of light gently drifting down a hill—final approach was a rather pretty thing when you weren't a part of it.

Liam walked into "Smiling Leo O'Bannon's" rental stand, a squat little corrugated bunkhouse, complete with smoky ambiance and fair share of early morning, twilight-type characters. He ambled up to the desk where a very agitated young man was there to greet him.

Sara waited outside with the luggage, overly obsessed with the notion of fresh air or some such thing. Early June and it was still straining to crack the forty mark. She rooted through her bag till she found a heavier woolen sweater. From inside she could hear the faint rumblings of what might have been raised voices—perhaps even Liam's in the mix. No worries, he was a big boy, probably just making friends.

She let her eyes drift around, soaking in the first snapshots of someplace new, the mind sorting how much the reality matched the hyperbole of a myth…. Very green and very cold, at least they were right on the first two counts. She took a seat on the suitcase leaning against the curb and pulled her sleeves long over her chilled fingers. Despite the shiver it was rather nice to see her breath in the cool morning air. Quite the game changer from the ridiculous steam bath they'd fled the night before.

She was a tall lithe thing—5' 9", nearly 5'10" if she did her good girl finishing school posture. She had an alert energy about her, and her long legs sat awkwardly off the curb like an impatient child who needed to keep moving. She pulled back her sandy blond hair into a tail and made a quick braid around. Her baby blues were a brighter shade that often picked up the finer points of turquoise in the morning before fading to a delicate slate gray in the small hours of evening. She thumbed through a copy of a *Let's Go* travel guide while the ever increasing sounds of some menacing vibration grew from within.

She looked out again past the edge of the airport property, as a small herd of cows ambled about a field of the deepest green, taking it easy in a postcard moment kind of way. Every minute or so another massive jet would come roaring over the outer markers just above their heads, a thundering boom that rattled through the bones; but they simply chewed their cud and blinked not an eye, 'til all was quiet again... A Zen cow roll call if ever.

To walk between the raindrops in this world was a bit of a mixed bag, a muddled misnomer. Too often the means justified the ends and there were always those who found this gift through the atavistic stylings of some hell bent pit bull.... But then there were others who found it down the end of the smallest of virtues. Sara was a rare breed, breezing through this dry, brittle world with a reservoir of grace. She was a third year, like Liam, although this one having actually finished the task at hand. In addition to her high-powered legal mind, she had already scored a Master's in Public Administration. That is to say, she was *educated*.

This little jaunt was, among other things, his idea of a fine graduation present for her.... Then again he seemed to inadvertently traffic in co-dependent abstractions. "C'mon, we'll get out of the country," he assured her, "break some shit, have a few laughs."

Shunning familial expectations with the flair and dash of her man, she would soon be taking her high talent legal bad ass self to West Africa, notably Sierra Leone, where she would hook up with Oxfam at the end of the summer, spending the next two years doing something other than helping carve up the world into finer and finer pieces among the Illuminati. That is to say she was an unrepentant *do-gooder*.

It should be said O'Shea had just a few misgivings when she hatched this little gem last winter. Lots of questions, lots of holes, and lots of air travel to places with less than stellar safety records. But on another level it aroused something in the deepest suspicions of his former hard scrabble background, something about the clinking glasses of champagne classes toasting one another in all their benevolent, beneficent glory.... These day-trippers reeked of something stale and unprofitable. But then again she was different, far different, a high-powered prototype, a smokejumper who went looking for the biggest fire she could put out. Besides, who was he to say anyway, he'd just called it a day at twenty-nine.... Not even a glint yet in the eye of some AARP database.

Everyone has a quirky way of coming out swinging at a world that's not meant to be understood, at least not from the dead-eyed, dead-end realism of the young man up in the rental shed white-knuckling his way through life. Some do it with a gentle word; some do it with a sword. The ones with a bit of *the shine* grift with a measure of both.

Moments later, O'Shea reappeared, rubbing his hands together with a catbird grin across his face. He lit up a cigarette.

"What happened to you?"

"Oh, nothing a little good old fashioned horse wrangling and a lot of bad noise couldn't solve."

He was tired, but the cold air felt good. He could feel his mind slowly coming around. "Well, they tried sandbagging us—my bog brethren. They'd have us *walking* into town." He took a drag, admiring a big Emirates 777 touching down, "Anyway, their computer shit the bed as it were.... Apparently it's hopelessly fucked. We're like the twentieth reservation he's lost this morning. It's a real siege mentality in there. Tourists storming off with all sorts of menacing talk of retribution—Molotov cocktails, shivs and zip guns...strongly worded letters to the tourist board. An angry exodus storming away to his competitors—but I chose a slightly different route..."

"So, were you able to fix things?"

"Most certainly."

"Did he talk you into something else, *bruiser,* or did you have to beat him?"

"I talked myself into something else."

"Oh yeah—what?"

He only shrugged.

Within moments a strong revving ginned from down the fairground way, startling the cows. And around the corner pulled a sleek black BMW Z4 roadster—fresh from the deepest jungles of Bavaria.... A rather elegant piece of machinery, and not one of those girly Z3 pacifist models, mind you. This was the new one, the one with the *grande huevos* and the monster engine which made the heads turn and scattered the wildlife. Liam looked over.

"Here it comes."

A catbird grin spread across his face as he admired the oncoming Beamer, not so much for the Diamond Jim peacock strut to it.... Although the bastard *was* nice. Rather, he wore that grin for something that spoke to the complete and utter inappropriateness of it. It was like his finer senses had come loose from their moorings, and instead of trying to right them, he merely stood at the edge of the pier and waved as they sailed past.

Maybe it was the strange glint in his eye that told the tale—one where late nights of drunken, drug-altered philosophical introspection make for mischievous little bedfellows—particularly when you felt your life was on the line. Now, safely back on Mother Earth with the unpleasantness behind him and only the residual boozy nicotine come down ahead, he could afford to feel a bit elevated. Out of his head and out of his element seemed like the place to be, and now they had the proper chariot to continue this mad overtaxed mishmash of a theme. He was, after all, fairly certain *something* interesting lay just around the corner.

The low-slung roadster pulled up to the curb across from them. A much older man than the excitable fellow behind the counter hopped out and started inspecting the car for any dings or bruises. He nursed a wheezing cough and reeked of one too many cigarettes. Along his face were the deeply etched lines of Christmas Future. After a quick once over he handed Liam the keys.

She eyed him suspiciously, "*Liam James*...chauffeured rides to the airport, first class seats, sports car rentals—were you planning on proposing?"

55

"…. Oh, that's rich—they were Business Class seats."

She smiled. "But seriously—have you lost your *Goddamn mind*?"

"Ouch." He looked up from the sleek lines of the car.

"C'mon, I played along with the limo to the airport and the 'surprise' upgrades, but this is a bit excessive—don't you think?"

"You could say that."

"This must have cost a fortune?"

He only shrugged.

"I can't split this with you," she said.

"Split? This is German, baby, not Dutch. Besides—I'm not paying for this…. *Handsome* is."

Oh hell, she'd heard this one before. She hopped off the curb and walked towards him. "Is that really the smartest thing? What happened to all the blather about being cautious with your money and taking things slow? Remember that whole speech about feeling *sheepish* about things?"

"Yes, well…what can I say—*I've evolved*."

"Evolved?"

"Yep. I'm afraid that poor cautious fellow died somewhere over the ocean. Putz was a bit too uptight anyway—but the new one is guaranteed more fun."

"Had a little epiphany, did we?"

"No, not really… more of breakdown I'd say—but that got me thinking—which got me rearranging things a bit. What can I say? Seven hours gracing the roof of the Earth can get a chap in one of those *expansive* moods—at least temporarily. So, in my temporary insanity of reprioritizing, a jet black roadster with the leather drop-top, 3.2 liter, 24 valve inline 6 cylinder turbo with 330 horses, suddenly became an absolute priority…. I even got the bigger engine—so we wouldn't be shown up out on the street." He laughed, before gesturing back to the bunkhouse. "These fine fellows here merely facilitated the reality of my unconscious revelations—therefore you can see the whole thing was a bit preordained to begin with…. So how about you jump in before I come to my senses and buy us a bus pass?"

She was obviously a non-believer. "So what you're saying is that you needed a BMW for equilibrium? I'd be scared to see what you'd need for perspective."

"Only my mother and my shrink know for sure, honey."

Liam continued, "Look, this car is not just some token ego accessory. I mean, do I look like some crass, bougie, yuppie apologist to you? Hell, we're going to *need* this," he touched the hood, gathering up the forces of unequivocal righteousness. "before this thing is over."

He paused, adding some Atticus-like gravitas to his voice. "You see *out there* is a whole world beyond our ken. Small, narrow, rain-slicked roads, festooned with wandering livestock and, worse, wandering bands of deranged hooligan youth, all doing the their best Eddie Irvine impersonations between lager flavored bouts of The Big Spit."

"Who the hell is Eddie Irvine?"

Liam cut her off. "So we'll be needing a getaway car with the emergency acceleration, tight handling, and proper coloring for all those last minute death defying sheep avoidance maneuvers."

She was hardly swayed, but his conviction was impressive. They were kindred souls after all. "You're a big boy, Warbucks," she sighed, "it's your money."

He grew serious for a moment "No, it's really not—and therein lies the fun."

"…. I don't know."

"Look, you're not splitting anything with me. I've more or less kidnapped you into this thing anyway—am I right?"

"Gee, Liam, that's a *romantic* way of putting it."

"Exactly, so c'mon, *bella donna*, hop in, let me whisk you away in this pride of The Fatherland. We've got to do this thing right…. Besides they know me here, there's a certain image to maintain."

"As what? A laboring jack-off?"

"Every village needs its idiot, my dear."

She was wavering, but it was time to fold. "All right, all right—persuasive as ever."

She came around to the far side where Liam was already holding open the door, "Let me just double-check something here—you never actually *believe* I buy any of this rubbish?"

"Oedipal musings and jet-lagged judgments aside—of course not.... If it makes you feel charitable, let's just say this car makes my dink feel bigger—how's *that?*"

She climbed on in. "Sick sick sick—you sicko."

"Sick? Maybe." He closed her door. "More of an American original, I'd say."

The agitated young fellow came out to see them off. He handed Liam his paperwork and cast a slightly nervous eye on the Beamer. It wasn't everyday he had to traffic emergency third party lease consignments for oddball Yanks with twitchy dispositions and sleepy bloodshot eyes.

"Ah, she's lovely isn't she? You need directions, Mr. O'Shea? Know where you're going?"

"Yep, downtown. But I thought I'd take her around the loop for awhile, open it up, get a feel for things." Liam could sense the man's exasperation. He thought to put him at ease. "Don't worry, you can relax—we're *trustworthy* people."

Liam was rising. He could feel the next wind of the morning coming on. He shot the young fellow with the suspicious mind a reassuring smile, and walked over to the wrong side of the $75,000 car.

"Where's the wheel?"

"It's on this side, honey."

".... No shit?"

He gave the rental man a sheepish look and started 'round to the drivers side. "Like I said, don't worry, we're *respectable* people."

He started up the car, eased it into first, revved it good, and headed out past the toll island towards the open road.

Christopher M. Basso

Chapter Six
Dirty Old Town

"Son of a bitch," Liam muttered, glancing down from the road long enough to smack the dashboard. "See if you can get this Goddamn radio working?" O'Shea had one hand on the wheel, a wayward eye on the sound system, and a spare eye on the traffic bearing down from the wrong side of the thoroughfare—a trinity of sensory overloads matching each ragged shimmy and shake of the roadster.

"May the road rise before you, and may you be in Heaven an hour before the Devil knows you're gone." Where had he heard that? An *evil* little chestnut of a prayer for the start of such an automotive adventure. He lit up the next cigarette of the morning and glanced again at the intricate array of whirls and dials along the dashboard. He could only fathom what half this stuff was for, but that's what you're paying for he thought—*The Show*. The accelerator was, for the time being, mashed to the floorboard with all the righteous zeal of an early morning dash, as the roadster sped down the frontage road leading them off the airport property.

These were some fine proving grounds, nice and empty, some twists here and there—*good straightaway*. He gathered there were only a few moments left to get his feet wet before the graduate course of Dublin's one real stretch of open road, the M50. He opened the car up, pegging the inlined six cylinders up to seventy-five in third gear—4900 rpms, just below the red line—nice pick up, good acceleration—can feel the blood *pooling* at the back of the brain he thought.... Just as promised.

"C'mon, give this thing a whack would you?" He shouted over the wind scream as she fumbled through her bag looking for a pair of sunglasses. "We need volume, clarity, bass! A nice counterpoint to the chaos–a *rising* sound."

Ever the granola girl, she already had her flip-flops off and was resting one leg beneath her in a half meditative Eastern crouch.

"All right, all right, Marconi, I'm on it."

The sun came out from behind the clouds as the last of the early morning fog burned off—a nice clean light on quick Irish morning. His focus shifted to the large roundabout coming up fast. Remember bear to the *left*—all things to the *left*...Damn, quite a little situation to find yourself in—bombing the early morning rush hour of a major metropolitan area where they drive down the *wrong* side of the road and don't give style points to the tourists—all this after you've spent a sleepless night abusing a cupboard full of booze and top shelf pharmaceuticals.

This simple primer for life and the Irish road continued rattling around his mind as they passed a steady stream of slower traffic. These first few minutes in-country were always a leap of faith for Liam, a crucible testing the grit, reflexes, and resolve of an otherwise American trained brain.... A not all together agreeable paradigm at that.

In the past this game would start out in the Dodge City meets Mad Max environs of North Dublin where he'd earned his road warrior stripes in his cousin's Vauxhall Corsa, with a clear mind and a good night's rest—not some drowsy early morning jetlagged barnstorming act into the nexus of Greater Dublin's traffic malaise, and most certainly not in a wickedly expensive, albeit fully insured, sports car.

He repeated the left leaning mantra in his mind a few more times till it began to feel at one and fully integrated with his *baser* instincts. Liam knew if they could just survive the first few miles all would be well. As always, his brain would start to remember and the deeper dregs of this shit would surface from the long recessed and repressed annals of his Celtic genome. Like a man waking from a dream his brain would remember bygone days of piloting some donkey cart down the left side of these same roads, dodging streetcars and runaway carriages, and from there the evolution would proceed *quite nicely*. His face caught a rush of the fresh morning air—driving as fast as the mind could think—this definitely seemed the way to go.

It must be said that this was the best case scenario. For now, extreme fatigue was causing a host of synaptic misfires making it ever easier for his noodle to miss the mark. The endorphins were swirling round his brain like the cavalry just over the horizon waiting to charge in and fill the gaps in dicey logic and random thought. But the commandant had blown them out the night before with a hell-on chemical binge that left nothing but a pleasant numbness in its wake—a fresh slate, divorced from the smarter instincts and fostering an early morning sense of the phony tough and the crazy brave.

While he pondered the fates, she was able to find the elusive route to the power switch and soon Dave Fanning's omnipotent RTÉ morning show was blasting through the ten Alpine speakers. Yes, louder, more volume—scare the *bejesus* out of these people; let them know you were back in town.

Besides, this was a vacation, one of those rare instances when it's ok to be that person blaring the radio—just for fuck's sake have some taste. Don't foul the sweet morning air with any of that poisonous weak-willed, radio friendly shit.... Hell, find the right combination of volume and wind speed and you might even reach those Bolshevik loving cradle robbers as they hurtled down the runway on the 8:10 back to America. The Brothers Gallagher snarling "Live Forever" at full tilt added a nostalgic poignancy to the giddy abandon of the moment.

"Shit," he mumbled as the cobwebs continued to clear. This bold little psycho-physiological experiment of impetus stealing the reins of logic was feeling more and more like a success. He soon banished, two times quick, any lingering furtive calls for sleep. A nice Ian Brown track queued up next on the Manchester revival—just the sort of ominous rising sound necessary for the moment. The stone was moved and the boy was feeling more than a tad resurrected.

Christopher M. Basso

He slipstreamed the ground-hugging beast through the left lane and briefly out onto the shoulder, before another quick jig back across the centerline ahead of some slow-minded Irish Telecom trucks, before gliding smoothly back onto the M50 proper.... Not the wisest of moves, but this was automotive Darwinism at its finest.

He could feel the reproachful once-over being shot his way, "C'mon now," he assured her, "It's the only way they'll respect you..."

.... *Right*. What color was the threat level on this one she wondered? And which was the bigger mystery—the all too happy glint in his tired eyes, or the odd, easygoing sense of propriety from a man whose father recently bought the farm in a fast moving sports car?

Liam downshifted to third for shits and giggles, red lining the engine again in a mad jolt of speed that would have made Chuck Yeager proud. Once again, a fine rush of blood to the back of the head and a quick flash of tunnel vision.... No hitch in this monster's giddy up.

The fascinating permutations of the moment boggled the mind, but Sara kept her cool. Not to say the whole endeavor wasn't a bit terrifying, but she took great pride in not showing it. Her hair whipped around slightly in the breeze as they sailed along the valley of the carriageway with tall lofty hedges bordering either side. Every now and then there was a break in the barriers and she could see out beyond the highway, towards the low lying flat land. A mixture of old sheep pastures and the new townhouse complexes which sprang up between them like testaments to the recent prosperity, or weeds sullying some former idyllic way of life.

She did break away long enough to glance over and see the most bizarre smile spreading across her boy's face. The same chap who'd just played an irrational, white-knuckled, chemically induced game of karmic chicken with the safest form of transport known to man was now weaving in and out of twisted little automotive showdowns with any lad willing. He seemed to be having a bit too much fun with it. Each gyrating squeal of the tires or hairpin shuffle brought about some new shade of wild gesticulation and a host of distinctly American gestures that made sure these foreigners *got the point*.

"My boy—ever the diplomat."

"They're like lions, they *sense* fear—you got to be firm with this crowd."

"Maybe they're just "nosing" the sick one from the herd....You know, the one that's acting weird?"

"That ain't me sister—I'm a man fully *in control*."

He moved again across an open lane, this time passing a large wobbly hay truck. They brushed close for a second and the drop top openness of the roadster brought faint hits of burning tire and summer hay into the car in a not altogether pleasant fashion.

She thought best to gain entrance into the warped mind wearing such a smile.

"Gee, Liam you look...happy?"

"Well, I think I'm getting my sea legs here," he paused, momentarily reflective. "A few more miles of this and I should be as right as rain."

"But how are you holding up?"

"I'm coming to, coming to…. Don't need this anymore," he handed over the large coffee cup ringed with small green shamrocks, purchased several mindsets ago near the baggage carousel.

"Want some?"

"I'll pass." She admired the tackiness of it, "Now all we need are some fuzzy shamrock dice for the rearview and we're set."

"Don't joke—I know where we can get those."

"Even at this hour?"

"*Especially* at this hour."

A terrible bit of bygone suddenly blared out the speakers—a Diddy back when Puffy, crimping a Sting long since the Gordon.

"*Creeping Jesus*, I hate that shit, makes my ears wanna bleed.... That was ear pain fifteen years ago—damn, some people should just keep it shut."

"I agree. How about some news?" She ran through the satellite stations before landing on the BBC World Service.

"I don't know about you, but I like to stay *on top* of things." O'Shea offered up between bites of a candy bar he'd snagged from the flight.

"All right then," she turned up the volume, "the comedy portion of our programming."

"*... If I were asked to use one word to describe the situation in Afghanistan today, I would choose the word–hope,*" *Mr. Wagner said, speaking in Amsterdam to the meeting on* The Tribunal, *the decade long plan to promote stability and development in the strife-torn country. "There is new hope that the people and Government of Afghanistan are overcoming these incredible challenges and working together to rebuild their country and their lives, after years of war, dictatorship and..."*

"No, no, no I can't listen to that shit—it's an epic downer."

She took another look at him.... The man was definitely *there*, but something else was going down, some sort of wild, thousand-yard stare in the eyes.

"You sure you're with it? You don't look so hot."

"What? I feel better than I have in ages. Don't let the slightly ashen, walking wounded thing fool you. I'm having *quite the time* over here. Not a care in the world." His eyes danced along the road before them, "Damn, I can't remember the last time I couldn't be bothered with this or that.... Might have been in utero?"

"Yes, well, some might say you've been a bit *uptight* in the past," she chuckled, before catching herself.

"No don't worry—couldn't agree more."

"Really?"

"You bet. Life's been playing me the sap for far too long. Longer than I'd care to remember."

"How so?"

"How so? Hmm, where to begin? I was born, I grew up, I went away, I fell into disgrace, etc, blah, etc.... Maybe a more modern Copperfield? I call my therapist, I think I feel a moment coming on, I am in catharsis, I have an epiphany—verse, chorus, verse."

"*What* are you on about?"

"I'm not sure yet," he smiled, "but you'll be the first to know."

"I think the fresh air put the zap on you."

"Indeed. I feel rather awake. Not sure why, but most likely it's a product of—"

"Your *evolution*?" She chuckled.

"Yep, all that guff is behind me now.... I'm setting the bar lower to go higher."

"Sounds like a plan."

"A man with a plan," he marveled. "I've never been one of those.... Unless worrying is a plan?" He was trying to light an uncooperative cigarette, "Do know what a drag it's been to have other people set the agenda for you? Feel like all that noise has stunted me somehow." He gave up and tossed it out the window. "I always knew I was missing out on something, but it's hard to think about windmills when the real world comes creeping into your wee corner of the sandbox."

".... Hmm, sounds a bit melodramatic to me."

"Well, *you* grew up with it. It is different."

She wasn't much in the mood for his power to the people act, "Well, only if you make it so."

"You grew up with it, I grew up *around* it—there's a difference."

"Maybe if you're a jaded bastard—but that's not you my friend."

Christopher M. Basso

"Whoa.... I think I sense a compliment coming on?"

"Well, yes—your sense of conviction has always been a strong point."

"Yeah, well, don't worry; this is just a little field trip. I'm not going too far up the river."

Liam dodged, bobbed and shot on ahead, this time past a bus, weaving right then left, trying to mind the gap before an equally nimble Jaguar did it for him. The speedometer danced across ninety for a few seconds before he reeled it back in. His eyes quickly spied the rearview for any signs of flashing lights but the coast was clear.

On some level O'Shea could take comfort that this was, after all, a place where you really had to *work at it* to draw the ire of the local constabulary. Unlike the rule crazy freaks back home these boys had better things to do than garrote the tourists for the occasional misguided burst of speed here and there...or so he hoped.

The M50 formed a long crescent arc that ringed around the city from north to south—a twenty-five mile drag starting around the airport on the northern outskirts of the city before reaching its end near the swank southern suburbs. They'd recently widened the entire thing, and he wasn't quite sure what the Irish would make of HOV's and eight lanes to hold you. But this was a nice upgrade all the same. Much better than the beastly traffic he remembered from way back when; the pastiche of donkey paths holding hands which the locals called *roads*. This was a clever if not delaying solution to the tangled web of Dublin traffic that'd only been given the occasional "rethink" since the first bands of nefarious Norsemen sailed in the river Liffey and wrecked shit up many moons ago.

This was progress personified, and a much more civilized way of doing things, especially to any overfed American accustomed to blazing from points A to B at top speeds, unimpeded by the constraints of history and narrow minded mores of civil engineering. They were soon zipping through the shiny new toll plaza at Clondalkin Road, when Liam hit the off ramp, swerving left and shooting up across the lights. The roadster hugged the ground like a pure hell-fire thoroughbred, doing the twin barreled cha cha through a smaller roundabout before evening out again. They were now moving east along the busy surface streets, following the signs for the Quays, Temple Bar, and the heart of fair Dublin City.

"You see," he began, "these roads are *killer*. No grid, no numbers, every street has a name, some streets have the same name, then there's lots of one ways—one ways suddenly changing directions, one ways just ending down some back alley—it's mad. Even the locals still get lost around here."

She looked up, "Sounds like a real mess.... How about it sport? Going to make it?"

"I feel good," pausing long enough to run another red light and ignoring the withering curses of Irish-inflected road rage. "Nice day out here, working on my second wind, straight shot to the hotel—I think. Anyway, we'll see."

The busy clip soon slowed to a crawl as the breezy rural feel around the fringe had shaded over to the looming frame of a traffic choked city. While this might have hampered the expeditious intent, it gave tour guide O'Shea a chance to reel off some of the sights which were rising into view.

Although, *rising* would have been a rather subjective term as Dublin was a low slung kind of town. But something was different, something instantly recognizable. In the near distance were close to a dozen massive yellow tower cranes looming large over the skyline. They were spread out across the landscape like ordered columns of infantry on a map. Big twenty-story boomers, each one some giant sentinel of progress. Impressive things to be sure, but they were also the scale dramatizing a local shortcoming.

"Not many tall buildings around here?" She said.

"Yep, poor ol' Dublin, it's a bit vertically challenged I'll give you that...but don't get all Shaudenfreuden on me—only the only the fallacies of Pharisees need tall buildings—and we Dubliners are very secure with ourselves."

"What we?" She laughed.

"I've got the passport to prove it."

"You've got the passport because you're good with

paperwork and have a tragic lack of hobbies."

"Never mind that; consider it an honorarium with the locals, or so they've told me—besides a short city likes its tall tales."

"And you've got one?"

"Really now—is that even a question? Anyway, my uncle once told me it was the Church who were originally behind it—a massive conspiracy along the lines of The Priory of Sion or the Illuminati. Except this one featured a covetous clergy wanting to make sure there was nothing taller than the steeples of the cathedrals, lest these pilgrims forget where the real power lay. Along the way throw in a fair share of collusion from the Protestants and their puppeteers back in Westminster; just the types who were more than happy to play along with this sort of crass logic, and you've got yourself a rather intransigent building code I'd say.... Hence our hunkered down fair little city."

"And you believe it?"

"Oh yeah, on the scale of pub room piss taking this would have to rank pretty low. But then again, that mad bastard uncle of mine thinks the Queen's been in cahoots with the Vatican and the Rothschild-Hanovers since the Battle of the Boyne fostering all the ills of the world."

"*Oh,* that would be your Uncle Fintan then?"

Liam raised an eyebrow, "Yes."

".... Can't imagine he's even seen the inside of a church."

"Careful—sounds like your drifting towards some slander over there. Besides he was just happy to be in New York.... He didn't realize that sort of thing was frowned upon."

"Really? Well maybe the whole incarceration, deportation thing set him straight...not to mention the dry cleaning bills."

"C'mon you're just pissed you had to see the inside of a police station at three in the morning. A little different than some kegger-fueled run in with the Cornell cops wouldn't you say?" He smiled, "*Besides*, all that time in New York and you'd never been out to Rikers."

"Yes, well, I'll always have the wonderful memories of a night well spent. Just hope his son is cut from some different cloth."

"Kevin Delaney? Why yes, much more of a poet's head on that one. Chances for incarceration are fairly minimal."

"And what of him, any word?"

"Nope. He's a hard one to track down, that boy, but he's got the dates and the hotel. I'm sure he'll turn up soon enough."

They passed another towering church; a façade of imposing stone carved with ornate reliefs and grinning gargoyles. All life, architecture, and function seemed to flow towards its doors. "Maybe that whack-a-doodle uncle of yours was on to something?"

"Aww, that's sweet of you to say, but the fellow *is* actually a bit of a wing nut—just another lost soul knee deep in his conspiracy theories.... The sad truth is this place was stone broke for so long that there was rarely any money to throw into something beyond the utilitarian and the functional, and what little was left was usually sent someplace else. But look at all these cranes—something's up."

He thought for a moment, "But the part about the Church having too much pull is sadly true. Maybe not as draconian as it used to be, but still nothing like you'd recognize. Damn, you couldn't even buy a *Playboy* around here back in the day, and *condoms*—it was probably easier to score heroin than rubbers.... Couldn't buy condoms or girlie mags, and your girlie mags and condoms often make for a guilty churchgoer fair. That's a chiasmus that'll lead you down a some dark roads."

"Gee, never thought of it that way—but obviously you have." She laughed.

"But of course my love."

He took a deep breath enjoying the crisp morning air, "Ah sure—Joyce said the bricks of sorrow built the bones of the Church.... That sort of guff would scare the straight piss out of some pagan Viking or dirt poor farmer, but how's it going to phase that guy?" He gestured towards a young fellow weaving past them on a speeding Triumph Tiger 1050, resplendent in a crisp bespoke suit, John Lobb Oxfords, and stylish urban man-pack.

"I don't know, crib his bandwidth?" She smiled, arching her back and stretching out in the seat, "Besides professor, it was—*Brothels are built with the bricks of religion.* You need to brush up on your Joyce, Mr. Home Team."

"There you go again, pedantic as ever! Hell, you'd have to be from money to have that kind of useless mash come rolling off the tongue."

For a few slow minutes they moved along the southern edge of Phoenix Park paralleling the river, both of them heading downtown as it were. The local bullshitenspiel trafficked in some nonsense about Dublin being a city of rivers—forty-four to be exact, but that would require stretching the notion of streams and puddles to some Munchausen proportions.

For the reality based community there was only one—the Liffey, which cut like a dull green knife through the heart of the city. He shot a quick glance towards the slow snaking waterway. Surely something beautiful back at bend of bay up in the Wicklow mountains to the south, but beaten up twice quick as it meandered its meandering self slowly through the growing chorus of man and his blind-eyed Lorax mischief.

They soon passed the rail yard at Heuston Station and crossed the Liffey, moving east now along its northern shore. Back across the river they could see the massive Guinness complex at St. James Gate, a sure sign they'd entered the city proper. Central Dublin lies across the Liffey as it makes its final turgid push towards the shallow silty estuary at the mouth of Dublin Bay. Traffic runs quick, along the quays lining either side of the river, in a fairly efficient one way, east-west layout. The *real* art would be figuring where to swing around to reach their hotel along the opposite side of the riverbank.

Next was the imposing Corinthian façade and faded green dome of the "Four Courts". The courthouse was a long time feature on the Dublin skyline—if you ventured up close you could still spy the odd bullet hole from Easter 1916. A regal beauty in this city of three and four story Georgian houses, warehouses, public houses, illicit houses, and townhouses. And just beyond that loomed the antithesis of the stately Four Courts; the sixteen story Liberty Hall building in all its ragged, reeking 1960's clergy defying glory—an ugly old bestial thing, whose busted functionality made a much more persuasive case for the stunted building code than anything The Church had to throw at them.

All in all not much to rub your eyes at, but a ground hugging city can produce the welcoming effect of eliminating the imposing sense of scale, and the claustrophobic feeling of being surrounded by immense buildings blocking out everything between the sun and the horizon. The small scale gave Dublin an open, sprawling feel—like an expansive stretch of one large uninterrupted neighborhood. It was easily navigated and highly manageable...on foot at least.

The traffic gods smote them again at the set of lights just past the Four Courts—no clever little slipstream scams here, unless the roadster had some amphibious capabilities they'd failed to mention. His burnt out mind might have been betraying him, but that sure looked a lot like their hotel just up ahead, rising up quick in the next minute or two. Some creative intuition would soon be needed, lest the traffic mill make a quick grist of them.

.... What an ignominious ending that would be—dashed into the juggernaut maze all the way back to the airport with his roadster between his legs. This would just about completely destroy his local bona fides, but that was airplane logic from another lifetime—he'd just have to roll with it and make due with the pieces.

For the moment there was no escape. He eased back in the low-slung seat, spying some Dubliners waiting under the shade of an old city oak for one of those lumbering double-decker coaches. His mind snapped-to in one of those abrupt, fitful recall moments; quick thoughts and cold sweat spent on those monstrous tin cans which were suddenly appearing like sharks sliding off on the periphery, growing closer with each passing street. Soon, the bastards would be in the proper mix of things and that would be some cause for concern. If memory served correct those boys made their daily rounds with the same burnt, steely-eyed abandon as a toasted foreigner who'd just stepped off a plane at dawn. *Bus Átha Cliath,* a formidable enemy

Christopher M. Basso

indeed.

Fortified for the coming battle, his mind drifted back to the young Dubliners milling about the bus stop, many smartly dressed; sharp suits and designer labels, trendy sorts, jabbering away on cellulars and fiddling with iPhones or BlackBerrys. O'Shea, for his part, had tossed his BlackBerry into the bed of a passing pickup truck a few months earlier, back Bermuda way.

A quick trip down to sell Handsome's sandbagger condo turned into a two-week jag of genteel island pleasures. Standing outside the Hog Penny Tavern late one night dancing with some pleasant thoughts, several sheets to the wind and, in a stunning moment of clarity, he gave that little pixilated demon the heave-ho. Life was too short for that sort of guff.

The lights changed and O'Shea fled this foul cluster of yuppish modernity with a stylish screech of the tires and just the right amount of flair for the occasion. The startled queue did a quick double take—well, *here we go again*—another dingbat tourist terrorizing our city streets. When were the powers that be going to do something about it? But perhaps her reproachful stare said it all.

"Oh, I'm just fucking with them a bit is all," he assured her. "Don't worry—*I'll behave*." It was a hollow mea culpa of the first order. His brain was zipping along far too fast to inject any sort of sincerity into the moment. But what was so *different* since the last time he'd been out this way—at least beyond the boom cranes and the burgeoning consumer lifestyle?

There was a palpable sense of it in the air, an energy, something slick about the way things were moving, something that had nothing to do with either of them, or the fast tracking purr of the Bavarian Beast. He'd been away, but he still had some sense of the place, something stored in the rainy day corners of his mind. He'd spent many a misplaced day down here in the city center, and with the exception of a Gaelic League sponsored riot or two, the place generally had all the hard charging bravado of a funeral—lots of sad eyes and dreams deferred. That kind of energy was a cancer, the anti-zeitgeist—and this poor place had always been rendered in some terminal shade.

Ah, poor dear dirty Dublin, he felt a great love and

allegiance for his titular homeland in these little reflective moments. Something about the perseverance and melancholy of watching life *slide out of view* generally appealed to the pampered foreign eyes of a straight-on day-tripper. Besides, to fancy yourself the righteous standard bearer for the downtrodden was an easy enough gig when you could buy a ticket and flee once the act got *too heavy*. But that brand of emigrant glibness seemed far away and out of step with the moment. The twenty minutes from the airport was all the proof he needed. The medicine must have taken 'cause these broad-beaming Yuppie jokers looked the part—bright eyed and well heeled, armed to the teeth with macchiatos and protein shakes—off to plunder whatever the day had to offer.

You could feel the sea change in the faces and you could *see* it in the Celtic style Marshall Plan which had taken hold of the downtown. It was in the chain link fences and drywall of a building site, in the ornate patchwork of scaffolding over old facades, but mostly it was in those yellow cranes casting their long shadows over the entire skyline. To look at it now, all bright colors, and reclaimed architecture—finally a reality to match the touched-up picture postcards and "Georgian Doors of Dublin" posters they pedaled at the airport and in the nostalgia shops back home. Jettisoned too might have been that tale of two cities vibe, which had formed the shoddy pillars for all the rot around here.

The Liffey was more than just a river to the locals. It'd helped to shape, define, and sustain the character of the city in some very drastic, lasting ways…. Which was funny in a sense because the damn thing was so small; never much more than a slight, narrow concern. The right sized stone and a strong arm could clear it easily in most places, but in the ways that mattered it halved this city as cleanly as a long stretch of some vast ocean. We've shrunk all the oceans in this world, but once upon a time they mattered. Ship captains from England and The Netherlands would sail up the river and whichever side they dropped anchor was the side that worked that day. A couple of very angry tribes staring across the banks at one another. Bad blood that endured; bridges would just one day make it easier to go after one another.

A simple geography set in motion all the pieces that cut across Dublin to this day—a working class northern shore full of real "Black Dubs" and a genteel dandyman's fortification to the south manned by *everyone else*; merchants, academics, teetotalers—Protestants. Maybe that's a crass generality, but generalities, like stereotypes, the only things collectively remembered and in that collective brain they carried the greatest wattage…and were the hardest bastards to show the door.

But they could occasionally, with the right kind of medicine, be sacrificed, blown to bits on the back of some new zeitgeist…. Maybe the Liffey had finally been rendered back to what it was, a somewhat charming if not derelict waterway—something for the tourists to take a few snapshots of and toss a coin or two to conjure the ironies of good fortune.

In one hot minute they arrived at the general confusion of O'Connell Bridge, where for once he made the blessed choice, turning quickly across the span, which promptly spun them through another roundabout, and left them finally heading west along the southern side of the river, now moving at a rugged clip towards Wellington Quay.

Within moments they pulled up to the stylish brick and sandstone façade of The Essex Hotel. O'Shea nudged the roadster onto the small shoulder near the main doors. As he hopped out on the good foot, one of those coaches whizzed by a bit too close for comfort. Undeterred he continued around and opened her door.

"Don't waste much space do they?"

"Shit, I'm surprised they gave us a lane." He said. Thought we might have to circle around a few times, pitching our stuff out the window."

A young man in a dark gray suit came out to greet them, while another wrestled the suitcases from a startled O'Shea's steely, kung-fu death grip and sped them inside.

"Good morning, welcome to The Essex—Sir, Miss, if you'd follow me to reception."

They fell in line behind the younger man while a third porter appeared, took the keys from Liam, jumped in and disappeared for parts unknown. The whole operation took less then thirty seconds, and went down with the practiced grace of a

Talladega pit crew, prompting Liam to whisper something about, "Either they're exceptional at this, or we just got jacked."

They walked into the churchlike stillness of a small lobby. The ambiance was decidedly low key; alabaster hued walls bordered at all points by light colored beams of oak and white ash. A palette rich in shades of blue, crimson and ochre offset the austerity around the edges. Tall slender widows of beveled glass flooded the foyer with a calm, brilliant light.

The Zen-like solemnity of the place was a welcome relief from the hellish mishmash brewing on the other side of the windows. He could see the tops of trucks and buses moving past, but they were silent and seemed suddenly very far away. The disconnect was drastic and put them both immediately at ease. There had to be some irony in this, finding a respite in the middle of the noise, finding the contradiction in the heart of things.

An attractive young lady with the high cheek bones and sharp blue eyes of some latter-day Valkyrie appeared from behind the counter to greet them. She snapped to work with a quick and breezy efficiency—name, rank, credit card, passports, wake up, turn down? "Is this your first stay with us?" Her accent was a lovely sort of honey, faint with soft notes.

"As a matter of fact it is."

"Welcome to The Essex, when we've finished checking you in," She gestured towards another genetic wunderkind who appeared in true *Stepford* fashion off in the wings, "Sebastian will give you a tour of the hotel."

"Thanks, that'd be grand," he said, before turning to Sara. "So why don't you take a spin around and let me settle up here."

"You don't want to see the hotel?"

"I'll wait for the movie."

".... All right." She studied him for a second. He had the same dreamy eyed expression as the rental lot. "Guess I'll see you upstairs then?"

"Indeed." He gave her a kiss on the cheek. She strolled off with the concierge, her mind somewhere between the slightly

Christopher M. Basso

curious and generally amused.

This was his in. He'd taken quick stock of the understated opulence of the place and got to thinking; the slightly malevolent tinge having returned to his eyes—taste, restraint, his better judgment they held no sway here. Between thought and expression *indeed*—Lou Reed seemed about a proper a co-pilot as any for a little stroll on the wild side.

He kept the third eye on Sara till she'd rounded the corner and was safely gone. Then leaning ever so slightly across the fine marble face of the counter, "Look, maybe you can help me? I'd like to surprise her."

The concierge led her down the hallway past the scent of fresh flowers and polished teak towards the hotel's bar—a striking eight sided room sitting beneath a large dome of frosted glass whose color could be adjusted to mimic either the bright shades of day or the dreamy boozy wantonness of the nighttime. The bar was empty, save for two Danish businessmen types chatting quietly over a beer in the far corner. The nighttime scents of stout and cigarettes were long gone, just the fresh buzz of the morning air and the slight whirling drone from a vacuum cleaner zipping along in some nearby room.

"This is our Octagon Bar. It's quite popular and tends to fill up most nights, but give us a call and we can always find you a table." He smiled as they kept down the hallway, "The Essex opened in 1874 as a modest inn and public house. It was especially popular with visiting clergy and councilman from the country." He opened the double sided doors to the restaurant, "There have been seven different owners in that time, the last, unfortunately, let it fall into a state of *serious* disrepair. The current ownership purchased the property in the mid-nineties, shuttered the doors for three years of renovations and reinvented the hotel as a boutique property."

They continued past a large fresco rendering of Europe in the dull white and green shades of a navigator's map. Ireland had been slid over from the ass end of Western Europe to a place of central prominence.

"We'll be closing again next year for another round of expansion and renovation."

"Really?"

"Yes, it's amazing, the hotel business in this city has become like the arms race—always escalating."

"Well, you've sold me, it's lovely. I like the stillness."

He seemed to grasp the implication, "Yes, this is quite possibly the *loudest* small city you'll ever come across—so we make an extra effort to keep things quiet."

He had a slight, but untraceable accent, "So, where are you visiting us from?"

"New York, well, I live in New York, but I'm from California…. How about yourself?"

"The Netherlands, but I'd have to say I'm from all over as well."

They kept down a long hallway, warm light falling through the transom glass along the walls.

"That's what I love about America you know," he zipped suddenly past propriety, into the realm of something animated, "*Movement*. Americans have no qualms about abandoning the past and reinventing themselves in some future. I grew up here, I see myself there, I make it happen."

His smile was something of a crazed Kerouac acolyte indeed, and definitely one too many movies had been shoved down the old boy's gullet, but it was a very sweet and earnest affectation all the same.

"Yeah, I guess that's about the lay of it," she smiled, "but that's kind of your trade too, the hotel business I mean. Must be exciting to meet people from all over the world?"

After spending the better part of the last year waiting on the perfunctory, to crassly rude, to occasionally deviant-kinky whims of the Euro jet set and bankrolled Subcontinent types; it seemed they were now sharing a mutually *fine* delusion of the other's latitude.

"Indeed it is," he leaned a bit closer, his voice shading to a conspiratorial flair, "*Actually*, everyone who works here is also from someplace else. I think the only Irish I've seen in this hotel are the ones who own it. Mix in our guests who are from everywhere else in between and we've brewed a nice little international atmosphere. It's a bit like *Casablanca*…were it always raining in Casablanca."

There was one more common room to visit—a smaller space set up right off the main lobby by the elevator. A beautiful high walled room, matched up with the same clean lines and Spartan minimalist vibe of the restaurant. Several leather couches and chairs were arranged at parallel angles with a long Mission style table cutting the room in two, continuing the theme of simple elegant Shaker wood work.

The long antique table was topped with a huge arrangement of Tiger Lilies—wildflowers which changed daily with the seasons. While the ol' élan factor ran strong through the place, there were also smaller touches that set it apart from the soulless eye candy monoliths raised from the void of some marketing team's dreams that you'd find in all the trendier cities.

Small nicks and imperfections dotted the woodwork, the quirky spaces and old world touches were all still there—all signs of a loving restoration mixed in with a fair amount of respect for the ghosts that had passed through these walls down all the days. It was a pile of bricks that embraced the notion of merely marking a space in time; content as a symbol of the moment and of the age.

When they reached reception several more guests had arrived and were queued up around the check in. The quiet lobby now fairly buzzed with activity, as the well-oiled machinery of porters and bellman moved suitcases here and there. They rounded back towards the Valkyrie behind the front desk.

"Mrs. O'Shea, your husband has gone ahead with the luggage, Sebastian could you please take her up to 508."

"No, that's ok—I won't keep you any longer. You look like you've got your hands full."

"Yes," he sighed, looking at the small line of people awaiting his services. "It's what I'm good at—well, if the hotel thing doesn't pan out, I might have a future in the museum business, or maybe a theme park?"

"I'd stick to the day job."

He smiled. "Please let me know if you need anything, Miss, it's been lovely chatting with you…. Oh, and I almost forgot, you'll need this." He handed her a small brass security key.

"What's this?"

"The key to the elevator; private floor."

Sara stepped into the tight space of the ornate iron cage lift and turned the key for five. A slow ascent up the old creaking frame, suddenly feeling very far from home, very far from life, and very far from the things she'd known. Calm austerity can sometimes breed a paranoia all its own.

Walking out on to the fifth floor landing she made a right down a long hallway lined on either side with heavy wooden doors. There was a faint but pleasant scent of lilacs and jasmine. Each of the old fashioned doors was a pale colored oak with shiny brass back plates and small pyramid eyepieces peering out at you. She rounded the corner to a smaller alcove and another sturdy door tilted slightly ajar.

Inside she could hear the sounds of Liam and the porters talking. Sara pushed back the door and stepped into a large, high ceiling suite of three rooms laid out in the fashion of a railroad flat, and arranged in the same minimalist Arts and Crafts style as the common rooms. The walls had a pleasant alabaster tinge, bordered with light colored wood, and finished with cool shades of blue and gold, highlighted in the carpets and linens.

Liam was in the sitting room at the far end of the suite with two of the porters, and the three of them were trying to get the television-computer hybrid up and running. A perplexed look sat across O'Shea's face as he fiddled with the controls. From where she was standing it didn't look all too promising.

"Christ, I'm a dunce."

"Maybe we should sit you in the corner wearing a funny hat?" She offered from the wings.

"Hey you—these nice fellas were just showing the

Luddite how to work the multimedia center. Did you see anything good?"

"Saw it all."

"And—what's the word?"

She gave him the thumbs up and slid across the room taking a seat on the steps leading up to the roof top terrace.

The apes clubbed the big black obelisk a few more times before the prompt screen appeared and they were off and running—cable and satellite were a go, movie library on demand, an Xbox—for *die kinder* of any age, high speed internet, an automated room service system, with spa options all at your fingertips.

"*Jesus*, why leave the room?" O'Shea muttered. He tipped both men and saw them to the door.

"I gave them five each, think that was enough?"

"I don't know. I suppose so."

She surveyed their new digs; a set of sharp leather couches faced on another in the sitting room, and a lovely pedestal desk sat near the large oval windows overlooking the Liffey. There were fresh flowers and various bits of esoteric artwork along the mantel; crisp air was on the heavy, and the whirl of a fully stocked minibar purred from behind a stately cedar armoire. A half drawn woven scrim filtered the Sun's light, letting in just the right mix of breeze, warm light, and muted distant energy from the street below.

"This is quite the pile of bricks you've landed on—good choice Liam James."

"Not bad—right?" He unwrapped a piece of chocolate from the welcoming tray, "What were you expecting—doilies and old lace?"

"I don't know—maybe more like kippers and a corpse?"

"Yes, well I have my moments," he looked appraisingly about the place. "It ain't your grandmother's pied-à-terre that's for sure. How about it—*molto bene?*"

A smile from across the room would have to suffice....

Hard to tell about that girl sometimes.

Sara left for a moment to make a quick call to her parents back in the Bay Area, Pacific Heights to be exact where God only knows what time it must have been. Needless to say, her mother appreciated such things. With no such pressing phone calls of his own, he set about to work.

In a flash, O'Shea was opening a mini magnum of Veuve Clicquot from the bar. He caught a flickering blue eyed stare from the couch as she finished her call. He poured a glass, and fixed a green eyed glance back her way, "Maybe *I am* proposing?"

".... I always pegged you as one of those wandering eye, wayward scoundrel types. Is it to be one of those marriages of convenience then?"

"No, one of conveyance. I expect I'll have to carry your teetotalling lightweight ass from place to place."

He poured another glass and handed it to her.

"Got your little drinking shoes on?"

"…. It's nine thirty there, Hank."

"What—have you gone all Mormon on me? Perhaps you'd enjoy a nice soft drink?"

"Well, I…"

"Look, I'll mix it with…" his eyes scanned the bar, "some *Fanta*—hell, it's *almost* orange juice."

She had a sip, "*Nice,*" and settled back onto the couch. "Did you tell the girl at the desk we were married?"

"Yes, how else do you think they'd let us *share* a room? Don't let the new paint and the shiny plasma screen fool you—remember the thing about politics and religion? Thought I'd just try to spare us the rude looks and crass asides saved for the unwed couple. Besides, I thought it would be a respectable cover for the amount of damage we might have to unleash on this place."

"Damage?"

"Yeah." He downed his drink and quickly poured another. "Relax, we're not talking about going all Uncle Fintan here—but a little bit of *Keef* throwing TVs out the window might be in order."

"Let em' know you're back in-country Liam?"

"Yeah, something like that, but don't worry—I've got some law school. I should be able to talk us out of any *situations*."

"Oh, it's *us* now?"

"Of course, you being my missus and all."

She sighed, "Well, so long as you draw it mild—but you know I hold the line at motorcycles down the hallways and setting fire to the Chippendale?"

".... Well, there goes Wednesday."

"Behave."

He shook his head sadly, "Jesus woman, did you think I was a savage? All I'm saying is for this kind of scratch we can expect the indulgence of a few *eccentricities*."

She studied the room again, "Yeah, so I meant to ask you, this set up seems a bit on the *grander* side.... I'm guessing this is not the Standard Superior then?"

"You Miss Moneypenny are on the proverbial *roll*. I left the Standard Superior back there at the airport with the two-door Ford Punta and the after clap of last night's karmic death." He glanced about the place with the slick-sheen bearings of some mad game show host, "This here is the Junior Bunkhouse Suite, 926 square feet of oakified feng shui with the soft lines and panoramic views of the city—all for your pretty self." He paused, "Junior? I said to the woman. How's the penthouse looking? But she mumbled something vaguely threatening about the House of Saud and how I ain't got the moxie to hunt with the *big dogs*."

"Why that rotten hussy." A supportive nature was one of her finer traits.

She put down her glass and gave him the rueful look saved for those not *quite* off the hook. His expansive, jangling mind quickly returned to the realm, "I know, I know—didn't have to do it. I know you'd be happy out there in a tent in the park, lying under Jerry-tinged skies listening to *Brown-Eyed*

Women—but I wanted to do something nice for you."

"Liam, you already do plenty of nice things for me."

"Oh yeah?" He stretched out on the couch, "Tell me about some?"

"How about graduation trips to Europe for starters?" She came over and sat next to him, "And maybe all the ways you've helped with my family over the last year," she grinned a sad grin. "All the craziness we've put you through…. All those nasty days when I felt like I was coming off the rails?"

He nodded, "Yes, well, I do have a saintly shade wouldn't you say?"

She smiled, "And you've been generous to a fault; so I don't want you feeling you *have* to do these things."

He hemmed a bit, "Well, I had been treating you to a steady diet of rain checks and what if's, you know?" His eyes flashed some of the sincerity that often waited for the words to catch up, "*Besides*, you're off to live in some tent for the next two years; you need a bit of pampering for the finale."

"It's not a tent and I don't need pampering, but you're a sweet boy all the same."

"Just paying back a gracious soul who puts up with a moody mess like me."

"Well, you have your moments." She started to smile, her eyes drifting over some of the finer furnishings. "But c'mon, is the boutique hotel thing really you?"

"No," he was now waving around a frozen Snickers bar, "rusted, bare spring mattresses and Top Ramen noodles were my milieu a scant incarnation ago… Besides, you should be proud. I talked myself out of the chauffeured Bentley service. Apparently, it comes with the room, like free socks or something."

Her eyes narrowed, "Liam, *how much* did you spend on this room?"

"Never you mind; let's just say the ailing Celtic Tiger just popped some Bennies, courtesy of the clan O'Shea."

"But two weeks Liam? This is going to cost you—"

"*A Lot*," he cut in, "but it's all relative. See this," he held up one of the small esoteric figurines from the mantle, "*haven't a clue*—but that's why they call it a journey—guess I'll have to learn."

She eased back, having another look about the place, an appraising grin spreading across her face, "*It is nice.*"

"Damn right Wheezy—come on, hoist a glass and let's give a cheer to Handsome Henry—the father of our feast."

"Just promise me you'll draw the line with the nouveau cheese—when you start name checking Baka pygmy carvings we're going to have a problem."

"Trying to keep me barefoot and ignorant are you?" He thundered, "Well—*screw* the television, I'd sooner throw myself out the window before I bought into that guff. This is just for some *breathing room.*"

".... Nice speech."

"Thank you." He scratched his head, "Baka?"

"Cameroon, love."

But he could sense he'd secured a kindred soul, "So, we're cool then? C'mon raise a glass to Henry then—poor fellow's been sent to Phoenix."

She laughed, "Jesus Liam, you've got a black soul."

"Yeah, black soul, lucky face."

He grinned his little boy's grin, knocked back his drink in one long gulp and slammed the glass on the table, "All right—you want to go out?"

"You up for that?"

"I would have to say I'm past the point of *needing* sleep. I'll either be fine, or just die out there on the street." A thoughtful look came across his eyes, "Just give me a *proper* send off—don't let them make me grist for the mill."

"Black horses and white doves?"

"Jesus, at least," he looked around at nothing in particular, clearing out the cobwebs. "All right rambler, lets get rambling."

"Ok, just let me throw something else on, I'm feeling a bit skeezy in these. What about you?"

He stretched out across the couch in all his rumpled, faded glory, "I'm comfortable in these." He closed his eyes for a brief moment to the low stir from the street below and the sweet smell of cedar and vanilla.

Christopher M. Basso

Chapter Seven
Dedicated Follower of Fashion

"Have a good one."

And with that the bellman swung shut the heavy doors at the back of the hotel and cast them out into the noisy world. While the entrance to The Essex sat smack ass in the middle of one very busy roadway, the opposing face was along a much more agreeable thoroughfare of the still and quiet variety. Eustace Street, which ran down towards the heart of the Temple Bar neighborhood was a narrow cobblestone lane which served mostly as pedestrian walkway—save for hosting the occasional confused visitor in the Hertz Emerald Isle special, or roving cop car on the make.

Back here the automotive bustle gave way to a continuously shifting stream of fairly interesting humanity milling about: University students mixing with the Babelesque rainbow of tourists, artists and street buskers of *varying* talents, hens and stags in for one last wanton fling, your occasional Thomas Wolfe jaded émigré type blowing through their inheritance, and of course, the Premier League hooligan aficionado—hell bent on terrorizing *them all*.... Which was principally a nostalgia thing around these parts.

A fine mash up indeed, but no one seemed to actually live back here—mostly day trippers and night crawlers, each claiming some measure of shade on the sun dial, with agendas that fell somewhere between the innocent and the atavistic. But even if you weren't all that sure of your agenda; not exactly certain what you were looking for—you simply *knew* that this was the place to be.

If someone had lit a fire under Dublin's ass, Temple Bar was where it was coked and stoked. The *Celtic Tiger* was a clever bit of phrasing, a euphemistic flourish which tried to paint a picture of the wealth and power a renaissance brings. But like any catch all, it covered far too vast a reality to entirely reconcile the differences—like the divergent paths which meant fortunes for some and a complete snake eyes for others. Not everyone on this little island had ridden the wave, but for the ones who were, the ones in the know, this was their scene. Down here in *The Bar* amid the rakish winds and the newfound glitter, they could still study the weathervane for the age and draw a straw for their place in it.

Still, there was an unmistakable energy in the air that summer. Imaginations dulled by a legacy of interminable concession were finally getting a chance to see the light of day. The Florentines had only to deal with the Black Death, the Borgias, and the marauding hordes, but *the English* had been another matter entirely. But this renaissance had commenced in earnest. In a removed sense—the long lens schema of things, it must have been a hell of a thing to find yourself moving through one of those upswings in history; walking with the king in a perfect confluence of moment and meaning.

A stroll walk down Eustace Street in the noontime hour felt more like the circus was in town, or at the very least, some mildly bawdy traveling sideshow. And since the circus was in town *why not* ride the vibe of hyperbole and rank embellishment hanging so heavy in the air? Seemed to Liam as good a time as any to roll out some local flavor, and the bullshit lore he'd spent his delicate years soaking up.

"So, let's get you up to speed—this is Temple Bar." His look bordered on the pedantic.

"And why's that professor?"

"Well, my heathen Californian consort, on account of

the first Temple in Ireland being built here," he pointed to a handsome yet utterly random building. "Right over there, if I'm correct.... Hence the *Temple* part—the *Bar* was the initial refusal of Irish Christians to let the Jews wander freely about. They actually needed Christian escorts to travel through the city."

She nodded, looking around, taking in the shiny renovations, trying to imagine a time when such cruel little scenes had played themselves out. Hard to picture the Shylocks and Antonios of ancient Dublin wrangling pounds of flesh against the pastiche of internet cafes, Johnny Rockets, and Swedish home furnishing boutiques. Although he had her intrigued with this one, "So what you're saying is these people are somewhat *prejudiced*?"

"*Hell no*," he shot back. "Just an unfortunate bit of indiscretion which was sorted out in due time. Irish people, after all, understand the vagaries of other people's hang-ups better than most. In fact, the Irish were in the vanguard of peaceful coexistence with their Hebrew brethren. Unlike on the Continent, where it was an Inquisition free for all, Jews flourished here in Dublin. They wove themselves into the local culture, held positions of power in the government, made their mark, made their fortunes—basically all that righteous guff we hold dear.... A great many even assimilated to the point of conversion, changing their names and submerging deeper into the culture, enveloped in their newfound Orishness," he caught his breath. "*Hence* the mixing of the darker Sephardic skin with those pigment challenged Viking leftovers and you've added another layer of intrigue to the 'Black Irish' thing."

"C'mon Liam, how many Jewish Irishman do you come across?"

"More than you think bubby, you'd just never know—like I said they've changed their names. Goldman's are Gallagher's, the Morowitz meets the Murphy."

"And let's not forget the Oppenheimer-O'Sheas?"

"See, you're catching on my friend. So, in a sense this tiny island was out on the front lines of religious tolerance.... At least when it was someone *else's* religion, but still."

"Yeah, so what happened?"

".... Well, the devil will play with the best laid plans. But still, there was very little in the way of religious persecution, unlike say, *your* ancestral land. That is at least before your family hopped the Mayflower and tore ass across the ocean, ready to terrorize a whole new set of faces."

"I'm only half English, *you idiot*—you know that."

"That's the half I'm worried about honey; keeps me awake at night, cowering in a cold sweat, thinking you're going to have a go at my floating rib."

"That'd probably be the *French* half my love."

"Naw, it's the French half I like," he said with something sly in his eyes. "Leave it to your old man to find the one *Fleur du Charme* wandering around Haight-Ashbury back in the day…. Anyway, it sure as hell wouldn't be the Californian in you."

"Thank you…I think."

"Well there you have it, a little ditty of our possible Jewish forbearers."

"That's wonderful Rabbi—clever story, but it's all nonsense."

"Come again?"

"I read in my trusty little travel guide here that Temple Bar was named for a family that settled here, shockingly enough—the *Temple* family, and it sounds like they were about as Jewish as the Swiss Guards."

"So they'd have you believe, besides, you going to trust a book?"

"As opposed to what? The truth?"

He smiled, "You're in-country now—the truth is never as important as how you get there."

They passed the arch near Merchants Square, "Besides, all that guff was the misdirection from my next point."

"Which was?"

"That in all likelihood Bob Marley was also Irish."

She laughed, "The Frommers Dublin doesn't cover that."

"It's a stretch granted, but no more so than you or I calling ourselves American.... Shit man, have you ever tried to find a *real* American?"

"I'm listening."

"Ireland and Jamaica are islands; both Ireland and Jamaica were conquered and subjugated—same good folks by the way. Lots of bitter pills to swallow, lots of songs of faith to purge, songs of salvation, fading out, rising up."

"And that means what?"

"Did you ever see one of those old navigator maps? Ever notice how badly they were off, tilted one way or another."

"Keep it rolling chief."

"The people who drew those maps were usually traders, and who you traded with influenced the way the maps were drawn. I can show you one in Trinity's library; Ireland, Spain, and West Africa all set perfectly down a straight line. There was something shared. Linear trade—carried west to the New World; then watch it become a triangle. West African slaves, Irish and Scot poor white trash in the Appalachian South, African musical tradition, Irish soulful dirge, brew, stir, add some heat.... Toss in a civil war, a hundred years of Jim Crow solitude—bam you got Elvis and Jerry Lee. Watch it tossed back across the ocean and then you get The Beatles, take it up a breezy junction on Highway 61 to Hibbing, add some poetry and you get Dylan; and a new triangle of sorts.... Old Bob Marley was just the finest high-powered hybrid of that grand tradition. *Ergo,* fine and proper to claim him as Irish."

They passed through the busy crowd in the square, and the impromptu open-air market set up along the periphery. Bohemian jewelry, arts and crafts, trinkets, and street musicians selling antique homemade tapes and cds of a questionable fidelity. Liam, ever the softie, bought her a small bouquet of wildflowers before starting up the incline towards Nassau Street and Trinity College.

"Gee, my little Trustafarian—I think you've missed your

calling, perhaps we should get you one of those travel shows? You know, catch the sights, with a little bit of history, and a touch of industry thrown in the mix?"

"Oh yeah, with my winning personality, it'd be great. No one's got a show where they go somewhere and abuse the locals. Just a lot of do-gooders on their best behavior, playing some silly self-deprecating game of grab ass with the Swells.... Hell, I'd have the boorish niche all to myself. They'd say who's your target demographic? I'd say, how about the jaded, thirtyish, morally challenged reprobate set?"

"Maybe you should throw the 18 to 34 Metrosexual into the mix?"

"What the hell does that word mean anyway?"

"It's the kind of dandy who pays $700 a night for hotel rooms and sips Bordeaux from his chaise longue in *Business Class*."

"$750, quiet as it's kept—and besides, I always thought those guys were called *wealthy*?"

"You wouldn't catch your boy Steve McQueen doing it."

"No, Steve McQueen was too busy being an actor—*that's manly*. Anyway, I always thought the cultural ambassador thing was overrated, especially in these prosperous countries. They seem to frown on civility. I'd rather represent the vacationing ne'er-do-wells."

"Well, you are off to a laser-like start."

"Good, I'd hate to think I was slacking."

They neared the top of the first hill, behind Dublin Castle, where some of the oldest buildings in the city still stood. From there they kept along the narrow cobblestone lanes, which were damn pretty to look at, but wildly uneven, and rough on the knees. He remembered them a bit shinier when he was younger.... Now look at them, gone to a dullish brown; weatherworn and beaten down by the insults and reductions of time...and stained with enough used Guinness and Saturday night street fighting DNA to fill the pages of a ledger from the head-hunting Cromwellians of his imagination to the Mate swilling, vegan Ashtanga enthusiasts of this reality—and perhaps a page for just about everyone else in between.

"You know, this used to be one *hell* of a seedy place when I was a kid," he surveyed the length of the road in either direction. "They've touched it up a bit—but I can still see it here and there. We used to come up here in search of various medicinal herbs and to try our luck getting served at a pub or two, but you had to be out of here by sunset—real bandit country after dark."

He caught her smile, "What's up freckles?"

"I just find it funny you have such a tangled little history with this place, it's like you know where the bodies are buried," she laughed. "Remember, before we went to visit my family, you said you'd never been anywhere except Ireland and Florida?"

"Yep, a pretty sad state of affairs at that."

"But yet you're strangely worldly?"

"Well, an only child and his library card were a powerful, mystical thing."

"I thought that was the thing about idle hands?"

"Yeah, that too," he added. "Besides, my people were kind of strange. All the older ones you know—they had some thuggish xenophobe thing going on, like they were only interested in the *native soil*. So they kept shipping me here, like some damn Louis Leakey expedition, off to North Dublin to gather notes on the *original strain*. Hell, I live in New York and I've never even been to Canada—but I could probably get a side gig working one of those *Baile Átha Cliath* bus tours."

"Jesus, so long as they don't let you drive."

"Yeah, well, *moving* right along—this was where the substance-challenged twilight crowd would wander around. Trinity and National are right up the hill, so you'd have the bohemian student types mixing in with the bohemian fringe types. Throw in some real *hardos* from the North Side coming down for a little street fighting man action, and you had quite a little mix—but that was something for *younger* eyes."

The crested over the hill onto the busy expanse of Dame

Christopher M. Basso

Street. "Yeah, I think I saw some Mancunians jump a Dutch mime troupe over there once. They were in for a visit and United had just lost to Arsenal," he shook his head sadly. "Like a phalanx of hyenas in the evening dusk, damn sad sight." His mind bristled at the chill of some long suppressed vision, "Real tombstone territory."

"Sounding a little jaded, aren't we?"

"I'm the freelance guide darling, I specialize in the *reality tour*. Although, I have to say, like most nostalgia it's bullshit anyway—the things you miss, well, most likely they just about sucked to begin with." His eyes fixed an appraising gaze. "I don't see who in their right mind would shed a tear for it. Fifteen years ago you couldn't even get a cup of coffee around here, and the only kind of food to be had was the deep fried, business end of some poor cloven hoofed beast.... Load up on grease and stout and run the vampire junkie gauntlet after dark—whew, damn, *them's* was the days. But look at it now; you want Sashimi or Iranian-Thai fusion?"

"I'm holding out for the Turkish-Greek I saw back down the way—*that's globalization*."

They marched up Dame Street heading west towards the main gates of Trinity College, and past the ornate Georgian façade of The Bank of Ireland. All that food talk was starting to sound about right. It'd been some eleven hours since the Tournedos Rossini in Madeira demi-glace back on the Rolling Thunder Midnight Revue, and the hodgepodge of booze and candy bars just wasn't making the nut.

At the bottleneck sway near the base of Grafton Street they spotted a nice enough looking place.... A take on the Paso Robles, Sonoma wine menu right in the heart of central Dublin? After a brief debate over the merits of such an experiment, particularly from the Californian, they wandered in past the large bay windows and were treated to a first rate meal. O'Shea washed down a fine plate of Steak au Poivre with a glass of a tasty Syrah, while Sara picked over the barbequed tofu and grilled artichoke. As she'd left her drinking shoes back at The Essex, a steaming pot of green tea sat between them.

An informal art gallery adorned the walls of the

restaurant. Exposed brick covered with all manner of mischief for sale—oil paintings mostly, little vignettes of childhood; smiling children, summer days, happy things. One in particular caught Liam's attention—two little girls, cherubic angels, flying kites on a sandy strand of beach; impressionist diffusion, their features washed in the beautiful constancy of the light—idyllic. He peered in closer...840 Euro.

Jumpin Jesophats, did they throw in a free Goddamn hat with that? The prix fixe on innocence had apparently been established. He ordered an emergency Sambuca straight away and pondered the foul meaning of the thing. It wasn't the mean experiences of life which honed your rage; they were fairly expected. It was when they came creeping in at the most innocuous of places that made you rotten. No one enjoyed being cudgeled with it, particularly over a nice bit of liqueur and a fine tiramisu.

It was a strange sensation being reminded from time to time you now had the means to travel down whatever roads may find you. His reaction had generally been the same—a fine blend of shock and awe, followed hard by the most pregnant of pauses, till a grim yet pleasant reality comes-a-knocking. And then all that's left were whimsical dustings of guilt with just the faintest touches of a hushed but celebratory coda.... Which of course fired up the shock and indignation beast again.

Good Lord, pictures on a wall could unleash *all sorts* of holy terror on the mind. Besides that bit of tenderfooting, the uneasy, creeping sensation that life was slowly shading to some bad Groundhog Day outtake. The wheels slowly spinning round and round, heady upmarket rushes followed by seedy, venal chasers down the mountain, as the swirling side of the brain dueled it out for a kind of moral primacy. But it was probably smarter to just try and forget this good fortune, lest you start walking around with your head up your ass, he glanced around...*like these people*. Better to be pleasantly reminded and mildly surprised. The bill was mildly surprising. He whipped out a newly christened platinum card which was just fixing for its fist top shelf workout.

Got to get me one of those American Express black cards, he thought, *The Centurion Card*—the one they give to third world despots and celebrities. He signed the bill, tipping generously, that 29.55% variable APR guff from his college days was over. The Swells fancied him respectable now.

After two hours of a fine Roman lunch they emerged onto Suffolk Street, into the calm of the mid afternoon. The temperature had crept up to a mild sort of pleasant, and all traces of cloud had left the sky. A bright sun and a cool breeze whipped along the zigzag streets; fortifying that fourth wind he was working on. O'Shea admired their sunny day, "We've got us a good one here, what do you want to do next?"

"How about we skip the folklore primer and go find a park or something?"

"Yep, right up there, at the top of the road—*Stephens Green*. You'll like it, plenty of trees and such. Besides, I've got to work that lunch off; damn wine jumped up on me right quick."

"That's what you get, abusing yourself like that. You're not quite the boy anymore my friend."

He smiled, "You can be harsh in the afternoon. Besides, no sleep, cigarettes, wine, adrenalin, I think this is a first for me—I'm starting to see *the patterns*, it's like I've achieved the astral plane or something. Nice if not a bit surreal."

"Sure you don't want to hole up back at the hotel marathon man?"

"Nope, sunny day like this is rare around here—let's keep it going."

".... Ok," she sighed. "Lead the way."

With plans faintly sketched they made for the top of Grafton Street beneath the warmth of the afternoon sun. She grabbed his hand, pulling him closer as they started up the steep rise of the hill.

Grafton Street is Dublin's premier "see and be seen" thoroughfare. About a quarter mile of controlled chaos from end to end, crammed with everything from the finest stores you could find in Ireland to the sketchiest of off-license betting shops. In between were a fair toss of pubs, banks, fast food takeaways, and knick-knack shops. It was a unique mix of the tourist friendly and the citizen practical, woven together in a way most large cities fail to pull off.

The bright red bricks of the pedestrian drag were a magnet for small-stand flower peddlers, "rare" Celtic souvenirs, and maybe best of all—the unofficial Juilliard of the Irish street show. If you were in from the hinterlands and had some act you were keen to busk, maybe juggling samurai swords, or a nice Portuguese David Bowie drag revue, this was where you could find a very simpatico crowd.

As always, the strip was crowded ass to elbow. Tourists milled about as a steady stream of Dubliners made their way from work. Soon the pubs would fill up and spill out into the streets on a warm, early summer's evening. In a few hours, a loud din would rise up and a steady stream of laughing, singing, shouting voices would carry up and down the breeze.

Liam quickly recognized the copper awning under which his long suffering cousin Kevin Delaney would sometimes set up his piddling Jag Stang-amp combo and thrash out his best Nirvana and Surfer Rosa covers—nice and low so the cops wouldn't notice. He could make some decent money in the busy hour. Enough to see the lads through a night of pub-life and running the hooligan thunder alley back North Dublin way. Yes indeed, guerrilla art at its finest.

The little memories were often the tenacious ones, unwilling to recede to those dark corners of your mind. A passing sight or the quickest of scents would call them back to arms, with a startling alacrity—just the low key snapshots of a life flying by. He had another glance at the rusted awning as they passed and wondered where the hell was that space cadet cousin of his, and why hadn't he called.... Family, sweet Madeleines one moment, and a *monster bad* acid flashback the next.

Up ahead a group of young girls were standing near the statue of Molly Malone, singing sad soft tunes in the Sean nós, an a cappella style, with the mournful notes bent long at the top of the range, sounding sad, like Arabic calls to prayer. The Irish could almost transcend every other shortcoming, with gifts like these; charitable laments to the ache of the collective condition. This was just the kind of civic-minded free enterprise no one

Christopher M. Basso

around here seemed to appreciate anymore. Even the tourists seemed a bit busy to pay much mind. Liam made sure to spread the wealth as they made their way up the road; lots of open guitar cases and bowler hats to think of.

But about halfway up Grafton Street things suddenly took a wild tumbling turn from the gentle roads of predictable nostalgia. In front of Kitty Parnell's, a well-regarded and occasionally moral pub, was set up what looked like the bastard trinity of Venetian carnival, Turkish seraglio, and Uncle Screwtape's pleasure palace.

Three parade floats draped in shades of red, black, and white were tethered end to end to end across the far side of the road, forming a kind of elevated stage where what must have been twenty or thirty people were getting their bacchanal on. A fourth and larger float of a pale greenish color sat slightly elevated from the others in a place of prominence. On each stage a fair mix of men and women running the gamut from weathered-aged to youthful innocent had been assembled. All in some manner of medieval dress, some wearing masks of crimson and gold, emblazoned in all the colors of decadent beauty. They danced around the fringes, playing to the crowd, blind eyed and dismissive of another troupe who stood beneath them, clad in somber shades of red and white. Their faces hidden behind the frightening masks of the grotesques, rendered in expressions of an all too human suffering.

And at the forefront, standing all by his lonesome on the red bricks of Grafton Street, was a stooping decrepit figure in tattered shabby robes and a hood of black, his pale visage, adorned with day-glo rainbow swatches, his scythe draped with beads and red velvet knickers. At his feet lay the broken shards of a balance, a sword, and a huntsman's bow. The poor boy had the sad pathetic air of some forgotten black sheep, wee-wee touching uncle about him, and the others made some point to mock him with relish. Rounding out the edges of this little gathering were a mix of circus performers; jugglers, clowns, and acrobats.

As there was no Sambuca handy, O'Shea lit an emergency smoke. "Well, there's something you don't see everyday."

Flanking the far side of the stage nearest Parnell's door was a full-on coterie of fife and drum, slapping out the heavy martial, marching rhythms that were so regrettably burned into the Irish psyche. Behind them on a small riser, two DJ's imported from parts unknown, worked a mixing board done up like the candy flipping haze of an Ibizan Methylene-dioxymeth-amphetamine sunrise. And while the drums and whistles might have ringed with something familiar, they'd been thoroughly subverted through some soundboard mashup wizardry to the point where they conjured up an uneasy, yet slightly riveting notion of what might have gone down had The Chieftains ever discovered psychotropics or House culture.

Liam and Sara took up a spot right across the way, surrounded by a larger congregation of curious faces. The crowd was building, adding on by the moment. This was *far* more interesting than the Viennese thrasher troupe breakdancing back down the way.

"*Shit.*" The boy exhaled, lighting up the next smoke from the last. "What the hell is this?"

"What, this isn't part of the tour?"

"No, this would be more my Castro Street tour."

A man in a ragged zombie's mask and Mad Max leathers did a running summersault right past them, leaping over a trim young lady in her bondage bodice wear and a powdered Marie Antoinette wig. Liam located his jaw somewhere along the ground, "I don't know.... Maybe it's the neighborhood outreach program, or one of those drug prevention PSAs? Look at that!" A pair of flaming whiskey spitters were trading body blows with some agile knife throwing dwarves, "Damn, they must have relaxed the blue laws around here."

Maybe so—there were a group of Irish cops, the *Garda Síochána* standing just up the way in front of the upscale Brown Thomas department store, but they seemed in rest mode, more concerned with cigarettes and passing skirts than anything the show had to offer. They simply didn't care. This town was as commerce minded as the next—as long as you had the right paperwork and put some asses in the seats, you could get as weird as your little heart desired.

Christopher M. Basso

Well, any good circus has a ringmaster; any good carnival its Mr. Dark—this one had both. A tall chap with a fierce mustache and the countenance of some throwback Viking Berserker sat up on the pale colored riser on what resembled a gilded throne. He sported a sharp Tyrian frock coat, rainbow psychedelic epaulets, and yellow sash to match. Rounding out this look were golden Rasta locks bent and set into towering horns, like if Darling Nikki-era Prince ever spent the winter with some of Goethe's darker impulses. Yep, this was definitely the power seat at this little happening.

There was a frightening look in that boy's eyes, a look lock in step with his wild smiling grin, like he'd spent the morning gearing up for this little Bonnaroo with a quick plunder of the local pharmacies, hammerheading all manner of feel good vibes.... This bunch was just a bit *too* fascinating for the moment. O'Shea's mind had been through the ringer over the last, who knew how many hours—bent and curved, taken out towards what test pilots called the structural limits; the thin air where the demons and the faeries live.

A whole lot for one brain to digest on a good day and this little slice of street life was starting to make the keel list. He had a look around for the comforts and certitude of his own, *his tribe*; surely they'd back him on this. But the Parnell regulars didn't seem to particularly mind. They'd occasionally stick their heads out the door between rounds, or peek through the windows and laugh. Not to mention the rank and file Dubliners strolling past with not much more than a raised eyebrow—from the suit and tie crowd to the hard chaw punter in his tracksuit.

They *glided* past this slice of street life with all the skillful grace of proper New Yorkers strolling past a dozen highly agitated Scripture screamers, dressed as Roman Centurions standing in front of Penn Station on a warm summer's eve. Basically, it was just the tourists standing there—awestruck, dumbstruck, and gobstruck; either digging the ride, or cursing out *the rabble* crashing their pipe and peat smoke Hibernian dreams.

It was then the slower witted, sleepy side of the boy's instincts finally caught up with him, and the sad dawning truth he'd been *had* by some new breed of renegade street art. He'd met the enemy and they'd done him over like some Joe-Bob hayseed mesmerized by perdition pedaling big city fancy stepping. Yeah, just as surely as Max the dog was a cowering congregate in the church of the growling vacuum cleaner.

.... Ugh, the little harpies had *had him*, on his nominal turf no less. All right, time to sound the retreat, head for the park, find a nice quiet spot, snort some summer dandelions, and brood over this sad state of affairs.

Some of the circus clowns were now weaving through the crowd, tossing out candy pacifiers and glow sticks, their faces done up in the foulest manner of grease paint renderings imaginable; all fangs and menacing blackened eyes.... Shit man, Clarabell was in the crypt, this was Pennywise at the rave. One brushed close right past them.

"Goddammit—I hate clowns."

"Who hates a clown Liam?"

"Anyone whose right, that's who." He'd had enough, "Dude, let's bail. This is giving me *the fear*."

"C'mon, it's kind of interesting."

"Yeah, lovely, but I can get this most days down in the West Village. Listen, I have to leave this place *immediately*, it's making my brain hurt."

"Well...all right."

"Trust me, it's for the better, there's something not right with these people. It's a classic misdirect—a Trojan horse for bestial avarice or something."

"Liam James, what the fu—"

"C'mon, to the park. I'll tell you under the shade of some old oak tree."

Liam started a slow, over-the-shoulder retreat from the festivities. He made sure to cover their tracks with eyes forward and shoulders squared, slow and steady, like making your way from some startled Grizzly. A steady stream of people drifted past, heading down the road to get a better look at all the commotion. From a distance the panorama came into view, of the risers and the large crowd that had formed around Kitty

Parnell's. Exhaled oohs and ahs rose up from the assembled, as camera flashes rippled through the air like a wave—it was quite a little happening in a dirty old town.

Maybe there was an innocent explanation for all this? Perhaps this bunch were just enjoying the succor of the public teat—The Emerald Isle, after all, lacked anything resembling a decent carnival culture. Perhaps these kids were filling some niche; just good industrious sorts out feeding the new found Keynesian Beast. Or maybe you could chalk it up to the giddy loopiness which rides shotgun with the fresh breeze of a new summer, like fine bits of dust carrying up along the spare wind.

However you sliced it this was the kind of thing that could *only* be sanely explained in the exegesis of the age. Twenty years ago, through the tired eyes of sleepy Dublin they might have been flayed and garroted—their middlings set adrift down the Liffey towards the dark waters of Dublin Bay. But for now, they seemed quite tolerated if not fashionable. The orphaned grandchildren of The Merry Pranksters had comfortably set up shop along the south banks of the river.

Which is not to say O'Shea was some teetotaler of the flesh. In fact, the notion of carnival always held a special fascination for him.... Perhaps it was that stirring of the pot on some of the bigger questions, the big ideas—sin, the flesh, the soul, rebirth, redemption. He'd even made the pilgrimage down to Mardi Gras once—*big* Goddamn mistake. Hell, once you got past the video starlets and every mongoloid from Alpha to Omega looking for love, past the free flowing body fluids, the random beat downs by the NOPD and precise shakedowns by the locals—fuck all if there wasn't much left in the *ideas* department.

This little Grafton Street affair seemed tame by comparison, but there was still something heavy around the edges. These people were just a bit too committed to some rote, albeit eccentric, idea. His brain was starting to hurt. Screw these deadbeat carnivals anyway. He had some bling now—why not head to Rio or San Raphael, walk among the kings who knew how to roll one of these things properly.

Within minutes they reached the Fusiliers Arch and the

Down All the Days

southern gate of Stephens Green. By then, only the distant beating of the drums and the piercing screams of the sacrificial virgins were still audible, but that too was dying like some odd conversation on the vine. None of the citizens waiting at the busy crosswalk had any clue of the strange brew sweeping over the lower half of the road.

Liam and Sara stopped for a moment to admire the massive triumphal arch near the entrance, an old imposing thing of broad limestone, worn gray over time. Just another sad, proud, and anonymous commemoration of forgotten heroes from forgotten wars—take another snapshot and keep it moving. To linger would be to care.

Once inside, the sounds from back down the way were completely gone. Stephens Green wasn't a large park by any means. You could probably stroll around the entire grounds in twenty minutes or so, but it was just the sort of permanent and unchanging respite his frazzled mind needed. Nothing ever changed in here. Just the same toss of gravel paths and iron benches, swans, ducks, and the occasional lagered out reveler sleeping it off in the cool grass—but nothing out of the ordinary.

They found a bench in front of the old white gazebo near the tear-shaped pond; the perfect vantage point for watching the swans slowly circle about, picking up bits of food from the children gathered along the banks. Liam made one slight concession to the day and placed his head across her lap, eyes skyward, his longish hair falling over the sides of his face. They passed the better part of an hour in this comfortable corner of old Dublin City.

Maybe it was the fresh air, or the Ziggy Stardust revival they'd just witnessed, but something had set her mind in an expansive mood. She was spinning along the brand of jazz where the words would often outpace the thoughts. Presently, she was free forming on the end of the summer, her impending exodus to the wilds of West Africa, and the two years of volunteer service which awaited her. *Oxfam* did indeed have a use for highly trained legal minds who'd pulled off a Master's in Public Policy when no one was looking.

Combined with her passable French, and she was

something of a commodity on the do-gooder circuit.... Which was not to say *he too* didn't have plans, but beyond assembling the crack team of ex-Special Forces to shadow her every move—an A-Team for his paranoid Z-gimping mind, he hadn't really otherwise delved into the miasma of this swamp.

This radical realignment of the stars was weighing heavily on her mind, and these many things which form the nerves, fears, inspirations, and aspirations that carry along a light June wind. Quite possibly her mind was moving *too* fast. She could zip along like an Osaka bullet train rumbling in the high gears, powered by equal measures of enthusiasm and sincerity—an intellect worthy of an athlete's grace, and a wonderful thing to behold, but it was that same breakneck pace which was starting to clutter the tortoise-gimping rhythms of his own. O'Shea was starting to *like* the slow gears, and the Buddha-like contemplations to be found in the smallest of things.

As he looked up towards the clear blue blanket of summer sky he could feel his brain shutting down, his emotions shutting off. If the last year had taught him anything it was to try and clear the decks of all the white noise, and all the dissonance which steers modern life down those darker roads. They might have been called *reality* in a former incarnation but the boy was, in the nominal sense, writing his own ticket these days.

Besides, heavy thoughts were far too heavy a thing, particularly on a Felliniesque afternoon such as this. He could feel his mind slipping into the rude, tired pantomime of some dotty old husband, absentmindedly agreeing on wallpaper swatches and divan covers. Generally this sort of detachment was a fine shield, a nifty little filter weeding out life's banes and drains. But every now and then, when he was in the wrong kind of mood, it would train the crosshairs on someone he cared about. He wasn't so far up the river not to notice these things, and when she was the mark, it hurt the most.

But this filter was an ethereal little gadget and certainly not *his* to control. He could no more deny air to his lungs than master the wanderings of a wandering mind. But avoiding these heavy thoughts often breeds them, and O'Shea was no exception. With a chill in the air and the shadows pulling long down the grass, he suggested they get on the good foot. There was still some grace to be had in the righteous burnings of a day.

But where to? The hotel? He was already a bastard, why be a geezer as well? More drink? Well, this was the place for it—but so soon? That might set off the bells and whistles for some manner of hasty intervention.... Maybe they should just keep with their stroll for awhile. His body was more or less still with him, no shaking tremors or bleeding eyes—and the idea of seeing just how far he could take this rough beast before *death* set in held a certain bent appeal all its own.

Well, the National Gallery was just down the road. She'd like that. Some Beckett, an ill-reputed and disputed Caravaggio, and some fine Jack Yeats.... *Then hit the bars.*

They left the park through the western gates and wandered past the large, well kept Georgian homes. This was a part of Dublin that, despite the historical privations, had never suffered from want. Everything else was just catching up with them. Nice and quiet up here, just row after row of neat, pretty brownstones, each greeting you with ornate fanlights, sturdy iron railings, and brightly colored doors. Handsome shades of yellow and green, orange and blue, lined the road.

"Such a pretty thing."

"Funny you should notice," his eyes grew large again. "The colored doors were to help drunken husbands find the right way home."

"Back when old Bob lived with the Rabbis?"

"Yeah, *especially* then."

"No, no, no," she laughed, "I've given up on you, remember?"

Christopher M. Basso

Chapter Eight
The Piano has Been Drinking

By the time they'd thoroughly toured Ireland's finest collection of bric-à-brac, it was nearly seven in the evening. They strolled back along the southern walls of Stephens Green, looking for the next bit of the "good craic," as the locals were wont to say. But mostly, they were just admiring the rumble of noise and people, and the fast moving traffic zipping along Merrion Row. The spectacle of a big city in its full flight madness could be all sorts of entertaining, particularly if you were no longer in the mix. Well, he thought, they'd bombed in on the morning rush and were now ushering home the evening crowd.

There was some talk of beating a quick path back to the safe confines of The Essex, where they could perhaps lick the collective wounds, take a nap, and order up a fine meal from room service. Sounded nice enough, but the lines at either cabstand near the park were about four abreast and wrapped around the corner.

"Shit," he muttered under his breath. Fuck all, if he hadn't seen everything now. He knew it was hellishly tricky scoring a cab in this city, but this was taking it out past the pale of his swiftly antiquing knowledge of his second home. Who *were* all these people and where the hell were they all going—at once? He tried organizing his thoughts.... Perhaps they'd still roll with some of that recent luck? He was with *her* after all, the herald of clean conscience and a fine purveyor of walking between life's

Christopher M. Basso

little raindrops. Maybe they'd come across one of those off-license lads, the kind of fellow who ran his own discrete livery service out past the narrow minded legalese of the day—but pinning your hopes on one of these boys was *bad bank* of the first order. They were something like a Hibernian Sasquatch—rumored to exist but rarely if ever seen.

This was serious. His tired, bone tired, legs were not up for the long haul back down the hills to the quays.... Well, they'd finally crossed the threshold. Circumstances beyond their control would be forcing them to stay out and cavort. And as the cavorting scale runs kind of narrow in these small rain soaked cities, they would soon wind up in another pub, where the drinks would flow and this filthy spectacle of burning the body to the bitter end would continue. However, if they were going down that road at least they could keep the venues classy. The imperial Shelbourne Hotel stood right across the way.

The Shelbourne was, and forever would be, the bulwark for Edwardian elegance gracing Dublin; even way back when no one would have this brutish little backwater of a city. In a way it was still the regent in this kingless kingdom, but her zeitgeist luster was fading fast like some formerly grand Bourbon lady, jabbering to her poodles as the barbarians stormed the gates. But hell, at least she *had* a history. In a transitory world that abandons all things with shocking ease, this continuity must have counted for something. Besides, there'd be no Lovesexy dragsters or flaming Mephistos in this haunt, and that would just about make up for the ungodly gaggle of tourists they'd surely find.

They strolled through the grand foyer, past the Lord Mayor's Lounge, and made a quick line to a slice of old Dublin—the stately Horseshoe Bar where Richard Harris and Peter O'Toole used to bring the seven kinds of smoke that would make lesser men grovel. Maybe he'd yet find some of those animated geezers who once ruled the roost, the old wizened fellows who could prattle on till the end of days.

But once inside and safely seated near the stylish curving bar the grim realities set in. This was definitely a scene of a decidedly non-local ilk. Nothing but a few mildly amusing Bostonians bitching to one another about just *how wrong* Frank McCourt had it, and a table of middle aged Dutchmen taking pictures of one another.

"We *will* be meeting some Irish people in Ireland won't we?" She innocently asked. O'Shea ordered up a Jameson neat for himself and a Chambord Martini for the lady as he dwelled on this question. A quick thought crossed his mind—perhaps the old Dub sorts had been completely purged from the scene, out priced and exiled to the hinterlands, or maybe hunted to extinction; all options seemed plausible. Even though this beast had once thundered across the landscape in vast herds, he'd fed primarily on a general sense of hubris and discontent. With his primary foodstuffs in such sort supply he might have just *faded away*.

Liam sipped the Jameson slowly, enjoying the bitter taste, the fine charcoal kick and the pleasant burn down the throat. Jameson was a fine drink, the kind of overwhelming foulness that could steel your nerves for the harder things in this life. It was an athlete's drink if you were athletic about your drinking. He managed to fit in a couple of glasses of ice water between rounds. For some reason the notion of hydration suddenly seemed key for surviving the rest of this day.

As such, they sat in the Horseshoe Bar, sipping their drinks, making small talk, and waiting on the next bit of signage as to where the day should lead…. The three "Smiling Leo O'Bannon" tour coaches filled with old age Germans disgorging into the nearby lobby seemed a sign almost proverbial in its providence. O'Shea paid up quick, thanked the barmen, and hit the bricks.

They emerged from the steely grace of The Shelbourne, back onto a much quieter Merrion Row. Most of the fierce bloodletting of the kamikaze hour had since passed, just a nice calm flow to things, and surprisingly, a brilliant kick of late day sun.

Daylight was a fairly perpetual thing in the Irish summer, and while it could trick the mind, it rarely got one past the stomach. The clock over Millennium Tower read close to ten, and dinner was sounding rather inevitable. Before long they were standing near the corner entrance to The Unicorn Café, another venerable granddaddy of the Dublin scene, and another address previously out of the O'Shea orbit. He'd walked by the place enough over the years, but now seemed about the right time to give it a try. A recommendation from their Florentine barman at The Shelbourne had sealed the deal.

They sat at one of the tables near the large bay windows facing the street. Once again, the bustle of cars and people seemed far away through a few panes of glass and the right kind of atmosphere. Just the genial, amiable din of the drinking glasses and the chattering classes making merry in the background. The Unicorn was something of a conundrum on the culinary scene; trendy places were supposed to burn with a short half life, but this one was gearing up for its sixth decade. Something admirable about those kind of legs, particularly since the décor still held that well-cast shine as though it were opened only yesterday.

Their clientele seemed on the nouveau side of things though, like the older, logical conclusion to the Young Turk n' gimp scene down at the bus stop earlier in the day. Just the tail end of *The Tiger* out on the town cutting loose with heavy expense accounts and lingering Celtic bling.... Liam could feel the subtle sideways stares coming their way; like the herd nosing the interlopers at the watering hole, and while Sara was beauty and grace incarnate, O'Shea must have had the look of a man who generally took his leave by the back door.

He wondered if the staff were fixing to give him grief for his scruffy look, perhaps some mothballed sports coat loaner from back when Thatcher was last in town, but they were actually quite gracious and all too willing to oblige. Unbeknownst to him, his foul and unkempt aspect was the new calling card for the age. He was obviously one of those new found cultural heavies who'd blown onto the scene like some trendy carpetbagger whistling Dixie through the postbellum South. Sitting there in a t-shirt of questionable provenance, faded jeans, and scuffed motorcycle boots—crass and classless to be sure, but just the type who could bring *an edge* to the place, maybe get another write up in The Examiner, or The Daily Mail.

"That's how you stay in business six decades," Liam offered up to the air. "Treat *the customer* right."

"What are you railing on now?" She asked over her menu.

"I'm feeling some heavy stares from these people."

"Oh, they just think you're handsome is all."

"Yeah, Metrosexual right?"

"Exactly," she lowered the menu. "You're looking pretty good these days you know."

"Moi?"

"Vous."

"How nice of you to say…. I've been feeling a bit busted of late though."

"Yeah, that's the part I like. You've got this rugged, unaffected thing going on. Like you could wrestle one of those Kodiak Grizzlies with your bare hands."

"And what—still be cool with a manicure?"

"Yep, that's the modern man," she said. "What every woman wants."

"What a rough beast indeed."

An afternoon of booze and finger foods at the Horseshoe didn't exactly portend for a large, elaborate meal, but the Tuscan menu looked too good to pass up. They ordered a couple of the Unicorn's signature dishes—hot and cold antipastos to share, which they tore into with relish. One bottle of Brunello di Montalcino *Biondi-Santi* with dinner sounded about right so he ordered two.... But as he stared down the last breaths of the second wounded soldier, a quick thought came to him—hit the brakes before the right kind of people started thinking he had the wrong kind of problem.

As the sun called it a day over the flat plains of Leinster they traded bites of dessert washed down with a sweet Vin Santo, before getting down to the brass tax of this little leg of their journey.

"Tell me more about this wedding," she said. "Feel like you're keeping me in the dark."

He took a swig from his triple espresso chaser, "You've got me—Kevin didn't tell me all that much. Seemed like the boy didn't actually *know* that much. Strange, considering he's an usher and all. I do know it's down south a bit, out in the country. Believe it's at some big old estate, one of those white elephants no one can afford to own anymore—even now. So they made it into a hotel and rent it out for weddings."

"And the odd Bar Mitzvah I'd imagine?"

"Yes, the very odd Bar Mitzvah."

"You were good friends with this guy Brendan?"

"Well, actually, Brendan and I are *technically* cousins, that is if you consider marriage part of the deal, but I don't really know him all that well. Truth be told, these people are mostly Kevin's friends anyway. I'd just rent them out for the summer. Although, more than a few of them have piloted my couch in Brooklyn over the years—yep, nice extended stays in my living room." He groaned, "…. Bastards probably got me on some INS watch list now."

"Don't worry, you've got some law school remember?"

"Exactly," he smiled. "Don't know much about the Bride though. All I've heard is that her father owns some manner of telecom company and Brendan boy works for it."

"Works for his future father-in-law?" She laughed, "Ouch, that's tight."

"Yeah," O'Shea soon joined her. "That boy better check his gumption and his stones at the door 'cause *he's done*."

It was a little past eleven when they settled the bill and started down the landing of the old brownstone. It was a Tuesday night, but the surge and swells of South Dublin were already rolling. Hordes of attractive well-heeled types had reclaimed the thoroughfares from all manner of deviant street art, and were now out and about vibing the high times in a swirling, churning mix. Lot's of wide-eyed, wound up looks, and a palpable energy itching to be spent—just as O'Shea was seriously starting to feel the riptide pull of a very long day. No shame though, he'd ridden the beast down to the bitter ends.

Liam glanced down the road towards the nearest cabstand—the longish line had grown again to an almost Byzantine complexity, now running all the way back towards the top of Grafton Street. You could time the light from fading stars on this one. These bastards were just *toying* with him now. Well, he'd had it. It was high time to weed out the non-hackers who didn't pack the gear to get a little dirty in the service of some iconoclastic clarity...or sentiments to that effect.

He strolled onto the shoulder of Merrion Row and conjured up his best Midtown hail—arm outstretched, two fingers towards the heavens, and the proper posture of a man accustomed to prompt service. Almost on cue, a green and white Toyota night flight special swerved wildly across the lanes, breaking protocol, and pulled over. O'Shea held the door open for her, whistling a few bars of *Luck Be a Lady*.

"Must be you," he offered. "They don't get many thundering 5'10" Amazons around these parts."

"5' 9", but you flatter me as always."

He shot a look back towards the glitterati milling about the cab stand—*so long suckers*. He hopped in and closed the door, thankful as all hell they wouldn't have to hump the mile or so back to the hotel. *Everything* and its bitch of a cousin were finally catching up with him. The walls were closing in and his aching brain screamed out for some peace, some rest, some sanctuary.

But then there was the driver to deal with. The Irish livery artist is a fascinating wild card of expansive humanity—always talkative and knowledgeable about a great many things. They ran the gamut from the highly educated, cultured sort who could reel off the history of Ireland from Brian Boru to Bertie Ahern with a shocking ease and less the pretensions of some nimrod PhD. That was Model A. Model Z was a bit of a throwback, a roughneck, a chancer.... The type who most likely would have beaten the trilly gobshite out of Model A for his spotty *feckin' studentness*.

Tonight's man was a bit of that tail end gamer and the big question suddenly became who had the highest BAC in the car? O'Shea thought he had it down cold, but the old man's laughing, swerving, and wild gesticulations might have given him the long money on the shortest kind of odds. He said his name was Charlie Burke, but they should call him Ray.

He made some excellent time, mostly by ignoring the whole rule crazy one-way schema of the city center, running reds and zipping down the streets marked up, but *always* flashing his lights and honking the horn—for safety's sake. He colored his barnstorming act with a vaguely endearing Dublinese patois of road rage mixed with useful sightseeing tips. This type of Doomsday-Bloomsday trip might have rattled some, but was just about lock in step with O'Shea's finer throwback sensibilities. He assured her there was *nothing* to fear. They rounded the last turn onto Essex Street with a stylish screech of the tires and scattering of midnight ramblers, but were otherwise delivered unharmed to the softly lit back entrance of The Essex. They paid the man and watched him tear off down the road, his lights glowing smaller and smaller till they were gone.

Another queue had formed along the sidewalk nearest them, as more of the trend kids waited at the entrance to the nightclub in the hotel's basement. The *de rigueur* pastime for this town had obviously shifted from having the good craic, to apparently *waiting* to have the good craic. But fuck it—evidently, it was *all good*.

They were at least thirty deep at that point. The gents were arrayed in a fine selection of Armani and brooding D&G with five o'clock shadow chasers and a French predilection for the cologne. And beside them, a lovely collection of wannabe footballer's wives; with all perfect hair and empty perfection. At the head of the beast, a couple of burly thick necked types with black suits and questionable antecedents manned the door. The Dublin doorman, another rarified creature of the elements—part judge and jury on high fashion, part time parolee phone-in.

Liam quickly sussed the scene, "Well, that looks heavy."

She took a peak, a sudden strange twinkle in her eye, "C'mon, what do you think?"

"What? *Are you mad?* No, listen, the jigs up—you got me beat woman. How about a nice nightcap upstairs.... Maybe one of those *special* messages I read about on the internets?" Yes indeed, a plan was shaping up. "I noticed some Patrón in the minibar. Ever done a shot of tequila and Santori in the shower, it's called a Rainbow Serpent—romantic, huh, right?"

"C'mon Liam," she teased, her eyes casting a grayish blue under the dim lights, "don't quit on me now."

She gently pulled him away from the door.

".... But the Serpent is calling?"

"Maybe we should make it warm brandy and a hot water bottle for what ails you old man?"

O'Shea was once again looking for his jaw along the ground. "Oh, *I see* how it is—wealthy white girls from Pacific Heights want to get their *real* on—all right my sweetie, game on." He motioned towards her. "After you."

They started for the end of the line, but were quickly intercepted by one of the hotel porters standing near the back door. It was the same fellow who'd sped off in the roadster earlier that morning. He offered to take them to the front of the line straight away—a special accommodation for hotel guests he assured them.

A long line of glaring, reproachful stares followed them to the front of the queue. One of the thick necked bouncers moved the heavy barricade to the side and shot Liam a fairly toothless grin, the grin of an expected gratuity. Liam obliged with a well-travelled tenner and they were ushered down the steps through the main door.

The first hit was of an old basement, mixed with a bit of the fun house darkness. There was a sweet scent of age and dampness in the air. Gas lamps cast a dim glow between the patches of shadows and the creak of the old floorboards underneath. As they walked down the hallway his mind flashed back to the scene at the door.... Strange, if you weren't looking for it, or getting off on it, a sudden dose of the heavy VIP treatment could leave one feeling a bit dirty. Maybe we're all just a material girl in a material world, but there was something cheap about jumping the line, something downright *un-American* about jumping the line.... Particularly if you dwelled on the deeper meanings of the whole set up; one hairless ape flinging dung at another just to let the poor bastard know which way the wind blows; and then ape three comes along with the free pass?

But then again, *fuck em'*. Night clubbing was still more or less an act of good old-fashioned Hobbesian free will, misguided maybe, but free all the same. And if you were the type of herdish dingbat who'd wait for hours to make the grade at some velvet rope just for the privilege of being fleeced, then you deserved any and all indignities that might come your way. It was *damn* hard to be a working class hero with this lot.

"Mr. O'Shea," the porter said, "next time, please let us know and we'll bring you around through the kitchen entrance."

"Uh, thank you…"

"Gerald."

Liam greased what he hoped was the last palm of the evening, but something told him there were still many a grift and graft yet to be had.

Gerald, the night man with the clever moves, took his leave through some mysterious side door buried behind the ticket window. Liam could just make it out, in the dark spaces where the light never shined—like one of those shrinking Wonka doors for some creepy hospitality sector Oompa-Loompa.

She shook her head. "Ugh, that whole business was embarrassing. Don't you think?"

"Yeah, I feel like I want to kick…my own ass."

"We've got to avoid that kind of scene in the future."

He perked up, "Yeah, but did you see the looks on their faces as we dashed by—all flashes of revulsion and wonder. Look dear we're *professional* assholes now."

Liam had another laugh when they reached the counter and had to shell out sixty Euro for the ticket to ride. The temporal favoritism ended at the front door apparently. O'Shea forked over the dough. A young lady stamped their hands and handed them some sort of drink cards. He glanced down at the stamping—1:49 in the morning.

From down a darkened staircase lined with siren red running lights, heavy sounds drifted up to where they stood; a deep growling sort of racket rising from within. Each thump of the bass reverberating in the mind as it rattled through the body; each step calling them a bit closer to whatever mischief lay just around the corner.

    Also drifting up from below were the faint sweet scents of sweat and perfume mixing with cigarette smoke and the sugared acrid smell of the herb. They walked down and around several darkened corners before coming out along a narrow catwalk overlooking a larger room of what resembled a slice of forgotten Britannia.

    Damn, if this wasn't *quite* the picture he'd painted in his mind. It looked more like a Victorian gentleman's club run amok than anything modern sensibilities would let loose, right down to the dark oak paneling, parquet floors, and the mix of antique brass lamps and French candle chandeliers. But there were some ready concessions to the age—an intricate lighting system was anchored up in the rafters and sleek looking DJ booth nipped on a riser behind the bar.

    It was an intensely, ridiculously, maybe even *dangerously* cramped space; packed with all manner of genteel humanity. Pretty young things mostly—talking, drinking, dancing in place, or just catching a breather on the laps of other pretty young things. There were several colonial fans spinning away in the rafters, but the air was of the still and oppressive variety; the kind only copious amounts of booze and the prospects for a little congress of the cow could camouflage.

    A sturdy looking long bar topped with a green colored stone ran across the length of the far side. Crescent shaped leather chairs and old world divans stitched in faded red fabric crisscrossed the center of the room, as the young and the beautiful of Dublin's newest scene lay draped across them. The loudest music rose from an adjacent room, just down the dark staircase near the bar—broken flashes of red and blue weaved together with twinkling points of white amid the darkness.

    O'Shea's eyes slowly adjusted to the light. There was literally no room to move, *unless* you had a plan—which the boy did. It was the bar and it was about twenty yards from the second star to the right and straight on till morning. That was if you had the grit and the pluck to barrel through all the punters spread before you.

    "I take back what I said about waiting in line," she

shouted to be heard. "That might not have been the way to go."

"You're a fair weather friend of the proletariat…. Think there's any chance of reaching the bar?"

"Listen Bukowski, forget the bar, there's a dance floor right through there, and I'm getting you on it."

…. The booze had obviously gotten to her. She'd only been tripping the light fantastic, but that might have been enough for such a lightweight. Never, never, NEVER, under any circumstances, save on pain of death, and maybe not even then, would Liam James O'Shea shake his moneymaker out on a dance floor.

"Me?" He laughed. "C'mon you know I'm afflicted with this damn slow twitch syndrome sense of rhythm."

"That so?"

"Yep, and this is an Irish shade so I'm afraid it's terminal."

"C'mon you can do it," she purred.

"Eh, chances are pretty slim."

Her eyes turned towards the dance floor, "Liam, look, there's nothing but Irishmen out there."

"Damn, I hope that's not your selling point—have you actually *looked* out there? Jesus, it's like a bunch of drunken, stumbling bucks in the mad dash of rutting season."

"They don't seem to have a problem?"

His eyes told a tale of incredulity, "*C'mon,* they'd sit wearing their mother's dresses, singing the score to *South Pacific* if they thought it'd get them some play—how do you think I met you? Besides, I *know* these people, in my bones."

"Now you're just being a baby," she'd taken his hand and was pulling him along. An occasional sanctimonious, persistence was an equally annoying trait. "You're surrounded by *your* people; you should feel at one with them."

"Yeah, but these poor bastards haven't been diagnosed yet." He had another look at them. *Sweet Jesus,* he wasn't that bad, not nearly as stuck in third gear as this garish collection of *dōmo arigatō's* and the slinky women they'd love to love.

But just as inexplicably he was sort of warming up to the idea. Put yourself out of your element—a bit tired, a bit buzzed, very far from home, and even the flimsiest of music in the sketchiest of clubs can honey the notes of something ethereal and sublime. Besides, a little bit of—hang the DJ—held a certain warped appeal for his current state of mind. As Johnny Marr was unavailable he'd have to do this on his own. He'd ravaged every other nerve ending, would one more hurt?

But while O'Shea had lost the war, there was still one battle he hoped to have.

"Look, I'm going to get out there, shake what I got, and suffer all manner of indignity and humiliation, but first—a drink?"

She eyed him suspiciously, "*One* drink?"

"To stretch out the muscles and loosen up the inhibitions."

She smiled, "Another drink and we'll be seeing your exhibitions."

"Hey, look at you, you made a funny."

But there was a sense of armistice in the air. A little bit of the give and take was what this was all about.

"C'mon honey," he said, "*one more* and I'll put these lads to shame. Techno, Jungle, Trip Hop, Acid, Ambient…shit, Ambien, Halcyon bring it on, it don't matter. Find me some cardboard and I'll breakdance circles around these chickenshit twilighters," his eyes were lit with a bit of the Charlie Don't Surf. "—I'm feeling huge!"

"…. Right," she started him towards the bar, pushing him along.

"That's right, *Liam James*, Lord of the Breakdance—where's my gear?"

But first there was the bar to achieve. He spied a narrow opening amid the fashionistas and glitterati, grabbed her hand, and made like Walter Payton hitting the seam on a thirty-eight

Christopher M. Basso

Toss Right. Within seconds they'd parted the sea of conspicuous consumption and sidled up to the long bar, where he fortified the nerves with another Jameson on the rocks and a club soda lime for the lady. They found a small niche for two near the end of the counter—a perfect vantage point for scoping the action. O'Shea was sipping a drink and bobbing his head to the music when something in the corner of the room caught his eye.

Two more of those no-necks, sporting something seasonal from the Saville Row Cave Bear collection were standing near a different door—one of those heavy, double-sash sliding things. Presently, the vault was drawn shut with the *heaviest* of intransigent airs about it.... Which begged the question: what might old Kafka have done with these Ripped Fuel gatekeepers?

"What are you looking at?"

"Over there," he motioned, "the Keymaster and the Gatekeeper."

"What's in there?"

.... Poor girl, she'd asked that question in such a sweet manner, chocked full of innocent curiosity and all the tell-tale tones of the sheltered life. She must have never come across one of these heavy scenes; burly cranked up men guarding a bunch of effete tossers who rated some sort of über-VIP enclave. VIP, a dreadful word, thought the boy, sounded like some sanitized shorthand glossing over the Janus face of some gross injustice, that or some particularly virulent strain of STD.

He smiled. "I don't know—come and see."

The man on the left muttered something into a walkie-talkie and quickly headed down the hallway and up the stairs towards the entrance—and then there was one.

O'Shea's eyes set on the last punter watching the door. He kept his gaze fixed and even, like some lion in the tall grass doing the math on a herd of passing zebra. And then it was time. A loud crash of glass; signs of an accident, or intemperate dispositions colliding rang from nearby environs. Punter two looked left, looked right, but no back up was coming. He begrudgingly hurried away from his spot.

O'Shea shook his head sadly, that poor sheep would

have never made the nut in the cutthroat crucible of clandestine ops...or the legal world for that matter—*never* leave your post.

"C'mon," he said, "let's go fishing."

"Beg pardon?"

"We're busting in."

Before she could raise the red flag he was gone.

They made their sly way back across the bar towards the now empty doors. An ominous sort of vibe still lingering in the air....But was all this guff really necessary? He knew those door monkeys would have been willing to trade a couple of discrete gratuities for the all access pass. After all, it was only a matter of volume with some people; amplify your sentiments with some cold hard filthy lucre.

But where would be the fun in that? Where would be the justice in that.... Where would be the *story* in that? A potential throw down with the no-necks and the *Garda*, getting thrown out of your $750 a night hotel, facing possible arrest and deportation; not to mention familial excommunication. The devil was certainly working overtime for these idle hands. Besides, fermented barley mash and self-deceiving freedoms could never quite compete with the mischief of a 2 a.m. mind.

When they reached the door the coast was still shockingly clear. In no rush and with a fine sense of grace and flair, O'Shea drew back the heavy doors, saw her through and replaced them with a strong thud—just to make sure they were properly announced. The outer hallway was still again, with no one the wiser. Goon number one returned shortly and resumed his spot at parade rest.

"I think I missed my calling," Liam muttered as they walked down a narrow passageway lined with bookshelves and dusty volumes. "I should have been door muscle."

"Well, you've certainly got the wardrobe for it."

"Hey now—be nice."

They kept down the hallway till they came to a larger two-storied room, quite spacious; with a calm refined air. This one seemed to dodge the Victorian-lite feel of the outer room and instead went full bore down the rabbit hole to the recesses of some forgotten imagination. It looked like a library from *Middlemarch* or *Jane Eyre*.... Except this one had a bar and a dance floor, some half-naked women shaking it on a riser, a couple of handsome gents making out in the corner—and copious amounts of blow being chopped up in the stacks on weatherworn copies of *De Profundis*.

"What is this?" Her voice the low whisper saved for tight confines with sleeping badgers.

"Beat's the hell out of me," he frowned. ".... Did you ever see *Eyes Wide Shut*?"

"Missed that one."

"Well, never mind."

But the boy could grasp the deeper implications; they'd wandered into the unchartered chum-filled waters where the Sanctum Santorum of New South Dublin seemed awfully...assembled. It might have been some manner of after-party, or primeval tribal function—who knew? The denizens sat at several small tables around the periphery, enjoying some pricey champagne and vodka table service. Strangely enough, they'd managed to up the genetics quotient from the previous room, which was running fairly high on the impressive side to begin with.

It's a strange enough thing to come across truly attractive, truly exotic people in your normal coming and goings; it's a *hell* of a thing to wander straight into the nexus of their collective gig, the very deep, very high end of the gene pool. These were the ones lesser souls turned their money into light for; walking, talking pictures from a magazine right before you. But there was something lost in translation. Up close, the greater the beauty, the more two dimensional that beauty became, like some savant with one heightened sense to the detriment of all others. It was a strange *mirror-mirror* sliding scale of karmic equanimity at that.... But perhaps this was giving these vapid sods a bit too much credit, although they were rather pleasant to look at all the same.... Wait, who's the sod then? Fuck it, mingle. Move confidently in their midst.

"Well then," her voice snapped him back to it. "Guess the Bonnaroo style never caught on around here?"

"Nah, I'd imagine the wealth has to sink in for a generation or two before you start pretending it isn't there."

O'Shea eyes spun around again, taking proper stock of the playhouse, "Their own private bar and disco?"

"So?"

"*So?* That chintzy little doorman bastard sandbagged us. Holding out on us just 'cause we're foreigners!" The Tullamore laughing gas had kicked in. "If I ever see him again, I'm going to eat his lunch."

"What are you babbling about you fool?"

"I don't know," he laughed, "just babbling."

"Well keep it down—you're going to rile the natives."

"Oh, I doubt that," his face was lit with laughter. "What the fuck have we wandered into here?"

"A wormhole I think. Let's make for the bar."

They had a seat at the smallish bar, surrounded by several bookshelves stacked with many old, dusty volumes. They were alone, save for a Drinkologist pouring some neon-colored concoction into a round of shot glasses. Orange Marmalade was the name they overheard, and a playful bit of banter between the servers that they were to be avoided at all costs. At that point one of them set a match to the whole business and strolled off with their flaming tray of mystery.

.... Obviously they'd stumbled onto the recreating Illuminati and Masonic set that Uncle Fintan feared so. But while these people looked *heavy*, they didn't actually look *dangerous*. That was after all what the muscle at the door was for. Rather, they just looked sort of bored and sort of rich—two states often noted for being sacrosanct in their equilibriums. And seeing as Dublin was a bit on the smallish side they probably knew one another far too readily, like some weird expat French plantation society where this type of inbreeding was tolerated if not quite fashionable. Outsiders, however, were cause for some interest. Liam and Sara could feel the ocular flutter tracking them across the room as they moved towards a table up in the stacks; but nothing critical, rather just *curious*.

In fact, in their defense, these people seemed relatively low-key. Maybe it was just the Orange Marmalades thinning them out, but there was something of a communal vibe in the air—a commune on the Sotheby's exchange, but one nonetheless....What a drag. The young Americans just pulled the wizard's curtain and found the bastard stone cold zoning. Which, truth be told, was fine with O'Shea, for in the annals of twisted boredom, the getting there had been half the fun. Not to mention his brain was sending smoke signals regarding the unholy terror it would be unleashing on him shortly.

He'd dodged the Cerberus at the door, had a peek around, and feeling that glow of an inner satisfaction, could repair to the home base and chalk this breathing cliché up to another tangle of overblown media myth.... Perhaps even dictate his notes to a receptive pillow? However, something now seemed to be catching *her* attention. She was watching the alcove back beside the bar, where through another passageway a smaller dance floor was jumping.... Damn, *nothing* escaped this girl. What were his prospects? Tight room, no windows, no egress or clever escapes in this episode for O'Shea. She gave him a smile and a tug of the hand. He was now walking that lonely green mile.

"Well," he muttered, "you ride till she bucks or you don't ride at all." He snagged an Orange Marmalade from a passing tray, waited till the blinding blue eye of Sauron was elsewhere, and sent that bad boy down the well.

Feeling ever so fortified Liam O'Shea surveyed his techno Waterloo from the doorway.... Well, money might have upped the ante on the gene pool aesthetic, but it certainly hadn't helped with the sense of rhythm—at least life was still democratic in some ways. Goddamn, what was it about his extended male brethren and the moving of the feet in time with the beat?

What a piece of work is man, can get to the Moon and back on a stick of dynamite, but can't keep 4/4 time with Kylie Minogue.... Damn shame, besides, they'd come so far in the last couple of years, it shouldn't be this hard. He'd have to show them. And as the first effects of the medicine had started to manifest, this might be easy.

Donning his best Vincent Vega face, he made for the floor, with nary the trace of skepticism in the soul, and just the right amount of attitude for the occasion. They found a spot near the soundboard and slipped into the mix with the ease of a practiced, decadent grace. At least for the Golden State Amazon, who was far better versed in such things, not to mention the one actually *leading*.... Shit, old Fintan would have his head on a Ballymun pike if he ever spied this scene.

No matter; the space itself was tight, ridiculously hot, and packed to the teeth with bodies moving quickly in time, synched with the great Ouroboros mind that forgoes the need for a rigid, pilgrim individuality. Just a synapse frying mix of beautiful women, ungainly sweaty men, and some quick-heeled Continental ringers management brought in to keep the milieu respectable. Notting Hill's own—Jimmy *"The Sazuki"* Rao—guest DJ, in from Lisbon by way of Mykonos was in fine form, squirreled behind his bulletproof bunkhouse riser, playing crazed conductor to one strange ass symphony.

But there was no such luck down below, where the wrong sort of angling had quickly moved them right beneath the double stack of amplifiers nearest the entrance. *The Suzuki* rolled with one hell of an impressive sound system—the kind of gear with enough pure raw wattage to ensure a ringing in the ears, and difficult conceptions for years to come.

But this general sense of chaos didn't seem to be bothering Sara in the least. Rather, it appeared to be resurrecting her sleepiest of fortunes.... This delicate desert rose, his venerable Dulcinea, the prim and earthy flower child of demure wealth and rarified zip codes, could seem to flip a switch and move her long lithe body with the reckless abandon of some patchouli-toking Salomé; all curves, hips, and elemental fire.

Her white shirt was soaked through, clinging tightly against her chest, a fine trace of sweat shined along the back of her neck; the excessive heat you see—a rolling swerve of all manner of possible intent, a bit of everything and a bit of nothing. His brain was leaving the realm of dilettantish hooliganism and drifting onto her late night finer points. *After all,* in a day of expansive inquisitiveness, she was still the ultimate curiosity of them all.

She moved in closer to Lefty Two Steps, her back pressing up against his chest, taking his hands and pulling them down along her hips. Her hands raised above her, the gentle curve of the back, his lips briefly brushing against skin, a taste of salt on the tongue.... The voyeuristic, exhibitionist politics of the disco; are they or aren't they, will they or won't they. A pleasant tension always worth the price of resurrection.

Loosen up you fool—learn to roll with it. Shit man, they write odes to such things...or at the very least limericks. Sex and violence, melody and silence; lost in some moment of driftless bliss, pressed hip to hip against her, surrounded by a hundred of your closest ghouls, raising Cain. Right in the middle of the contradiction was the safest place to be. But just as he was getting the faintest hang of the thing if only in his mind, the faster music cut out for something slower.... Unbeknownst to him, the Suzuki had to see a man about a horse.

Sara shelved her sudden wildcat predilections, turned towards her boy and fell in a step closer, her arms around his neck, close together now, moving slowly to some trance-like "come down" music. A fine little interlude before the next wave came crashing over. A perfect moment to hit the jacks or fortify yourself with whatever grease got your wheel turning. Either way, there was suddenly some room on the floor. Not much, but enough to gently sway in place.

Whiskey epiphanies, wino revelations, her beauty bordering on the grace of a religious solemnity, all the fortunes of the world suddenly before him—the rest, half a world away.... It was said angels would trail a conquering hero, gently whispering in his ear—all glory is fleeting, thus the glories of the world pass.

But as the gate crashing humility of the seraphim's was in short supply in the basements of South Dublin, the couple next to them would have to suffice. Couple? Perhaps that was being a bit too old fashioned-quaint with the term; that they were exploring the sacred depths of one another's adenoids implied little more than the introductions had been made...possibly. And as quarters were tighter than a Tokyo subway, this felt like something which needed a rather *deft* touch of perceptive intervention.

"Get a room!" O'Shea shouted into the windstorm of decibels and spent monkey sweat.

"Liam!"

"They can't hear me.... Shit, I can't hear me." The Orange Marmalade was waxing quixotic.

...Well, such judgments might have been a *triffle* harsh. They could have been sweet sorts in the clean light of day? Not too much to reveal otherwise. Nice threads, a few tats and piercings here and there, a bit of an edgy air about them—anarchists without the anarchy. Yep, nothing *too* untoward, with the exception they were now about one base shy of a very public congress of the crow—once upon the midnight dreary *indeed*.

The music stopped for a moment, then switched gears to something even slower, an almost dirge-like rhythm, simple drum and bass, as an eerie feeling of carnival déjà vu briefly crept in for a moment. O'Shea downshifted accordingly. *Bold* in his repertoire, the boy took on the exaggerated, almost comical stylings of a fellow who mixed his Kabuki theater with four-to-the-floor nitrous whippets.

"Jesus, you're a bad dancer Liam," she laughed.

"Yeah, I've got a signature style—*impressive,* right?"

"Lucky you're handsome, or I don't know if I could be seen with you."

She had her arms around his neck; in her Boulevardier heels they were almost eye to eye.

"Good looks are the shortcut to all originality.... Just ask these folks."

"All your failings swept under the carpet?" She smiled.

He laughed, "To the last."

There was a fine cast about her, like some pleasant echo down from the hallows of the first night you ever lock eyes with some major force in your life. If you were lucky that quick rush up the mountain was covered by a sheltering sky to help ease you along the rest of your middling days. If you were *very* lucky, the bastard still reared its head once in a while; like a quiet chapel the mind let you pray at from time to time.

His eyes grew heavier and heavier.

"My boy, requiem for a heavyweight?"

He smiled, "No, just the coda."

Liam glanced over her shoulder, the baseball fans were still at it—now one whispered hush from what might have been…actual penetration. *That,* would be a rare step indeed.

"All right, he's getting waved home—let's bail."

The elevator doors closed with a pleasant rush of air from below. He glanced around—any cameras in this thing? What was the Big Brother factor in a place like this? Hard to say, but then again once you've rated your own floor key, they were probably fairly tolerant of most indiscretions short of the sacrificial or bestial. O'Shea leaned against the doors watching the lights track from floor to floor.

"Man, I'm burnt."

"And it only took sixty hours."

"Yes indeed, Le Mans, here I come."

His tired eyes settled on her again…. He had one last hurrah left in the remnants of what used to be his mind and body. She was looking good, with all the powers of womanly mystery and sway at her disposal; yes sir, an alchemist's touch to turn his lead to gold. He looked her up and strolled over, the space between them gone, a forearm up against the wall, leaning over, leaning in, good and proper into her business. She eased up, her back resting against the wall, her heels in her hand now, several inches between their eyes.

"Hey stranger."

She laughed; knowing this peacock's strut all too well. "That's *impressive*, two days in the valley and you've still got a filthy wanton look in your eye."

"Youth's a hell of a thing."

She reached down, her hand now fully in his business, "Well, something's still working—why Liam, planning on having your way with me?"

"Is that what they call it?"

"No, I think they call it fucking."

"You kiss your mother with that mouth?"

"I'll kiss a lot of things with this mouth."

"Why miss, are you propositioning me?"

"More like…pre-positioning."

She pushed back from the wall, catching him a bit off balance; an aggressive imp-like grace was another hidden talent. The biting of the lip and the pulling of his hair were a nice touch as well. He picked her up and slammed her back against the wall, wrapping her legs around him, his hands slowly running up along her thighs, feeling the soft curve of her breasts through a wet, sweaty T-shirt.

"Goddamn, I do like a fast woman."

"I'll bet you do," she tightened her legs around his back; a bit of a *violent* move, the rather sudden shortness of breath most pleasantly pronounced.

While still in their element, the car stopped and the doors opened to a still and quiet hallway, only the smell of rose of hay and bergamot rising up to greet them.

"C'est la guerre," he smiled.

…. Nearsighted, intransigent Dublin building codes had doused many, many, *many* a worthwhile endeavor. He threw her over his shoulder, lest the point had been missed, and started down the hall.

"We'll just have to find taller buildings." She said.

Out the large windows at the far end of the hallway, night had slowly started to mingle with the first shades of an early Northern morning. The day's burn was considerable indeed.…Perhaps some reinforcements were in order?

"Tell you what, let's order up some drinks first, maybe a quick bite to eat; after all I've got to feed the beast to jag one of your limber marathon sessions."

"It's those cigarettes son; they rob a man of his youthful vitality—his *finer* talents."

"Not this one darling—this machine runs on a pure high-octane, weapons-grade mix—one part cock, two parts fear."

He fumbled through his pockets for the room key.

"Just can't have you *fading* on me cowboy."

"*Shit*, I'm just getting started—where's the camcorder?"

"Why Liam James, you little whore."

"What? Your mom said to take some pictures, remember?"

"Behave."

He laughed, "I'm no better then old tonsil *boy* down there," finally getting the key in the hole, "just a bit savvier with my moments."

O'Shea was on the phone with room service in a flash. A cool breeze was blowing through the windows and you could hear the sounds of traffic moving along the quays. He ordered up a feast fit to make a resurrected Elvis weep—the savory canapés of course, a cheeseburger deluxe with extra everything, a tomato and mozzarella baguette, two heaping plates of chips, and a fairly caramelized Crème Brulée for the finé.

"Don't forget the water!" She called out from the jacks where she was having a piss in the communal fashion of her Ashram forbearers. He leaned back for a peek—her stylish jeans rolled down snuggly along her long legs—a cute pink butt as fair and magisterial as the regents of the sun.

"Oh, bella vista, that they might not beteem the winds of Heaven I visit your ass too roughly."

"What?" She called from within.

"Nothing dear."

Liam shifted the headset from ear to ear, "What's

that—no, not you chief, listen, we're going to need a couple of big and I mean decidedly *large* bottles of water. What? Yeah, mineral water is fine." He scanned the menu one last time, "And how about some beer, some Heinekens?"

"I don't want one!" He could hear her shout.

"Right…better make that two."

He hung up and walked over to Mission Control. How did those boys fire this thing up? He studied it for a moment; a daunting bit of reverse engineering was surely in order. His head ached at the thought.

"That's quite a little snack you've got going there," she'd come out of the bathroom and made a line for the couch nearest the window. Her shoes were gone, but she was still dressed, "You plan on eating all that?"

"Damn right. You should see what I can do with this mouth."

"That, my friend, is hot."

"Well, didn't want the man to think I penny pinched my nightcaps; besides once you start down an impulse road things just tend to snowball."

"Well, don't be wasteful," she seemed fairly serious.

"Don't worry. I'm famished."

She noticed the blinking light from across the room, "Phone's flashing. Must be your boy Kevin?"

"About friggin time. Was starting to think I'd have to track that squirrelly bastard down," Liam checked the machine while she rummaged through her bag for a bottle of aspirin. "….Oh, it ain't Kevin," he frowned. "It's Cameron von Summer…. How the hell do your spacey friends find us here before my own blood?"

"What's she got to say?"

"…. Ah, can't tell. Complete gibberish," he handed the receiver over. "Is this even English? It sounds like Esperanto, or some magic language twins teach each other?"

Sara shot him a dirty look.

"I mean shit, is she hitting the Valtrex too hard, or just phoning it in from Mars?"

"No, France I think. Don't worry, I'll call her tomorrow." Sara started to fiddle with the sound system that had so beguiled him.

Liam strolled the long hallway of the suite several times. A slight dizziness had suddenly jumped up and taken hold of him. Just need some food he thought, that'll reset the clock, maybe help with this ringing in the ears. He lit up a smoke from the last of his pack.... Yeah, ringing in the ears, smoke in the lungs, booze on the brain, and a blast of red meat coming down the pipe for el corazón—wonderful—kick the ballistics on *that*.

In short order she'd mastered the beast, and a softly crooning Sinatra drifted gently through the suite and out the speakers along the terrace. A voice which understood a bit about all this useless beauty, but could offer little to remedy it. He went out to join her.

"Well, well—aren't we talented?"

"You're just jealous, Stone Age man."

They had their meal out on the terrace. The doors were drawn and the curtains swayed in the soft currents of the breeze. A little after three, and the first rays of light were gathering over the shadows of the dark Irish Sea. Five stories down were the faraway sounds of delivery trucks moving quickly along the empty quays. He looked across the span of Dublin and at a sleeping city never really asleep. Ireland was big sky country in the middle of the night; expansive, drifting, sliding off toward the lines at the horizon, the bend of the Earth just perceptible over the Leinster plains. Thousands of lights dotted the landscape, most of them solitary, untended things. He looked over and noticed his lovely, lost in her own, taking in the same view, from the same angle, with the faintest of smiles across her face.... He might have made her happy at that—*and that* could almost be enough.

It was a fine meal and as promised O'Shea ate every damn bit, including what she couldn't finish. Sinatra cycled back through the mix as the first bars of *Summer Wind* came on low and bouncy soft.

"Good one," his weathered mind suddenly rather clear. "Sixty years later and the guy's still making thunder.... Think about it, our grandparents were getting it on to this guy."

"Probably our parents too."

"In the Seventies? No, those were Frank's wilderness years—too old to be relevant, too young to be resurrected—a blue eyed Moses at The Sands."

But then he furrowed the brow, his weary brain connecting the grimmer dots. "*Besides*—my father never touched my mother."

"Were you a virgin birth then?"

"I'm still holding out for adoption."

"Liam! Tsk, tsk—what a terrible thing to say."

"It's just a joke. Man you Episcopalians are a touchy lot." He laughed.

"Coming from the Irish Catholic I'll take it with a grain of salt."

"Yeah, well…touché I guess."

The cordless on the balcony rang, startling them both, "Who the hell could that be?"

"Answer it," she said.

"…. Creeping Jesus; it's not like it's the middle of the night or nothing."

"Hello?" His voice was guarded, before suddenly cutting loose, "Motherfucker, it's about time."

Young Sara was willing to take it on faith this wasn't one of the hotel staff. She got up and wandered back inside.

"You ignorant slut, what are you still doing up?" O'Shea's thoughts gathered for a dim-bulb second. "More importantly how'd you know you wouldn't be *waking* me up?"

"How's that? You're just *getting* up…. Fuck man, do you work in a bakery or something?"

Christopher M. Basso

Apparently Kevin Delaney had risen early, as he did most days to get a jump on his non time zone specific graphic design gig; and the witching hour was last call for any clients left on Pacific Time. The cousins parlayed for a few minutes in the best free forming, ass grabbing tradition which did this country proud, before setting a plan in motion. "All right tomorrow morning....Uh, better make it late morning there chief."

He hung up and walked inside. Where'd that girl go? Time to test the limits of an elastic fantastic mojo—that old *love* was in the air. Maybe if he phoned down they would send up some Al Green or Barry White—something soulful.

He sauntered down the hall to the bedroom, only to find her already asleep, sweetly curled up, still wearing her party clothes. He strolled over and pulled the covers up over her, gently lifting her head beneath a pillow and turning out the lights.... *Sui Generis*—to be innocent when you dream. At least those rotten Jesuits had taught him something other than bedrock fear and loathing. But what of yourself, he pondered, still feeling fairly spry, sixty-two hours and counting?

He searched his bags and found the crumbled remains of an old stale pack, bent and twisted, barely holding together, but technically still qualifying as cigarettes—that'll do. He walked out to the balcony for what he promised himself would be the last, the final, the finito smoke of the day. He climbed up onto the parapet, his body leaning slightly over the edge, arching his back in a tired stretch—a fine vantage point, right on top of things. Not too much ambient light to muddle the stars over fair Dublin City. A long arc of them still lingered just before dawn, watching you, watching them.

Interesting how a very real five stories seemed far safer than the wholly imagined perils of your mind, at least when you were the one behind the wheel.... Airplanes were *deadly*, drunken hangs on the top of tall buildings were not. A neurotic superhero of sorts, a fine paranoia for the age.

It was quiet now, save for the odd drunken shouts from his fellow late-night malcontents down below. Just kindred souls out burning the wax to the bitterest of ends, equally gone with the same relish as the one watching from above; fairly content with the lay of things and their place in it.

But for all the light decorating the city, it was still rather dark along the river's edge, just the neat line of street lamps casting shades of muted yellow and fading white. Most of the shops and storefronts were still shuttered and shadowed. A descending lull met by the colors of the ascending sky, but still too dark to bring the old waterway fully into focus.

The tide had come in, pulling the Liffey high along its ancient walls. He watched the dark waters flow under the soft lights from the Halfpenny Bridge on a slow path to the sea; the darkness briefly lit along its latticework frame. Just enough to capture the faintest movements in the current and the slight eddies of the give and flow. He drank it in, the gray blue sky, the bright lines at the horizon; all the elemental things one could burn into the mind; regarding them with utter bewilderment, trying his best to breath in the essence of the things never to pass through this life again…. And a poor minds attempt to remember the humility due life's rare gifts.

A strong memory was something on the plus side of his uneven ledger, a mind that worked in snapshots, absorbing as much as possible, hardening the levee walls against some unstoppable advance. His waking mind had always been weighed down in the abstraction of confusing pictures; but his foggy foregone mind always sharp in the divination of the moment, in that midnight prayer clarity which always seemed to light the best way home…. Trying to paint pictures for rainy days was a fleeting, uphill push; a rush always tempered by the simple sad acceptance that these were only yours to borrow, but never yours to keep.

Applying a bit of elbow grease, he tossed his smoke off the roof and watched its still orange ember spiral down on the wind till it disappeared in the dark mulling waters below. He closed up shop and crawled into bed next to her, with the lights off and the Vidiwall lulling away in the background; the shiny glare from Mission Control as warm and reassuring as his ThunderCats nightlight. A fine bit of ambient noise for those not altogether fond of the silence.

Christopher M. Basso

Chapter Nine
The Sick Bed of Cúchulainn

Kevin Patrick Delaney stepped off the tram near the corners of Abbey and Capel Streets, just up North Dublin way. He filed past all his fellow punters smart enough to leave the cars at home and give this new light rail system a try out. Blackhorse to the city center in just under twenty-two minutes—that had to make you feel proud to be Irish. Right down the way were the low arch and gray spires of the Ha'penny Bridge. His step was light with a sense of bounce and purpose. He paused near the junction of Ormond Quay only long enough to light a cigarette and button up the front of his coat. *Bloody cold* in this damn city, he thought. You could still see your breath on the June air, not a good portent for one of those rare Irish summers. Not to bother though, at least not yet. Chipper up, still a long summer ahead—enjoy it.

Two young trim things drifted into his orbit for a moment as they waited for the lights to change. Remembering his manners, "Morning ladies." For his pains he took a downturned frown and a quick little smile. One for two—that was good enough for a balmy if not bracing morning. He started up towards Wellington Quay; his vintage Adidas trainers cut a silent path along the rough stones.

His tall, nearly 6'2", lanky heroin-chic frame moved, or should we say propelled itself along at the quick step in great purposeful strides. He had a lean, rawboned look, like he might have been perpetually food or sleep deprived, but was neither. His eyes, a dark piercing shade of blue, gave the impression of a man who rarely slept and was always, fully, awake.

Twenty years ago he would have been considered one of *those* people, the ones who zoned all day at the feet of O'Connell's statue. A generation of blameless cripples, thrill seeking their next fix; the children of another dream deferred. In some ways he very nearly was, the trajectory was there as they say. But a fine public school education, courtesy of The State, and a timely bit of patronage, courtesy of the Benedictine Brothers, carried him to higher things. This and a passing interest in art and computers led to a burgeoning career in graphic design, the perfect sort of gig for reformed Bohemians looking for a fairly stable piece of the action. At least you never had to wear a suit to work, which suited him just fine. In fact, he'd recently designed some of the glossy billboards and posters for the light rail he'd just stepped off of.

He paused in front of one for a moment; a smiling moonfaced montage to forever remind him of how he spent his long nights…not too shabby—but if he *ever* heard the phrase, "Try the Tram," again he might have to load stones in his pockets, stroll out to Poolbeg, and take a half gainer into the sea…. But then again if only his saintly grandfather could have lived to see such things. Thirty-nine years in a coal tinner so that his progeny might spend his days staring at pixilated light, and make more in a day than he did in a month—something to be said for being born at the right time.

The clock over the Millennium Bridge read two minutes past eight. Right on schedule and that was, after all, important. Unlike some of his older relatives, this boy had a prompt, organized sense of time. It was shocking how many of his Celtic ilk had only the vaguest constructs of it; with something almost Newtonian in their elasticity. For many Irish, time was twisting, something dancing around the fringes like an ever expanding and contracting contradiction—Dubliners were like jazz men, shooting for the edges of the beat, not caring if they hit the mark square. At least that's what they told themselves. So when yer' boy Paddy Fitzpatrick said eight o'clock, he was really drifting more towards an eight forty-five varietal. It was an abuse so flagrant, so woven, so omnipotent, that offense was rarely if ever taken.

Well jazz men didn't keep the trains running on time....*Sweet Jesus*, did he really just draw the water on that grim bit of judgment? Modern times had his brain drifting in Judas rhythms, but maybe these gray hairs would learn something yet. Punctuality was key—especially when it helped facilitate and exacerbate the torturing of family members who were most likely sleeping off savage burn-on's nearby.

And that was his mission of the morning—locate said cousin and his girlfriend who'd slipped into the country only the day before, track them down and perhaps fuck with them a bit—and, as no other welcome wagon had been dispatched, it seemed about the *least* he could do. But where to start? Call up Visa and report those cards stolen, dime him to "The Guards" as a known drug mule.... perhaps phone in a bomb threat to the hotel? No, that was for summers past; time to be a bit more practical about things. Showing up four hours early and on the tail end of a vicious bender would have to suffice for the mischief in these graying years.

Despite the chill there was a nice bit of sun creeping out from behind the clouds, falling across the old buildings and quays in slants of soft light and golden shades. He always liked the early morning hour in Dublin, when the last of the spewing stragglers and corporeal chancers had quit the drink and angst-fueled rages, abandoned the corruptions of the night, and crawled back into their beds. Everything was fresh and new; last night's sins, the mortal and the venal, all the petty dramas and intrigues washed away by the cool dawn cull of the morning rain—at least until the great beast was fired up again.

The Essex Hotel, his ultimate destination, was coming up hard and fast on the right. Though not as traditionally handsome as his cousin, the youngest Delaney fell somewhere in that handsome, in a peculiar way, category.... like some old school Merseyside rock star, or otherwise sun-deprived person who could wrangle a distinct kind of attractiveness out of looking like they've been propped up on death's door. He flashed a pair of dark blue eyes, shaggy black hair, and cheekbones of some prominence. A rather sublime look, an angler in the truest sense—from one end projecting a preternatural beauty and at the other revealing something that might actually spook the children and the grannies. He had a coiled energy about him that only served to underscore the features he was given, and for that he wouldn't complain—who gets to choose their own poison anyway?

But those were appearances and they can be deceiving—for as wound up as he looked, his personality was five bars down the measure of easygoing; happily drifting through this life with a fine sense of the ironic and the absurd. An added bonus of this off kilter alchemy was that once the nervous sorts realized he wasn't going to have a go at them with some concealed jailhouse weapon, they would often feel an instant sort of peculiar camaraderie and trust. His was a strange jujutsu, meant to throw the Burghers off balance—it was a stealing from the thieves of the highest order.

Several shades down the temperament scale stood his cousin, Liam James. And while they may have been born three hours apart during the same miserably cold winter, back when polyester was worshipped and disco was king, few similarities remained. Theirs was a metaphysical ocean to match the literal one separating their births. That's not to say O'Shea wasn't well liked, but he was certainly more the keep your hands from the cage regressive model—a bite much worse than his bark as some of those North Dub types might say.

As such they were content with simple pleasantries and cutting him a wide berth whenever he might shade over to the Dark Side.... Although rumor had it he'd dropped some of the Shōgun serious act, grown out his hair, and was presently on some manner of extended get away. *The Family*, in the royal sense, thought it best to check up on the boy, make sure things were still on the up and up. The slumbering Golem in question was presently off in the land of the faeries, some five stories up when Kevin Delaney rounded the last corner onto Wellington Quay and made quick for the hotel doors.

As he reached the entrance of The Essex, he noticed along the ground a great many cigarette butts, uncrushed and smoked to the bitter nub. Ahh, he thought, this must be the place. He strolled in with the easy going airs of a man who could still remember when this posh pile of bricks was shuttered fast, one missed payoff to the Council Chieftains from being fodder for the wrecking ball crews. He smiled at the thought—a railing whinge at those who might fly the flags of entitlement had always been considered a civic virtue around these parts…at least till the place went condo so to speak. But in the currency of true Dubliners to have shown yourself impressed would have been to show yourself too much.

After some bad noise with a strange Belgian who tried jumping him for his coat, he was free to roll up to the pretty fair-haired girl behind the desk and dispense with some meteorological pleasantries before rolling out the million-dollar question, "Perhaps you could help me with something?"

She seemed a bit hesitant to ring the suite unannounced. The maid had been chased away at dawn by an irate man fumbling with the Do Not Disturb sign.... They had some *real* chancers staying in this place from time to time. But Kevin thought to assure her. "Oh, I promise no trouble—we're blood. Besides, I'm not the paparazzi and he ain't Sting." She placed the call at once.

He stood in the foyer light letting his eyes drift about the place.... Kevin Delaney tolerated his own brothers—mainly out of some fearmongered biblical sense of familial propriety, but he actually *liked* his cousin. Perhaps all that came with the relaxed rules of men who were close, yet never in direct competition; never trying to spear that same piece of proverbial mutton off the table during those hungry formative years.

His mother Angelina would host the butcher boy at their Ballymun home some summers, which was all fine and good. But better yet were the summers when Kevin would escape the rusting backwaters of North Dublin and into the largesse of American suburban life—video games, cable television, towering eighteen screen megaplexes, not to mention the 2 a.m. pizza deliveries and the endless stream of GAP jeans and Air Jordans down at the mall. That all these things were now par for the course in his backyard was irrelevant, a young set of eyes viewed them with wonderment once.

That the whole thing might just have been an exercise in

the crass, tasteless perils of addicted "ownership" society was equally spurious. Nostalgia had since washed away the stain of an almost original sin. He thought about it as he scrolled through the messages on his iPhone; a good education in hindsight, and a *fine* primer for life on the big rock candy mountain.

Three hours forty-nine minutes and twenty-two seconds after he'd gone off to join those faeries in the happy hunting ground beyond the sun the phone nearest the nightstand rang with a shocking clarity, scattering the stardust and snapping him right back to attention—a rather jarring and generally annoying way to rejoin the world. O'Shea nearly fell off the bed lunging for the ringing whose simple amplification had grown to a lion's roar.

He thought best to compose himself, this was a nice place after all.

"Yes?" He croaked.

"Of course, I'll be down straightaway," he paused. "Yes. Why thank you."

He rolled over catching sight of himself in the long mirror.... Lazarus out of the tomb. His black hair was in his red eyes, as he struggled mightily to focus on what his watch was telling him. His ears were ringing, and his tongue had the fine pallor of warmed over death.

"What's going on?"

".... Dirty bastard's downstairs," he looked around. "Jesus, did I really sleep in my clothes?"

Most certainly—in fact, scanning the room, he'd gone a long way towards remaking the elegance of their suite into a rather swank hobo junction; mounds of crumbled clothes, flowers in the minibar blender, and room service trays now far less elegant then the horse they rode in on…ugh the cruel light of day.

He started for his pillow again, "Putz, let him wait."

She rolled over, seemingly unaffected by such things, "Liam go down and get him."

There was no movement from the departed. With a deftly aimed foot he was shoved off the bed and delivered floor-wise with a loud thud.

She peered over for a moment, studying him as he stumbled about the room searching for his shoes. "Bit of a hangover Liam James?"

He smiled, "More of an inexplicable headache really...Must have got a hold of some bad ice."

"Right."

He looked back at her, his eyes starting to focus.... Well, now she'd gone and done it—a wholly unintended lasciviousness invited to this innocent morning scene as she lay there wrapped in the sheets in all her statuesque jaybird glory. A comfortable hippie throwback flashing forward in some sort of new age amalgamation of the Erica Jong ideal without any of the hold ups. And as gone to death as he was his eyes still did a gyroscope spin—she'd be quite the hit when they found the warm waters of the Mediterranean.

"How am I supposed to concentrate with this kind of smut floating around?"

She threw aside the white sheets, arching her back in a bit of an exaggerated stretch, leaving little to his imagination, "I'm sure you'll manage."

.... Well, in some circles propriety still counted for something. He stripped off the sweat caked t-shirt and rummaged through a bag for the next of his cleanest dirty shirts. The heavy motorcycle boots looked too ominous in the light of day so he sported a pair of canvas flip flops and camouflage cargo shorts. He popped a couple of Excedrin and strolled down the quiet hallway towards the elevator.... Her West Coast rhythms were starting to rub off on him for sure. Looking somewhat the bastard love child of Hank Chinaski and Jeff Spicoli, he pressed the button for the lobby and leaned back against the cool wood of the elevator trying to gather his otherwise scattered thoughts.

The doors opened on three, a man and a woman walked into the tiny car with one of the bellhops and several bags. They all gave O'Shea a slight sidelong look, but otherwise kept to themselves. He had the rank stink of the Irish cologne about him and his bearings, at least the ones he could bring to bear, were something most foul. But whether he realized it or not, that same comportment was once again the secret Masonic handshake of the age; a calling card, if you will, where new found wealth's naiveté dovetailed quite nicely with a bored ninth generation's currency of practiced indifference to most things.

Without the legend to the map most strapgawkers would defer to the default mode—if the bastard looked like he didn't care, he simply *must* be someone. And ergo his sweat pored whiskey stank and Guinness cheese-chaser were merely the colorful accoutrements to the act…like their Louis Vuitton bags he very nearly tossed his cookies on.

"Good morning."

"Morning."

The boy's head was still loose from the moorings, swimming in that bone-tired, jet-lagged, hung in a bad place kind of way—but on the prayers for forgiveness scale this one wasn't *too* bad. No spins or piercing death rattles—hallucinations to a minimum, nothing that a little acetaminophen breakfast could make right. Pair it with some grease to mend the throb in his brain and the ache in his belly and we'd be right as rain. Yep, not too vicious all things considered.

You could always gauge the quality or severity of the hangover by the night it's answering for, or at least the day it answers to. There was a bright clean light shining through the transom slits in the glass, just enough to briefly spy the Heavens as you made your way slowly back to Earth.

He found his cousin perched astride one of the green leather chairs in the study near reception, smoking a straight Marlboro Red down to the withers; another bit of America that had colonized his mind—but to each their own. Filter anything through the haze of some pleasant peripheral memory and watch it gain all sorts of acceptability. How else could one eat blood sausage and deep-fried candy bars with a straight face?

Their reunion caused little fanfare, no whopping, hell-raising, or general carrying on. A simple handshake and a hug, like two old men—too bored and familiar for any song and dance hysterics. Besides, the wild displays of histrionics were best reserved for those insecure types who have to gauge their affections by the sheer crank of volume, back slapping, and bloodletting. These boys had been to the mountain together, after that not much else mattered.

Liam crashed down in the soft club chair across from him, bleary eyed and half slumped. "Why Kevin lad, you're a bit ahead of schedule," he smiled. "I'll be getting you for that one you sheeplovingsonofabitch."

"Weren't *you* the one always singing the virtues of being prepared?" Kevin leaned back, studying the state of the man, "Put yourself through the ringer Liam James?"

"Does it show?" He chuckled. "Give me one of those."

Kevin lit the match for his cousin and watched him settle back…. Looked well enough, nothing outwardly odd or discernible.

The first jolts of nicotine seemed to bring him back into focus. "It was epic," O'Shea offered, his eyes lighting up. "49 hours on the piss, 38,000 feet, 500 mph, 6 types of distilled something, 5 time zones, 3 packs, 2 continents, and that's before I'd even cleared Customs."

"…. I've seen it better."

"Really…and what, then you came to?"

"Heathrow to Sydney, 22 hours in the air, consumed the entire contents of one beverage cart, smoked off a tin of these—back when such things were permissible—tattooed a concubine on a Bangkok layover—44 hours in Sydney, torched The Mercer, and woke up the following Tuesday in an Aboriginal camp outside Darwin, resting between Warrun Willy and Narrah Ned."

"Friends of yours?"

He nodded appreciatively, "Two of the old fellas…saved me from the crocs and the gillas when I was off my tits beside myself."

"*Shit*, Huckleberry," he exhaled, "you've never even *been* past London."

"Right—but what I'm saying is that's how it would've gone down you understand?" A broad smiled crept across his face, "But fuck man—it's good to see you!"

Liam nodded, "You too."

One of the hostesses came by and took their order, one coffee as black as the night, and one Earl Grey as queer as the Queen. Liam frowned—quiet as it's kept around these tea loving parts, but O'Shea *hated* tea, hated it with a passion akin to air travel with circus clowns.

Kevin Delaney's eyes drifted around the room, "Jesus boyo—this pile of stones must be costing you a mint?"

"How indelicate of you to ask," he smiled. "No worries though; I gave em' a fake credit card—yours to be exact. I'm running a felonious burn on this place."

Kevin eyed his cousin for a second, but good-naturedly let it go.

"How you settling in?"

"Ok, getting my legs back you know."

"Been awhile hasn't it."

"Seven lean years my man."

"You've been busy," Kevin said.

"I've been under a rock," he smiled. "But that's been sorted too…. Anyway, what's going on around here? Has the place gone fucking *mad*."

He shook his head, "Hasn't it though…. Government plan, *rebrand* the place—The Square Mile meets The Left Bank, with not quite the charm of either and more than the shitty weather for both."

"Well…that's a damn shame."

"Oh you have been away too long O'Shea." Kevin smiled, glancing out the windows towards the clearing sky, "Anyway, they took a hammer and nail to the place, couldn't mend everything but they rezoned the better and bulldozed the worst."

Kevin Delaney lit up another for himself, "So, croppy boy, tall tales of travel and civil engineering woes aside, when am I going to get to meet the missus?"

"Oh, you wanted to meet her?"

"Thought it might be appropriate."

"She's getting dressed I think. She said to bring you up presently—but remember, no drooling you swine."

"She's a looker then?"

"Well, she's rockin' a full set of teeth and two sets of chromosomes, so I guess she's excelling by those Delaney standards."

"Eyes of the same color only add to a woman's allure," he smiled.

"A strong pulse and no bleating—you might be a wee bit crestfallen."

The hostess had returned with the coffee and tea just in time for that jem.

"Naturally, he's kidding of course."

Liam smiled and shook his head, "Could you put it on room 508 please?"

He motioned to his irate cousin, "C'mon let's go."

They strolled out to the lobby and into the lift.

The acetaminophen had yet to kick in and all this early morning drama left the boy in need of a hand. He propped himself against the wall and counted backwards from ten as they ascended the skeleton of the hotel. His was a pantomime Kevin understood all too well.

"Look at you O'Shea," he shook his head sadly. "Where did it all go wrong?"

Liam closed his eyes and conjured up the ghost of a smile.

"Sure they must have slipped you a dirty glass," Kevin

said.

"Yes, I've been unlucky in that way, thank you for your concern."

"Where'd you go anyway?"

"Nothing too heavy—but it was that flight, got it rolling on the flight…saw no real point in stopping after that."

"Aye, sure."

"Anyway, after that it's sort of a hazy, tourist-themed blur."

He nodded, "Well, you have to get it out of the way."

"Trinity, Grafton Street, Stephens Green, the…"

"Look, Leopold," he interrupted, "I'd really like to hear about your epochal *Frommer's* Dublin wanderings some time, but get to the good stuff…. Pick it up where you started to look like this."

"Oh, I see—well, to the best of my recollection it went off the rails somewhere just before midnight. I made the regrettable decision to leave the wine and return to that rotten Jameson."

"Well, that would do it."

"We wandered around a bit, finally wound up in the club downstairs."

"…. The Flaming Colossus?" He sounded a bit concerned.

"Jesus, is that what's it's called?"

"Unfortunately…. What'd you think?"

He shrugged. "Looked like some good Catholics idea of bad night out."

Kevin laughed, "Hardest gate in town right now you know," he thought about it for a moment. "How'd you get in?"

"Shit, I got pull."

"Handjobbing the bouncer ain't pull."

"…. No, I would think that's more torque—but then

you'd be the authority on that." O'Shea tapped his fingers along the railing, "…. Besides your sister beat me to it—no pun intended."

"Your cousin might I remind you."

"…. Oh yes—perhaps I'll just smack myself?"

Kevin smiled, "Good to see you boyo."

She'd left the door to the suite cracked open.

"Sara!" He peeked his head around the corner, "Get decent, we've arrived."

"Be out in a second," came a voice from the bedroom.

The suite was a bit of a mess, suitcases half open with their contents strewn about the main room, several room service trays sat on the far table, a couple of empty bottles of mineral water and one fairly full bottle of wine. The faint hint of French fry grease and vanilla cedar armoire lingered pleasantly.

His cousin gave an appraising once over, "Nice place." He raised an eyebrow. "Must be costing you a fortune?"

"Don't worry. I have a generous benefactor."

Sara strolled out from the bedroom, her wet hair pulled back from a quick shower. She was sporting a pair of slightly frayed blue jeans and a black, fitted shirt. She looked bright eyed, awake, and strangely girlish in the early morning light. She knew the fine line between her limits and the undiscovered country which lay in wait. As such she rarely tempted them, and even on the rare occasion she did, it was with the deft touch of an angel who always knew the precise moment when the wax would melt.

A proper yin to the yang of her man who specialized in a kamikaze mantra of spinning rooms, mad dog ravings, and ulcerated banshee wails. The banshee wail in question was presently standing in the doorway; the corrosive burn of the night before still lingering in the eyes, with the spent jet fuel trash penance hovering on the tongue…. Standing there with another such degenerate, both smiling the same strange catbird grin.

"Liam," the slightly taller of the degenerates spoke. "You

haven't done her justice. She's *lovely*."

She smiled the smile of pleasant apparatchik, towing The Party's *feel good* line; her Boxer/Feinstein raised ears having never quite heard herself referred to in the passive sense while still actively in the room.

She regrouped quickly, "He rarely does me justice—I'm Sara," she shook his hand. "Nice to finally meet you."

"And this hobo would be Kevin Delaney." Liam grabbed his shoulder and shook his head sadly, "Somehow, somewhere down the gene pool from myself...down the shallow end *most* likely."

"And you'd already know this sad specimen used to be Liam O'Shea—we rarely see him out in the daylight anymore."

"Sounds like you boys have this all figured out," she smiled. "Have a seat Kevin, can I get you something, some tea maybe?"

"Yeah," O'Shea chimed in, "Bars stocked all to hell. What do you want?"

"No, no—it's your *vacation*," he gestured to Sara. "Let's you and I have a seat—my better half can do the honors."

His better half was still playing around, trying to get his eyes to focus, "Sure, by all means—righto."

He located three fresh pint glasses and peered into the fridge, "What of it," he shouted to his cousin. "You still on your love affair with The Priest?"

"No, wheat grass shakes these days I'm afraid. I've had to fortify myself Iron Man style of late."

"Trying to keep the herpes under control?"

"No, more like the work week. I'm putting in a steady sixty or seventy these days."

"What do you do?" She asked.

"Web design mostly, some freelance commercial graphic work as well."

"He's the technosexual Gigolo Joe of the Celtic rising

sun," an obnoxious voice emanated from within, "hustling his Apple scruffs down along the waterfront."

He smiled at Sara, "Grumpy before he's eaten isn't he?"

She smiled, "You'll have to excuse him, he has an inexplicable headache."

"Oh, that's ok. I've had one or two myself.... All right Liam James," he shouted back, "Serve me up a jar of the good stuff!"

"That's what I wanted to hear." He cracked open two cans of Guinness and a tin of orange juice for his beloved. Spying the still half filled demi of Brut from a scant sunshine ago, he poured the rest into each glass. *Voilà,* two Black Velvets for the local boys and a gentle Mimosa for the wayfaring import."

He could see Sara and the miscreant Kevin Delaney out on the balcony getting to know one another. They were looking over the balustrade as his cousin pointed out something down along the river.

Good, he thought, getting along, just as hoped for. The misanthrope in him hadn't much time for most people and most things. That his two favorite people in the world were seemingly hitting it off in that crucial thirty second window between like or loathe, love or hate, was a pleasant affirmation of the grander plan. Add a little alcohol, stir, and we should be home free. He returned with their drinks on the tray, and an oversized Gideon Bible for the benediction.

Kevin offered up his glass for a small toast, just a few words bordering on the touching if not charming, at least until he dredged up the foulest bit of vice he could affix to his cousin's head. After all, amongst the Dubliners to show yourself impressed would have been to show yourself too much.

Liam lowered his head. "Lovely speech Kevin—bless."

He nodded with a smile. "I've got a beer goggle, late night eloquence about me—you'll see."

It was then decided breakfast was in order. Within twenty minutes they were walking out the back door of the hotel, retracing their steps along Essex Street from the night before.

The Essex, while a fine pile of bricks, didn't quite specialize in the type of grease laden throwback the moment called for. A homeopathy of local shades was more in order.

Just around the way from the juice bars and sushi shacks was a rather nondescript, almost condemnable, looking storefront which only Irish eyes would have recognized as open, let alone a restaurant, let alone a local treasure for just this sort of time traveling repast. Paddy Dignam's Social Club was well...social; crowded out with the early lunch and late morning straggler crowd.

They took the table nearest the window. O'Shea sat with his back to the wall, Mafia style, just out of reach of the sun's rays creeping across the table. There was some pointless perusing of the menu. But he knew exactly what was needed, and as it was really the only thing old Paddy served, they were blissfully sacrosanct in their hog jowl union. A *real* Irish Fry, like one of those witch-hazel remedies that poisons you a bit as it delivers the cure.

Within minutes O'Shea was staring down a plate that would've made Dr. Jarvik gasp. Four eggs over easy, big strips of Maybell bacon, rashers, baked beans, stewed tomatoes, thick slices of Irish brown bread lathered with something decidedly not margarine. The ubiquitous brown and black disks of mystery offal were delicately skirted off to the side.

Despite his wholly reasoned local bona fides, he'd never quite gotten the fascination these island people had with grinding up the strangest parts of the animal, stuffing it in sausage casings, and fraternally serving it up to one another in what must have once passed for dares, or tests of manly resolve. Necessity might also have been the hobgoblin of providence once, but now it was decidedly something else.

Not content with the mere heart attack on a plate, Kevin Delaney went for the Ulster Fry; a nebulous concoction which made the Irish Fry seem more like a South Beach salad plate....Rumor had it the government kept a roving team of cardiologists and laptop defibrillators prowling the city on emergency flight line standby—who said socialized medicine had its drawbacks?

For an hour or so they had a chance for a bit of catching up, getting acquainted, and generally watching the ebb and flow of Dublin drift by Paddy's grease caked windows. The youngest Delaney was quick to regale them with the most sordid tales his cousin had tried his damndest to forget. Once there was a rude etiquette with these things. You could pull a little Clockwork Orange now and then, but any and all record was expunged at the airport curb for the flight home…. Long winded tales of fights, flights, and late nights spent terrorizing the denizens and the architecture. What happened in Dublin was supposed to stay there, at least until ingloriously resurrected like dirty laundry blowing loose in the breeze. Kevin lad was obviously in the vanguard of the new transparency.

"…. I don't know about you," Liam offered up over a fresh cup of stale coffee, but family are some of the most vicious people I know."

"Like Dobermans," his cousin smiled before checking his watch.

"Late for a very important date are we?"

"My apologies, I've got to be going," he winked at Sara, "the man beckons."

Liam held out his hand, "That's why he's the man."

Kevin smiled, "Oh to have the life a gentleman. Sara it's been grand," he gave her a kiss, "and Liam, as ever." He put on his sunglasses and grabbed his urban rucksack. "Try to get some color back into you; you're starting to look like me…. Wedding is in three days, I'll be in touch."

And with that, the miscreant Kevin Delaney took his leave. Even the slim constraints of the unstructured lifestyle reared their ugly bilious head now and again, and when they did, even stoner Surfa Rosa types had to answer the Batphone. In short order he was out the door, bounding up the street in his quick energetic way, where he met the *Bus Átha Cliath* at the corner, jumped in and was gone.

O'Shea's expression had grown a bit quizzical, "Did he seem normal to you?"

She was stirring her tea, guesstimating the proper

number of sugar cubes local etiquette allowed for, "*Silly*—how would I know? I just met him."

"Right," Liam was watching the empty road where the bus had been.

"Did something seem wrong?"

".... I don't know."

She looked up from her tea, "Why Liam, usually it takes a few generations of wealth before the paranoia sets in."

"It was a bit odd when the check came. He damn near speared me with his fork for it."

"Yeah, what was that about? If I knew you two were going to get frisky I would've given you some privacy."

He looked ahead, leaving his troubles with a smile, "Must be a family thing…"

A tender look crossed her eyes, "I know you meant well, but maybe it hurt his feelings—he probably feels like you're his guest?"

Liam laughed softly, folding the bill between his rough-hewn fingers, "Yeah, I suppose I'm still getting the *hang* of this?"

She finished sugaring her tea, ".... Does he know about your condition?"

"*My condition*? Sweet Jesus—is there something I should know about?"

"Stop it…. You know what I mean."

"Oh that," he smiled, "yes that."

He leaned against his chair and ran his hand along the back of her neck; the morning light, clean and diffuse, picking up the strands of gold in her hair. "Well, he certainly knows Handsome Henry was shown across, but I'm not sure what else he's heard. We haven't talked much in the last year, but there are a lot of scamps around the campfire, you know? C'mon—Uncle Fintan? I've probably been the topic of some interesting conversations."

"And you're ok with this?"

"Well...it is what it is," he smiled, straightening up. "C'mon, let's hoof it back to our $700, excuse me, $750 a night bunkhouse, maybe alert the minions to summon up the Martin Bormann pimpmobile and keep up the low key, inconspicuous act…. Maybe some sightseeing? *Lovely* country just south of here."

"Sounds delightful."

He smiled, rapping the table with his knuckles, "Vamanos!"

Christopher M. Basso

Chapter Ten
Rain Dogs

     Three days of rain are what followed. The sky opened up and let loose with one of the worst thunderstorms any Dubliner could recall. Strong gusts of wind blew along the natural alley of the river, as the flashing lights of some tropospheric pinball game played itself out.... Great, casting sheets of rain began to fall, straight down the chute at first, then slightly slanted to the side, till finally driving east to west; like the furious descent of their last end, upon all the barely living and the recently functionally dead. Maybe the ferocity was to make amends for the dearth in frequency, like nature was out to provide a friendly reminder that despite the gloss, man's dominion over this world was a rather tenuous thing at that.

     The fury came rolling in with a ferocity not all together known around these parts, turning the sky a frightening shade of black and then a more ominous, if not slightly ironic, shade of green. O'Shea watched the emerald sky approaching from the terrace of the suite—a bad twinge went through him. Green skies meant tornadoes.... Tornadoes in Dublin? Complete rot, no twisters here—only man made calamities around these parts.

     He stepped back into the suite and cracked open a cold G&T. His precious was sitting on the couch, wireless keyboard on her lap, staring up at the huge plasma screen, typing away in a

Christopher M. Basso

flurry of instant message chitchat and the occasional email. He had a long pull from his drink and studied her for a moment….Oh well, everyone has their idiosyncratic ways to ride out the storm…presently his own were calling. He walked back onto the terrace, lit up, and took his catbird seat near the ledge.

He'd since cultivated this gargoyle perch as his own. A fine spot amid the stained green copper awnings and white pigeon middlings, the broad expanse of fair Dublin City before him, and a sanctuary where he could light up with impunity. There was a strong breeze blowing from the west down to the east, channeling the alley of the river, a wind whipped fury getting right with its mojo, scaring the straights and foreboding the portents of something wicked just around the bend.

"By the pricking of my thumb…" He mumbled to no one, as an old Verve tune cycled in the background.

…. The rain felt good in Ireland. It was a reaffirming, expansive thing. One that was generally laced with something—be it the bad omens of consequence or the pleasant tidings of providence, which launched a thousand voices speaking or a thousand pens a blazing. It carried up in the warm air from the arc of the Gulf Stream, Caribbean skies bestowing one last waning favor before they turned somewhat brutish for the Portuguese coast.

Occasionally lightning would strike out in the distance, illuminating the gray-green sky for that briefest of moments, capturing the city in some eerie, overexposed snapshot. All the majesty of things he'd never understand…the Lightning Rod Man was creeping up for sure…. Cigarettes just about fucked moments like these, or at the very least sullied them. Booze was ok, a rather victimless crime at that, a self inflicted wound. But addiction called, so he lit up another under the far side of the terrace, where he could look through the glass and see her on the couch, and the reassurance which came when she was in sight.

He stepped down from his perch to enjoy a bit of the rain. He held out his hand and let it fall on his arms, along the back of his neck, his hair turning a cooler shade of wet, and watched as it traveled down the faded awnings, to the ends of the stone parapet before falling onto the street below….Quite pleasant the first day, a bit wistful on the second, somewhat tedious by the third, and shades of *Here's Johnny* by the fourth.

".... When the fuck's this going to stop?"

"Talking to ourselves again?" She called out.

"Yes, I keep the worst sort of company I'm afraid."

"What are you muttering?"

"Nothing. Just talking to myself.... It's one of the first signs of cabin fever, don't you know?"

"Should I be worried?" She inquired. "You know I think the Donner's started out on vacation too."

"Well, I don't think we're quite there *yet*, but we gotta to get out of this place."

"The hotel? I agree."

"No, the country," he paused, "and *soon*."

She stopped typing and looked up, "What are you on about? We just *got here*. We're supposed to stay for two more weeks."

"Yeah," his face took on that malevolent, not quite benevolent tinge, somewhere between patently thoughtful and slightly insane, "not so sure I see that one happening."

"Why?"

"I don't know," which is to say he did. "This place kind of...blows."

He leaned in the doorway to the balcony with the ominous green sky lit up behind him.

"You're kidding right?"

"This place—it's gone off the rails. A bunch of hopped up crack babies *way gone* on binge buying and image lifting," he shook his head sadly. "I suspect some of my friends and relations have taken the soup as well."

"Liam," she reigned in the disbelief. "This is called a glass house and you're standing in it...would you like a stone?"

"What?" He looked a bit hurt, "C'mon, this business is

an *experiment*—a bit of play-acting…but these people—these mugwamps have let it go native!"

She thought about it for a moment. Usually his moods, even the erratic ones, were fairly predictable, but this little chestnut had jumped the fence and was just about off the reservation.

"C'mon, you're just letting the weather get to you."

"Nope, not this time. I'm pretty sure about this."

She nodded, "I understand…. I might even have to agree—this was *nothing* like I pictured. It feels like we never left home actually."

"Exactly!" He shot back, before crossing over to the club chairs near the windows. "That's what I'm talking about."

He cracked open another G&T, "Here I was thinking we could expand the horizons, give my missus a bit of a show, and what do we get——the confirmation of my deepest fears and suspicions."

"…. Well, *despite* all that, I think we should stay a bit longer. We've got this wedding, and your cousin and your friends want to see you."

He thought about it for a moment, "Yeah, well, *things change*." He was smiling, "I think they'll understand."

…. Liam O'Shea, back like a mule, heart like a wheel, and the quixotic fantasies of a gent, but by the bye, interpersonal relations were not a strong point.

She studied him for a moment, was this a joke? "Yeah, I'm sure they'll understand there Chesterfield." She enjoyed playing along sometimes. "So, where we off to next, Okavango safari…a bit of white water down the Blue Nile?"

"No—better." He'd been making his slippery way from the door to the chair to the couch, gradually getting closer till finally he was sitting next to her, hijacking the keyboard. "Let me show you."

He let his fingers do the walking and within moments he'd pulled up the main page of the *Palio di Siena* in all its bright, garish, glorious colors.

It took her a minute to grasp what exactly she was looking at. "You want to cut out—to go to a horse race?" She paused, "But you don't even like horse racing?"

"No, I hate it—bad for the Lilliputian, worse for the horse. A time bomb profiting only atavistic assholes paying for the hay and the gambling mainliners laying down the odds; all the reward with none of the risk…. Sport of kings my ass."

"Are you through?"

"Look, my friend," he continued, "this isn't just some afternoon out at *The Aqueduct*—this is a centuries old mad dash through the center of Siena, the heart of Tuscany. They throw down a dirt track for the day, erect massive crash barricades on the turns; three laps around the *Piazza del Campo*—no saddles, no starting gates, no rules. Shit, no riders—only the *horse* has to finish."

"And they do this because?"

"I don't know…bragging rights I think." He thought about it, *"Apparently,* these fuckers take this thing as seriously as the plague. It's daggers and shivs in the dark, neighbor vs. neighbor—real old school Medici and Borgia street violence and intrigue on a truly dangerous level. And after they bury the hatchet, they bury the hatchet; everyone sits down to a giant communal feast."

"And where did you get this one from?"

He was silent.

"Right—I should have known."

"*What* do you have against my lawyer, nay, dare I say *mentor,* Fred Dewan?"

"Nothing, except he might be, dare I say, the legal world's version of a Goddamn carnival barker."

"…. That's a bit harsh don't you think?"

"No! He should probably be *disbarred*."

"He's a bit quirky, I'll give you that."

Needless to say when it came to matters of ethical propriety, or the lack thereof, the bohemian flower child went out the window, and in its place a frothing Rottweiler let slip the dogs of war.

"All right," he said, "his interpretation of the law is a bit *elastic*. But he's had plenty of good advice, and he certainly hasn't tried any shenanigans."

"Jesus, I would hope not. Is that the measure then? He hasn't broken any laws...yet?"

"—Hey glass houses? How about you come down off the cross, we could use the wood."

"Whatever."

The phone interrupted them.

"Yes...what, ok hold on please," she looked at him. "Did you schedule the masseuse for after three?"

".... No, I scheduled the *masseuses* for after three—good looking out right?"

She frowned. "Ok, please tell them three would be fine."

".... You're welcome," he laughed.

She cut him off. "What does Fred Dewan know about horse racing in Italy anyway?"

"How should I know? I think he used to *romp* there back in the day."

"Lax extradition laws?"

"Ha, ha—that's a good one; glad to see you're keeping yourself amused."

She gave him a measured look; there'd be another time to argue about Fred the huckster. "I think you're off your rocker. What's so special about *this*?"

"Shit, I don't know." But then again he most likely did. "It just *seems* like the right thing to do, like that little voice that tells you which road to follow."

"So you're hearing voices then—is that what you're saying?"

"Give it a rest smartass…. C'mon it'll be interesting. A bunch of hopped up Sienese duking it out for next year's bragging rights…. Hell, it'll be a damn sight more interesting than watching a bunch of bloviated Dubliners spending their ducats like they were wallet kryptonite."

He said it with such delicate sincerity, full of hyperbole and rank illusion. He'd obviously never been knee deep in a heavy scene where ideas matter less than realities.

She leaned forward, honing in on the finer print, "Liam, it's *this* Sunday."

He exhaled deeply, "Indeed."

"The wedding is Saturday."

"You are correct Mish Moneypenny."

"Would you stop calling me that," she said. "Why do you keep calling me that?"

"It's was the name of a horse I owned once," he laughed

"You want to skip the wedding then?"

"Whoa, I didn't say all that—I'm not a *beast*, but look," he summoned up an awfully assembled random presentation, "the wedding is most of the day, and knowing these bastards, most of the night, but the race isn't till around dusk on Sunday."

"And?"

He looked at her, "…. Where's your sense of the absurd? Need I remind you that this is Beckett country—and he too couldn't wait to get the fuck out of here."

She studied him with a quizzical eye…obviously *not* a Beckett fan.

He smiled, "We go to the wedding, booze, shake, parlay into the wee small hours…the *very* wee small hours, mind you, and then around three or four we bust out. It's about an hour to the airport, hop on the six a.m., get to Rome around eleven, pick up the car…"

"Let me guess—a Ferrari Enzo?"

"C'mon then, there's no need for all that—*Anyway*, from

the airport it's about a four hour burn up to Siena, where I have," he quickly changed screens, "taken the liberty to rent this lovely Tuscan farmhouse."

"Wait, you already rented it?"

"Hell yeah. Blew some mad coin on that bad boy…they told me da Vinci slept there once."

She looked at the furiously assembled accoutrements of his presentation, not quite sure whether to be impressed with its speed and precision, or rather concerned with the general back alley insanity vibe which seemed to be driving the beast.… In the end she was a bit of both—a balanced nature was perhaps her finest trait.

…. But then there were questions.

"What about Scotland, I thought Scotland was next?"

"Trust me, it'll still be there."

She gave him a long look, "C'mon Liam James—drop the nonsense," she was leaning forward in the chair, "How about a little bit of the truth?"

"The truth?"

"Yes the truth; royal, ragged, or otherwise."

His mind was racing under her watchful glare. He blurted out the first recycled convenience which sprang to mind.

"I've had enough of schizophrenic, ego-centric, paranoiac, prima-donnas?"

"Nice try, but not even *He* can help on this one."

"Uh…snoochie boochies?"

"*Get real.*"

O'Shea looked beaten. Expeditions into the privations of the soul rated somewhere right above bamboo chute pedicures and just below QT in the bastinado.

"All right, the truth?"

"Yes, or some halfway home version of it."

…. How best, he wondered, to explain the vague terror

166

seizing his mind with each passing moment in this town? How best to articulate the notion that history—the local revisionist brand—had just been run through the cosmic soak, wash, and spin cycles with a vigor bordering on a the Nuremberg ideal.

As such the complete revolution, evolution, and devolution of a memory had violently come to pass. And it didn't need tourist anachronisms like him standing around listening for the echoes. That these private requiems should be measured from such a set of jaded eyes only had to make matters worse…but how to explain such things, to the fresh baby blues meeting his?

Honesty might have been the best policy on this one; thoughtfulness might have come in handy, but when have either gotten in the way of expediency. Instead he rode the first strange bit of bucking bull out the chute.

"Things never used to change."

"Beg pardon?"

His brain was unwinding now, the words more or less found themselves.

"When I was a kid, I liked it here, mostly because everything stayed the same," he paused, "between my borderline incarcerated father and my lovely, but spacey mother, this place was like some kind of oasis—cold, raining, and hyper-aggressive but an oasis nonetheless." He paused again, suddenly caught in just the sort of cringe-worthy memory lane podunk he'd always cursed to flames, "Shit, guess you don't realize those things till you get a bit older?"

He met her eyes again, "Given all the miscreants I've subjected you to so far this might seem hard to believe?"

She chuckled, "You could say that."

"Yeah, but see—even the sketchy shadiness was as dependable as a Swiss watch. Nothing ever changed, the cousins, the friends…that shit-tiered pile of bricks out by the airport which the Delaney's called home." He smiled, "Kevin could be counted on to be the scammer, his mother was the doting aunt, his father the reliable town crank straight from Behan's pen, his brothers a pack of wild animals, and his friends just one shade north of criminal—but generally *really* nice people once you got to know them…"

A wistful look now crossed his eyes, "A predictability taken for granted…regrettably I guess." He grinned, "But it was *nice* all the same—*Quite* different from where I was calling from."

"…. And now it's gone?"

"More than gone—like it never even happened."

She looked sad for him, "That's how it seems to go, though doesn't it? Life's a lot more forthcoming about the things it's willing to take away from you."

"Yeah, I used to think that—at least until I drifted into this tax bracket."

"What do you mean?"

"Up here in the playpen you get to paint a bit more of the picture than down there…shit, you even get some say in the colors."

"That's hardly the truth."

"Ah yes, you were looking for the truth. Here's a truth—my bladder hurts, so you'll *have to* excuse me."

He went snorkeling with the door open as so they might continue this jabberwocky fest.

But she remained quite adamant about the essence of the thing.

"Still working on the truth huh?" He shrugged, "Well, it's not hard and fast, but it's close enough to plant your flag on….Besides, I can vibe that. Why shouldn't they want to change?" He looked about the tasteful appointments of his suite, at the Zen-like splendor of his surroundings which were reset daily by helpful unseen elves, "Damn, they'd say I've changed a bit…. Anyway, they seem a whole lot happier than I remember, and I'd feel more than a chump if I sat here and bitched about my nostalgia in the face of their getting somewhere with their lives. But fuck man, when a symbol stops being a symbol, why hang around? Bad food and shitty weather?"

"Won't argue with you on that one."

"Well, how about it then? Let's take this little show on

the road."

He had a strange look in his eyes; miles from the sarcasm and cynicism which was always just within reach.

She leaned over and gave him a kiss on the cheek, "Well Geezer, you've moved the stone—I'm in."

"Are you raining down on my epiphanies you *evil* woman?"

"Nope, I just don't necessarily *believe* them."

She thought about it for a second, "How are you going to explain this to *your people?*"

"Oh I think they'll understand."

"Well…it does seem kind of rude, maybe even a bit shallow?"

"Yes, well I've cultivated my fair share of goodwill over the years—but if not, I'll just have to live with it I guess."

"Maybe we should stay one more week?"

He shook his head, not to be dissuaded, "The clocks running backwards to zero my dear. This is your life, and like the man said, it's ending one minute at a time…. Hell do you know I found a gray hair in my ear this morning—can you believe that grossness?"

"That's hot."

"Yes, well I shudder to think *where* is next."

He looked at her, the deal nearly done. "C'mon, you're on *vacatio*n—time to play act at some wickedness, very far from home…very far from the things you know."

He stood up.

"I'll deal with the brood," he smiled. "Besides, propriety can take a back seat in the annals of our days—we got windmills to nuke."

He started over towards the door. "Well, I'll leave you to it," he glanced at the long IM trail down the screen. "How's ol' Cameron doing anyway?"

"She sounds fine, a bit scatterbrained as always, but fine…where you off to?"

"The bar, for a fresh pack of smokes and a wee spot of fruit juice."

"Don't be too long," she smiled. "You wouldn't want to miss the masseuse, excuse me—the masseuses."

"Right, wouldn't want to miss that…. think they offer the Happy Ending?"

"Gross—get out of here."

"Don't worry, I hear they service both sides of the great divide—you'll get your's today…that's what four stars is all about."

He turned serious for the thinnest of moments, "So, we're still on for this Cameron thing when we get back?"

"Uh-huh, I told her we'd be back around the third week in August. Sound about right?"

"Sure."

"She said she's excited to meet you."

"Yeah, the mutants always are," he mumbled.

Be nice, you haven't even met her."

"The phone experiences have been enough, not to mention the bead-jagging Bourbon Street YouTube clips…feel like I know her better than her OB/GYN."

"She's sort of a free spirit—I'll grant you that."

"That's probably being generous, but like I said I'll leave you to it."

Chapter Eleven
All in the Golden Afternoon

He eventually found the bar, after wading through some sort of fashion-themed soiree for which he didn't quite have the ticket to ride. He took a seat near the crowded wall, next to someone he was sure he recognized from the movies, but couldn't quite place the name.... He thought he'd handled the native Exodus with just the right bit of tact and flair for the occasion, but he *must* have crossed those hands of fate because rain, in all the glorious shades of inclement clemency, blanketed Dublin City for the next two days—God working overtime, as old Fintan might have said, stretching out the slate blue and charcoal grays in the palette. Arrangements by turns, from a fine gentle mist that made you sit up on the balustrade smoking your smokes and admiring the gray-green constancy of the sky, to the bullet launched rivulets of cold steel-jacketed rain that drove lesser men indoors to perfect their effete modern man survival skills.

Namely, ordering up strange sounding, vaguely unpronounceable, items off the room service bill of fare, and availing of whatever manner of contemporary life, easy living distractions the hotel had to offer. Regrettably, the masseuses were of the thick, eastern European "Olga" variety who could probably lift a Mini Cooper as soon as they could work their way down the delicate alleys of your spine. And of course there were always the less painful distractions, a freshly stocked bar, fine cotton slippers and soft terry robes, hydrotherapy baths and sauna/steams; hell, even pants pressed while you wore them—why not? The hospitality industry was like the space race indeed.

But he hadn't come 3187 nautical miles to stand on a hotel balcony, pissing into the breeze and admiring the mist. Umbrellas were acquired, a rain slicker procured for his lovely, and they boldly ventured forth from the hotel.

As degenerate pub-life held only so much interest for Sara, they were soon left looking for something else to fill the void. Food? Too much consumed already; time to start pacing himself or they'd have to roll him onto the plane home. Museums? Quiet as it's kept; they were almost in the same league as a steaming cup of tea for the boy. Perhaps shopping? Lot's of slapdash trinkets and otherwise useless shite out there to separate him from his money. Some folks even call them "gifts" and Sara Connelly had an eye, if not the disposition, for such things.

They hit most of the one-off shops throughout Temple Bar, but the suburban American Bloodhound in her eventually nosed out the enormous Stephens Green Center near the top of Grafton Street. The stylish steel and glass behemoth was a sort of quasi Irish stab at the proto-Midwestern mall experience, but with a scaled down, stripped back *local* flavor. The inside was bright and airy; three floors stocked with a strange mix of the chinsy-kitsch, the functional practical, and a smattering of the über high-end brands that had only recently crashed these prosperous shores.

Liam dutifully followed behind, watching her buy gifts for her three sisters, her parents, grandparents, and even her spinster Auntie Deborah from Chico. She slowly loaded up young O'Shea like a pack mule readying for an assault down the narrow chutes of the Grand Canyon. As he struggled behind, he had himself a laugh about the relative grace of all this useless beauty. And then the slightly hazy realization that his own list of forget-me-nots was looking awfully threadbare these days.

Parents—gone. Grandparents—sent hither. An only child left to ponder this rather thin list…law school friends? That made him chuckle. His best friend? Strolling up ahead, refusing to take anymore of his wayward charity…. Max the dog didn't need

172

a new Blancpain "Fifty Fathoms Diver", so he bought one for Kevin Delaney instead; in case the bastard ever got the urge to wade out into the Irish Sea for a bit of the scuba. He had the fine timepiece wrapped and would take nothing less than an effusive thank you for an answer. With one last gift in hand, they made their way back to the hotel.... That wee punk bitch, he'd best appreciate it.

The wee punk bitch in question had briefly dropped by the day before, but it became readily apparent that he wasn't kidding about the Jamba Juice wheat shakes and twelve-hour workdays. *The Man* had indeed locked him into the burgeoning chains of the American Samurai work week. And while the Irish had always been the sorts to work themselves like a gang of rented mules, it had always been someone else behind the traces. That they were now at the head of the reins must have put quite the zap on them, gearing up the collective mind to push it even harder, as though it all might still be taken away one day.

This could of course account for Kevin Delaney's dazed and confused look of late. In addition to his late night techno Bob Cratchit act, there was his side gig assisting with the upcoming nuptials of his cousin—fast approaching this weekend. The *perils* of agreeing to a spot in the wedding party were only now coming to light, as he scampered away his free time dodging about Dublin on mad little errands, and cutting into his already dangerously depleted REM happy time. Shit, he might have been laid back, but he wasn't laid out.

Yep, these people were still clearly in the lean wolf phase of the ascension, where all the focus and energy was razor sharp on the prize. The Caligula-fueled orgies and sequin jump suit Vegas bloat were still but clouds on some distant horizon. Presently, Kevin had that lean wolf ethos cranked to about eleven as he cut across Dublin towards The Essex for this, several times delayed, night out with the visitors.

He dodged through most of the after work crowd along Nassau Street, weaving in and out of the bustle, with the heavy stares and long doleful faces of the wildly successful rising up to greet him.

.... Nearby, in the bar at the Essex his cousin was of a

similar verisimilitude of opinion regarding this craziness—Had all this modern times rubbish turned these gentle folk into a marauding gang of Ripped Fuel Capitalists? This was still *Europe* after all, home to the larded and guarded thirty-five hour work week, not to mention the robust seventeen weeks of mandatory vacation.... No, most likely they were some strain of Mercedes driving Communists—switch hitters playing both sides of the same moral equivalency.

O'Shea could actually *feel* himself drifting a bit too close to this particular orbit...wretched thoughts indeed. He ruminated over this sad state of affairs as he sat near the hotel's octagon shaped bar within earshot of three Hugo Boss bespoke fop banker-types, trolling some bad brand of Hugh Grant foppishness in the general direction of their comely waitress in a not so subtle invitation to join the fava bean and muzzle mask set.... He sipped his White Russian and pondered the filthy meaning of the thing while he waited for his lovely to descend from the suite, his cousin to find the hotel, and the restaurant to fetch them a table.

When all were accounted for they adjourned to the De Valera Room, where they were seated in a slightly hidden corner near the back, which the maître d' made a point of repeatedly assuring them was generally reserved for any celebrity that might drop in. Refreshingly *underwhelmed*, they settled into their stylish seats; affording a fine view of the former Edwardian ballroom, beautifully reborn as one of Dublin's premier eateries.

Over cocktails, O'Shea presented his cousin with the sturdy rosewood case. A first-rate timepiece for the young urban overachiever on the go, wrapped in a finely offensive shade of shamrock emblazoned wrapping paper. They collectively admired the watch for the politely observed gift giving window.

It was a very elegant, stylish little trinket of a thing; the finest hands in Zurich must have bled for this little gizmo. But in the end what was it really, particularly in the circular rhetorical flourishes which kept the boy awake at night? A code word as much as a timepiece? And if you didn't speak the language, there was no room at the table, no matter how much you humored the gatekeepers.... But bless these two seated with him, in all their graceful ignorance of such things. Only the admiring maître d' and one of the Hannibal bankers seemed to grasp the bad cosmic uptake of such an item.

The youngest Delaney, understandably miffed by this dire breach of manly etiquette, went all hyper Irish on him at this point and politely tried declining the gift, which in turn forced Liam to make his intentions clear to beat him senseless with his own shoe should he continue with these idle, foolish, protests. Which in turn proffered up the final gambit allowing Kevin Delaney off the hook, with the firm yet polite threat the check was his, and he'd marlinspike with the butter knife, any hand that tried to stop him.... This sad exchange perhaps put to rest any quibbling debate whether Phil Lynott was more the cultural anthropologist than his day job had ever revealed.... The Californian in the bunch simply sat there wondering, though politely demurring, *what the fuck* these two oddballs were on about?

As it was their penultimate night in town, a fine bottle of something celebratory seemed in order. A bottle of Krug '88, recommended by the maître d, went down a damn sight better than the supermarket varietals he'd always made do with. This was followed by a very mellow Spanish red which set the mood right for rest of the evening. Because, after all, in the annals of our days the lubricated soul made for the tallest of tales.

Most painful: a flashback to a boozy rainy night in the late nineties, a cab fare dashed on the Finglas Road, an underage trio in flight, and a buzzed Kevin suddenly slow of foot. Sanctuary for the lagging was under the works of an old Fiat Punto as the cops and the cab man searched him out. Forty-five minutes of these hophead Clouseaus standing right next to him, cursing the *bastard kids* these days—so close he could see the brass buckles on The Guard's shoes as he had a slash in the gutter next to him.

O'Shea and Brendan boy just over a nearby fence, sipping the korova milk, eminently safe as the collective weight of their pursuers approached that of a water buffalo. And with it the priceless peace of mind that comes knowing only the good Lord himself could have miracled their asses over that wall.... The lads gave Kevin a wink through the cracks in the fence and made a break for it, whooping, hollering and raising as much hell as

175

possible in their wake—drawing their fire as it were.

Leaving Kevin Delaney, a rain soaked, grease stained Kevin Delaney, to slip out in the confusion and break the other way. Thirty short minutes later, Liam and Brendan were regrouping at the boot of Paddy Frank's mobile Fish n' Chips, each trying to outdo the other on the sphincter scale of auditory imagination…. And Kevin, rain soaked, grease stained Kevin, his new *Arsenal* jersey looking like it'd spent the night under an old Fiat Punto, lay low in the alleyways of Drumcondra, drinking his wine and biding his time till the coast was eminently clear.

"What did you do?" Sara laughed.

"What could I," Kevin smiled. "Out in the sticks like that? I called another cab and went home."

But droogie misadventures aside, their meal was excellent, elevating the discourse from crude nights of misspent youth. Over dessert they had another look at the nearly $4000 hunk of glass and metal which told time.

"Consider it your future wedding gift," O'Shea assured him. "Now we just have to get you to stop playing grab ass with the doormen."

Kevin smiled, "Well, I would give you a kiss, but you're a terrible human being you bastard, so instead—I'll just thank you kindly," he raised his glass. "Cheers!"

It was after eleven, but they still had a bit before Kevin had to be back one of his many rock pushing freelance gigs; this time running system checks on the RTE's national servers. Hardly the kind of work requiring a temperate steady hand; tracking employee porn site usage and chat room blather wasn't exactly the tech world's version of laying a crippled F-18 on the deck.

So they made their way across the alley to *The Burren*, a dangerously touristo themed pub by day, but on this fairly chilly rainy evening, the place had a hauntingly local vibe. Hell, maybe they even knew these boys were coming—this being one of the first places to ever serve a couple of intrepid sixteen year olds, back in the days of Tony Blair, before New Labour got old.

There was a traditional session in for the evening, which

had the more phlegmatic side of young O'Shea rolling his eyes. At best he was just the type of lout to cherry pick the bits of his ancestry he found most intriguing and then disavow the rest with an equal measure of a zealot's flare. For some reason, the fife and whistle had never quite caught his fancy.... Which of course made for the dodgy proposition of venturing into the rain forest and expecting not to get wet.

The music varied from the upbeat tap your foot and pound the table tunes, to the long mournful dirges of the *Fonn Mall*—sad notes played alone on uilleann pipes, or with the lonely voice of a young girl. Most were just laments, or the thin sketches of songs, many old enough that even the words had been lost—just the pulse remained. A heartbeat cadence, revealing something far deeper than any complexity would allow. Tonight's queen of the dirge had a fine voice, rich and deep, hitting all the right plaintive notes for the departed. A powerful voice wrapped in a little wisp of a body, casting out strong into the world.

He listened to the sad, surreal, surrender, his mind halfway to someplace else, running a mental tally of all the things which presaged tomorrow's great escape. He'd packed their bags before they came down to dinner. Tomorrow would be a marathon to be sure, ending some nine hundred miles away in the bed of a nice Tuscan farmhouse. But for now, he could glance over at the two of them talking in the half-shouted tones of the pub, fast friends having quite the time. That could be enough for him...too much guff and not enough grace amid all the useless beauty. He checked his watch and discretely signaled for the bill.... Loves labors lost in those annals of our days, and all on a 13.75% AmEx too boot.

Kevin looked over. "Why are you so quiet?"

"He smiled. "I'm just enjoying the show..."

Christopher M. Basso

Chapter Twelve
Rock the Casbah

It was with no small fanfare that the galloping ghost of the Greater Bay Area, the poster child for unwitting co-dependence and the arbiter of clean living, cracked open one of those clear blue eyes and caught the first warm rays of sunshine casting down through the windows; slanted shafts of light held up the fine twirling particles of dust carrying through the air. Her eyes traced the path along the floor to where they met in falling crisscrossed patterns against the wall. Out past the windows the sky was a perfect shade of cerulean, clear, and not a cloud in sight...this was unexpected.

"Open your eyes," she tapped his shoulder.

.... His brain was off again with the faeries, swirling their own brand of stardust particles around the sun. That was a fine bottle of Krug '88 indeed.... Why, good Lord, why, had he introduced fiery agave to the gentle Loire grapes? Now he was left to contend with these vicious Patrón dragons, breathing fires of citrus and sodium gunstones with all wasteful vengeance attendant on those who would dare fuck with them.... And what was this terrible gibberish trailing off on the very edge of dissonance? Complete claptrap, pathetic, bad rhythms...maybe it was the garden gnomes come to finally collect the bill...were there no six-shooters available? Never mind, need sleep.

But she wasn't one so easily dissuaded. She proceeded to dig into the rib cage of the slumbering beast with a great dexterity, in the furtive attempt to realign the liver and expunge any lingering fermented spirits.

"C'mon, rise and shine *you thug.*"

…. Not much of a response, but then again she knew where the chinks in the armor lay. She leaned over and bit the scruff of his neck right below the ear which reduced the vaguely menacing form of O'Shea to a bitch in the whelping box.

"Hey! What's going on here?"

"Welcome back," she said, caressing his face, studying his decrepitude. "Well, at least halfway."

The engine had nearly turned over, some of those synapses were starting to make the jump as the great blackness shaded through the penumbra, on its final journey into light—though not without some struggle.

"Look outside you pathetic tourist you…you'll notice the sun has returned?"

He cracked open an eye and looked around at the beams of light before him, and gave her a—"Ah' sure tis' grand it is," in the best Culchie from the Boglands brogue he could summon up from the time fog, and pulled the pillow back over his head.

She promptly grabbed the pillow in mid-retreat, beating him to the punch, and slapping him upside the head with his weapon of choice.

"Liam James, open you eyes," she shook him. "The power of Christ compels you!"

No response. She had a real catatonic on her hands. "Liaaamm…" she ran her fingers through his longish hair and leaned in. "Liam…" she purred, "roll over so I can blow you."

The synaptic flush was immediate.

Bam! The *mere words* had set off a fusionable reaction that only the Fermi's and Oppenheimer's of the world could fully divine…. Clever girl had played the trump card and played it well. The one word that hits the adrenals like a ragged Pit Bull in heat lust after the mailman's lagging leg, or some degenerate grabasstic frat boy on an overcharged Bourbon Street wet T-shirt-bead wilding jag.

He rolled over as told, one eye cracked open peering

down while she playfully ran her tongue along the length of his torso, moving slowly down his chest before stopping just below his waist, her hot breath a fine wake up call at that—whence she kissed the brass ring just once, for good luck and long life, before jumping up, hopping out of bed and bounding down the hallway.

"Uh, darling, where you off to?"

"Silly rabbit, Trix aren't for kids."

She gave him a grin as she strolled away, pulling his borrowed T-shirt up over her shoulders, a fine long back and the Sun kissed curve of her breasts in profile. A lusty Hyperion his blood shot Satyr. The white cotton knickers soon joined his shirt on the floor as she kept along her catwalk gait, all hips and evil exhibitionist intent before strolling off to the shower.

"You swine," he mumbled.... Damn, even Santa left a lump of coal.

"All services rendered are performance based," she called out from the bath. "You've got some law school, remember? You need to work up your billable hours first."

".... You know *this* is why people hate lawyers."

"Oh, there's probably a few other reasons we could spitball if we tried," he could hear her from the bath.

"Lovely—try not to use words like spit or swallow or any manner of ingress-egress for that matter."

"Try counting backwards from a hundred, I hear that helps."

"Yeah, wonderful, how about you save me some cold water in there, 'kay?"

She stood in the doorway, just off to the side, "What can I say? You just have that kind of face that makes my thoughts impure, unchaste."

He ruminated for a moment, "I can think of some fair trade sort of barter we could work out?"

"I bet you could *mad dog*, but hitch those spurs for now. Need I remind you we're checking out in a couple of hours?"

"Oh yeah, I knew there was something on for today.

We've got a little bit of a wedding don't we?"

She came out to grab one of the robes from the wardrobe, "And a bit of a marathon jag down to Italy, courtesy of yourself."

"Righto," he watched her walk away. "Miss Sara Connelly, mmm, mmm, mmm, La Reine Soleil, hate to see you go, but love to watch you leave."

Holdover hippie parents were a fine blessing indeed—indoctrinating their children well against the closed minded atavistic pratfalls of a token Sunday morning morality and cheap puritanical inhibitions.... That she had an ass which could find magnetic north was an equal blessing—like some manner of divining rod leading straight to his guttural instincts.... A blowhard, atavistic Irish Catholic father swimming in a sea of token Sunday morning testifying taught his boy something *else* entirely.

O'Shea sat up in bed, perhaps he should shut up while he was ahead—Once adjusted he could see what she was on about—the sun was still fairly low in the sky, but it was bright and constant, trailing off into a brilliant blue cloudless sky. A cool breeze drifted in through the windows and he could hear the sing song calls of the gulls perched on the awnings. O'Shea shook out the cobwebs a bit.... That mutt Brendan Delaney *must* have paid those faeries himself. It was shaping up to be an exceptional day at that. The clock near the bed read 7:33—some four hours till the festivities commenced proper-wise.

Within the hour O'Shea found himself perched, half slanted and slumped on his stand up bag in the lobby, fashionably decked out in black for such a sunny day. A pair of sunglasses shielded his eyes from the churchlike rays of light shining through the tall beveled glass. His damp hair and fresh shave almost bringing him back to a moderate respectability. The roadster was being summoned, the credit card being readied and the best route out of town being mulled...but then there was the bill to deal with. A *massive* thing, not entirely unexpected, but fuck man, they'd needed two envelopes to slip it under the door. That alone should have put *the fear* in him. He sat there reviewing it—truly shocking in both scope and breadth...the sheer number of itemized zero's drifting across the page were enough to resurrect the head spins.

Who-the-hell called Juarez? Did Patrón even make a Black label tequila? His eyes scrolled down the page—*Gran Patrón Burdeos Añejo*—apparently so. And then there was something called a Capri Twist...bad mind fog—a cocktail? Something with the masseuses? Something with a bit of both? The possibilities abounded.... At what point had his sorry peacock trutting ass ordered up a magnum of Louis Roeder's finest to compliment his Johnny Rocket's "Texas Burger" and side of hombre fries—why 4:35 a.m. of course—that was just about the right time for idle hands to go to work.

The exchange rate added an extra shot to the solar plexus. Goddamn, what's this world coming to when the greenback was just one shade north of the finest outhouse paper you'd ever come across? He chewed over the geopolitical machinations of the thing as he waited his turn to sign for his sins on the dotted line.

"Well, *Hank*," he muttered, "let's take this up a notch, shall we?"

Within moments she joined him. He thought best not to mention the wee triviances of the check out procedure at least until they were good and far from the scene of the crime...like back across the ocean.

Out near the curb sat the low lying roadster, idling in the taxi lane with the passenger door already ominously open. O'Shea made a quick move for his own bags—all the glad-handing was *seriously* starting to creep him out. He narrowly beat the bellhop to the trunk, tossed in his gear, slapped him a fiver for old time's sake, and jumped in the driver's side next to Sara.

He toyed with the mirrors for a moment, checking alignment on the dials and for proper modulation on his quadraphonic Blaupunkt—looking preoccupied and official, but at the same time working up the proper balance of fear and rage necessary for some driving around this town.... Needless to say, it would be a bitch of a drag to trash the roadster the last twenty hours in-country.... but then again, sounded just about right for the nasty karmic footprint of his forebears—better keep a clean nose and watch the plain clothes. He lined up his shot into the maelstrom—*daylight* was just ahead.

Mr. O'Shea, Mr. O'Shea," the voice carried nervous and quick, "you forgot your paperwork!"

It was a full, proper bellow that put the kibosh on his back door man act. The young manager came running out to the curb, a bundle of papers in his hand, and a bundle of papers which were deftly, if not politely, snatched up by his erstwhile companion and hotel registry approved wife.

"Hold on," he muttered and jammed down the gas, spinning the tires, and successfully tearing out into the fabric of things with a flair suggesting more of a controlled opportunity than any random act of desperation. They were soon moving at the good clip along the N11 motorway, far removed from the hellish mishmash of downtown Dublin, and entering the former "landed gentry" country just south of the city.

The last of the new strip malls and massive intersections were safely in the rearview, and the ragged peaks of the Wicklow Mountains were rising up to greet them. Hell, they might even catch a fleeting glance of the Liffey back near the source where it was still a blue and pretty thing. But for now, the sun was out in a pitch perfect sky and a warm breeze whipped through the car.

"Man—this is the way to travel," he shouted out over the windscream.

"Yes, yes, lovely."

He glanced over, "Something on your mind angel?"

"I just can't believe the size of this bill."

She grabbed it from her bag for another look.

"Did you think you were back in the youth hostel?" He smiled.

"No, but—"

"Did you have fun?"

"…. Well, *yes*."

"Good," he said at length. "Then that's all that matters

isn't it?"

With that he went back to his breakfast, a bit of Cadbury's local finest with a Coca-Cola chaser, a wild confident look in his eyes, croaking along to a ramshackle torch song tune under his breath.

.... *Yeah*, she glanced over, time to start keeping a closer eye on this one for sure—that and some singing lessons for Christ's sake.

The scenery quickly shifted gears again to the type of lush, low country, you'd expect to see in coastal Britain or France. And once off the clear boundaries of the motorway it was deep into the narrow abyss of hedgerow country, where tall stone walls lined both sides of the narrow road, and bright purple and red flowers grew in bunches between the barren thorns. It had a strange beauty about it, like some inadvertent work of art; the cover dense enough in places to pass for a delicate tapestry woven with ancient spindles and draped over old heavy stones.

Yes, truly lovely till one remembered that just inches behind the gentle canopies of ivy and bougainvillea were some *seriously* unforgiving old school walls. Many a car 'round these parts had the tell tale scarring of red, green, and black etched in their fenders, as they too had drifted a bit too close to the sun....So, not much room to operate here if say—a massive British Petroleum tanker should meet you in the rye, like the one chugging its wobbly ass way down the other end of the strip, a clearly deranged thrill seeker to be sure, but one rapidly closing the gap at that.

Now, the roadster had many fine attributes, as did occasionally the driver, but playing chicken with four thousand gallons of Bedouin tea wasn't one of them. This was that proverbial line in the sand. O'Shea pulled over into one of the gate breaks between the fields, where some congregating cows gave them the once over. The tanker inched by at a fairly tension filled five mph with about just as many inches separating them. Close enough on either end to get a good hit of Ivy and wild juniper, exhaust and petrol fumes.

"Like I said, the only way to travel."

"…. I can't say I enjoyed that."

He threw it back into gear, "You leftist heathen—thank your American stars you live in a place where you could drive three of those down the street sideways and still clear a few cement mixers."

"Yeah, I'll count my blessings when I'm lathering up the 2000 SPF."

"Suit yourself," he shrugged. "…. Fucking roads will be the death of me."

Once cleared, he stepped on it. Successful gaming theory said something about limiting your time on the battlefield. Luckily, there were no more tanker-themed run ins, just a few sheep grazing on the fringes, but they moved quite nicely for unlicensed shiftless types. They flew through the small village of Enniskerry, and were soon before the massive gates at Dunamore Estate, their final destination wedding-wise.

…. *Jesus Marimba*, the massive stone gate house alone suddenly gave The Essex all the glitz of some flea rollicking, pimp hostelling crack den. Not to say this place was huge, but it had its own separate zip code on the national postal grid. They crept past the gatehouse and its imposing gothic turrets staring down on them, and slowly made their way along the winding drive. Past the fields of barley and golden summer wheat, and along the boundaries of a small apple orchard, till the next bend revealed the distant profile of the main house—which could ride most stately euphemisms from the antiquated, "castle-like" to perhaps the more with it, "Wayne Manor". The *house* sat imperially at the highest point on the grounds, which sloped gently down in every direction for several hundred acres.

The Earl's of Wicklow, Beauregard and Luke, had slowly cobbled the place together over a leisurely century or so. And like many a crazed wealthy European of a certain age, they had paid visit to the original mad hatters—the Bourbons, and their massive flaming phallus at Versailles. Where they of course divined the fine idea that they too should carry a bit of that megalomaniacal fairy dust back to their own Plutonian shores.

A potentially *dangerous* game of ostentation that had cost more than a few demagogues their powdered heads.... but unlike those ratty Bourbons, Irish nobility had a bit more sense than that. Riding the help till they were Frankensteining your ass with pitchforks and torches was never a smart way to go.

Unlike them, the Earl's of Wicklow got to keep their heads; which over the course of many decades would come to realize a truly striking balance of architecture and landscape engineering. There were formal French and Italianate parterre gardens flanking either side of the manor house. Along its southern exposure, a broad, gently sloping hill ran down towards a small lake where the pitched pavilion of a Japanese tea house sat between the Bonsai and Magnolias just beyond its shores. And well in the distance near the edge of the grounds were the small stone spires of the family chapel. Tiny white points ringed the church; the final resting places of the many hands that had stirred this stew.... Even their pets were accorded a small touch of eternity; a cemetery beneath the shade of a line of willows near the stables, offering all the grace a sheltered perpetuity could confer.

But like all massive works that dwelled mostly in the imagination, this one too had outlived its original intention. And even if your business card read media tycoon, or mad Russian oilgarch, Dunamore might have been more the expense than it was worth. As such, it had slowly reverted to one *very* opulent ward of the Irish State—which had run the place as a museum for years, but were now taking the plunge into the high end resort business. And if you had the scratch you could rent this mother out for conferences, retreats, and the occasional four to the floor wedding that would've had Jay Gatsby reaching for his Swedish penis pump.

They crossed under a long line of massive oaks, passing from the sunlight beneath the shade of the canopy, until they reappeared on the other side, now immediately beneath the looming shadows of the house. The misdirect had the desired effect. A sudden wondering sense of shock and awe were upon you as you took in the sheer scope of your surroundings. The main house was a neo-classical behemouth cast in shades of a dark heavy stone. Imposing mansard towers and graceful pinnacles ringed the roof, while the façade wore a weathered sort of permanent defiance to the elements.

 A small brigade of catering trucks was lined end to end in the drive: Bloom & Boylan's, floristry of note, M. Furey's Bakers of Enniskerry, and Lenehan and Corley's tent rentals of distinction. Pulling up along the main house they briefly caught a glimpse of the far side of the property. Three large tents sat on a broad even rise overlooking the sloping hill and the massive stone staircase that descended along the incline to a portico at the base of the lake, guarded by a coterie of marble horses and a bronze statue of noted Gaelic badass Cúchulainn, slaying the Hound of Culain.

"Jesus, would you look at this?" He muttered.

"It is something."

"Right up your alley I'd imagine?" He smiled.

"I wouldn't know, my parents got married at *Hog Farm*."

"Yeah? Was that before or after they bought it?"

"Well," she flustered, "…. you needn't go there."

He laughed as they pulled into a spot on the crushed stone drive right between a Mercedes and a gleaming Bentley Flying Spur. The roadster, fresh from some off-lease bog testing and slick sheep avoidance maneuvers, looked a bit ragged in this league where all things were geared towards the angst of inadequacy which dwelled within.

"Now, you sure you're ready for all this noise?"

"Liam, it's a wedding."

"Oh no," he assured her. "That's just the kind of thinking that'll sink you quick. It might *say* wedding on the invitation, and they'll certainly be some manner of church, chow, and chance in between, but make no mistake—the Irish wedding is just a bit longer than Mardi Gras and just a hair shorter than death."

"Please."

"What?"

"Would you stop your *bellyaching*, I'm game if you are."

"Fair enough," he smiled.

It was a mad scene in the main lobby. The space was crowded and the vibe was unmistakably tense. Wedding guests were transiting in and out, and the small army of caterers seemed to be using the front entrance for some reason, causing a great many guests to dodge a tray of hors d'oeuvres here and a bouquet of wildflowers there...and then there were others, older highly-agitated pasty skin types, who seemed to be dressed like...like extras from some vaudevillian stag revue.

But on closer inspection this was just the rusticating Burgher set, out to the hit the nearby links. The Irish Government, in a deft attempt to squeeze a bit more water from this stone, had gotten in cahoots with the Saudis who'd just opened a Greg Norman championship property across the Highgate Road on what was once the stud farm for the Earls of Wicklow.

Funneling the well-heeled across the road was now a top priority. Regrettably, the lobby is where these disparate worlds clashed. O'Shea watched the uber-Cauco plaid and pleat brigade suffer the fools and handmaidens of the merely wealthy as they took it across the road. Truth be told, O'Shea fancied the links about as much as he liked the ponies...which was to say, slightly better than a mug of tea, but a *highly* risible endeavor all the same. He found it a rather unseemly, unmanly abdication of youth and, George Carlin rantings aside, the kind of thing you did when you'd just about kicked the can on what that queen Teddy Roosevelt might have called the vivacity of being in the arena.

For his part he planned to face the oncoming decrepitude of age in the more measured Papa Ernesto tradition of an empty bottle and a loaded gun. Or so he liked to tell himself.

O'Shea soon recognized a few faces passing through the lobby as some of the people from the *way back when*. He started over to say hello to one of his Aunt's neighbors from Finglas when a rather large and slightly demented looking man lunged at him from behind the potted Rhododendron, and placed him in a steel cage death-clamp bear hug, lifting him over his head and shaking him side to side.

Sara jumped back a bit startled—this was a manner of check-in she was unfamiliar with. But O'Shea kept his calm, as if such things were par for the course. He pivoted, getting a better grip and swung around on the bear-man; shifting his weight back, ensuring they both went down to the mat with a thunderous crash—a no win proposition, but then again eating a piece of floor was sometimes the only way to even the odds with a bear.... The golfing set wore a mask of pure repugnance—but then again they were the ones wearing plaid knickerbockers and high socks.

The stranger shook him a few more times before finally letting go. They slowly rose to their feet, evidenced with the same shortness of breath of those who abuse themselves before they abuse each other.

"O'Shea, you little tosser—let me see you—you look like a fey man in your buzzard Baptist's finest."

".... Ryan O'Neill, well, well, well—looks like the penicillin's finally made the nut. You're looking good."

Sara softly cleared her throat.

"Sara, my dear, this is Ryan O'Neill." He put an arm around him, "A more honest man you'll not meet, unless you tap a stranger on the shoulder."

"Don't listen to him darling, this bit of failed humanity used to be Liam O'Shea that is, till he abandoned me all those years ago."

"I lost my passport."

The bear man adjusted his ill-fitting suit from the fall, "*Riiight*—lying on a church day; you'll *burn* for that one."

"Ah, Ryan, whimsical as ever," Liam looked back over his shoulder, suddenly remembering this was generally a package deal. "Where's your brother?"

"At the bar, in the bag."

"And your father, how's he keeping?"

"About to retire, then it's off to Mallorca. Me and the kid are taking over the business."

He looked at Sara, "Their father Norman runs a garage out by the airport. He's the one who taught us all how to drive."

…. A good upbringing and humble pilgrim's soul allowed that one to pass unassailed.

"You all checked in then?" The bear man asked.

"Come again?"

"Your room for tonight?"

O'Shea shrugged.

"Jaysus, did that silly bastard cousin of yours fail to mention the Bride's family has rented out the entire place; we've all rooms in this fucker for tonight."

Liam shook his head, a high beam headlight rictus smile in place, "Guess it must have slipped his mind."

Ryan shrugged, "Well, go get your room, and I'll grab that squirrelly bastard and sort him. I saw him running around down here a few minutes ago." The Bear Man disappeared once again, behind whatever Rhododendron suited his fancy.

…. It must be said he could feel the eyes before he heard the voice.

"Yes?"

"They *rented* us rooms and we're leaving?"

"Yes well…life is quirky like that."

O'Shea went to the desk and was quickly through the check in motions.

She tailed him over, "Still feel right about cutting out in the middle of the night?"

"Uh, hells yeah…. I'll send them another asparagus steamer if it makes you feel better."

"You've got a mean streak in you sometimes."

"It's more a camouflaged charity my dear."

"No, what I'm saying is—"

His nerves were staring to fray. He chose his next words poorly, "I guess we could always send them a fine case of twisted martyrdom, we seem to be running a surplus."

A cold look met his rising smile.

"Right." She took the room key and started towards the elevator.

He watched her walk away…*ouch*. To have more offenses at your beck than thoughts to put them in made for the worst sort of mischief. Where'd he read that…*Maxim* probably.

Before he could dwell on this latest bit of misanthropy, Kevin appeared under the watchful wing of Ryan O'Neill. But talk of wedding etiquette and a spurious forgetfulness quickly switched gears to some manner of nuptial crisis.

"What's got your knicker's in a bunch?" Liam greeted his cousin.

"Can you fucking believe this—I need to go back to Bray for some of that Plumtree's Best tanning shite."

"What?" The wrestling enthusiasts said in unison.

He looked at them, "Not for me you spanner twats—the Bride's mother. Wants to look her WAG finest I guess."

"How'd you get roped into that?" Ryan laughed.

"I made the mistake of asking what was wrong."

"Well, I'll drive you." Liam said.

"No, that's ok, I'll drive."

"Kevin, your car's a piece of shit, we'll never make it. We'd be better off on horses."

Ryan looked on, "He's right; it is a piece of shit, sorry."

"Fuck the two of you…. All right let's go."

They started out the doors, "What about your missus?" Kevin asked.

"She's gone up to the room, wants to finish getting ready."

"What about you?"

"What are you trying to say?"

"No tie?"

"It's out in the car. C'mon on you momma's boy."

The two gents hurried down the walkway and out across the crushed gravel path towards the drive. The light crunch of the gray stones gave up a pleasant sound underfoot as they moved along at the good pace, for a moment almost feeling like boys again, at least till the bastard offered him one from his pack....And then he could see it, in the eyes, just for a moment, the first creeping signs of age in a face you've known forever. A slight chill ran down the spine, wondering if that weatherworn expression was just the mirror back to self. Hard to say, it's subtle but it's there, there for good, like a hangover face that just ain't going away...

"Is she ok?" Kevin asked.

"What?"

"Sara, I ran into her upstairs. She looked a tad—off."

"Oh...well, she might just be a *wee* bit pissed at me."

"You, Lash La Rue? *Shocking*. What have you done now?"

"No it's more like what haven't I done?"

"Ah, even worse than what you have done."

Liam gassed it down the drive and out past the iron gates.

She's a bit upset we're bailing tomorrow."

"Understandable, even by your standards I think it's a bit fuckin' *mad*."

"Ha—that's the pot calling the kettle black," before wincing, "well she might also think I'm just a tad frivolous with money."

Kevin Delaney looked around the car, "Sports cars and bunkhouse suites in four star hotels, now why would she go thinking that?"

"Gee, I don't know. Personally I think she's grasping."

He laughed, "I'm still convinced your old Da' was in the mob."

"Handsome Henry, a Westie?"

"Why not, he had the bearing for it."

"The disposition too," Liam laughed. "…. No, he was just lucky I guess."

A sort of quiet hung in the air for a moment. William Henry O'Shea had always been a "go to" punch line in these moments, but even the whelps would not speak ill of the departed. Kevin politely shifted gears.

"Well boyo, I can see why she's pissed. Not only are you dining and dashing, you're going to miss the Bride and Groom's day tomorrow…. the *only* measure that makes one of these things bearable. *Goddamn*, an extra day of merriment, minus the formality and glad-handing—it's bliss." He thought about it for a moment, "…. You swine."

"Swine?" He looked over, "Listen, you truncated paraquot, how dare you—I got to get out of here. You people and your wicked ways are making me wretched."

Kevin chuckled, "*Lightweight.*"

They passed the junction near the N15, making good time for a busy summer's day. Liam checked his watch; this would still be close. He kept the roadster on its toes, weaving in and out of things with a general sense of disregard he was rather coming to enjoy—that and the lack of anything remotely resembling *The Authorities*. No speed checks here, just a freedom of expression unknown back across the pond.

He glanced over at his cousin who was turning a shade of green just slightly darker than the hills they were weaving through. Perhaps some small talk would put the boy at ease.

"Hey, cosmonaut, how's that lady friend of yours?"

"Which one?"

"Why Alison of course."

"She's good, she's good. Just got herself a promotion. Going to buy a Harley and race it across China I think," he smiled. "Not like I get to see her much anymore though."

"Yeah, where is she?"

"Working."

"On a Saturday?"

He sighed, "It is what it is."

"Suppose so.... How about the rest of them?"

"Keepin' out of trouble you know. And how about you boyo, everything going ok back in *Westchester*? You chasing tail with Clinton yet?"

"Oh, can't complain. I moved into Henry's digs about six months ago, but I'm sure Fighting Fintan told you that?"

"Yeah, said you were living up in the country like some kind of queer sultan, squired behind high walls and armed to the teeth."

"Yeah, well Handsome was the Sultan—I'm just the caretaker.... but I do got arms—so beware."

Kevin looked out the window for a moment; he and his cousin were two for the ties that bind but never much for the words that mattered. Although sometimes they were called for, "I was sorry to hear about him, we all were. Terrible way to go."

Liam kept his eyes on the road till finally a small smile crossed his face, "Why Kevin, are we having a moment?"

"Good Lord—you're a harpy little bastard."

"What, what do you want? Thank you, thank you—*there*. You've said it about a dozen times already—after a while it's sort of hard to process."

"I know you know, but I just thought you should hear it from me, face to face." He smiled. It was a bit tricky ashing out the speeding drop top.

"You should have seen how worried my parents were about you...they were going to send me over to keep you company."

"Keep an eye on me?"

"Something like that. I told them to relax, that you were a strident little shit. Glad to see I was wrong."

"*You,* watching *me*? Holy shit—that would've just about done the trick; two addictive, borderline types, running around New York with unlimited credit. We'd need a rehab from our rehab."

"Yeah, probably so—what the fuck were they *thinking*?" He laughed, "Older generation you know, their faculties have gone to pot."

"Yeah," his grin was something frightening. "Driving skills too apparently."

Kevin shook his head, "You *evil* fucker."

"Well, don't worry too much; I think I'm holding it together quite nicely."

His cousin fumbled with the matches in the strong breeze. "Then *why*, did you quit law school…and with only two months to go at that? We had high hopes for you, you bastard, free legal advice is a rare commodity."

"Shit man, I can still hook you up, but you never know, they might just be the idle ramblings of a madman."

"More like an ass I'd say," he finally got his smoke up and running. "Anyway, that's my mother talking—had to ask for her you know?"

"Yes indeed," before gathering the gravitas and tossing it back Kevin's way, "and what do *you* think?"

"Oh, I think you hated it to begin with, and were just going through the motions 'cause you thought it's what everyone wanted," he paused, finally tossing his uncooperative smoke into the wind scream, "but that's just my unvarnished, opinion….Couldn't really see you as a lawyer anyway, fucking criminals. Besides, you don't glad hand well and you seem to prefer your deceptions on a strictly personal basis—family mostly. You would've gone mad."

Liam smiled, "Say hey–who knows me best?"

O'Shea swerved towards the broken divider, pausing only long enough to think about yielding and then gunned the car again. His dark hair pinned back in the breeze, "Nice day for a drive isn't it?"

"Grand."

It felt like the roadster had only missed the dividing line by nanoseconds. Kevin Delaney discretely checked his seatbelt and thought to compose himself. His cousin hadn't actually had any crash ups, at least none he could remember…but then again there was the boy's odd fascination with Steve McQueen to consider.

They crested around a bend and eased up a bit behind some slower traffic. It would take Speed Racer a minute or two to find the next sling shot window. Sensing a lull in the chaos Kevin lobbed his cousin the million-dollar question, "So, what are you going to do with yourself?"

To which his cousin flashed back the evilest of twenty cents looks.

"Keep your eye on the road you bastard!" Kevin shouted, "Jesus man—I'm not prying. I represent curious parties is all. Shit, *I'm* curious at this point."

O'Shea shrugged, "I don't know man…buy a Mondrian day-glo bus, call it Furthurest…maybe start a band with my obnoxious kid brother and hot enough for incest sister."

His cousin shook his head, "That's not an answer."

"Kevin lad, c'mon get happy."

"Piss off."

"Why Kevin, when did you become so *inquisitive*?"

"Well, when you roll into town in this ox tail ass of a car and start renting suites atop The Essex—it gets me to thinking. Something, I tell you, something's up with that boy," he smiled. "I am perceptive if anything."

"That's you in broad strokes my friend…. Anyway, I'm just riding my missus' dime. She's the loaded one."

"So you're a gigolo now is what you're saying?"

Christopher M. Basso

"Shit man, that makes it sound so crass. I prefer a kept man."

He looked straight ahead, "Well, that explains it then."

"You bet."

"And that's it?"

"Jesus," he shot back, "you sound like an old lady. Sure the Plumtree insta-tan ain't for someone else?" Now, c'mon, that's about as much thought as I can put into it and drive at the same time. Would you prefer I shifted my attention to these inner turmoils?"

"No, Christ man, keep your mind on the road, we'll pick it up later."

"I'm sure we will."

.... Now Kevin Delaney could recite most of Yeats' *Sailing to Byzantium*, and he'd even run a five minute mile once, but a subtle tact would often escape him, "And what about the lovely Sara—is that serious?"

O'Shea was instantly annoyed, annoyed in the way only family can make you—just because the fuckers knew you, didn't automatically grant them some divine right of proprietary Tourette's, as they let it ride indelicately in ever so delicate matters.

".... You know me—all things are serious."

Kevin wasn't amused.

Liam's eyes kept ahead, but a thoughtful look washed across his face, "Yeah, hell yes, it's serious."

He paused, "I mean, I feel pretty good about things, but I think..." His voice trailed off for a moment before breaking out into laughter, "Who am I kidding—I know she's a bit frustrated with me."

"Well, I like her. So try not to bog it up, right?"

".... What am I, short bus fodder all of a sudden?" He raised an eyebrow, "Somehow I've gotten this far, what with feeding and changing myself—and while all this has been a great challenge, I'm still here."

Kevin though about it for a moment, "She's frustrated? Beyond what—I mean besides the obvious that you seem off your tit?"

"Oh, where do I start...let's see. She didn't quite see the inherent genius in walking away from law school with forty-nine days left, not like you anyway.... Then there would be the drinking."

"You?"

"She seems to think I do too much of it."

"No more than the rest of us."

"Sadly, that's not saying much."

"What?" He feigned a fine indignant.

"She grew up out West. She's a *Californian*. They're a bit more clean living than you or I."

"Ah..."

He winced, "Anyway, between reserving my room at *Betty Ford* and keeping an open line of reconciliation with the Dean, she seems to be of the opinion I've strayed off the reservation a bit."

"Would you agree?"

"Strayed? Shit man, I've jumped the fence and stampeded clear for the horizon," he sighed. "Which raises the problem of how best to delicately explain to her that I *like* it out here."

"Yeah?"

"Fuck yeah, it's groovy."

Kevin smiled, "All right boyo, I can wait till your feeling a bit more earnest about things."

"You might be in for some wait there chief."

There was a slight bit of friction drifting through the roadster as they made the next hairpin spin through hedgerow land, clearing the last of the hills, and revealing the faint arc of the pale Irish Sea...but nearly thirty years of the shared brain had to count for something. A silent, though understood, détente had been reached.

Kevin looked about, ".... Well, speaking of faux alcoholism and problem drinkers—let's crack em' open shall we?" He reached back to the rumble seat and fumbled through a bag for the Red Bulls and vodka.

"Ah, Mother's Milk, if the woman didn't love ya…. Do you have a drinking problem Liam James?"

"Why no, do you?"

"No, 'cepting when I can't get one." He poured the vodka cordials, liberated from the hotel minibar, into the fluorescent brew, "Cheers."

"Cheers."

"Want one?"

O'Shea was drifting towards a yes, but the seraphims flashed a fleeting thought back to Handsome Henry and Max the dog, and he quickly thought otherwise.

"Uh, let me hold off till we're nearer the church; that's about the last thing I need. I have enough problems driving sober."

"Suit yourself," he took a long slug. "See—you don't have a problem."

Kevin Delaney raised his drink and made the sign of the sign of the Cross with his trigger finger, "*Ad Deum qui laetificat juventutem meam*—To God, who giveth joy to my youth."

Liam smiled, suitably impressed, "Good thing your mother gave you to the Benedictines; at least something's rubbed off on you."

"Yeah, the leg of the priest if I was lagging."

They crossed the river Dargle and rounded into the slightly faded seaside town of Bray, and made a hasty stop at the raggediest looking pharmacy/smoke shop that this little corner of the world had to offer. They quickly located a batch of Plumtree's Best spray tan and were back in the car, burning a path to

Dunamore. Liam checked his watch; serendipity was on their side to be sure.

They crossed the river and tore back into the hills, but almost at once the road began to take on the shades of those bewildered, but not quite ready to admit they were lost. After a few bends through the hedgerows, they rounded a switchback curve and were suddenly looking down again on the pale Irish Sea.... It was agreed between the cousins that those bastard culchie faeries must have been working overtime.

Kevin Delaney, cheap rental car company map in hand, fluttering madly in the drop-top breeze was trying to sort things out. A look of great concentration sat across his furrowed brow as he sipped his foul brew and pondered their options.

"Jesus—you don't have a fucking clue where we're going do you?"

"Shut it boyo, I got a fine sense of things."

"Oh yeah," Liam laughed. "That's why history's littered with the great Irish navigators."

His cousin looked up over the map, "You looking to get your ears boxed?"

"All right, the hell with this. I got a plane in sixteen hours. Reach back and grab that GPS thing out of my bag."

".... Where?"

O'Shea started to reach behind the seat.... Which of course meant they'd arrived at the next savage fork in the road, and one poor boy hadn't noticed that the lights had changed.

"Liam!"

The rest was silence....

.... Once upon a time, deep in the jungles of Eastern Cameroon, a young pretty thing, long of limb, blond of lock, and buxom of bounce, was walking with two of the local *Baduoue* guides along the western edge of a ridge. Their mission: a head count of the African Gray Parrot; part of a biodiversity survey of protected rainforest, and not a bad side gig for one's study abroad program.

The midday heat was well past the point of oppressive when the sky opened up and let loose with the rain and the thunder. The wet foliage on a hillside ravine gave way, and a guide's errant machete went a' wackity-whack with it—and a fine two inch gash was opened just a cat's whisker from her Ulnar artery, the ragged oft-forgotten stepsister of arterial players, but one that would kill you quick all the same. And while this might only complicate your day if you were standing, say, outside the Vascular ward as Mass General, it was a whole 'nother beast entirely when one was out in the rainforest 200 miles from anything resembling the medical arts.

That is to say it presented a bit of a problem.

In her stunned and broken Patois French and the guide's equally horrified Cameroonian Baduoue, they collectively decided in a crystal clear lingua franca that this was one bad fucking scene indeed. Guide one, François called, stripped off his *Charles In Charge* T-shirt to use as a tourniquet, begging the question: Did anyone ever think that bad boy would be out saving lives in the equatorial rain forest?

…. Perhaps not, but it was a vastly reaffirming notion that whatever your viewing habits, the Lord moved in mysterious ways indeed. They double timed it back to the logging road, with our damsel shotgunning a jug of water and several packets of salt, as the guides furiously hailed down a bush taxi along the red mud road leading back to somewhere better than here.

The *Bush Taxi*—an open top Toyota Land Cruiser usually rocking no less then fifteen souls at a time, not including the chickens, sheep, and Belgians—and a driver generally taking the pock marked, moon cratered "roads" with all the ornery grit of Tony Stewart on a bad day. Now plowing along to somewhere, with the ashen faced *Jeune Blanche* in the back, her arm elevated, her clothes a blood stained mess, much to the horror of the locals just looking for a quick, uneventful ride home.

After much barnstorming through the bush, they arrived at the remains of a Belgian lumber camp at dusk for greetings and salutations with a half in-the-bag spawn of Mr. Kurtz who nervously owned up to his position as camp foreman, chef, and resident medic. And who, after a lot of bad noise and threats from the guides, agreed to sew her up with what they kept on hand for all the lovely, bloodied foreigners who wandered in with the evening breeze: a low grade anesthetic akin to Neosporin, and 1/8" grade filament that would have given the strongest of Marlins a run for its money. But the fishing line would prove to be the emerald offering in this triage of mystery, which featured a nervous hand, several shots of $400 cognac left by the camp's owners, and a strap of full grain leather to bite down on.

Cue the scene: Early evening's dusk light, equatorial rain forest, Belgian lumber camp, King Leopold's ghosts all around, a kitchen table, a dim light, a crowded room, twenty or so grizzled bushmen types, aghast as the medic's nervous needle darns the pale pink skin—yet not a word arose from the one being darned. Steely nerves, patient penitent—deep down, women are far tougher than men any day.

Seventy-two hours later she of the long limb was sitting in the office of Dr. Bob Roberts, Chief of Vascular Surgery at Columbia Presbyterian, as a calm bit of Neil Sedaka Muzak filtered through the waiting room.

"Amazing."

This was the assessment. Never before had Dr. Bob seen such a fine example of low-grade field stitching—probably wouldn't even leave a scar at that. And he would know—long before his cushy "hand guy" gig, Dr. Bob had been rocking a world of hurt; his office, the Mekong Delta circa '67; his waiting room, a rice paddy of no particular import.

"You're a *very* lucky young lady."

Ain't that the truth…. It was six days before her twenty-third birthday.

…. But then the fog cleared and there were suddenly other voices. The galloping Bavarian was half spun out in the median, idling quietly, about 4 ¾ inches of already borrowed serendipity separating them from the massive grill of an oversized

Christopher M. Basso

BP tanker full of Bedouin Tea—*still* looking awfully lost on these roads.

So, what had a certain roguish wandering penitent sort learned on the cusp of The Great Reveal? That the most interesting bits of life flashing before his eyes belonged to a Miss Sara Connelly.... A nasty bit of Déjà vu, or some savage brand of irony? Either way, bummer that.

The driver of the tanker thought to answer first as to its providence, "You feckin' edjit! What's wrong wit ya!"

Liam just stared at the man. His brogue was thick, almost unintelligible, somewhere from the deepest of backwood bogs. His cousin, however, was on the problem—as well as the hood—in a flash, "Shut your fucking mouth! What they hell are you doing back here anyway?" Kevin Delaney, not one to let a four thousand dollar watch and a subscription to *Mens Journal* dull the edge on his hard-wired street fighting skills.

O'Shea was still clearing out the cobwebs; authoring such mayhem had momentarily fried the circuits...all he could think was these Germans really knew how to throw a car together—the fucker had responded quite nicely to the split second go around, spinning out in the turn, and gripping what was left of the road with a steely death vice before coming around to a screeching halt. The smell of cut grass and cow manure was in the air...wouldn't have been a bad way to go—could think of worse....Jefferson was on to something—the agrarian life was the way to be.

But then there were particularly *loud* voices, a machine gunning of expletives that quickly snapped him back to attention. Kevin Delaney was already well into the meet and greet.... Liam noticed he was somehow now standing on the hood of the car, gesticulating wildly, and waving the seemingly innocent looking energy drink slash fatally damning evidence bomb, should the local Guards ever rear their pointed heads.

"All right, all right take it easy you bastard." Kevin finally said to the agitated driver.

Liam, having now returned to Earth, thought to join the negotiations, "Calm down buddy, it was an accident—"

"Yeah, you heard him Padraig, where's your sense of sportsmanship?"

"Go fuck yourself!"

"Fine, fine, get it out of your system." Kevin said.

"Clackers! Cunts!"

"Grand. Listen, glad you're working it out, but would you know the way back to Dunamore?" Kevin asked.

…. A sudden calmness enveloped the tanker man. There was a distinct brand of Irishness which could return to a perfect civility after having just visited the depths of primal rage with frightening speed. It was a fire that outsiders would probably never understand. "Yeah, down the way you'll hit a church at a crossroads, make a left, follow it straight until."

"Bless."

"Listen…might you know the way back to the N11?" The tanker man asked rather sheepishly.

Within moments they were away from the scene, leaving just another quiet, charming junction in a country full of them. O'Shea thought to break the silence.

"Whoa, we had a real nut job on our hands."

"He was a bit hot."

"Shit, man I was talking about you. Nice to see you still got *the rage*."

He smiled and shrugged, "Just working things out was all. No harm no foul."

Liam shook his head, "That's a very Zen-like way you have of going about things. Back home, that long a string of blue would've had someone reaching for their steel—*somebody* would've had to go."

"Yeah, well, you lot are the bastion of vicious savagery, that much is understood…. Shit, at least we keep our hyper violence on the political bent."

"Yeah, the politics of soccer I suppose?"

"Touché." He shrugged. "C'mon, we're late for a wedding."

True to his word the tanker man had them back on track, the mountains were once again on the proper side of things, and the faint outline of the manor house was visible through the rise of the lower valley.

Kevin had a wide-eyed, wild look about him, "*Damn* son—we almost died." The adrenaline high having frozen a clown paint smile across his face.

"It would seem so." He looked over, "Kevin, you didn't spill your drink. I'm impressed."

"Yeah, well, priorities."

Liam kept the roadster clipping along at a more reasonable pace and brooded.

"Jesus, almost died for a tin of Insta-tan—ain't that a B?"

His cousin laughed, "Try puttin' that on a headstone."

O'Shea suddenly felt fully awake for the first time in a long time, the gimping of near death having been better than anything found in bottles or pills.

They soon pulled back onto the grounds of the estate. From the drive they could see some of the assembled already making the slow procession down to the small chapel on the far end of the property.

"Damn shame," Liam concluded, still chewing over their little mishap, "I think I will have some of that nastiness."

Kevin nodded, "It's only reasonable. What's your split, 2 to 1?"

"After that? Better make it 1 to 2." O'Shea's eyes scanned about the car, "Where the hell are the Altoids?"

"I don't know, with the GPS?"

He dropped Kevin near the front and parked the roadster in a small field behind the chapel. The sun was still out in full force, affirming once more that Brendan boy was a lucky bastard indeed—who knew what manner of Faustian trade off was in play?

O'Shea had a look up at the beautiful old chapel; a pretty whitewashed stone, gothic angels and gargoyles, all the fates and the furies staring down from on high. Salvation or damnation, pill or poison, take your pick. His eyes settled on one of the angels; there was something he recognized from another time. "Stop your looking at me," he croaked. There was no reply, ".... Want one?" He slunk low in the seat, enjoying his pick me up as a strong gust of wind blew past. He reached back into the bag and found the bottle, shaking two small orange pills into his hand....Xanax with a Red Bull-Grey Goose chaser out on the grass at Dunamore sitting in a BMW ragtop...five, ten years ago, who knew?

.... Life's a strange mutha. Mundane and tedious all your days and then, suddenly and just as inexplicably, cutting along at the speed of light.... Where will we be in another ten? Floating around the South Seas? Drinking white rum in a Corsican bar? Stone broke, working the lines on a fishing trawler, snorting one's father's ashes—the only thing not pissed away in the preceding ten, as you try your best to kick that black tar sweet tooth, while trying not to get shanghaied into some ragged *Montagnard* army, sticking heads on pikes deep in a jungle of mystery...the permutations were as terrifying as they were laughable. Well if the whores hustled, then the hustlers whored—better gird the clackers to meet them both. He chased the pills with the last of his drink, winked up at the seraphim winking down and toasted, "All right then—to all the old familiar places?" There was no reply. Never mind, a couple of mints were the proper finé for those young rascals in the know.

He popped a few, chewed em' good, and made his way around the stone path to the front of the chapel where the congregation was milling about. He found Sara out by the steps of the rectory talking to a young couple he didn't recognize...which therefore meant they were with the Bride, which therefore meant things could go either way. The chances of being tackled or otherwise assaulted were fairly minimal...but then again, known commodities were sometimes the best.

"There you are, Liam, this is Jason and Brooke," she smiled, "They're in from The States."

"Wonderful. Vacationing are you?"

"Actually, we just moved here."

"They work at the American Embassy. Jason's just finished his M.S. at the Foreign Service School."

O'Shea had to jog the memory of his former life a bit, ".... Georgetown, right?"

He nodded, "Just finished last month."

"And Brooke's been telling me about some of the work she's done with Doctors Without Borders. Similar stuff to what I'll be doing.... She was even in the same part of Africa I'm going to."

He gathered up his best shade of sly, "You two wouldn't happen to be *lawyers* by any chance?"

"They *are*," Sara grinned. "Berkeley."

He smiled, "Very impressive. Listen, if you'll excuse me for a moment, I'm helping out with things—got to go find the keys for the *Prima Nocta* belt."

"The what?" Brooke asked sweetly.

"Oh, local tradition, you'll see." Whence, he ambled over to join the safe confines of the merely human crowd to have a smoke and brood. Fate, it would seem, had a funny habit of taking the long way for a joke.

Liam found a discrete enough distance, had a seat on a stone wall, lit up a smoke, and watched some of the more entertaining aspects of the wedding unfold. While it was only a short walk down from the main house to the chapel, that would have made for some piss poor theatricality—therefore with all righteous intent, a trinity, a fleet if you will, of white stretch Humvees were employed to ferry the Wedding Party from the front gates of the property, slowly through the grounds, and down along the winding path to the chapel. Three of the buggers, 69 feet in all of tropospherical death, were slowly rolling down the long promenade with the backdrop of the mountains in the distance.

.... He imagined they used to roll this kind of largesse with a bit more dash back in the day; teams of pale colored horses pulling ornate, elaborate carriages, coachmen in morning coats drawing their teams with all the rigid formality of a military review. But that sort of action was increasingly for those with one foot in the grave. Modern times called for modern means, but for the moment this unholy trinity was momentarily stuck trying to navigate a particularly sharp turn between the old stone walls...shit man, at least a horse could take the corners a bit better. However, with great care the matter was sorted and the revue soon arrived at the Chapel.

Brendan and Kevin were the first to step out. They looked about as confused as a couple of spare pricks at someone *else's* wedding. The concept of a large, watchful crowd and the actual appearance of one could make for a very jarring disconnect. The lads were on their own with this one. O'Shea ashed out his smoke, found Sara, and filed into the chapel taking a respectful seat near the back of the congregation.

He made the sign of the Cross towards the altar.

"Nice touch," she whispered.

The last of the guests filed in. And while the organ music was pure Handel formality, there was something else in the air, something a bit more bouncy, something much more keeping with the temperature of the age than anything from the dog eared Irish copy of the Vatican II playbook.... Maybe it was just the Xanax kicking in, or the general lack of sleep, but somewhere, if only in his mind, he could hear the faint jangle of Van Morrison's *Everyone*, as the delovely Bride filed past and Kevin Delaney slowly pulled the heavy chapel doors shut.

A few Starlings were up in the willows singing songs as a Grasshopper chirped on the rusted iron of the Churchyard gate. A warm, alive sound carried along the summer wind, from the hills all the way down to the sea, before snapping back like a thunder clap across the ocean, all the way to Maison du Henri, where a green light sat atop the old stone wall near the drive, and where many many creatures waited for their new master to return.... A transcendence was in the air. Thoreau was right as well—why run when you can walk? But perhaps old Trimalchio had been most spot on—Piss warm and drink cold, because our mother the earth is in the middle...

Christopher M. Basso

.... Suddenly the peaceful magpies scattered.

"A lovely service!" Miss Mary Morkan shrieked as the heavy priory doors swung open. Brendan and Kevin's aged neighbor from Ballymun had managed to find an amplitude only space station astronauts could have missed.... Although there might have been one who hadn't registered it.

"Liam," She hissed, "Wake up!"

He stirred a bit, "I'm awake."

"Your eyes were closed."

"Who you gonna believe?"

He leaned forward a bit, bright eyed and refreshed.

"Did I miss anything?"

"Don't sweat it chief."

"Well, then.... I'm Starin' Marvin over here. Let's get our food on."

Now that the solemnity was through the real festivities could commence.

Chapter Thirteen
Trimalchio

Hand in hand, Liam and Sara filed up the long graceful slope of the hill back towards the manor house. They were offered a ride in one of the Humvees, and while difficult to pass up such a rare treat, decided it was far too grand a day for such things. The reception was being held under three large white and cream colored tents, impressively lined end to end to end in a display of grandiosity that would have made the Pasha's caravan feel like wee lesser men. From the reception line on the far end, to the three ice swans nearest the tennis courts, there were some three hundred souls in all; spanning the entire southern terrace of the great manor house. The Wedding Party and their extended families were already into the formal meet and greet when Liam and Sara arrived.

The cocktail hour had started properly enough. A thirteen piece wood and string ensemble were lilting through some gentle standards, as waiters and footmen in white coats and black ties moved expertly through the crowd carrying trays of pâte à choux and flutes of chilled Ponsardin. The Bride, Groom, and their attendants soon disappeared for photo time deep in the reaches of the manicured gardens, leaving their guests to mill about the tents and terraces with that strange wedding air of complete strangers, trying to feel one another out.

Things seemed innocent enough, but the right kind of hound could scent the mischief in the air; a fine sense of brewing rebellion to all the forced niceties the first half of a wedding compels you to...this was perhaps the regrettable downside to a

211

culture which placed too high a premium on form over function. The notion, long espoused by grouchy puritanical sorts, that moderation was the better part of valor just never seemed to catch fire with the natives 'round these parts. If someone struck a match the kettle might just boil over.... O'Shea breathed it in deep, like the fine aromatics of napalm in the morning. He had a few of these under his belt already, never *this* elaborate, but then again that was merely a function of volume and amplitude—certain things were most likely, and inevitably, par for the course.

But until the fireworks commenced proper-wise he was content to let his eyes wander a bit. Each tent was arranged in such a way that all things would flow towards the center of the action, that is, towards the impressive bamboo floor they'd jerry rigged over the short grass in the center tent. And before it, rising up over the congregation, was a long dais of dark sturdy oak, branded and embossed with some sort of heraldic shield.

Since the clan Delaney could claim only the Guinness Harp for some manner of family crest, O'Shea guessed this one was from the Bride's side. It was a *mad* set up meant to evoke the divine right of kings, but on some level it worked. If image was the currency, and currency was the gospel, then this was one high flying holy rolling hosanna of money well spent.

Within the hour the bridal party, all eighteen of them, returned and took their seats—ergo the next level of *Inferno* meets *Brides* was activated. At the head of the elegant dais sat the Groom. Liam nudged his cousin in the ribs and motioned up towards old Brendan boy, orbiting celestially on his throne. In his morning grays and stylish tails he had the mad bearings of some effete Bogman gone straight.... But there was definitely a look of *fear* in that boy's eyes, like the dawning sense of dread when one realizes just how far over their heads they've drifted. Not to mention the filleting that awaited for any and all filial transgressions.

Along each of the girders crisscrossing the tents were elaborate strands of woven light; points of soft white wrapped in trains of Ivy and Polo roses. Wrought iron chandeliers filled with candles hung from the center arches, shining a faint golden light over the assembled. A slow but gathering chorus of laughing, shouting voices began to carry along the warm summer air, mixed here and there with faint notes of music and the sharper dissonance of cutlery and glass. The long bar opposite the dais was in full-press, packed end to end with those not to be bothered with mere champagne and white wine table service. These were the hardo's requiring the stronger drink of a vicious fortitude. That is to say this was the Groom's side of the aisle and slowly but surely O'Shea was recognizing a few faces from the way back when.

Two overworked barmen manned the center tap, as a sea of Saint James Gate's finest was flowing amid some heavy, if not entirely suspicious, stares from the extended clan. If it wasn't Guinness or some manner of barley-based libation, it might as well have been garnished with the faint unmanly airs of a criminal capitulation. Cosmopolitans, Mojitos, Caipirinhas; bright colors and strange names of exotic provenance didn't sit too well with the congregation. For the moment they seemed content to swill their stout and make odds and ends about all the no class *put-on's*.

The two cousins and Sister Sara were standing in by the out door when Liam noticed the ocular flutter vibing from this particular group.

"I know," Kevin added. "Like moths to a flame. We're going to have to get these people to *mingle* some."

"Get the skiffle band in," Liam shot back. "That'll warm them up."

Kevin Delaney shot him a dirty look, then set a kinder eye to Sara, "See, here's the thing…in America a fella might see another man living in a big house up on the hill and think to himself—that's going to be me one day. In our little patch of green it's more like, when you see the fella living in the big house up on the hill, the first thing that springs to mind is the best, most expeditious way to tear the bastard down…. Think of it as the blueprint from which all things *flow*."

She looked at Liam and grinned; they were obviously in on the act *together* now.

"Oh, he ain't kidding blondie."

Kevin gave her a reassuring smile before heading up to his seat, "Just keep your hands behind the screen, you'll be fine."

The cocktail hour, like any decent wedding's cocktail hour, zoomed by way too fast. Just as soon as you were settling into the rhythms of the thing, the band cut out and you were being gently but firmly encouraged to wander off and find your table—which was no small task. Kevin Delaney made for his perch on the far end of the dais as Liam and Sara were seated near the dance floor with a fine and utterly pleasant group of complete and utterly random strangers. Within a few minutes they were able to gather this was by and large the *singles* section—that bastard afterthought of the nuptial seating chart.

This particular collection of nomads seemed to be straggler friends of the Bride mostly…. *Strange locale* for such an esteemed late addition and his plus one, but then again Brendan was an exceedingly strange guy. But at least there was that nice young couple from The States seated across from them. Sara immediately fell into conversation with these two, reducing the recently retired O'Shea to a gadfly on the wall in a milieu of heady idealism run amok…. Liam buttered up a roll and made a mental note to add old Brendan boy to his dead-to-me list. Retribution would be swift and forthcoming.

They brought out the potato and leek vichyssoise first, which went down well on a warm summer's evening, followed by the bronzed sea scallops and dusted porcini risotto cakes.

"Mmm, this is excellent," she said having a sip from a fine Tasmanian Riesling, "don't you think?"

But his mind was elsewhere, "Sure, wonderful…. Let me ask you, why do you think he sat us at the straggler's table?"

She frowned, "I don't know, I've never met him."

He sighed, "Could be worse I guess—could be the hard up table."

"The what?"

"Over yonder," he discreetly pointed behind her shoulder, towards the mutant revue, half out the tent near the spikes—a Van Diemen's Land of unruly third cousins, obligatory business considerations, and ardent enthusiasts of the three whiskers on the chin mole aesthetic; the mean of which might otherwise upset the more gentle sensibilities of decent folk, appearance-wise.

He thought about it some more and smiled, "Must be Brendan's idea of something *humorous*." He looked up and spied the man in question, shaking his head sadly, "I've always suspected that boy been kicked by some manner of ruminant."

She grinned, "What, cows and such?"

".... Well, he's still got most of his faculties, so I'm thinking something smaller…donkey perhaps?"

"Next you're going to tell me he's cross-eyed?"

"No, interestingly enough he *was*. I suspect that donkey sorted things out for him."

She gently patted his hand, "Well dear—straight from the ass's mouth."

"Thank you. Perhaps that's why we're sitting here? Anyway, two mules for Brother Brendan—I sense a toast coming on."

He ordered another glass of the pleasant Shiraz he'd been dabbling in. The Groom's problems with the local livestock were only so riveting, so he let his eyes scan about the room for a bit till they landed on something of bit more interest.

"Listen—I'll tell you a good one. See that wizened fellow sitting over there?"

She nodded.

"That's Brendan's grandfather, Rory," he quickly surveyed who was within earshot. "Rumor has it that back in the day Rory was knee deep with the local Provos up north—doing all manner of shady things."

She gave him a quizzical look.

"Good lord woman, did you not hear tale of *The Troubles* out on the Left Coast?"

"You mean the I-R-A?" She might only have been louder if she'd grabbed the microphone near the ice swans.

215

"*Jesus* woman, Ixnay on the I-R-A-stay," he glanced around nervously. This was not the sort of ice-breaker this crowd would altogether dig. He leaned in, measuring his words, "When not working as the occasional bagman, he used to run guns in and out of Dundalk, the little border town where they lived."

"So, what you're saying is, he was in that—organization."

"Not quite…more like a groupie than straight with the band. Rory's brother Terry however *was*. He's still in Long Kesh—*the big house*— serving out his twenty-five to life. Anyway, during the summers when they were kids Rory used to get the boys—Brendan and his brother Jackie in on the act. They'd go out to the bog lands and play buried treasure." He frowned, "…. Some bizarre take on quality-time I suppose."

"Buried treasure?"

"Yeah, buried treasure, which generally involved the old man digging holes and burying the types of things that needed burying for awhile…but he'd always throw some shiny Queen Elizabeth Silver Jubilee coins down the hole, so the lads would be properly motivated to find them later." He chuckled, "A bit of a *deft touch* with irony that must have amused old Rory to no end."

"…. Damn."

"Damn right. Except Brendan was so shanked by the donkey that he went around telling anyone who would listen what he and his granddaddy did in their spare time. Anyway, the local Provo chieftains paid Rory a visit and buried treasure came to an end." He paused for some gravitas, "In a very nearly permanent way I've heard."

Sara looked over at Rory, a happy looking older fellow, festooned in some fancy sashed martial-like garb for the day.

"Don't worry, he's quite retired. Most of them are. There's no action in that business anymore."

"None?"

"…. Well, there's a few Masada Jews who'll ride the rock till the bitter end, but *Goddamn*, look around, ice sculpture swans and champagne fountains—blood grudges aside, what's the point?"

"History's a hard thing to let go," she said.

"History's a thing best swept under the rug," he shot back.

They brought out the Filet Mignon and smoked celery root puree, with a nice side of blue cheese whipped potatoes to finish things off.

She stared at her plate sadly, "Hard being a vegetarian in this country…"

He laughed, "Downright impossible."

"So why aren't you touching yours carno-boy?"

"Don't know, have less and less an appetite for it these days…. I think you're finally starting to rub off on me."

She smiled, "That's what I like to hear! Unfortunately, free will has already left the building on this one."

"It would be a waste, wouldn't it?"

"It would."

He picked up the blade and set to it, "True, true….Besides old Rory might start giving me the stink eye and shin me with that shillelagh."

There was a clanking of the glasses as the Bride's father got up to make the first toast of the evening. Declan Fineas McManus was his comically kismet whale of a name, to which Liam-James-Fintan-Bailen-O'Shea, quiet as it's kept, could relate to almost at once. It was Declan who was the father, chief, and high priest of this particular feast, and a feast it was—369 guests, 3 tents, 3 stretch Humvees, 23 wait staff, 170 dozen roses in shades of yellow and white, three guest bars, a five course meal, a five tiered cake, ice sculptures on either end of the concourse, and comped accommodations in the manor house for half of County Clare—and all on his dime. And what a *fine* dime it was. Declan had the foresight, way back in the primordial soup of the Reagan-Thatcher transatlantic blight, to realize that someday, people would just be falling over themselves to talk to one another on little portable phones that you could slip into your pocket.

Sounds rudimentary? Maybe to a gaggle of Facebooking-Youtubing-Iphoning heathens, but try selling that to a bunch of flat Earthers, back in the Jurassic wilds of 1986 when the only cellulars were about as pocketable as a Cadillac El Dorado, and required a loyal team of pack mules to move from place to place.... Yes indeed—a bit of *sand* that old boy had.

So *now* he could stand up on the dais, busking his best Flamingo-era Sinatra pose, and reap the rewards of the last twenty years of hard work, as he saw off his first born lovely in style.... The moment called for a bit of Demosthenes, but Demosthenes he was not.

Not to mention he'd been *at the bar* as they say...hell, almost under it, and it fairly showed—now lubricated like a fine Swiss timepiece off he went on a rare sort of rambling obvious jag, commencing around Genesis 1:1 and leaving off somewhere in the parking lot with some advice he'd offered the limo drivers.

This was a man rather *keen* on himself.... And hell, he might have even recognized this bloviated failing of personality—but dammit if these sycophantic suck ups, these *freeloaders*, were going to smile through their teeth at him, drink the free Veuve from his tap, and eat the caviar blinis off his trays—then they were gonna damn-well-listen!

Liam's eyes began to wander. A slow pan around the assembled, all the way from side to side. Names were gelling with the faces. There was of course Ryan "The Bearman" O'Neill from the lobby and next to him the wiry visage of his brother Jimmy—the one man with the *intrinsic ability* to get them all incarcerated this evening.... The brothers O'Neill were an odd match; fraternal twins who hadn't shared a thing since their mother's womb, with the exception of a childhood littered with blood letting and piss taking, yet were inseparable in that strange blood oath-death match kind of way.

Despite the wrestling predilection, Ryan was a rather serious fellow, thoughtful and restrained, the cosmic shining light of conscience to the dark star of his seconds younger brother, who generally strolled in through life's out doors, and who once got stink-eyed enough to proposition a cigarette machine in the dimly lit hallway of a Dublin jacks. Not the easiest of things to live down, but Jimmy was a *hell of a gamer* and someone you most definitely wanted in your corner if things got dicey.

Presently, they both worked for their father's garage out near the airport. Ryan was being groomed to run the place while Jimmy was, of course, being trained not to burn it down. Yep, the Jeb and George of Ballymun to be sure. But Jimmy was well regarded in the tight insular world of North Dublin, where his eccentricities were hosanna'd as virtues, and he was a tolerated if not beloved civic treasure, like some Gaelic Punxsutawney Phil—if Jimmy popped out and saw his shadow there'd be six more weeks of the *Guinness Fleadh*.

.... Just down the way from them was Eveline Conroy, a fine looking girl who grew up on the same North Dublin street as Brendan and Kevin. She deep-sixed the rest of the council urchins to gimp along their private Frank McCourt reduxes, and headed down to Trinity College, graduating near the top of her class. She rode that thunder all the way to Oz where she earned an MBA from Stanford, and had recently returned to a job as a junior analyst at Deutsche Commerzbank. She was as they say *driven*.

She had a waifish Andrea Corr look about her, and a fine Palo Alto tan to play up her dark feathery hair. She seemed to be growing even younger and more beautiful than he remembered—perhaps this was the real Faustian bargain in the mix? The final painful proof that the rich only seem to get richer. But good genetics and Mephistophelian antecedents notwithstanding, she was considered a *point of pride* to all those who knew her.... Seated across from the beneficence of her beingness was Michael Dempsey, who was not a point of pride to most anyone.

O'Shea grimaced—*Damn,* if he had gotten through this life without ever seeing the little tosser again he would have considered it a success. Liam slouched low in the chair in a preemptive gamble and every bit the prayer that their sightlines might never cross. Friggin' wedding—big enough to need a map, and small enough to fail the safeguards of a blissful anonymity....*Very* difficult to be around the type of insufferable spare-pricker who in his resentments managed to be both poncy *and* elitist—a metaphysical act of Bikram contortionism that could drag you down into the morass if you let it. He too was one of the council urchins from up the way, and he too had managed the escape of a higher education, but the fiduciary enlightenments of an art school edification were limiting, unless of course your antecedents were the ones already buying the art.

Let's just say that in this new paradigm of the quick and the dead he was a well read, well spoken analog player in a crassly vulgar digital world. To be able to quote Wilde and Shaw for a living was a fine gig for college professors, or bedrock street crazies, but to be caught in the mass median was to be truly stranded on a desert island. Lord only knows what the uppity quotient would be on him this fine evening surrounded by the positively freewheeling platinum card Chav set of Greater Dublin.... Shit, at least he could define irony for them.

As the band played on, a touch of grey drifted across the evening sky. O'Shea took heart that by this time tomorrow he'd be under the warm Tuscan sun, shoulder to shoulder with the drunken Sienese, eating mozzarella di bufala, drinking Brunello Montalcino, and watching some rampaging horses get a bit of revenge on the paisano chumps who thought clever to kick their kidneys and whip their withers.

At that moment there was a pause on the revolving mike grab at the dais. Declan had finished his brief history of time with a belligerent shout out to Miss Mary Jane Rottencrotch of wicked County Wexford who'd once had the pleasure of a finger themed carnal knowledge under a talon August moon back when Frampton really did make them come alive.... Oh well, *not quite*—but someone *wisely* thought to hit the faders on Declan's mike before we traveled down those dark roads of discourse. Besides, there were a slew of other punters in the on-deck circle; the tribe would have their say, in what was slowly shaping up like slam night at an Al-Anon fandango.

"Oh, Jesus," Liam groaned to no one in particular, "this is why these things last three days." Good Lord man, had we sunk this low in the conversation? Even in the subconscious subtext these fools were just piling on. The endless spiels, reminiscences, bad jokes, and sexual innuendoes being summoned from the nostalgic time fog were chilling, a conflagration fixing to talk an army of glass eyes to sleep. The foul rhythms were brutally clear, escape was the best option.

The waiters were moving about the tables laying out the intermezzo; lemon sorbet with just a splash of chilled champagne, as a steady stream of people made their way to and from the bar. Michael Dempsey was now on his feet, wandering about the place with all the joie de vivre of a man about to test experimental parachutes. Presently the daft little bugger was drifting a bit too close for comfort…time to get on the good foot.

"You'll excuse me," Liam politely interrupted the do-gooder confab. "I've got to take a powder, be right back."

With fresh drink in mitt, O'Shea slipped past the tent flap and onto the old stone terrace overlooking the gardens on the south lawn. Acres and acres of descending bands of colors and geometric patterns, gently sloping down the hill to the large lake framed with Bonsai trees and a tea pavilion. A gracious symmetry which helped to order a wandering mind. Framed high above the gardens in shades of dark green and wild purple were the looming jagged peaks of the Wicklow Mountains, standing sentinel in a stark and rugged *otherness* which served as a fine counterpoint to the well thought out balance and proportions of the gardens. There were the barbarians at the gate and wolves out at the edge of the darkness; the demarcation could not have been clearer.

A bronze bust and plaque near the end of the terrace commemorated that the Earl Charles Sommerton, Vice-Chancellor of the Realm, and the original father of this three legged tripod nod to self had indeed modeled these grounds after the Court at Versailles…. It went on to ramble some other blowhard bits of John Locke getting bedbug queer with his inner Hobbesian, all in the service of the grand delusion that these grounds should be, "A testament to the establishment of order and the fullest expression of man's entrusted dominion over nature."

…. Uh-oh, this type of guff made the boy uneasy. He looked at it again…the testament to the establishment of order? Holy shit man—the mad rumblings of half crazed Ahab sensibilities; screaming sea shanties into the maw of a driving storm, pissing in the funnels of the harshest winds and wondering why it's raining. These egoists made him none too pleased at that—time to *calm* down though and take another belt of the medicine. Generally speaking, O'Shea liked his sensibilities delicate, but not when they burnt the edges on all things one could consider *reasonable*.... Which is not to say the boy played exclusively to those Grandpa Rory fanboydom instincts. He could imagine a copy of Herodotus or a pool cue each making a fine weapon in a pinch—rather he was just suspicious of such graces on the balance.

He rested his drink on the Earl's head and marveled at the mountains off in the distance...no humbling of these, no debunking the unbunkable. Man's fragile grasp over the things he ruled never so apparent. The Earl of course, being several rungs up the free time plus madness diaspora, had given it a valiant try. Although once you chewed it over a bit there was actually something *admirable* about that—like those Tibetan monks who spend months building the most intricate of sand paintings only to destroy them the moment they are done.

This was something similar, only the sandbox was bigger, and *your* proverbial ass was what was scattered to the wind....Perhaps Ahab sensibilities and pissing into the wind were overlooked bits of recreating at that. Perhaps it was time to get in touch with that Man from La Mancha who dwells within us all. Perhaps it was...*perhaps* it was time to shut the fuck up before saner people came 'round after him with nets and soft canvas shoes.... It was *this* lovely wheel which was spinning round and round when he suddenly realized he was no longer alone.

He glanced over to the far side of terrace where standing in almost the same manner and attitude as himself was a lone figure; just another hapless reveler out measuring his share of these local heavens.

They acknowledged one another with a pleasant nod through the shadows and seemed content to leave it at that. But unbeknownst to O'Shea the stranger had kicked his pack, and noticing the orange light of a cigarette thought to wander over and test the verisimilitude of the kindness of strangers. He crossed into the shadows on the far side of the terrace and reappeared in the light; a tall, thin, form somewhat older than himself. He was handsome and even in the countenance, his fair skin tanned and bronze with slight weathered creases at the eye, measuring wear's slow advance; the devolution of what must have recently been boyish looks.

"Evening there. Mind if I bum one?"

O'Shea, for his many faults, had always taken a Boy Scout's zeal to preparedness tobacco-wise, "Yeah sure, no worries."

"Sure you don't mind?"

"No, not at all."

The stranger struck a match against Sommerton's ear, lit up, and tossed the fire to the damp grass below. They hung there for a moment in the eternal smoker's dilemma—was this merely the transactional or did some polite conversation etiquette apply?

The stranger solved this for them, "So, how are you tied to this nonsense?"

O'Shea thought about it for a moment, "Friend of a friend, I suppose…but no real way at that." He chuckled, "How about yourself?"

The stranger shrugged, "Let's just say, my sister's making one hell of a mistake."

O'Shea's eyes lit up. Was this to be the first honor-dusting of the evening? The Delaney's kept a pool on this kind of thing, and paid handsomely for the first scalp of the night. "Oh, don't care much for the Groom?"

But there was something regrettably disarming in the stranger's manner, a lightness which diffused the sting of any ill-chosen words. "Ah, not too bad I guess…seems a bit tossed around or something—but a solid man all the same." He laughed, finding the distilled essence in his mind, "Seems like he can't do much harm either way." The stranger flicked some ash on the Earl's head, "More the institution I don't care for, not in this day and age."

"Not the marrying kind?"

A thoughtful look crossed his face, "Lousy proposition—good for the man, utter bunk for the woman—and *that's* the pinnacle…. Give it a bit, eventually becomes bunk for the man and downright intolerable for the woman." He shook his head sadly, "Shit man, I spend most of my days dabbling in fairly potent strains of opiates and even *I* know that." He caught himself and glanced down for any sign of an anchor around the boy's finger.

"Sure, you might be of a similar opinion?"

"Well, *not quite*—but I can see some of the wisdom in that."

He smiled, "You'd be one of those hope springs eternal types then? I dig that."

"Well…thank you. But then again, I'm American; it's a bit more *legalistic* where I operate." O'Shea tossed his smoke out onto the stones below, "Optimism and rigid legalism, it's a vicious little game."

"Well, better than this bunch, they revel in a brand of fine bullshit fantasy mostly."

"…. But, aren't they?"

"Family? Yes."

…. The jury was still out on what to make of the stranger. He'd taken a seat against the railing, his white linen suit looked the part of wealth on relaxed means, though somewhat unkempt, like it'd recently seen the balled up inside of a suitcase…. He was perhaps the older stoner brother you looked up to, that is till he finished school and landed back in your parent's basement, took to building MacGyver-like superbongs, and trolling past the high schools that weren't on the way home…. To have articulated such things would have been the acme of foolishness—rather, he just let the boy preach on.

Almost on cue he produced one *extremely* well packed bowl from his suit pocket; an ivory and silver plated device that had the provenance of far flung lands. He balanced it in one hand and his champagne glass in the other. And while he might have been a bit too crocked for a verbal discretion, his social graces were still intact.

"Where's my manners—care for some?"

"Na."

"Mind if I?"

"No worries."

He lit up. The sweet acrid smell hung lazily in the warm summer air. The toker fixed his gaze on him again, "You know, I *thought* you were American...but the drugs and the time zones can confuse things."

"Yeah?"

"Sure, give it another hour and I'd swear you were speaking Ji Lu Mandarin.... You on vacation or something?"

"Yep."

He sighed, "So was I, at least until this thing called me back."

O'Shea laughed, "You don't sound too enthused?"

"Three days ago I was laying on a beach in Brazil, surrounded by a group of topless, morally indecisive women, growing more morally indecisive and topless by the minute, and now I'm back *here,* chasing Will-o'-the-wisps in the freezing bogs, breaking bread with the clan, and staring up at...Bleak House." He caught himself in mid harangue, "Shit, sorry about that. Thought the pot was supposed to keep me on a pacifist keel?"

"Well," O'Shea offered his support, "Maybe it's just the jet lag monkey-wrenching your vibe?"

"That's very kind of you to say." He looked up, "Sure you don't want a hit?"

"Nah, I'm driving."

"*Driving,*" he let out a hearty laugh, "that's a good one."

O'Shea wasn't quite sure what to make of that. He thought best to smile and nod.

The stranger shook his head after a particularly harsh hit, "Bit strong." He coughed, "They call it *Sneachta.*"

"Gaelic for NyQuil isn't it?"

"It is." He banged the bowl against the railing and held out his hand, "Colin McManus."

"Richie…Richie Cunningham."

Another strange pause hung in the air—as they'd officially run out of transactional niceties. But in death, the horsemen pass, and men were men. "Well," he slapped his knees and stood up, replacing the pipe in his pocket. "I've got to keep moving. God forbid they put the arm on me. I'll have to give a speech or something." He held out his hand, "Nice meeting you Cunningham."

"Same."

And just as quickly he was gone, shuffling along into the dark shadows down the lawn…perhaps for a nice nap against one of the Bonsai? Then suddenly he turned and shouted back, just barely audible over the wuthering breeze, "Postscript—avoid entanglements at all costs!"

"Sure, right, thanks." Liam smiled, "Hey, they'll be wanting that glass back."

"Not after I'm done with it," he shouted back.

"…. Right." O'Shea looked the Earl Sommerton in the eye and shook his head, "Whack-a-doodle."

He watched the tall figure sashay his Jack Sparrow way back down the lawn. Yep, that was just about enough rusticating for the evening…. Time to see what was going on back in the Big Top. He started up the lawn again and glanced down at his watch—half past eleven? Shit man, was this thing still on East Coast time?

The growing sounds of voices and music rose up to meet him as he poked his head through the tent sash. The woodwinds were gone and a massive sound system was up and running. There was an amp rack about every nine feet, and enough speakers to make contact with the dead.… His eyes drifted across the tent. His missus was still in deep conversation with the do-gooder confab, while a quick scan of the room revealed his cousin pinned against the bar. He had a pained look across his face, well into a discussion with some long lost relative, an excitable fellow, regaling him with tales of the hotel business in Torquay.

.... Oh, if *this* wasn't just too much fun to stick around—so he didn't. He slipped out the side and made his way along the edge of the far tent, towards the last of the guest bars. He found a deck chair overlooking a glimmering pool, decorated in a sea of floating candles and pink water lilies.... Peace, or a piece of it anyway, a small reprieve despite the decibels rattling through the topiaries. He was quietly nursing his beer, admiring the stars when his serenity was shattered by an abrupt run in with the natives.

It was a smaller, rowdy group of what he assumed were friendlies—or at the least neutrals. One of them, a slightly older, somewhat cuckoo-puffs lady, soon had him pinned by a cabana table full of empty champagne bottles near the waters edge. Their exchange, while brief, went swimmingly.

"What do you do for a living?" She shouted over the music.... This seemed to be the crass leitmotif of the evening.

"Pederast."

"What?" She smiled, leaning over, her breasts pushed up against him. Robbie Williams, *Rock DJ,* was shaking the trees right above their heads.

"Pediatrician."

"Oh that's nice for *you*," one could almost hear the whettening of her knickers.

"Isn't it though?"

The boom rattled through the trees—Robbie was *feeling* it in the chorus.

As was she...a hand had past Checkpoint Charlie and appeared to be going for the groin.

He put his empty bottle down, "Uh, you'll excuse me if I take my leave, I heard there was a young boy inside in need of some massaging."

"How's that luv?"

"Medicine, the boy is in need of some medicine," he gave her a reassuring smile.

She touched his arm, slightly longer than necessary, "That's very sweet of you."

"I try."

"Well, it was nice to meet you—listen here's my number. If you're ever…"

"I most certainly will." He grabbed the card, gave a wink, and made like Moses across the Sinai.

He moved back along the near side of the house, weaving in and out of the shadows, wondering what manner of David Lynch-Frank Booth outtake lay just around the corner…. But then again, perhaps that was a bit too harsh. What, after all, had these gimps done to him other than sour his meal, crass his reflections, and grope his junk….Maybe *he* was the problem? Perhaps he should get that stick out from the dark place, drop the fussy pretensions and join in the fun—perhaps see what other millions of mischiefs he could get into…. Ugh, maybe he could tell them the one about the Priest, the Rabbi, and the Pakistani who went to Heaven. Better yet, maybe the one about his alcoholic party clown father who used to beat him like a rented mule with his big red and white clown shoes…. Behaving boorishly was more fun than he imagined—not to mention just the Jujitsu response the situation demanded; amp it up to keep one step ahead of this pack of aberrant humanity.

With a renewed heart, and only mildly lingering paranoia, Liam strolled back to main tent where much to his relief they'd already cut the cake; that is *the cakes*. The show pony of the evening was a towering $20 a slice charmer of light chiffon and lemon finished in a white butter cream…. Damn, it was almost too pretty to eat—well almost. He snagged a piece off a passing tray and got down to business.

Meanwhile, the Broom Hilda stepsister, *the traditional cake*, was also making the rounds…. It was a foul goblin of a thing, three layers of whiskey laced fruitcake and sweet almond paste. You posed with it for the pictures, assaulted your guests with the first two tiers, and then stuck that sucker in the freezer till the Christening of your firstborn, whence you wheeled it out again and laid into any remaining family members with it. By then it had cured to the fine consistency of a well traveled meteorite.

God forbid they gave a taste to the gumming newborn—then you could understand why pain and penance comes early in the Irish experience.

.... He could see its generally uneaten remains on various tables, but there were always a few exceptions to the rule, particularly amongst the gray hairs who seemed to dig it. Shit, old Rory might have even gone back for seconds. Ugh, then again they ate blood puddings and seasoned entrails of their own free will and volition.

Kevin came up beside him, "Thing tastes terrible today—imagine what it'll be like in six or seven years when our lad finally brings himself to do the deed?"

"Shit, he's got to figure out what the deed is first, before he even thinks to try it on."

"Fair point."

Liam laughed, "Worse for you friendo—you're going be the one eating it."

"You won't be joining us then?"

"I'll be conveniently indisposed I'm afraid."

"You'd do that to me, wouldn't you, you bastard?"

"A big ocean comes in handy—don't worry, you can mail me a chunk."

Kevin looked at him, "Where'd you wander off to anyway?"

"One of the hopheads in the band said there was some fine scag to be had down by the gardens; thought I'd go forage a bit."

"Well, he's wrong, best scags behind the bar—c'mon, let's set you up again you're looking a bit low."

In short order the cakes were cleared, the tables bussed, and the dance floor was up and running. The cousins found a spot along the crowded brass rail where they could take a breather and compare notes. From the corner of his eye he could see his lovely still safely shuttered in the same intense conversation with Eveline and that couple from New

York....From the sheer levels of divine sincerity radiating from the table he imagined they were knee deep in a game of Model UN or some such thing earnest types did in their free time....*Damn son*, shit-can that rude talk, virtuous people, and their virtuous deeds, were a good thing. Feeling a bit expansive, if not corrected, he set his sights on those who were not.

By now a great many guests had dropped the pretensions of formality. This was the *Magic Hour* of the gig; the time when nervous rigid energy loosens and just before The Collective's inner Id was let loosed. Once that wheel started turning it was every man for himself. Then would come the inevitable splintering, jelling, and general whittling down of the guest list. There would be fractious factions, new friendships forged, blood feuds born, and passions purged. And there would be yet *others* jockeying that strangely perverted sexual charge which rides shotgun whenever weepy wedding vows and copious amounts of booze are shaken, not stirred.... Shit man they should put a *warning* on these things.

Good lord man, who *were* these people? He could feel the wavering nerve of a subtle panic start to grip his mind. He drained the last of the Golden Goose. *Get a hold of yourself* you Sally-boy, don't go all wobbly on me now. The medicinal rush instantly steeled the nerves.... He began running through the escape scenarios in his mind when the music shifted gears to something more ambient and ethereal. The dance floor was momentarily pulsed, but quickly figured out the new rhythm. Not your standard wedding fare, but something interesting all the same.

He'd heard Declan had flown in his own Johnny Fontane, a spinner of some note from London; which would've impressed him greatly had he cared about such things. That was till he glanced up at the elevated DJ booth beside the dais and the impish man under the Kanga bucket hat.... Holy shit, it was The Suzuki!

"Otis, my man!" Liam shouted.

"Easy killer," Kevin looked up over his drink, "don't rile the natives."

".... Good point."

Sometime after midnight they rolled out the second dinner. Waiters in elegant whites run ragged from a long night's work reappeared wheeling heavy silver carts, one after another in a long procession, each laden with finger sandwiches, pastries, and candied scones. If that didn't make the nut, each multi-tiered tray was adorned with an assortment of artery clogging, waistline assaulting, heavy creams and marmalades. There were powerful brews of the beloved tea and by the bar a twin piston espresso machine was up and running.

The crowd descended en masse on the lovely spread and picked it clean in short order.... These people were *serious*. Food was taken not with pleasure, but with the earnest discipline of world class runners, power loading for that 26th mile. In the amped up vibe of a Mad Hatter's after hours, the maintaining of strength was essential. There were a group of them already double fisting shots of espresso by the bar, ignoring the palpitations, and assuring one another that this bit of booster rocket was just what the doctor ordered.

As feared, this thing was rapidly degenerating into the Le Mans he had dreaded; an epic jag testing the celebratory grit of all involved. The midnight hour had culled the lightweights and day trippers, and in the process the numbers had shifted toward Brendan-boy's side of the aisle. Who, while vastly outnumbered, were a powerful one-brained Chimera.

Shit, even old Rory had lost the shillelagh and was cutting a rug out in the center of the floor, letting his inner freak speak to a high powered Kanye West track with a young woman most definitely not Missus Rory. There was a broad smile on his face and a twisted look in his eye as he seriously contemplated showing that poor girl where the horse had bit him.

Well, that was about par for course.... But *far* more pleasing to the eye; Sara and Eveline had stowed the chit-chat and were now out in the mix, doing that voodoo demon shake, that many a prim white girl shaded over to after they'd toked one too many Cosmos over the line.

Then of course, right nearby, were the freakish dance stylings of Jimmy O'Neill who seemed to have the uncontested

Christopher M. Basso

patent on all his moves—a sort of wide ranging, all inclusive-never exclusive free form that suggested what might have happened if rave culture ever met the Ken Kesey set. Ah, lovely Jimmy, his eyes were a wild, pie-sized shade of glazed, so egregiously gobfreaked that he'd probably lost the plot and slipped the roofie into his own drink…. *Cad*, served him right.

Several times these various miscreants tried collaring O'Shea into the action, but his fondness for untoward activities involving rhythm and movement were fairly well documented around these parts. Rather, they collectively took the hands off approach, cutting him the wide swath generally reserved for royalty or the criminally insane. Every now and then there was a gentle coaxing to come out for a brief spin, but always with enough lead to let the boy retreat to the sidelines and the shadows where he could indulge in his *other* extracurricular wedding activities…. Which was a fine plan if not for *his lovely* throwing a monkey wrench in the works, sweetly grabbing him as he wandered by, only to be foiled by his slippery raggedy man act.

Kevin Delaney had his own problems…. He too had a run in with the Hibernian Mrs. O'Robinson, who in her day job was also known as CFO of Declan's cellular empire, and a Kilkenny cougar of rather questionable repute. Kevin had once again made the mistake of a general decency and that was all it took. She soon had him out on the floor, her hands around his waist, moving with a witch-hazel nimbleness south, till she had equal handfuls of Grade A Delaney rump chuck.

The Suzuki could just make out this terrifying scene from over his riser…. Yes, he was sure of it now—definitely time to sack his agent—fuck money, this was his *last* swindler's ball and pervert's gig…. *Jesus*, the DJ's face was a mask of pure repugnance, was this any way for a grown man to make a living? Better put on some Manilow, he reasoned, that ought to cold-shower this lot…. On second thought, old Barry might only fire these weird fuckers up—better try some *Goodbye Horses*; yep, old Buffalo Bill's swan song—with any luck it just might make them suicidal.

O'Shea was of a similar opinion as the impish DJ, but *unlike* the Suzuki, the hazy memories of an eight a.m. wake up call, deep in the throes of a physiological horror, were still fresh in the mind.... Poor Kevin Delaney—the son of Jor-El would kneel before Zod on this one. The cavalry was going outside for a smoke.... Forty years in the desert, forty minutes more in the parking lot.

Liam had since distilled his act down 1 to 1, water to cocktails. The sheer endurance of the thing was just beginning to dawn on him, as this was only the first act in their day. He weaved through the quiet lobby and out the entrance before tripping over a bag of golf clubs left in the drive—*which,* he promptly delivered airborne over the shrubs and blue bulb Marigolds to the Cotswold perfect pond below.

"Au revoir gopher," he grumbled rubbing his shin.

He briefly slipped away from the mad action and cut a beeline for the slumbering roadster. There was a bright starry sky blanketing the Earl Sommerton's fields and pastures. All the ambient light from Dublin now far and faded, just a long, dark blanket dotted with brilliant points of white light.

The crushed stone on the drive felt good and sure under his step.... A transcendence was definitely coming on, as the ghost that marries moment with memory had arrived. These inconsequential actions at inconsequential moments that become seared deep into the gray matter for nothing more than their own simple, uncomplicated beauty. A collection of these for when you are old; remembering this and nothing else from a night long since gone to crowd the stars. This was a manner of gift one could never be at odds with.

He reached the car and ran a quick inventory of the trunk: luggage—check, passports—check, boarding passes—check, half a pack of smokes…regrettably—check, withering writ of karmic culpability—most definitely check. Once he'd finished he ran through it again just to be sure. The bitter herbs of a cruelly regimented parochial school education were fully on display. No wonder so many a good Catholic was arsed with the OCD—too many plays in the playbook. Slaving to a rigid detail might not bring you closer to the Lord, but that kind of guff would keep the trains running on time—ecumenically speaking.

On that note—when Pope Julius II was looking for an artist to paint the ceiling of the Sistine Chapel he asked prospective suitor, and paint thrower of note, Michelangelo di Lodovico Buonarroti, to give evidence of his talent. The young man from Arezzo responded by drawing a perfect circle in free hand, and shortly thereafter the gig was his. The moral? Well, none really at that…but fuck it, fuck perfection, and fuck Michelangelo too while we're at it—it was time to light this candle! *Next up*, slip back into Declan's Big Top and commence with the delicate extrication process.

He closed the trunk and started away when suddenly he noticed the faint light of a flashlight leading out from behind the house near the tennis courts…coming right at him it would appear. *Christ*, what manner of misfit was next; three-fingered harpy Huns dancing with the butcher's sons…this was more than he could handle.

He crouched low behind the trunk for a moment, peering back at the light which was moving slowly towards the first of the large gardens leading down the hill. Fair play, well enough, lay low and this too shall pass…but his errant pint glass had another agenda; sliding slowly down the edge of the fiendishly waxed hood and landing with a thud on the crushed gravel path.

And in an instant the faint illumination of a wandering flashlight was trained his way; catching the boy in the full glory of some vaguely compromising position hunkered down behind the boot of a very expensive sports car; looking somewhere between laid up and laid out…either way it had fairly sideswiped the regal airs of self-regard he'd just been dabbling in.

"Hello? Somebody there?"

The voice was English, he was sure of it; the soft proper lilt of a Devonshire belle…at least that's what the movies had taught him…. And before he could catch himself for indulging in such speculative claptrap rubbish, the voice crossed the near side of the lawn and appeared from out the shadows, standing beneath the faint light of the drive.

She clicked off the flashlight and smiled.

"You ok down there?"

He could just about make her out in the grayness; a tall, slim girl with dark hair, high cheek bones, and a pale, flawless countenance that almost seemed to glow in the half light. Even in the shadows her eyes flashed a stunning shade of green as she stepped closer. She looked confident; and a strange sort of elegance hung about her from almost the first instant.

Sensing the threat of imminent danger at a minimum the boy quickly regrouped. "Yep, all's well...just checking the tires you know?"

"Well certainly," she chuckled. "You can never be too safe."

She had come around the far side of the car and was now standing more or less across the way from him, though the light still gave her a certain bit of shadow that was strangely disconcerting. But in the grander sense of introductions she seemed to be waiting for O'Shea to proffer the opening gambit.

He stood up dusting himself off. "So, uh, you part of the festivities?"

"Strictly a guest...bit of a shoe gazing third wheel actually." She studied the stars for a second, ".... Unusual wedding though; I really had to get out of there. Those people...those people are *strange*."

"Yeah, rather grim isn't it?"

"Oh, it's well past grim my friend; I'd say it's hovering about two feet above the bestial."

"That good?"

"I guess that's what we've been reduced to these days; the level of dumb beasts."

"Well, at least animals have the sense not to abuse themselves," he took a smoke from out his pack and offered her one.

She hoisted her own up from the shadows with a smile.

Her look suddenly took on a more serious bearing. "Actually, I'm a bit of a rescue party, my escort for the evening seems to have wandered out into the shadows."

".... That wouldn't be the tall fellow in the white suit—goes by the name of Colin?"

Her eyes picked up. "Oh, you know him?"

"In a manner of speaking; he bummed a smoke a while back, made some vague threats about catching a nap down by the bonsai."

Her next tell was quite interesting, in that if the looks doth proclaim the woman and neither a borrower nor a lender be...but then again the boy's boozy brain did digress—her *next* tell was that she was not in the least surprised, shocked, or enraged, but merely took the news with the calm airs of a soul who's heard it all before.

"Yes, that sounds about right for him."

That this somewhat trifling breach of saner wedding etiquette produced little in the way of exasperation or surprise was perhaps the final sign that this was one of the level headed friendlies on a rather scorched playing field.

A second of mute recognition hung in the air for their mutual disregard of this strange scene; but then she seemed to return to the task at hand.

"Well, I should be going, this could take a while." She stared down into the darkness of the gardens; a predawn game of find the pothead whack-a-mole in the moors held little in the way of appeal...but the thing needed to be *done*.

.... O'Shea could then sense that regrettable instinct of "gentlemanly obligation" sneaking up like the mad little voice that leads one to perdition. He ran a rather patronizing equation quickly through his mind—returning the sum that the aberrant collection of mutants back in the Big Top seemed capable of just about any and all manner of Grendel-themed queerness out in the dark with the lights gone low. He would have to offer.

"Listen, uh, I don't mean to be forward, but I'd feel better if you let me come with you." He smiled, assuming the forbearance of a mutual understanding, "Not the safest of places for a young lady to be roaming about."

"Is it now?"

"Indeed." He could feel the nerves loosening up, the bullshitenspiel coming fast as fancy, "Why do you think I'm out here? Courtesy service of the betrothed…they obviously know their guest list well."

She cocked her head to the side, "So that's your job then?"

"Yeah, rescuing defenseless women is part if what I do."

She let out a hearty laugh, "Well, I can only suggest you find one and rescue her."

"*Look*," he said at length, "all nonsense aside; this place is where the wild things roam…. I'd feel better if you let me escort you."

She studied him for a second; her gaze suddenly direct, as though this was the first time in the exchange she'd looked at him rather than through him.

"Actually, that's probably the nicest thing I've heard this evening."

"…. Strangely, that's not saying much."

She laughed. "Yes, but at least it's saying something."

She walked over and extended a hand.

"Claudia, Claudia Sommerton."

"Liam O'Shea."

"My goodness; all the chivalrous speechmaking, I was expecting Bruce Wayne?"

"Give it some time, the night's still young."

"Very well." She smiled. "…. Shall we?"

She clicked the torch on and they started down towards the gardens…. It was fairly evident from go that this was the right call. Out past the gentle lights on the drive, the grounds were reclaimed by nature at the quick step; just like the jackanapes on the plaque had planned it…a quick and impenetrable descent into a rather rarified heart of darkness.

"By the way," he whispered," don't let the chivalry fool you; first sign of trouble and I'm off like a gun."

She smiled. "Good, I'll know who to hide behind when the time comes."

They made their way slowly down the path leading into the vast expanse of gardens and orchards; the faint glow of the flashlight cutting like a silent sentinel through the blackened hills. They passed through a small grove of olive trees, so narrow they had to squeeze between them; as the heavy canopy grew denser, and the perfume of the hedgerows rose up to greet them.

"What were you doing back at the car?" She asked.

"Just loitering, making a fool of myself really…the usual." He ducked beneath one of the tall branches. "Needed a bit of a breather."

"I know, I'm afraid to go back." She laughed before following past the same crook in the path. He helped her over the small stone rise leading down the next tier to the lake and the Japanese tea pavilion.

"What's your tie to this thing anyway?" She said.

"I grew up with the Groom, he's sort of a cousin."

"…. But you're American?"

"I am, but much like the prodigal son, I return." He caught her out the corner of his eye, "What about you? Sounds like I'm among the English?"

"You are, but don't hold it against me." She smiled. "I'm just doing Colin a favor."

"How do you two know each other?"

"We were thrown out of Oxford together."

He shrugged, "…. Well, it's the ties that bind they say?"

"Isn't that the truth."

"So you're accomplices, is that it?"

"No, I'm a fairly self fulfilling prophecy as *they* also say…but we have formed a kind of standing pact to accompany one another to these mutually retrograde family functions; few and far between as they are."

"That's nice of you."

She shook her head; "Don't even like it here really. Weather's dreadful."

He frowned, "Worse than England?"

"Don't like it there either.… Spend most of my time in France these days; probably the closest thing I'd call home."

They had rounded the last turn near the tea pavilion; the night's creatures were in full song from the nearby pond…

"Don't get back much then? To England?"

She shook her head, "Births and deaths; about the only things that'll get me there these days."

"Fair enough.… So where do you spend the rest of it?"

"Traveling mostly, seeing new things," she looked up at the stars again, "new things till they become old things; then I move on."

"Sounds sort of lonely?"

"No, not really.… More liberating than anything."

He seemed vaguely interested.

"It's a big world," she said, "new things to see, new people to meet; it would take you a hundred lifetimes to run out of it.… Until then, this particular little arrangement will have to do."

"What about yourself?" She said.

He shrugged, "Insurance salesman; whole life, radical limited; triple indemnity—the full bit."

She frowned, "*Doubt it*. Given this wedding, you look more…no wait, I'm good at this—junior investment banker, wracked with guilt, by the strains of a dying boyhood liberalism?"

"Oh Miss, only in my dreams."

239

Christopher M. Basso

"Was I close?"

"Only if to hurt my tender sensibilities."

She smiled some devil smoke, "Well, what do I know? Does it look like I work in a carnival?"

He laughed. "You know, I could be *offended*, had I not suffered so many indignities already this evening."

"No, I don't think so..." She sized him up. "You've a very pleasant way about you; a very forgiving personality I suspect." She stated this as far more declarative than question.

".... Well, that might just be the nicest thing I've heard this evening."

They came out near the garden path leading down to the edge of the lake. Out in the fields again, with the eyes having found that happy middle ground between the dark and the light, he was finally able to get a better look at his travelling companion.

She was about his age he guessed, and while her beauty was already apparent, the clearer light shifted his appraisal to something of a deceptive loveliness; like a hazy image slowly coming into focus, and with it a greater wealth of beauty revealed in the finer details.

She was dressed rather elegantly, more so than most, yet there was something in her manner which made her seem more scandalous, and conversely far more *dangerous*, than anything swinging back in the Big Top.... And yet in the apparatchik dynamics of some grand misdirect, her appearance and transcendence thereof, produced a third quality for *the prestige* that was wholly unexpected. She seemed to carry herself with the sure, clear understanding that she possessed the indefinable sprinkle of "otherness" that many spend all their days flailing in the dust to achieve; and that she was completely aware of the same.... He imagined it a fine bit of armor at that.

It was probably also a rare enough thing in this world to run into someone rocking a full-on megalomania vibe; it offered something of the same impressive adrenaline jolt of standing near the lions in the zoo at feeding time; and rejoicing rather thankfully at the moat in between.

.... Yes indeed, a strange twisted rush that made one quite happy to have planted their flag with the antipodean libertine back in the house; most likely plotting some Birkenstock themed airlift deep into the forest fire *du jour*.... Well to each their own and all that.

He paused soaking up the rank introspection of the first, before dim-bulbing the sudden deeper implications of the second; when from out the bushes nearby came a sudden rustling sound; a sound that grew with each passing step.

The rescue party shared a look of bemused terror for a moment as they stood near the edge of the tea pavilion. They'd wandered deep into the calm stillness of the Japanese garden, and it was only then that Liam noticed the intense beauty all around them; the intricate arrangements of hedges and blooming flowers, the rows of pine and sugar maple, and the sound of water falling over stone.... This was a calm piece of it indeed. A calm piece broken only by the sudden appearance of a maniac in a crumbled white suit, stained with five thousand miles of slacker indifference, barreling from out the bushes shouting, "Banzai!"

The beast's eyes were wild with wombat lust and he stank of a Munich Biergarten gone to orbit. He lunged towards them; rather crazed, one foot on Jacob's Ladder and one foot in the fire. Thankfully, he tripped over one of the stone walkways and came stumbling into O'Shea's arms, coming to a halt just inches from the boy's face.

".... Ugh, Dr. Livingstone I presume?"

A bright flash of recognition shot across the interloper's eyes, "Ah, Cunningham...we have to stop meeting like this."

Claudia stepped forward, "Colin, what are you *doing* down here?"

"Looking for the beach luv, couldn't seem to find it."

"Do get a grip my dear; we're taking you back to the house."

"Why on Earth? It's lovely down here; the sun, the moon, the stars…"

And with that, the old boy more or less cashed his chips; not quite drifting off to the Happy Hunting Ground, but suddenly requiring the steady shoulder of borderline alcoholic to steer the best path home…. And so it went; phase three of Liam O'Shea's observations on a wedding, carrying a more or less grown man back through the Earl Sommerton's gardens towards the house; having to listen to intermittent shouts of vaguely menacing gibberish and a few bars of "Show Me the Way to Go Home" in between.

Liam smiled under his burden. "Guess he's been thoroughly retrograded for the evening?"

"Actually he's quite entertaining in his element…regrettably, this is not his element."

"I'll take your word for it; bastards heavy either way."

He carried him over the rise of the footpath leading back to the drive; the sounds of the wedding still in full flight from the other side of the house, and Colin McManus singing right along with it.

Liam looked over, "I thought he just smoked some weed?"

"He did, but the boy likes to armor-up on occasion; soaks his wares in Ketamine now and then."

"Bit of booster rocket?"

"To be sure."

"…. Wait a minute, son of a bitch tried giving me some; *Christ*, I'd be under the table right now clawing my eyes!" He momentarily thought to roll humpty dumpty back down the hill.

To which she could only shrug. "Didn't anyone ever tell you not to take candy from strangers?"

The dénouement to the affair came rather quickly. They reached the crushed gravel drive and picked up a good tailwind heading towards the side entrance of the manor. There were a few other dissipated revelers messing about the drive who stopped to watch the events unfolding with something bordering on the smug; *which* considering whatever Faustian shill they had perpetrated to afford $400 a night hotel rooms should have given them all the humility necessary to revisit the word *hypocrite*.

Miss Sommerton, who generally cared little for the opinions and propriety of this sub class of humans who hide their vulgarities in broad daylight, graciously thought better on the reputation of the future heir to Éire Telecom. She motioned to the doormen for some help and sought to wrap things up quickly.

"I think I can manage it from here."

"Excellent; the old boy's killing me."

He passed Colin off to two of the waiting porters who seemed eerily practiced in addressing such tactful matters.

But then the old boy suddenly sprang to life again like some ginned up jack-in-the-box. He reached over and kissed Liam on the mouth, "Good bye Cunningham—you're one of the good ones! Insouciant tripe's, meandering fools; don't let them tell you otherwise!"

…. She watched them lead Colin away, shouting all the while, before fixing a long smile on the boy, "Well, thank you Cunningham; you *really* are one of the good ones," and extended her hand again. "Looks like you get your merit badge for the evening?"

"Well, maybe it's more the karmic one…evens out all the mischief I've done in the end."

"*See*, that's the spirit. Put it in the perspective of some Roman wedding run amok and the whole endeavor can almost even seem…quaint." She had that habit of phrasing questions in the declarative.

"…. Gee, never thought of it that way. But uh, thank you, Claudia this has all been very…illuminating."

She smiled. "Then it wasn't such a waste after all." And with that she disappeared back into the shadows of Bleak House just as quick as the devil smoke she'd been conjured with.

…. He admired the collectives' departure for a moment and marveled briefly at the strange élan of grit, grace, and grovel which had heralded it. He then looked up at the large portrait of the Earl Sommerton hanging in the entrance; his weary mind missing the greater implications of lineage, but content to share with him his assessment of the night's proceedings.

"Fucking clown shoes…seriously."

He started back along the side path around the house and under the massive porte-cochère towards the growing noise from the terrace and the tents. The sounds of chirping crickets and cicadas quickly gave way to the heavy, rising thump of drum and bass. The set list had time traveled back to 1984 as the Suzuki jigowatted a steady stream of Culture Club, Wham, and Duran Duran—your basic late night wedding fare the world over—'cause from Kalahari bushmen to prissy London bankers *everybody* knew "Karma Chameleon".

By now it was just after 4 a.m. and even King Hamlet's ghost had quit this shit and gone to bed. The respectable folk were tucked away in the splendid Louis XIV rooms in the main house, as was surely now Colin McManus; peacefully off to the land beyond the sun; his mind on the skimpy thong set along the Copacabana strip, his arm around a throw pillow named Gisele.

While in the center tent an already limited crowd was growing more limited by the minute. The Bride and the Groom? Long since gone…. He could regretfully picture the scene upstairs—a dark room, soft music, the Bride weeping gently in the failing half light; her make-up a shade of bewildered raccoon, the Groom apologizing profusely, reassuring her between the wracked sobs that he just wanted to *see* what it was like to wear a $9000 dress…. Ah, bliss—50-60 years sail by like a flash; welcome to it child.

His eyes scanned about; just the misfits now, the vampires and long tongued liars, the beer goggle chancers…and Declan. *Truly* working at the bottom of the barrel wedding-wise….Good Lord—did he really just think that? What *evil* aside was this—straight from the cerebral cortex sans the roguish charm and smartass smirk that usually flavored his harmless odd man act. A cold chill ran through him. Where had all this animus come from? Shit man, there use to be a beauty inside of him—where'd it go?

He'd felt normal enough when he woke that morning....Must have been the Xanax; that shit was a grouchy blowback personified. Yeah, add a little alcohol and some energy drinks; he rubbed his eyes, like poking a sleeping lion in the ass with a stick—unwise at any speed.

Well, sod it. He'd make amends to all people when the moment was right. In the meantime, cut another check from the karmic-friendship IOU book—his credit was still good...mostly. For now he grabbed two bottles of Bud and took the Nebuchadnezzar high chair on the empty dais next to Kevin Delaney, already in the King Solomon throne. Reunited at last, mutually surveying the now defunct trappings of what had only recently been a very elegant and stylish affair.

Kevin seemed to read his mind, "Well, you know what they say about money buying taste."

O'Shea laughed, "Yeah, I just might be the walking proof."

The youngest Delaney took a long draw from his beer, "It don't buy taste, and it don't buy life." He nodded, "Yer' boy Bob Marley said that."

"Kevin lad—you getting all existential on me in the wee small hours?"

"Just thinking about our little vehicular adventure this afternoon."

"*Close* wasn't it?"

"Like horseshoes and hand grenades," Kevin smiled.

At that moment the Suzuki appeared to dodge a shoe aimed for his head—to his credit he kept spinning, although crouching a bit lower on the riser. A brief pause hung in the air, "You were out checking the car weren't you?"

O'Shea shook his head, "*Busted.*"

"You predictable fuck," Kevin laughed. "Those Jesuits ruined you."

"A small price to pay for such fine book learning."

He cousin nodded, his eyes drifting out past the silent gardens, out past the noise, "You know where you're going after this?"

"Sort of."

The longest of silences hung between them…but there must have been something in the air that day, 'cause the O'Shea heart grew three sizes they say, "Shit man—why don't you come with us?"

Kevin laughed, "You, me, and Sara. Where'd we go boyo—Niagara Falls?"

"Yeah, wander the earth a bit; c'mon I'll even let you drive."

"Well thank you, but I've got too much going on here."

"Like what?"

"Well, for starters, I've got to hit the pawn shops tomorrow; got a *fine* watch to move."

Liam chuckled, "Don't take a buck less than $175."

But by then a small commotion was rising up from the floor below. The lads had been going shot for shot with the Tullamore Dew and the ugly results were beginning to manifest. Jimmy O'Neill was rocking nitrous whippets behind the bar, and Declan was doing something *unmentionable*, though technically anatomically possible, with one of the ice swans.

The cousins studied the melee, "…. Fire hose?" Kevin Delaney finally said.

"Ever the optimist," Liam smiled, "I'm thinking tear gas."

Fortunately cooler heads prevailed. Declan was urged off his avian paramour before he could do any irreparable harm to his reputation and something resembling normalcy briefly returned. The cousins took this as the intermission, and lit up a pair while waiting for Act III to commence.

The slow dissolution of the collective mind was leisurely playing itself out, when Liam O'Shea offered something up from of the deepest corners of left field, "You remember the summer when we were kids, my mother took us up to the country, and we stayed at that horse farm? She had that friend who taught us how to ride?"

"Hell yeah, one of the best times of my life—one week and I was like Butch Cassidy riding tall in the saddle."

Liam frowned, "Shit man, I sort of remember you falling off all the time, screaming bloody mercy to a horse named Dutch?"

".... Well, just seeing if *you* remember."

Kevin paused a moment before laughing, "What here's got you onto that? Besides, you never talk about your mother."

"Vehicular misadventures I guess."

"Nonsense," Kevin said, "That sort of thing usually amps you up."

O'Shea ignored this somewhat dismissive judgment, but couldn't quite bring himself to look him in the eye, ".... You ever think this life has any chance of getting back to that?"

Kevin shook his head studying the scene, "Well, maybe not quite *this* good, but..." he grew somber for a moment, "I don't know, I like to think it will.... But then again what do I know? I still like to think my right leg will turn into a thunderbolt and *Real Madrid* will come a calling."

O'Shea took some comfort in this evasiveness, "So the jury's still out is what you're saying?"

"Something like that."

Kevin Delaney was on the verge of something a bit more thoughtful, when there was an audible gasp from down below as one more late arrival reared his head...Declan's joint was officially out for the meet and greet...the mashed potatoes would not be safe. Needless to say, the crowd cut him a clear path on his way to the buffet table. His youngest son Aidan was chasing his father down with a blanket, the family honor was *clearly* at stake.

Kevin thought about it a bit more and sighed, "Ah, loyalty. They say that's why you have children, but I don't necessarily buy that noise.... It's a vicious lifestyle swindle engineered by the Church and the disposable nappy companies." He shook his head, "Sure, those precious little millstones—they'll start you ageing in dog years." His cousin was just hitting his stride, "Besides, it's a fool's paradise to even try. Life's a kicker, a great beauty and bilious insult, often in the same moment—but you've got to take what it gives, what else can you do?"

"Why Kevin, I wouldn't have thought you so the...pragmatist?"

"That's the secret. The more dull and pragmatic you become, the easier it gets. You aim lower to go higher."

".... You lost me son—never mind it's just midnight booze talk anyway."

Kevin sat there quietly for a moment...the machine-gunning of Dr Phil platitudes had been rather breathtaking in all their ham fisted glory. O'Shea having given him the conversational equivalent of a golf clap didn't help matters. The youngest Delaney hated the notion of an unturned stone and this very much felt like one. Big picture items were often best rendered in well worn sound bites; they tended to dull the demon-sting of things never destined to have an answer. There was a momentary lull between the music and random acts of violence and desecration from below.... No better time than now to pull one from your *own* twisted bag of smoke.

"Do you remember my grandmother?"

Liam smiled, "Of course—great lady, real pisser."

"To be sure," he laughed. ".... Do you remember a few years ago when she got sick?"

"Yeah, I do."

"I used to go sit with her sometimes, when she was getting bad, you know...and mostly she was quiet, but every now and then she'd find the strength to talk...for a moment it would even almost seem like old times." He grinned, "You remember how the old lady liked to mix it up?"

"Hell man, she threw a shoe at my head once; thought I stole her cigarettes."

"Did you?"

"…. That's immaterial."

"Don't worry, aerial footwear meant she liked you….Anyway, what I'm trying to say is the fight was still there to be sure." He shook his head, "We'd have some crazy-ass conversations in those days, just riffing on this and that, gossip, neighborhood nonsense…anything but the unholy terror creeping around the room."

O'Shea understood this at once, but thought best to remain silent.

"…. And I don't think I'll do it justice, but there was something beautiful in the woman near the end. Like she was able to cast off all the small minded filters a person spends a lifetime throwing up, all the blind rule obeying that's drummed into you when you're not even looking…. And in its place there was a clarity, a liberation from all the thoughts you're not supposed to think, all the words you're not supposed to say."

"Are you talking about some kind of peace?"

"No, maybe more like a truce. A truce with yourself, where maybe you can leave all that other shit on the battlefield….After that, there was a kind of singularity—a radiating grace that…. Shit man, you could almost *feel* it shining off her. And you remember Granny wasn't some doily queen, she was a hard chaw North Dublin crank—not the most sentimental of sorts even in the best of times."

"I won't disagree."

"Yeah, but this…sorry gran, but even this crass, hard-on of a woman, could find the most eloquent bit of a poet's head in her final days."

"How so?"

"Well, you know, she'd ramble on a fair share of nonsensical things, but once or twice she cut through it and said something that only an honesty with yourself could bring…. she likened all these moments in her life, the torments and the pleasures, to tears in a driving rain. And they were leaving here, and then they were gone." He lit up another cigarette, trying to keep these random thoughts in order, "…. Needless to say Granny didn't tow the company line, dogmatically speaking."

"I'll say."

"That ain't even the kicker. She'd lay down these heavy markers, these bedbug terrors, with all the ease of working a well worn joke—not a trace of fear in her eyes…. And there I am sitting at the foot of the bed, her grandson, the straight-piss scared out of him by this megaton intrusion on the glorified patch of sunshine that was his life." He chuckled, "Like she was now in the know of one very exclusive punch line."

O'Shea sat there, a suitably impressed look across his face for his shoe throwing nemesis.

"So, seeing Granny rocking such a brass pair, the glorified patch of sunshine felt ever so emboldened to ask: Was she scared?"

The mind fog cleared for a moment, the sheer terror in the order of words froze him for a second waiting for his cousin to finish his thought.

"And she looked at me, these old eyes I'd watched fade for years, suddenly finding some way back to the bright warmth I'd remembered as a kid, reassuring me, that in the midst of an unanswerable question, all could still be well." He let it hang there for a moment, "Of course, then she put the wind up it—said something like life was the demons pulling at you, tormenting you…but once you made your peace with the demons, they became the angels who'd lead you to Heaven."

"Jesus man," Liam shook his head.

"Not quite, but something close."

"…. And now, all that's left are the echoes," Kevin Delaney grinned, "—Chilling isn't it?"

The penitent traveler next to him gave a faint smile.

"I don't know man, atheists and their foxholes get a lot of play, but it can't be easy flipping fate the bird so close to meeting it," Kevin tossed his beer towards the bucket near the stairs. "But back to that original question—I haven't a clue if anything gets you back to that…. It's probably silly to even try. But in the face of a great unknowable, I take some comfort in communing with those who've at least had a toe in the water."

He looked up, "…. Meaning what again?"

"…. I don't know, but I like to think the old lady gave me a gift—to try and get the hang of these things, the angels and the demons, before the issue becomes an issue."

O'Shea was genuinely impressed; that miserable Delaney clan had been momentarily redeemed. He slapped his knee and gently placed the empty bottle of Bud next to the slumbering Michael Dempsey; asleep near the edge of the riser…. Always a pleasant feeling to be surprised by the things you thought you knew.

"Kevin lad, you're a fucking strange one, but…thanks."

"Ah, no worries—cheers then."

"Just as well," he added. "None of that shit means shit anyway, but I thought it would keep you quiet for a few minutes." They laughed at this momentary bit of maudlin psychosis quickly returning to the barley-based stasis of chop-busting reciprocity, but it was too late the damage had been done.

Life's about a lot of things; equilibrium, balance, moment—though some might say it's about knowing just when to exit. This ship had reached the high water mark; to linger, would be to drift out with the tide…plus Declan had found the ice tongs. He was running around the far side of the pool gird in something vaguely Speedo-like, chasing any and all girls of a tender indeterminate age, screaming *Piranha* at the top of his lungs.

Kevin sighed, "We should probably get out of here. This can't end well."

"Yeah."

"Let's go find your lady."

"Where's she at?"

"Up in the house, I saw her walk back with Eveline a little while ago."

"Smarter than the two of us."

"Sadly that's not saying much."

Christopher M. Basso

They walked up the stone pathway, the first bits of light still hiding behind the dark shadows of the mountains, a golden light gathering out over the Irish Sea; the sins of the last, the mortal, venal, and otherwise, about to be washed away anew.

They passed through the dark, sleepy lobby, and found the two of them having tea in the old library. There was a quiet stillness, as a bit of Neil Young played softly in the background.

Sara looked up and smiled, "Time to go?"

BOOK II
No Direction Home

Christopher M. Basso

Chapter One
Zenyatta Mondatta

The crickets chirped in the long grass as the Manchego cows rustled about a nearby field. There was a fine stillness all around, and in the sky, a faint patchwork of stars lit the near dawn crescent moon. Nearby, an old hacienda road cut across the lonely Aragon countryside. Crooked crosses lay in between, and the Pyrenees stood softly in the background. At a lonely, forgotten railroad junction the lights and bells suddenly came to life.

The heavy white and black checkered arms slowly fell across the tracks, as the red lights whirled about and the bells rang out their warnings to no one. Hanging on light posts near the approach and retreat were dullish ultraviolet lights that cast a faint mix of purple shades and black shadows. They bled off, smaller and smaller till they melted into the darkness and the great effusion of life which lay beyond...Son of a bitch was old—*Generalissimo* old you might say.

At once, a great, long train tore by at the good clip, kicking up all manner of dust and wind with it as the gates and lanterns shook and swayed. As quickly as it came it was gone, and all manner of dust and wind went rolling with it. The lights stopped, the white and black checkered arms drew up to rest. Within moments, all was still and quiet in the antique shades of the Spanish countryside on a warm summer's night, crickets chirping and all manner of life cast about.

Already around the next bend, the long train sped through the darkness; some thirteen cars in all: two locomotives at the fore and rear, pushing-pulling a cobbled mix of ageing postwar-era cars, and shiny new Eurostar liners. On the lead locomotive were the twelve stars of the EU flag painted boldly across the side, its bright lights casting a path as they hurtled down the tracks at a fairly terminal velocity. The notion of a world unto itself, and a thoroughly connected continent, were alive and well—for a few hours at least.

It was sometime in the early hours of the morning when they finally slipped into the shadows of the great mountains, the very hour when saner types have dimmed the lights and sought out sleep.... But here and there you could still spot the makeshift quilt of random light sailing past. These were for the *restless* ones, the ones in need of a never ending distraction. Bits of light gliding past the frames of the window, a pause in the darkness, before another quick flash sailed past; each repetition, the choppy, staccato rhythm of some old movie reel laboring to get up to speed.

The train cleared a bend in the break and the grade evened out straight and flat. They picked up speed drifting somewhere near the century mark as the wandering eye struggled to settle in. Each flash of light revealed the corridors and compartments of the train, illuminating a sleepy late night journey colored in the faintest hues of ultraviolet blues and purple. Many miles from nowhere you'd recall, and somewhere east of what seemed like forever since leaving the *Santa Apolónia* in Lisbon.

A smallish clock overhead at the far end of the car could tell you the time—were it to work. But it's a bit of an *antique*, like most things on the older cars. No matter, a seeker could be content with a fair guess—maybe some three go arounds since the witching hour past? That seemed about the safest of bets.

All around a mix of whirls and bangs weaved in and out of the sleepy silence. The old air compressors cut in and out on a humid hazy night, as the narrow slats in the glass let the wind whistle down the length of the cars in a low rumbling hiss. One of the conductors drifted down the corridor, pausing here and there to peer into closed compartments, stamp an errant ticket, or replace one of the stubs along the overheads.

He moved steadily from car to car, an oversized set of

keys jangling from his hip, gradually working his way back along the length of the train. From the rickety, upright cars of the *Marquis de Sade* low budget specials near the loud engines, to the four across couchettes in the center, till finally the sleeper cabins at the very rear. From the rickety and cramped cars near the engines that would have done the Marquis de Sade proud, and the slightly roomier four across couchettes in the center, to the opulence of the sleeper cabins at the rear.

In the roaring boom near the engines a real *twilight* crowd had assembled. American and English college kids mostly, backpacks hanging down from the overheads, with that wild charged look of youth in their eyes. A few of them passed a bottle of communal libidinal diplomacy, with a couple of like minded souls.

The rare charge of youth indeed, bright eyed and awake in that once in a lifetime kind of way. Youth being served and youth being watched. Attentive eyes of the midnight marauders, pickpockets, prevaricating roustabouts, a Peter and the Wolf kinderspiel, slowly unwinding in the predawn hours. But so goes it on a midnight run down the back alleys of some foreign land; overfed enfants terribles, riding shotgun with a slightly *heavier* element that likes to travel on the fly as they kept it on the low.

All was life and noise in these last two cars where no one seemed to sleep, and then off in the windswept connector, something to warm the very cockles of the heart. A kind of oldest school currency exchange, featuring two blond, blue-eyed youths in their Dartmouth Crew shirts and low riding corporate jeans—some horrible Bruegel tableaux ginned up courtesy of the Abercrombie lifestyle. Observe said youths endeavor a bit of shuttlecock diplomacy with a seen some better days, Marseilles night walker type…. Her sigh tells it all, as this evening's suitors with the Visine eyes and Spicoli timbre have a hard time reigning in a wicked case of the giggles…. *Poor lady*, what was the value-status of this gig anyway? Quick easy cash? Maybe a slight cut for the laissez-faire minded conductor? No worries though, pacifist crowds at these high speeds, and gentle as lambs these ones were—easy money…. Not quite your high roller days, back with David Niven and Serge Gainsbourg along the esplanade in St. Tropez, but *then again,* the last decent refuge when you've lost all your pull with the syndicate men and the respectable environs will no longer have you. Slight solace though, now staring over the precipice of some great unknown, before the final slink and sink into retirement. Or worse the foul bestial demimonde of some Tangierian Kasbah....c'est la guerre indeed, as one of the laughing boys produced a Platinum card.

The wandering eye departs the budding capitalists, the streetwalker fair, and the rest of the *Nessun Dorma* crowd; all crazy dwarfs and mad carnival clowns anyway. It's a rare thing in this life to meet a living, breathing, fully functional Tom Waits' song—so meet it. An easy decadence swirled about as shapes lose their form on the canvas of youthful vigor and a well-oiled criminal avarice. Life comes at you fast down in the sweaty confines of rambling steerage where they occasionally, though not exclusively, rotate the passengers along the outside rails of the train, but still show the good graces to take it slow through the turns.

The conductor passed through to the next car and the better grade of the couchettes—a refuge for the casual, thirtyish, train dilettante with a bit of money to burn, who've generally lost their mirth for casual solicitation and petty larceny. Ten compartments to a car, set back in fairly nice, sometimes quiet, glass booths with two rows of three seats facing one another. These could in theory fold down to quasi-beds in the wee small hours, but *only* if you were lucky on the draw; no reservations here. And therein lies the rub—*inclusiveness* seemed to be the euphemism bandied about in the brochures. The trick here was to look shady enough to float the general vibe that *you too* could live inside a Tom Waits song. If just to put the wind up the odd thieving type and keep the occasional stragglers moving on down the line.

One's acting ability was key in this proposition. Play those cards falsely and your gentle gamester of an ass would be rewarded with nineteen hours of the upright sit, staring at some gimp of a stranger, the better angels of your nature cursing the worser failings of your grit. Seeing stars in the time it takes to get from here to there, softly cursing this oddball twit who at best was some atavistic shill and at worst some raving mad dog lunatic. Your back aged a year for each painstaking hour of this rubbish. Such was life…. the conductor's jangling keys kept a jangling.

Then came the rarefied air of the sleeper car—not like anything seen in the American mind since back before the Pullman went the way of the Dodo. But here's where you found the super exclusivity, the kind where you'd easier jump the fence at the White House then casually stroll past the Kafkaesque gatekeeper sitting by the door all night, waiting for just this manner of outlandish intrusion. *Gang swarm* was clearly in his eyes, as the propagation of this cruel fantasy sailed along. *This* is what the Burghers on the other side of the door have paid for—*the show*. And what better way to roll for the latter day well-heeled paranoid set than a discount Versailles on wheels.

The gatekeeper nodded as the conductor passed. It was quiet and still inside the bunkhouse; six cabins, each a cocooned world unto itself. The air worked just fine in this car. The windows were sealed tight, revealing only the quiet hush amidst the noises all around. The harsh spotlights were dimmed to just the track lighting along the baseboards as the conductor shuffled past the cabins. Past the Airbus engineer and his wife heading back to Toulouse from their Algarve walkabout, past two spinster sisters down from St. John's Woods who came to see the windmills of the *Castilla-La Mancha*, and past yet another, where bathed in the fine moonlight of a cloudless night, the well travelled bags of a wandering young American. And finally, past the last cabin, where a portly latter-day renaissance man of means and "his nurse" kept the disgruntled staff on their toes with a never ending string of demands.

The conductor slipped through the wind-whipped junction, hit a lever and slid past into the sleeper's dining car—the end of the line for this particular round. He nodded towards the barman, reversed course and started back; his Sisyphus styled gig would run this way for the rest of the evening.

The dining car was a small sea of empty tables, red and green leather seats, and white tablecloths with the breakfast settings already in place. In the foreground of this dreamy little background were three people snugged into one of the low-slung booths at the far end of the car. The two in the nearer seat, a man and a woman, with their backs rudely set to the wandering eye,

Christopher M. Basso

sat across from the darkly silhouetted form of our boy, sitting, as was his custom at the time, with his back to the door. He was dressed in dark jeans, a blue *The La's* t-shirt, and a sharp black dinner jacket. Earth tones were his friends. Presently, he was clinking the ice in his drink and running an inner monologue on just how he'd arrived in this moment, and what might have been the easiest means for a casual disengagement.

The wandering eye crept up along the faded tiles of the narrow aisle, like a predator in the tall grass, low and slow, past all the empty booths till finally swinging around to have a pursuer's look at tonight's guests. Or perhaps revealing this evening's hosts? Liam laid down his glass, his sleepy eyes settling on the two before him. Where had they come from, this perfectly complimentary mismatch of meandered souls? Were they even real? Flesh and bone in the moment, or just the pixie dust kicked up from a bad batch of John Jameson's finest?

An older gentleman sat across from him. He was a bit more than fairly heavy set, with the riotous features of a riotous life, cut across his deeply furrowed ridges and brows. A wild mane of sandy colored hair flailed loose and a deep, booming Welshman's voice that could cut by turns to a gravelly Nick Nolte lineage. He smoked Dunhill Internationals right down to the nubs. He *was* old, but merely in that annoying chronological sense of the word, and it was quite obvious he took great relish in making sure it was known to the world that he still had some lead left in the pencil of life.

Exhibit A sat just to his left, on his arm as it were, keeping the aisle safe for her man. She was a *considerably* younger woman, fair of skin and dark of eyes, a true Southern stunner in that Henry and June let's get right with the all sorts of wrong expat way. She too was Welsh, but with a side tour down the back hills and valleys of Basque country. A fine confluence of the gene pool found expression in her dark raven hair, deep green eyes, and the soft, delicate features of an unnerving grace…. Just a trim Jacqueline Roque stand in, sweetly hanging on the words of her man and his huge hill of flesh.

Her name was Alessandra, but he called her Mia Dolce. She favored the filtered Capri's of a slightly tamer if not saner crowd…. Yes sir, this was a fine pair staring down at him in the old bar car, done up in shades of somber reds and muted greens. The dark inlays and casings were casting sleepy shadows far and near. From time to time, Liam caught himself watching the smoke from their cigarettes drifting up through the air, holding in the yellow glow of the gas lamps and capturing the firefly beams of a great disturbance in the projectionist's light.

Two waiters sat over at the pocket bar near the door, watching the replay of Real Madrid beat the living schadenfreude out of Bayern Munich. They seemed quite pleased with how the evening was unfolding, despite the heat, long hours, and the sweat running through their dress whites; the black ties long since abandoned. They shouted in strange joyous bursts of Castillian Spanish here and there. One of them noticed the gabachos at the far end of the car were running low. Five rounds and counting, he started over—don't these people *ever* sleep?

"Same again?"

The big man spoke up first, booming in Liam's general direction. "No more whiskey for you. You're too young to be drinking whiskey—it's an *old man's* drink for old man's problems."

Liam shrugged. "Yeah, you might be right."

"Let's lighten you up a bit," the old man added.

As mixed drinks were a rather dead art on the Continent, even more so on the ass-end of some train hurtling through the Spanish sticks; perhaps some advice was in order.

"Can you recommend something?"

"Patrón Añejo, Cointreau, and a bit of orange," the fat man said. "I call it the Volga Boatman.... but for the life of me I can't remember why."

"Sounds good."

"Very good—one *Volga Boatman*, a vino tinto for the lady." The waiter shot the gravelly voiced man with the sandy hair a somewhat derisive eye, ".... and a Purdey's Elixir Vitae with the Johnny Walker Blue chaser for the Señor."

"Put this one on my bill," the old timer shot up. "John Oldcastle, bunk cuatro."

"Thanks John." Liam said.

"No worries my boy."

The waiter walked away.

"I don't think he likes me," the old man said at length, with an eye wandering back over his shoulder.

"Don't be silly Johnny." The lovely one spoke, her dark eyes gave him a tender gaze. "You're too much of a whirlwind for some people…. I think you *frighten* them," she laughed. "Besides, most of humanity doesn't travel with its own brand."

"Well, that much is true." He glanced back at the two by the bar. They were muffling a general sort of blatant sniggering—which might have been the Rolando goal in the face of Rolf Emmanuel—or perhaps it was something far more…. local.

"Indeed, I think they're having fun at *my expense*." He groused.

"Pay them no mind." She smiled. "They've just never heard of such a drink before."

Purdey's Elixir of life and Johnny's Thunder Blue—Oldcastle had boarded with a steamer trunk damn near full of the stuff. He asked the barmen to store it for him in the cooler. When they had the temerity to object he told the stewards in no uncertain terms where he'd locate some room if not in the freezer…. A decidedly intimate if not indelicate locality. Now little metallic bottles of silver and gold festooned the galley of the dining car, packed into every nook and cranny they could find. In the polyglot Babel of EU co-dependents and Iberian night trains, *volume* was generally the clear decider when all other manner of translation was failing—or so Oldcastle believed.

"Anyway—I shall keep my eye on those two…. Where was I?"

"Carnival." Liam said.

"…. Yes," his eyes glazed a bit, "which one again?"

"Uh, the one in Nice I believe."

In the wee small hours, catching that third wind on the

262

fourth time around, who could really keep track of such things?

"Right.... you're off to *Nice*. Any chance you might see the carnival?"

Liam nodded—damn, this might get tricky yet, riding shotgun with the Abbott and Abbott of the Swansea and leek set. The drift from the moorings had only begun in earnest on the last round. Prior to that, they'd been able to keep things much more on the convivial and topical.

Oldcastle and his missus invited themselves over some time ago, after noticing the young man sitting like a lonely Nell back down the way. A nod and a handshake later and they were off and running—that was somewhere just outside of Madrid. By the time they'd sailed around the low ring of the Casta le Libre, they'd been steady tipping the mash for a good two provinces. That is to say, if this moveable feast had been stationery they would have been asked to *leave* some time ago.

"Carnival." Johnny Oldcastle said again, raising his drinking hand in a fine, if not entirely steady, benediction. "Carne, carne levare—to take out the meat as it were. The flesh, the taking of, and the giving of," he stared off into space, his mind bending spoons somewhere in the time fog. ".... Did I tell you I was in the seminary once—training for the priesthood?"

"No, actually, what...."

"Well, 'twas, brief...." He shot back, casually tapping his dockman's sausage finger against the reddened weatherworn nose, and then to the fine looking assemblage of womanhood next to him. "Not really for me if you catch my meaning," his gruff baritone laugh boomed through the car. He didn't want to brag, but with Burton long gone and Anthony Hopkins off in Malibu, he was currently in the running for Greatest Living Welshman.

"Looks like you made out ok though?" The boy asked.

"Well, dissipation is a final dereliction for the filial desperate."

"Don't be *modest* Johnny," she said. "You'd think he sat around all day baking bread and casting candles." Alessandra leaned in, clearly devoted to her man's gig, "And it wasn't a seminary, it was Oxford. He spent four years studying theology with Sir Fredrick Norman. Not to mention his friendships with *both* Lewis and Tolkien. He knew Lewis well in fact."

Oldcastle feigned a shyness that seemed almost genuine.... almost, "You're too kind to me my dear."

"She's right though. I had the pleasure of knowing both of those fellows, not so much Tolkien, but Lewis used to employ me for a time as this sort of.... mad errand boy—had me running all over Oxford Town on crazed bits of this and that," he laughed. "Such was the price for the proximity to greatness. Post his mail, gas his car, make a run to the grocer.... Hard worker though. *Christ*, sometimes the man would get so wrapped up in things he'd have me scurrying pints back from his local.... What was it called?" He rubbed the gnarled whiskers on his chin, "The Crane...no—*The Bird!* Good Lord, surprised I remembered that!"

He chuckled to himself, at the afterglow of some diminishing memory come back to burn brightly for moment. "But that was Lewis—an odd tosser of sorts, but a sweet bear of a man."

The waiter returned with their drinks.

Liam smiled his own. *Damn*.... Some things could still shock you from the methadone metronome of this life—C.S. Lewis' Johnny-on-the-spot right here in the flesh, the ample flesh. He watched the portly penitent play around with his elixir of Kentucky Blue, ginseng, and yohimbine, taking great care and diligence with the mix like some fussbudget winding up the atomic clock.

It was O'Shea's turn to scuff the short whiskers on his chin and marvel how the most interesting moments in this life had been the ones most improbably scripted, and the ones most improbably played. They'd appear like delicate apparitions, as fragile as the wind, and if only you turned left when the best action was right, or maybe rubbed the grouse too long from tired eyes they'd almost certainly be gone; slipping back into the ether from where they came. How else could these two have been conjured up on some hazy, sleepy midnight run across the windmill strewn high plains of Spain?

Well, no matter, ignore your mind and the wild permutations and circular rhythms you've fallen victim to—just focus in. Besides, revel in your time, 'cause pixie dust or not, these were just the sorts you'd never trip across back home. Shit, did they even exist back there in the haze?

.... Somewhere down those Kerouac traveled roads and on the broad backs of Sandberg's fancy.... Hell, maybe they were everywhere—everywhere and nowhere, Tom Joads, the left over Whitman camerados, the morally exacting Twains of the national superego, out there somewhere laying low, Tsavo lions in the tall grass waiting to strike, waiting to exact some measure of revenge on the fatal and the fallen.... Nope, far too fucking generous. Probably just a raggedy band of shell-shocked gimps drifting around the edges of an egg timer culture, hiding out in the sulfur weeds, flashing Masonic handshakes on the low, grousing pot luck dinners in Bill Kennedy's basement, or bonging Amyl whippets, on stale, fruitless pilgrimages to Woody Creek—because the last thing an atavistic culture with its collective finger fast tracking the remote needs are some nervous, poncy collection of smart asses telling it like it is. Shit, they'll roll a stone and see if you float for that kind of action. Clearly, there was no use for these hamwitted pricks.... Modern life was rubbish, a cheap fuck all with a nice patina on the surface. Hell, if you were lucky only a pillar of salt was waiting over your shoulder. Just a doom struck saga of choruses, dueling echoes in the dust, too many hands towards the Heavens, too much looking for the Baby Jesus under the trash—never quite on top of the notion, espoused by some, that what frees the mind might well kill it too.... Nope move this stone and ye will be revealed a steady diet of peg-legged gimps, shady movers, blue blood scions, psychic cripples, and reality show contestants waiting to happen.... And lastly, one nimrod, on a fast fleeing train, throwin' punches 'round and preaching from his chair.

"*My boy*, you look like you're drifting on me?"

".... What?"

The old fellow smiled at Alessandra. "Must have been the *Boatman*," and added sadly, "I don't know—whelps these days can't seem to hold their spirits."

Liam laughed. On what most nights would have passed for a bilious street fighting insult, rolled off Oldcastle's tongue in the brogue of a spotty old Tiger who'd earned the right to pass judgment on all. He sat back and marveled at the old timer with his grand tales of times long past, and his lovely dark eyed lady of the lake. If anything, he'd at least one upped Lewis on this account. To live life well might have been his gift, but was there a secret to such things? Something in the gravitational pull about him?

Liam hadn't even thought twice about signing up to join the party; it just looked *too interesting* to pass up. To live well and out of all compass some might say. Corpulence, elevated to some fine blend of lifestyle choice and rarified art form. O'Shea lit up another from a dwindling pack, the click of his Zippo right in time with the rumble and shutter of the train.

Hell, why not? He sank back in the booth, with a fresh jolt of nicotine and a good stretch to chase away any lingering calls to sleep. Exhaling a trail of smoke up into the lights, a smile crossed his face. He looked comfortable enough in his skin—his newly golden skin, sporting a healthy tan you could read like a map. Six weeks of the jobless roustabout will do that to a fellow. His hair had grown out a bit, the Black Irish kink starting to wave and curl at the edges.... Which brought out the *Paisan* in him he liked to think.

Oldcastle mixed in a bit more of the black bark and ginseng brew with his Scotch and took a long healthy slug, which seemed to revive his fortunes almost immediately. Liam watched as his eyes jumped back to life, as though some inner mystic had channeled the foul brew like some warped Barfly Phoenix.

Oldcastle caught his eye, "Beat's Benzedrine," he shrugged. "Besides, helps the circulation, I have bad legs."

The old fella, found his train in vain again, it was about to leave the station and the carnival was still on his mind.

"To be a young man again going to Nice." His eyes trailed off to the happy place around the sun. "Too bad you weren't a few months earlier, you must really see the carnival, if just once."

"Funny—I think I just saw a carnival."

"Forget those *Brazilians*." He roared back.

"Well, actually...."

Oldcastle wasn't paying attention. He was in full-bore ragged glorious flight. "One's not enough for them, they make *two* weeks out of it, these Niçoise, these Italians masquerading as Frenchman—floats, parades, fireworks—but nothing *too* outlandish, not like the Brazilians, with the sex out on the street.... Although that could be an art all its own I suppose. But these Niçoise add a fine little *twist* to things."

"How so?"

"Well, they start with a simple series of parades, your standard fare I suppose—floats heaped with Provencal flowers cruise down the *Promenade des Anglais* hauling the local beauty queen, or whatever silly ass politician is running for reelection. Between the floats there's a sort of controlled pandemonium—bagpipes, flamenco dancers, flag twirlers, commedia grotesques and all which that entails." He smiled. "Then they take it up a bit."

The *grosses têtes*, literally, "fatheads" are unveiled near the end of the first week, enormous, magnificently crafted puppet-like personages to herald the commencement of the floral battles. Costumed helpers aboard the floats toss a cargo of flowers to the crowd, gardenias, rose water, tiger lilies, and yellow mimosa blossoms, the pleasant scent of which will linger in your mind years to the day. Leading the procession of the grosses têtes are the towering effigies of the king and queen of the carnival. The crowds lining the road toss back confetti, wave bouquets of flowers, and cheer for their favorite floats. Weaving between the floats are stilt-walkers, jugglers, and street-theater troupes dressed in phantasmagoric excess who leer at onlookers and tease smiling children. Imagination reigns, no image is too extreme, too bizarre, or too extravagant."

He took a slug from his drink, "But then, and for my part this is what set's it a cut above, the French understand the *theatricality* of the thing."

Liam listened in.

"The King is the guest of honor at every carnival, the father of their bounty as it were. But he is also the sacrificial lamb, ensuring their bounty remains. And so he goes to perdition with all their sins. Sin and rebirth are still the essence of the tradition, and even as we hurtle forward in this charmless age, symbols can still be invested with something of the mystical, something of the redemptive—wouldn't you agree?"

"I'd have to—"

"On the *final* night," he roared, "the crowd leads the king in procession to his doom at the water's edge. The festivities take on an almost solemn air, torches line both sides of the avenue, right down the esplanade, onto the beach facing the dark waters of the Mediterranean.... Finally, the crowd thickens along the shore, the streetlights dim in a moment of chilling silence, people crowding out along the water's edge. From up on high *The Negresco's* faded orange dome, the mob takes on this Roman shade, the solemnity gone, almost twitching and salivating, on the cusp of vulgar expectation."

Alessandra gave him a rueful look as he stared down into the swirling pestilence of his drink. "All right, *perhaps* I'm guilty of a certain hyperbole.... but good Lord, I'm not far off!"

He composed himself. "A parade of torchbearers in friar's robes cut a glowing swath through the crowd till they reach the figure of the king, where their fires lick the hem of his dress and he bursts into flames. A set of lines are pulled, and he is cast out to sea, where he burns till he burns no more.... A silence falls over them for a moment, then a cheer, really a primal *roar* rises." Oldcastle paused for emphasis. "Then fireworks, from barges offshore, burst into the night air, confetti colors stream over the waterfront—And the party's over.... at least till they've built their sins back up to a suitably penitent level."

Oldcastle finished his tale with a bit of a forlorn look in his eyes, like some wounded hellcat on the final mend, of times long since gone, and now way back when.

"You know the worst part about getting old?" A grin spread across his face, "Is getting old."

"C'mon Johnny, you're not *so* old." Alessandra said as she laid her head on his shoulder and started to sing softly, "Out of smokes, out of jokes, feeling sad and on the ropes." Which in Basque-flavored English really sounded more the prayer than any idle midnight rambling.

"Too be old and fat is to be damned," he muttered to himself.

But maybe he sensed the millstone vibe he'd suddenly danced into their midst. As such his mood seemed to lift a bit, which seemed almost genuine.... almost. "Yes, not so old.... Well I should *damn well* say so," he laughed. "Forever with one foot ahead of The Man, the Preacher, and Father Time." He rattled off each on a plump finger before pausing, "Probably why I like trains to so much, they function more or less on my *bandito* schedule."

It was now Liam's turn to take the piss, "Damn, John—sounds like you've got this one all *figured out*."

But the old man grew somewhat rigid. "No, you don't really figure it out.... it's just a happy evasiveness, something you can measure by degrees."

"Of what?"

"Movement mostly, halfway 'round the world and back, words vomited out like some stay of execution as long as they keep coming." He looked out ahead, the broad smile returning, the clouds having lifted. "Every day you're taller than the flowers is a gift," he rubbed his hands slowly together. ".... *Sometimes* I can even *believe* that sort of tripe.... But back here on Earth it's still all too easy to be so much like yourself, your flawed self that is."

"Yeah," Liam chimed in, "sounds like something my unborn Hazelden sponsor is gonna lay on me one day—cribbed off the rehab wall of fame."

"I know not your particular mode, young man, but I know the type. Platitudes you can stick your stamp to and daydream down the letter box." He smiled, "And wipe your ass with—should the urge to move ever strike."

269

Christopher M. Basso

O'Shea nodded, duly impressed. Oldcastle might not have had the keys to the kingdom, but he at least seemed to grasp what it took to jimmy the lock.

"But for my part," the old man said, "you take your pleasures, all pleasures, when and where they come.... If you live long enough you might yet find the wherewithal to pare them down, to weed out the static and the rot, and all of *this*," he pointed to his massive, sweat shined fivehead. "It's a wicked little enemy that resides within—and its shadowy counterparts out there." He groused a bit. "And all of its wicked intentions, all of its false meanings—a triviality next to the sweet blessings of a subtle humility, of God's gift of the wind in your lungs, the sun on your face.... and an unencumbered pair of firm young breasts strolling down the beach in *Beaulieu-sur-Mer*." He had a whimsical look. ".... If the rascals had not given me the medicines to make it love again, I would have been done with for sure."

He gave her a wink, "The eternal questions troubling the mind—but then again, nothing a little blue pill won't fix."

Liam laughed.

"Yes, indeed, sights to see where you're going," he thought about it. "Saw my first carnival in '71, the first one after de Gaulle died—*Le Roi Juste,* the just king, they called him.... And my last the year Mitterand—*le Roi Médiocre*, deemed fit to follow."

What the hell is he on about now, O'Shea wondered, trying to catch the barman's eye for a refill. "Sounds like a blast John. You say you haven't been back since?"

He shook his head and said softly in a low rumbling voice. "Noooo, I am in the parlance of times past, *persona non grata*." He settled in. "Live as long as I have, live as well as I have and they'll be a few doors, a few haunts, a few *lesser than sunny* dispositions you will entangle along the way." His flourish was a pure mutant Welsh-Don King hybrid. ".... *Nice*, the *Cote d'Azur*, the entire *Alpes-Maritimes* for that matter, are such environs for me.... A plague on me courtesy of a good night at the baccarat tables in *Monte Carlo*, and a bad morning for some ponderous Corsican who couldn't seem to grasp that in this life we don't deal the cards, but only play the percentages.... He threatened me with anatomic infeasibilities I dare not mention or imagine."

Oldcastle feigned a good despondent. "What can I say, bad company, generally my own, has been the ruin of me. We like to think we paint with our own colors, but life often has a way of doing the courtesy for us.... I liked to think mine was a touch of Cary Grant in *To Catch a Thief*, but spin the wheel for reds and invariably you land on blacks.... and wind up something more like *Bob le flambeur* in the end."

Alessandra nodded. She seemed to understand this well.

"For prudence sake, I'll just keep my head down when we change trains at the *Gare de Nice* for the infinitely more welcoming environs of the Amalfi coast.... Where the air is warm, the breasts are firm, and John Oldcastle is always welcome."

The lights from the sides of the track were shining through the car, playing tricks with bleary eyes, flashing in and out, wavering between shades of red and green, moving from light to dark. It was about then the waiter came around to announce they were at long last turning off the grill.

"I care not for food, but where the *hell's* my ashtray you *culero*?" The old man mumbled not quite under his breath, all but begging a predawn international incident.

O'Shea quickly tried to get things back on track. "Good story John—I liked that one," he said, swiping one of Oldcastle's smokes in the process.

"A heavy tale indeed—I guessed you might." Oldcastle smiled. "When I saw you sitting over here, staring out the windows with that heavy look across your brow, I said to Alessandra—that ones working on some ponderous tale of his own."

A sheepish smile came across the boy. "Well, I don't know about *all that*. Might just be the booze coloring my little bit of grist—I have been *manning* this booth since about Lisbon you know?" He said this as a point of pride, refuting earlier untoward comments about an implied lack of constitution.

"No, there's something else," Oldcastle said. "You've got that look all over. No matter, that's why we came over, we were a bit *concerned*."

Liam shifted around in the red leather seats.... A bit stiff in their newness, but still on the comfortable side of things.

"How's life treating you young man?" John Oldcastle coaxed with a pleasant smile.

O'Shea could feel the inner gonzo rearing up. "Ok....how's life treating *you* John?"

"Taking forever my boy, it's taking forever, and it's slipping away."

Liam smiled and dialed the bathos warning system down a notch, "I don't know.... maybe I'm just tired is all. I've been out and about for a while now—it might be getting to me."

"What did you say you were doing on this train again?" Oldcastle asked. "Memory's the *second* worthwhile thing to go you know."

"Well, I was home, feeling a bit boxed in by things....and then I came into some money. So I thought maybe I'd do some traveling."

"Interesting, how did you do this—if you don't mind my asking?"

"He's American Johnny," she set he eyes on Liam, "Probably won a *game show*."

"No, reclusive caped crusader wealth," he shot back. "The *high side* is excellent—but oh, the nights are long."

Oldcastle's eyes grew large; he smiled and looked at his mistress, "Doesn't sound like a very taxing line of work?"

"Oh, you'd be *surprised*," Liam assured him. "Some of the heaviest lifting I've ever done."

"Well it takes all kinds I suppose," the old man grumbled into his drink.

Despite O'Shea's fondness for the no give and take, the big man with the space oddity countenance had a gruff warmth which just about took all the fun out of this kind of rubbish. He looked again at the two sitting across from him. Dark stars trolled past the speeding glass, and evil thoughts all too often become the evil deeds. Mock the devil and watch him flee? Perhaps, but one thing was for certain—Oldcastle and his minder-muse would soon be shading over to those vast hosts of the other world....Why not?

"My father passed away last year."

Oldcastle eyes took on a look of concern, a genuine expression interwoven with the jangling jester's glare. "I am sorry to hear that.... Was it cancer?" His voice rang with a note of alarm.

"No, traffic accident.... Just outside his home actually. Bad piece of road, car slid down an embankment, rolled, and crashed along a stone wall." He could feel the warmth in their eyes, which rather annoyed him at the time. "Close enough to see the lights from his own porch.... Can you imagine that?"

"That's terrible." She said softly.

"Yes," Oldcastle added. "Were you two close.... if I might ask?"

"We were not." Liam shrugged. ".... Wish I had something more redeeming for you, but that's the way that one went." And then with a trace of something not quite himself, "He was kind of a stranger, bit of a prick.... Not altogether there if you know what I mean?"

"I think I do," he stirred his Cornish health shake with the end of a matchstick.

"My *dear own* back in Newbridge, was a bit of a yarble himself.... Been dead forty-one years now. Probably still an ass," he sighed. "But I still hoist a glass to him now and then," he raised up, nodding in the eternal gesture of the great surrender. "Because in the end, you just forgive them."

Liam met his gaze but said nothing.

Oldcastle leaned in, "*Trust me*; there is really no other choice."

Liam could only nod.

".... You look like a smart boy—you must know that to be true?"

I should probably be better than this, was all he thought to say, but instead, open mouth and insert rote reply, "I traffic in an angry studied silence that's often mistaken for intelligence."

Oldcastle sensed he was poking sticks in the hornet's nest, and besides raw nerves *never* made for a simpatico audience. He left the boy to the silence he'd wholly earned, and tiptoed out the minefield to engage in his third favorite hobby—discourse. Discourse about anything about everything, the shock of the lightning, the color of the sky—a veritable vomiting of words that always seemed to keep *the beast* at bay, and as long as they kept coming all might be well. As he drifted further and further down this road, with that foul potion of his riding shotgun, you could sense how more correct and ordered his thoughts were becoming.

As Liam and Alessandra propped themselves up with weary elbows, the old man began, with shocking command and alacrity, kicking the tires on everything from Faulkner to Woolf; bending Nietzsche to Kundera's will, eternal return and chaos theory, Los Alamos, Oppenheimer, Bertrand Russell, The Second Coming, The Waste Land, Wellington, Waterloo, New Orleans and Sun City, Reagan, Thatcher, Bagism, Shagism, Ragism, Tagism.... An intellectual *tilt-a-whirl* which was starting to make the boy ill with its nimble dexterity.

The train had shifted north towards the French-Spanish border. From the high vantage point on the plains one could just make out the Mediterranean in the distance, and creeping in the first slanted breaks of day far out on the horizon.

A confluence of moments not lost on Oldcastle. "I can see the morning coming on fast," the fat man remarked. A raggedness finally getting the better of him. "I'm a bit drunk and a bit old, and a bit young."

His eyes took on a soft expression. "Maybe it's time for us to roll up our recoverables and call it an evening, or a morning—or *a hold* for my young friend."

She kissed him on the cheek. "Sounds good my sweet old man."

"We take our leave of you then my boy, back to the domiciles of the demimonde. Thank you kindly for your time and your table."

He started to rise, "Alessandra, my dear, lead the way."

Liam watched him amble away down the narrow aisle taking great care with his steps, like some proud old bull Elephant, who so many years later, weathered and worn, accidentally noses out the place he was born. Each movement one step closer to the end of the beginning. He skillfully executed the best kind of exit, quick and permanent, no falseness or pretension, no awkwardness, and no future—except maybe in the next life. The door slid shut and they were gone.

The car was quiet again.... What now? It used to be nice to *have* to leave—gave you some direction at the very least; maybe a bit of pushing, shouting, hard stares from the men with no necks—the closing time melee. Just the type of edge work to bring out the best in wayward youth.... But no such luck; the two gents on the far end were watching the game, paying him absolutely no mind. He looked around again; obviously he'd have to play the *heavy* on himself this evening.

On the crisp linen tablecloth sat a single candle in a small oval glass, burning with the faint scent of bergamot. The second of the evening, as Oldcastle had talked the first to death. It sat in center, casting delicate shadows against the shape of his hands which he held up close to the flame. He fanned his fingers back and forth across the light; tracing patterns along the rough edges of his skin.

In his other hand a forgotten cigarette slowly burned away. All around him, ascending like cloudy bands of angels were rising wisps of smoke. Crass equivocation? Perhaps—but the more assailed your brain, the more fogged your perspective, the greater the poetry found in life's vulgar things.

O'Shea's brain slowly drifted up from the time fog....John Oldcastle, a tumbling tumbleweed and a fine assemblage of life at that. One leaving much in its wake; perspective, possibility, joie de vivre, la vie en rose, the ethos of the Eros—and glancing down at the plastic slate peeking out from the champagne bucket...and his bar tab. Liam glanced over—$213 dollars. That seemed about right; a fair price for a night's lesson.

Christopher M. Basso

Although, he'd be *sure* to yell "fire" outside Oldcastle's door in about an hour, fair was fair after all. The only real debate was whether to greet him with a locked and loaded fire extinguisher. Liam smiled, at *least* he hadn't tried to lift his wallet.... He put his hand down and felt the reassuring bulk and his wallet wedged next to it—to be young indeed.... Where *was* that girl? Ah, sleeping back in the cabin, yes, a lower and slower tolerance in her of late for these late night, early morning award tours. Where were they anyway, France? Hard to tell out these windows. A slight daze running through him—the ignominy of having been drunk under the table by your grandfather.... All right, cut the silly banter, go get some air.

He made his play to rise, but the knees were uncooperative, a mix of stasis and the things you do when staid.... Fine, regroup, recover, you've got some time. First, the nicotine. He lit up in earnest and motioned the barman over. He kept his smoke perched between the fingers, turning it gently while he waited, still fascinated by each slight alteration causing the white lines to dance and drift in new unruly, wholly unpredictable patterns.... Fucking cigarettes, campish affectations piloting you to an early grave—a mild bummer at that.

They'd long since killed the AC, and a warm sleepy stillness had settled in. Anything to clear out the grosse tête with the booming laugh. Now it was just the faint grumbling, rumbling constancy from the train grinding along the tracks. Well, one more for the road seemed about right, the barman arrived almost on cue.

"Could you make me another one of those—tequila, Cointreau, and a bit of orange juice?"

"The Volga Boatman?" The waiter smiled.

He gave the man an affable smile, but made no small talk; Oldcastle had more than sullied his communion with the staff, damned by association it would seem. He left Liam to it, and went back to the galley to sort through the small mountain of Purdy empties left in the old boy's wake.

O'Shea cracked open the small bottles, pouring in equal measure the makings of his drink. A fine unison illuminated in the faint light and orange hues gathering in the dim glow of the candle. His eyes trained on the undulating end of the flame, a pleasant fire cast back across the green in his eyes, sparkling with flecks of orange and gold. He turned his glass about, the clink of the ice, the pleasant sound of a casual perversion.

His hands were rougher, more weatherworn than he remembered, but a *nice* kind of worn, less the labor and the angst, with something of too much sun and just enough sin. He'd taken to sporting a clunky silver Claddagh ring. A little something she'd bought him before they'd left the land of the faeries. The tradition said something about luck, providence and just a bit of fidelity thrown in the mix…. Sod it, he could use all the friends he could get.

He stared in a few seconds more, elementally lost. He'd heard vague rumors of bending spoons with the mind, of roads of excess leading to the palaces of wisdom. Sounded like real *fringe work*—just the sort of endeavor for an occasionally spotless mind…. That was until the barmen sideswiped his delicately calibrated plans; landing the bill before him with a loud thud.

"Good evening señor," the man grinned heavily.

"About that time then isn't it?" Liam smiled.

He started to stand, his knees *far* more with the program this time around. But it was still too early for cashing out. Perhaps a bit of a stroll was in order? Make sure everything was copacetic in this strange little Mxyzptlk universe. He blew out the candle and made his way towards the door, feeling the slight sway and buckle of the car. Damn, the old man was right, life *was* better on a train. Shit, it made more sense at the very least.

He started down the thin corridors of the train, past the gatekeeper nodded out, head against the glass, his arm like a pillow. Nothing stirring here. And down into the couchette cars, catching bits of sleeping faces behind the slightly drawn curtains, little trains within the train. Past the slightly tipsy conductor from the Lisbon station, the one who'd been channeling his inner Gunny Sergeant back on the platform barking orders to the tourists. He now seemed to be summoning every fiber from within to keep his equilibrium, not mention his dinner, in check as he balanced against the open windows to catch some air.

Christopher M. Basso

O'Shea found a quiet perch near the end of one of the couchette cars, by the open windows with the pleasant breeze rushing past.... They were still a good ways from Nice, probably some four hours as the drunken conductor flies, on what would be the final stop for the marginal mystery tour. Four hours and six weeks removed from the dine and dash in the Dunamore meadows, and what was there to show for it?

A mad romp through the streets of Siena; running for horses but tangling with bulls. Just a *few* scuffles with the juiced up locals over liberties taken from liberties never granted.... Flee the scene *post-haste*. Back to Rome; ancient footprints everywhere, dodging lions wasting time. Venice, Prague, Copenhagen, and a beastly dopamine-charged journey to the darkest corners of the mind, courtesy of the good folks behind the *Centraal Station* in seedy Amsterdam. Emerge from the tomb three days later, short hop it back to Paris for a French TGV bound for Waterloo Station, passing from the sunlight at Calais, and onto massive London.... Too massive—hopping a midnight flight for Madrid, smoking a cig beneath the statue of Cervantes in the Plaza de España, his beloved, a fine Dulcinea in her pretty summer dress; admiring *Guernica* in the Reina Sofía; all genius born from some slight madness.

On the balance, cutting *quite* the swath across the continent, and like that long list of marauding invaders before them—Vandals, Goths, and Saracens—keeping themselves busy. Barcelona, Granada, Seville, the Algarve, picnics in Oporto and perfect sunsets framed.... An epic piss-taking session in a Lisbon bar, some drunken wagers and one-off dares landing him in the belly of a rickety Air Portugal turboprop, 500 miles out into the Atlantic to lonely Madeira. Juggling terrors through a low level thunderstorm, her calm demeanor the only thing averting a complete meltdown, bar room courage melting quickly, like wax in the hot sun. Terror *averted*, hopping a chartered fishing rig back to Lisbon. Three days on the open water, a better cure for aviophobia you will not find.... A crazed sprint through Lisbon, weaving down the side streets of the Bairro Alto, offering the cabman a double sawbuck to beat the evening rush to the Santa Apolonia, mad dashing it down the platform, deep breaths, an exhausted measure of the moment, take a seat at the back of the dining car, rustle up a drink, open your eyes you have company.

He lit his last near one of the open windows, the long corridor empty now. The howling wind buffeted the thin panes of glass, as the grey and black of the hills flashed past at a sleepy, steady hundred mile per hour blur. The wind felt good against his face, each hit a bracing rush. He held his cigarette up in the breeze; watching the orange embers grow and burn a fiery color, catching his fancy as he played with it, lost in it like a mischievous boy, far removed from the foibles of a man.

O'Shea could feel the train starting to slow, the slight hiss of the brakes, the wind easing off his face, till his eyes caught the coming twinkle of lights sprinkling down a hillside, and a small town rounding into view. As they passed the last of the bends, a sudden firefly trail of slow flashing red and blue led them in processional as they drew up slowly to the station. He tossed his spent smoke out the window, watching it kick out sparks along the stones. "Ask and ye shall receive." He made for the nearest door.

There were no platforms at the smaller stations, just a set of retractable stairs the conductor would kick down at each stop. *Quaint touch*, but not for the unsteady night man, who unleashed some strange rumblings when he divined that somebody actually intended to use it. A vague look of incredulity quickly shifted to a rising, risible sense of contempt.

"Mister, train only stops for five minutes—just clearing traffic." His English was about as good as O'Shea's Spanish.

"I'll be quick."

"Got you passport?" He laughed.

"I hear you, I hear you."

"This ain't no subway *cabrón*, next train tomorrow."

"Good looking out—God bless!" O'Shea shouted as he lit out.

Overhead, an old wooden placard swayed slowly in the breeze, the name hard to see through the shadows, but slowly it came into focus: Port Bau. The red and yellow flag nearby meant they were still on the Spanish side of things.

Well, despite that fool's protestations he was off.... Poor bastard, O'Shea thought as he made for the station doors—stone cold worrier. Obviously, he just didn't get the angles and paradigms of this life.... To be sure, the Lisbon-Nice run was not some glorified cross-town local, that his lack of passport, ticket, or anything resembling bona fides would present all sorts of interesting conundrums to a Rosetta Stone challenged man-of-means out in the Spanish sticks at dawn.

Besides, anything worth the doing, was worth doing well. Hell, Cervantes got off the train; he split form the whole program.... But then again, the poor bastard spent five years in a Barbary prison, so pick your poison.... Not to mention, but did that pendejo say a *few* minutes or two minutes? Faulty hearing among the many casualties lost in translation.

He wandered into the small, brightly lit station where not much was stirring; just rows of old wooden seats, and a few stragglers here and there. A pair of ceiling fans stirred a weak breeze as he crossed the faded blue marble inlay floor which fairly reeked of high grade bleach and lemony sweetness in the early morning calm. And just as quick, O'Shea was through the far set of doors, out to the dim gray of the town square.

A few teenagers were still out in the plaza, bouncing skateboards across the stone benches and grinding marble walls, slowly taking apart a few centuries of fine Catalonian architecture. Something that most likely earned them a righteous clubbing in the waking hours, but here in the predawn stillness, they were relatively safe to go about their business. They scarcely even noticed O'Shea cutting right across their path.

Somewhere nearby Liam could hear the sound of the water breaking along the edge of the coast, and the faint scent of baking bread from one of the buildings in the square. The sum of which ushered in a fine, early morning clarity. Getting off a fast moving train at dawn in some faraway corner of the world you'll never see again, a head full of hop, a skin full of bogeymen; feeling the clean cull of dawn, the stars moving through your mind—a fine place to call yourself a moment.

Nice thoughts, but no time for it now. It was going to take a slim bit of luck to find what was needed to steer this star. Not to mention the creeping flashes of killjoy oversight dancing through his mind; the ones registering that while he could *feel* the train through the high plaza walls, he could no longer actually *see* the thing. A fine incentive to be quick about your business.

But for the first time that evening fortune served up a very clear hand in the shape of an all night-early morning smoke shop just past the thrashers in the corner of the square.

He loaded up on nicotine; one's never enough, how about two, why not three? A bit excessive, but no telling what other manner of foul, cruel hearted philosopher-thief he might run across between here and the warm currents of the *Côte d'Azur*. He grabbed some crisps, a new Rolling Stone, an old New York Times, and a Vogue for the missus—for which there was *no way* to properly explain oneself to the grizzled old Spaniard giving you the stink eye.

A few bottles of Diet Coke, and an excess of Altoids for his foul, Volga Boatman *sum* tobacco bearings.... And just for good measure some trinketry, *I was there,* type bullshit to commemorate the occasion. Complete claptrap garbage for which he dropped about sixty Euro all together.

He slowly made his way back through the station and found the waiting train—although cutting it closer than one might have liked. They would have been dust down the tracks for sure if not for a brief skirmish in the sleeper car with one of the conductors and a grossly intoxicated, portly passenger and his daughter, causing a slight delay in the schedule.

He jumped up the three steps of the ladder and into the train, making sure to give the exasperated *puta madre* a fine grin, all teeth and the like. "*Buenas noches.*" O'Shea nodded, before slipping back to the rear car, where other than a few loose Purdy's bottles sliding along the corridor, all was silent and still.

He arrived at the door to sleeper number three just as the car began to move, lurching quickly up to speed like modern trains will. He leaned back against the wall of the corridor in a meditative catcher's crouch contemplating the merits of one *more* cig, 'cause as anyone who's ever battled the perils of addiction and the hubris of denial will tell you; the beast *always* needs to be fed. He lit up and rested his head against the glass, listening to the rustle of the wind between the gaps, feeling something like an anxious boy waiting to get called in on a warm summer's night.

Shapes gathered in the light out the windows, shadowy forms coming into focus. Along the horizon, lovely little bits of antique Europe streamed past; hounds to the hunters in the face of a relentless modernity, anachronisms, uses unknown, slowly drifting off towards a gentle oblivion.... And a mind and body drifting along to meet similar fates, the natural order of things.

But also a growing, gathering sense, there was no one out there tending the light on the far side of the Big Reveal, and that there were fewer and fewer remedies for such a certainty, including the lovely one who had tended him so well.... They say if you get far enough away, you'll be on your way back home. He tossed his smoke out the window—time to find out.

He opened the door and gently slid into bed, not bothering to undress, and taking great care not to wake her. He came to rest in the small space up against the glass, his elbow a fine pillow, where he would have a fine view of that pretty light as they made their way down the track.

He reached over for her hand and when he could feel her fingers in his he closed his eyes and relaxed. She smiled ever so slightly and nestled closer to him in that pleasant sleepy way one never remembers in the morning.

The last of the moonlight was giving way to the first colors of the day as they turned east again, racing along the French coast. He watched the light with sleepy eyes, surrendered to the ebb and flow of a peaceful constancy. Out the window the calm expanse of the sea offered something close to solace, all coast from here, good omens to sleep by.

Chapter Two
Waterloo Sunset

The strange wisp of a man in the periwinkle suit threw open the heavy Cossack doors and stepped inside the grand old house. A faint hit of bottled air rushed out to greet him, "Well," he said, "...been awhile."

In the courtyard Liam and Sara stood admiring the doorway to their new digs, as the sounds of birds rang from the trees, and the gentlest hints of gardenia and orange trees drifted in from the garden.

"Please, come in." The man under the eaves gestured to follow him.

Monsieur Henri le Fleur from "the company" was how he'd introduced himself at the *Gare de Nice* earlier that morning. He had a friendly enough smile and was seducing the bleary-eyed travelers with the promise of an air-conditioned car out in the drive. What exactly "the company" entailed was not all together clear at the time, or for that matter of much importance. Having spent the better part of the summer being moved from place to place like a couple of very pampered zoo Pandas, they'd learned the golden rule—the less you asked, the better off you were. Having only the vaguest constructs of the gig was something to wear like a point of pride.

After wandering off the train at dawn smelling, and most certainly looking, like a man three days in the tomb, O'Shea was greeted on the platform by this fast talking little oddjob. He was somewhere on the wrong side of forty, with a fine weathered tan, fair hair, and bright blue eyes. They followed him to his waiting Citroën C6 where he proceeded to drive like a man two seconds from death along the jagged cliff roads of the Riviera coast, over perilously steep hills and barrier free blind turns, till they drifted out past the saw grass and the demons spins to the quiet peninsula just east of greater Nice.

Then again, he could have been driving them to Canterbury for all the boy knew…. in fact, who *was* this curious little fellow, and why had they so blithely jumped in his car? If the recent O'Shea karma held true to form they were surely headed to some *Alpes-Maritimes* dungeon for a little game of "it puts the lotion in the basket".

Well, it went without saying that he'd either have to garrote the poor fellow and make a bleary-eyed break for it, or have faith that this blistered carbuncle was somehow in the employ of his trusted benefactor and all around *arranger*, Fred Dewan.

The Great Man had swung this deal for Liam courtesy of the magical mix when robust credit lines meet the wonders of the Internet. To be a purveyor of the finer lifestyles of Manhattan, London, and all points east was a rare talent indeed. Not to mention old Fred had *romped* down here once in another mainline era, back in the halcyon days of the Nellcote summer and the Exile on Main Street era jag…. Rumor had it he used to roadie for The Stones, running gaffer lines from the mobile down to the basement, back before he found adulthood, or at least before it found him.

"David Niven lived here once," Mr. Henri snapped the boy out of his thoughts as they walked up the angled stairs beneath the heavy colonnade doors. "Three months while he was making Casino Royale in *Juan-les-Pins*."

His young clients stared back at him, expressionless, eyeing him with something that was either severe jet lag or complete befuddlement. He seemed to grasp the disconnect and leapt forward about a generation.

"Posh and Becks stayed just down the road—back when they were locals so to speak," he glanced back. Now they looked like they just didn't care.

"Right, follow me please," he swung back one of the tall doors and ushered them inside.

O'Shea arrived in Nice at the end of his tether; worn out, drunk out, and courtesy of some scoundrels in Amsterdam, a touch drugged out. The rolling thunder party revue, which had been lit with such vim and verve back in Dublin, had wound its way across Europe, before finally making its way down the yellow brick road to the Côte d'Azur.... And all that had seemed like so much lightness, was rapidly morphing into something a bit heavier around the edges; as though the mind and body really *did* have capacities for these things, and that testing those limits was becoming an increasingly unnerving game.

Pulling up through the gates of the villa only moments before, she'd nudged him out of a pleasant daydream. "Open your eyes," she gently whispered.

When he focused, his eyes set on a lovely, if slightly faded, Belle Époque villa sitting gracefully beside the sea in, what was later explained to him, a respectable, yet not especially *fashionable* part of this tucked away little universe.

Run down and less than fashionable was not quite how this morning's tour guide and luminary suck up would have painted it—in fact quite the opposite. Henri le Fleur had the sad, genteel airs of a man coasting along on the fumes of an idea long after its genesis had passed. He was clearly still impressed with the opulence of the Côte d'Azur and all that it entailed, but was frequently and ever increasingly, depressed with the bland cut of his clientele.... Opinions might have averaged him as a bit of a judgmental git; but then again, how serious can you take a man who looked like he was wearing Capri's when he wasn't smoking them.

But oh the *tales* the old boy could tell. Christ, when he started this gig back in the summer of '85 the place still had some *spark* to it—Hollywood jet setters, European royalty, the occasional vacationing Third World strong man…. Now it seemed like a never-ending stream of British telecom speculators and German venture capitalist; computer geeks mostly—flush with more cash than the Romanov's even in these depleted times. They paid they bills, but hardly fueled the hedonistic imagination…. Hard to gauge these two though—down here Americans were wild cards of sorts, too polite to be anything interesting and just annoying enough to be something ruinous.

Monsieur Henri and his young charges walked along the southern edge of the property, with the grand man speaking in slow deliberate sentences as he gave a leisurely tour of the grounds and villa. He always made sure to mix in a bit of history and dash on these things for good measure. A touch of the reverential show was the least he could offer for these prices, and besides, this villa *had* a past. The Cossack doors were not merely ornamental; a Russian duke from Vladivostok had dragged them clear across Siberia, when he built the place for his mistress.

He kept her squired out here for nearly two decades, living with his wife and children in the larger compound across the road…. Not quite intern in the West Wing risqué, but daring nonetheless. That was until Mrs. Russian Duke from Vladivostok had enough of the Mormon-Turkish free for all and sent the both of them heel-clicking not to Heaven but the *other* place.

Since then the house had passed through the hands of extended sundry families, some great, some not so great, with just enough hints of rusticating movie stars and vacationing dignitaries to keep things risible and visible.

Liam stood beneath the ivy trellises on his portico, staring at the sea staring at the sand, taking in all he could. Given the weatherworn look of the place and atom bomb hit on the Amex, he couldn't quite tell if his new friend was being honest or perhaps just a little bit *interesting*. Old Fred had warned him about a certain brand of nimble-kneed raggedy man that flourished in the dry air, hot sun, and loose antecedents of the South.

These were the ones Fitzgerald shredded in prose and Ray Davies called out in song; a spurious varmint in any age….But then again, it could have just been some poor man's Somerset Maugham routine, something the boy would later learn was a dime a dozen around these parts, where the highest of premiums was placed on how finely you'd calibrated your act of not being what you seemed.

This was a clusterfuck on life's sincerity ledger to be sure, but a vastly entertaining one all the same. *Besides*, the last two weeks of Iberian swordfights and windmill charges, where the *lamehuevos* lay the odds and the house never bets the bull, had left him a bit worn out and in need of the sunnier side of life, the *slower* side of life…hell, perhaps even the *feminine* side of life.

Monsieur Henri wrapped things up with a brief explanation of the security system: a complex mixture codes, nodes, and diodes which gave the boy a headache; not to mention a strange bit of foreboding, as this otherwise interesting little show had been suddenly sideswiped by such rude waves of fear and paranoia in the encore. Well, the boy figured, to each their own.

…. And just like that, with a double-tap kiss goodbye for each of them, the Gaul with the gall was gone. The heavy gates swung shut as Monsieur le Fleur tore down the drive, scattering the various wildlife about the place as he made his way back to Nice. As the little gimp lit off down the road, O'Shea suddenly remembered that he too had a fast tracking Citroën C6 on reserve with the rental people back in town. After an amazingly brief inner debate he called and canceled the car. Quickly scanning the back section of *Les Pages Jaunes* he located a Ducati dealer just down the road in Sainte-Hélène and, putting his lovely's Cameroonian French to use, ordered up a hellishly fast, retard strong Monster S4, with the proper mix of flash and getaway power the assignment called for. Cars were a bit passé anyway, not to mention a dangerous luxury on the cluttered roads of the quick and the dead…. Nope, this gig would be on cab, foot, bike, and one freakishly nimble ground mawing Italian motorcycle.

Henri le Fleur was but a fading memory when O'Shea stepped onto the terrace above his kitchen and marveled at the rich tableaux stretching from his door to the unbroken line at the horizon…. Fairly satisfied with his new latitude he repaired to the indoors and commenced with his own private tour of the new digs.

Despite its size, the house retained a sort of intimate, immediate feel. It was a low-lying two-story affair, a Provencal villa in the truest sense. The walls were stone of a burnt red that had faded over time to a fine weatherworn pink. The terracotta roof had fared no better, baked to an elegant shade of disrepair by the many decades under the sun and the relentless wear of the sea which assailed its walls night and day. Off the sun porch on the western side of the house, a small English garden sat under the eaves and overhangs. Further afield, a long stretch of lawn ran the length of the property before melting into a tangle of rock and shear cliff walls that zigzagged as they wound their way down to the sea.

The rooms were neither large nor small, but all seemed to catch a certain kind of light that made them feel spacious. The furnishings were tasteful and restrained—even sparse. It felt like a house you could sleep in and for a man of deceptive good humors that seemed the greatest compliment he could imagine.

O'Shea went down to the bar and fixed himself a Kir, a local's drink for the local sun. He found his missus and they made their barefoot way down the long sloping lawn towards the water.... Twenty-nine years and change, and he'd somehow failed to notice the recuperative powers of a barefoot walk through the grass. Any lingering train lag disappeared and he felt revived almost at once.

They followed the path down the stony pass to the water's edge, where they sat along a small corniche above the black stone beach. In this small bit of seclusion, hidden amid the brambles and sea scrub, they passed the drink between them and watched the procession of big ships head in and out of the harbor.

".... Well, what to do with ourselves?"

"Maybe a swim?" She said. "Water looks nice."

"Perhaps, perfect the art of the freestyle hip stroke?"

"Cool your spurs, jangling Jim," she smiled. ".... I should really call Cameron, let her know we're in town."

"Ah yes, *her.*"

"Got your phone with you?"

He handed it to her as she took a piece of crumbled paper from her pocket and placed the call.

Momentarily free to roam, the boy's mind drifted out to the harbor and the big boats swaying softly in the breeze. He closed his eyes for a moment, imagining the many ships, the many flags that had sailed in and out of these waters, ever since the great tribes of antiquity nourished their curiosity or simply fed their greed.

.... It was still an exclusive society in more ways than one; a loose affiliation of millionaires and billionaires who at some point in their lives simply became the palace guard. And when you've taken on *that* kind of weight no one comes around knocking you didn't already invite. This was a party atmosphere to be sure; one written *large*, in big gaudy letters across the sky; inviting you to punch that freak ticket; just as strange and outlandish as you please...that is so long as your credit could cover you particular brand of public kinkiness.... Jeezum Crow, these were some heady ruminations indeed, heady ruminations interrupted only by loud shouts into a cell phone.

"Wait, what, what do you mean she's not there? Where is she...*Mykonos*? What's she doing there?"

Liam could feel the cockles of the heart warming as sure as the bright sun beat down on the smooth rocks beneath him. He could leave the miasmas of antiquity and avarice to Spartacus and his dingy—where were his swim trunks?

Sara clicked the phone shut.

"I can't believe it.... Cameron is in Greece—she won't be back for a week." A look of sad bewilderment swept across her face, "That was somebody named Rain.... I said, can you give her a message, or give me a number? She said—no she travels light.... What the hell does that *mean*?"

"Never try to understand intrepid wealth dear."

".... What the hell does *that* mean?"

"It means she's on a vacation from her vacation." He stretched out on the warm rocks. "Must be the life?"

"Careful there, Liam James, remember that thing about glass houses?"

"Yeah, something about stones, but I could never abide those assholes anyway."

She looked out towards the harbor, "Ugh, I can't believe her—we come halfway around the world and she *flakes* on us."

"Uh, not to split hairs, but isn't a certain level of flake her MO?"

"No, not like this." The surreal shock was still palpable. "We've got a week left and she's gone."

"Yes," he shook his head sadly, his brain someplace very far away.

"Haven't seen her in three years…"

He leaned up again, nearly spilling his beverage, "Look, you need to get your mind off this, these betrayals of the heart are always the worst…. Let's go for a quick dip, make a fine Rum Swizzle punch and fall asleep in that hammock over there. Then tonight when it get's a little cooler out, we'll go into town? I'm feeling a wee bit tired all of a sudden."

"…. Yeah, you look beat."

"I didn't get much rest last night."

"What happened to you anyway?"

"Two little gremlins down in the bar car; I fed 'em after midnight."

"…. *Whatever*, look, I'm pissed!" She hopped up and headed back towards the house, "I'm going to text her nonexistent phone and send a few choice emails to her forgotten laptop—let her know where it's at!"

"Yeah!" He shouted. "Ungawa, beat her like a rented mule honey! I'll be down in yonder hammock if you need me."

In a flash she was gone. The faint hints of righteousness trailed behind her like falling stardust. Liam ambled over towards the old hammock slung low between two Olive trees and slumbered off the last of it; promising himself *never* to talk to strange men on trains again.

.... The road to Nice had been a long one, fraught with a summer's worth of excess and wonder, but here at the end of the line, with a scant week to go, things were suddenly on the cusp of a great *wind down,* the moment where the mind and body try to recalibrate for the coming normalcy. As always, the paradoxes of this life were amusing to behold, because just as they were going under Nice and its environs were suddenly coming to life.

August *was* the season along the Riviera, and this meant droves of people arriving by the day, as all of Europe seemed to descend on the coast at once. Old Fred had thought ahead and secured them a place out past the madness of the crowds on the little peninsula of *Saint-Jean-Cap-Ferrat;* as quiet and hidden a locale as you could find. A shuttered zip code of *huge* homes and high gates with imposing stone walls and just enough ivy trained over the sides to find that nice balance between the charmingly aesthetic and the vaguely menacing.

But leave this little slice of peace; venture out into the elbow to elbow throngs of Nice proper, and you'd find crowds running the gamut from stressed out Parisians and old age Gallic pensioners wishing the German, English, and Dutch families packing the sidewalk cafes, swilling *Fanta* and eating minute steaks would just discover the *Costa de Sol* and be done with it. The English in particular have always had an affinity for the place; they pack their cars onto Chunnel trains and descend en masse, throwing an already dicey traffic schema over the edge to full on crisis-meltdown mode.

And it must be said, that was the *upside* of this little sandbox. Attendant on all environments which draw their water high was a fair share of transients; a remora trail of pickpockets, petty thieves, and shills of every shade.... Then of course there were always the *outliers,* the degenerate schadenfreuders, like young O'Shea, content to spend their days watching rampant tourist tempers flare as they scoped the pert and alert, rest of the best, in European womanhood enlightening or depressing the topless scene down at the local beach. Such cads were equally content to spend their nights sipping wine behind the tall stone walls with the shades drawn; laughing bitterly at it all.

Christopher M. Basso

There were even a few *Americans* here and there. A strange, disparate mix of curious college age backpackers with dog-eared copies of the dusty books they'd taken for disaffected generational gospel, to down the other end, jaded industrialist billionaires jockeying fortified compounds ginned up on an ego scale that would've made Hitler's left nut weep for its right.

.... In the end, this little slice of Earth was what you made of it. Throw on the horse blinders to the rampant excess, atavistic intent, and overwhelming kitschiness and you might yet crack the bone and get to the marrow. Our boy O'Shea liked to think he occupied some strange ground *in between*; too old to backpack, too young to go all Woodrow for some Albert Speer monolith moment—and most definitely, rocking a full brassy pair.

Besides, standing on the edge of the small harbor in *Beaulieu-sur-Mer* at sunset, or walking along the gently crescent curve of the *Promenade des Anglais* where the sea met the land, made it more than bearable in the end. If you could just look past what man's ragged claws had cut across this land in its excess, you could still, see what drew him here in the first place. Something of burnt umbers, rose violet sunsets, and the glimmering shades of olive trees flashing silver points of light to rival the sun; the fresh scent of salt in the cool air as you slept, listening to the gentle waves against the darkened rocks, and the heartbeat, rhythmic cadence from where all life begins.

This was why the Greeks, Romans, and Saracens all thought it a fine place to set up shop for a millennium or two....O'Shea finished his drink, leaned back and closed his eyes. The wave was coming fast. There were worse ways to kill an afternoon than a sleepy hammock facing a quiet sea.

Chapter Three
Where the Water Lilies Grow

"Let's shag ass." Liam called up from the front steps of the villa towards the open windows and the pale ivory curtains fluttering in the breeze.

Within moments she was out the door bounding down the tall stone steps. A lovely cornflower summer dress fit snugly against her skin, her hair falling over her shoulders picking up points of flax and strawberry red from the sun. She flashed a quick smile, the smile always easing an otherwise irascible condition; a sound and fury in the apprehension; and these, the moments that could always knock him on his tail wondering when the curtain was going to be pulled on his charlatan act.

"Whimsy my dear...I must say."

"What?"

"Nothing, you look lovely."

"*Whatever.*"

"No, truly, I must have been born under a lucky star." He held out an arm, "Shall we?"

The villa gates clicked shut behind them. With some purpose they started down the winding road, as the light from their first day began to fade. They crossed onto the *Promenade Rouvier*, a red brick path hugging the eastern edge of the cape—down past some of the Belle Époque behemoths peeking out from behind the high walls and overflowing gardens. Further to the east, the long vista of rugged coast stretched past the twinkling lights of Monaco, and with the right kind of eyes, clear down to the Italian border.

Midway between the villa and the road to Nice sat the small chocked full o' yacht harbor of *St. Jean*—where they stumbled across a run down little brasserie with a fairly twilight countenance and a fine view of the sea. *Le Select,* in all its faded glory, seemed right about up the O'Shea alley. At any rate, it looked a fine enough place to stop for a bite and to play meet and greet with the natives.

It was later explained that Marcel Rochambeau, an intrepid young chef from *The Cordon Bleu* set up shop on the beach right after "the Big One", once the Germans were gone and the Vichy had melted back into the hills. And for the three generations since, his crew had run the local gastronomy with something bordering on a similar absolutism. From the patriarch's stern hand, thru his son's slightly freewheeling '68 ways, right on down to his grandson's current Ducasse inspired no nonsense attitude. Institutions which had reached a certain shade of *venerability* could now afford to play fast and loose with the little things…like decorum and ambiance. And what they lacked in these they more than compensated for in attitude.

But in the end it was estimably redeemable that such a place could thrive and survive, even amid the local hubris that demanded all their pennies shiny and new. The assembled coterie of excess must have found this strange pile of bricks at their door fairly charming, and well, rather bohemian. O'Shea, itching to break the chains of the former, found the place, with its odd collection of bric-à-brac and crusty wharf rats, immediately to his liking.

They sat in the smallish courtyard sheltered on each side by the crumbling bricks and reddish walls. The whole affair seemed held together by ivy, bougainvillea, and a mad dash of pure gumption. Across the walls was a smattering of old, tattered postcards from around the world, as several tables stretched across the small wooden deck hugging the very edge of the beach. The tide was in and the sea looked close enough to reach out and touch.

Liam sat back in his rumpled cargo shorts and Bill the Cat t-shirt and marveled at the scene. Hot climates like this weren't especially friendly to the subtle charms of Irish whiskey, so the boy shelved the national treasure for more local fare. The Rochambeau's signature mix began making the rounds; a sweet tinged Limoncello and vodka concoction, which the owners swore the Romanov's bequeathed to the local culture to staunch the wounds of exile.... Which made sense on *some* level he supposed—better than the jive strange men pushed on midnight trains at any rate.

The sun left them; ushering in a bright full moon hanging low at the horizon. Crickets chirped from the hedge brush lining the road as the last of the swimmers rolled up from the beach. By their final drink an interesting mix of regulars had drifted in. Fishermen mostly, girding up for a night spent out on the bay in trawlers, dragging for sand crab and langouste after the glitterati had passed out or gone to bed. They spoke a dialect that might have given them trouble up in Alsace or Brittany; an almost French patois with some Italian thrown in for good measure. Sara, however, had a wonderful ear for it, another sign that fate and fortune were on their side.

Night descended fully on its last and the whole eastern coast was lit in reds and whites, ranging along the avenues and snaking down from the villas lining the hills. Liam had a double shot of Patrón Silver with a fast talking man from *Antibes* before taking his lovely out on the creaky deck for a slow dance to the strains of some long forgotten Yves Montand tune.

When Rochambeau *die jünger* produced a bottle of dusty prewar Absinthe, a fine Dien Bien Phu vintage from the cupboard, cooler heads knew it was time to go. Even the young American had to agree; to have come all this way to be laid low in their backyard hardly showed the grit and spirit this thing set out with. Besides, a fool's errand was a fool's reward—as a portly certain someone might have said.

O'Shea forged ahead, wobbled ahead more precisely, down the red bricks of the promenade before hitting the Pont St. Jean and the main Nice-Monaco junction, where they hung a turn real westerly like towards the village of *Villefranche-sur-Mer*. Just close enough not to bother with a cab and just long enough to deaden a penitent's hard won buzz.

They soon rounded the last of the dimly lit curves along the sea road and descended a broad hill onto the crowded beachfront esplanade. Apparently Friday night *was* the time for these people, the ones Fred Dewan warned about; the polo pony bowls and key party mischief set. Good credit and pretensions to horseplay seemed the only prerequisite.

It was a bit jarring at first, like being wakened from some pleasant stupor by the business end of a hot poker come a calling. All around was a sudden sort of controlled chaos, swirling voices, rude words, a chorus of Babel tongues striving for primacy.

Cars lined both sides of the narrow road and traffic sat at the standstill as couples and families, stragglers and ramblers, strolled the boardwalk and streets of the tiny horseshoe shaped village.... The young Americans reconnoitered the perimeter a bit before settling on *Le Cosmo*, a jumping little harbor front café with a zeitgeist vibe, and a lax attitude about late arrivals.

Regrettably, they made the mistake of sitting at the bar, where a booming mongo of a woman, with the voice of Gilbert Godfried on hormone replacement therapy, and the social niceties of O.J., was rambling something about all the Goddamn no class tourists, and the wogs and bogs that needed to get their asses back to Africa.... Liam felt like flicking his spent cigarettes at the ample target of her head, but suddenly thought better...lest they ship *his* ass back to Africa.

But that was the Rubicon of the lifestyle, cross it fully and you might be lost forever. Drawing breaths with every alligator skin pill box hag running a Friday night peacock strut was a small price to pay to plug yourself right-proper into the *nexus*, the living breathing zeitgeist of the times. It was a balance-ledger thing, or perhaps something like karma: meet a few nice people; come across a few louts—a typical weekend night along the Riviera. They discretely moved the rambling shindig to one of the tall tables along waterfront.

From his deck chair O'Shea had a clear view, over a freshly tilled Volga Boatmen, of the harbor and the hills across the bay. He brooded over his drink as Sara quickly struck up a

296

conversation with a couple of trust fund, hippie castaway types, currently on the low from life.

Amazing how these types could seemingly find one another on the spot, like fraternal Masons flashing secret signs down dark alleyways. They were soon over the soapbox making lots of bad noise about local fishing rights...or maybe it was the declaration of the rights of man? Who knew? An over earnest brand of righteousness was often lost in translation, and while not quite louche PBR hipster country, also not the sort of thing to sustain a hard won buzz.... In fact, it might have even sobered him up a bit. He frowned—a mental dexterity in the service of self-aggrandizement was a sinful bit at that. Shit, even a pre-alkie in a Bill the Cat t-shirt could spot that one.

Besides, such radical talk was never a healthy thing when one was riding an escapist vibe. He merely nodded thoughtfully every now and then, dropped some bollix he'd filched from freshman poli sci, and let his attentions otherwise drift.... That is, until he noticed something out in the harbor, something catching his fancy the way house cats eye the passing birds and arrogant squirrels. Out past the workman dinghies, bateaux de pêche, and rusty trawlers sat some truly epic bits of nautical life bobbing about; massive yachts and full rig cutters, sleek, resplendent...and utterly unguarded.

And the germ was suddenly in his mind, a plan was hatched, the scales balanced, the judgments weighed.... What if we were to just *borrow* one? How could they ever call it thievery when the borrower led with such an honest heart? Yellow cake and baking soda had sent lesser sorts to war.

He had another look at the hippie boys raging away....Yep, it was getting about that time, time to ditch the social activism, not to mention the thin-skinned euphemisms—*borrow*? Hell that was for tenderfoots who planned on returning things, he'd flat out have to steal one. Having already played with several fringe behaviors on this trip, nautical kleptomania seemed about the logical progression of things

.... Could get messy though—securing bail, formal inquests, escorted to your waiting plane in a pair of manacles....Might be best to just *crash* some swanky party raging

297

on one of those "big boys" in the harbor. Yep, one of those massive things with the Arabic nameplate on its ass, side scanning geometric stabilizers, and the dual use disco-helipad. They might know where the good craic resided. What were a few more revelers at that point anyway?

.... Seemed weak in the final analysis though; the basest panhandling to the masters of war. Besides, the allure of tearing down the coast in some extremely stolen property had a mad savage bent that was hard to let go.... He'd have to place a call to old Fred back in his Amagansett love shack and make sure there was bail money on the line, ready to wire at a moment's notice to the Gendarmerie post of his choosing.... Roger that, capital plan, capital indeed. Another Volga boatman to steel the nerves, and Houston we'd have a *go*.

.... There's an old maxim about the virtues of honor among thieves, but such graces rarely confer down the narrow alleys of lovers. Alas, they keep the home fires burning but tend to extinguish those lovely bonfires of the vanity. So it was that Miss Connelly dropped the boom when it became clear things had drifted past the idle liquored banter of the late night hours. That is, once she could *see* the exact levels of booze and sincerity swirling across his eyes. Strangely enough, she wasn't moved by the declaration that this would be an *enlightened* statement—something that might have made Locke or Rousseau proud.

The two activist types listening in were clearly vibing his line of reasoning though, gradually building up the same sense of classist outrage.... Which was quite the delicious irony in itself, but just as well—trust fund rabble were a highly expendable commodity anyway; this generation's *Banzai* charge, ready and willing to take one for the Emperor.... Give me another twenty minutes, O'Shea reasoned, and he'd have this whole bar ready to storm the harbor shouting, "Sans-culottes!"

.... Fearing an international incident, what with her hopped up boyfriend, two borderline eco-terrorists, and the ominous foreign flagged mega yachts in their midst—Sara took charge. Grabbing Liam, she politely excused them from the deck before quickly leading him out the door for what she promised

Down All the Days

was a "reconnaissance sweep". Once outside she was gently able to talk him down—but just barely.

She trailed a step or so behind her man as he walked along the harbor's edge, cursing plans of what might have been. Better to hang back and keep an eye on him, she thought, as they put some distance between themselves and the Bolshevik rabble back at The Cosmo. Monitor those wayfaring ways, as he sought his next tequila windmill to slay; far gone on lime-sucked poetry and saltshaker courage.

She sighed; he'd become quite the bored boy these days, his vibe having drifted out past the mild vandalisms to something a bit more destructive. And what was that thing he'd been rambling about of late—shades by variation of degrees? Or perhaps one of those erudite, logical tangents he'd spin out right before breaking something. Yep, that seemed about it, he'd finally stepped inside one of his own wacky parables for a test drive.

…. But then again the worst of his transgressions were almost always limited to himself, and he *seemed* happy enough. She watched him up ahead, his arm around an Isadora Duncan statue near the harbor, singing some sort of garbled tune…. Best to wrap up this little lost weekend soon though, before he started talking to the furniture.

A forlorn O'Shea stared into the harbor…foiled again. There wasn't much left for him in this town, disturbing the peace, terrorizing the tourists, burning the locals—his job here was done. He wobbled down the strand, past the crowded bars and the elegant gaming houses with their flashing lights and tuxedo men who lured you in to venture a pull or two on that shiny love handle…. Gentle gamesters, clasped hand prayers, all fellow pilgrims on this strange journey back to the Lord; wild moments lost in the witching house haze of a complete synaptic flush. Liquor and location were the *key*, only in such environs; fortified with mash courage, would sane men drop their guard and start believing they could somehow steal from the house.

Might he be one of them? He had the cash, that much he knew…. They might object to the cargo shorts and unseemly cartoon t-shirt, but the Centurion AmEx and a heady dose of

299

attitude would surely make his intentions clear…. But what would *she* say? Avatars of clean living and moral resplendentitude usually ranked games of chance low on the list—somewhere above kitten smuggling, but certainly say below kitten juggling.

Besides, that boat thing seemed to really put the zap on her. Hell, she really thought he was going to try it on…. Not a very high opinion of the old boy at that. Christ, he might have *banged* on a few hulls, carved a few L.J.O.'s in some mizzenmasts, but out-and-out criminality required *some* planning. He'd learned that much in law school.

O'Shea stepped into the road against the signals, and was nearly clipped by one of the many scooters tearing down the thoroughfare…by a whole sea of them actually. They were comical almost childish looking things to an American geared mind, that was, until you realized they could have just as easily been the end of you. *Damn*, your last sight in this world; some Italian girl flipping you the bird from the rumble seat of her man's orange Vespa; as their matching Rafael Nadal chestnut locks flowed lushly in the breeze.

That sort of ignominy made a plane crash look good…but the pure sight of which, like your old granny working some joke Richard Pryor blue, had him suddenly laughing. A short kind of giggle that built each time he tried putting it back in the box. The boy was soon doubled over on the curb with the tears running down his face, making a mess of poor Bill the Cat.

"Dude! *What's* gotten into you?"

He looked up smiling, "Just making an ass out of myself honey; it's a time honored tradition down here."

"Well dial it down—you're going to get arrested!"

"I doubt that," he added rather soberly. "C'mon, no harm, no foul."

"…. Get up you fool."

"Let's go, sing it with me—he lit into some manner of sea shanty, or at least what he considered righteous for the occasion. His voice like a glasscutter scattered the seagulls, taking one woman's chi to the breaking point.

All right—time to sound the retreat. She quickly hailed one of the shiny Fiat Bravo's that cruised the coast all night, ferrying a very similar type of wayward clientele back from the foul brutish rhythms of Nice to their quiet villages and gated homes out on the hinterlands.

.... The lights at the *Casino Place du Manion* were bright, and the smiling men and lonely rainy day women beckoned, but they would have to take the proverbial rain check. There was enough static in the air without the spark of a full on public meltdown. He did as told and climbed in.

He stretched out in the back seat of the car, resting his head against his lovely and staring a night dreamer's gaze out the window. Their driver was an older man, quite pleasant, but not much English. He smoked a pipe and the sweet scent of tobacco drifted through the car. This proved a bit much for Miss Connelly, who cracked open one of the windows as her man zoned out to the cool bit of breeze rushing across his face.

As they climbed the hills the whole of *Villefranche* shimmered in fine pointillist hues, drifting in and out of a dream. Gas lamps snaked along the water's edge, casting soft yellows and whites, just enough to light the boats swaying softly in the harbor. The cab roamed slowly through the dimly lit roads, each turn growing quieter and darker than the one before, till the last of man's sounds died away. In his place, a full-throated bellow of the night's creatures came to life. O'Shea could just make out the darkened shapes of the homes and villas dotting the hills—flashes of light here and there, standing like sentinels, half obscured by the canopy of trees and the dense cover of sweet scented magnolia and cedar lining the road.

They soon reached the small sea road junction; almost unrecognizable in the darkness, with just a few spare lights here and there to remind you civilization still existed.

"Drop us off here, ok my friend?"

"Yeah boss."

"What's up?" She said.

"Feel like taking a stroll?"

"I don't know, will it involve carrying you at some point *my friend?*"

"Only if I lose my nerve darling," he said hopping out. "Only if I lose my nerve."

The cab's lights slid slowly off into the distance, growing fainter and fainter till they were gone.

They started down the road to their faded house on the point. The scents of flowers drifting up from the gardens along the alley greeted them at each winding turn, carrying sweetly like fragrant notes on the cool night air. Too much city living had robbed the boy of these simpler pleasures, the names and shapes now gone to memory's mystery, but he could still *sense* them. Like serenades for wind; one would hold the air for a moment, then gently mingle with the next, before surrendering completely in the sweetest of vanquished phrases. The sing song crickets and the gentle roll of the surf rounded out his waking dream....Prettier moments there might yet be, but none would ever be this again.

He shot a fleeting look her way. She was slightly up ahead regarding something off in the darkness. The canopy had grown denser, almost cutting the moonlight off completely. The faintest of colors muted to a recessed opacity, visions now off on the very edge of perception. She suddenly felt as light and far away as whatever it was which caught her fancy.

.... Ah, I have behaved like a bit of a bore this evening he thought, no revelations there. Mea culpas? Don't think so—can't quite ring with an honest sincerity when you've had the semblance of control all along. Active choices those angels might say; victimless crimes the devils could rejoinder.... Sod em' both, *she* would forgive all transgressions in the end.

But was it saintly patience, or simply trying the patience? Small mercies, small mercies indeed; feeling like a bit of an ass these days.... Lots of miles for these smiles; hard to be an ambassador of good vibrations when you've grown so tired in your skin. Laugh though you fool; you had a beauty inside you once—where'd you stick it? And with it, the savage, saving grace in knowing your fragile bit of ground was in no way unique to this world.

.... Ah fuck it then, revelations over—revert to boorish form. How about a bit of ladish poetry across the bow? Turning shapes in the fading stars of a swirling drink? Worse things could sail in a pinch. Freed from the graces and niceties, an unencumbered mind could race from vision to vision, with all the colors to match the masters.... And all around him the kind of buzz where you can *hear* the visions and *see* the sounds. The mind painted in a tipsy van Gogh on a warm summer's evening, Cezanne for the pretty girls, Monet for the butters, a vulgar Gauguin for the boorish hand coloring them all.... *Scandalous*, but you're just looking after all. Why's an eye to wander when it has perfection; because sometimes perfection's too bright too bear for rhetorical fools who dare tangle with it.

His sober mind moved in shades of wholesome Wyeth, stark and simple, with just the vaguest hints of the depth which lay beneath. But that was for some time long ago, now way back when. Was this how the Dutch king did it he wondered? Making his penniless way down here to find the colors out on the edge of the imagination, walking the fine line between visions of the divine and the scarred depths of the chasm.... No poor fool, just some bad timing; born of the moment but born at the wrong time. No psychopharmaceuticals to keep the beasts at bay, just rock gut absinthe cut with turpentine—that would have anyone going for the ear two times quick.

.... Guess the old boy didn't have a Centurion card and the proper shoes? Regrets, regrets—ah to be famous *after* you've turned to dust; isn't *that* the business? Poe, Dickinson, Turgenev, Kafka, poor van Gogh...society never let's you live that one down. A vicious brand indeed, all strong spirits and shaded pain, like the kind John Oldcastle might have favored before he *got straight* with The Fates.... The tedious and routine brewing with sad genius and angst, a potent Bitches Brew if ever...

"Liam—where the hell are we?"

".... I was hoping you knew."

She looked a bit annoyed, "I've got to pee."

"Yeah, me too," he looked around. "How about here?"

"You're kidding?"

"Doubt it." He walked over to one of the high prison yard walls, replete with closed circuit monitors and several *Chien Mechant* signs, dropped trou, and proceeded to let loose with nature's business along this edifice to inhumanity.

He was autographing his *nom de guerre* with an extended flourish that would have done old Pablo himself proud.

"It's ok," he said in a calm, lawyerly tone. "Look up there, the camera's turned the other way—you're good to go."

…. Unfortunately, reason was never going to be the victor in a struggle with necessity. She sighed, wandering out a few feet further, crouching between two Jerusalem Pines and studying him; a contented smile across his face, as he sent the Volga Boatman further downstream for their consideration.

"You're a whack-a-doodle."

"That's why they pay me the *big bucks* darling."

"Boat thieving, public intoxication, destruction of property…*urination*—What's gotten into you this evening?"

"Petty larceny is in my blood, vagrant misdemeanors too…does that make sense?"

"About as much as you checking into hotels as Steve Dallas and Vic Ferrari, but that doesn't seem to stop you."

"Well James Bond was taken," he said zipping up. "C'mon, before they release the hounds."

They kept along the darkened road till it met the red brick junction of the promenade. There was levity in the moment that the place sort of *fostered* on you, where most things seemed permissible if not downright encouraged…but O'Shea delusions aside; there was also something slightly off in the mix, *their* mix more precisely.

He thought again about his night's transgressions, with a bit of mawkish shame at first, but looking out on the riotous lights and the black expanse of the possible sea, his guilt began shading to something else. Guilt was a sad item in this world, better than circus clowns, still worse than cigarettes—but unwanted all the same…. He cast a sad eye to the source of his guilt, the barometer for this night's transgressions, as a quick thought drifted across his mind making him instantly uneasy.

.... For all his catalog of faults, for his many garden-variety sins he was always aware of the durable ties that bind. Always keenly aware of the way his culture sold a blow dart notion of the uniqueness of self. Each of us a special vessel cutting through our one moment in time—an advertiser's trick to divide and conquer, to keep you perpetually alone, always in search of the *next* rush to fill the void.... But he couldn't help but thinking, for the first time, this fine evening, that her vibe had become the roundest and heaviest of millstones. He quickly lit up another smoke reminding himself that ponderous thoughts were for ponderous times past.

They left the dimly lit road entirely and made a slight turn back up the way.... Jesus, if it wasn't *dark* back here, he thought, like the edge of some great jungle, so rich in greens as to almost be black. They walked along the ridgeline, beneath the heavy canopy and fragrant hedgerows, slipping back into the heart of a very exclusive and reclusive jungle.... Mr. Kurtz suddenly sprang to mind, but alas it was only Mr. Berlusconi. The jungle talk was apt enough however as each step met the low rising chorus of bird and beast alike.... And then suddenly, faintly at first, a soft guttural rumbling, followed by a full-throated roar—one that sent the chimp with the Centurion card and the fancy shoes scurrying for the nearest tree.

"Did you hear that?" He half shouted.

"Uh, how could I not."

His mind broke badly for a moment, ".... Do you think they slipped something in our drinks back there?"

"Stop it!" She hissed.

He peered into the darkness, "Jesus, these oddjobs have skipped the dogs and gone straight to lions!"

"Get a grip," she said. "One of these bloated *maniacs* must be running some sort of wild animal menagerie."

"Think he's availed of some cages for ol' menagerie, or is it a come as you are affair?"

"I don't know," she said, "*you're* the lawyer; try explaining to them about punitive damages and billable time."

"Yeah, that worked like a Goddamn charm in the Coliseum."

After a few tense moments of tip toeing through the brush they crashed through a small grove of olive trees and back onto the familiar red bricks of the promenade. A scant fifty feet down the way, they came across the signs for the *Cape Ferrat Zoological Station*, inviting any and all to visit their collection of big cats and sundry predators of the African savannah.

A bequeathment from King Leopold II of Belgium the sign said. A *regular* round these parts back in the day apparently, and a man who liked Africa *so much* he made sure to ship as much of it as he could back to Europe.

"Mystery solved?" She smiled.

"Fuck 'em." O'Shea intoned, reading the dedication plaque. "…. Show off."

"Quiet you; you're lucky you didn't do your business on some electrified fence back there."

"Well, that would have changed the complexities of the trip, now wouldn't it?"

Soon they were alone again, with just the katydids, crickets, and the distant roars of the lions to light their way back to the tall spires of the villa's gates…. It must be said, the gates to his new home were alone worth the price of admission; massive iron railings, backed with thick bronze plates and capped with fierce pickaxe spikes that would have given the Kaiser a fright. These gloomy monsters were anchored fast to the heaviest of old, ivy covered stone that looked like it could withstand a direct hit from a variety of frightening objects.

Several inscriptions were etched in the bronze, which looked like poetry, though it was hard to tell, the letters having worn to a fine illegibility…. Didn't Shelley used to romp down here as well, he thought? He came for the waters they say…see how dandy that turned out *for him*. Though what would he think of the place now, where a sweeping paranoia grips the day and the palace guards are all retired Mossad and ex-KGB shade balls? Sad state of affairs at that.

Liam stood at the keypad and studied the flashing red light of an unwatched camera. He could barely remember the numbers before forgetting them completely.

"What did that periwinkle geek tell us?"

"I thought you were listening?"

"Hold up…" he started to say, his voice trailing to a fine exasperated, when a loud crash came through the nearby brush. It was from their neighbor's house, the only other house you could actually see. They listened in…but nothing. Until a much louder crash, which had O'Shea diving again for the nearest wall.

"Jesus, the lions got them!"

"Would you *stop* it!" she hissed. "…. What's going on over there?"

"Didn't Charley Manson retire down here?" A voice came from behind the bushes.

"No, San Quentin—keep it up and you can tell him all about it."

There was another quick barrage of what sounded like plates crashing and then the sounds of a man's low moans rising from their neighbor's house, which mixed with the general disharmony and angst until O'Shea could make it out clearly…. It was the sound of music, a low baritone aria rising up through the dissonance…sweet and plaintive, until the *next* round of plates went crashing in the night.

"Jesus, let's get inside," he groaned. "Everyone here's a Goddamn *madman*."

"Yeah, I hear you," she said stepping over to the keypad. "Let me try something."

She punched in the three-digit address of the house and the gates slowly swung outward.

"…. Nobody likes a friggin' know it all, my dear."

"Then learn something and you won't feel so alone."

307

Christopher M. Basso

.... They bypassed the house and proceeded immediately down to the pool for a bit of nightswimming; where so impressed by his rugged untoward ways was she, that she demanded he *take her* on the portico facing the sea, with the wide expanse of Heaven and Earth before them. A fitting background to accentuate their primal, sweaty rantings, and the dark jungle come to life with the full-throated bellows of man and beast.... And then he could hear it, clearly now—a bit of the Glorious Ninth, Ludwig Van, ringing out from his plate throwing neighbor's house: *Freude, schöner Götterfunken, Tochter aus Elysium!* The delicate union of a ferocious peril rising up as the wind whipped through the willows*: Alle Menschen werden Brüder, Wo dein sanfter Flügel weilt!* She spun around from the railing, arching up, her hips resting on his. Her teeth sinking into his lip under the canopy of stars, with the sounds of the water and the waves and the ginned up crickets all around.... Or maybe *something* like that, save for the fact she'd already gone to bed as said Lothario lounged on the chaise lounge, catching the 2 a.m. replay of SportsCenter. To be lucky in life was not to be lucky in all things; a remembered phrase playing through his mind as he chomped on a bit of cold pizza; the room spinning, the clocks ticking, and the world still counting backwards to zero.

Chapter Four
Two Shots of Happy, One Shot of Sad

It was the low rumble that woke him, one of those hard to capture hard to place sounds frightening man and beast alike, at least until the beast gets its bearings. He cracked open an eye...fucking airplanes.

The sound intensified, a rising growl before a lowering boom, which cleared the high hills of the coast and crossed the bay towards the far side of Nice. The engine's roar was just enough to resuscitate the brain, just enough to bring the mind back to the television jammed on a volume only a passed out man could have sanely ignored...well no longer.

Adding insult to injury, last night's *Yojimbo-Ronin* twilight double feature was long gone, replaced by some soul-crunching Eurovision song contest. Amateurs murdering a fairly jumbled slice of French Pop—which was of *dubious* pedigree to begin with so this hardly helped matters.... Strange how these French had their Little Jack Horners ass deep in all things culturally viable, but had missed the boat entirely on pop music. Johnny Hallyday, Jordy Lemoinem, Jacques Brel—what the hell kind of cruel, gimp-fisted society would let these creatures see the light of day, let alone export them?

He aimed a motorcycle boot at the set, but his coordination still compromised with drink, missed badly and said boot went sailing out past the Oriel windows, presumably into the garden below...but quite possibly into the pool as well.

Christopher M. Basso

"Ball four," he muttered in a low voice, straightening up a bit. The first wave was coming. Well, this would be it, he thought. To make the commitment would more or less set a vicious chain of events in motion. He swung over the side of the old sleigh bed, planted his feet firmly on the cold stone, balanced himself, and strode over to the set gently turning it off.

The boy dry-jawed a packet of "English Bob's Headache Powders" from the nightstand, as he pondered the paradox of extreme beauty before his eyes and the vicious terror between his ears.

He moved towards the tall beveled windows and stood there; a full glorious view of the eastern Riviera rising up to greet him. It was a clear day all down the coast. The sea was a calm glassy blue with hardly a cloud in the sky. A large sailboat drifted slowly past the lighthouse and the beach in Beaulieu was already alive with a morning crowd…. It smelled like wealth out there, whatever that meant. He leaned an elbow against the sash and admired the scene, ass naked as a jaybird in the morning sun. No need for modesty down here on the water's edge, only the curious wildlife to see your comings and goings.

He stepped back for a long look at the view and the room framing it…. He could get *used* to this. You could just feel the healthy qualities inherent in these slow rhythms. This was a fine place to recalibrate the mind if not the body. But then he slowly finished his turn…which room *was* this? It didn't much look like the one he'd set up shop in yesterday. Besides, wasn't that one facing the lawn? He turned back towards the bed…where was *she*?

A vague terror seized his mind…. Was this the right house, or had he pulled a Goldilocks on one of his uptight, armed to the teeth neighbors? He gingerly made his way back across the room in yet another of these damn "shock of the lightning" mornings moments. He creaked open the door, covering his virtues with a throw pillow, and stepped across the hall to the adjacent room, slowly peering around the corner…. But there she was, slumbering peacefully…. Seemed the leitmotif for that one he groused.

He closed the door, backtracking it across the hall where he caught a glimpse of his tussled hair and Lazarus-stink in the tall Jacobean mirrors.... How could she have passed *this* up? Well, pay no mind; you've bigger fish to fry. He located his bags and proceeded to get his sorry act together. Last night's rumbled cargo shorts, a light blue button down shirt, and some flip-flops—preppy chic, to throw the burghers off the scent, or something like it. Only his freeballin' commando ways could betray his true freakish colors. He grabbed his wallet and gently closed the massive doors behind.... Time to *provide,* as it were.

The sun rose to greet him in a particularly vicious fashion. He pulled a baseball cap low over his eyes, skipped the scene down at his gates, and jumped the wall on the far side of the property. On a fine August morning he followed the reddish brick road to the sleepy harbor at St. Jean.

The promenade was fairly empty, just a few joggers and rollerbladers shuffling past—health enthusiasts who most likely assumed our boy for one of their own, smiling and greeting him in a variety of languages. That he'd forgotten his smokes only added to the subterfuge.

There was a small stretch of beach to his right, where an early morning gathering of lovely young ladies had shed the crimson inhibitions governing much of Western life to capture the generous sun in all the ways nature had intended.

He made sure his peek remained on the mildly coy, if not slightly creepy side of things. It'd be a *damn* shame to be made as a tourist so early in the game. But twelve year old thrills aside, he had to admire a place where the Hapsburg stick was so far removed from the collective ass, as to make narcissistic exhibitionism seem almost quaint.

He arrived at the quiet harbor of St. Jean; a charming strip lined with several restaurants of a scraggly bohemian pedigree, but patroned by a certain customer neither scraggly nor bohemian. This place first got its legs as an artist's colony, and the über-burghers seemed to like to keep a few of them around for ambiance sake, that or perhaps just a frozen charitable stasis to make them feel a bit better for having been so successful in life. O'Shea hoped the long hairs were at least stealing from the thieves; there'd be some poetry in that.

O'Shea passed the shuttered *Le Select,* and the demon Limoncello-vodka concoctions which had launched last night's tailspin odyssey, till he found what he was looking for—a small bakery with this morning's efforts still hot from the ovens. He fell into an easy conversation with the owner, a salt and pepper haired hippie throwback who spoke impeccable English, and had probably seen more of America than he had. The baker was shockingly enough a tobacco enthusiast in the national sense, and generously let the worse for wear young man bum a few smokes.

Liam provisioned the Maison du O'Shea quite nicely: fresh crusty bread, pain au chocolat, a cheese and egg brioche, and something called a "pomme de terre galette" that would have to pass for greasy comfort food. Suitably armed, he headed back for the point.

As he made his way along the promenade he paused near the gates for the Cape Zoological Station, the scene of last night's road tripping ignominy, and took a seat on the stone wall facing the Mediterranean. He lit up his Lucy and watched the calm waters, making sure to take it all in, as a portly man of means once advised.

A lovely view.... He took out his phone and snapped a few for posterity. That they would register little more than a fine blotchy grim was immaterial, the *memory* would remain. He continued for a few minutes with his shutterbug gig, but the boy suddenly couldn't escape the feeling he was being *watched*.... He finally turned, real Josey Wales like, to his left and there, perched on the retaining wall, was just about the damn biggest house cat he'd ever seen. An orange and white dump truck of a thing, staring at him with a look of massive indignance, with a possible indifference chaser to boot.

".... Well, hello there big fella."

There was no reply.

"You, uh, come here often?"

Big orange let loose a low wattage, "Oop ack thbbft!" belch that probably said a whole lot in cat, but to lesser human ears sounded something like a stick up for whatever he had in the bag.

"Well, I think I can help you out sporto," O'Shea said, rummaging through the bag—ciggie perched from his lips, as he eyeballed this fat fellow who seemed to be claiming this spot as his own, and *very much* in charge of the negotiations.

Liam produced a few pieces of the brioche which he placed on the broad stone of the sea wall. The big man loped over in several great strides and proceeded to chow down with apparent delight, having dropped the attitude, and seemed quite content to let Liam pet him. And so they sat there, till O'Shea finished his smoke, and the fat man finished the better part of the boy's breakfast.

Finally, the busted orange cat gave him a satisfied look and started back towards the retaining wall, where he had just enough runway to launch his oversized self up to the ledge before disappearing into the oleander and sea scrub.

"Well, I see how it is," he smiled. "You're welcome!" He shouted back up the hill. And with that Liam hopped off the wall and eased it on back down the road—*hunger* was starting to get the best of him.

O'Shea reached his gates with vague memories of breaking glass and discombobulated opera, but was still none more the wiser on how to work the damn things. He was about to jump the wall again before realizing it probably appeared a far better thing to be breaking out of one's home, than breaking in. So he followed the hedges down the far side of the property, past the line of orange trees and the sweet scent of the sea, to the water's edge. From there he could see the large homes perched along the hills above Beaulieu and Eze Bord-de-Mer.

They all seemed to share something, whether it was a frayed newness meant to emulate the old, or a painstaking resurrection to recapture something shiny and new.... There was a strange sort of desperate architectural *neurosis* afoot that even to a daytripping layman seemed categorically appropriate for this scene.

Then he stole a glance between the palm and eucalyptus to his own pied-à-terre and understood almost instantly why they'd scored the place for a song. Good Lord, in the clear light of day the place looked something of a dump. Not necessarily falling apart but just sort of...dusky. There was a certain slow decrepitude creeping in around the edges, as an unweeded garden literally grew to seed. The pale pink wash of the stone probably burned a fine red once upon a time, and the terracotta roof had certainly seen some better days. Several of the heavy trellis shutters were also on the way out, covered in nicks and cracks. One of them was now loose from its moorings and water stains crept down along the basin plates on the far side; all victims of the strong wind and the relentless sun.

.... O'Shea looked at his crumbling house, slowly finding its way back to nature, and suddenly liked it even more—a ragged survivor amid a sea of shifting plastic. He took a rather certain pride in having the foulest house on the road.... *Screw* propriety, he thought, and started to scale the stone facing.

As he sat atop the wall he glanced over for a better view of his neighbor's home; a two-story Moorish-Castilian villa, a pile of bricks far more stylish and elegant than his own. It sat at the other end of the point, a fine sunflower color with dark green shutters, brown tile roof, and a well-tended English garden that spanned most of the back lawn.... And then he *saw them*, his plate throwing, muffled moaning, opera enthusiast neighbors. He ducked down just out of sight.... They were two older gentlemen, both wearing sun hats and decked out in gardening attire. One was working on a bed of hyacinths as the other stood by, resting his arm against a shovel.

They appeared about as dangerous as a couple of old ladies at a Fort Lauderdale Canasta table. And then suddenly, almost in unison, they looked up and noticed the scraggly young man straddling the stone wall to the house next door, looking more vagrant than lord of the manse.

"Morning then!" O'Shea shouted, waving to them with the authority of man who'd merely misplaced his keys. Playfully enough, they waved back. He shot over the wall and back up the lawn to his faded seaside home.

From the foyer he could hear the sounds of the radio

drifting down the stairs. As he moved closer he could hear the running water and the still fainter sound of the blissfully bashful, singing in a low soft voice as to not be heard.

He made his way quietly up the stairs before pausing at the door to the bath for a moment; his generally guttural mind divorced of all voyeuristic intent, just listening...a song he couldn't quite remember in league with a voice he'd not soon forget.

He slowly peered around the corner. She was laying in a bath of cream colored stone; the only light, coming through the large iron windows, scattered in silhouettes falling through the room, creating the kind of beauty where only nature could transform a Provencal gents into something of a church.... She would look up in a few seconds from the washcloth gently tracing along her arm, singing sweetly, softly off key, and the spell would be broken.... Take a snapshot in the mind, snapshots for a rainy day. Just a few seconds dancing through one's brief history of time.

He stepped back in the hallway and down to the base of the stairs; just close enough to seem far away, "Oi, Sara—I have returned!"

"Hi Honey!" She yelled down.

"Got us some breakfast. Meet me on the terrace when you're ready."

He swung by the kitchen, grabbed some plates and silverware, orange juice and champagne flutes, and a bottle of Ponsardin he'd noticed in the fridge. The hair of that lousy dog was about to bite back.

He wandered up to the terrace above the kitchen. The sun was already beating down as he laid the food and drinks across the sturdy pilgrim's table. He poured himself a mimosa and took a seat facing the sea. With a bit of fortification in the blood, the relentless sun didn't seem all that bad. He tossed his hat over the railing and laid back, letting it shower his pigment challenged Gaelic ways with warm rays.

There was a slight breeze coming from the sea and he could feel the soft palm ferns swaying about. From just down the

Christopher M. Basso

way he could hear the sounds of a Jet Ski cutting through the water, too far away to be anything but a pleasant bit of white noise. He sipped his drink, waiting for his girl.

.... Simply lazy, he chided himself, always failing to appreciate the gift of beautiful things, always questioning the intent, the inherent expectation—until you've wound yourself tighter than a screw. Setting yourself up in this quasi Shangri La, then wondering when they were going to come at you with the Billy clubs. Life was going to pass you by, no matter how hard you tried to monkey wrench it...silly bastard. No, just sit back, deep breaths, breathe it in—from perfect sunsets framed, right down to the elemental and molecular. Just keep telling yourself such things...hell, they might even work.

Yeah, a nice brand of bullshit, *le charmant*, but utterly useless.... Too much of this senseless guff to keep smiling through with a straight face, especially late at night, when the moonlight creeps and the floorboards creak, and where the wild things are free to groan.... Think *they* want to hear about carpe diem and self-actualization rubbish.... What did that dingbat cousin of his say about atheists and their foxholes? Nah, hold that cynicism close to the bone, it's like a shield, a talisman, the only way to fend off the beast—and the cold chill of alone.

"Dreaming again Liam?" She gave him a kiss on the cheek.

"Dreaming, ruminating, rusticating—you name it."

She was wearing a long cotton robe; her wet hair pulled back over her shoulders. Her eyes picked up the twinkle in the fresh morning sun.

"Here, let me help you with that." She took the plates from twister two-thumbs and started serving breakfast. She loaded the boy up with a fair heap of extra, just the way he liked it but was casually *loathe* to admit.... Carol Brady, Marisa Miller, and a bit of Anaïs Nin all rolled into one—yep, she'd make some lucky fool a glorious fifty-year distraction at that.

He tucked into his egg and cheese brioche, or what was left of it.... Beauty and grace versus the subtle dominion of the unknowable? Best to line up with the forces of the elemental and eternal, or spin out as gloriously as Elvis in a Cadillac Coupe, tearing off into a fried bacon and peanut butter banana sunset, when hell was on high and the worm had yet to turn.

"Well," she said finally, "I *tracked* down that little von Summer scamp."

"And?"

"And indeed, the flake is in Majorca. She'll be gone till next week."

"Do tell?"

"Yep, got her on the phone this morning—which was a chore. She's going to try and get back sooner, but I don't see it happening. We'll see her next weekend... maybe."

.... He wasn't sure how he felt about that. Well that's not true, he was quite sure how he felt about that, but *unsure* of what he was willing to reveal. Cameron von Summer—the mere name conjured sparks jumping through the driest of tinderbox, as fiery a tempest as the New World had to offer.... She was of course filthy rich, and by filthy we mean dirty; old money, blue to the cerulean core: Hotchkiss booster, Dartmouth legacy, post graduation stint down in the bars of Kangooland.... Rehab Southern California, rehab Northern Minnesota; Bali for communion with the monks and now Europe for a dash of culture; a cosmic-karmic joke on her robber baron family—a black sheep—everybody's got to have one don't you know....Next stop failed marriages, ice storm scandals with the local tennis pros, and then bingo; *rehab*—third times a charm. Finding the fates, finding Jesus...didn't realize the old boy was lost? Any and all, six of one, half-a-dozen of another; then, who knew, perhaps The White House? That's where her type generally found their sea legs.

.... Cameron stories had always been interesting in that tabloid-ish killing time in the checkout line kind of way...except they made *those* stories up. Now they were due to meet the beast. He'd better get right with the holy water and sharpened stakes.

He poured himself a fresh mimosa without the orange juice. How did the saint ever fall in with the sinner anyway? No doubt another of her youthful leper reclamation projects gone

Christopher M. Basso

awry. His mind was suddenly snapped back to attention.

"Whatever will we do with ourselves till then?" She was still smiling.

".... I don't know."

They laughed a moment before the slightest tinge of fear drifted onto the portico, a pause that hung in the air like the last few seconds of *The Graduate*. Twenty-four hours in and it was already apparent this place served up inertia best. Inertia and the lascivious pursuit of wholly atavistic endeavors; which was fine, but generally in small measured doses.

"C'mon," she finally said, "this is pathetic—let's *do* something."

They dressed, packed some lunch, and hopped on two of the old pedal bikes he found in the gardener's shed. Much like the house, and the man, they were a bit worse for wear but would still do the trick.

"These will get us into town," he assured her.

The man at the gas station patched up their tires and recommended heading down the coast towards Monaco and the beaches of the *Cap d'Ail*; nice and uncrowded, he assured them, even at this time of year. Then she remembered one of the hippie boys raving on and on about the hiking in and around the villages—said the place to go was out past Villefranche towards the even sleepier Eze Bord-de-Mer, and climb the "Chemin de Nietzsche".

"Yes," those borderline ecoterrorists had castigated O'Shea, *"That Nietzsche."*

"You mean crazy Nietzsche of syphilitic fame and deity loathing renown?" His rejoinder was pure fear and loathing.

They merely gave him a dirty East Coast look before explaining that Ol' Fritz used to romp down here back in the day, whenever the humours, or perhaps the syphilis, got too much to burning. He used to hike up the winding trail each afternoon to the sister village of *Eze* proper; a two thousand foot doorstep up along the cliffs, built long ago by Saracen pirates for whenever they wanted to lob a few cannon balls out into the bay to make their intentions clear.

.... A short hour later they were standing the base of the Chemin de Nietzsche, looking up the winding, rocky path which seemed to point right straight up the brush to the sun kissed cliffs.

"Jesus," he muttered with a newfound respect for die Übermensch, "a bit more angle and we're going to need harnesses and a rig." Liam hadn't the burn, but there were some other poisons to purge.

"Lace up the dancing shoes Geronimo," she smiled, "we've got to clean out your blood."

"Me?"

"Yeah," she laughed, "*the humours* seem to have gotten the best of you."

O'Shea, never one to shy away from such challenges, laced up and took the lead. After all, despite illusory rumors to the contrary, it was *only* a pack a day habit—not the *true* viciousness of a fully armed and operational Bukowski-Cassavetes lifestyle. Nothing that couldn't be cured with a little good old-fashioned red-blooded American *boyishness*. And besides, surely the man could resurrect the lad who'd once bitch slapped the fates and hit for the cycle against Penn back in the day.

But as they rounded the fifth of the winding switchback curves, the one with the small marker still reading: Eze 1 km, O'Shea had to pause against the rocks. He struck a pose that might have done Edmund Hillary or his man Tenzing proud if not for the bloodied elbow and the wheezing gait.

He waited as she stopped for a couple of pictures of the sea below and took a few deep breaths, trying to regroup. His skin was a fine shade of crimson, but a clever boy could hang that one on the beating sun; the gasping wheeze was another thing altogether. Rough beasts not so easily pshawed away by the vagaries of meteorological indifference.

He caught sight of himself in one of the shiny reflective plates around the narrow bend.... Handsome Devil, sinning your way back to salvation and all—how's that working out?

He finally caught his breath and it seemed a fairly ominous cardiac event was averted.... Wear all your sins on the inside, he smiled, something old Henry might have said. Yep, somewhere up in an attic there was a portrait of young Liam aging rather horribly.

She turned around, "Ready?"

"Hell yeah girl, I've been waiting for you."

He was able to keep it together till the summit; the last thirty steps a brutal up close and personal of mind over matter, like one of those Bikram yogis stretched over a bed of nails. But with one last desperate push he propelled the bag of bones over the crest and was suddenly standing on the smooth stones just outside the tourism office, looking up at the ancient village.

Most death defying monster climbs usually rewarded you with little more than scrub brush, titmice, and maybe a couple of those fuzzy spectrometers, but Eze was something else entirely. An entire medieval village perched between a series of rocky outcroppings and sheer cliff walls. Sturdy old stone homes, lovely gardens, and orchards growing right out to the very edges of the cliffs, almost hanging over them. Small winding streets snaked through the fortress town, where there were few people and even fewer cars. Other than the tourists, it probably took a steely sort to make their home up in billy goat country.

So much so that everyone from the Saracens to the Grimaldis had given it a try, only to split when life demanded more than just a pretty view. The place had been largely abandoned until modern means figured a way to pump water up from the lands below. Eze was now enjoying its latest incarnation as summer tourist mecca and winter artist's colony; worse endings were entirely imaginable. Lonely and lovely, perched straight up the cliffs almost a half mile above the sea.

.... Lovely indeed. He rested his weary bones against a stone wall and studied the town. Surely these good folks had what he needed.

"I think I see a café over there. I do believe a couple of cold Peronis might be in order? Bit of a reward for our efforts?"

She smiled, "Ready to go down?"

"…. Come again?"

"What'd you think we were doing, recreating?"

"Well, you know, a view *like this* doesn't come along every day."

"Don't worry, it'll still be here—you might not. Like I said, we've got to clean out the blood."

"Clean out the blood?"

"Posthaste!" She smiled, bounding down the path back to the sea, "C'mon, the going down's the easy part."

"…. You know, you're a very self righteous person!" He shouted down the hill, but she was already gone.

Self-righteous? Maybe. But she wasn't done with the boy, not by a damn sight. Her newfound corrective zeal was based in some part on her own nimble fate challenging ways. She was a fine example of the species to be sure, but also quite the little athlete—a gymnast till she grew too willowy tall, then a college track star till she grew restless and bored. This little jaunt up the mountain was a reminder of how much she missed that former incarnation. Besides, some physical activity might do the boy good. Six weeks of touring the provinces sampling all manner of foul, Earthly delight was no way to plan for a thousand years.

With von Summer retiring brain cells along some Majorcan beach, there was time to kill before the next social reprobate-miscreant came a calling. It was the perfect storm lining up, the chance to breath some life back into this withering vine. The sun, the warmth, and the dry air all made for the perfect accomplices.

They rented a sturdier class of bike the next day and headed down the coast—all the way from Beaulieu to Menton; up along the old Roman corniche where the sun met the sky, and back through the meticulously kept streets and gardens of

Monaco. They left the principality and kept along the sea road, down narrow paths lined with Aleppo pine and lemon trees, and heavy with the sweet scents of wild Jasmine and Lavender.

And finally down into the harbor at Beaulieu; past the cafes and the silver wisps of olive trees, and past the strange, burnt to a crisp, jewelry laden women and their prissy little French dogs, replete with Napoleonic complexes and anger management issues.

"Merde chien!" O'Shea shouted as they nipped at his ankles. "Even the fucking dogs are xenophobes!"

She could only laugh at the fine sense of diplomacy inherent in the boy. Clearing the Poodle strewn esplanade at the far end of the village they circled round the smaller square near the water's edge—O'Shea, a latter day Lizard King himself: shirtless, hair grown out, peddling around town, a pervert's pair of aviator "tea shades" resting on his nose and a ciggie dangling from his lips, hanging free.... A formerly "wound" man reset to Jell-O, and most likely cresting what must have been his Gauguin day.

.... That was till the Poodles went for him again.

"Peddle faster!" He shouted. "They looked pissed!"

They met the last bit of rise before coming down the bend to the *Plage des Negres*, where they tossed their sweaty clothes on the sand for a running jump into the cool waters. After a brief swim and a game of topless/bottomless Marco Polo scorned, it was back to the villa where he collapsed exhausted.

She mercifully left him alone to go shower up for dinner. O'Shea had foregone the bathing routine completely, preferring the manly musk of days well spent. He retired to a couch in the solarium and stretched out. A cool breeze drifted through the room, and already the faint sounds of opera were rising up from his neighbor's house—they of the straw hats and plate throwing acumen. He could hear it quite well now, Puccini's *Tosca*, an endless stream of it.... Which *must* have been John Bonham loud in the room, but was reduced to a faint and pleasant echo by the time it'd crossed the lawns and gardens.

They ordered some takeout and planned for a quiet low-key evening. Liam met the Vespa man down at the road; where after much erudition he finally solved the riddle of his gates. With a fine Vietnamese *Com Bo Luc* feast in tow he met her by the back of the house. They carried their meal down to the table at the far end of the garden, under the shaded trees with a commanding, hidden view of the eastern cape.

Sara lit several candles and soon the childhood scent of citronella was woven with jasmine honeyed night air.... It was a fine thing to have a meal like this, before a view like this; humbling in the expansive way of remembering where you found yourself a short year ago, humbling in the ways of the wonderment of fate; a gentle or rude door that swung both ways.... That was until you saw your plate-throwing neighbors rolling what appeared to be a moveable bar down the length of their lawn. He sighed; maybe it wasn't as bad as it looked?

From their hidden perch near the rocks they had the drop on the strangers. O'Shea peered in again, *Jesus*, that was a bar they were piloting down the lawn—one of those large unwieldy things that you were meant to roll from room to room, not take on extended excursions into the great outdoors. But they seemed to have a rather deft, practiced touch with the thing, navigating it gently down the slope of their much longer lawn to a bed of crushed stone right beside the sea.

At that point the gig was up; they were now within perfect sightlines of one another. The two men, one with a dark tan, the other a bit fairer, caught sight of them. O'Shea suddenly felt a bit sheepish, more the child than Handsome Henry's Blingmaster General, who'd just had his fine repast trod upon.

But the older of the two gentlemen, a sandy haired man in his mid-fifties, thin as a rail and seemingly evident of grace and form, waved to them first.

"Hello there."

.... Sounded like an English accent?

"I hate to interrupt, but perhaps you'd like to join us for a drink?"

.... Civility? They'd seen many interesting things in the last few days, but a gregarious impromptu courtesy had not been one of them.

"Yes, do join us," the other one slightly slurred.

They already appeared to have gotten a heady, head start on things.

"*Sure*," Liam shouted back. "Be right over."

"What are you doing?" She whispered through her smile.

"I don't know...just act natural, no big sudden arm movements."

The strangers introduced themselves in the royal collective as *Ed*, that is—The Two Ed's. And before Liam could wonder how to keep things straight the younger of them, a well-formed man of medium height and exotic complexion, offered they could call him "Shirley" with the assurance that everyone does.

.... After one round with the Ed's he understood why they traveled with their own bar; hell, after one round he was surprised they didn't cook their own gin. The rolling set up was all the better to facilitate the making and shaking of truly epic, towering cocktails.

They had foregone the narrow, old-fashioned martini glass in favor of the increasingly trendy supersized stemware, first made popular in shillish-foul corporate themed restaurants, then co-opted by the *hep* world like the first thing had never occurred. Well, cultural anthropology aside, the Ed's stood a "round" with a glass you could have taken shelter under if ever caught in a passing gale.

As stated, they appeared to be Englishmen at first, speaking in slight, crisp Oxbridge accents and affecting an Englishman's correctly observant passivity to most things.... But they weren't English, unless, on some far out tangential Loyalist reckoning you still considered Philadelphia part of England. No, between the lines of the Merchant-Ivory act these two had the faint twang of upper Montgomery County; yeah, probably out by the King of Prussia Mall—but they'd tackled the English affectations with the same zeal as the Material Girl after she lost the plot.

Liam watched Ed the Elder measure out nine jiggers of Old Raj for his martini, and in what must have been either some aesthetic flourish, or mad form of denial, topped his *mug o' gin* with a twisted slice of lemon.

Drink in hand, Ed the Elder took a seat and began recounting the time at The St. Regis, Bora Bora, when he got into a row with the barmen over the amount of alcohol he was imbibing.

"*Eight* shots to a drink the barmen insisted." Ed took a bracing sip, lubricating the vocal cords, "Eight! I shouted—are you mad! This is my fourth drink; I'd be dead if that were so!"

And he looked out to the sea, "But he *did* pour them out…and indeed it was closer to ten."

Ed the Younger, aka Shirley, didn't have quite the wooden leg, but to compare him to his better half was like comparing Sham to Secretariat. He was probably rocking something closer to seven a glass. Bringing up the rear on a very wobbly pair of knees was a sheepish Liam O'Shea, probably working three a glass. And picking daisies in the rearguard was Miss Connelly, who'd left the field entirely for some cranberry juice from the mini fridge on the SS Moveable Feast.

Jesus, these two were *animals*, Liam thought; the Yoda and Obi-Wan of the juniper berry thrill-seeking set, with just a thimble of Vermouth now and then to keep a certain lifestyle delusion afloat. But the *highly* respectable part was they were still frighteningly correct; monkeyshine drunk to be sure, but by all AMA standards they probably should have been dead.

…. The Ed's didn't scream money and their overall welcoming demeanor was a sharp departure from the high hedges and imperial gates which ruled this scene…. But for not *showing* money they sure must have *had* an awful lot of it. Most of their tales revolved around extreme bouts of drinking and traveling—like if Frommer's ever ran the ultimate transient Barfly forum….Europe, the South Pacific, Rio, Cape Town, Japan—*Easter Island*—where the hell was that anyway? And then like clockwork, every Christmas in Bermuda, holding court at *Henry VIII*, drinking nine merry jiggers to his six wives of woe as they assaulted a fine holiday feast.

Just the two of them Sara asked? Sadly so; with both their families having long since swept them, and their whole host of curious affectations under the rug, or under the bus if the accuracy of savagery was your intention.

.... O'Shea, the finest product of a more then mildly dysfunctional home, took a great interest in these two. They couldn't have been kinder or more gracious to their guests, but as the drinks flowed and the dirty pastoral-comical continued, they would occasionally lay into one another with the fervor of a couple of *bender* men who think they're alone but are actually shouting in a crowded bar. They seemed to hate each other with a real *zest*, and yet loved one another with a fated grace and familial acceptance he'd rarely known. At least not back at Handsome's version of Wuthering Heights, otherwise known as Watery Bottoms. Almost at once the boy could grasp the cause of all things that had been going crash in the night.

Society wasn't built to deal with this manner of mutant prototype. The cruel, beady-eyed Bushmen and their Stepford Rotarian ladies had long since carved their own golden calves. *God* was barely invited to their party, why would these two be? And the Grand Inquisitor? He wouldn't even hear the case. He knew all too well the vagaries of the thing, but he had other matters to attend to—the trains, real and otherwise had to run on time.

The two Ed's and their ilk had been so thoroughly thrown under that bus that they finally took to the rails, zipping along now on a bullet train of wonderment, perpetual intoxication, and bohemian wanderings. That they rolled *so large* was probably the only thing saving them from some mix of quiet fear and somnolent disrepair. After all, even a freed cage bird could still go mad.

.... Which must have been in part the allure of *this* place. In a closed atavistic society all manner of personal indiscretion fell along the lines of a sliding scale. It was a finely honed *Lord of the Flies* for bored grown-ups; a complex equation of weird wealth, divided by kinky predilections, versus just how much the Palace Guards were willing to tolerate. Generally, anything short of bedrock murder could keep your act afloat; an equation in essence running ad infinitum. But it was quite obvious why these two needed the non-stop booming opera; they might kill each other without it.

In the end, when families have cut you loose, straighter society has shunned you, and social pariah hypocrite types have called you out...*well then*, if life was the kicker, the best revenge was to paint your masterpiece well.

And *well* The Ed's seemed to have nailed it.... A perpetual state of Angst and Zen, ginned till it no longer mattered. Having it wailing banshee *large* on the private beach beside your grand seaside home. No judgments, no equivocations or recriminations—just stone cold entertaining. And you know you'd been at it good when Ed the Elder asks Sara, three sheets to the wind and on the fourth time around, "Have you ever been to Bora Bora love?"

"Not since the last twenty minutes you asked her!" Ed the Younger interjects. "*God,* you are such a bore sometimes..."

Variations on this theme consumed the better part of the night, with reams of invective and affection coloring the cool night air.... It was hard to say when they parted ways. O'Shea had vague memories of taking his lovely's arm as she led him back up the way; the unsteady, wobbly way—as the faint strains of Papageno's aria from *The Magic Flute* carried playfully down the lawn from the grand villa next door.

Christopher M. Basso

Chapter Five
Queen Jane Approximately

"I thought I saw you there."
"But you didn't."
"…. I would have liked to."
"I know, I would have too."

The next thing O'Shea clearly remembered was lying on the lawn, a fine gingham blanket beneath him, and the sheltering sky above. Sitting next to him, Sara sketched a few drawings of the sea in the spare pages of an oversized journal she kept. His eyes glanced over at the page; faint delicate renderings she would later fill out with color.

Yep, a fine steady hand, another of her many hidden talents. O'Shea's best talents were what presently laid him low. While the body might have been functioning continuously, the mind had only caught up moments ago. The sun hadn't quite reached its zenith and all brutal signs pointed towards mid morning.

It'd been some eight hours since their run in with the Two Ed's. Eight hours since wandering back up the hill from the beach, with vague memories of banging his knee against the small statue of Bacchus at the base of the garden steps…evil little fucker. The pain was clear, but the exactness of memory was forever committed to the time fog…. Having one's elders consistently drink you under the table was becoming a rather recurring, if not humbling experience. He might not yet walk with The King…but then there were more pressing concerns.

"Welcome back…" There was a definite hint of malice in her greeting.

"My God…did I die?"

"I bet you wish you did—*mug*."

He pulled himself up a bit, "I remember leaving the beach, lots of shouting, and," reaching down, "busting the *hell* out of my knee."

"You picked a fight with a statue—guess who won."

"Yeah, but how's *he* looking?"

"Remarkably the same…. Anyway, I patched you up. You should be able to get around."

He reached down, felt the bandage and the sudden rush of pain, "Did anyone survive?"

"The Ed's are fine. I saw them bright and early having breakfast out on the patio and working in their garden."

"You're kidding?"

"No, lightweight."

He sighed, "No lightweights here darling, only deadweight."

He pulled himself up against the small tree behind them and shot a look out to sea. Perhaps he'd taken it a bit too far last night? Partial blackouts were rather new to the rusticating equation. Either way, the vibe out at the point had suddenly become a bit *excessive*. And though his mind was scrambled, shattered, shot—some strange bit of clarity suddenly shone through.

"Let's go to Nice today," he said. "How about it?"

"Really? You going to be ok?"

He shrugged, "Yeah, it's nothing. I'll get dressed."

He hit the house while she sketched; drawing a triple shot from the Bitalli espresso lifeline and bringing it with him up to the shower. Within no time he was back on the driveway kick starting the yellow and black beast for its inaugural run into town.

Liam felt good and sure on the bike. French roads were tricky, French drivers not so good, out-of-towners on the tricky French roads with the not so good French drivers made for something downright frightening. A small nimble bike mixed with the proper shades of steely nerves and reckless abandon would just about make the nut he figured.

Moments later the Ducati was tearing out from the point, heading west along the Nice-Monaco junction. She leaned forward and dug in tight around his waist as they navigated the narrow winding roads hugging the water's edge. Back through the harbor at Villefranche, and stray, rambling memories of epochal boat thievery or some such thing; then past the long *Cap du Nice* with its lonely lighthouse sitting out at the end of the harbor wall. From there it was a straight shot down the hill into Nice along the *Promenade des Anglais*.

Nice sat along a gently curving crescent bay which ran about three miles as the kept gigolo flies, from the lighthouse at the harbor, to the airport runways on the far westerly end. From the water's edge the city rose along a low, sweeping set of hills which framed the town; from the tourist mecca along the strip, to the middle ground of modest to drab apartment buildings, till the last stretch of vista where the city's old elite dwelled magisterially in the *Cimiez* neighborhood.

Belle Époque mansions and the grand hotels of Nice lined the waterfront along the Promenade des Anglais. The promenade was an enormous thoroughfare, on a scale which reduced the likes of Grafton Street to something of a piddling alleyway. The interior was a dual carriageway for auto traffic and across the palm-lined dividers, nearer the water, was a pedestrian walkway spanning the entire length of the coast. Past the boardwalk was a long stretch of beach made up almost entirely of small uncomfortable stones and festooned with hundreds of blue and white beach chairs and umbrellas.

Christopher M. Basso

The young Americans made their way at the slow traffic crawl till they found a break and hitched the Ducati to a post near the old Negresco Hotel; the same address from whose faded red dome Oldcastle's carnival revelers would watch their paper king burn to renewal.

With a guide book in hand they set out, hearts full of vim and minds brimming with curiosity; sieves for the enlightenment of experience.

.... The Greeks had rolled up first of course; the temperate lands, sheltering skies, and a green thumb for olive orchards were their calling.... Followed of course by the Romans, a notably *ribald* bunch who generally crashed your party for a bit more than the postcard moments and horticultural delights. Hannibal and his elephantine hubris would pull a drive by on their way to meet the fates on the plains of Zama. The Saracens, Berbers, and Moors would all come later. Russian Czars and movie stars would bring up the rear—all finding the place and its climate more than agreeable. This perch had seen it all; war and strife, excess and plunder, a broad vista which swept out for two millennia.... An anathema of creepy moments, borne back ceaselessly from our past, projecting forward in the new currencies of easy decadence.

But perhaps this was just a wankish poetry of the first order...more bellyaching from a man who suddenly had sixteen rooms at his disposal for the storage of socks, and a limited edition AmEx Black that could make troublesome hookers disappear faster than the Romanovs at a May Day parade.

Just maybe that elusive proof was right in the pudding; that is to say, the young Americans presently hoofing it down the *Rue Jean Medicin* like a couple of sheep with a wolf at the door, beating a quick path back to the safety of the bike.

"Damn," he shook his head, kicking the Ducati into gear, "Can you *believe* this friggin' hole?"

She just shrugged, "Like bizarro Vegas...on psychotropics."

"And I fucking hate Vegas." He added, edging out into traffic.

She thought about it, "You've never been to Vegas."

"Never investigated the Queen's skivvies like Sir Walter Raleigh either, but I'll trust my instincts in these things."

".... I don't think I've ever heard a waiter use the word 'pig' when taking an order," she mused. "That was *massive* restraint you showed by the way. I've seen you go Bonzo over less."

He gunned the engine, "Yes, well, discretion is my new goal to soul."

They'd hatched this plan of exodus about twenty minutes earlier standing in line at the closest thing to a Starbucks, surrounded by a bunch of bewildered tourists types perhaps contemplating the same. Sharp elbows, dirty looks, and cheeky service were the red lanterns to flee this place with all attendant haste.

Nice was a strange place indeed. From up on high, right down to the Rorschach test which greeted you as you slouched into town. One man's pomp and glitz was just as soon another's bad trip down the ladder on some Mescita Sunshine Gold.... If the essence of all things was truly in the eye of the beholder, then quite possibly this place *was* the primal scene; your mother's *vagine*, bearing down on you deep in the REM cycle, with the "Guernica" flaming horses and shattered spears.... Well, that might have been stretching it a bit, but in every hyperbole was the grain of truth.

But then again, that was only if you let the place *get* to you. If you had the knack to roll with it, it could suit you well. But for that certain someone who finds a modesty in their excess this place might have been the equilibrium of delusion—wedged up nicely between a world of vast inequity.... That or some strange time warp-time share back to the pre-Crash, pre-Axis of Evil, end of the century crowd, when the worse thing to sweat was a couple of extra zeros on your computer's clock.

A case could probably be made it was a fine and decent place in the off-season once the marauding herds had thinned,

Christopher M. Basso

but on a hot humid August day there were better things you could be doing with your "vacation" then dueling blood matches for overpriced tables at a café, and angling for airplane quality elbow room along the Promenade des Anglais.... You say you want the beach? It's only footsteps away; just gird up with some jellies for the stones, or take the hedonist's route and freeball it—orthopedically speaking. Don't feel bad to call it an ugly thing, only a broke dick dog or a hedonist would embrace such vagaries with a smile.... Would you like a chair? Bring some Euros 'cause the blue deck chairs aren't free, and for that matter neither is the beach; at least not in the stretches where some pretense to glitz has cordoned off a patch of rock to keep out the undesirables, which may or may not mean *you*. Don't let it get to you though; with Heinekens running $15 a throw this is a hard won buzz.

    It's that sort of atavistic set up where temporal, spatial inconveniences are only exacerbated by some Gallic assclown with his hands knuckle deep in your pockets at each and every break of dawn and bend of bay. That's why those *in the know* avoid this place at all costs, or at least kept it to the occasional excursion up the river now and then before retreating to the small towns and villages ringed along the fringe; where everybody might not know your name, but at least the sodomy comes with a kinder gentler fist.

    .... It's a strange place the Riviera; to quote a man, "where the absurd courts the vulgar." A culmination of disparate images revealed only in steely little moments of clarity. But what was the point of stressing *that* the boy thought, as he steered the bike out of the downtown and pointed it laser quick up towards the highway; this was a *vacation* after all, not some heavy power to the people/working class hero expedition. Hell, that kind of noise would just about kill anyone's buzz, and with those Heinekens running $15 a round it was a precious buzz at that.... Best to look the other way; and set your blameless gaze to sundry fields afar.

    But what's the eye to make of the general incongruity to things? A glance across the promenade was all you needed: middle class families vibing some sunshine, North African immigrants busting their asses in the kitchens of the sidewalk cafés, and all the while, young beautiful eye candy stripped down to bare tops and dental floss bottoms, draped across the decks of the Illuminati's yachts out in the harbor, twenty feet from the sunshine vibing families, swilling overpriced Coca-Cola's and minute streaks, hootched up by the hunched down immigrants in the sweat sheen kitchen of some French snack shack, one step ahead of *the authorities* hell bent on shipping them back to some hellish Kasbah to answer to the local mullah.

.... Every soul under the judgmental gaze of another; appraisals, revulsions, envies, fear and loathing; the cosmic gamut of all naughty niceties bankrolled out past the point of questioning...fucking whacky indeed. All the more reason to scope the blinders and keep it right in front of you, sipping your $15 beer that this astronomical planetary debt has brought about. But *enjoy* your bit, the place was tailor made to sweep the clarity under the rug if only for a bit longer. Best to just do your business quick and nip back to a hidden seclusion, sipping your wine with the shades drawn, thanking your blessed stars you're not out there, riding bitch, on life's privy.

.... What did old *Fritz* make of the scene he wondered? Little bit different back in the day, particularly in the dental floss ass-wear department, but a sliver of song remained the same. Moody bastard that Nietzsche, came down here eight winters in a row they say. But if that leidernitz and his crotchety syphilitic drip could make heads or tails of this scene, maybe there was something to it? Some heretofore unseen clarity that might tie the place together like Lebowski's pee stained rug.

O'Shea pointed the bike north, tearing up the hills through the city, past the detritus mingling with the glitz till they hit the main highway just north of town. He paid the toll with what amounted to a good night's take at the blackjack tables and ginned the Ducati to its true Thoroughbred potential. Blessedly, all traces of city ended almost immediately as they lit out on a western tear through the sunshine and wide-open spaces towards the heart of Provence.

He kept the bike straight down the centerline, restraining any urges for a little shake and bake with the traffic; instead preferring to take in the scenery. The Provencal Massif was rising quickly to greet them. This massive limestone "shelf" was something of an attraction down here. It ran from Avignon in the North all the way down to the edge of the sea. Woven in between was a massive system of canyons, rivers, and gorges that the French could in all good conscience compare to that rather large hole out in Arizona.

The stone ridges were a wavering darkish color with tufts of wild grass, white moss, and lichen growing out from the rock faces; this as a whole, mixed with the tricks of the sun, cast the Massif in an almost purple hue which ran from one end of the horizon to the other. To have seen the Massif from the air would have revealed a broad expanse of canyons and steep gorges, with small rivers and streams snaking in and out, cut through the heart of tall sentinel walls.

That was the horizon. In the near ground the action came in fits and starts. Just flashes of color here and there, as the traces of man's busy hand began to fade. By the time they'd reached the little village of *Salernes*, the beauty of the country had revealed its truest expression; burnt fields of red and orange clay lined the valley on both sides of the road. Dark rich soils, freshly tilled for the coming year, hedged against wild tufts of sea grass and meadow, and in between a palette worth of wildflowers and bramble woven in delicate ochre's and Castilian reds.... All of these things were but a lovely overture to the endless fields before them covered in dark purple lavender.

Lavandula dentata, Provence's bread and butter, aesthetically and commercially speaking; probably a good twenty thousand acres of the stuff—the lavender growing capital of the world. But the brain was only used to dealing with God's purple in small, measured doses; little dots of Blue Aster and Wild Jasmine here and there, but nothing on this scale. Confronted with endless vistas of the stuff, stretching from your hand to the horizon, required a reordering of the senses—a very pleasant sort of reboot letting you know you'd arrived in what one could call *good country.*

The scenery was almost too much to take, especially at a crisp seventy-five mph or so, too much for the eyes to focus on, too much for the brain to focus in.... This could in fact be the penultimate moment to the sensory overload of the last few weeks; the near penumbra to the shadows of a weathered brain. The gin and juice were but the grease for the skids; this rush of the natural kind might just push the spiritual teetotaler in O'Shea right over the edge.

Luckily man had an answer; rising up quick from the dusty hills near Aix was the "Carrefour hypermarche". The suburban kids in them couldn't quite resist the siren's pull of the massive French supermarket; calling to them, like some commercial megalopolis amid a sea of tranquil, desolate beauty.

Raised right on Elysian Fields, they could only avoid what was burned into their nature for so long. They roamed the vast aisles loading up on cheese and bread, some olive oil, and a few bottles of the fine local vintage before lighting off again—the Ducati's saddlebags stuffed with their take.

They quit the highway near *Manosque* and officially entered off the beaten path territory. A series of picture postcard moments began drifting past in the wind scream blur; a small village at *La Verdière*, the fragments of a Roman road across the Verdun, and the ghostly spires of a railroad trestle dynamited by the retreating Germans during the time of the great unpleasantness.... The land froze all these things, be they sin or sanguine, into something which merely incorporated their limited narrative. It was a bilious insult to the hand of man who thought he tilled the rudder on such things. But here he was merely passing through, smited by something which regarded him with a fated, elegant indifference.

Outside of *Valensole* they bought homemade honey from an old woman who sold from a stand in the dusty road beside her farm. A large truffle sow sat in the shade nearby, keeping her company and sniffing happily the will o' the wisps carrying on the summer wind.... Agrarian life—Jefferson said it best, too bad no one really listened.

At a petrol station trapped somewhere forty years in the past, the man working the rusted pump recommended keeping down the eastern road, through the small village until they reached *Moustiliers* and the massive system of gorges along the Verdun River.

Christopher M. Basso

"Just like the Grand Canyon," he said proudly in friendly, broken English.

"He made us as Americans." Liam shouted over his shoulder as they tore down the road.

"What do you think gave it away?" She shouted back.

But the old codger wasn't playing around. When they cleared the small rises near *St. Marie* the first panoramas came into view; sheer vertical walls and jagged granite cliffs shooting straight up into the sky…. Humbling stuff from below, but must have given a king hell fright trapped up in the mix. He would be finding out soon enough.

Lonely trees and wildflowers dotted the cliff walls, shading them in strange patterns and random bursts of color, with bits of lichen and white moss dashed across the rocks in nature's approximation of a Pollock free for all. A bright turquoise river snaked through the base of the gorge, like a shade strangely out of place, resembling something more at home on a beach in the tropics. But the sheer scale of this enterprise only came into view as they rounded up the last narrow lane, with nary the guardrail separating them from either the rustic beauty of nature's finest perch *or* some absolute bit of Euro-themed terror—depending on which way your thrill seeking door swung.

Now *this* was more like it, he thought. The kind of adrenaline you just couldn't contrive. He leaned into each nasty curve and roller coaster chute with the focus of a man sure and right in his chosen element; not merely a series of empty gestures calling themselves a life, but quite literally the expression of the fine line between life and the *other* thing.

Though that was not quite his to say, and *true* free will was the dominion of lonelier men indeed. Rather, he steeled the nerves and took an extra measure of care guiding the bike and its precious backseat cargo through the demon hills along the tail of a dragon—caught somewhere between silly, ass-tickling abandonment and the sad realization of the tosser he'd become…. But a more pleasant resignation he would never know.

Finally came the reprieve, a broad piece of flat rock just above the dark waters of the *Lac St. Croix*, the effluent where the fine turquoise of the river resolved to the deeper shades. High along the eves, with the grand sweeping views all around, they laid out their picnic lunch on a stretch of tall grass wedged up against the canyons walls. A fine piece of land overlooking the tributaries and a series of descending pools, all slowly working their way down the canyon to the lake below. A *swim* would definitely be in order.

With the fresh scent of Earth and flower all around them, the crisp light of sun and chance in the mix, this seemed about the place to be; pain au chocolat for the gullet and ripe French cheese for the nip; the bottles of *Chateau Virant* smartly shelved till later that evening. Caffeine and nicotine would have to make the nut till they reached the safety of the other side.

Liam almost always had the nervous appetite of a wolf, tearing quick into his food like it might be his last, failing to find the pleasure in the leisurely contemplation of these things.

"Slow down," she would scold him.

"It's my nature," was often the charming reply through a mouthful of bread.

And to his credit, or detriment, this was not far off. A nervous mind, always looking for the next distraction to keep the larger contemplations safely on the horizon…. Had he appeared twenty years later, the Dr. Spock's of the world might have dosed him with enough Ritalin to put the freeze on Mandingo, but in yet another age, a kinder gentler age, they might simply have billed him a curious man of infinite industry and gone on their merry way. But his mind, whatever the disposition, could still find the narrowness of purpose, particularly in matters of want and expediency. And at the moment those cool waters below looked awfully inviting.

After dispatching the last of the Bûcheron and baguettes they waded out into one of the sheltered pools for a quick dip. Liam went down for the hollows, rubbing his hands along the smooth stones at the bottom. Nice and cold, just the type of thing they might have called *bracing* back when refrigeration and illumination were on every Provencal bumpkin's wish list; a

Christopher M. Basso

primer which would more than steel the nerves for the wind whipped dry-down awaiting them on the ride home. A bit chilling at that, but no matter; merely another manifestation of the *true grit* vibe he'd been rocking since about Amsterdam, when a great many of these effete, charming things suddenly, and rather inexplicably, ceased being altogether charming and effete.

Since then it had become a bit more of a contest, a contest to strive for that something just out there, just beyond his grasp; or so he thought as they splashed around the small pool with the grand view. An itch you could never scratch…bad odds tanglin' with that kind of noise—diversions were needed.

Fine enough spot he thought, taking in his surroundings, the mind quickly going guttural, perfect place for a little game of bury the hatchet where the nail won't rust. He glanced over at the patient…but she seemed blissfully unaware. Just as well, he sighed, doubtful it would have come to pass. Yes, he was definitely in the bad place, that strange middle ground of knowing you've sinned, but knowing not just…quite…where.

And what's one to do when their vibe has become a bit stale? Not the most polite of things; dragging others down into the morass as you take a walk on the wild side…. To be the blackness reaching out for the blackness; a proud yearbook caption this was not.

She suddenly broke the sad boy jamboree with a quick sneak attack from the side, taking him by the shoulder and sending him down to corruption, before he spun about and quickly returned the favor. They came up and shared a glance for a moment, a bit of the friendly *High Noon* in their countenances, but there was something missing in her eyes, the something that forever underwrote the silliness of it all, something always offering the penance…. And so maybe these things just come to pass; one perfectly at home in the moment, the other forever in the apprehension thereof, and in a greater sense perhaps the overtures of innocence keeping that intimacy of trust forever safely on the horizon… What an epic bitch when you've misplayed your hand on a *cosmic* level.

As they left the pool for a bit of sun time she noticed something in the distance, his Saint Christopher's medallion floating on the water, drifting with the slight riffles in the current, moving ever closer to the ledge and the steep drop below.

"Liam, your necklace thingy."

Had she been regarding the fine trees, the sweeping view, or the mad dog bulge in his trunks she might just have easily missed it. For his own part, the boy wouldn't have noticed till the rare occasion he occasioned the shower those days. No matter, he shot back across the rocks like a fey man fast stepping orphans for the last boat on the Titanic, dodging the gaps and making for the ledge, but by now old Saint Christopher had crested over the side…and the very reverent Liam O'Shea with him.

Sara could feel her heart drop as she raced back across the slippery rocks, frantically scanning the walls of the vast canyon below; her mind flashed in a frozen terror…. But there, about six feet down, with back up against the rocks and the fast water rushing over him, sat the whelp. One foot to the right and he could've added iconographic BASE-jumping to his many varied vacation talents. His general state was hard to suss through the runoff, but she could just make out the faintest of smiles as he held up his hand, adorned with one errant bit of iconic belief.

She reached down and helped drag him back over the top where he came to rest under the shale overhang near the ledge; now safe from all things including himself. He held the medal close to his chest for a moment, cursing something under breath, before carefully placing it in his pocket and lying back on the stones.

"What were you thinking?" She shouted.

"I wasn't."

"You almost went over the side!"

He looked up from the daze, "I thought I did?"

She stared at the boy for a moment, her voice softening slightly, "Look, I know that thing means a lot to you, but you've got to be more careful—you're going to get yourself killed."

"Don't worry darling," he smiled, "who's got a thicker skull than me? Hell I could fall off *ten* of these."

"Not funny." She sat down taking a deep breath. "You don't need a medal, you need a minder."

He rubbed his knee, suddenly on fire, "Patron saint of travelers *my ass*."

"Jesus Liam, you're bleeding."

He'd opened another nice gash just below his knee, matching the other from last night's playtime with The Ed's. A steady stream of crimson ran down into the water resolving to a dullish brown.

"…. You ok?"

His eyes trailed off a bit, "Well, I've been better." He studied the small pool of blood forming in the still water.

"Working on the stigmata?" She smiled.

"Yeah, halfway home."

"Get over here, let me clean that."

He turned to his side and felt the first twinge of shooting pain; the pleasant comforts of shock would soon be a memory.

"Lay it on me woman, I can take it."

Regrettably, mobile triage on the side of a French mountain consisted of a bottle of Purell and a few stray napkins. While this was still a damn site better than her rain forest days it was going to be ugly all the same. She patched him up as best she could; at the very least she stopped the bleeding.

"You want to head back?" He finally said. "It's going to take awhile."

"All right…. You sure you're ok?"

By then the rosy vim and ass grab jowl had returned to his step.

"Don't I look it?"

It was a straight shot down the other end of the hills to the coast. No more of this silly, death defying, curve-themed business. He gave her his sweatshirt for the chill, kicked it into gear, and pointed home. The howling wind scream helped staunch the wound quite nicely, and what the wind couldn't mend, hypothermia took care of the rest.

As the vagaries of chance would have it, the route through Cannes was the quickest way back to the Cape. He put the spurs to the mule as they tore back towards the growing chorus of evening lights along the coast, and by the time they hit the first row of lanterns on the *Boulevard de la Croisette,* O'Shea was feeling right as rain. They slowly cruised the main drag in Cannes, past The Carlton and Majestic; the grand hotels dominating the pretty skyline, and past the casinos and harbor, all immaculately neat and ordered. The sandy beaches had cleared out and a steady stream of people were filling up the bars and cafes along the water.

From the center of town it was a quick 5th gear burn back to the outskirts of Nice. This was the point of the day, or the endeavor, when the kick of elation has been spent completely, and the rush of wind from a fast moving bike becomes little more the tedious chore of moving from A to B. He kept the Ducati rambling along at a steady clip down the Promenade des Anglais, back through hell town, till they reached the more civilized environs of Villefranche once again.

With the soul sucking grime of Nice properly off the skin, and the Negresco safely in the rearview, he could feel himself winding down a bit; all else fading to a pleasant stillness as they rounded the last bend into Villefranche proper. The village was beautiful in the early evening, uncrowded with an easy breeze, and a small farmer's market set up along the old square by the waterfront. He parked the bike along the sea wall and headed into the Esso Mart for some aspirin and a couple of Red Bulls; the fruits of thrill-seeking gimpdom were coming on fast.

Sara wandered off into the market near the back of the square. She slowly strolled the aisles of neat and ordered stands, each sheltered under blue and white striped canopies, past bustling arrangements of flowers and honey, perfumed soaps and marzipan candies.

Christopher M. Basso

Liam reappeared from the Esso Mart, *vice replete*, and stopped to pet a German Shepherd puppy tied to the railing outside. Eager fellow was wagging his tail and seemed very much in need of a friend so the boy took a seat to keep him company. He popped his aspirin and chased it with the high-octane caffeine before leaning back on the railing to take in the scene.

A street artist type sat beneath a shady umbrella near the water's edge surrounded by a collection of rather excellent sketches. Liam studied the older man for a moment; a fellow in no particular hurry to sell his wares and looking rather at ease under the sun in a floppy oversized hat.... Obviously not a volume-generating gig here, but the look of contentment on his grizzled suntanned face spoke to something else. It was a look the boy envied, but one he could probably never share.

He thought to go over and buy one of the drawings. They were stills mostly, some of the local countryside and many more of the tableaux along the coast. He could buy a few and ship them home; something that would always remind him of this place, if not quite the way it made him feel. Sadly the man didn't take credit, only gold, and the boy rolled a bit light in that anachronism these days. But he made a mental note to find this man again before he left.

.... He wasn't so quick to rejoin her though; time to let the mischiefs and medicines do their thing. Besides, O'Shea was happy enough to be alone; a tried and tested milieu for an only child, no fear in the solitude, only peace.

He sat back as the happy pup nipped at his fingers, but always keeping the beloved just within his sights as she passed along the edges of the *Place Amelie de Polanais* market; a gentle expression flashing through the blue and white shaded shadows and the bits of failing sun.

He set the shot in his mind; her walking past the flower stands by the church at the water's edge. He worked best in pictures, they made him happy or at the very least not sad. They were simple uncluttered things. His mind otherwise struggled with these overworked circadian rhythms, a cluttered mojo of explanations laboring for the source; looking for that screaming wing nut back in the prime numbers.

Life was a fair amount of screaming into the wind tunnel. The last few years had given him that one. He liked to keep it simple these days; the still and simple honesty of an image held a special place for him. Otherwise, what was left; a sense of dread brokered by a greater sense of reverent propriety which kept the worst of it on the inside, and the only expressions deemed socially acceptable were wanton acts of a most disorganized recklessness.... Which at worst made him seem an unmitigated loon, and at best gave him the tragic airs of a failed nobility. Neither of which were the stuff of lordly headstones.

With a cool and easy precision he froze the moment in his mind—the way she passed through the market in the clean sunset light, the flowers and the scents of peppermint and lavender; a smiling, knowing look on her face and some secret all her own. A snapshot he hoped to recall some distant day; when snapshots would be the only things left.

Hindsight's an Achilles heel; *premonition* was the only way back to blessed Ithaca.... Another of Fighting Fintan's eloquent barroom non-sequiturs, the ones which usually earned him a free round, or the polite insinuation to leave the pub. His nephew trafficked increasingly in a similar sort of static; from standstills in the tempest, to the rambling jazz of being naïve enough to still embrace the very demure of being so immature. Hindsight's a dog; the harbinger of perspective, a gruff and grizzled thing, hand me down generational harangues from once lovely souls gone to pot with the weathered advance age; ugly souls wrapped in too much drink and too many cigarettes.... But not in memory, not in snapshots. Keep your eyes closed a bit longer, a life of ripples on a clean blank shore.... Everything perfect in a dream.

Nearby, several men from the Beauregard Hotel were out along the short stretch of beach raking the sand in nice clean lines for tomorrow's crowds. Had to hand it to these little towns, he thought, they truly took a certain zeal in keeping things orderly and presentable. Unlike the dubious charms and hot weather jungle rot of Nice, these trendy outlying villages prided themselves on a prim neatness. No trash or graffiti, no chaos—just order, commerce, and a charmed aesthetic.

His eyes flashed briefly to their table at the Cosmo from the night before; bad rhythms suddenly entering the mix, vaguely sinister memories of Brigadoon hippie know-it-alls magically appearing to entice innocent souls into degenerate boat thievery.... Jesus, was this his life? Perhaps just the proverbial youth being served?

But what to do when not so youthful? He glanced out to the harbor and had a laugh. Shit, maybe he would've tried it on at that? Well, perhaps not—but damn man, at least take it right up to the edge, show these bourgeois swine you mean *business*.

At the moment several of said behemoths sat superciliously out in the harbor, any one of them making a fine candidate for a quick trip down the shallow rocks. Big bastards; the kind that might've made the Pharaohs blush, that is, if those crusty fuckers sailed.... The brass plate on one in particular caught his eye; *Erebus*, in shiny arrogant cursive along the side. An arrogance abetted by a small horde of buff deck boys who emerged deck side sans tops—hinting at a whole nether level of hubris dwelling behind the pulled shades of the velvet jet set mafia which ruled the place like the Borgias with better fashion sense and a finer set of toys.... These dirty old cats generally liked to "refresh" the crew at each new port of call; usually loading up a mobile narcotics lab and enough Benzedrine to electrify the field at the Kentucky Derby.... And gold stars all around for being the seediest players on an already seedy field.

"Well well well," Liam muttered to himself, over his pervert's shades and under his own *below deck* peccadilloes. Just keep looking the other way, everyone does.... Yes indeed, the absurd courts the vulgar—take a swig of the foul energy drink and pet the innocence at your feet.

She came up behind him cradling a small bundle of wildflowers and a straw basket full of bright red strawberries.

"For dessert?" She smiled.

"Hmm, sounds about right.... Who we going to call on tonight?"

"How about some *Pissaladière?*" She accented Frenchwise, knowing O'Shea's grim horror for the local favorite of anchovies and caramelized onions slathered on thick pizza dough.

"Ooh, sounds like a winner…" He rose from the curb bidding his new friend a quick goodbye, "How about that Spanish place then, the one I read about?"

"Still on the Iberian kick I see?"

"A one star Michelin tapas takeaway—what's not to like?"

"What's not to like indeed."

"…. Yep," he took a deep breath of the fine sea air, "you can't beat this place."

"I'm going to miss it." She agreed in a not so agreeable way.

He basked in the glow of the setting sun, "Let's just make us a pact never to leave?"

"Sure," she said, "We'll just stay here forever."

"Really?"

"Yeah, we can open a pottery shop with the Two Ed's."

He frowned, "Pottery…can they drink the clay? I was thinking more a nice winery up in the hills?"

"The three of you? We'd never produce a barrel."

"No c'mon, we'll call it…*Château du Mal Voisin*. It'll be grand."

"Let's just start with dinner and maybe we'll work our way up to the Scott and Zelda fantasies?"

"Ok, so long as I get to be the drunk one."

In short order they emerged from the Casa Bardeo with enough Andalusian goodies to orbit the far side of La Mancha. Now clearly overburdened with bags and booze, a quick decision was made to ditch the bike till morning and hike back to the point. Sunlight and sobriety would hopefully remedy any of the directionally challenged misadventures from earlier in the week.

Christopher M. Basso

Walking down the old quay road was like entering the quiet shadows of a rather loud buzz—laughter drifting in and out from the cafes, the low clang of boats in the harbor and the sounds of children playing out on the sandy coves lining their path. They kept along the sea wall until the last of the palms and tall cedars were behind them.

And then, almost at once, the whole of the coast was revealed in panorama; a massive crescent shaped illumination that stretched as far as the eye could see. The breadth of which was something beautiful, but maybe more so was the thought, *the knowing*, that a whole lot of "something" was going down—the life and energy of thousands of random souls colliding about, and you were but a small part of it.

A Zennish sort of Gestalt piece that could keep you chipper-humble about your place in things…that is until you crossed the Pont St. Jean and drifted back into the high walled stillness of Mr. Kurtz country, where the AmEx cards cut the stillness like rusty machetes and the used Botox needles were the pikes for the "taken" heads…. Navigating along the paths of a quietly enforced stillness was to be caught between the devil and the deep blue sea, at least until they hit the friendly environs of their open minded hippie ideal out on the point, where they would be enveloped by the sheltering sky and the strange paternal Ouroboros embrace of the Two Ed's.

But amid the setting sun and the heady sense of righteousness there was but one remedy for such an incongruence of want versus wantonness…

"What the hell is wrong with you?" She asked, nervously looking about.

"Have a slash, you'll feel better for it."

"No, I'm housebroken actually."

Liam, who had taken to urinating on his neighbor's property when the coast was clear, and even when it wasn't—pulled over to a large Cyprus and did his bit with an enviable Rudolph Nureyev grace and nary the wasted drop. Such trips to the sandbox were met with a withering eye and rising anger from his beloved who kept watch nearby.

"C'mon, lighten up," he assured her. "Think about it—you've got Italian media potentate types living in French mansions guarded by German Shepherds—it's like the Goddamn Vichy crew all over again."

There was no reply from the peanut gallery.

"I can only take that silence as a sympathetic nod to your Teutonic forbearers?" He zipped up with dramatic flourish, "Still some blood from that stone which needs *repaying*, if you catch my drift?"

Which was met with a stony silence; a stony silence not broken till the tapas were spread across the balcony table and the loving cup started flowing. The boy had grabbed a nice bottle of white from the man in town; a bright crisp Vignoier, from deep in the heart of van Gogh country. His sins were apparently many and his penances regrettably few, but within no time they were back to their old chatty selves; the sun, the moon, the stars, whatever discourse might cross their fancy.

They stayed out on the balcony till late in the night, with the good crisp wine and the pleasant scents from the garden drifting up through their house. They played a few hands of Hearts and watched the fisherman head out for the night, as the faint strains of *Nessun Dorma* carried across the lawn from the Two Ed's.

Sometime after midnight Liam was out by garden shed tossing bags of trash into the nifty stone bins when something sprung from the shadows to give him a wine addled start.... For a moment he pondered the terrible possibility that one of the pee stained grocery clerks had come to collect the bill, but the boy quickly regained his senses, breaking it down to a fine crouching tiger pose that would've done Elvis' "Senpai" black belt proud.

"En garde bitches!"

He peered hard into the darkness before easing off a bit.

".... You again?" He smiled at the big orange cat, "Shit man, you almost gave me a heart attack."

Sara wandered out onto the porch, the sounds of struggle and a crashing in the bushes having roused her from her magazine.

"Who's your friend?"

"I don't know, he *accosted* me the other day down on the sea road—held me up for my egg and cheese brioche."

"You gave a cat eggs and cheese?"

"Does that look like a cat do you?"

She sized him up, "That's debatable I suppose."

"Yeah, he came at me from the garden this time, yes sir, I thought was a goner...like one of those African lions; gets you from the *trees*."

"Those would be Indian Tigers—Monsieur Animal Planet."

"Whatever."

O'Shea kneeled down and gave the old boy a scratch under the chin. A slight guttural wheezing purr ensued.

"A homeless cat on the Riviera," Liam smiled. "Don't know whether to feel bad or envy you?"

"Careful Liam," she cautioned, "he might give you the plague."

"Bitosh," he said to the malcontent spewing wisdom over his shoulder. "I thought you WASPs *loved* animals?"

"Only when they aren't out to *get us*, look at him—he's kind of busted."

"He is at that."

The busted cat jumped up on the old moss covered wall, looking about, unabashed and utterly unashamed.

"He's got personality, I'll give him that." She said.

".... What do you say my man; you want to come back to New York? We'll clean you up nice." He then offered up the sweetest of carrots, "You won't have to be French anymore." He almost sang the last part.

"Ugh, I don't think the plane would get off the ground."

Liam looked over his shoulder, "Well then, we'll just take a boat—and *everyone* can be happy."

She studied the cat a bit longer, "…. Poor bugger does look kind of hungry?"

"Yeah, I bet it's been a good ten minutes since his last."

With that, O'Shea stepped back in the house and returned with the remains of their meal; a rather expensive little potpourri of cat treats: chorizo in sherry, salted cod, patatas bravas, and some Manchego cheese—all on the fine bone china of course.

"Mr. Henri would have a coronary if he saw that."

"That's what I'm counting on dear."

The fat man tucked in heartily.

"I think you've just established a regular here," she said. "What'll we call him?"

Liam studied the cat, "I'm thinking—Bruiser?"

"*That's lame.*" She smiled, "…How about, Crookshanks?"

"Yeah, why not just Garfield then?" He shot back. "How about Oldcastle?"

"What's that?"

"Just has a nice ring to it."

"All right then," she said, "Oldcastle, the busted cat."

"Well, let's leave him to it."

They walked back inside leaving the screen door slightly ajar; should Oldcastle require seconds, or perhaps the use of Mr. Henri's Chippendale chairs to spruce up the claws. O'Shea was suddenly happier than he'd been in ages, finding some manner of crudely elegant equilibrium along the Riviera.

He killed the lights and started up the stairs as Oldcastle the cat—John's spiritual brother from another mother sat along the low stone wall; plump and busted, chowing a feast of salt cod and sherry chorizo, laid out on the finest of East India Company china, under a blanket of stars that fell from the clear bells of the heavens to the unbroken line at the horizon.

Christopher M. Basso

Chapter Six
Beetlebum

There was static at first, just a din in the background that slowly came into focus, and then there was sound. Two men stood in the anteroom of a tall gilded bedchamber dwelling magisterially over the decaying bones of some industrial wasteland; the glorious red wash of a fiery sunset spilled through the windows behind them.

"*I would have expected you sooner?*" The older man spoke first, a slight trace of fear in his voice.

"*.... It's not an easy thing to meet your maker.*" The younger man stared him down, his eyes burning cold shades of blue.

"*There is nothing to fear here,*" he smiled, "*after all, what am I if not you?*"

The young man cut him off, "*Can you repair the things you make?*"

"*I have that power yes,*" his demeanor stiffened, an imperious arrogance returning, "*slight corrections here and there.*"

"*.... I had in mind something a little more radical.*"

"*.... What's the nature of this problem?*"

The young man smiled, "*The nature? Why, death of course.*"

Christopher M. Basso

O'Shea's eyes shot open from a quick dilation to the finest of points. "Goddamn," he muttered looking about the room. He wiped the sweat from his brow and drew hard for a breath, but nothing's there, nothing would come. He shot up in bed, righting himself against the headboard, determined to ride this thing out. And then it arrives; the next moment; the one where an unknowable expectation runs its course and the stillness returns. The wind blows gently through the room, the television drones away in the corner on the late show is getting later, and one man regains his footing so to speak. He clicked off the remote—quite a thing those first few seconds of terror straining to remember where you are...decaying villa, deranged Mayblossom senility, the South of France—affirmative.

He looked over at Sara, turned on her side facing him, studying her for a moment in the pale ghostly light; her face the content expression of a private grace somewhere very far away....As for his own, the breaths were still shallow in the coming; like a body remembering how. Steady yourself boyo, hold the center, the rest will come.

He gently slid off the bed and into his sandals and headed downstairs, stopping only at the window's edge to blow out a forgotten candle. He kept his footsteps swift and still as he made his way through the silent house; arriving in the dimly lit kitchen. The boy swung open the heavy doors to the Sub-Zero and peered in...with not much peering back. That lousy cat had made off with the best of it. Just some artisan crackers and a bit of the Manchego cheese left to set a feast.

That would have to do. He grabbed his snack and searched through the drawers for a knife.... *Manchego*; from the milk of the La Mancha sheep—supposed to be Cervantes favorite...where had he read that? The La Mancha Dairy Cooperative no doubt—but pay no mind, try to ignore the winsome bits of rubbish the 2 a.m. mind traffics in.

He sat by the windows facing the sea, half-heartedly spearing bits of food with a few sips from a cold Heineken in between.... Lovely out there he thought, bright night, hardly a cloud in the sky, moonlight casting the waters in a pale greenish hue; the whole of the coast lit from his window.

The tall cedars rustled in the yard; their shadows casting enormous on the walls behind him. Nearby the sound of wind chimes danced softly in the breeze. From across the bay he could see the outlines of the airport and the approach lights flashing in silent rhythmic precision.... Shades of renegade film noir all around; saturated colors washed to their essentials, mingling with the dark moving shadows of a vaguely reassuring grace...a rare night indeed.

Well, that about settled it then. He shelved the snack and rummaged through his nearby bag, looking for his smokes but finding something else. Feeling a tad *invigorated* he slammed his beer and slid like a pair of ragged claws silently out the door and down the long face of the lawn.

From down by the water the old villa looked peaceful in the night, the stray lights from within cast in diffuse shadows along the darkened walls, as the sounds of crickets chirped in the darkness. Several candles from dinner still burned along the edge of the balcony, the faint wisps of flame swaying ever so slightly in the breeze. An unwavering stillness had settled over his borrowed home; just the fine and perfect rhythms of cosmos and creation in harmony. A calm interrupted only by the darkened shape of a man strolling out from the shadows near his garden.

O'Shea started down the long edge of the lawn, past the tall trees and lush gardens, with just the faintest etchings of a half moon drifting in and out from behind a cloud. He walked past the edge of his pool, lit bright from the footlights below, only the slight whirl of the motor audible above the sounds of the surf against the rocks. With each passing step one grew louder while the other trailed off to a fainter and fainter disregard.

He kept down the stony path with only the faint purple light of the shade globes to guide him. From the water's edge his dark silhouette cast its own shadows against the slate colored rocks as the scent of orange trees and wild jasmine rose up to greet him. He looked back to the house and across the small inlet separating his and the Ed's villas. As pro forma, their lights were all a' blazing and their lawn strewn with last night's West Egg for two detritus. No green lights on this pier though, just the faint sounds of Puccini; the low wattage lullabies to their high-octane lifestyle.

Christopher M. Basso

"…. *Eccentric mothers,*" he mumbled.

And from his own house, just the dying light of a few faint candles, all else a darkened quiet stillness. The half crumpled portico, the weary face of resignation, the rows of ivy draped down the sides, the measured expression of a timeless contemplation.

He kept a steady hand along the smooth stone wall. Just a slight slip here, a hasty misstep there, and a storied introduction to those twenty centuries of stony sleep waited below. He peered over the side down to the water's edge…. Something beautiful and ominous; black grayness and the dim blue light on the horizon, the water shading through warm to cold and back again…the elemental elements lining up—beauty and a cold brutishness, fear and liftoff.

To the east he could see the low lights of Beaulieu and Eze-Bord-de-Mer hugging the crescent arc of the coast. He let his eyes wander up the mad philosopher's trail, straight up to the mountain perch at Eze, and wondered how he'd ever hauled his weary bags of bones up it…. Further out, a sea of flickering lights, Monaco, maybe even Menton; casino stragglers, midnight riders, long tongued liars—no one sleeps to be sure.

He stripped off his shirt and sandals and dove in with only a pair of cargo shorts and a healthy sense of self. A forgotten pack of cigarettes and a silver flask bearing the heretic heraldry of the father of this feast dwelled nicely within one of the twenty-six or so pockets.

The boy was in a *fine* mood, tumbling down into the dark blue-green waters, reveling in that bracing shock that reboots the senses. He shot up from the first blast, quickly corrected, and had a look about…. Yep, he could hear it clearly now—*Pagliacci* rolling down the lawn from the Two Ed's:

Ridi, Pagliaccio,
sul tuo amore infranto!
Ridi del duol, che t'avvelena il cor!

He swam back to the water's edge and found footing on the smooth stones ringing the tiny pier. The lights from below cast the sea in bright green shades tinged with the elemental and ethereal. He had another swig from the flask and stared in dumb wonderment up the lawn towards his neighbor's house...wafer moons, gestures of formal farewell, and large havin' it motherfuckers.

But then his mind returned to the matter at hand; humid night such as this, what with these warm currents...might just be time to go the Full Monty? But then again, what to do with the flask? Leave it on shore? That went without saying was something of an impossibility; besides, lots of o' room in these shorts for such things, and for some reason extra space seemed critical at the time.

Who knows, maybe just lash it around the old wedding tackle—*guerilla style*. He deftly pondered the anatomical feasibilities for a moment, feeling about ready to bestride the colossus, but once again vastly overestimating his own, uh, *shortcomings*.

John Holmes? Maybe not, but he could smile the warm affirmation-confirmation from within at having dodged the *true* Irish curse.... Man, that would have been a *drag*, certainly limiting your unfettered co-ed nightswimming possibilities at the least. He briefly dwelled on the horror.... Well, a man had to have priorities. He placed the flask in his pocket and dove in.

But self-congratulatory wanks aside; this whole train of thought rang with something patently unsound. After all, only the morbid ones would even feign interest in being shown across with exactly what they had coming in. But that wasn't the point of this gig anyway...or was it? He shook his head—c'mon now man, are you going to get on with the job or stand around talking circles? He gave his watch a gentle toss back to the stone jetty, watched as it landed softly on his shirt, and started out.

Liam was a strong swimmer...at least he *remembered* it that way. He had a physique like old Marlon boy before he took it to a cheeseburger Valhalla; all broad shoulders and a back like a mule. And just like some Gaelic Kowalski, he could withdraw by turns, into hidden versions of himself, finding the smallest space to reside, but always ready to cut loose with a bit of the physicality the situation might call for. Tonight was such a night to put away those finer graces.

He kicked out with the violent grace of movement and energy lost to some previous incarnation; an athlete's body, which could still snap out the drink and smokes quick to recapture some of that lean energy. Maybe with a bit less of the automatic frequency youth takes as its own, but these old strings still had some play in them yet.

He kept on the quick stroke working up a good head of steam as he cleared the last lights from St. Hospice Point and out into the dark waters of the bay. Out past the last of the sailboats and pleasure cruisers and into the *real deal*; where one could watch the fine points of light growing ever smaller only to reveal a great tableaux in its entirety.

He took a mouthful of the briny Mediterranean water, rolled it around like some far out sommelier, and spit it back into the drink. A fine bitter taste on the tongue; a pleasant vintage, but they could keep it. Better tastes waited back on shore; a thousand variations of jest, the infinite possibility of earthly delights, or the fine salt lick between her thighs whichever came first.... But oh, there you go again with the *vulgarities*. Best to keep your mind on the task at hand boyo; lash those baser dogs gone to hunt—purpose the *nobility* of your task.

.... What had those Jesuits taught him so many years ago—sure we're all from the same elements great and small; *Ad majorem Dei gloriam*—all for the greater glory of God. Feel it in the spirit, feel it in the bones—can taste Rome, Carthage, Siracusa in these waters—elemental things, risen, razed, and gone.

He paused, letting his eyes settle on the random patterns of light spilling down the hills to the water's edge. The Promenade des Anglais snaked like some great serpent in wavering shades of red and white, yellow, and twinkling points of amber rose. But then his ears settled in and suddenly he was no longer alone.... Jesus, three in the morning and the place was *still jumping*. He could hear bits of conversation from the shore; songs and shouts from the beaches and cafes where the last of the midnight ramblers were just packing it in. These were the fortitudinal types—*his types*, out taking their personal weirdness to the bitter bitter ends.

.... But then he could register something of a far greater immediacy; the sound of an outboard cutting through the water nearby. A faint first followed by a second and then quite possibly a third.... Good Lord man, it was quieter back on shore with the seraglio blaring away from next door and the late show on the tube.

The Niçoise fisherman did a brisk business at night in narrow 33' trawlers dragging lines across the bay from east to west, then reversing course in the morning. They would stay in fairly close to shore, hugging the shallows as they went about it, hauling in bundles of langouste and shellon. The pleasant din of the motors filled the air over the sounds of the wind and the water.... He could catch bits of their voices, the inflections of a story, the pause, and then the chorus of laughter; just men busting each other's chops, some things the same the world over.

The voices sounded French, but not quite French. It was the local dialect; a more Italian sounding tongue, with just enough French to leave the delicate sensibilities of the national character intact. Either way, it was a pretty patois; a pleasant counterpoint to the rhythmic sounds of the water and the slightly labored exertions of his breath.

Each of the fishing boats was fitted with a small red light at the aft. As he glided along the rises the lights would disappear behind the swells only to reappear in a comforting sort of fashion, something that even became predictable after a while; until finally he floated out past where he could see them at all. He was pushing towards the deeper waters now, just the circular arc from the lighthouse beam still visible with any honesty or clarity.

He made his way towards one of the old steel buoys leading into the harbor—seemed like as good a place as any for a bit of drink and a rest. He wrapped an arm around the cast iron base and gently swayed in time with its comings and goings. The pendulum bell rang softly with each bit of sway, as the bright green light cast an eerie illumination below. He fished out the flask and took a few long belts, sizing up the situation—glistening in the moonlight, set under the bright blanket of stars, fixed and constant, only swaying about with the tide's intentions.

His eyes trailed to the west, towards the airport, and the flashing columns of approach lights over the water; powerful kliegs burning fiery bright on the inbounds before slowly dimming to a complete darkness, repeating this silent ballet every few minutes or so.

He lingered for a bit, careful to stay out of sight from the fishing boats, lest one of them "spot him" and bore in for the rescue. He laid low till the sounds of the engines and bits of Niçoise French disappeared completely. And then it was quiet again between the waves and swells, like the whole bit was never more than some slight alchemy of the mind, the random ghosts in the machine. Until finally there is peace, just the water cutting across the skin, a bit of reverb on the breeze, and a noise he tells himself is only in the mind—swirling in booze, wrapped up in the echoes of some night and place long since gone…. French Patois? Keep up the good stroke boyo and you'll be hearing Berber Arabic soon enough.

Wet cargo shorts avec silver flask were however weighing him down. *W.H.O.* initialed in a regal cursive along the side; the perfect accoutrement for the Bonnie King Charley set…regal indeed, just the mad maleficence for the meager mind. No matter, didn't need any extra drag on a gig like this. Besides, flasks were never a proper thing; who the hell still owned one anyway—upscale derelict drunks who sandbagged the living and the clownish grave diggers who swindle the dead.

He did an artful summersault beneath the surf and came up with his shorts, balled in a dripping scrunch and tossed them around the rigging of the buoy. And the fine silver flask he placed gently between the iron grating at the base. He patted it thrice for an obsessive's good luck and started out again.

Soon the soft green light from the buoy began to rise and fall between the swells, looking smaller and smaller, fading in the distance. He must have been out past the two-mile mark by then, but hell, who knew, maybe he was closing in on three. The vanity of the vanities hadn't quite rotted the planks yet. Nope, not bad at all…but then again, a *dangerous* business leaving your humility back on shore.

He switched over to the backstroke for a bit giving the forearms a rest. His new latitude provisioned a rather grand view of the heavens. The sky was a blanket of white points laced with flashes of yellow and green. His eyes, so used to city light, were genuinely taken aback by the brilliance; as the gray-blue strands of the Milky Way snaked lazily across the sky dreamy and indifferent.

His brain, the lower functioning survival instincts anyway, would kick in now and then reminding him of the great peril he'd availed them of; well out to sea with a head full of hop and no real plan save for pressing on.... But once you were able to ignore the fear, did the semantics even matter? Oceans, rivers, shallow puddles, salton seas; anything out past the ankles was just taking a roll on the good graces of providence and the fates....And if it was all just *shading* by matters of degree, well then, he was more than willing to push that envelope a bit.

The colors blurred towards the horizon as he hovered in a momentary breather, focusing on the small points of light from shore.... Remembering back to a time, monkey drunk on a Brooklyn rooftop, *sanctified* in the most Rastafarian of senses—eyes locked on the flashing red lights from the tallest buildings in the distance; keeping them fixed in his view till the sickness passed, till the fear abated; back in a time when innocence was still relatively innocent.

Just lock onto those finer things with that kind of laser-like precision and you'd be ok.... But what a *vicious* business it was, these beastly moments of clarity intruding on the otherwise fine fantasy world you've ushered in. And so we beat on, boats against the currents indeed.... Like some whingeing nag who wanders in on the most pleasant of dreams to remind you you're not really who you think you are. To remind you that despite the patina, life rarely imitated art and *imagined* art even less.

Inner monologues which bit with such bite were usually the first and finest signs to sound the retreat, drag your ass back to shore, crawl up into bed, roll under the sheets and pretend the whole thing was just some wicked midsummer night's folly....But for the hardier ones, the ones with *the ganas* to match the megalomania, it was merely the invitation for a quick pause to gird up those limitless limpid jets of love and ride it out till that fourth wind rose up from the deep wellspring within.

Being cast from that slightly *finer* grit, Liam James turned away from shore and started out again with a renewed energy into the vastness of the sea. Remember boyo, just keep kicking till you see the lights on the other side, could even be there by dawn—catch the inquisitive tangles of Arabic here and there and the friendly Bedouin fires that awaited. Surely they'd dig his oddball act, an endeavor of the most righteous earnestness.

Then for no particular reason he took a deep breath and dove down; down as far as he could into the cool dark waters, feeling them out, but nothing there...until silence. He finally found a bit of peace and quiet, that is till the lungs reminded him of the frailties of evolution. He shot back up to the top with a deep breath, and the green light from the buoy still smiling back at him in the distance.

The moon drifted behind the clouds as the dark canopy of stars dove down to meet the horizon. His thoughts drifting back to a booming voice in a booming town, many incarnations, many lifetimes ago...

'Cause these were after all the same stars that shined through the lattice work windows and across the fine sheen of James Quinn Esq.'s desk back on the Upper East Side, and the same ones creeping in through the big windows of his father's somewhat deserted homestead.... Max the dog cries softly at the door to be let out, the cats lounge lazily in the old man's study—just another night up round the way. And that same light from these stars would shine over that lonely 6'x 3' piece of perpetual ownership out at Ringsend Road, where all the greater capitulations went to sleep untouched and untended in a garden of stone; an unweeded garden growing out to past.... And even a bit of this lovely light, this same blanket of finely pointed stars, cast over a small patch in Hyde Park and a place that should never be visited too roughly again.

.... And maybe even the sad bit of moonlight falling over the poor tener of Hindu Kush he bought from those rabble trust fund hippies back on shore. That same tin of weed he should have brought with him.... Why not, could have packed it like a wad of chew, might have even worked.... Clear the mind of this rubbish; get the soul straight with the fates. Nothing worse than being trapped as your own captive audience; a late show that never ends.... Bummer that.

Brave talk but look where you've put yourself you fool. Then again, no need to worry, hell, learn to relax, it was actually kind of *nice* out here.... All things being equal not many places he'd rather be. Out in the deep water all things felt on the up and up.... Like he'd finally found the equanimity of the here and now.

The honesty and clarity of the moment cuts right through once you've left the clever, bipedal, prehensile, walking upright business back on shore—no more of that guff to hide behind. Yes, you've certainly gone out too far; no phones, no lights, no motorcars—out into the warm embrace of the *great equivocator*. A moment out past where the knowing meant anything.

Being tuned into the equalities of the world—a good thing. Lingering out where the fish now had the advantage; maybe not so good. His mind flashed back to that tasty salad Niçoise from lunch. A fine meal polished off with several glasses of a pleasant *Château Les Valentines* Rose—91 points from *Wine Spectator* don't you know.... Some knowing jokes with your Spanish waiter at a burgeoning brand of knowledge proving more useful with each filthily enriching passing day.

Squint through those Bvlgaris though and catch the slight rueful looks from your beloved, and nary a second thought to the unwilling guest of honor on your plate, and nary the third to the first order sorts of things. He was sorry, but as they say the world turned, and humility and compassion were hardly the bromides for such a meal.... Pleasant thoughts as the poor fellow went a progress through the guts of a halfwit.

Have a chuckle with it boyo, it seemed a rare thing in this life to be caught in a full on moment of unknowable revenge and atonement. A peg for a leg, a whale of a tale, and bitter and bruised dragged down to the leviathan depths—a level playing field once again.

Send all manner of thoughtless, indifferent cruelty a mark and others would come to collect. Fair play, I've done enough to them...although, sharks would be a *drag*. He wondered what the Jaws quotient was like out here? No idea—complete claptrap gibberish; just the juniper berry follies talking again. And while not quite in the terrordome neighborhood of 35,000-foot avionic flameouts, cashing your check as a morsel of well-heeled chum held an altogether perverse appeal for the finale which was hard to ignore.

Yep, checking in with a bit of the messianic complex and checking out as a tasty bit of midnight bait; a coda that had to be right up there on the shod scale—the Chevy Impala of ignominious endings. Nope, no glory there, keep paddling...just remember though—*smack em'* in the snout should they come a' calling.

He kept his ear tuned for the booming music and an eye peeled for any greased lightning fins, but the rest of him was free to sweat those pesky fates. More so, the capricious nature of the fates; the small tilts here and there, the slight shifts and forks in the road—all which held the possibility of some greater capitulation.

…. Capitulation, a far politer euphemistic flourish then what awaited back on shore. No, *at best*, they'd call him shark bait. Suicide they would say. The meaner ones would laugh indignant, "What no stones in the pockets for the young lad?"

The gentler ones might wax poetic, "Hell no officer, we saw him going out into those dark waters, but shit, we all thought he loved himself…. What's that you say, was he a reckless personality? No…more stupid than vain really. Yep, that was him in a nutshell Monsieur Gendarmerie."

A nutshell *indeed*. Well, cut, print, and check the gate—there was the eulogy. Vicious business this life; even in the equivocations they might shred you to death, but then again who'd be around to complain? No, in the end they would never know. He'd just float out with the driftwood and the jetsam; a curiosity, till an enigma, till nothing more than a memory.

Then he too could join the pageant, Liam James, *last* of the family reserve—safely back on the reservation…. And maybe someday, some other commingling soul brother from another mother could drift out past the saw grass and the breakers on a night such as this. Wander out monkey drunk, laughing to themselves, perhaps take a hit of the briny water, taste the honey on the tongue and know what it meant to be alive.... And just maybe wander back on the lives and times of the dearly departed.

.... What would it feel like to be part of a memory? One of those gathering twilight shades, risen up in a great brief fury, then cast back into the darkness? But those were arrogant Earthly concerns. The only noble equivocation out here was to sink like a flamed out stone—instantly, organically rendered thus. Back at one with the eternal return, or some such vaguely comforting thing. He closed his eyes to the stars and listened.

Drip, drip, drip—the sound of the water on the tin outside the window; but do you remember it well. Aunt Margaret makes us tea, a long lost cousin tells of a fond memory to lift the room a bit; time is static, time is still—the silence that comes to a house when no one can sleep.... Ah waiting, waiting, waiting yet again...fuck-all with this waiting.

Ever is as always, always was forever, always forever is now.... And so I hanged back a measure, stayed in a quiet spot and watched them lower her into the ground; bastards, thieves, robbers and robbers to be, kept under a watchful eye, cursing their blood, cursing all they would ever have.

They all want something you know.... Why didn't you just say something? Your silence was selfish, a selfishness that was deafening.... So much better at all this in death than in life; but late to the table yet again, always so late. The best of fireman after the house has turned to ash.... But ah, the small mercies, the small mercies offered for today.... Meander a bit, try to push it down, smell the flowers, taste the honey, feel the sting—blah, blah, blah, verse chorus verse. I am here now, an irrecoverable, incontrovertible...and strangely irrevocable fact.

.... Sitting in the sun one day as a child playing in the dirt of my mother's garden. Turning up the rich black soil with a spade, playing rough with it as any good boy should. Stab down into the ground, the violent thrash of Earth, turn it over in my hand; a small green salamander caught in the blade, almost severed across its back. It struggles for a few seconds until it

Christopher M. Basso

struggles no more. I run to her crying.... I watch them lower her into the grave.

.... Ah, small mercies, small mercies. They are all gone, I am still here; the sparks of flame gone to dust on a warm summer's night.... I pour a bit more, I study the labels, I am exacting if anything...pop pop pop down the gullet.... I wait for the eyes to glaze over, small mercies, small mercies indeed—linger a bit, waiting on the judgment, as ever.... My poor salamander daemon; twenty-five years now gone to dust. I am still here.

.... The calm glassy eyes watched the flashing lights from an airplane make the pretty arc down the spiral chute into Nice. Terrified safely in the air, perfectly at ease drifting out to sea, but reason and logic were never your strong suits.... Fear and loathing, hot headed scorn, and a healthy contempt for a growing list of Pharisees—these were the things of tougher stuff.

He arched his head back a bit.... What about the practical? Who foots the bill on one of these massive search and rescue gigs? Not to mention the repatriation of the remanded remains, and the special plane ticket home for the dearly departed? At least there'd be no need for the Xanax-Grey Goose cocktails and Nicorette snorted swizzle sticks.... No, this would be an eternal "power hour", an ersatz George Bailey rocking the *forever* buzz down in the belly of the beast. Egads, this was a fool's errand indeed.

.... And then there would be the *paperwork*; the escrows, the accounts, the fights, the Quinn's, the wills, the bills.... Ah the bills, coming in fast now, thick as thieves—Amex, Cirrus, Visa; the sexus nexus for the Lexus.... A slow drip at first, matching the timidity of their new found master, but get a bit *dry* behind the ears and watch the great rolling wave crashing into his accountant's office.

Why just the other day, Fred Dewan, erstwhile moral conscience and financial advisor extraordinaire rang up the batphone as O'Shea waited on a Lisbon platform for the evening train. He glanced down and hit the mute button. Avoid the call—all calls for that matter; a hateful thing a ringing phone....

His thoughts were briefly interrupted by a bellowing fat man, his smoking hot daughter, and an army of shell-shocked porters passing by. Check the flashing light once the coast was clear, wait as the honeyed voice retrieves the message, listen to the gruff familiar baritone it finds.

Hmmm, what's the old boy got to say? $1,100 for the good people of Reid's Palace Hotel in lovely Madeira. Something about $2,000 fishing charters back to the mainland—loud shouts, bad noise, boom goes the dynamite. Old Fred takes his job as the divination and the light quite literally. Liam arched an eyebrow—too bad *he* doesn't actually sign the checks.... Listen closer, $28,346.74 in the hole for the last six weeks.... Light another smoke, stare ahead, just remember everyone's on their way to Heaven; act accordingly.

Take a deep breath son, *calm down*; this was more holistic update than exasperated ultimatum.... Although last year's salary at the law clerk office gone in the time it takes the Cubs to break spring training. Hell, probably more than your old Grandfather ever made in a year.... $28,000 in the drink and you haven't even *left* Lisbon.

He flashed behind the waves for a second, briefly losing sight of the shore.... An *astronomical* sum from a lifetime prior, but one that still made him quake in his birthday suit. For the realization was a far from instantaneous thing, only coming on like the warm enveloping sense of security when the liquor cracks the blood and spreads the joys of absolution and approbation.

But that much? Really? He shrugged; hideous exchange rate was to blame—free fall, the Greenbacks gone to hell....Blame it on the echoes of that asshole Lone Star crowd. Good thing you've gone *off the grid*. They'll never find you here; they wouldn't even know where to look.

But then again they say the hottest places in hell were reserved for those who in times of crisis remained neutral....What evil, guilt-binging, soul-sucking bastard had the stones to troll that sort of guff? Had such shoddy fools ever found themselves drifting out on a high sea of peril? Doubtful. But then again, these were just the vicious voices in his head, the same echoes from many moral equivalences ago. Obviously such scoundrels never had to manage the machinations of vast, ill-gotten gains.

And what do you call it when your ill-gotten gains were already ill-gotten? It was a moral laundering of the first order, spinning wildly in the wrong direction. Was there no way to make this shit clean? Such things might even make a mind check out before its time; nothing left but hazy memories of Ava Gardener's once firm ass in your hands, pulling at your two foot beard with your nine inch nails, as a perpetual loop of *Ice Station Zebra* blares away in the background...a curiosity, till an enigma, till nothing more than a reclusive memory.

He was somewhere out past the lighthouse when the second blast from the magic flask hit him, catching the boy square on, he could feel the mind expanding and contracting—ushering in the pleasant calm from within.... Something like déjà vu all over again; back to another warm night in the water, down Bermuda way, on the trial run for the Lost Weekend template. Just slightly out to sea that night, never past the reefs or the wave breaks, drifting along the warm Gulf waters, the wide Sargasso Sea not far for those with ambition; and the easy times of shallow pleasures.... Cuban cigars in the bar at the Hamilton Princess, sunning on the rocks by Tucker's Town.

He even thought he saw James Quinn Esq. zipping by in one of those little golf carts; just another plaid-gird Boomer out spending his billable time well. O'Shea almost gave his cabbie a heart attack as he jumped from the moving taxi, all the better to chase Quinn down.... Come at him low like a spider monkey from the Bermuda scrub pine, grab his sand wedge and show him a new interpretation of *prior restraint*...but alas it was only Silvio Berlusconi, and *that* was from some other mainline era, long since removed from the foul brutish realities swirling about the warm waters of the Mediterranean under a snarky moon for the misbegotten.

But what was this greater feeling? Was it guilt; was it propriety...propriety for the sake of guilt? Most likely a bit of each mixed in the bouillabaisse. Lovely to be in league with those who wrestle the foul burdens of managing the bonhomie of large inheritances...you dick.

Down All the Days

He should spend *the rest of his life* on an airplane, shotgunning Earl Grey with chatty circus clowns, listening them talk about their golf game; absolution was too good for you, you lout.... Ah, self-deprecation; they say it eases the burgeoning entitlements of the ego don't you know. At least they'll cut you some slack for the effort...you dick.

But what to *do* about it—drift further out into the metaphysical sea? Or maybe just take charge of things—go the monkish warrior route? Rid yourself of all soul sucking encumbrances—lose it, ditch it, give it all away.

.... Well let's not be rash there Chico man; he spat out some water as the warm currents tickled his wayfaring nether regions, for in the heart of every generous man is the cracked looking glass of a selfish beast, who gives to see but the reverence in himself, or so at least the younger slightly jaded Jesuit model held dear.

However, there was some currency to this idea of expiation...up to a point. Jacob wrestled the angel and all he got was this lousy limp—sounded like a T-shirt he could do without—besides some of this guff was too much fun. So sidestep that noise, perhaps divine your own blueprint of sorts; dollar for dollar, a present pleasure easing a mortal pain. Might assuage any of that lingering culpability and give one the license to behave badly. That or at least earn some of those karmic-cosmic chits which might just keep those Friendly Skies friendly...you dick.

Perverse pleasures, guilt drenched expiations, just another man about town lingering between the here and there. Lingering on the people he'd never meet, living lean in far flung lands, the ones who were gonna roll it large from the cheese wheel of shared guilt and revelry.... A nice slice for every happy endings massage he might come across and for every ruby red stripper's knickers there to be enriched—*philanthropy,* making it rain on a scale that never felt so admirably...piquant.

But all that felt like jumping the gun a bit; after all this was a boy who still felt a vague sheepishness ordering a nice spread from room service. Perhaps those simpler pleasures would have to wait. At least till the semblance of his newfound

369

Christopher M. Basso

normalcy became too much the freaky cross to bear, and the only natural order of things would be to keep your roll on the wild side; seeking states of grace down all the back alleys the lifestyle had to offer.... Yep, long nights and demon days of cruising airport restrooms; toe-tapping, glory-holing anonymity through the partitions of men's room stalls, or seeking higher office, whichever came first.

But to be *free* from the spurious jaded wants and perversions of this world...free to create *your own* jaded wants and perversions—now therein rested a liberation as liberating as anything.... So, ever onward, excelsior, keep moving, even if just in spirit. And if you sink like a stone *even better*, more of the larder to pass about—*lot's* of worthy people stand to gain when you've had the prescience to insure yourself like some Saudi racehorse.

But no stud fees for today, just one young fellow drifting slowly out to sea, riding the fine pageant crest of a dreamy mind and body rocking his birthday suit; his lungs and legs in a race for the bottom; just a bag of bones for the irate fishies—perhaps they'd serve him with a *Château Les Valentines* Rose—94 points from Wine Spectator, don't ya know.... Black humor, gallows humor, a lifetime of it, who cares, you don't.

Besides would you even sink free and clean, or did you rate the Ivory soap of midnight marauders? Give yourself a little credit, no witches here, you'd sink sure and even indeed—clean again, at the beginning, right to the bottom with the Roman Triremes, Spanish Galleons, and all other manner of perversion preceding you.

.... My poor salamander, gone for decades now, and poor peaceful memories and attendant grace which sails with it. Soft Earth and dreamy summer days, drifting next to the stripper ass-candy grime of some dime store pipe dream—was there any justice for a twisted mind? Being reverent or being honest; no one's mind is a cathedral; act accordingly. The cruel, hardy nimbleness of the fates standing sentinel, the mind awash in the bosh, wandering in and out of the profound and the vulgar, almost by turns, hand in hand, lock in step.

It was surprisingly easy for the uninitiated to slip into a velvet morning existence, especially when you were one of those meticulous, well-researched types. The type who understood that "knowing" was half the battle, at least when it came to replicating *the lifestyle*. A life of collected images about how this was *supposed* to look. Shit, anyone could pick up a copy of *Maxim* or watch *Gossip Girl* and get the hang of this.... But then again, $10 of mosquito netting could save one of God's delicate creations in some far-flung land. Try finding that in *Maxim*.

And he was if anything a creature of the culture, dosed on just the right levels of Elysian Fields, material excess, and sensory overload since shortly after birth. A *futureshock* of sorts, but even Toffler might have been amazed at the sheer levels of fear and loathing his three decades had rode shotgun on. Living the dream seemed less the coinage of the realm and more like a *threat* in the context of things. The fashionable beast of the 5th seal who would leave your untanned, doughy ass in the brimstone, gunstone dust.

And this Recession-Depression talk? Hmmm, would that be the perversion of every generation creating a calamity of self-aggrandizement and then having the temerity to act shocked when the perversions come home to roost.... 1929, 1956, 1974, 1987, 2002, 2008—bagism, shagism, ragism, tagism indeed—WTF? Market adjustments? Social Darwinism? Horace Greeley might have been more apt: go west young man, there're always a few more brown folks to be had.... Shit, on the big rock candy mountain we should all be sporting twelve-inch Johnsons or lusty 32D's, and all the bankers would be strung Mussolini-style from the nearest tree with piano wire, but *regrettably* none of these things looked quite on the horizon.

.... Had O'Shea's grandfather really left part of his knee and all of his innocence back in some Okinawa jungle for this? Apparently so; for every generation throws its villains up the pop charts to explain away the werewolf within, and we forgive our children for many things. You could almost set your watch to it; the pissy avarice of the drinking classes out *getting theirs*.

.... Handsome Henry is beastly dead, $2.4 million reasons later he is gloriously resurrected. Noblesse Oblige for all—thank you kindly numbnuts.... Sad to say the boy had crunched the math even before Quinn was through pushing those funeral baked meats.

Christopher M. Basso

A *mind-boggling* thing—masturbatory monopoly spoils; twisted just the like the culture in the hot lights of some payola game show—a porcelain veneer toupee entreating the young Donkey Boy to, "Come On Down!"

He'd have frittered away nearly forty years in the bowels of some lowly DA's gig to generate that kind of scratch. Sixty grand a year was after all the going rate for the pro bono público back in the metropolis; just enough to lay low and stay respectable in the eyes of the chattering classes as they piloted the next generational catastrophe.

60K, pension, free parking, that vague douche bag air of law enforcement entitlement, and a golden ticket for all those late night DUI runs with the Blue Fraternity—no worries, professional courtesies; just the tight knit fragments of his Fenian forbearers.... And *best* of all: a free pass back to the walls of a sturdy 5.25% mortgage, complete with warm body, modicum of respectability, and the cheap thrills of a purely recreational ED pill popping lifestyle.... And if you *still* had a bit of that fiendish roll in your stroll, there was always the suburban penumbra where Friday night's key parties became Saturday morning's soccer matches. Yes indeed, feel those walls closing in.

Keep those eyes fixed to the box; more shite, reality shows, game shows—the cranial Pablum reaffirming you're only slightly more elevated than some sub-group of fragile maniacs....More rubbish, more commercials telling you to stay on top of the purely recreational ED pill popping lifestyle. Sometimes those walls can't close fast enough.

.... And perhaps the coup d'grace; that fearful Jesuit strain which would have kept you from the big ticket corporate Wonka Bars, respectful and resentful to the last of some fey notions of ethics and accountability.... But to who? The mutants in Theodore Rex's arena architecting the next societal implosion they can lay at your feet?

You can spend all your days toiling away for an ideal tangled up in shadiest of souls.... Victims who are criminals, criminals who are victims, where does that one end? And the people? Can't stand them never could—Mad dogs, glad rags and handbags, sociopaths and deviants...and then there were *the clients*—Bad jokes, lawyer jokes, gallows humor, a lifetime of them.... And the perverse comedy of it—sixty thousand dollars a year, 98.7% percent more solvent than the rest of planet Earth, but back in Gotham the *futureshock* crowd was ready to throw nickels in your cup like some broke dick hobo derelict...hells bells, only in America.

And then the phone rings, and a perfect stranger hands you your life's work in an afternoon. Pick your jaw up off the shiny desk, add water, shake, and watch the sidesplitting guffaws ensue.... But who's to complain, you wee Jesuit, not you.

And the *numbers*, numbers he couldn't even comprehend in the meager heretofore—game show winnings, a whole new secret vocabulary to learn. Floating now in the wispy-waspy truisms which had meant so little drifting through a week-to-week lifestyle. Suddenly your money was off making money...rude of it not to even tell you. Just statements filtering in now and then, exponential jumps here and there—8% in the first year alone....Fearful paranoia, joyless loathing; hoard the top shelf spirits for equilibrium; give those rotten O'Shea Overachievers a king's share, give Monsieur's Wilson and Heath the pennies right off your eyes and you were *still* light years ahead of an honest days work.... What was a closeted Kesey-Kerouac acolyte wannabe to do...hells bells, only in America.

The waters had cut a bit chilly down that last stretch and a timeout was in order. He kicked his heels to Heaven and pointed headlong towards the other place; diving down, down towards the shadows; peaceful down there, just the soft pounding sound of the blood in your veins; keep it moving. Shake away the shrinkage of this life, man up slacker, walk unafraid.

Come up *reborn*, smiling the smile; embrace the interloper you've become. Like some snarky Bud Fox hustler, with a shiny Hong Kong Rolex and the ethics of a jizzbooth carny—the type of chap who could hit the right notes on the right occasions, wear the burnished uniforms of the day, and infiltrate the infiltrators with a special king hell sort of talent—a real *joie de vivre* for the thing.... Though that too might have required a bit too much blurring of the lines for his tastes.

Christopher M. Basso

But as he looked back towards the shore, at the brightly burning lights cascading down the hills, he could sense he'd finally hit it; the Neural Cortex—the epicenter of the contradiction. And that above all else, *this* was the place to be; the right place to chew over the dynastic implications of this mess.... These people, *especially* these high rent Euro carpetbaggers, held fast and dear the notions of tribe; tribes of race, class, ethnicity, whatever—all in some loose exclusionary cohesion, but all under the same banner of self-aggrandizement.... Although *tribe* might have been a bit too crass for these Beauregard peacocks; too primitive a thing for their collective Superegos to handle. Go for the latter day semantic parlance—*a network*.

Be it dynastic or otherwise plant a seed and watch it grow, but careful though, strange roots take hold. The miasma can drift either way; carefully mapped out ascendancies: Borgias, Rothschilds, Kennedys; little fiefdoms built to stand the test of time, or left to flame out spectacularly in the hands of idiot heirs with one finger on the ATM and the other steadying the rails of charley across some model's ass.... He chuckled, or maybe just *sink* to the bottom of the sea like a mossy Irish stone?

Yep, Mark Twain said it best: Right in the middle of the contraction *was* the place to be. Wise words indeed for a newly minted, rifting, drifting midnight rambler; a lovely mossy stone if ever.... But then again the ol' tribe might not even want him, for he had the rank stink of it, the scent of some doom struck interloper cheating life with a 7-Eleven scratch and win, or some blue haired granny who's pulled the lucky slot at the Pig in the Poke in Reno.

Sad to say, but *these* ass goblins were now his spiritual kin—and in a perfectly practiced way the dynastic Von Summer's of this world, would eventually see right through it. See you trying to back door your way into their clubs, drink all their booze, and donkey punch their bored pouty daughters; all the while having the temerity to not even tell them *you're a Jew*.... Or was that just some movie he saw once? He was, after all, a product of the culture; green-lit piers, six-toed cats, and the deepest of Southern melancholy were all at his disposal. Modern Life, if you weren't still fighting the mosquitoes for it, was just a slim series of storylines aped from somewhere else.

374

He paused for a moment to contemplate his latest failure; his thoughts swirling in the bright stars and the strong drink.... The slow stroke to Africa afforded all the time in the world to dwell on these things.... Damn, his wasn't even a *respectable* piece of ascendancy—one of those Horatio Alger tales of kicking darkness till it bled daylight. People loved that shit; hell, *he* loved that shit—that brand of rising up from the swamps of diminished expectations and sticking it to the swells of this world.

But he'd failed them, the *royal* them, on this account. He couldn't even lay claim to the other end of the American wet dream; that hazy predawn breaking the bank at the Bellagio Pisgah vision.... Nope, *sensible* people would draw the wagons and hide their bored, pouty donkey punching daughters when they saw it coming. No one respected the idle hands of inherited wealth, except maybe those in the same listing boat.... Truly an evil thought that this crew of halfbrights and fuckwits were the closest thing he had left to a tribe.

The chop had given out some and the currents faded to little more than a pleasant pull in the here nor there. The scent of brine and a cool mist hovered just above the surface; his breath little more than a shadow in the moonlight, just the sounds of the sea and his exertions in it. In the stillness he could feel his strength building again with each cut through the water, his mind sharpening in the calm as the phony tough led the crazy brave.

The lights from shore took on a fine distant crispness through the breaks in the swells; only the sounds of the pull, a rising crescendo, each to its own.... No fear out here, just a warmth between the pockets of cold; huevos like a lion, heart like an alligator; just keep going, always keep moving—stay still and you'll sink like a stone.

Dynastic fools, penny ante fiefdom rubbish, they could keep it.... He could well be proud of his peasant's name—*O'Shea*. At least he always imagined it a peasant's name. A good solid handle from back the deepest perils of the original dark and bloody ground. Stone Age throwbacks down to the last man. They didn't come much more original than that.... Joyce's sad sunken cunt of the world; Eire, a wandering flock with no shepherds left to strike. Now scattered out on the bitter waters, drifting the high seas of this world; set forth for greener pastures in the first of many westward expansions.

Pissers, scrapped all the way from the green-jawed stains of a former life, somewhere back in the old country, deep in the bowels of landless County Sligo, or in the cholera laden back alleys of Limerick.... *Fine jewels*, the townships of their day. Board the coffin cruisers; watch the collective soul transmigrated.... A powerful loaded word *transmigration*, a word for the body and spirit; dust, scattered to the four corners, trading one paddy Soweto for another.

O'Shea; a name no mistaking, nothing but the original article there—and his none too bright forbears refusal to part with it.... *Fools*, they could have just *anglicized* it a bit. How about the Shelley's or the Shepherds—would've had an almost respectable sounding ring to those 19th century Puritanical ears, throw em' off the scent lest they think you were some acolyte off to shine the Pope's ring behind their backs.... Silly bog bastards, a little subterfuge would've gone a long way, might have even spared you from the savage mentality of the day...but you missed the proverbial boat on that one. So bite the bit and settle in for a long undulating string of the most mean and menial sort of West of Eden lifestyle gigs—call it O'Shea 101.

Wait though, watch and learn, *lay low* in the weeds for a generation or two, maybe three...let it permeate, let it burn into the identity; gets in the blood that way. A Sun Tzu blowback on the chattering classes; the art of war vis-à-vis the name, that foul hardscrabble name marked with the caul of it.... Indeed, enough betrayals, upheavals and capitulations would breed a fine line of hardscrabble scrappers; long-lank Kentucky studs ready to run.

He laughed at the thought of it; trading your donkeys up for thoroughbreds left you with something of a mule. He spit another jet of sea water into the air as a ghostly band of clouds made the arc overhead shadowing the moon for several minutes; the reassuring brightness gone, the scene suddenly a bit heavier than he cared for.... Octavio Paz perhaps said it second best: Solitude, that profoundest of human conditions; to be the only poor buggers on this rock who know they're alone.... But the clouds passed and the moonlight returned, reassuring in its breadth as ever. His body still felt with him and there was work to be done.

Besides, spoiled contemplations of original solitude were not on the docket for this evening, as this was not quite a remembrance of those things past. Hardier sorts would have to steer this thing from the maudlin, steely ghosts conjured from the shared collective of dreams turned to dust. And like the plough horse that finds its strength in the traces, his kind had come to America and laid in the weeds till the time was upon them.

From the foothold of slumish tenement flats this was an army which fled with all attendant grace into the arms of a young nation's industrial age: Youngstown, Allentown, Hagerstown…up the Hudson, down the Allegheny, Monongahela, Susquehanna. Riding out the first waves in the ironweed claptraps of the Northeast, fighting The Kaiser, pausing a breath, fighting the The Fuehrer. Booming home to abandon the derelict chorus of a growing rust belt, embracing the life of white collar, Chinese lead, silicon based obsolescence. Homesteading with a bit of: I like Ike and Just Say Hey for JFK, to There's No Way with LBJ and Getting Sick of Tricky Dick…. Make you mark, make your move, burn a draft card or two—twice a century was enough. Flee the ghost towns and burning cities, squire a country home, squire a country wife, or three, *embrace* your inner jellybean eatin' wannabe cowboy, keep buying, keep moving….

Hard charge it right up that ascendant arc, and in some final cackle of irony, return to the thing it once beheld—landed gentlemen farmers, sashed in the titular orange of the day. Indulge yourself a contrition for your pains, a noblesse oblige for all; roll yourself a treat for a job done well, buy a Range Rover and then zig when you should have….

Transmigration, a powerful word indeed…*illumination* an even more powerful one; the reclamation from sin, the opportunity to start anew. Lowlife old world criminals, pimps and dogfighters from back deep in the bog country; The O'Shea's, surely the last to ditch the outhouse and start shitting indoors…probably in their sinks, but you gotta learn to walk before you run.

Christopher M. Basso

Slow bunch, bestial sorts, vile wicked people...*ah family*; but choose em' well as they regrettably tend to define you. Yes sir, play this strange game to the end of the beginning, long enough till you're the one with the respectable sounding handle cracking the whip on those with one too many vowels in their name...hells bells son, only in America.

Indeed, almost 150 years of the stuff playing itself out with a dizzying sort of methodical ascendancy, so much so that the latest production model could sit back on these plutonian shores, on a lovely beach filled with a scantily clad sea of the finest in European womanhood on display, sip a cold cerveza, and gimp chuck the *deeper* meanings of things.

.... But with the right kind of eyes you could almost still see it; like some Pisgah vision out on the horizon, a place alive in the apprehension, but never to be achieved. It was a line always on the northern trajectory, never on the cyclical...well until maybe now with this one out splashing in the deep waters. Maybe the clan had finally crested over the mountain, and was now looking down the other end—to the place where all steady ascendant leaps go to die, and the grass grows long covering all disrepair.

And with this profound release—this elevation or prostration, depending on which way your door swung, he could only stop, stretch his tired arms, and lament a bit for all those poor bog bastard O'Shea's who'd only made the mistake of being born at the wrong time.... And for all of them a bit of genuine reverence mixed in with the tall tales and blarney bullshit; a line handed down from the faded daguerreotypes, through the muted jaundiced Kodachromes, to something finally rendered in brilliant pixels of digital light.

Phineas O'Shea—a florist of note. Phineas the florist, his right leg crushed by a runaway flower cart on Eccles Street in Albany, summer 1882, les fleurs du mal indeed.... Could modern eyes imagine a gashed leg and a couple of weeks in *the hospital* would kill you dead at 27? They laid him a fine bouquet of a wreath though, in a time when the nurses were still Whitman's poets, and penicillin was just a shiny glint in Pasteur's stick.

James "Jimmy" Stone—roustabout and bricklayer. Wise enough to lose the name, but not enough to duck the Hun's shrapnel.... Ring around the rosy—septic death, met with the dysentery, one of the waning military deaths of it's kind...but at least he got to tour the Continent as well. Dead, The Somme, 1918.

Patrick O'Shea—AKA Handsome the Elder, a successful line of the branch. Toll booth collector, fathered six children, fifty-nine years of marriage, all to the same woman.... Peaceful quiet life, dignified reserved passing—a rowboat on a lake, trout in the bag, the embers of the setting sun to show him across; *la mort heureuse*—a happy death.... Completely boring fucker.

And right down to his progeny, the always ironic, never iconic Son of Erin himself, Handsome Henry—murdered by a slick patch of oil and an Englishman named Captain Beefeater....Sly boots that one—only got to enjoy the largesse of his labors but for a moment. A flameout if ever, an Irish Bodrick-Bodkin tailspin in the truest, meanest sense of the phrase...it was even a *Range Rover* that got him.

.... And what of the prodigal son, version 2.0, drifting out on the high seas of peril? Who'd be out here mocking him one fine night, many moons from now—once the ballast of this life had jettisoned his poor ass into the Horse latitudes of an indifferent sea...confused and bewildered, watching the firmament drift away.

He could already hear the whispers—silly ass fool...bit of a laughingstock really. Fuck man, less than a year, a veritable *Irish tailspin* in the truest, meanest sense of the phrase.... No, most likely they'd get the whole bit wrong, misconstrue it in the most convoluted of ways, cast it as nothing more than some doom struck jaunt into the never- never, thus sandbagging the poor boy in advance.

But this wasn't that, this was a *celebration*, a wee bit of singing that body electric.... Then again, a simple stupidity had done in far brighter bulbs than he.... Well, heroic musings aside, this was a bit too much gibberish for the mind to take and certainly more than the fragile ego could handle. He might have hit from the rough on smarts, but he drove long on a little thing called wisdom. Indeed, perhaps it was time to turn this mothership around. Mrs. O'Shea didn't raise no dummies.

But there was one whingeing; bingeing nerve that just wouldn't let go. Meeting The Boatman on the service end of some vague, ambiguous finale had a nice epic *ring* to it. And immortality in the right kind of hands could resurrect all sorts of dimwits and misfits. The beloved, back in her bed at the villa, would be more than apt for that sort of action...the perfect caretaker for his memory.

She'd roll those doe eyes, "No, I'm sure he went out there to save some orphans and shut-ins from the charred hulk of a sinking battleship." She would spin it up as well as others could tear it down. It would be a fine epitaph from the pretty lady of the rocks.

.... The Tibetans divest the body of any special meaning once the soul has moved on. The monks break you in two, cinch you in a sack, and leave you out on the mountainside for the vultures and the wild things.... We leave it to $6000 silk lined caskets and monuments to ourselves that would've made the Romans blush. Whose madder I ask you? Our boy to be sure; he already had one in mind, a fine twenty foot obelisk out at Ringsend Road; an enduringly endearing phallus, casting long shadows over the old man's piece of immortality just down the way.

.... And what of the *in loco parentis*? Poor morbidly life challenged duo that they were. The bad vibrations had met the calamity of insanity in those vows. The best of intentions transmigrated by the worst of results.... Maybe they were the same thing though, these perversions and enlightenments—which in the end is what they both became; paying off like ghoulish piñatas.... But what was the etiquette? Did she avoid him in the Afterlife? It would be the smart play after all—that foul beast, the chewer of corpses.... Ah, the shameful shades you conjure when floating out and about. Can't help it, try to stop and they grow even squirrelier...must say something about you, you *sicko*.

Oh there'd certainly be good souls who'd chafe at such things; an ambiguity of the spirit that might be downright vulgar in more civilized circles, but he had no hand in the plan.... Who could know; like the old shaman once said, it's all a gamble when it's just a game. The First one greased the skids of culpability for the Second—and the funeral baked meats...well, we get the point, we understand; it goes without saying. One gives you your sorrow, the other your release, with just the echoes left to testify.... Heady musings indeed as one endeavored to get straight with the fates, amid these strange mumblings, strange rumblings on a naked moonlight dash to the Algerian coast on a hot August night, stranded as it were on the eve of a new decade.

The boy smiled...when did you meet that fool anyway, '71, '72? He heard Handsome regale the peanut gallery with the stories now and then—My father saw my mother across a crowded field at a "Save the Yippie" peace rally near the University of Albany. Now the old boy wasn't a peaceful fellow mind you; rather he was on his way to the Chanticleer Public House for communion with a shot and a beer when he hitched the wrong turn and wandered straight into the brouhaha.

....Guerilla street theater, Puff the Magic Dragon "smoke-ins" and Dadaist pie throwers; not your typical *comfort* environs for a guilt tinged draft dodger and armchair Green Beret.... The big fella was about to start "moving" some people when he caught sight of her coming down the stone steps by the library; and he thought he'd seen an angel.

She was about twenty at the time, a willowy girl of medium height and fair complexion, with dark raven hair and bright green eyes that captured the finer points of the sun. Eyes that lit the light in a smile and childhood freckles forever giving the curious shine of the lovely girlishness.

But those angels were in league with the devils as she quickly passed out of sight. He waded through the crowd as only Handsome could till he caught up with her around Eustace Street near the banks of the Lafayette Canal; watching her from a distance but never close enough to be seen.... Generally, young Henry had the ego of a troika of Trumps, but there was something about her that stopped him cold in his tracks that day, as though he sensed his was in the presence of something greater than his own fey, high-stepping Diamond Jim act.

Christopher M. Basso

But he had a look down at his fingernails crusted dirty from the machine shop, and the general overall bearings of a man about ready to tangle with a shot and a beer, and knew at once *things* needed to be done. He slipped into the Woolworths' gents and went about pumicing those digits and pomading the wild hair. He bought the closest thing to a respectable pair of shoes and paid some longhair $5 for his McGovern button—new habits of skullduggery would apparently die hard.

He caught up with her on a park bench along the river where he proceeded to put his best, most gentlemanly, and most nervously sincere foot forward.... The old man was a chancer to be sure, but he did have *the gift*; a natural storyteller, if not something of a charmer. Generally, he put these talents to more nefarious ends, but not that day and not in that moment.

Sometimes, even the life challenged among us can recognize when they're in the presence of something transcendent; of an ethereal quality conjured in the mind but only occasionally invested in human form. And when we see it, we covet it, not necessarily in any mean or evil way mind you, but merely to stand in its warm shadow if just for a little while. Old Hank found his way into one of those shadows. It could be said he was quite smitten indeed.

They spent the better part of the afternoon there, basking in that moment, the first one, when all things seem new and eternal; a young couple sitting in the shallows staring out into the premonitory wash of a sunset.... This was the genesis, yet this would be the requiem; this same river who's high wind swept banks would one day shade their eternal rest....... AND *scene*.

Or perhaps merely the conclusion thereof, out here in the deep waters, some three decades later drifting in the Med in the middle of the night.... Life, when you weren't still fighting the mosquitoes for it, was one strange, funny, *evil* mother at that.

Liam's eyes broke along the edge of a swell as he watched it roll towards the shore.... Maybe that was just the joke of it; this cleaving of the soul, this ever-present reminder that time is something holding us and time is forever after us.... But perhaps it was more wicked than anything in the end, at least at getting its watchful kicks with a bit of pleasure spiked with pain.

…. They say one of the first sights burned into the infant mind is the image of its mother's face; like a road map back to the Higher Hand himself. And in this regard the boy had always thought himself the luckiest of sorts. It would be maudlin though not inopportune to say his mother did indeed have the face of an angel; a countenance allaying childish fears and making all the unkind things in his world go away. But he imagined this was how most remembered their own precious memories; their own bits of angelic regard.

He stretched his tired muscles in the sea; the stars in the sky now crossing paths with the ones in his eyes. For a second he even thought he *saw* her in those dark waters. The smiling face from his childhood; one of Big Wheels, Stone Age Atari, and candy left over from Halloween…. Must be the *fast twitch* reserves going, he chuckled, the last endorphins bearing down before you went belly up. He looked in again till he was sure it was gone.

…. And the greatest illumination was to found in the smallest of contemplations; yes, he seemed to remember those Jesuits beating something like that into him once. The shit and straw of a provincial manger was their leitmotif, but the point was clear. Greatness could be found in the minute, in the happy meditation of the moment…. Beauty in vulgar things was beautiful; it defied the cheap image sellers and societal shills who'd tell you otherwise.

Vulgar things were often your last sight in this world, could a deathbed be anything otherwise; but you had to be hep to God's design, you had to find the beauty he'd hidden in the attendant grains of sand. A deathbed could be a lovely thing; a lifetime of reactionary beauty could flow from its pains, fresh roots in the ground for the ones you leave behind.

But only in their measure to create order from chaos, to apprehend beauty from pain, only then can they whip back the beast…. He took some pleasure in this reckoning; the sometimes misfiring proton-neuron casing atop his shoulders was occasionally a soul-fascist killing machine of the first order. A fierce weapon that saw through his failings in the waking world…but one no more equipped to get to the heart of the matter.

Christopher M. Basso

His mind raced to ground covering his own brand of experience in these matters. Old cats tend to wander off for a safe, quiet place to meet their end; humans it would seem are only slightly different in this regard. The Darwinists might call it a vestigial instinct, the Evangelicals would surely play the line of a divine apprehension; the naked boy on the moonlight mile considered it a little bit of both.

But he could remember her eyes the most; his poor mother's eyes. Once the bright green fires had gone it would take only sixteen months for the rest of her to follow. A quiet decline in a back room at their house, television blaring away at all hours; the sitcoms of her youth, Jackie Gleeson and Lucille Ball playing her gracefully home.... And once the curtain falls what do you have left—faded memories, vivid memories, the snapshots of a life sailing by. And *objects*, dead things, even more so without the light that gave them life; clothes, books, photos...shiny little medals you wear around your neck.

Poor Sara, that sweet Episcopalian would never understand the twisted iconography involved in being willing to sail over the canyon cliffs of this world for these keepsake trinkets. It was a distinctly Catholic vice or virtue.

.... But he could still see it around his mother's neck; this one nod to the stern theocratic miasma her old world brood enforced with a martial rigidity. The same brood who would have been delighted with her being little more than a walking talking blarney cliché—a human Pez dispenser, who when not larding it about, would be free to wear those rosaries down to the nub. Well, not that little green eyed monster.... Quiet as it's kept; she was the *original* black sheep, long before her only son was off halfway around the world making it vaguely fashionable. She was a willing devotee to the left leaning conflagration of her day; of stopping a war, of test driving this *love* thing, and of an idea of a nascent community not based on threats of eternal recrimination.

But she'd always liked the story of St. Christopher ferrying the infant Jesus across the bad waters; a catcher in the rye by any other name. But as for the rest of it, the dog heeled dogma of her family; she wanted nothing to do with it...until her deathbed. She'd folded, down in the narrow hours, when individuality meant little and rebellion even less.... It broke the boy's heart to think this iconoclast, this idolater's idolater, a woman who did good things for the virtue of its own reward, had been laid low by the small minded hocus pocus of her tribe.

She'd tried leaping forward a generation or two before such things were permissible. And like many a wide-eyed pilgrim soul, her reach had simply exceeded her grasp. She was still too close to the throwback models; locked and loaded, loose and lean in the scarred ways of former times. There was no world in these people, only a vicious circle of vice and virtue, contrition and redemption.

.... But along came the strapping young man with the dirt caked fingernails and a mind full of grand ideas; a handsome fellow of infinite purpose, if not questionable antecedents who hosanna'd the stars with a passion she'd never seen in her world. And so she took a chance, stepped forward, placed the apple upon her head, and closed her eyes....

.... Liam opened his own and quickly looked about. It had gone completely quiet out in the deep water and, he realized at once, this little endeavor had only become frightening when it finally became silent. He squinted through the salt water burning his eyes and could see a faint halo of light at the edge of the horizon; out somewhere in the distance between reality and a mirage. It would have to stay that way. He drifted a few minutes more under the grand canopy of stars before finally starting the long journey home.

Christopher M. Basso

Chapter Seven
Rue St. Vincent...la Fin

".... Oui?"

"Non..."

"Qu'est-ce qu'il y a?" *(what's wrong?)*

"Ce n'est pas toi c'est moi..." *(it's not you, it's me...)*

  It was in the quiet predawn stillness along the *Plage de la Sale Massage* when Rafael pressed his hands up underneath young Monique's fine white knickers, attempting to Rubik's Cube one hell of a stubborn bra clasp; *but no go*. Monique lays back along the dark sand and smiles; a pert, shapely girl fine and firm with a bit of come hither witchcraft in her eyes...and truth be told, quite the kinky *git* of these French kids to be wearing clothes on a beach.

  A bright blue light settles along the shore as Rafael mulls his Waterloo sunset moment with Victoria's Secret and quickly regroups; this boy's a player with some *game*. He jaw corks a bottle of *Château Les Valentines* rose and queues up the "intimate mix" on his Bose-travel setup lying nearby. Soon a heavy bass sound is kicking down the waves to meet the Roman Triremes, Spanish Galleons, and all other manner of foulness preceding him.... Artful Rafael is soon rounding second gearing up for the headfirst dive into third, when out the corner of his wondering eye what should appear, but the naked blurry visage of a man coming near.

Christopher M. Basso

.... The boozy predawn hormone amped mind wasn't equipped to deal with these sorts of primal scenes; the juxtaposition was just too rapid, the mind simply tripped some manner of default/overload switch. The startled beachcombers shot up just as a nice Jacques Brel track cycled through the mix. But the naked dripping man, rocked out with his cock out like Adam in the Garden, seemed to grasp this as well and thought to put them at ease.

"Carry on," he smiled, through some exceedingly bad French, before trotting up the Hibiscus and Oleander strewn path to one of the grand homes along the hill.

Book III
Monkey Man

Christopher M. Basso

Chapter One
El Mañana

"He's a terrible human being!" the voice carried long and lean over the ocean, "And if I *ever* get my hands on the son of a bitch, well, I don't know *what* I'll do!"

.... Click.

Liam silenced the BBC running stream and returned to the "ambient" playlist on his MacBook Pro.... Legions of angry (212) hausfrau's enunciating in fierce-like detail just what they'd do to the shamed junk bond Ponzi king being sentenced that morning was a bit more than the proverbial line could tow....Not that the boy didn't approve the general drawing and quartering of such scoundrels; in fact, *hell*, he'd probably do the honors himself if ever given the chance, but on the morrow such cantankerous intrusions were a tad heavy for the apathetic therapeutic vibe he'd been rocking with the diligence of a Shaolin monk.

O'Shea sat in the sun of his garden, on a creaky bench, beside the lovely hyacinth and snapdragons rising tall all around him. Before the boy sat a small sketchbook perched on an easel with its back facing the sea, and a mismatched box of pastels by his side. On the balance; the bearings of a fellow quite engaged with his work as he quietly sketched his youth away. Blissfully unaware of the sunflower sentinels peering down his shoulder, studying the hunched over figure furiously having a go with the creative life; ever polite with their critiques, ever reserved in the judgments, but of a *definite* opinion all the same.

Christopher M. Basso

Up along the stone wall his laptop ran quietly through the motions, a fine counterpoint ambiance lit with a low wattage softness. Within moments the irksome News of the World was gone and the reassuring cackle of the old Walrus himself, Dr. Winston O'Boogie, merrily broke the silence.

A righteous vibe of a time gone by if ever, and one ushering a pleasant half hour or so of utopian consonance into the sunny early morning proceedings. Fine, well enough; paradise regained or something in the neighborhood thereof. He had a slug off the nearby triple espresso and tried concentrating on his raggedy efforts.... But the morning's events crept back to the forefront. What of it, did the old biddy with the newfound Barbary Lust shouting at the newsmen really have a leg to stand on in the end?

Quite possibly, quite possibly; after all many a good, honest soul had just been fleeced with all the delicate consideration of an impish virgin at a prison rodeo.... And who knows; perhaps if those proverbial seven fat cows could sweep the sand of the seven lean years all might be well again...but then again maybe not. Reading Pharaoh's mind was never an easy thing, and creatures of a generally self-serving obligation tend to be spot on in their ability to screw the pooch anew like a Phoenix rising from the ashes.

.... Ugh, this was a heady morning mouthful at that, the kind he imagined best avoided. Besides, that blue haired Once-ler loon would've steamrolled all the Truffula Trees and Bar-ba-Loot chutes for a few extra nickels on the balance sheet anyway. Whole swaths of American flyover country have been razed by these grabasstic Beelzebub's who act as innocent as sheep to another's slaughter.... Old Cruella was never in it for a fair fight anyway, so why doth the lady protest now? Perhaps for the same simple reasons those Jacobin and Girondin heads went a' rolling down the Champs-Élysées once upon a time, but we digress; modern life was far too civilized for such crass wanker contemplations in the end, and fine Côte d'Azur mornings had no use for them at all.

.... Yeah, well bummer that. He reached for a smoke but then thought better. The moment seemed not to want it, and lately honoring the moment seemed about the wisest of things.

Rather, he shifted in his seat and brooded on another of the endless nameless dime store aphorisms visited on him of late like some unkempt, contemptible—yet roguishly sexy—Buddha who suddenly rocked the humility thing with all the joie de vive of a Frenchman eyeing a stick of Old Spice.

But then again this *was* the place to learn; the epic heart of the Antinomian contradiction, a bling'd out Dagobah system gimping along on songs of experience with a grizzled array of jewelry laden, Hermès totting Yoda's out to tin your ear in the many garbled tongues of the Dark Side.

He smiled, set his questionable efforts down and stared hard into the sea; one of those prescient moments of hellish self-reflection suddenly washing over him as they sometimes would.... At least he'd run the self-cleansing morality train on his own ass; that still had to count for *something*, even in the clutch of these demon days.

The boy laid back on the bench and felt the warm sun against his skin. He looked down at the almost finished sketch and looked over at the fully finished orange trees; a sort of heaviness cleaving the soul; the virtuous light keeping the uncomfortable equivocations a million miles away and the guileless summations a million pleasant more.

Liam placed the pastels in their case and set them on the bench. He pitched his half empty coffee onto the lawn and started towards the house. He shuffled up the stony pass, his sandals giving way under the crunch of the soft fieldstone, the stylish white boxers and trailing terrycloth robe giving him the mad bearings of one of the "end of the empire" inbred Caesars.... The heat was the principal culprit of course, but the more comfortable one grew with the lifestyle, the more an excess of clothing seemed a trifling extraneous thing.

A cool sort of breeze kicked up from the rocks below; the clouds had sapped the sun of its strength, and the bright colors of the villa and the gardens took on the muted tones of neutral shades. The general appearance was of a quiet and peaceful reserve.

The boy nipped quick into the kitchen and reloaded caffeine-wise before starting through the maze of his faded seaside home. The open windows framing the pleasant scents of the garden and the crisp salt of the sea with a languid loveliness, a languid loveliness interrupted only by the sudden ringing of a phone from somewhere deep within the bowels of ol' Brokedown Palace. A shrill shrieking racket cutting through the stillness like it always does.

The boy sighed; he knows the call, he always has—one of those clarion trumpets that rattles deep to the bone. He took a breath and counted the measures till it passed.... Hateful business a ringing phone; never good news, always bad, the friends posing thus, sharks and interlopers, ghouls and geisha; he let out a grim cackle—one's penultimate deliverance unto the paranoid waves of the sheltered strange and wandering weird.... That or perhaps just the Tandoori takeout down at the gate; but who knew, and the not knowing was the crude essence of the thing.

O'Shea stepped into the foyer with just a vague notion of answering the little beast, but once again thought better. Rather, he suddenly caught full sight of his open-robed truffle shuffle in the elegant fin de siècle mirrors adorning the great hall.... The revelation in profile was a less than aesthetic delight.

"Bit of an Oldcastle going there Liam James," he gave the gut a friendly shake, "Good Lord...any more and we can name it."

He slid over to the opposite side of the glass, sucked it in, and offered the thinnest of retorts.

"Well, they say insecurity is in fact the best kind of security—besides think of it as padding—*strong like bull.*"

The boy slowly let the air out of the tire.... Not so bad, not so good; wholly on the balance with the Madame George in her paler shades lifestyle, with perhaps just the faintest hints of fully caped rhinestone meltdowns hovering on the horizon.... He figured he could live with that.

He grabbed the jelly once again, "*In revelation illic est verum.*"

.... The Jesuits would never understand of course. There would be no way to properly explain himself to a gang of hymens who generally kept it to the pilgrim's progress with only the occasional vino veritas themed freakouts to rekindle the Phoenix. Luckily, Jesuits around these parts were about as rare as a natural face over forty; on the balance he should be just fine.

But luckily the shrill shrieking ceased and a calm normalcy returned to his faded seaside home; with just the delicate scents of the garden and salt of the sea to ring the grace notes once the charmless charmers have finally fucked off. The boy dialed it down a notch and returned to the kitchen where he raised the stakes on his Illy dark roast blend with a bit of the Jameson-Kahlúa fortifier; making sure to alm a measure for the angel's share lest anyone doubt his sincerity to the cause.

He sipped his rocket brew by the windows, admiring the shape of the gardener's skull down below, when the perturbations of the last ten minutes suddenly gave way to another sort of sound drifting from the upstairs of his faded seaside home; something soft at first, almost too faint to register, but slowly unwinding through the valleys of his mind. He craned his head skywards towards the Girandole balcony and listened…a song, a gentle voice carrying the most pleasant of tunes. He smiled and slowly started towards the second floor; taking care to cinch the robe and stow the hut; now codenamed "Nick Fury"—such calumnious transgressions were probably best left to the undiscovered country.

He made his way quietly up the stairs before pausing at the door to the bath; his penitent's mind suddenly in league with the most solemn of inhibitions. And a song he couldn't quite remember in union with a thought he was quick to forget. A strange unease crawling up the skin, the calamity about to assault the walls of a perfect day. Ah, psycho my psycho, the apprehension alive as ever, quick to the chase even when all else of evening's empire has returned into sand.… No matter, it was a lovely song indeed.

He peered around the corner, eyes carrying over the threshold; settling on the graceful shadows and a languid vision of…nothing. An empty bath, a solemn song, and the silence that comes to a house where no one can sleep. He smiled, stepped over to the long pedestal tub, climbed in, and stretched out. His legs crossed, resting against the cerulean Moorish tiles, the finest of southern light falling across the delicate mosaic designs, and the snows falling faintly and faintly falling across the universe...oh well. To be lucky in life was not to be lucky in all things after all; or some such noise. He rested his head against the cool tile and let the music slowly take him someplace else.

.... A beauty and a vision given unto him, but thoughts never far from the sturm und drang of the last few weeks; his mind never far from the coffee shop of the Côte d'Azur international airport; thirty-six days ago to be exact.

A mainline time from another era, but the boy was no longer the minder of such retrograde exactitudes. Time had shifted to something of an expansive commodity of late and minding the ledger was the most unpardonable of sins these days.... But the impetus of conscience was another beast altogether. And that same impetus was still at a loss to answer the whys he should have boarded that evening's freedom bird to back to America and the one very persuasive reason he did not.

"You sure you're going to be ok?" Her smile was as reassuring as ever, though no longer privy to the new wisdom of the quick and the dead.

"Of course."

"It's not too late Warbucks, we can still get you a ticket?" She waxed in her whimsical way.

"What, and miss the rest of opera season with the Ed's?"

She sighed, "Just trying to look out for my broken ladder."

"Getting to be a real chore for you."

"It's what I'm good at; the points to go to Heaven kind of thing."

He returned her smile; a hollow bit of empty at that, dressed up with all the joie de vivre of a Soviet May Day parade.

"This is no country for old men; isn't that what the poem says?"

"Sounds like fine advice if you're slightly insane, or a man of means. Where'd you land that gem anyway?"

"Men's Journal...or Yeats; I forget which."

"Well, that says it all then…"

He rubbed the back of her neck, "…. Just a few more weeks and I'll be along; I promise."

"I worry about you." There was something uneasy in her voice.

"And that's why I love you my dear…but I think this is something I should do."

"Still trying to make this flake-out seem something noble are we?"

"Well, at least it ain't evil; besides I'm starting to rather enjoy the endurance aspect of this thing; like a deviant marathon."

"…. It is what it is."

They shared a smile that was somewhere between the gentle understood chiding of family, where all was bound to be forgiven, and the nervous tension of youth, unobligated by blood and just narcissistic enough to seek its own path in all these greater glories.

Indeed, maybe it was the sunlight or the warmth of the breeze, but he'd certainly found a firm footing in these Judas rhythms of late; and regrettably the young lady to his left, bound for New York and then the wilds of some far flung African outpost, had nary the clue she'd just been cast the unwitting Ingrid Bergman in one man's private *Casablanca* moment.

The den mother was already taxiing down runway 46C as he hightailed it back across the city to his newfound existence out on the point; and whatever attendant mischief might follow on its heels…. But then again those were just the squirrely thoughts of some dream best deferred…perhaps till the stars fall from the sky and the ol' hidden wisdom flows like grace.

The simple sun returned to his eyes and he sat up again, nearly spilling his beverage and reminded himself that these little betrayals of the mind were still permissible so long as they didn't translate to those of the heart…or something to that effect. And perhaps the summa grata consolation of this particular passing fancy was that while guilty he was probably somehow *technically* still innocent.

Either way, it was time to get his mind off this....Perhaps go for a quick dip in the lovely blue waters, make a fine rum punch, and pass out in the old hammock down by the beach; assured once again in the ultimate divination of these moves.

But in a flash those imperial thoughts were gone and his mind returned to the same uneasy stasis of a man who knows he's transgressed in some deep, profound, and lasting way, but alas was unsure of just…quite…where.

The young penitent ambled down the stairs and out across the lawn towards the old hammock slung low between two olive trees to slumber off the last of it; his head still unmoored from last night's tangle with the Volga Boatman, promising himself to never sell the soul too short, to follow the lemonade springs to where the bluebird sings, and *never* listen to the wisdom of strange men on trains again.

Around dusk the boy woke with the sudden urge to fill this newfound silence with something a bit more *substantial*; perhaps even throw his own two cents into the millennia long brouhaha? He hoped on the Ducati and motored over to Bonnie Prince Charlie's *Imports of Distinction* in Sainte-Helene with thoughts of purchasing the bike outright. The logic being; anything worth doing was worth doing *well*.

The Bonnie Prince was a loud Scottish expat with a huge gut, nuclear winter tan, and a fine eye for the best in Italian ego-stroking machinery. Liam had struck up a casual friendship of sorts with the old codger, based on their seeming mutual zeal for destructiveness codified by the measure of another's means. The Bonnie Prince was in fact one of the many wharf rat regulars down at Le Select, and the two had sealed the May-December friendship over several shot gunned rounds of thirty-aught-six Limoncelo-vodka death; followed of course by the peering in the leering way, at all the comely young ladies out along the surf.

.... But such a cordial familiarity didn't curtail the epic horse wrangling session that ensued. To be a man of some means was not to instantly confer the status of a rube-like chump, meant to be *done* on any and all fronts. The ownership of the bike was now on the table, and the boy was in no mood to be trifled with by another wannabe Gallic assclown.

After a considerable amount of bad noise and threats of recriminations of a rather personal nature, the bike was his; and for a very choice price at that. As Smiling Charlie waited for the paperwork to clear he assured the young man he'd made the *right* choice.

.... Clever fellow, old Charlie, but was he clever enough to divine the true wisdom of this move? Was there even any? A quick and the dead brand of nimbleness had certainly enveloped the boy of late—a sort of pervasive action and reaction type of lifestyle that might have just been the new wisdom of things, that road to the palace of wisdom as it were.... He sighed as he signed along the dotted line. In the absence of an anchor such drifting gin addled rubbish would have to suffice.

He pulled out the dealership with some complimentary racing stripes and helmet decals, fairly pleased with himself as he headed back to the house on the point. He had many plans yet for the bike; she would prove much the Rocinante daisy on the many long rides he had still to make all over the South.

Nothing but fine, head clearing days with little more than the same pair of clothes on his back, crumbled cigarettes in his pocket, and a platinum card which he wielded like a gun.... Broad open stretches of road laced with treacherous curves and stomach churning switchbacks; just enough to relax the mind and just enough to remember you were still alive. But as clear as the mind could feel, it sat forever moored beneath the firmament, that bitch of an anchor which measured how all things must pass.

He ginned these same thoughts several nights later, returning from the Provencal hills, and his daylong test drive of the new low-end theory. He was drifting along the *Promenade des Anglais* in Nice, through the slow gears, with grand plans for a relaxed bender back at the ranch. Locate a sixer of lager and some deep-dish pizza from one of these Continental shills who might have actually spent some time in America, and he could call it a night.

As for the rest of it; perhaps keep it simple, try not to push your luck. The kind of grandiosity you can conjure up idling in neutral in the warm embrace of a failing sun tends to wither badly under the lonely specter of someone missing at the table.

…. Pathetic though, you're thinking way too small boyo. Ditch the bike; get yourself an Aston Martin, rent a tux, and head over to the *Grande Casino Monte Carlo*. Perhaps try your luck at *that* wanker fantasy? Cozy up to some wily Grace Kelly redux and test-drive the Cary Grant lifestyle in the fullest sense, now that the last whingeing vibe of scrupulous moral constraint was gone.

But by the time he reached the big set of traffic lights in front of the Hotel Negresco he'd burned through most of that bad air. He hated gambling with a passion and rental tuxes never fit him right through the shoulders, not to mention Monte Carlo was the one place that even the locals considered a bit too *far out* to be handled on any meaningful level.

He sat there idling after the green. Unbeknownst to the boy, this was almost the same spot where Isadora Duncan had met her grisly end nearly a century earlier, courtesy of a flapping silk scarf and her touring car's graceless tires. This was no place for the weak indeed. He admired the long white pergolas lining the Promenade, catching shades in the in the sunset before gunning the beast eastward.

A few hours later and he was sitting back on the stone terrace at the villa, with the last of his Peroni six-pack and an empty pizza box. It was, after all, these simple pleasures that were still the best. Not the loudest, but the quiet ones, for they required the least amount of effort and that was key.

He felt the crush of the can in his hand and watched it sail down into the pool below, fully satisfied he would soon turn into *that* neighbor; a fellow ready to gleefully dive head long into that finest brand of filial depredation and degradation. Well, as long as you didn't tip your hand too far, this bunch was probably ready to tolerate your act indefinitely. He did make a gesture to the anchor of civic normality that night and had several loads of laundry running down in the basement. It had, after all, been a while and even the palace guards have some limits on free form personal hygiene.

But however busy you were in the midnight hours, the morning would still come crawling back with the foul ponderings of how to fill another day with an artful bit of the next dodge. The practiced only child in Liam could take to the solitude scene quite nicely: more swims, more dreams, more of everything and a fair share of nothing.

His tale could read like a sad compendium of the stuff....Getting in Dutch with the newfound barfly friends at the Papaya Lounge in Villefranche; wandering through the lively little villages at night, lit loud with a whole class of high rollers who always stake the matador and never bet the bull...perhaps brood a bit on the unjust nature of it all over your seventh limoncello-Grey Goose mashup...then maybe score one for the little man as you defile your neighbor's fortress walls, wandering home late in the night, slightly lost, thoroughly deranged, and badly in need of the loo.

Indeed, falling backwards unto the strange rhythms of a place could prop one up with a fair sense of normalcy; buy your bread from just the right *boulangerie* down on the esplanade, load up on useless wines from some postcard vineyard you've found out in the country, get to know the merchants a bit, a hello and a goodbye, some commendable attempts at broken French.

But there would always be that restless vibe kicking around the shadows, the one that rides in shotgun whenever the calm waves of repetition rear their ugly head and then it would be time to split. You might find yourself standing down at the pier in Villefranche one day watching the big boats drift around the harbor and then all of the sudden it *comes* to you—damn, if it wasn't time to hit the high seas.

Indeed; get yourself a fine ship and a star to steer her by, liquor up on Ahab courage and Starbuck mash, then sail that fucker straight into the maw; right around the bestial hell of Cape Horn, through the pirate infested waters of the Chilean Straits on a savage burn to the beauty of the South Seas.... *Society Islands*, they might be nice this time of year? Maybe meet up with Fred Dewan at the St. Regis, Bora Bora for a few drinks, pull a

Christopher M. Basso

Fletcher Christian on his killjoy Bligh loving ass, then start the whole bit over again. Just keep rolling son; keep moving, remember, they can't catch what they can't see.

.... Papa Ernesto's lions running down the beach will never find you here, you've outlasted them, outrun them all; around the world and back.... Just the rosewater sherbet scent of the gravity bong confessional and the sweet burn of the pipe...inhale, exhale, exhumation, exaltation. Lovely was life in a daydream, but the downside always awaited, the moment of cresting over the mountain to that well trod place where all ascendant leaps go to die, and the grass grows long covering all disrepair.

.... And such strange, sad scenes could repeat themselves with the verse-chorus-verse perpetuity of the seasons, until one day, you find yourself laying on the beach of some far flung atoll, splayed out big boy style, like some mad Tahitian Brando after he took it to a cheeseburger Valhalla. Stark naked under a blanket of stars, not a soul for miles, only the quiet sounds of the surf on the beach and the wind through the trees to keep you company.... Your body corrupted by the accumulation of excess, your marbles turned to mush by the vanity of self.

But those were just the rumblings of an idle daylight fancy, and everything looked better in the day, even if it felt better at night. A nighttime of weak knees and shaky spirits, of the walking wounded. Forget the rabbit hole, those were for gentler times, it was all about a full bore tilt down the K-hole these days; of whatever turned your mind to ether fastest.... And all around the spinning whirls and buzzcock sounds, shape shifters who come to you as friends, ghouls, the chewers of corpses.... You should really lay off the recreational opiates my boy—that shit's a paranoid gateway, or so they say.

In two shakes time you'll be taking bumps off the rude tiller; lost, balls-deep, in the ontological riddles of our time....Hot tinfoil burns the nostrils; deep breaths, Xanax for the fear, Rohypnol abbreviates the brain, Librium takes away the pain....Till finally you wind up mad as a hatter, bending spoons with your mind, setting imaginary places at the table like some doss wee girl with her first tea set.

And there was always that evil little Screwtape sat perched on your shoulder to consider, the one that always seems to show up in the midst of some personal hell, vicious withdrawal, or backbreaking litigation. Probably best to just avoid the fucker on many levels; practical, ecclesiastical, and otherwise.

.... Boredom; rustle about your Provencal summer home, lifting latches burning matches, till at last you find yourself digging through that red box of memories. Standing with her atop the *Torre del Mangia* in Siena, the rubia Dulcinea smiling on the stone steps in front of the Prado, a quiet moment under the warm Madeira sun.... Absence has always made the heart grow fonder; like a mawkish line of nostalgia rendered gloriously anew in brilliant pixels of digital light. Windy winding traveler's tales; boring as all hell, but her smiling face still makes it somehow seem worthwhile.

.... Boredom; rustle about some more, dig out the *other* tapes...cause it goes without saying that the deviant beast has to be served every now and then. Fire up the high definition camcorder; hook the auxiliary to the sixty-inch plasma, large and larger star of stage and screen.... The pause of a blue-green screen before it jumps to life.

O'Shea manning the camera, straddling the parapet of an ornate oriel balcony, panning out to the Eiffel Tower, bathed in glorious orange and yellows, his lovely standing in the foreground, her smile mixing with the sunset of the city of light.... Go on then love; give us a bit of a show. What's that? No, we won't tell a soul; burn the tapes when were through we will, scout's honor.

Everyone is a voyeur these days anyway, exhibitionists laying low in plain sight; a generation of kinky Scorsese wannabes caterwauling their double fantasies as they turn money into light; marrying moment with the memory... Hold up that tush now, watch the Dutch tilt on the long shot; get ready, this grindhouse feature is about to go tent pole epic—cut, print, check the gate!

.... Exactly five minutes and thirty six seconds later these thoughts return to more family friendly fare; the camera capturing the blur of an artful tableaux sailing by; The Coliseum, The Rijksmuseum, Big Ben, Versailles; each time capturing the smile,

Christopher M. Basso

the smile you take with you when you go.... Till finally the camera is turned on the boy, a broad sort of grin across his face, contentment in the eyes, innocent to the last...his well-tended crusty playboy act sideswiped by the soul that was once, creeping through the darkness, slouching towards the light.... Where the hell did that one come from anyway? Skullduggery to be sure—better burn the tapes...no future in louche hipster cynicism with that one drifting about.

Click off the power; a blue screen again, just the crickets in the tall grass, a boat motor's hum in the evening distance, and the wind through the willows. For each man kills the thing he loves, yet each man does not die... or some such rubbish that steeled the nerves once.

.... Utter boredom; take your act for a stroll through the ins and outs of this faraway land, with the tourist crush slowly fading the subtle colors start to shine through; interesting fancies abound. A small market just inside the gates of the old town, hear the cries of the sellers in the street; strange sights and sounds, no French here, Berber Arabic; the shadows of a mosque falling gently along the ground, leading further down narrow back streets; the muezzin's call to sunset prayer carries a lonely song on the evening breeze.... A street peddler apothecary with his jangling cart of goods slowly passes by, the scent of food nearby, strange aromas, spice and flower, Morocco and Algiers; days spent like this, Moorish highs, beastly lows, stranger in a strange land.

.... Lost in surrender, the eyes sink slowly in the happy warmth, a shiver in the trees signals the evening wind; travel around the world and back if only in your mind, but all things are of a temporal fancy, all things an illusory grace falling back unto themselves; the moment passes, only the memory remains.

.... But then such were the perils of riding shotgun on your own burning bush act. And what to do when you've lost your co-pilot? The one last thing that kept *the voices* in check....Go to sleep, start fresh in the morning. To be lucky in life was not to be lucky in all things; a remembered phrase playing through his mind as he chomped on a bit of cold pizza; the room spinning, the clocks ticking, and the world still counting backwards to zero.

And so it came to be that he awoke on an innocent enough Thursday morning several weeks later, in the solarium, with a spate of hunger for a thirst he'd foolishly quenched. He squinted towards the welcoming sky; and the wages of sin were paved with a bright sun and a bad heart for those who took the wrong path indeed. He dressed and wandered down to the village at St. Jean, but all the shops were closed for no apparent reason other than the locals really did seem to take this notion of comfort over commerce to heart.

Scores of summer people were drifting out by the day now, as the slow exodus of conspicuous consumption began in earnest. Many, hell, maybe most of the large homes and villas dotting the point and rising up along the hills were shuttered for the winter. In a few weeks all that would remain would be the few straggle-hards—ginned up Euro bluebirds, and the odd mix of security contractors and caretakers...Maybe it was *time* to finally make his way back into the haze and grim of Nice? After all, life was getting just a wee bit suspiciously beautiful out there on the point; maybe it was time for the milieu to the match the man—not to mention score himself some grub.

In short order he hopped a gypsy cab and made his way back into the maelstrom; the stomach a bit sour, the mind a bit warped from last night's hobo alley cat wanderings, and the soul in need of a touch of the beast to mediate that humbling perspective back to a healthy stasis. Besides, the mind could only take so much hubris and salvation was forthcoming.... Eggs, cheese, bread, grease—it was a plan elegant in its simplicity.

That was till you found yourself arguing with some French teenager 'cause you've just slipped into the *Rue Moulins* Golden Arches at 11:04 a.m. and the lunchtime Gestapo just burned you to the tune of no Mcgrease, precipitating one boondoggle of a clusterfuck that just sabotages your shit utterly and entirely.

The scene at the counter quickly turned standard trim, ugly American. O'Shea's brain, having rummaged around the Continent for months now, had finally waved goodbye to that last shred of gracious diplomatic restraint. There was simply no consoling him. A string of heated invective was suddenly flying across the counter; ranging from snide remarks about the whip marks from the jockey on the "McChevalier", to what the fuck was a "Croque McDo" and why would he want one anyway?

This sad *mise-en-scène* dragged on for a few tense minutes ultimately involving several of the line cooks, the manager, and some bilingual locals whose civic pride might just have been insulted—that is till they had the boy safely hustled to a booth near the windows at the rear of the place, hunched over a complimentary McCrispy and coffee black, pondering this foul reversal of fortune.

…. What did these yobs expect anyway; if the fascists were gonna rule the counter with an iron hand they should expect the odd bit of withering jingoistic abuse now and then…. No matter, pay no mind; the demon days were back upfront, and with that grim bit of reality sorted he was free to enjoy the hard charging caffeine rush and the parade of humanity sailing by the windows.

He half-heartedly glanced at his morning copy of the *Nice Matin*; the French learning had seemed to stall somewhere between kindergarten babble and the guidebook conversational…a stone cold bummer that. He tossed it in the bin and focused his energies on a bit of people watching. The boy sat back in his chair and surveyed the scene running down the long expanse of the *Rue de Russie*, and what seemed to pass for the high street in this rather beaten down part of Nice.

Before him lay a collection of rather seedy real estate concerns; of fading buildings and the washed out colors of the *Belle Époque* propped up by the garish storefronts of the abandoned Médecins. These poor old places had started to imbue that same burnt quality of the land, these things waiting for a fresh coat of gentrification. But from this little perch it held a fine vantage point over a city on a hill and the long steep dive to the sea…and the sea of graceless faces passing by.

Liam braced the senses for another day of nothing in particular; of haughty boredoms of the first order, of eyes stretched to the horizons of these shores as it were…that was till life suddenly zigged where it had most often zagged. And with just the slightest ocular flutter catching the eye, like those spectral ghosts off at the edge of perception, that certain something clicked and one of life's little doors was kept from closing. He straightened up a bit, searching for the bearings, focusing his eyes under the sun...but where was it? Somewhere.... There.

A tall dark haired figure moving along the silhouettes of glass and sunlight, several paces down the way. Back turned, but no mistaking, it had to be her; his playmate from the gardens of Dunamore.... Well, kiss my grits. Three months, half a continent, and a healthy dose of mirthful sloth later and he was suddenly back in the Irish countryside carrying a drunken Gaelic scion through the midnight topiary.... This was simply too delicious a thing to let pass; he had never been part of some random collision of chance and circumstance. To have spited it, and returned to his happy meal, would have been the acme of eschatological rudeness.

But what was the next play? She was presently cutting along at the good clip, moving down the street towards the *Zone Pietron*. Better jog that memory quick or a memory this would have to stay.... Constance? No...*Claudia*. All right ropey boy, you've gone long on the daily double, but now what? He leaned back for a moment; sipping his complimentary coffee and pondered the karmic curveball the fates had just tossed his way.

Another fine crossroads indeed; just toasted enough to grasp that life's little moments don't drift along all too often, and yet fully cognizant of the creepy outcomes often bred in the detritus, madness, and fairy dust of a moment.... Open doors weren't always the best things to bull through; a jaded surety assured him, no guarantees of anything—redemptive, worthwhile, or otherwise. Though he could sense that bitch's brew of butterflies and giddiness laced with just the faintest twinges of trepidation rising up in him. Like that big jet lumbering down the runway for liftoff, the kind of last ringing nerve which must be silenced before you could fully commit to the leap.

He leaned back fully in the chair, soaking up the foul milieu of stale air and week old fryer grease, and had another quick look out the window. She had passed. His eyes scanned down the street. From his booth he had a fine view of entire intersection; a jumbled little tangle of open air cafes and one-off shops; a combustible mix combusting. A sea of faces he would never know, moving about in the random half crazed energy of the morning. These were the mystical booming voices in the booming town that that mad old uncle of his had wanked on about; none of them aware they were now playing periphery characters in this unfolding little drama.

He ditched his drink and made quick for the sliding doors, stumbling out into the sunlight, and nearly tripping over the curb. A few tense seconds passed before he spotted her again, looking through the sidewalk stacks of a used bookstore along the *Rue des Invalides*. He made his way closer, hanging back in the shadows of the overhangs, keeping his distance as he sorted out the possible greetings and salutations.

She looked good...*damn,* better than he remembered in fact. Yep, that should just about complicate things properly. Her dark, very dark, straight hair was wrapped over a smooth, porcelain complexion, like some vampire who scored a day-pass in the sun. How the hell did you stay so fair traipsing around down here anyway? A fine question and a delicate mystery indeed.

In the midst of his machinations she'd given up on the bookstore and started down the avenue in the general direction of the *Place Massena*. He loitered under the eaves for a moment, still not quite sure where this little kinderspiel was headed.

After all, solitude had been bliss, just as silence had been golden.... Retreat back to the villa on the point, the angel on his shoulder entreated, safe behind the tall walls and parapets...perhaps order up some takeout? A little Niçoise comfort food for the pledge, a little Internet porn for the turn, and an inspired foxtrot with the old hangdaddy for the prestige—not necessarily in that order, but a *decent* evening all the same.

.... Either way this inspired bit of predatory stalking was starting to make him feel a bit grime-soaked, like the busted storefronts and weatherworn walls under which he loitered. The boy pulled back at length, content in the end to mind his manners.

But still, that one twingeing nerve just wouldn't let go—not that that was any real surprise. Songs of innocence would always lose the trumpet call to those of experience; why should this little bit of scorched Earth be any different? Though maybe he'd just let the fates decide, the same rotten little bastards who'd ginned him into this mess could be the same ones to lay the final judgment. He'd hop the next bronze and gold tram car heading down the road and hop off wherever seemed about right. If providence should find her again, then he would have his answer.

He spotted the carriage making its way down the hill and jumped on near the Cathedral de Notre Dame. The old car slowly snaked down the avenue, cresting over the rises, the downward tilts affording fine views of the *Baie des Anges* on a slightly cloudy day. The Mediterranean waters lay still in the distance, blending coarse and even at the horizon.

As the tram made its way down the avenue, he kept his eyes straight ahead, past the stores and cafes; there was no need to cheat the luck of a perfect draw. The large bells of the cathedral started to boom, a deep bellowing sound you could hear clear across the whole of Nice, signaling the high noon call to Mass. Maybe that was the sign? He'd never had much luck with it anyway, but it seemed about right...that and the conductor making his way to the back of the car. Ticketless young Americans bereft of exact change were an easy mark for one of those 200 Euro on the spot fines.

He rang the bell for the next stop, hopping off near the northern edge of the vast *Place Massena,* near a small bosquet of palms and stone pines he didn't quite recognize. Well enough, he thought, and started for the open space of the square. The *Place Massena* was an old school European square in the grandest sense; a vast openness of fountains and statuary, tree lined esplanades, and monuments.

It was a space meant to conjure a sense of awe, or merciless ego, and when wedged betwixt the cramp quarters of the rest of Nice it only served to heighten a dramatic effect. Versailles it was not, but certainly a step up from the venal Golden Arches on the proper dramatic scale of *occasion*.

Christopher M. Basso

He stood off to the edge of a smaller courtyard and studied the general sense of combustion and humanity before him. Hundreds of em', hell maybe even thousands, milling about the vast expanses of stone and grass, and yet no sign of the day pass vampire.

He leaned against one of the sturdy iron gas lamps nearest the courtyard wall, hunched in a fine catcher's crouch, and exhaled at length. At the far western side of the square, a glass and gilded Ferris wheel turned silently like the slow wheels of a clock, each ornate car swaying gently in the breeze; its soft lights flashing of a regal world long since gone.

He studied this empty scene, confident, though a bit annoyed he'd made the right choice yet again; and suddenly quite at ease with the notion that all things are utterly and irrevocably preordained.... That was until she rounded out of the boutique tin shop on the opposite corner, a pack of Boyton Reds gently tilling against the palm of her hand.

A slight twinkle of questioning flashed across her eyes followed by a welcoming smile of recognition.

"Bruce Wayne, right?"

Chapter Four
Supersize Me

Camus died in a terrible car crash at a place called "Le Grand Fosard" near the small town of *Villeblevin*. In the pocket of his coat was an unused train ticket to his ultimate destination; a ticket he had foregone for a little Sunday jaunt through the Burgundy countryside. A bad choice? Perhaps, but a seemingly poignant one all the same, considering he once said dying in a car crash was about the most absurd way he could imagine checking out.

But scheduling mishaps aside; what did he see in those final moments...the ones where the mind no long matters, when all the defenses are laid bare? Are we brave in the breach, staring down the wrong end of the abyss, or quick to renounce the vanities that have defined our lives? Life after all is a measurement, a study in how we handle the unknown, in the sudden curves that in the end define our story.

So how is it we handle the "Grand Fosard" of running across some attractive stranger in a faraway land, burnt to a crisp and at the end of one's rope? Particularly after you've stalked the poor girl for the last six or seven blocks on the sly? Do we stand there making pleasantries about the weather, current events, or the entire spectrum of things slightly less interesting than the price of tea in China? No, that was for weaker souls. Venture boldly forth, "So, you a dainty top or power bottom?"

Restrain yourself crazy man, that's the talk of lesser souls. Hold fast; go for the middle ground, remember—grace under pressure.

"Hello there...Claudia."

".... Fancy meeting you here," she smiled. ".... I'd have thought you long home by now?"

He shrugged, "What can I say; Europe's grown on me."

She smiled, studying his weathered tan and fine barfly beach demeanor, "You've gone native I see?"

"You like it? It's the latest in hobo chic."

"It suits you well."

".... What are *you* doing here?" He asked.

"I live here—maybe I didn't mention that?"

"You probably did, but I can't remember, I was fairly in the bag that evening."

"Weren't we all?" She leaned in a bit closer like she was about to share a secret. "By chance, did you stay around for brunch the next day? Apparently, the Bride's father started a full on row with the caterers; some perceived slight with the Hollandaise or something...*quite* the scene I'm told."

"No I split before dawn, one night of the Irish wedding was enough for me."

".... So, what have you been up to since?"

"Just travelling around. Went to a bunch of places. Though, I've been down here slumming it for like a month now."

"A month?"

"Hells yeah, rented myself a house and everything."

"You really have gone native."

"Right down to the baguettes and berets."

"God, I hope not." She laughed.

He studied her for a second. "So, what about you?"

"Oh, traveling as well. Though, like I said, this is my home, well, was my home." Her expression soured, "My family just sold our home up in the hills; I've been on a sort of farewell tour of the place ever since."

"I take it this wasn't a happy thing?"

She sighed, "It'd been in our family three generations; since the *Twenties* in fact. Hard to let something like that go, you know?"

The clan O'Shea had never really embraced the whole "manse of the manor" thing, but he politely tried to play along, "Yeah, guess so."

But then the winds suddenly shifted and they arrived in the land of Non; into that slightest of moments where the shock of recognition has worn off and the exchange of pleasantries have been exhausted; the point where a kind of *awkwardness* informs the next move. Do you sandbag the moment and hightail it on your respective paths, or dig in hard the heels and ratchet things up a notch?

Maybe she sensed it too, the exhilarating rush of the unknown, even if your intentions were as clean and unfettered as the angels…. But then again, by the turns of the screw, that same innocence always held the portents for an embrace of something a wee bit, well, darker. And for a tender moment, there hung the split second where the possibility was alive for either.

As he debated himself to death, rambling ad infinitum these perversions of the mind, Claudia Sommerton let him off the hook with the slightest shrug of her shoulders.

"I was heading down to the marketplace for a look around…want to go for a walk?"

"Uh, yeah, sure thing."

And so down the avenue they went, slowly angling east, along the narrow labyrinth of ancient streets; the kind which required an elephant's memory, rather than map or reason to navigate, till finally they reached the ramparts of the oldest part of the city; the *Vieux Nice*. This was a truly strange and stunning neighborhood of crumbling terracotta roofs and colorful low-lying apartment flats, its entirety measuring time in some blissfully elegant state of disrepair.

The cramped, somewhat derelict, alleyways were often no wider than the span of a man's arms. Daylight barely crept in between the lovely old Baroque buildings, weathered in colorful Mediterranean shades; their ghostly wrought iron balconies standing sentinel over the unending procession below.... In fact, the argument could be made that the *Vieux Nice* was really more of its own separate entity, clipping along nicely on some level of aesthetic disconnect from the generally drab functionality of greater Nice.

.... Which is not to say the place wasn't a viciously over cramped tourist trap in the high season. O'Shea had wandered in a few times, generally in the altered state of the wailing banshees and entropy faeries, only to come across more Americans than a Saturday at Churchill Downs on Derby day. His buzz rudely put to rest as he mingled with the masses, shelling out fifteen bucks for watery double espressos to mediate the ache behind his eyes, and matching wits with the Gypsy street urchins who'd deftly lift the wallet from any and all hung-over *bête touriste* should they lose the plot.... But you gotta go there to come back, or so they say; and such paranoid ramblings were for another day.

Hunting season had passed and a calm sort of circadian rhythm pervaded the scene as they rounded the last switchback alleyway and descended a steep staircase of faded ochre stone till they were delivered into the broad open air of the *Cours Saleya* marketplace; a place that had a controlled bustle you could hear, smell, and feel before ever actually setting eyes on it.

It was an anticipation richly rewarded. The expansive tree lined courtyard was filled with tents, cafes, and a bustling crowd; even in this last gasp of what one could still call summer. Each of the tents was filled with vendors manning stall after stall of fresh flowers, olives, wine, fruits, and vegetables... and quite possibly the entire detritus bric-a-brac of the Alpes-Maritimes; as though the whole of the Niçoise coast decided to empty out the attic one night and see what grandma's old bits could fetch.

Each of the canopies was shaded with white ribbon, offset by solid shades of reds, blues, and greens. He wondered if the neat uniformity of the colors held some deeper meaning in the processional of things? He even thought to ask, but something else had caught his attention. Subtle at first, the kind of thing which makes you take a breath and question whether you had spent too much time in the sun...but then there it was again.

Between the wanderings and conversation young Claudia would occasionally reach over for a quick sampling of whatever caught her fancy; a bit of fig here, a dash of lychee there. Just a minor helping of the wares, particularly when the vendor's back was turned or otherwise distracted.... Either this was how it was done round these parts, or he suddenly had a real *viber* on his hands. She hadn't actually mentioned what they'd come down here for in the first place, perhaps she was brushing up on her own street urchin skills?

After lifting a small bunch of flowers with the dexterous hand of some scamp who would have done Dickens proud, they turned towards the small church at the far end of the courtyard. This little chance encounter didn't really seem to be obeying the scripted arc of such things anyway, why stop at a wee bit of thievery? They passed beneath the dome of St. Raoul's and, with a lull in the conversation, a smile passed between them.

"What were you saying about your family home?"

"Oh, well, my parents, my aunt, and my uncles went through with the sale last week.... Sort of a family scandal really, half of the brood wanted it, the other half didn't; the kind of thing that drives some families apart." She grinned, "There's going to be blood before this one is settled."

Again, the O'Shea cupboard was rather bare in matters of inbred, intransigent inheritance battles, but he tried to play the chipper git.

"Bad huh?"

".... It's going to get worse before it gets better."

"Where is it, this house?"

She pointed back up way, "Up there in the hills; the neighborhood is called Cimiez, a pretty old place of grand homes and gardens."

"Sounds nice."

"It is, but that's sort of gone now, no longer me." She paused. "They finally got around to signing the papers last week, no family, just a room full of lawyers…billed the sale, signed the contracts, and the movers scraped away the last of it yesterday."

"C'est fine?"

"More like, *détruire entièrement.*"

She had exhausted his French, but he nodded sagely all the same.

"Despite all this, I can't say it's not that bad…. Quite the opposite, I've had this extraordinary sensation come over me the last couple of days."

"What's that?"

"Just sort of a strange realization that I'd outgrown the place…sort of a requiem for the past I suppose."

She twirled the small bundle of rockrose in her hand and stared ahead. "You ever have the feeling you'll never be returning to a place?"

"All the time." His mind flashed to this morning's culinary adventures; or a half dozen other grievous injuries these Europeans had visited upon him, "I can think of the few."

"No, I mean a place you know, a place that's meant something to you."

"Well, in that case no, probably not."

"Sort of bittersweet parting; like somehow, in the end, you've maybe mutually wronged each other."

"Sounds more like a premonition; that I can understand."

She smiled, "Well, these premonitions tell me I've grown to truly dislike this place; the grime, the soot, the crime, the crowds…I think maybe I always have."

He couldn't help but agree.

"Maybe more so, the way it knows me, the way I know it. You can become too familiar with a place; know each other's secrets too well. It's not until the prospects of an eternal departure present themselves that you really bring some clarity to the equation."

She had in fact lost him again, but her pretty voice made it worth the listening. She had a soft accent, a gentle lilting thing; something warm and knowing, something that belonged down here with the sunshine and the blue sky, far from the reaches of any bloated Cockney bombast.

"I've always thought," she continued, "that if you could weather the insanity of a thing, if you had a piece of something to call your own, then you would never feel so alone. A legend to your own map."

"And now it's gone?"

"And now it's gone…lose that bit of the rock and get a clean look, your first clean look, and an entire opinion can change overnight…. Necessity has an ugly way of clearing out a rose tinted view of things."

She smiled again, "Not that I'm *bitter* or anything…. Anyway, I just thought the place deserved a little farewell of sorts."

"Is that what this is then? A sentimental journey?"

"Well, we each face the prospects of a growing past and the reality of diminishing future; so maybe it *is* sentimental."

"Or perhaps madness?"

She smiled, "Something like that."

They kept moving as she led them down a set of stone staircases and side streets till they suddenly seemed very far from the bustle and crowds of the market. Soon they were walking along a pathway of crushed, faded stone towards a lovely little *parterre* garden hidden amid the haze and grime of Nice.

"I come here to think now and then," was all she offered.

417

Christopher M. Basso

They walked past the Aleppo pine and Fern palms before stopping to admire an old wooden pergola, set like the sheltering firmament across the broad open courtyard. A lovely thing of silver oaks trained across a white skeleton maple shoot; sad and frail in the morning light, with the first leaves of autumn warming shades of orange and red along the ground.

They took a seat on one of the faded iron benches lining the path, as a gentle breeze passed through the ivy branches of the pergola, and the sounds of the city faded to distant concern, removed from the here and now. She was on a role with the trip down memory lane and he was more than content to listen. She'd picked up where John Oldcastle left off with a little jangle about the Niçoise carnival tradition; describing in detail the true rhythms of the beast; when the looming clouds rolling in from the sea finally made good on the threat.

A light trailing mist quickly shifted gears to a steady driving rain. The eaves under the pergola offered some protection, but the weather was picking up by the minute. They made a mad dash for an abandoned colonnade that sat near the far side of the garden; old and faded but offering something in the way of shelter.

By turns the sky over Nice quickly lit up in bright flashes and a distant rumbling grew ever closer. It was a full on beast, one of those rare but frightful storms that lashes the South from time to time, the kind of thing the locals either rejoice at in its provenance or curse for the rude intrusion. Claudia seemed to be of the latter opinion as she stood in the stone archway as the winds began to pick up. She stared apprehensively skyward with a look that seemed to be in the grips of a planning strategy.

The colonnade was old, well past its use for these sorts of things, and in no time they were both fairly wet to the touch; shivering a bit in the sudden storm.... But a touch of the rain, despite its inconvenient failings, has a fine way of stripping down the pretension of such occasions; of finding the elemental and the honest hidden amid the hubris of calculation and design.... And while Liam, ever the empiricist at heart, seemed perfectly at home in this wet equation, Claudia was one of those rarer sorts who took great comfort in the acquisition of things which gave her distance; folly was never her cloak of knavery, as some might say.

But at the moment it was her Waterloo; and realizing she was soaked through, with her dark hair lashed across her fair skin, she sensed the utter futility in maintaining appearances.

"And I tried so hard to look pretty today." She offered with the subtle smile of surrender.

"Yeah, me too."

She looked up, "I know a place we can get out of this," before casting him an eye. "You game?"

He shivered in his rain soaked t-shirt and flashed fond thoughts on the hat he almost brought. "I'm game."

They made for the steps leading back up the hill towards the alleyways of the old town. Through a few close thunderbolts and the perils of the shaking earth it was a quick dash for the warren of narrow streets and the shelter of the covered eaves. Overhead, the old wooden shutters of the Baroque homes rattled loudly in the breeze.

And from whence the mad monk dash had commenced, a few wet minutes later they were in the vestibule of a tall, well *Niçoise* tall, building that looked rather like an old apartment house. Claudia led him towards a damp and musty stairwell leading up to the sixth floor. Liam craned his neck skyward through the long maze of iron and stone balusters.

"Didn't think I'd let you off easy, did you?" She chuckled through a wet grin.

Christopher M. Basso

Chapter Five
Fluorescent Adolescent

They reached the top of the landing, six flights of stairs behind them, and Liam winded as a ragged sail. Something which was not lost on his fellow smoker who was taking the whole bit rather jauntily in stride.

"You've got to look after yourself my son," she advised. "Life's all about the climbing."

"Thanks chief," he grasped the old brass handrail, like a clown crying on the inside, "I'll remember that."

"Well, we're here."

"You sure? Maybe I could go back down and tug up some furniture or something? Maybe a nice piano...perhaps an armoire?"

"Stop it—it wasn't *that* bad."

Claudia led them down the far end of a long hallway lined with casements of dark rich wood and heavy ornate doors before reaching a small concern with nothing to announce its presence other than the faintest etchings—*Grenier, Nombre Soixante-Six*, weatherworn into the faded embossing above the door.

She looked back at him playfully and then did the St. Jerome knock of the five angels a tuneful seven times, before entering the foyer with the sure and graceful authority of a woman who simply knew she belonged. The inner door rang a quiet warning before clicking open. Claudia pushed through past a smaller vestibule where a man in a sharp gray Seville Row suit and sinister looking black Aristotle Onassis glasses glanced up from behind his desk and copy of the *Nice Matin*.... For a moment he looked as though he might make a move to garrote them for the intrusion, but a quick look of recognition swept across his eyes and alas that one never came to fruition. He merely watched them drift past and casually returned to his business.

They left the Brigadoon charmer to his foul demeanor, fine suit, and morning paper as they pushed on to door number six. O'Shea glanced back over his shoulder at that oddball...that's what you had to dig about this place on some surreal Dadaist level—you simply never knew if the cat you were sailing by was just some far out doorman or some twisted Muammar Gaddafi billionaire type, waiting on his next call girl to drop down a deep dark hole. No one was ever what they seemed, and that seemed to suit the natives just fine. It certainly kept the tourists on their toes at least.

The last door opened onto a surprisingly bright and well-lit space; a long strangely angled formal room cluttered with several ancient wooden tables, brass lights, and heavy shelves crammed with worn and dusty volumes of French and Russian provenance. He was immediately drawn to the place. It had a spooky *vibe,* from the stranger than strange Masonic-Illuminati entrance to the wide plank floors, stained and abused by each encroaching generation to a beaten and honeyed lived-in look.

Each of the smallish tables was tiled with Moorish plates of dark green and dull white set over heavy ornate iron bases. In fact, the whole of the place sang to a scuffed beauty and a darkness which was rendered something angelic by the enormous beveled windows which illuminated the proceedings to something of a decent Vermeer knockoff.

The proprietor seemed to know Miss Sommerton and was over in a flash for the small talk and pleasantries of transactional acquaintances. He listened briefly as they rambled on in a fast paced French that would have taken a few lifetimes for his tin ear to sort out. Rather, he left them to it and breathed in the space, the old woods, the green-coppered alchemy, and the faintest scents of age and permanence buried down in the mix by a sleight of hand and perhaps the things you only wanted to see.

In the stillness of the afternoon's lull they took a table for four near the tall windows by the front which allowed them to spread out a bit. One of the waiters did them a solid and cracked open the glass to let in the faintest hit of the breeze and the soft sounds of the rain against the clay flowerpots on the sill.

They had a fine view from this little perch, which crept just high enough over the top of the dense and cluttered mishmash of Vieux Nice, to reveal the wide and sweeping arc of the coast and the sea—all the way from the lighthouse in the harbor down to the beaches of Cagnes-sur-Mer. O'Shea surveyed the scene—cigarettes, ashtray, lighter, liftoff.

Claudia had been minding to her own excavations. "Well well," she finally said. "A stroke past noon, and with it goes the guileless guilt…I think I'm having a drink. How about it Liam, what's your penance?"

"Oh, I don't drink."

She smiled, "Now you're just trying to make laugh."

"Nope, *complete* teetotaler I tell you."

"I doubt that," she cast an appraiser's eye on him; "You've either got the obnoxious confidence of youth or quiet desperation of a much older man."

"Thank you."

"…. Deep pondering over-thinking type," she kept the eye on him, "That would make you straight scotch or whisky," which was delivered with a certainty that was hardly a question. "And since I'm scotch, you *must* be whiskey."

He leaned in. "How do you know I'm not of the crazy rambling extract; drinking hemlock moonshine and Absinthe currant mixtures?"

"Well, I'm not getting the insanity vibe."

"How about the metrosexual one? What's the Crantini, Lemon Drop action like in this place?"

"Grounds for expulsion I think."

"Wonderful, in that case I'll have a beer."

She turned to the waiter, "A *Dalmore* for me and a beer for my friend."

The nom de jure around these parts was a bowl of salted olives or some nuts, but the waiter seemed to know her habits and simply laid out a second ashtray and a book of fine gilded edge matches. The boy's hunger would have to wait and the detritus of this morning's foul wanderings would have to continue a bit longer. But a cold G&T would suffice for the moment.

The rain had picked up a bit, tapping softly against the glass and the low strains of music drifted up from deep behind the heavy kitchen doors. With the booze on the way, they lit up their smokes with the simple grace of a couple of degenerate pros. To the blessedly initiated there was a certain "book of tells" in the nicotine lifestyle, little affectations, variants of artistry and deviancy, or maybe just the personal kitsch which were revealing as anything in a Rorschach.

"When did you start that filthy habit?" He asked borrowing the torch to light his own.

"I think I was…13."

He chuckled.

"And yourself?" She asked, a slight incredulity in her eyes.

"Let's see, I was—22 almost 23."

"Sort of late to the game, wouldn't you say?"

"Statistically speaking I just about missed the game—they say if you can make it out of your early twenties without ever starting you most likely never will."

She didn't seem to be buying it. "Who says that?"

"The royal *they* I'd imagine."

"Well…that one got blown right to hell didn't it?"

"And never looked back."

"Tragic," with the same mock indignation, "And you were *so close* Liam, what happened?"

"I was bored one day, thought I needed a hobby."

"There weren't any stamps around?"

He winced, "Not as much fun as they say."

"What about heroin?" She asked, "There was always heroin—it's a bit more fun."

"More fun than cigarettes?"

"That's what they tell me."

He thought about it, "Well, I guess I probably didn't need that much fun in my life—just something between stamps and heroin…. Besides I'd have a problem with the whole needle thing."

"There's more than one way around that."

"I bet there is. Chased a few dragons have we Claudia?"

"Nope, *complete* teetotaler I tell you."

"Now you're just trying to make me laugh."

"Why Liam, what do you *take* me for?"

"Something of a mystery I'd say."

The waiter arrived with their drinks and maybe sensing O'Shea's desperation, a bowl of cured black olives and bread.

"Well, dammit now you've got me all sorts of curious" she said, "why'd you *really* start with cigarettes?"

"Why's anyone start? Stress…depression maybe. Besides, you don't really start—one day you're just doing it."

"Yes, that sounds about right," she nodded gravely before adding, "Why were you stressed?"

He smiled, "America is a stressful place. What about you?"

"I needed a hobby," she purred, "and all the good ones were taken."

"Stamps and such?"

"Numismatics would be a little more my speed." She said.

Christopher M. Basso

"I bet. What was it really though…it wasn't stress I'm guessing?"

She looked puzzled, "I'm *European*; it's kind of like a birthright. You've got the Second Amendment; we've got a tin of Dunhills."

He laughed, "And so it goes."

She excused herself for a moment to talk with one of the waiters who seemed greatly interested to ask her opinion on one thing or another. She obviously had some *pull* with the management.

O'Shea sat back in his chair, drinking his beer and smoking his cigarette…ah, peace. Just the foul and bitter confluence of a pernicious assault on the senses working their magic again….Old friends come home to roost, sad bastards opening wide the door, elevated serotonin, increased deadening of the musculature and the senses….Less work than a dog and better companions at that; a fine line playing out an ageless trick.

His mind expanded, Prousting a bit, but no sweet Madeleine's here, just the sudden creeping memories of a Dave Matthews tailgate in the Foxboro parking lot; many foul and garish incarnations ago…. And the strange rumblings-mumblings of one of his lame poseur friends from college; all prep school whiteness and dreadlocked wealth, "—*True* Rastas," the boy intoned with the solemn, bloodshot eyes of some ragged Trenchtown mystic, "don't drink alcohol—tis' da poison flowing up through da veins like a man been embalmed."

The assembled seemed suitably impressed at the time, as the orator returned to his can of Pringles and haze of Hindu Kush behind the van…. But perhaps the greater implication was that youth was a funny thing indeed, particularly when age was just some specter on the horizon, and inscrutably speaking, that shit made *perfect* sense at the time.

…. The slow embalming of the living. A grim image indeed, one which only ramped up the nasty scale the more you chewed it over in your drug addled mind; the booze freely flowing through your dead man's veins.

Yes indeed, for a brief moment out there on the cracked

asphalt with *Dancing Nancies* blaring from the Volvo's low-fi speakers and all the pretty horses in a row, that boy with the sensimilla flair seemed to *grasp* something.... But just like the rest of the best and the brightest from that grim space-filling generation, the Rastaman traded *I and I* for a $200 cut and color, a Wharton MBA, and the general BlackBerry-Grey Goose assholeness of his spiritual forebears.

O'Shea suddenly looked over at the returned Claudia, herself looking out the windows at nothing in particular.... This one seemed just about game though; and true avatars of fringe work were a rare find indeed.

"Apropos our mutual foul habit..." he said, which perked her up a bit, "I came across one of those Internet life expectancy calculators a few months ago, you know the ones?"

She nodded.

"Punched myself in for a laugh, taking into account all these rank and unnatural vices...41 more years it said—49 if I cleaned up my act. Almost twice my age but, eternally speaking, it doesn't really sound like all that much, does it?"

"My, you *have* been bored?"

"Yes—well French television truly does leave something to be desired."

He lit up a fresh smoke and continued, "So this whole thing got me to thinking. The first 18 years or so are not really your own, their just some extension of your parent's lives, so in a sense you've only been living a "real" life for the last 10. In that sense those 41 to 49 more years are along the lines of five more adult lifetimes...and I was thinking well, fuck all—that might just do. Besides, all the science and what not they'll have by then; might just blow that curve to hell, curing your maladies in a moment.... Remote sensing doctors, generic recombination matrices, zygote enriched organ farming—hell, they'll keep you alive longer than old Walt Disney frozen in the Tiger's cage, racking up the years like one of those Old Testament patriarchs.... But then on the flipside, what about the vicious quality of the maladies they'll have cooked up by then—UV decimation, water logged coastal bugs, flesh eating skivvies, mad cows, bovine bird flu warriors? That'll be child's play for the mutant nasties roaming the Earth by then.... Ghastly business; rats on a listing ship when the bill comes due."

"And then what, the ship sinks?" She seemed charmingly quixotic in her puzzlement.

"Exactly."

"So...what you're saying is?"

"I'm never really all that sure," he sighed, ".... Maybe just light up, drink deep; and keep the penance true—it'll all be sorted later."

"*That's* the kernel of wisdom you gleaned down the end of the tunnel?"

"Hey, I never promised it was profound, just that it was my own," he paused, "Besides you don't look like the type that buys into a one size fits all cure for what ails you?"

"Who said anything ailed me?"

He chuckled, "Maybe *you* do need to chase the dragon."

"Now you're just projecting a bit."

"Oh, let's not flatter me too much. How about we leave it at a fatalist; with a whingeing bit of hope flailing on the end?"

"We'll let you off the hook with that I suppose."

"And you? Where are you falling down that fine line?"

"What if I just pushed that half empty glass off the counter and went on my way."

He laughed, "As you leave to minister to the orphans and shut-ins?"

"No, to take their homes and souls—"

.... The black tie waiter returned with their drinks; thankfully or regretfully interrupting the elucidation of that finer point. He made a small show of presenting a bottle of Puligny Montrachet 1995, which Miss Sommerton had slyly ordered off camera.

"We're going straight for the grape I see?"

She nodded, "Ordered it when you staring out the window; you seemed to be trailing off a bit?"

"Yeah, I tend to do that..."

The waiter offered the first taste to Claudia.... O'Shea, it should be noted, while an avid enthusiast of The Drink, didn't care much for the theatricality which sometime occasioned it. As Claudia "Frenched" the finer points of this particular vintage with the man, Liam took another glance around the room, his eyes returning to the genteel strangeness of the set up.

"What is this place anyway?"

"It belonged to a friend of my grandfather." She said.

This was a fine, bald-faced lie on the surface of things; the surface of things being that which was best obfuscated and obscured anyway. A Sommerton family virtue to say the least, and considering the Sommertons had held title on the place since DeGaulle was in knee highs, her grandfather might well have been proud how well she'd learned the company line. The greatest trick the devil ever played was convincing the world he didn't exist—old landed families slouched along on a similar ethos.

Claudia lit up and looked the old room over, "They call it *Le Grenier,* which sounds a bit exotic, but is just French for..."

"The attic?" He cut her off.

She smiled, "Have you been studying your French Liam? I would have pegged you for the ugly American, Graham Greene type?"

"You know, that's something of a point of pride in the circles where I operate."

She ignored him, "You notice those doors over there? It's a quick drop to the alley and then a straight dash to the port below. During the war, the Great One that is, the local Resistance with the help of cloak and dagger bespoke tweed suit types like Llewellyn Sommerton, used to hide all manner of mischief up here.... Weapons, cash, transients and partisans, you name it; all sorts of interesting things being channeled from the border at Menton through to Marseilles and vice versa. Real old world intrigue...or at least that's what I was told."

She raised a pedantic finger as she ashed out the last and lit up the next. "That's the story they liked to tell...who knows, maybe even some of it is true. What I do know is that when the war ended their little warehousing operation did not. The Germans left the door open for the gendarmerie and the taxmen to return.... Which I suppose in some ways was even more of a bother. Plus the space was just too good for hiding things; the networking and the implicit complicity involved were too conveniently entrenched.... Anyway, this old attic stayed down that road for a few more decades till somebody apparently divined the risks were no longer worth the rewards."

He shrugged. "Or maybe they just became satisfied with the reward?"

"I doubt that type is ever satisfied with the reward." She smiled before teasing him, "Such a charming boy; you're about as clean and provincial as this old place."

"It's the ugly American in me I suppose."

"So let's see," she said, "it's been a dusty old attic, a wartime liberté, égalité, fraternité smuggling operation, and an entirely for profit post-war tax dodge, before settling into the much more relaxed visage you see—an English dining club, for the boozy expats to come and remember home now and then."

She had a full pull of the Puligny Montrachet, "I've never entirely understood why my people are so hell bent on recreating some little corner of Britannia wherever we went."

"So, is he still around?"

"Who?"

"This friend of your grandfather."

She'd picked up his lighter, studying the silver plated *Bill the Cat* emblem, before resting it at an angle and spinning it along the axis with a quick snap of her finger. "Nope, he's kicked those heels to Heaven."

"Sorry to hear."

"All of them actually. Too many cigarettes maybe—guess

they didn't consult your tables," she looked a bit wistful, "Notable and notorious families just wither and die sometimes. They might have been scoundrels and deviants, the lot of them, but at least they were colorful...can't say that much for the ones they left behind."

"Their heirs?"

"Yes, it's still in the family. One of the grandsons has plans to gut the place and turn it into a *martini bar*—lights and sounds rigs, $500 a throw table service, heavy door muscle, and repressive guest lists that would've made the Germans proud—a cliquish abomination *at best*; a charming little slice of New London for the wrong kind of Renaissance Russians."

"Ah, that's a shame."

"Isn't it."

She clicked shut the Zippo and fixed a slight sidelong glance his way, which flattered the ego but lingered just a wee bit too long for his better judgment. She had an appraiser's eye, you could feel her sizing you up before she punched your ticket. He'd caught that same glance many shades ago, on that fine moonlit stroll down the Dunamore gardens.

Disconcerting to say the least. But then again they were at least a *lovely* pair of inquisitors' eyes, bright and alive yet revealing very little. And it goes without saying that under such circumstances all transgressions and trespasses can be forgiven.

He imagined life pretty much sailed that way for her; a lifetime's pass on a lifetime pass. The confluence where a dangerously high octane blend of looks, station, and intellect come together in some triple threat of deviant talent and talons. Should she ever cast it to fairer uses the world would be a better place, but even should she remain forever in idle disconnect, it would keep something charming and unique as it withered away on the vine.... But maybe that was just the prosy of a ring, or better yet the opening gambit of Puligny Montrachet waxing idyllic. A straighter eye might have pegged it for what it was; an energy where a werewolf's ethics prevailed and all inner convictions go to die.

A slight tinge of the self-righteous courage coursed

431

through his judgmental veins; hell, he might yet be working on a sanctimonious hard-on for his pains. Present company made it pleasant to be sure, but what kind of foxhole spiritual mendicant could look himself in the eye if he let some shade ball off the hook but for the simple graces of her genetic lifestyle lottery?

To be slowly taken in by the statuesque trimness, the inquisitor's eye, and the pull of a pert rack through a tight t-shirt was to know a spiritual defeat; a defeat only more pronounced as the grape and vine kept those scales across the eyes.... It was a spell that must have been another perk of the lifestyle, he imagined; a free pass brokered through the awe of something dynastic and gracious, only to reveal itself in twists and turns as a thing tight and sinewy coiled; a beast waiting to strike.... Perhaps it was time to crack the bone and get to the marrow?

"So, tell me more about yourself," Liam said, feeling rather artful in the deflection.

"Will that be on your published rates?"

A coy look crossed her eye, like a meter registering that fine line, and whether or not it was worth the effort to cross.

"I was born, I grew up, I am here."

"And what about the in between, my little Copperfield?"

"You want the war paint?"

"Why not? My rates are cheap."

"Well, let's see.... Claudia Sommerton, Capricorn, twenty-nine years of age, really just a polar bear's whisker from thirty.... Pretty conventional upbringing I suppose...summers at my Grandmother's villa in Luzerne, winters at our little place down on the Congo.... My father was a relentlessly self-improving import/exporter type, who drank like a fish and often made mad claims like he invented the cathode tube and Mahjong." She shook her head sadly. "...But when the old boy really found the depths of the bottle he'd take the heads of the Congolese natives in his rage and stick them on pikes outside our compound; at night he would read them selections from Kipling and Robert Ludlow.... If we were insolent, our mother would beat us and throw us down a tiger pit, where my sisters and I would have to engage in feats of strength for rewards of sustenance and escape," Claudia took a long drag off her cigarette, "Pretty standard stuff actually.... Needless to say, I escaped those eccentrics, ran back to England, slept my way into Oxford, slept my way out of Oxford; but unfortunately the needle and the damage were already done; years lost to the avarice of drugs, a haze of skinny skiing, nightswimming in the broad daylight, bullfights on acid, group—"

"The paint woman," he rapped his knuckles on the table, "Not your lucid dream fancies." He shrugged. "You could have just simply demurred you know?"

"Where would be the fun in that?"

"Whatever."

"All right, all right, here's one—I'm actually a *half breed*...bet you couldn't tell?"

"Oh really?"

"Yes; my father, a decent enough man actually with no thirst for heads, was from suburban Philadelphia. He came to London some time back in the death throes of the Love Generation; he was by then a slightly older fellow on a younger man's scene—a bit of a draft dodger, a bit of showman, a bit of a swamp runner. He marshaled those God given talents and opened several cabarets and gentlemen's clubs across East London."

He laughed, "You mean strip clubs?"

"If you must." She smiled a forgiving gaze, "But you understand that sort of thing was still strangely frowned upon in the social circles he wished to grace."

"You don't say."

"Anyway one afternoon, early in the quest for ascension, he was walking through Belsize Park when he caught sight of young Dahlia Sommerton sitting on a bench under the shade of a willow tree. Well, one look at those high cheekbones and the smooth white skin and I think he was done. A graceful moment...that or just the hunch he'd found himself the willing partner of a well bred, perfectly delightful trophy wife."

"Willing for what?"

She seemed all too eager to tell, "My mother came from a very boring very stratified world where nothing much really happened from generation to generation.... Daddy was a showman, he had a bit of money from his family, but not much of a past."

"So?"

"*So?* That sort of thing still had some currency in old money, old school English circles. Those people launder ancestry like criminals launder money."

He laughed, "Is that true?"

"Yes indeed. Anyway, my mother's name helped ease the old boy's gentle condition."

"Sounds like quite a match."

"Yes, between the two of them they've managed to mangle at least five lives with a rather deft touch."

"Five?"

"Their own—my brother's, my sister's and occasionally my own."

He thought about it, "Well...occasionally is a start, right?"

"There! An optimist, just like I suspected."

"Well, not get ahead of ourselves." He lit up one for himself and one for her. "Brother and sister, where are they now?"

"Sister's in Manhattan—runs a glass blown bead boutique on Mercer Street," she paused momentarily in some hellish resignation. "My brother is unfortunately right here, trying his luck with venture capitalism; nightclubs actually."

"Doesn't sound so bad." Liam offered.

She shrugged, "*Egads,* maybe you do need the heroin. To me working and *living* are two very different things. For most people there are so few options that they're forced to coexist, but I wouldn't say it makes for something happy."

Friends were in short supply these days so Liam cleared

the morose hick out of his voice and choose his next words carefully. "Would you say you're happy?"

She pondered this with that same bent of hellish reflection, "I'm free…if that answers the question? Comes and goes I guess," she paused for a moment and took a long drag of her cigarette. "You want to know the real kicker about my father? He was actually a terrible businessman. He never paid attention to the details. Each of the cabarets, each of the strip clubs as you so eloquently called them, eventually flamed out in some spectacularly humiliating fashion." She crinkled her eyes, "…. But for all his faults he always managed to hold onto the real estate, and in East London that became about as sure as printing your own money."

She seemed suitably pleased with her deft rendering of the family reserve. "And the post script to the whole mess? Letting someone *else* set the bar, the worth on your failings. They can either strike oil in your backyard or throw up an asbestos plant across the street. But the important thing is—you did absolutely nothing to deserve it either way. Get your head around that one Liam O'Shea."

"Damn…I liked the severed head thing better."

"And that, in essence, is the family reserve."

"Gee Claudia—sounds like a real *scene*."

"How else do you think I can *relax* in a place like this?"

"Is that's how it's done?" He laughed. "Amp up the carnage back home?"

"Yeah, and then take it on the road… But what about you?" She smiled, "Goodness—I've told you *far* too much already. Not too many jet setting American pragmatists come drifting into my orbit. At least, not while things are vertical."

Liam laughed, "I can't top that kind of tale."

"Well try, even if you have to make it up."

"Trust me darling, I don't have to make it up. It's just not so, let's say…poetic."

"Middle America sitcom laugh track bad?"

435

"Lady, *I wish.*"

"What—am I on to something?"

"Yeah, you've painted me in bold strokes."

She studied him for a moment, "I doubt that's true." She smiled and slapped his hand, "C'mon Liam, own up, you're one of us now *remember?*"

He stiffened, "Hardly. Besides, I wouldn't want to bore you with my simple tales of woe."

"Don't worry, I don't mind," she perked up. "Every raker down here likes to talk, but they never have much to say—I think I'd find the whole thing sort of refreshing.... Besides," she added with a smile, "we're all *Americans* here after all. At least partway."

"All right, where to begin let's see.... I was born, I grew up."

"Evasiveness. I like it."

"I try."

"How about you start with the childhood?"

"My childhood? Let's see, my childhood...my childhood was like Mad Max...Mad Max without the leathers and the assless chaps."

She thought about it, "Are you implying *mine* had the assless chaps?"

"It sounds like you people didn't even bother with the chaps."

"Point taken; all right so you have the whole Thunderdome thing going on...then what?"

"I *was* going to be a lawyer once you know?" A flash of thoughtfulness crossed his eyes.

"Ugh, don't tell me those things."

".... For a Sinaloa drug cartel."

"Better."

"See this is boring. The truth is *boring*, the kind of thing that's best left safely in the past.... The bullshit is much more fun. Amp it up with booze and its downright ace."

"C'mon, try me."

"Well. Let's see…grew up in New York, just outside the city…no bona fides to speak of unless you consider a wicked matchbox collection a point of pride. No brothers or sister, parents got along fine, Christmas, birthdays, and all that business. In fact, I was living a downright extraordinarily ordinary life until I came into some money." He smiled in confirmation, "Now I live out at the villa, drink my wine bide my time, and make the occasional trip to the ATM to pray for a little atonement." He was smiling, "Look I'd like to get deeper into this sordid tale, but I have a bit of a problem."

"*What?*"

"I had some trouble scoring breakfast this morning, are you hungry?"

She shrugged, "Yeah sure."

"Want to order something?"

"Here? Good Lord no."

"No?"

"Well, I'd drink here but the food…" She trailed off.

"Bad?"

"Well, it *is* a little slice of England."

He smiled, "Do you know a place?"

"I know *many* places."

She stood and handed her wares for Liam to carry, "C'mon."

"Nearby is it?"

"Just out the way," she purred over her shoulder trailing off down the hallway.

Christopher M. Basso

Chapter Six
Chateau of the Golden Calf

Within minutes they were sitting in the back of a black Mercedes gypsy cab, tearing ass up the busy *Grande Corniche*, and making fine time along the main east west motorway. In Claudia years *just out the way* obviously meant a ride clear over the top of Nice and up the steep wrapping inclines and nerve wrangling switchbacks to the tiny mountain perch of Eze village.

She made her intentions for prompt carriage and lack of otherwise tourist themed bullshit understood to the driver. Her pitch perfect patois French had an eerie inflection that might have lingered on the sinister. At the very least the man understood that the tall brunette in the back seat riding caravan with the sleepy looking drunk wasn't some rube in from the hinterlands ripe to be trifled with.

For his part the sleepy-eyed drunk's mood improved considerably once he'd sussed the final destination. This was *de facto* honorary O'Shea country. Nothing to fear here, no more callous miscreant burger-boys, no more oddball men in fine bespoke suits who looked like they might have a go at your floating rib. Just the fine mountain view, the sun and the sea, and the gathering possibility of actually scoring some food—at least that was his plan.

As the Mercedes tore across an old Roman arch, with the mad man driver at the wheel and the daypass vampire in command, O'Shea had the sudden feeling that his morning's journey had all become somewhat rather...arranged. The boy's attention turned to the steep ravine below.

"Damn, that's quite a little drop."

She looked over from behind her sunglasses and added rather mischievously, "It's called, *Le Pont du Diable*."

"Is that supposed to mean something?"

"I thought you'd know?"

"What can I say; the French, it comes and goes."

She smiled, "Well look it up sometime."

"Sure, whatever."

The taxi left them off at the bottom of the *Place de la Colette* for the short walk up to the main part of town. Most of the narrow winding streets in Eze are impassable to anything wider than the donkey carts and carriage grooms they were built for. You pass between the steep and crumbling avenues which wind along beds of cobblestone and weathered brick, and pass the old stone facades and dull canvases, all brought to life with the effusion of wildflowers growing along their old skeleton frames.

A very pleasant sort of symbiotic give and take, of a dead thing rendered beautiful again. It was a place that set its own pace, indifferent to the demands of modern opinions.... Which presently afforded O'Shea the pleasure of watching well-heeled hotel guests having to trudge their *Hermès* gear up the donkey paths towards the reception office.

Claudia's final destination, the Chateau de la Veau d'Or, sat at the far end of the village. The swankish hotel was perched atop the very edge of a cliff; with its gardens and infinity pools but an iron railing away from the precipitous half mile journey to the environs below. The grounds wrapped around the old stone buildings and the castle keep in a very tight crescent arc that met up again at the steep edge of the mountain.

They walked towards the largest of the stone buildings, an old neo-gothic monster with two turrets and a garret bell tower in between. A stone cistern carved with the heads of medieval grotesques marked the entrance to the check-in. The scene at the front desk was instantly familiar to anyone who's ever watched the falconer wait on the whims of the falcon. Great wealth and even greater ego have little patience for the things they find inconvenient; and quite a few of the guests were already laying into the staff for the unexpected climb to the hotel....They were about fifth in line behind a group of angry Belgians, but then fortune smiled again when the staff suddenly recognized Miss Sommerton.

The young concierge ditched the Belgians in mid-protestation and came over to greet Claudia. They exchanged the pleasantries of an air kiss, and whispered something low to each other about all these lousy tarted up foreigners, before the young man lead Claudia and Liam down an ornate stone staircase to what O'Shea sincerely hoped was the dining room.

They passed through a lovely space of white Moroccan flourishes set under the gaze of a French colonial firmament; a motif accented with soft Lycee couches and heavy wooden shutters, propped open to let in the afternoon breeze. The exited the far side of the room out onto a broad stone terrace; perched up against the edge of the property on the steep escarpment of a cliff.

.... Apropos a certain fear of flying, the boy's therapist had once suggested that his particular problem was a rather manifest fear of heights; a manifest fear in fact hiding something far *deeper*.... Maybe so Kojack; but the why's of a garden variety psychosis were never all that comforting; particularly when you were staring down the 2,000 foot business end of its incarnation.

The outdoor terrace was lined with small sitting alcoves, set between the cubbyholes of old stone risers and faded red terracotta bricks—bits of ivy and flowering trellises of bougainvillea colored the gaps in between. They sat at one nearest the bend in the arc; a very private bit of real estate, and quite possibly the finest view of the coast below.... Claudia Sommerton might have been some ramped up space oddity but she was rapidly proving herself the shit; a young lady most definitely in the know and somewhat more connected than the Petronas Towers...which were quite possibly somewhere down the line in the Sommerton portfolio.

Soon they were sitting across a low set table, the glass littered with white Azaleas and small seashells burning fragrant oil. Liam took a spot in one of the low backed rattan chairs nearest the wall, while Claudia opted for the white divan across from him. A complimentary Moët aperitif and a small plate of upscale bar treats arrived, and with them, triumphantly, a set of menus.

O'Shea nibbled some brochettes, had a sip of his drink, and took in the killer view. A calm sea with the Cape riding out like some lonely interloper on a sea of perfect blue—all regarded through the spiraled balustrades of the black iron railings.

Just below them was a small grove of olive trees, clinging to the narrow sloping hillside with a heady mix of strong roots and maybe something bordering on the faithless faith. One in particular caught his eye. Growing at the very edge, its branches angled over the precipice, hugging the last bit of soil with the tenacity of a Billy Goat, the one right before the fall.

…. The better angels of his nature told him to ignore such things; so naturally, he leaned forward for a closer look….*Jesus tap-dancing Christ*—that old familiar vertigo tinge kicked in—the harsh one, the one that shoots right up the spine, and stammers the brain….It was the same fine view from row thirteen on the window; strapped in on the bumpy final approach; wearing the rosaries down to the nub—a vast drop into the sea of tranquil green, of stark stone, and the reds and orange of the terracotta village below. Alcohol was essential. He downed this weak local novelty and signaled immediately for stronger drink.

"What's up chief?"

"…. I don't much care for heights."

"Prefer depths do you?"

"Something like that."

"Sure you don't want the couch?" She patted the cushion in a rather taunting way.

"I'll be quite all right thank you….*smartass*."

"Suit yourself." She didn't quiet lay across the couch, but rather *splayed*, in a somewhat alpha sort of way which gave her the vague bearings of some mad Caesar.

"Comfortable?"

"Very."

He had a look around the joint. "Spiffy place.... Might your family tree be in cahoots with this one?"

"No," she smiled. "This one's just a hotel. No intrigues, no guilt-stained past, but pretty good food—try the duck and truffle *parmentier*."

"French huh?"

"We are in France Liam."

"I know, but I've been deftly managing to avoid this stuff for the most part."

"*This stuff?* "You're in the epicenter; in one of the great culinary zeniths on this little blue melting marble and that's what you'll have—this stuff? C'mon, live a little...here try the *Boudin aux Pommes*."

He scanned the menu, "I don't see it."

"It's off the menu, but they'll make it for you."

Boudin aux Pommes? His brain drifted around the Rosetta stone.... Something about blood, sausage, and apples...all signs pointing to a pass.

"I'm not feeling all that adventurous, despite the seven acts of contrition this morning. How about the *Pizza Américain* and a big—and I mean big ass plate of the frites?"

"Ugh, maybe they could Supersize it for you."

The service down South was notoriously slow. Even the Michelin stared places took a rather laid back approach to things; nicotine would be *key* till the booze arrived. He reached into his pocket for his lighter, but noticed she already had it in her hands. She lit one for Liam and then herself, resting back on her couch and for the first time, he noticed, she was actually taking in the view.

443

The sun had since come out for good; the early Mistral winds having blown away the last of the clouds revealing a sky of perfect blue.... A lovely young lady on one of the private balconies overlooking the pool had since lost the top half of her two-piece. She laid across a deck chair, the soft shape of her chest, as natural as the setting—all this time down here was giving him a fine detector for such things. Proper form he thought; far enough away to show some decorum but close enough to still hold the eye. Some bits of France were redeemable at that.

Liam looked out across the water. Quite a thing; the beauty of the Corniche Pass and the Baie des Anglais, Beaulieu and the beaches below, and farther out the snaking arm of the Cape. He strained his eyes a bit, "I think I see my house."

She looked up from her menu, "You snob; would that be your *villa?*"

"*Please*...my rapidly dilapidating summer rental more like it."

"I don't know," she shook her head in mock sadness, "Lot's of shady types down there on that point." Her eyes drifted along the profile of Cape Ferrat; at the avenues of impressive villas sneaking out from behind the tall trees, at the well tended jardins and fortified grounds. "This century's robber barons they say; Russian oil tycoons, third world despots...the 116th Iraqi palace." She laughed, "Anything down there is grande money or grande sin," before squinting a bit, "I don't make it out there much myself you understand."

"Ethical considerations?"

"More like a shrinking invite list, but I'll take the former."

Then she added, "You like it down there?"

"Oh yeah," he shot up between the mouthfuls of rose bread he'd heartily laid into.

"Ooh Liam, now that's *hot*..."

But his mind still dwelled on the horror. "Yep, nothing like hopped-up HGH, ex-Mossad security types pulling the gang swarm on me when I go for my morning coffee." He paused between bites, "Italian media potentates, living in the French mansions, guarded by the German Shepherds...it's that damn Vichy crew all over again. Aside from that, it's a delightful place."

"Sounds like trouble with the natives?"

"Shit, I'm lucky just to be here...no sense of humor on those people."

"I don't think I want to know." She kept her eyes on the drink menu, "Starting to have some issues with a life of leisure are we?"

"Making me a bit cynical I think. Or rather, more cynical than before."

"My poor old man...you know, they say unless you become like a child, you'll never enter that old kingdom of Heaven?"

He glanced nervously over the side, "Yeah? Who said that?"

She took quick stock of the man. There was definitely something a bit off about him, something of *the fear* suddenly clouding his heretofore easy mix. Like that quick rush up the nicotine mountain, married with the lack of strong drink, was starting to play some wide-eyed gonzo game with him. Softer types might have coddled such a delicate sort...but for those whose mothers drug-muled the Percocet on the nannies when they travelled; the world was made of infinitely harder stuff.

"Look at you—you're a stressed out mess. You need to *man up* my friend. No room for wobblies around here."

"Any ideas?"

"Take a few deep breaths, find a happy place, and we'll keep shooting the breeze in the meantime." Her demeanor stiffened slightly, "Reinforcements will be here shortly.... If that doesn't work, I'll just spike your drink with something when you're off in the jacks?"

"Sounds good—just make it something strong is all I ask."

"For your troubles?"

He sat back rigid in the chair, angling a boot against the edge of the table.

"More for my present pains."

"Well, unfortunately I'm lacking in the special medicine at the moment. Talking might just have to do."

"Lovely, what do you want to talk about?"

She thought about it, ".... How about me? How would you *size things up*; given these tall tales and all?"

He laughed, "Where would I begin?"

"Begin by not being polite, 'cause point of fact we may never cross paths again, and so few people are willing to tell you what you need to hear rather than what you want to hear.... So don't hold back."

"I didn't know I was."

The drinks arrived. O'Shea took his Jameson down the gullet in one long draw. He immediately ordered up another. Just relax and wait for the cavalry he told himself—that drag strip courage would be along presently.

He fixed his gaze on her; "I think you're an...*interesting*, obviously quite bright, attractive...uh...rich girl with a lot of free time on her hands."

She looked a bit annoyed.

"What, too much with the rich part?"

"No, not that...*interesting?* What am I, a Goddamn op-ed piece The Economist?"

"Well it's..."

"Stop it; the hole you're digging is already deep enough." She smiled in her subversive way. "See in the life of leisure, candor is the thing, and embellishments are the kicker. I would have gone with something more along the lines of: an artfully mixed up Eurotrash type, cursed with just the faintest hints of dispossessed American carpetbagger.... A spiritual mendicant, bored with herself, up for anything, just passing off the tedium of her days as the seemingly profound, when she's probably just waiting for someone else to shed their mortal coil and recharge/enrich her Phoenix act."

He looked at the table and then looked at the sea. "Well that might have been a bit rude."

"But we're *friends* old boy. How could that be rude?"

Just about then the fermented backup arrived; the rush of blood to the head came quickly; the synaptic cavalry on the charge…why not indeed?

"All right then, play time is over. In the grand equivocation of things, having a chat with you, the bellwether for this foul and terrible place, has been quite fascinating…. But I can't help thinking that you *just might be* the horrible manifestation, the symptom, of the modern mind left to wander."

She looked hurt, "Oh Liam, what a *rude* thing to say."

"What I meant was…"

She laughed, "Relax, I'm fucking with you."

"Well I might be a bore, but at that I'm not *charmless*."

"You sure know how to flatter a girl either way."

"Straight talk always has an upside, a kind of frankness to it—how's this—what if I said that you wore the mad buzz of modern times with… the forgiving gaze of the best social graces and the free pass of a well rounded ass?"

"Well, at the very least, you've just made my afternoon."

The waiter returned with the next round, which O'Shea thought to handle with a bit more care…. Where had that bit of mad dog Tourettes come from? Such boldness was several "lets" down the line. She *lets* you woo her, she *lets* you compliment her; she *lets* you flirt with her…then you're free to comment on those various body parts. Hell, he'd already skipped the first three lets; he might as well have just gone ahead and taken the Pepsi challenge while he was at it.

"Talking about my ass," she demurred in her proper English lilt. "I *barely* know you."

"This might be as well as you ever know me. You said so yourself."

"So what are you saying, you wanna *go for it* in the bushes over there behind the forsythia?"

"I was thinking more the potted fern."

"My virtue is on the line."

"Is that off the menu too?"

Before she could answer the food arrived. Provencal haute cuisine wasn't the first thing you'd look for to sate a driving hangover, but this would almost do. Liam tucked into his Pizza Américain like a raggedy man in the dessert. Social pleasantries were clearly out the window. They had, after all, actually broached the topic of botanical fornication. Besides, once you got past the effete presentation, this was some righteously decent food.

Claudia on the other hand wasn't much for food, haute or otherwise. She seemed to be rocking a steady diet of air, cigarettes, and more air; picking around her plate when she touched it at all. People like her never seemed to be big eaters. Like it might somehow be at odds with the wolfishly observant eye and the natural *preternaturalness* they brought to bear. There's a certain school that buys into that dignified abnegation of things…usually they're called monks, but she might have been an exception to the rule.

On some level she might have been an adherent to the idea that a hungry thing is an attentive thing and a bloated thing had a use unknown. He watched her from the corner of his own ravenous eye, watching him from the corner of hers.

Midway through their feast, the hotel manager, at or least a dapper older gentlemen who might have been the hotel manager, came over and exchanged pleasantries with Claudia.

"Is there anybody around here you don't know?"

"Plenty…I just cultivate the ones I do."

For the rest of lunch, him eating and her smoking that is, he managed to steer the conversation away from the revealing and the personal. Preempt her questions with his own. He asked her about all the places she'd been and the list was extensive. To listen to her, she been just about everywhere twice. Strange shots in the dark like, "Ever been to…Rangoon?" Were met with the even stranger, "Just last year as a matter of fact."

She'd abandoned the harsher stuff and switched to some odd red concoction. Vodka and some bestial elixir, probably the closest thing a piece of steel from the Essex midlands would even come to a cocktail.

"What is that?"

"Just a little something." She smiled.

"Off the menu?"

"More like off the books. Try it."

"…. *Jesus*, that's harsh."

"It's an acquired kind of taste. I picked it up in *Rangoon* don't you know…"

"Ugh—I'm going to need some water." He motioned to the waiter.

She quickly shifted gears; after all drinking games were well and good, but a steel-trap mind wasn't so easily dissuaded, "So—seeing as you've sized me up; ass, brains, and otherwise—why don't you tell me something else about yourself?"

"Uh oh, this game again."

"Start small—like what brought you here?"

"An airplane."

"Maybe a bit broader."

"A green airplane."

She shook her head. "Let's try a different tack you dodgy little bastard—how about what's keeping you here? You've no love affair with the place—*that* much is obvious."

He fidgeted with his lighter, "I don't know…. Shit, do you always know why you do things?"

"You do things for a reason."

"…. It's that easy then?"

She shrugged, "It could be."

He lit up a fresh one. This back and forth was sort of fun. He realized it'd been a while since someone asked him a question he really felt like answering. Maybe it was the tenacity she brought to it; maybe the way she threw her voice from the soft notes of The Queen's proper, to the bawdy drawl of the urban savvy. A talent that deserved to be rewarded or at the very least not trifled with.

He ran his hand through his hair. "Well, what can I say...I had a life—now I have something else. He signaled for the band, "Cue the strings by the way."

"Yes, touching."

"Now I live out at the villa; sleep too much, buy my bread from a hippie refugee named Paul and my wine from a lippy sort named John." He smiled sadly, "Sometimes I get bored, head to the ATM; use my dead mother's birth year for the pin; which I suspect keeps me honest on some level. Take that bit of angst for a wandering stroll—it's all good. Just try to embrace the...fakeness of the place. It can't hurt what it can't see."

Claudia smiled and slowly intoned, ".... This is not my beautiful house? This is not my beautiful wife?"

"*See!* I knew you were gonna bust on me."

"Rubbish—show a little backbone though." She looked a bit tossed for it, "Try having that same fakeness as your only nostalgia, your only memories, and you'll see what a *proper* mind fuck looks like."

"Fair play, fair play."

Liam took a drag, leaned back in his chair, and studied her for a moment. She looked very pretty, her dark clean features set against the blue backdrop haze of the sea.

"Let me ask you," he finally said, "I've been all over this cheese-laden continent for the last couple of months rubbing asses to elbows with every expression of budding yuppie, arrogant flat-Earther, and wannabe bohemian wastoid.... So my question is this; how'd you escape with the clever chops intact?"

"Why Liam was that a compliment?"

"Shit, now *you're* the optimist."

"No, you're just too down-heavy is all. Anyone can see it; you wear it through the shoulders. You need to relax…to be honest, you sound like one of those *bored* people who doesn't quite know what to do with themselves. In my experience that's either the mold of old money rotting, or the guilt pangs of some new found prosperity."

"That a fact?"

"It ain't a fancy."

Her smile was perhaps the most annoying aspect of it. Nothing like some dissipated, albeit clever, type who thinks she has you all sorted out.

"It's not so bad really."

"Careful, I'm a delicate sort."

"Why? What makes it so particular with you?" She asked.

"Who said it was a problem?"

She shot back, "You did! I said, 'starting to have some trouble with it?' And you said, all affable boy charm, 'Oh just a little'. So what's the deal then?"

He smiled, "Well maybe a *little* trouble."

She cast a sly eye, "I don't know, you seem right about at home in it."

"…. You're still fucking with me right?"

"Afraid not," she smiled, "Liam, my dear, have you ever stopped to consider that you just might not be as deep as you think?"

"Every day in fact." The autopilot shot out. It takes a minute or two to process such a broadside shot to the testicular superego. Claudia helped fill the space between.

"It's a bitch of realization really—but once you own up to it—life, oh life, becomes a much *nicer* gig."

"Sounds like it's worked lovely for you, but what's it got to do with me?"

"Well, in the two hours we've spent together I can already see something of the change..." She smiled, "Or maybe it's just *grown* on you since we last met."

"Is *that* a fact?"

"I'm a decent judge of things," she assured him, "That night at the dreadful wedding; you had something of a shy decent quality about you. I don't think you were out in the drive *checking your tires* anymore than I was out looking for that fool to bring back to the house. We both reached our tipping points on entertaining that monstrous perversion of a religious solemnity; and while we might have had different triggers, we wound up looking for the same thing."

"And what was that?"

"Sanctuary would be an apt description. Watching you mope around the drive like that I felt compelled to come over. You couldn't have looked more uncomfortable if you tried."

"Me?"

"Don't give me that *ME* rubbish," she laughed. "Unless hiding out in the driveway, smoking cigarettes, is your customary habit?"

"Maybe...but what about you? Hell, you'd beaten me to it!"

"I was just having some down time, trying to smoke a spliff, when the Bride's father suddenly tried to make my *acquaintance*.... But that's a whole other story I suppose."

One of those long strange silences drifted up in the air. It was hard to divine if this was of the shy or hostile variety. But the fairy dust blew from the left to the right and they were able to share a smile.

"So what are we then—Merely Lame or Antisocial?"

"Nonsense," she said, "Just two people who like to avoid the crowds."

"Well, that's relief, here I was starting to think I was strange."

"No, you *are* strange, but it's for entirely different

reasons."

"Such as?"

"Well, going with my theory about you being a fundamentally decent sort, I find it strange that you're content to spend your time down here; in this epicenter of an ugly organizing principle."

"Travelocity must have skipped that part?"

"It's almost kind of...charming, or kind of sad. You're seeking some sort of sincerity in this world and you've come to one of the most genuine examples of a place built on murderous insincerities. I mean, where do you think the straw men of the world come to play with their ill-gotten gains? Everything here radiates from those poisoned roots."

"Well, someone once said that right in the in middle of the contradiction was the place to be."

"Sounds like an idiot to me."

"Some enlightened idiot perhaps." He chuckled.

"Tell *that* to the half of West Africa that was destroyed to build most of that bougie point you're shacked up on."

Her act of indictment was almost convincing, that was until you realized she was truly part of the scene, and therefore some manner of Judas to be vilified by one side of the equation and treated with a deep and abiding suspicion by the other. But, in the fairest sense, maybe she was just trapped with a foot in both worlds, her protests echoing something which was once sincerity, or conviction.

She glanced over the escarpment down to the blue waters of the bay, "Look out there...any of those yachts, any number of them rendered from the broken backs and burnt out hovels of faraway lands." Her eyes told the story of a different set of gears now working the machine.

"It's a mad fucking world. You've got the dim sheer luck of birth types down there, but there's also the ones who, through some sociopathic series of machinations that would've done Macbeth proud, are sitting there free from want, inured to penury, and downright worshipped through the looking glass.

Worshipped, or at least feared, by the very people they're working over."

"Yeah, that's fascinating but," John Jameson had clearly seized control of the wheel, "What makes *you* any different?"

She didn't seem fazed, almost relieved someone had *finally* asked.

"Not much really, but at least I can see the folly and the pathos in it—that's about a revelation better than most of the people who can afford this view. At least I can, with good conscience, loath what I represent, and then in time maybe move on—rise above it...like old Nietzsche sprinting up that trail. I suppose the worst expression of my laziness would be to just casually *walk* down the hill...a bit of birth, a bit of luck, and a bit of revelation having freed me from caring."

He straightened up, "What a bunch of bullshit..."

"What are you on about?" She smiled back, "I don't think you've even come to the first revelation yet."

"Well—that might be because I've been too busy *living* it, to sit up here thinking about it."

"Don't go all wobbly on me now Mr. O'Shea. I'm just making a point—if it makes you feel less threatened; an *observation* that I think I've seen the king "fuck all" joke down the end of the tunnel, and it involves an ostrich limberness, affinity for beer ponging $500 bottles of Louis Roeder, and railing lines of charley off the asses of rented mules.... This is the life of all those third and first world reprobates moored out in the bay."

"So...they're not all sadly misunderstood sorts, generous types with fine sundry graces and hidden wellsprings of karma?"

"I never said that...harmless was I think the *buzzword*. There are the harmless ones and then there are the not so harmless ones. Besides, don't sound so innocent...the great Shiva didn't miracle you up here to throw down €23 whiskeys and bicker with me. Free will is somehow still free I think?"

"Preach on sister!" He exalted. "I have seen the light."

"No, but you will."

Well into the next round a few of the regrettable regulars began drifting onto the terrace. The suitcase and donkey path connoisseur with the narrow heretic's eyes set up shop at the bar, ordering the staff around with a Zen recalibrating vigor that might have made up for his earlier inconveniences. Across the way, a young doughy-pasty John Phillips banker type and his gene perfect trophy lady dove into the infinity pool and began with the kind of racket one makes when they are indelicately announcing they have *arrived*.

"Let us depart then." Claudia said suddenly. More of a declarative than anything else, she was already up and along the breezeway past the commotion in the pool and out towards the gardens.

Liam looked around for second, paused, and started after her. He caught up with her near the fountains. "What about the bill?"

"What about it?"

He kept checking back over his shoulder. No signs of trouble.

"Dine and dash then?"

She smiled, moving confidently among the azaleas but saying nothing.

"I thought you were all about cultivating the natives?"

"I am...but not these ones." She could sense a bit of hesitancy on his part. "You need to live a little." She grabbed his hand.

".... Right."

Maybe she had a point. Any trouble with the locals and her family could buy up the mountain and exterminate the cheeky brutes.... But all the same, he was new money, with minimal credit, and no cache in these parts. The small sign for the *Chemin Nietzsche* crept up around the next bend of bay, and they hung the sharp left heading down to the coast. *Smart plan*, he thought, no one would ever think to look, or more importantly, *pursue* a couple of dine and dashers down the damn side of a cliff. They'd rounded the first crick in the path, passing from the perch at Eze.

Claudia seemed quite pleased with herself, "Think old Fritz would be proud?"

"I think Nietzsche probably paid his bills."

"Nonsense, he was famous for this kind of thing. He'd pay the gypsy kids a few kroner to fake a fit in the lobby of the Negresco and haul ass out the linen door when no one was looking."

They took their time piloting it down the mountain. No rush here. In this game of patently deceptive conjured realities, expectations were artfully low. All that remained were the things that caught your fancy on any given day, in any particular moment, and in that space of infinite energy. The air coming down the pass was thin and dry, entirely in sync with the greater instincts to press on.

About midway down the mountain they came across a break in the clearing, at a low stone wall that formed a kind of natural viewing point. He glanced up towards the circular ramparts of the village, perched quite some ways in the distance, looking for any signs of a Michelin-starred Gallic posse making their way down through the saw blades and switchbacks...but all signs looked clear.

He joined her already sitting with legs dangling over the edge of the stone wall; still high enough for that particular breathtaking view of the sea, but already obvious that the scale of things was coming back in line along a more human order. The trail was quiet and empty, no signs of man, just the small white butterflies sailing, drifting from flower to flower. They rested here for a while, not sharing a word, as the late afternoon sun drifted lazily into the western sky.

By the time they reached the bottom he was a ragged mess, short of breath and a bit ropey in the knees. It was time to summon up that next reserve of borrowed energy. At the base of the cliffs sat *Eze bord du Mer*. Perhaps the most laid back of these charming little seaside towns, sheltered by their proximity, grace, and utterly draconian zoning laws from the foul brutish currents of greater Nice. They stopped along a quiet street where Claudia picked up some ice cream from a soon to be hibernating *Gellataria*.

They found a seat along the boardwalk that looked out on the western sweep of the bay. The first bits of setting sun gathered near the horizon and across the narrow road a string of seaside cafes were coming to life. He watched the waiters as they moved from table to table, lighting small hurricane candles, trying to keep the wind from blowing them out.

"All this staged beauty wasted on us?"

She smiled; the sun a fine backlight to her delicate features.

"What's next?" He asked. He could see the lace of her black knickers through the white shirt. "Want to go for a swim?"

"Trying to get me out of my clothes now?"

"Saw right through that one didn't you?"

She nodded. "How about instead, we just sit here, see what happens."

He looked back up the cliff, squinting at the tiny dot of Eze. "I haven't jumped out on a bill like that since college."

"That so?"

"Yep—an Albany Denny's, 2 a.m., underage and over served, couldn't find my wallet with the fake id, two redneck cops sitting down the end on a shift change, looking twitchy, waiting to pounce. I waited till they were knee deep in their Lumberjack Slams and flew out the Goddamn door, never looked back."

"A thing of beauty is a joy forever." She smiled.

"Tell me about it."

Then it was silent again. Had they drifted into the land of pauses and gambits, or was this the prelude to a longer nothing?

"Let me ask you something," he said, "seeing as were friends and all…. All that talk up there, the yachts, the generosity, the nihilism—you don't *really* go in for all that nonsense?" He smiled, "I mean, speaking for myself—I get a bit lit up and like to talk. But that's all it is—*talk*. A fine mix of insecurity and bravado, but I'm usually just fucking around in the end."

All the talk of asses and potted ferns were about to sail away.

She looked out towards the sea, "I don't think you are. Maybe you were once, and in your head maybe you still are—but you're right *here* in the middle of it...like you said *Hobbes boy*...free will is still involved." She leaned in," Have you noticed we're the *only* ones here, everyone else has taken it on the road. They're lighting sea shells for customers who aren't coming, just us and a few old age French pensioners." She straightened up, "Tell me that's not some ragged dodge.... Life is elsewhere, life is passing us by."

"Well, *I* can relate.... Even if you can't."

"Yeah," she smiled, twirling some ice cream on the spoon, "You keep telling yourself that."

"All right, look, you might be right about *some* of that—but that doesn't mean you can't understand, or be bothered, or care about feeling empathy for what someone else is going through."

He could sense she wasn't buying this line of reasoning, "Listen; before I was this half-burnt bit of toast *fabulousity* you see before you I was piloting a whole other agenda."

"Finally, here comes the real story..."

"Right, thank you—can I *continue* here?" He turned, staring intently enough to make her shift along the bench. "Back when I was in school I had a variety—a regular cornucopia if you will—of shitty dead end jobs that helped pay my way through college."

There was a mix of wonderment and revulsion in her faux socialist pampered expression that was almost, but not quite, endearing.

"It's an American thing," he explained. "We love that shit; think it builds character or something, and the fouler the gig the better. Anyway, among my varied bits of rock-pushing was a summer job at a rank little Upstate gas station."

"Yes, sounds like the Dickens."

She was rapidly getting on the nerves.

"Let me tell you something else about America Claudia—nobody likes a smartass."

"Ooh," she bristled, "now, *that* was hot."

"Anyway, I used to see these guys come in every Thursday afternoon, right after they'd cashed their paychecks...pickup truck-contractor looking guys mostly, and they'd round up and buy handfuls of these $2 scratch and wins and stand by the microwave scratching out a good chunk of their paychecks. I used to sit behind the register and watch these cats over the top of my *Rolling Stone* with this heady mix of fear and loathing.... What the fuck were they doing? They didn't look like they had pot one to piss in and here they were blowing $40-$50 on fucking lottery tickets...and God forbid every now and then one of those tossers would win $50 or $100 and it was like all hell had broken loose; the terrible affirmation in the nobility of their quest, and they'd only come back with a greater vigor than before.... In the end though, I got to tip the fuck out of that backwoods Podunk town and they stayed behind to work the third shift."

".... And now, almost ten years later and that whole way of thinking seems a world away, hell that whole life seems a world away, and what started out as the real burn of empathy just sort of fades to the arrogant fancies of a young man with too much free time on his hands." He smiled, "That's the prosy part I like to tell myself—but the better take is it's just the ramblings of *any* young man before he's been slapped around a bit, before he's had the chance to dangle at the end of some rope. Once you get a bit of that under your nails you can revisit that scene with a bit more than just the *pretend* empathy from a book."

"Now that is some self-pitying bullshit."

He smiled, "You are *definitely* getting on my nerves."

"Why—cause I'm calling you out on these things?"

"Calling me out on what—what the fuck are you talking about?" He straightened up a bit, "What's the alternative? Not to give a fuck about other people at all?"

"Maybe."

Christopher M. Basso

Exasperated, he ran a hand along his chin whisker stubble. ".... Lady—I think the sea salt and wacky weed has rotted your works. *Why* shouldn't I care about them?"

"Where's it going to get you?" She asked. "Or better yet, what are you going to do with it?"

He could feel his blood rising; but she shot the gap first.

"You're here after all, not there.... I mean really, if that was your game you'd abandon all your material things, live a life of quiet contemplation and...I don't know pass through the eye of a needle," she laughed. "But you haven't; in fact *you* just stiffed some working men on lunch." She smiled and her green eyes softened. "C'mon, it's an egregiously high standard to measure oneself against—a predetermined failure, dead in advance. You just stir in the guilt for a healthy dose of loathing. Life's much easier down at the shallow end of the pool."

"Fuck that." He sighed.

"See—*that's* where I'm going with this," she said, "What good is that story to me? Think it's going to change my world? Look around this place. Think anyone cares about it here?" She had stopped smiling. "No, you're pissed at me because I'm not letting you off the hook. What am I your therapist, your priest? Come unburden yourself and I'll give the benediction on your beneficent ass for a clean soul and a job well done—without ever actually having to, God forbid, *change yourself?* Shit, I'm giving you a better deal. I'm not even charging you the $200 an hour and you don't have to sit on my lap—you're making out ok here."

"You're assuming quite a bit."

"*Really?*"

He thought about it for a moment, "Yeah, well, fuck all that noise—at least I've been *in the mix.* Jesus, three hours of listening to you and I don't think you'd know a Goddamn shovel from a spade." He smiled to himself, pleased with this clever dig. "C'mon—gene pool breeding, class laundering, and Vichy collaborating. *Shit,* at least I'm still the virgin in the room," he laughed, "You're in Dutch with the cunts still writing the book."

"Now, look who's assuming things a bit."

Down All the Days

"Yeah, it's not very pleasant is it?"

The vibe had definitely grown tense; somewhat malicious in fact. But for once, O'Shea didn't quite feel like making the best peace.... Claudia Sommerton was already a foregone conclusion in this regard; the best peace had left her a long time ago.... But still, there was something redemptive, something of shouting these things into almost...a mirror. But before he could reconsider, she pulled the trigger for him.

".... Maybe I should be going."

Yes, the vibe had very much just gone off the rails, but the old boy was a proud sort, an intransigent Irish mule not fond of giving ground unless he was the one initiating it. He had but one road.

"Yeah, I suppose I should too."

Though the well was soured it was not quite poisoned. He thought to try to save the last remaining fragments of good nature between them.

"You around much longer?" He asked.

"For a bit."

He shrugged, half-laughing; "Maybe we should do this again sometime? Maybe leave the talking points at home...and the bill hopping...and maybe the mountains too."

She grinned.

"Let me give you my number," she looked around quickly. "Don't suppose you have a pen?"

"No."

"How good is that memory?"

He chuckled, "These days?"

She walked into one of the cafes and quickly reappeared, "Give me your hand." She took his hands in hers and etched her number with an oversized flourish.

There was a strange lull in the air, not quite a conclusion but rather an impasse. He thought to act before it became a solid thing.

Christopher M. Basso

"Let me flag one of those taxis for you," he walked out into the street and signaled a passing cab, "I've gotten good at it…. The key is to look pissed off—watch."

The cab pulled over and Claudia slid in. She leaned out the window and gave him the French double tap.

"How about it, still friends?"

"I don't know," she smiled crinkling her eyes. "You hurt my tender mercies."

And with that, she was gone.

Chapter Seven
Loving Cup

It was early evening when he reached the edge of the villa. The sun was just starting to drift around the margins, ushering in the pleasant orange and red of the evening sky. He jumped back over the wall to his property. Gate was busted—hadn't worked in a week. He made his way down along a trail of spent Heineken keg-cans and other various bits of trash lighting a breadcrumb path to the door. Met with more bits of trash on the other side of the door, clothes draped about, spent rocket trash, crude bits of pornography and all the other sure signs of a full blown bachelor lifestyle. Jesus, did any *men* live up in this motherfucker?

Sad bastard. What to do with another evening? Maybe conjure up some *real* food, give your dialing finger a rest, try making something...but what? He went to the cupboard, but the damn thing was bare. Boredom *and* hunger. Maybe give Fred Dewan a call, have him overnight some Ramen noodles and a fine Louisville Slugger with a crate of pristine Rawling specials. Tee em' up off the back terrace, loft a few out to sea. With any luck he might even tag a few of those no class yachting bastards as they sailed past. Though with the O'Shea deluxe karmic package he'd probably just take out a pod of dolphins rescuing children from the bands of marauding sharks.

He ambled over to the Sub-Zero like Gladys Presley shucking banana-bacon fry ups for The King and rooted around for some Gallic version of frozen living. Even this was too much effort, as these inertia "things" tend to gather strength in waves. Sod it, he thought; keep it simple.

A cold brush of fear all around, revealing itself by degrees, a party of one, this has always been a party of one—best that way maybe. Strange memories fog the haze, drifting back to the teenage miasma; the way you looked at the lads a few years older than yourself. Wide-eyed, like fucking rock stars making the scene at the local Taco Bell parking lot on a hot summer's night. But then something gummed the works.... What was that moment of utter and total *transmigration*?

Now look at them. IKEA nesting birds, grasped firm and *snipped* high for their own good, simonized cohiba stainless steel range tops, a very practical Chrysler Town & Country, thirteen seats and a stow on the go with Captain Bligh piloting the S.S. Lowered Expectations.... Sweaty palms chewing over the shortcomings in The Master Plan, sweaty palms leering at the young girl's trim asses and g-string peekers at the mall, as red rose petals fall faintly through the universe.... Decrepitude; worse than old Roy Batty's, the light that burns brightest burns half as long. He felt a queer mix of fear and loathing for the lot them, as he mined the Nutella jar with an index finger.

Maybe the libertine was right. Hunker down, bunker style. No more of this God awful wandering nomad transient nonsense, of wanting to go home. No more going home. It's a way to cheat time without cheating death. Delude yourself long enough, till you actually buy it. Then, at just the right moment, you jump the gun, hit the Percocet and Demerol like the Tupelo Thunder himself and let yourself go mad as a hatter. Fold before *He* makes the call. Play it right and you can string enough of these moments together to call it a life.

Grand plans to be sure. Grand plans suddenly and rudely interrupted by a ringing from the mobile in the next room. A ringing phone is a hateful thing indeed; hardly ever worth answering...let it ring. Six rings gets us to the safety of voice mail oblivion. Two rings and counting. Who could it be? Run down the list of the usual suspects—Fred Dewan? Calling to tell him he's finally gone broke? Mr. Henri le Fleur calling to rage on the young man's latest destruction of real property? Or *perhaps* it was even the Bay City Roller herself; calling to remind him that all glory is fleeting and of his many failings therein.... Four rings and counting.

He sauntered over to phone by the long mirror in the hall, stopping for a moment to admire the shape of his skull. In his best world-weary voice, he answered.

"Yes?"

He could hear the loud crunch of potato chips through the receiver.

"My, don't sound so *enthusiastic*."

".... Claudia?" He croaked.

"No, it's the ghost of Christmas future."

The fog was quickly clearing. "Uh...how'd you find me?"

"I told you; I know many things," crunch, crunch, crunch, "cultivate all sorts of people."

He rubbed his eyes coming to.

"Actually, I lifted your phone when you were off in the jacks, got the number...hope you don't mind?"

"Mind? No, well, not at all."

"Good. Listen, I feel a bit bad about how we left things. I think I laid into you a tad thick.... I have been known on occasion to howl at the moon."

.... Some chick pulling the "it's not you it's me" dodge? Did this then make *him* the chick? Who was this oddball anyway? Hang up the phone, his wiser mind might have said, keep all fantasies in the purview of a fantasy. But maybe, just maybe, this one was worth the ticket. He shifted the phone from one ear to the other and listened.

"So, dinner? You can pick the place.... My treat, I even promise to pay this time."

"Well—with an offer like that. What did you have in mind?"

"I leave that up to you."

Christopher M. Basso

He thought about it for a moment; the litanies of the day lost in the sudden desire to fuck with her a bit.

"I think I know just the place."

The time, place, vibe were sealed, all that was left was—

"Liam, wait!"

"Yes?"

"Take a shower."

Click; she was gone.... He put down the phone and stared into space, slowly contemplating this strange and perverse reversal of fortunes. He cracked open a Red Bull and made a mad dash for the bath.

He arrived at the brasserie a bit early, as was his custom, to find Claudia already there, sitting in the last table by the bar with her back to the wall. He stood in the old stone entrance for a moment pondering this crude sandbagging if his finely calibrated power play act. The smallish restaurant was packed tight with a very *authentic* looking crowd, as the pleasant smell of shallots drifted through the air.

The main room was ordered around a massive zinc bar which ran the entire length down the far side. Above, old glass orbs hung from ancient fixtures over narrow tables set for two, but pressed tight with three and fours. In between a row of enormous Belle Époque mirrors cast quiet reflections along the yellow tiled colonnades. The walls were filled with poster prints from the *la grande foisson* and engraved daguerreotypes of who and where he did not know.

Claudia was already talking to someone. A young lady of indeterminate age with her back turned to Liam, half sitting on the table's edge, shooting the breeze over something which seemed to have the both of them fairly animated. He stayed in the shadows a bit longer, letting this scene play out, if not for anything but to study the beast in its habitat. He'd been starting to wonder if she actually had interactions which weren't based on some middling levels of servitude, debt, or fear.

The mystery girl kissed Claudia on the cheek and started down the length of the bar in Liam's direction. No point in it now, the gig was up. He made his way towards the table, passing her about halfway down the bar. She was an attractive girl, dark skinned and petite, with lovely Spanish eyes. As she passed they shared the faintest of smiles.

He kept along the white and yellow-checkered tiles to the orbit of Miss Sommerton who'd eyed the whole thing from her catbird's seat. She failed to rise and greet him, rather she smiled and kicked out a chair gesturing him to sit.

"You think she's pretty?" She nodded, gesturing towards the door.

He took the bait. "She's cute...friend of yours?"

"Yes, Isabella, from Lisbon."

"And where was pretty Isabella from Lisbon off to so animated?"

"A get together up in the hills."

"Yeah? What's the occasion?"

She shrugged. "I don't know...Thursday?"

"Maybe we'll stop by later." She added.

"Maybe we will."

His thoughts turned to the mundane, "Find the place ok?"

"Yes—but I remember this being a bakery.... Must be new." She sniffed.

His eyes scanned the aperitifs menu. "Must be."

"A *vegetarian* brasserie Liam?" The wince on her face was a pure strain of revulsion. "Now I think I've seen everything."

"Well, I thought we needed to broaden your horizons a bit."

She studied the place for a moment and laughed. "Well, maybe so.... Too much red meat in my diet anyway."

"Look at it this way; manhandle one vice you can righteously backslide on the others."

He whipped out a cigarette and struck a match against the brass railing.

"A head of righteous vigor and a heart of clean living as he strikes up another one of those." She smiled.

"I try to keep the self-flagellation confined down the narrow aisles of this vessel if you please...but good looking out Claudia."

She watched the smoke trail up into the air. "I can see." She laughed. "Give me one of those."

"You bought a pack this morning?"

"And I smoked a pack."

"*That's* heavy."

"I've got the constitution for it. Grandmother Victoria smoked for sixty-four years, lived to be a hundred and two." She lit up, "It's in *the genes*."

The sound system was set on overdrive, Moroccan Sufi hip-hop seizing that slim bit of space just above ambient noise of a crowded restaurant. She leaned in a bit closer to be heard. "I took the liberty of ordering a sampler from the grazing menu. Hope you don't mind."

"Fine by me."

Within minutes, drinks safely in hand they were working on a spread of hummus, dates, and flat bread. She studied the table for a moment.

"You realize of course that Hitler was a vegetarian?" She smiled, "Goebbels too I think..."

"So was Gandhi, what of it?"

"Nothing. I'm just saying you find it in the strangest of places."

Yeah, and I bet old King Leopold's ghost rocked a steady diet of rib eye as well."

".... Touché"

"You said you needed to work on your empathy skills." He said. "I thought we'd start with animals...or the lack thereof on your plate."

"I don't remember saying that." She laughed. "Stand me another of those Reds would you?"

He smiled. "I could have sworn you did?"

She lit up and pushed back from the table, most decidedly over the repast.

"How'd you hear about this place?"

"You're not the only one with minions.... Actually, I just walked by it the other day. Been wandering all over this beastly city for a month—this seemed one of its more redeeming venues."

One of those pleasant pauses hung in the air between them. She leaned across the table, resting her head on her elbow studying him for a moment. Her black shirt offset the fine white of her skin. She looked rather beautiful in the soft light of the bar.

"What?" He smiled, slightly embarrassed.

"I thought to pay you a complement—you look good for a man your age."

"What age is that?"

".... I'll tell you when I know you a little better."

"This could be the best you'll ever know me."

"Rubbish, we're locked at the hip.... Here, give me your hand."

He recoiled slightly. "You're not going to try and read my palm or some mad shit like that?"

"I could blindfold darts at a board and divine your mysteries." She smiled. "I only wanted to see your Claddagh ring."

He held out his hand.

She studied his rough-hewn hand, busted and mangled, scraped from a recent Ducati themed run in with an uncooperative retaining wall.

"How'd you get such rough hands?"

"You don't want to know—I'm a *very* lonely man."

She was in fact reading palms, just like some gypsy shyster.

"Want to tell me what it means?"

She then switched gears. "It's a lovely ring.... The hearts turned in?" She smiled.

He studied it for a moment, "It is."

"See, you're a sentimentalist. I knew it."

"Say what?"

"Well, you're either quite alone and still holding on, or you're one *hell* of a shady bastard. And since I *can* read palms, I'd figure you for the former.... Some patron saint of the lost cause?"

He nodded, a bit annoyed, "Yep, that sounds about right."

"I understand perfectly." She smiled and added, "Want to tell me about it?"

"Nope...just the same old same old you know."

She leaned in closer. "Tell me something *interesting* then."

"I can recite most of *Blonde on Blonde* from memory."

"I said interesting not humdrum.... What were you saying about your father before?"

"When?" His mind flashed an absent blank; railing on old Handsome had become as memorable as drawing air.

"Sitting on the boardwalk—in mid-tirade about my inherent touch of evil. You said something about your cheap father.... What did that mean?"

He smiled, "I thought English people were supposed to be reserved?"

"I'm a half breed remember. The *other* part is all talk show confessional."

"Yeah? Which is better?"

"Ever seen the Windsors handing out free cars?"

He laughed before another bit of silence drifted in.

"I came into some money."

".... You came into some money?" Her eyes flashed again, as much a compliment as an accusation. "You find it in the woods or something?"

"Yeah, a bulrush basket floating down the river."

"So, how did you really come across this loot?"

"My father passed away a little over a year ago. He left me some money."

Perhaps she was expecting something more along the lines of wizened grandfather, Vegas cash out, dowdy old aunt, or any number of purely bullshit spiels she'd seen spun down round these parts. The immediacy of confession seemed to shock her back into some form of default *Englishness*. Her bearings were suddenly quite restrained, with an air of gravitas and the slightest hint of E. M. Forster humanist correction.

"Unfortunately, that's how it often is."

He suspected she knew of some things far more sinister than his own.

".... Yes." He grinned. "I suppose so."

He braced himself; chances for the ancestry follow up were always about fifty-fifty.

"And your mother?"

He didn't wait a beat; to wait a beat would be to wait a lifetime. "Same as my father."

"Both your parents gone?" A genuine feeling crept into her voice, something strangely different than her own.

"Cancer, the Big C…cancelled the poor women of her charm."

"I'm sorry to hear that."

"Well…unfortunately, that's how it often is."

She smiled with the black humor charm of someone whose pleasures had known a bit of pain. A heaviness suddenly gathered over the table, a metaphysical hangover in advance of the real one. "Jesus, Claudia, hide the knives!"

"I'm sorry I brought that up...I had no idea."

"How could you? Dodgy little bastard that I am."

She still seemed unsure, wary of some transgression.

He thought to put her at ease. "Don't worry; you're off the hook..."

".... Want to talk about it?"

"I don't know." He cringed. ".... It's a mind fuck all around. The reality is still too much for words sometimes." He let the autopilot kick out the reflective platitudes which often filled the space where his heart was once. "Death's a one time shot, no auditions necessary—and it takes all comers."

"There's more to it than that."

"I know, I know." He could feel the honesty building in him, the kind you can only conjure with complete strangers. "I guess it was anger at first, anger then annoyance, annoyance that I'd even been dragged into any of it."

"Who were you angry at?"

".... All the shit I couldn't put a face to. So I put my father's there instead."

"The Angry Son?"

"Yep, just like the fucking horse in the story."

"You two didn't get along?"

"My dear, that would be an understatement."

".... Can I ask why?"

"It's a long story."

Unfortunately she looked interested.

".... Well, in a nutshell he was never around...the man just sort of abdicated the role." Liam paused wise-like. "Which, you know, is fine in a strictly wild kingdom sort of sense; a rambling man's gotta keep on rambling.... Dr. Darwin might have even had a name for him, but I digress." He looked at her, truly pretty in the saw grass evening buzz, "C'mon you really want to hear this?"

"Yes."

"Prodigal sons usually lay it on a bit thick, don't you think?"

"Yes they do."

He smiled. "Point taken.... Besides, lately, it's getting harder and harder to see only the contemptible things in the departed."

"There's no point in it." She threw in her own two bits from those bitter Fergus waters.

"Damn right." He slapped the table.

"In the end, it turns out to be one of the nice things."

"What's that?" He asked, lighting up the next.

".... Pleasant memories."

"—If you're lucky."

She watched the smoke trail up towards the rafters for a moment. "What was he like, your father?"

"It's complicated."

"Then let's uncomplicate it."

"All right...where to begin?" He mused a bit; weary of stories about Handsome, but with one still left to tell. "Right after my father died I went up to his house in the country. This was a place I'd never been before, an eerie place, sort of like a bad museum.... So I'm walking around this eerie snapshot come to life, at this life that I should have known, this life that I should have shared." He paused to signal for another round. ".... I can't get comfortable in my skin though, you know? I feel like the walls are closing in around me; some sort of bad energy filling the house."

He drummed his fingers along the table. ".... So naturally I get *lit*."

She smiled, "Of course."

".... And then I start to ruffle around the place.... I'm in his office digging though his desk, past the Cuban cigars, past the betting stubs, the old issues of *Hooters* and *Hustler* and all the other detritus of a life oddly spent...all the bullshit I've learned to expect from this ne'er-do-well."

He shifted his weight forward ".... But then I'm finding all these *other* things—thank you notes from old friends, people he'd helped out of a jam, tax disclosure receipts from animal shelters, a civic medal from the St. Rose hospice he'd been supporting.... A photo of the old boy with the deputy director of the New York Meals on Wheels Program—Holy shit! What *the hell* had I wandered into?"

She nodded, "What did it mean to you?"

".... Right then and there?"

"Yeah."

"That it's a long strange fucking trip indeed.... From a rather despicable chap lost in some strange narcissism to...I don't know, maybe just a broken man who lacked the courage to rise above a few despicable moments, and all in just one evening."

She patted his hand. "It's quite a thing when all your certainty becomes uncertain?"

"Yes," he nodded, ".... But this was something worse." He gathered the courage of a fleeting thought. "The anger I could learn to live with, even the guilt of never making things right....But then I felt something else that night. Guilt that I was happy. Guilt that I was *free* from *all this shit*."

"It's a strange...nice feeling isn't it?" She smiled a conspirator's smile; slightly surprised he'd made that journey across the Styx.

"It certainly is.... At first I thought it was just the fifth of Scotch I had keeping me company, giving me that monstrous courage of my convictions, but then I understood, I was free, free from a certain brand of craziness that had defined my life." Liam smiled and ashed out. "Yep, I took his $3000 faux Baroque floor globe, doused it with some lighter fluid from the grill, and torched the fucker right on the lawn."

"You didn't?"

"No, I didn't...just passed out on the couch actually. But in spirit I had a bonfire, a grand bit of flame to send all those boogeyman off to Valhalla."

She raised her glass, "Here's to scoundrels then?"

"May they rest in peace."

Christopher M. Basso

Chapter Eight
La Fée Verte

They left the relatively pleasant confines of La Zucca Brasserie a little after midnight. Regrettable as that decision might have been, this *was* the lifestyle, and it dictated the rules....Too much of a good thing was most certainly just a bad thing waiting to happen; and with that they lit off down the road in search of something with a bit more of the grindstone grit. They walked along the main drag of the Old Town, trolling a few of the bars and clubs enjoying one last gasp before they shuttered their doors for the winter.

With the tourist herd culled by the first chilly winds of autumn, only the skells and the skullduggery beasts remained. Nice was a strange scene after dark, a place where you might want to ditch the sunscreen and avail yourself of some manner of firearms. The Mafia still owned the place of course. From Nice right on down to Marseilles a very strange breed of flashy, rather corrupt dodgers loitered in their gold chains around the edges of the finer places along the esplanade and the Port du Nice.

Among the demimonde of hard burned locals was another group, represented by the indentured servitude set of young girls. Mostly nineteen and twenty year olds, mainly from Eastern Europe, places with names like Belarus and Estonia, places for which this most sadly must have been some sort of Faustian upgrade. They're blackmailed into coming to the land of sun with the promise of cheap but relatively honest work. They are greeted by the waiting wolves, the only deliverance is their passport into the hands of one of these beasts, held hostage, while they are quickly introduced into a milieu of ill repute.

You could see them, standing along the *Zone Pietron* in the half-light of a humid hazy Riviera evening, a haunted vacuous gaze under the gaze they are aspiring to. Their Cezanne pimps drifting around the periphery of the green and yellow gas lamp glow.

Sad stuff indeed...but not when you're living *the* charmed life. Claudia and Liam zipped past this slice of street life on their nonstop jag to troll the bars and clubs lining the Rue St. Vincent.... Noted dandy boy Edmund Burke said something about the only thing necessary for evil to triumph is for good men to do nothing—but he was most likely an unrepentant mama's boy straight from the squarest of Oxbridge whelping boxes.... No *grit* on that type.

Which went without saying that the newly christened toxic twins were chocked full of the stuff, and it also went without saying that Claudia Sommerton had an encyclopedic knowledge of the haunts, nooks, and crannies of this foul sulfur ash realm. They soon set up shop by the bar in *Pravda*, an upscale, low moral, new money joint by the water. From their perch they had a fine view of the Odessa oligarch set dropping $800 on top shelf table service, as young woman shimmied in steel cages swinging from the rafters.

It was politely billed as *cabaret*, but the vibe was unintentionally Dadaist. All that was missing were the flaming spears and the trapeze queens. Yep, they'd just about *nailed* it; that hellish carnival air the old knight on the Spanish train was railing about. Except this was something worse, the heady sense of atavistic abandon, the apex, the pinnacle, the spirit of the age.

Neither of them was much in the mood for this nonsense. They'd crested up the mountain of a fine mutually shared weirdness that day, and they weren't particularly keen to let the jabberwocky fest devolve into rubbing shoulders with a bunch of poseur hucksters.... And with this, the sad, gripping realization that try as you might there was no way to properly mix with the exact depths and depravity of this lifestyle without a healthy dose of irony.

This scene was simply too naked, too vicious, too bare, for even a Welsh cut piece of steel like Miss Sommerton to unwind properly. There was something in her wisp-o-the-willows glance that he understood at once. He could he see it in himself, shining back across the same eyes, the same eyes that had watched the dear dirty Dublin of his youth burned to ash in the fire of some Phoenix.

"This town isn't what it once was." She sighed. "At least the lads had a bit more dash back then."

"This is some God awful music." He remembered saying, as if on cue.

"It's Techno." She said. "Is there any other kind?"

"Point taken."

"Let's jet." She said. "This place is giving me The Fear."

They high tailed it out of little Siberia with something bordering on joy, free from the beastly subterranean clusterfuck they'd wandered into. Any further assaults on the finer senses would necessitate stronger reinforcements. Claudia had at least one of those bases covered…. She produced a half-mashed spliff, rolled and forgotten, from her jean pockets. A few passes between them was all that it took. Claudia rolled in a league that harvested from the potent, well-tended fields of the Lord. Feeling better for it they started up from the old town, still in the mix for something to keep wandering minds from idling.

"We need to get our hands on something heavier." He declared.

"Is it time for The Dragon?"

"Not *quite* that heavy."

"Speed?"

"Too fast."

"Vicodin?"

"Too slow."

Christopher M. Basso

"How about some...Absinthe?"

His eyes lit up like she'd just discovered fire.

"Now we're winning.... Where can we get some?"

"Anywhere—it's *legal* here you rube."

She thought about it. "But I know just the place—they make it their business to know the real deal from the swill they pawn on the tourists."

Within minutes they were sitting in the rafters of a converted, deconsecrated church turned fun palace, looking down on the dance floor below. They sat in a small table along the railing sharing a beer and catching their breath as they surveyed the scene below. A huge stained glass window sat over the center floor, backlit with strobe lights, casting eerie shapes and shadows over the congregation.

Claudia excused herself with the vaguest rumblings about needing to see a man about a dog, a declaration which took on a multitude of meanings in the urban slang tower of Babel. But with his best distraction gone, attention shifted to the people gathered along the upper reaches of the scaffolding walkway. From this perch he had an excellent view of all the exhibitionist action below...

Claudia returned, one step ahead of a waitress balancing a silver tray loaded with the wares. She had a smile across her face, and had he looked up a second earlier he might have noticed the slight wolfish rub across her lovely teeth. She sat down and the waitress set the silver tray next to her. Miss Sommerton would take it from here. The tray was filled with pirouette shaped glasses, a carafe of water, some ginned up looking silverware, a small bowl of sugar cubes, and one very dusty black glass bottle embossed with elaborate cursive lettering.

"You said you wanted it, here it is."

"That's quite a set up."

"It's quite a drink...ready?"

He waved a hand, "Proceed."

Down All the Days

She placed one of the small sifter glasses front and center and poured a few drops of an amber colored liquid down the side, watching the slightest streaks of green running like contrails through it. When she was satisfied with the vintage she poured the glass one-thirds full. She placed one of the heavy silver spoons across the rim of the glass, forming a bridge. The spoon was perforated in the center, forged with gilded cuts of elaborate fleur-de-lys. Across the openings she laid two cubes of sugar.

A few of the more observant eyes around them watched the proceedings, suitably impressed, with her diligent reverent hand. In some circles, this ritual still occasioned the religious solemnity of a priest blessing the altar.

Next she took the small carafe of cold water and began to slowly drip a continuous stream onto the sugar, which slowly dissolved though the gilded fleur-de-lys into the Absinthe. Each drop of sugared water slowly traced a band through the greenish liquid, drip by drip, till it gradually shaded to an almost milky color.

"Viola." She announced, gently pushing the glass towards him.

His eyes went down to table level, studying the strange brew. She could sense a bit of trepidation on his part. To some, Absinthe was one of those things which sounded far better in drunken theory than the actual application.

"C'mon then," she assured him, "pacing a little green faerie is a damn sight easier than chasing the big red dragon."

"I don't know man...looks like carny jizz-booth streaks."

"Well, you'd be the authority on that Guv."

"And what's this supposed to *do* exactly?" He cut her off.

She shrugged, "Only one way to find out."

He raised an eye. "That helps."

"I can always order you a Shandy or something?"

Calling into question a man's already assailed manhood could overcome any personal predilections. "Give me that."

481

Christopher M. Basso

He grabbed the glass and took it down the gullet in one long belt. "Booyakasha!"

"Whoa, careful there—that's not the fake business they pawn off on the college kids."

His face was a contorted rush, spasmodic *and* demonic, as he worked to get around the strong rush. "Ugh—tastes like…"

"Decaying licorice, I know." She took the glass from him.

"Well that was suitably awful." He slammed his fist on the table. "Stand me another."

"Ah, wait a second there."

"*Fine,* I'll do it myself." He poured another quick draw from the old dusty bottle, forgoing the whole sugar and water bit, and took it down in one long green belt.

He looked at her. "What? You need some training wheels my dear?"

She shook her head, slowly sipping her own…. The *Américain* would soon learn the hard way, why the green faerie was never to be slammed, shot-gunned, beer-ponged, or mainlined. This foul and evil little drink was barely legal for a reason. Psychedelic or not, most quality brews hovered around 150 proof. And Claudia being a high end purveyor of the low end lifestyle never went for the watered down Absinthe-Lite shite from Western Europe.

She went right down the rabbit hole, for the *Boshkie*, a particularly virulent strain from the deepest, darkest recesses of the former Soviet Bloc. The *Boshkie* was brewed by a lusty sort up in the Hartz Mountains, mad monks who stirred their brandy with a nail and made it a point of pride to lace their vintages with enough Thujone to kill a whole army of Oscar Wildes and a legion of Ezra Pounds.

…. The flight of angels began almost instantly. A clean bracing shock wave sent right down the spine and launched back to the brain. The music started picking up a bit. A stream of bad Techno filled the room—was there any *good* Techno indeed? Strange shapes started to slither down on the floor. Goddamn mutants, cast in serpent shades, square pegs about to miss the mark on the roundest of holes.

Then the next rush hit him, a clean, warm sort of clarity, not at all expected, and something one could enjoy.... But there were stranger things at work than silly old licorice brews. Strange things like the spurious little bit of spliff from her pocket, toked a mere twenty minutes ago outside the club.... The one which she failed to mention had been dipped in liquid Ketamine. A strain of which could take down a whole army of cocky Hartz Mountain bootleggers.... A booster rocket if ever, whose foul powers were slowly seeping in to find their *level*.

Feeling confident about another spirit bested he struck the match for another cigarette...but there was something wrong with the flame. It burned a soft blue shading to green, snaking out from his hand like a silver contrail; strange bands conjured from the tumbing bend of bay. He tossed it back on the table lest it grab *him* next.

"Damn," he sat up straight, "Man...I hate to admit it, but I think that stuff jumped right up on me."

"Best to just ride it out." She smiled, her eyes bright points. "Hold onto something and steel the nerves."

The glass in his hand was expanding at the angles; the silver spoon taking on the shape of a gilded dagger. Mad thoughts assailed the mind, colors of ochre and pale greens, little dragonflies buzzing through a field of lazy daisies.... And green eyes across the table burning even greener, till they were burning, fiery points of phosphorus white...

".... Perhaps some fresh air is in order?"

"I agree, I hate the music here." She smiled, and started to rise, heading for the door.

"Wait, what about your drink."

A sour look came across her face. "Absinthe? Are you mad? I never touch the stuff."

Christopher M. Basso

Chapter Nine

The Samaritan

The *Rue du Dismas* sat parallel the corner of the *Avenue Portinari,* somewhere near the faint lights of the train station and somewhere far from the artifice and edifice of daylight's passing fancy. A sleepy moonlight draped across several centuries of mismatched roads, cutting at odd angles here and there, into a patchwork maze, which forced one to make a choice, and as this was Claudia's show, she made one—nipping quickly down the darkly lit entrance of the forgotten quarter.

They followed the narrow skeletal tracks of a long gone streetcar, its cable riggings still lining the way, snaking lazily like the overgrowth deep in the reaches of some jungle. A slight bit of dusty wind kicked up to greet them on a still warm Indian Summer night.

The length of the street was empty, just odd bits of paper rolling along like Yojimbo tumbleweeds. From the far side of the way, the lonely dogs and alley cats might have caught sight of them in the almost spectral glow, their shadows lit against the stark green and dull purples of the cheap ultraviolet lights lining the path.

The rot between the glitz, he smiled.... Drift a bit from side to side, and watch it reveal itself—graffiti, French and Arabic scrawled across the flimsy walls, ramshackle corner shops steel shuttered for the night, bad vibes all around, feels unhealthy, a sunny place for shady people indeed.

"How you doing Liam James? Holding up?"

"Better than ever." He smiled. ".... Where we going?"

"You'll see."

They kept down the dust bowl road for what seemed like an eternity. Past the low-lying tenement flats, faded and falling....Rows and rows of old wooden shutters fastened shut, bits of rust stained walls caked with a thick layer of soot. It appeared as though time had simply forgotten this small corner of Nice.... But as beat up as it looked, one glance up the nearby hills revealed the sprawling gardens and Beaux Arts mansions of Cimiez, and one glance back over the shoulder sat the beautifully tracing arc where the sea met the land. This was obviously some nasty piece of conspiratorial real estate purgatory...but what were *they* doing back here he wondered?

Liam might actually have felt a bit more at home here on some echo-like metaphysical level, a certain kinship with those having been left in the dust.... But his practical brain, the fight or flight one, reminded him he'd since crossed the threshold, and that HE was now very much part of the problem.... Maybe best to keep the footsteps fast because in his present state there'd be no proper explaining to the natives where it had all gone wrong.

.... Which was to say the foul mix of opiates and spirits the she-devil had plied him with had only recently sounded the retreat. And till the last of that foul goblin was gone, all manner of ghastly hellish apparition was still on the table. He looked at her, a smiling innocence shining back, pale green eyes still a bit aglow in the brutish wash of the chemicals cock-whipping his brain...and one may smile and smile and be a villain yet.

"We're here." She said at last.

He looked up. "Here?"

It was a fairly nondescript, slightly sturdier looking red brick building, the last door on a dead end street.... Maybe it was still the drugs ginning up the works, but even in the beatific light of morning this place still looked as busted as a Chevy Camino shedding isotopes on some fine Kentucky cinderblocks.... Shit, condemned might have been politer. The only hiccup to the faded beaten *chi* of the place were the few high end sports cars lining the street nearest the door. The shining glitter horribly out of sorts with the general back alley ambiance of the surroundings...that or more ominously right at home.

The effects of his most recent power-hour continued to shed their intensity. And once her eyes stopped glowing that hellish shade of green he was able to address her properly. "What the hell is this?"

She slid back the heavy iron outer door along its tracks, pressed the buzzer and smiled. "Your reality, my working class hero."

"Here?"

She nodded.

"As what—machinists? C'mon, I meant an *interesting* reality."

"Oh, it could be interesting. Just depends on which way the wind is blowing."

A small security camera overhead trained on them, its red light slowly blinking. The door buzzed and they past through.

He noticed an old gated elevator at the far end of the building. A charming antique of a thing, and from the look of it still quite functional, but she instead opted for the stairs and this strange theme of drugs, air, cigarettes, and exercise continued.

He followed dutifully, down the hall and up the stairwell, running wild with the detritus of some abandoned *Blade Runner* set... It was the unifying theme of rotting decay that really tied the place together, like Lebowski's rug, and any attempts at consistency had to be admired on *some* level.

But how many more of these strange moments could the brain endure? This seedy, pointless, yet highly entertaining wandering.... Foul nights and fucked up mornings, relieving yourself on the imperial registry of your neighbor's ornate gates, and twelve hours later arguing with every fiber of your mo' at some French teenager about a spurned Happy Meal. This was a crass dilemma to be sure.... A Moses without the mission was usually called a bum.

".... People live here?"

"Yeah...kind of like a cooperative of sorts."

She pushed on past to the fourth landing, the final floor.

"And you know these people?"

"As well as you know anyone."

"All right," he caught his breath. "Here's the million dollar question—how do you know them?"

"I have friends all over this town, remember."

Something then clicked in his head. "This isn't where you've been *staying* is it?" He looked around and laughed, "Damn Claudia...not much of a going concern wouldn't you say?"

She said nothing.

"Actually," he grew a bit serious, "This fucker looks a bit *condemned.*"

"Does it?"

"Hell, I made you for eccentric—but I never suspected *hardcore.*"

"I'm flattered...I think."

They continued down the hall.

"*Hardcore.*" She let the word roll off her tongue with relish. "Now, see how much *better* that sounds than smart and interesting?"

He took another gander at the place. "Add *stunning* to the list."

"Well, you know what they say about looks? Besides, it's more for appearances, keeps the curious at bay."

"Curious?"

"Never mind—I'll tell you later. Here hold this while I find my key."

"Whose place is this anyway?"

"His name's Влади́мир Ильи́ч Ле́нин...but you may call him Bob."

"Is he here?"

"No. He stops by now and then, but even he has a limit on the eccentricities of his youth.... Actually, he has a lovely cream colored stone mansion down in your neck of the woods."

Interesting, thought the boy. He wondered if he'd perhaps scent-marked this poor chaps gates late one night.... It was then he noticed another set of security cameras training on them, not to mention the series of heavy deadbolts on the door lining the hallway. She could sense his trepidation. "Again, those are just mostly for show. *Actually*, this is probably the safest place in the whole of Nice...or for that matter maybe the whole South of France."

"Bob's got that kind of action?"

She smiled, "No one steals from Bob."

They arrived at the final door, their destination. It was one of those heavy slide-sash things, formidable on any occasion, but this fucker looked downright bombproof. She was able to slide it open with a little help from O'Shea. He had slipped behind her, his chest briefly brushing up against her back as they pulled the heavy door along the track, caught in that strange innocent moment when we know *we can*.... A bit of warm breath on her neck, cigarettes and alcohol; a fine Sodium Pentothal—the wasting wastrels pheromones of choice.

The door clicked back along the mechanical track, revealing a massive open room that most certainly was once the floor to a machine shop or some such thing. Acres of sturdy exposed brick, stained and cured with the whitewash of the day, faded now to a dull but neat shine. Above them, a row of windows ran across the top of the furthest wall, each pane a well-tended set of perfectly opaque frosted glass, offering the peace of mind that comes with the talisman charms of a complete and total anonymity. An orderly system of ductwork kicked out a steady stream of cool air on the still warm coastal morning.

On the main level, there was little more than several old couches sat between the fading and chipped columns spaced every twenty feet or so. And resting beneath those busted old couches and astride the chipped fading columns were several rugs, dingy Persian Santar prints in shades that had seen better days, warming the cinder stones of the cold floor.

Christopher M. Basso

A few tables lined the wall near the entrance, piled high with booze and empty boxes of Tandoori takeout. Several open laptops whirled forth, a tracer line running from one to a stack of Marshall speakers, each the size of the average Frenchman's car, blasting out the some of the Moroccan hip hop the boy was learning to enjoy.

There were no other doors leading out, no terraces, no fire escapes; a perfect boxed in box—no one enters, no one leaves, save through the blast door out front. A single cast iron grate staircase ran up the near wall to what might have been a foreman's shop overlooking the floor below.

And even after all those decades, the vague scents of oil and diesel still hung in the air—commingling of course, in a passing of the torch kind of way, with the sweet reefer and tobacco air of the current occupants.... There must have been twenty or thirty of them, draped across the makeshift furniture and along the alcove window slats, like scattered bits of casual human existence accented here and there.

Some of them were standing around the makeshift bar, while several others gathered round a large table for what looked like some sort of high stakes mancala action. But there were others still, drifting in and out of unseen rooms in the back. Might have been bedrooms, perhaps a library or a nice conservatory.... But then again, it might have been Uncle Billy's Red Dragon Shooting Gallery for all he knew. *Whatever* it was, privacy and a wary covetous of it seemed key. Lot's of tense vibes had greeted their arrival, and for a crowd on the edge of doing a whole lot of nothing, they seemed awfully intent on studying absolutely everything.

And an odd bunch they were, all the colors under the Benetton flag working some strange angle on an early September morning. There were the young and the pretty, day trippers from a set Claudia could once upon a time most likely have called her own. Thrill seeking rich kids he imagined, the type who liked to run with a heavier element, but would damn quick click their heels three times if the scene went heavy. The heaviness was courtesy of several hardo looking types, North Africans mostly, still fighting the Battle of Algiers on some lousy level, and a few serious looking Tartar gents plucked most certainly from the

490

deepest steppes of Mother Russia.

O'Shea's eyes scanned the room with their usual mix of paranoia and self-righteous fervor as he ran the ballistics on the scene. He was rather enjoying his Crazy Joe Clark routine till he eyes regrettably settled on several of those legally kidnapped girls, newly arrived from every corner of that collective Diaspora we call "the sticks", and now trapped in the maw of something they never saw coming.

There was the loud thud of music, but nothing so pleasing to the ear. A few languid bodies moved in the center of the room, but no one seemed to be having any fun.... No, the vibe here was far too tense, too paranoid, too cagey for such things.

Such was the scene when the youthfully diluted O'Shea, and the Kensington Garden Libertine wandered around the foyer and made the scene properly.... All that was missing was the sound of a record being scratched to a halt in the collective pause to welcome the newcomers...or that is to say, *the newcomer*.

There was no mistaking it, their arrival was poorly timed.

After what seemed a rather *longish* pause, the eyes of the actively paranoid and the thoughts of the merely curious returned to whatever had been occupying their fancy. First impressions had been a bit of a bust, but once passed, a subtle if not strange sense of détente crept into the air. Perhaps a strange face mixed with the familiar had put them at ease...or maybe it was one of those dozing afternoon lion bits, biding their time, drinking their wine.

And looking around the room it seemed a rather fair trade off.... Certainly not the most *at ease* crowd, but once they seemed to sense the lack of any immediate threat they became content at the margins to simply ignore them. And being a fine ray of sunshine in his own right, this little transactional indifference suited O'Shea just fine.

"Quite an assemblage you have." He whispered.

"Don't be a snob."

He looked hurt. "Hell—I'm no snob."

"Sure about that?"

".... Mostly."

"Besides, I told you this bunch was fairly laid back."

He studied the fine tableaux of physical graffiti strewn about the place, ".... Oh really?"

She looked at him, he looked at her.

"That's the central fallacy with you tightass, straight thinking types—even the oddball vampire gets the urge now and then for a low-fi evening."

"They don't look especially low-fi."

"Well, I did say for the *most part*.... But then again if the lads are in the mood, then things can get a bit jumpy."

She made only the most cursory attempts with greetings and salutations...not that anyone seemed particularly put off with any transgressions of form and etiquette. Rather this was just the smoke and mirrors which run with the hierarchal confirmations that often need to be established or reaffirmed. Her introductions-interactions were genuine, in that they genuinely made it known that Liam was *with* her and all which that favorably conferred, or perhaps ominously implied.

"Listen, you stay here." She said. "I've got to make a phone call, be right back." She started up the iron stairs towards the head screw's lair. "Talk to no one, touch nothing." She chuckled.

"You don't really have to make a call, do you?" He called up after her.

"No," she smiled and disappeared.

O'Shea strolled over to the makeshift bar and poured a Grey Goose neat, before turning to greet this rather seedy slice of lifestyle art. Good folks he assured himself.... Mingle—move confidently in their midst.

He took his drink and started the gatecrasher party circuit—a slow leisurely stroll around the periphery of things looking for any gamely takers. Not much there though. Of course, it must be said, you haven't really lived till you've been on the business end of some vaguely threatening rumblings, uttered under the breath of some midnight foreign tongue.

But his eyes soon locked with one of the young Russian girls, a delicate pretty sort of no more than twenty. She was petite in frame, but with a proud countenance that seemed to raise her up in stature. Her dark black hair was streaked with shades of auburn and very fair porcelain white skin. She was rather beautiful actually. She looked like the ghost of a Russian princess from a story.

But there was something haunted about her eyes, eyes too young for looking so old. It was something he thought he understood from his own, the resentment of things, the resentment for the virgin graces you can never get back.

They exchanged a brief, wholly innocent smile…. Maybe she sensed something kindred in the eyes. Maybe she'd made his gate crashing act for what it was, and had some sympathy for the simple fool who's drifted into the deep end of the pool.

Regardless of its provenance he started ambling over to her, but at that moment one of the shotgun-shogun types casually pulled her away towards the hallway leading to whatever dwelled in the back. He watched an indelicate hand lead her away and seethed a bit. Just a bit more of the poor bad timing that had informed his evening apparently.

He wandered over towards the windows and found a free seat…. It's quite the nightcap to stroll into some heavy drug milieu particularly when you weren't one of the imbibers or suppliers….Doubly worse if you're the stranger in the strange land menacing around the fringes like some unknown quantity. But as long you weren't *actively* a threat, say some undercover narc, or some hard up retribution gimp they'd burned along the way—than you could be tolerated, and in these parts that just about passed for civic minded hospitality.

But through this confusing sociological mess he'd watched the Sommerton carry herself with the strangest of bearings, an almost regal confidence, that defied and subverted the various hard-on types as she'd ascended the staircase. Without so much as a word they'd dutifully and expeditiously cleared a path, a parting of the sea for which no one's ego looked worse for the wear. No one seemed to find this a bit strange save for the horse-vibing, gnome-fearing Yank watching this bit as he stood there nursing his vodka…fairly confident that this was the *second* damndest thing he'd seen that evening.

She played the room with a fine bit of rum, sodomy, and the lash that was as English as John Bull, Sheppard pie, and shitty weather. Like some maestro running tremolos from the white keys to the black, utterly and totally convincing them they were rightly gauged in their assessment.

He'd made like a good gatecrasher and wandered back towards the bar, to a nice if not limited selection, and poured another bracer of vodka neat, and thought best not to inquire about a twist of lime. By way of the bar he'd drifted over to the orbit of the long table and the high ante mancala stakes match….Finally, elevated tensions that he played no part of.

He was content to watch the scene, admiring the languid singsong chant of the many languages not his own. *Splendid,* he thought. Much more his speed. He scarcely noticed the libertine gone.

That was until he heard some strange bit of tongue, reflexive and a bit more aggressive in the phonetics, but certainly a question all the same being posited somewhere…. And there it was again, this time a bit louder.

"Mais qui diable tes-vous?"

He turned back towards the table and noticed one of the natives had come out to greet him properly.

"Mais qui diable tes-vous?" he repeated again, an agitated face, a somewhat unpleasant tone.

…. Hmm, didn't sound too friendly at that. Didn't need Noam Chomsky or Henry Higgins for that one.

O'Shea thought to break the ice, "Come again?"

He now spoke in English, slow, condescendingly accented English.

"Who…the…fuck...are...you?"

An ugly silence lingered the air waiting for some

494

remediation.... Liam, *way* past the point of giving a fuck, thought to break it. "Ask me again."

The last traces of green faerie dust and horse tranquilizer kicked back into the wind, a hard aspect returning to his eye, and looking a bit tougher than he felt.

The greeter man stood from the table, knocking his chair over. He appeared to keep rising, and rising, and rising.... Which was to say he was a rather *large* fucker.

Jumpin' Jehoshaphats, son of a bitch looked like a Goddamn Wookie.... A crazed Wookie that had been chewing on fresh pineal gland.

They stared at each other rigid and stiff, caught in that weird tipping point moment. There were too many eyes on them for the big man to back down.... O'Shea figured he'd have to go low for the kneecaps.

"Cool it, he's with me." Claudia said calmly from behind his shoulder. She had watched events unfold from the staircase, waiting for the proper moment to make her point.

The big man seemed quite agitated. He walked closer to the bar, which was to say closer to O'Shea, who was already formulating a plan to enlighten the interloper with the realties of an Adamantium berserker rage.... Shit, there was no shame in street fighting with a Redwood.

The greeter was polite enough to switch to English, "I should have known." He turned to Claudia. "What the fuck are you bringing these skells around?"

She had reached the bottom of the stairs and was starting over. Heavy vibes were some of her favorite things.

O'Shea, confident he'd made the right play, and most confident that she was about to make the wrong one, started closer across the floor beating her to it.

"Turko the terrible, you got a problem with me, you talk to me."

The greeter seemed a bit confused with the rapid fire English, but the feeling behind the words was easy enough to grasp. He stared hard in O'Shea's direction.

Liam smiled. "I can show you better than I can tell you my man."

Claudia chimed up coming between them, a tall girl looking suddenly rather small, "All right, everybody just calm down.... Liam's going to go get me a drink, Kahil and I are going to have a chat and everyone is going to be cool."

Liam and the Wookie slowly started the fine peacock strut of disengagement. Claudia and the greeter drifted over to a corner of the room. Her back was turned but she said something which seemed to change his whole program rather quickly. The slightly wild look of "touch and go" was replaced in a flash by the ashen faced quality of someone who's just had the fear of God put into him.... Or maybe in this case the fear of Bob.

Lesson learned he skulked away, righteously pissed, and a fairly defeated man. His crew, who had only moments before been angling for a possible gang swarm, had no choice but to collectively look the other way.

Claudia rejoined Liam by the bar, sizing him up with that same cool look in her eye.

"And what was *that?*" She asked, slightly agitated.

"Beats me." He shrugged, "I was having a drink telling a girl about a horse I owned once when that loon pushed up on me."

"Yes, well Bob tends to retain the fairly motivated high strung ones."

"For what?"

She smiled, "If you have to ask, you'll never know.... It's better to leave it at that."

"Of course."

"All right, that was enough excitement for the three o'clock hour. Besides, I think I just cashed my last check on Bob's good name with these boys." She smiled. "Come with me."

Chapter Ten
By the Stone

Up and away they went, to the relative stillness and peace of the second story. The vibe of the downstairs having returned to the merely tense; downgraded from the actively hostile. Liam trailed behind as they passed through another set of heavy doors, the status light from the pass code key flashing a muted, dullish green.

In the midst of the Wookie scrum he failed to notice she'd ditched her heels and was walking along the cool red tiles of the entryway. Something seductive about that, and an ankle tat of a thing he couldn't quite make out, until he looked closer.... *Le Gros Serpent*—and God created woman indeed.

She led him further down the hall through another set of doors. Once across the threshold the old boy was somewhat stunned by the sudden and drastic change in latitude. The grit of the pauper court having transformed to the Zen stillness of palace guard. They were now standing in the breezeway of another oversized bit of reconverted factory, tastefully reimagined, into some artist's studio retreat.

Cubist prints sat balanced along the walls, none hanging, only resting, tilted at easy angles, some draped with throw cloths, others out to admire, but each singularly rendered by the sure and steady hand of someone who could be fairly proud of their work.

The nighttime lighting was low wattage simple, helped by the shafts of clean moonlight casting down from the cathedral glass ceiling set gracefully over this bit of backwater grime. The shadows revealed the casual disarray of easy living, elegant bits of jet fuel trash, pictures draped and covered, expensive bits of furniture chipped, nicked, and generally beaten down. Two comfortable looking worn leather chairs sat beneath one of the massive windows with a decent view down to the water and the faded orange dome of the Hotel Negresco.

Along the far wall sat a row of antique coin and spring slot machines, dusty and worn, with names like *Triage Diable Les Derby* stenciled across the side; entreaties from long silent ghostly sentinels. An old roulette wheel sat beside them in the corner, half covered with a drop cloth and a fair share of clutter.

Liam walked over and gave it a spin. "Bob a gambler?"

"No," she smiled, popping her head out from the kitchen, "a *degenerate* gambler."

She lit a few candles, setting them down on the faded cloth layout next to the still spinning wheel.

"Bob also fancies himself a Renaissance man." She looked around the room, at the fair jumble of easels, sketches, works achieved and works in progress, "Most of these are his." This was a statement which rather impressed Liam, but seemed to bring out the withering critic in her.

"Amateur hour—strictly."

"You know about these things?"

"I know a little bit about something.... Besides the rapidly calcifying bitterness of my own failed attempts has made me quite the astute commentator."

"Well—how sophisticated for you." He fell back into one of the deep weathered armchairs under the moonlight.

She kept about the place lighting candles. "He uses this place occasionally when he's too lazy to drive the five miles back to his house.... But who understands these wealthy people."

"Otherwise he lets me use the place when I want." She finished the last of her mood setting. "You want a drink?"

"I don't know about you, but I think I'm done with the

booze for a bit."

"How about some tea then?" She called from the kitchen, her voice suddenly sweet with a genuine inflection.

"Yeah…sure."

"Wonderful. I've just the thing."

He could hear her rooting around the pantry doors.

"No Ketamine or Angel Dust blends please."

"Relax, like I said, I've got just the thing."

He continued with the inspection of Bob's fortress of solitude. Besides the main room, there was a small kitchen and a bath off to the side. Through another door he assumed was the bedroom. An equally comfortable looking couch sat in the far corner. He felt a bit sleepy in the old chair. Maybe time to close his eyes for a moment, just till the brew was ready.

He heard the once remembered, long forgotten crackle of the needle to the grooves, and then Nina Simone's rich baritone drifting out from the time fog.

He snapped back to it. "Damn, is that what I think it is?"

She nodded. "The genuine article."

He hopped up and walked over to where she was standing. Sitting by the door to the small rooftop garden was a perfectly kept Steepletone record player cased in a heavy red leatherette—shining like the day it was new.

"I haven't seen one of these since I was a little kid."

"Yeah," she said, "I know. I was in a vintage shop recently, saw an 8 track, and thought I was back in the womb."

He ran a hand along the smooth skin of this strange technology. Seemed like it should be easy enough to get it working, but he couldn't quite remember how. That is to say he could work the nanotechnology on his iPhone blindfolded and manacled from the bottom of a bathtub, all Houdini-like, but *this* was reverse engineering of the highest order.

She handed him a cup of steaming tea.

"Here's to technology." She said.

"Yeah, and getting back in the womb."

They headed back towards the armchairs by windows. A nice breeze had picked up carrying the old curtains softly in its wake. She was totting along a small wooden box under her arm. From it she produced some rolling papers and a very sweet pleasant smelling tobacco. Before he could say Depp, Claudia had taken to rolling a pair.

The voice from the record was hushed, a whisper, but with a presence that filled the room. *My Baby Just Cares for Me,* Nina Simone's torch song, sung with a conviction that could easily have put Frank to shame.

"Are you a fan?" She asked.

He nodded.

"You know, she lived up in the hills near *Arles* the last few years of her life.... I saw her once having coffee and a cigarette on the garden terrace at the Hotel Ritz. She looked the part too, a very elegant lady, sitting at one of those old tables, drinking paint thinner strong espresso, smoking her hand rolled Blanchards. She had...that certain something."

She shook her head sadly. "So, it's fair to say Nina Simone is responsible for some of my vices." She handed him one deftly rolled Blanchard special. "And to think, I was actually mulling the idea of quitting at the time."

He smiled, "Yeah, I know, passing the nicotine buck is one of my favorite pastimes. It's got the fine ballast of Catholic guilt with just a touch of the soul crushing heaviness of your finest existentialists—really the best of both worlds."

"That's right—what was your boogeyman trigger again...stress?"

".... No that was all a well-tended lie. It was just good old fashioned peer pressure in the end." He thought about it for a moment. "Twenty-two years old too. So late in the game. They should have beaten me for that."

"Are you sure it wasn't a woman Liam?"

"It just might have been." But not the kind she thought.

"The fantastic lies of possibility." She smiled. "I think even Nina Simone would have agreed...had I ever seen her in the garden terrace of the Hotel Ritz having an espresso and a smoke."

He laughed. "Well, you've got your legend to live up to and all. Such things are permissible."

"Rubbish, I've got antecedents and a decent skill for acting." Then she smiled and lit another. "You know they say it's far harder living up to a reputation than living it down."

He studied the sky for a moment. It was one of those very bright full moon nights, the complete arc of a day which went from a sad grayness in the morning to this pitch perfect evening. Strange days indeed.

"Well, they do talk a lot don't they?"

"Indeed. But if you don't spice up your life with these things, if you stick with the same fortune you're born into, you'll go mad." She smiled. "You'll wind up *down here* shoplifting trinkets and dodging lunch bills."

"Sounds terrible."

"Don't laugh—I gave you the easy tour, bit of petty larceny here, dine and dash there—child's play to some of the things that go on around here."

"Really," he perked up, "like what?"

"Let's just say—most everything I've railed on today, has more or less been some manner of an artful, practiced dodge, offered with just enough clarity to keep from being a total fabrication."

A rueful look swept across her face, something of almost embarrassed nostalgia. ".... Little sins which were more fun than I should admit to."

He smiled. "Lucky me, I've only been saddled with the really big ones," and then added. "All right, you know so much, how about it then, the truth?"

".... The truth?"

"Sure why not."

There was a long pause as the steam from her tea drifted up.

She looked a bit perplexed. "Were you really expecting an answer?"

He smiled. "Cultivate one why don't you."

"Ah, a bedtime story," She grinned. "Well once in the land of Nod, just east of Eden."

"I think I've heard this one before."

"Will you settle for *A* truth?" She finally asked.

"Yeah, guess that's a start."

"All of this, all of these things, all these distractions—they cure nothing, solve nothing, fix nothing. In fact all this place gives you is an embarrassed aftershock; sheepish mornings answering to sing song nights, where you've carried on like some priggish golden goose tosser...making an ass of yourself looking for something you'll never find. And all because you've convinced yourself you'll *eventually* sin your way back to the salvation of your former graces.... All because *you*, with all your time and privilege, have divined some path back to the light."

"Shit," he mused, "sounds pretty bleak."

"Doesn't matter, a few years from now you'll barely recall anything from this night—that's how memorable it is."

"Oh, I doubt that."

She cut him off, "You wanted a truth, and there it is."

"Harsh stuff." He smiled.

"What about you?" She laughed. "Harassing me as you are.... All you've told me is how you fell down the nicotine hole and some vague protests about your family...which for this sad generation ain't exactly a *distinction*."

"You're right, I've not been fair.... What would you like to know?"

"Finish that thought about your father, from the restaurant."

"Shit, I thought I did. He's taken easiest in short, controlled bursts—trust me."

"Then tell me something else about your childhood. You don't talk about your mother, I've noticed."

".... Momma issues."

"No shame there," she said. "Everyone has those."

"True; but mine are a little weirder."

Her eyes lit up.

"No, not like that." He smiled. "I got along fantastically with the woman." He rubbed his hand along the chessboard. "But then she left me, left me far too early."

He had briefly mentioned this to her earlier, but like so many things that day, it was either lost in the whirlwind of frenetic action, or buried beneath some layer he considered the safest of obfuscation. There was no easy dodge in this small room, three feet from a very intense set of eyes now focusing intently on his every word.

"Do you ever talk about it?"

"Now and again, but I usually pay someone $150 an hour for the privilege."

"Consider it a bargain. Mine are more like $300."

He shrugged. ".... At this point, I just sort of remember my mother in terms of pictures, nice harmless images. It's much easier than the reality of the thing."

"How so?"

"Keep it simple and you get to pick and choose. Little snapshots that cover a lot of ground with the least amount of pain."

".... Tell me one."

"Maybe when I get to know you better."

"Why, Liam," she smiled. "This might be the best you ever get to know me."

He thought about it for a moment. "…. When I was very young, my father, that fallen fellow of note, leased this small working farm a couple of hours north of Manhattan…. And he, my mother, and I lived out there with some cats and dogs, horses and donkeys, and a few Alpacas for good measure."

She looked perplexed as to the provenance of this.

"It was the early Eighties," He explained. "*Woodstock* was still the ghost of an idea…. It was still a very popular notion at the time, this back to basics thing, particularly if your marriage was sinking faster than the sun; and particularly if your wife wanted this more than anything…. When you can't stand each other and all else fails, pull a Thoreau and get back to nature I suppose…. Anyway, we lived out there for a couple of years, out with the rented horses and the farm animals, really way the hell in the middle of nowhere—and I loved it." He smiled. "Dandy man appearances aside, I am much more agrarian close to the bone."

"I'll bet." She laughed.

He ignored the nonbeliever. "Yep, we were all pretty happy out there actually." His eyes lit bright for a moment before turning a bit darker. "Well, one of those happy days I was sitting out on the stone wall in front of the house, playing with my Hoth ice planet action figures when I noticed this woodchuck making his way down the hollow and across the road…. We lived on a quiet road, which probably made it all the worse; the animals didn't really see enough of humans to be properly afraid."

She nodded.

"So I'm sitting on the wall and I see this little guy start across the road…. I guess he never really had a chance. I saw him get hit, roll under the tires…and then I remember how he stumbled for a few seconds, trying, I think, to get back where he came from. But then he fell to his side and stopped moving, a bit of blood ran down from his nose."

He lit a quick smoke off the end of Bob's marble chessboard. "The pickup that hit him never even stopped. Disappeared around the corner, having played his part…fucking redneck cliché."

She was leaning in, listening intently.

"He was the first thing I ever saw die.... Wonderful, yes? One of my first memories and it was of death."

She nodded. "They say that kind of bad break builds character."

"My mother must have seen it too." He cut her off, now deep in his thoughts. "She came out on the lawn right after. She'd seen that I'd seen it.... Little children are untouched you know, which in their innocence makes them as sharp as a knife. There's none of that bullshit to muddle the radar, to cloud the band."

"Singularity of thought." She said. "The likes we never get to know again."

"Exactly. So, in the moment the thing that hit me most was the idea that that poor animal was just trying to make his way back to his home, and that he was never going to make it there now.... I thought if he could just get to his home he'd be safe."

"The other upside of being so young," he added, "was not *realizing* what you've said. But it put the mark on my mother. She started to cry right there. She had two very soft spots in this world, her son, and animals."

Claudia smiled.

"I asked her if we could move him to the woods; so he wouldn't have to lie out there on the road. So we carried his little body way back into the woods and left him in a hollow covered from the sunlight in the shadows, made sure to clean the leaves and twigs from his poor broken body. The blood from his nose had dried and I remember a vacant hollow look in his eyes. I hoped there would be someone to watch over him."

"My mother, much to her chagrin I'm sure, was still something of the Catholic—no prayers for the animals.... But I think we said one between us as we walked back across the fields to our home."

This was a revealing enough image for Miss Sommerton, one which said a great deal about this man who seemed to relish the art of the misdirect. So it was this very directness which made it all the more surprising when he busted out this little gem.

"My mother died at night...I know that."

Claudia froze, looking up from her happier thoughts.

"Cancer, you know?" he smiled, *"Peacefully,* as they say." A rueful harshness filled his voice, "After all the bullshit they put her through, at least it was merciful in the end, letting her go in her sleep."

She looked at him, saying nothing.

"Small comforts and tender mercies—they fill you full with that sort of guff, the transcendence of things." He smiled. "But what the hell do I know." A haunted note entered his voice. "She'd died to me well over a year before."

There was a gentle look in Claudia's eyes, "I'm not sure I understand?"

"I guess it's taken me all these years to wrap my head around this limited notion of life, yours and mine, being this collection of moments; random, chaotic, sloppy, that as a sum add up to some kind of central theme.... Waiting around for that theme to reveal itself is tedious and boring, a fellow can drink himself to death down here in the meantime. But my brain's always been trying to find some shortcut to that clarity, to the simple distillation of the things that frighten me most."

He thought about it some more. "My last time home with her she gave me one, a moment of clarity, and I've never been able to shake it."

It was Claudia's turn for a fresh cigarette.

"I was home for the Easter break," he continued, "she died later that April.... Being a dutiful son, I'd dragged myself home for another bout of pins and needles. You can put your best face on, but in the end it's all a bitter, delicate thing.... But late one night, *after* I'd put my game face away, she came round my room, and just stood there in the doorway. She was weak at the time; it was a great effort to do this." He said this with an emphasis making sure she'd understand.

"She must have thought I was asleep, but I wasn't." He smiled, *"Hell,* I was just a teetotaler back then, a light sleeping fancy boy..."

"She just stood there, watching me, you know? And for the first time in my life, I felt the paralysis of not having some-way-out.... So, I just laid there listening to her in the doorway, playing possum like a good son should, listening to these heavy breaths, the strength I could feel draining away from her."

Claudia eyes cast downward. Her heart was something too hard by now for easy sympathies, the greatest compliment she could offer at this point was respect, respect for a very genuine emotion she could no longer feel. O'Shea's heart hadn't built up such walls yet, but he was already sizing up the effort and space needed to. The tears still dwelled behind the eyes, but to give them expression would've brought the whole house of cards tumbling down.

"She just stood there for what felt like forever. And I just lay there, like this scared boy I've never shaken. The best and the worst of it.... I remember cursing her under my breath to go away—I've got nothing left to give.... You let your heart die for someone, that's about the best you can do."

Claudia reached over placing her hand on his. Her slight and unsure way was something close to endearing. No matter, it no longer really mattered what she thought. He could feel the strings of a very limited choir all around, but then again, handholding wasn't much of a virtue anyway. Each soul walks through this door alone.

"Then she left. I could hear the steps shuffling slowly down the hall, back to the den where she used to stay in this big old chair." A faint smiled crossed his eyes.

".... And she'd listen to these TV shows all night, *really* loud. Old sitcoms, Lucy, The Honeymooners, Jackie Gleason booming through the house, cranked to eleven.... Little moments drifting up through the haze...the things that must have taken her back to when she was young."

He nodded. "I've already got my shows picked out for when the time comes—you should try it, it's the strangest of parlor games."

She smiled.

"Anyway, the next morning I was gone. Back to school. I never saw her again."

She said nothing.

"That night was the last time I cried.... Damn, I think it might be the last time I'll ever cry. Failure to *do something* is a hell of a millstone."

His mind broke in mid trance. A nubbed Boynard had just about burned his fingers. "Never really put that night into words before." He let that realization find its depth.

"What are you supposed to do?" Was all she could offer.

He thought about it for a moment and smiled. "Don't know. If I did, I probably wouldn't be here...no offense."

"None taken. I'd be somewhere else too I suspect."

"Yeah?"

"You think I'd be here, with the Cossacks and the thieves, listening to this? I'd be somewhere doing something...respectable."

They shared a bit of a laugh, a momentarily lifting of the mortuary's bells from Bob's elegant crash pad.

He grabbed one of his own from the nearly empty pack. "Christ, I heard her joking with my aunt one day, when it was getting really bad—Death was so close, she said, it had become boring." He looked around the room and smiled, ".... I think I'm starting to get the joke."

".... God's got his phone off the hook?"

"Nope. The only one to blame for such things is yourself.... So you see, in end, nothing really frightens me anymore. My failings are so pronounced, so profoundly manifest that the only thing left to fear is the last thing."

"How about you?" He looked up. "Got any crazy primal scenes, so to speak?"

"Not really, I'm probably too foregone for that." She looked something almost sad, trapped amid the potentially angelic might of her own monstrous convictions. "All this, all my life has...inoculated me from a lot of things."

The vibe had steered past heavy and right into grim. The boy thought to get things back on an even keel. "You know, I think I will have that drink. Want one? I noticed ol' Bob has some fine single malt on the shelf."

They walked over to the small bar by the large windows looking down towards the sea. Liam poured them both a drink, but she was in another place. The view was expansive, taking in the whole sweep of the crescent bay, from the bright lights of the coast to the dark austerity of the mountains rising behind them.

"It's a strange life down here." She said.

"Vegas," he shot back, "Without the stretch pants buffet and the hospitality culture."

She laughed, as they clinked glasses. "To a brave new world my friend?"

…. She had a lovely look in her eye, for a moment all of the cynicism coloring her act was gone, he wondered if she saw the same in his. For a moment they stood there, their eyes locked in an embrace, and for a moment seemed on the verge of actually saying…something.

But then there were *noises*, noises rising up from the floor below.

Christopher M. Basso

Chapter Eleven
Bullitt

"What *is* that?"

The low grumble racket from downstairs was just a bit more than one could ignore. She smirked and strolled over to the windows, her lovely profile caught in the shadows between the light.

He put down his drink and slowly drifted over, joining her by the windows overlooking the main floor.

"What is that?" She said again.

The downstairs lighting was very low; it was hard to make out things in detail, but several of the Berber-Russkie boys from the Mancala match were standing around one of the beat up couches arguing with all manner of gusto and the seeming fanfare of violent intent. The small slight figure of one of the young girls was draped across the couch, looking in a very bad way.

When he squinted O'Shea could just make her out; the ghost of the Russian princess. Her eyes were closed, her chest barely moving, a slight line of blood tracing down the side of her face.

Before Claudia could form the thought to speak the words Liam was gone. Grabbing his coat, wallet, and out the corner of his eye...Bob's cricket bat–should he have to make his intentions clear.... But as fate would have it not his keys, sitting idly on the kitchen stand. Getting comfortable had its price.

The after-hours crowd began gathering around the

periphery of the scene. There were concerned looks, but more in the manner of self-preservation than any level of empathy. This was after all a potentially rather rude intrusion on their own graveyard pleasures.

In the end the only crimes on this type of jag were stupidity, of not handling your wares, and the final judgment was expulsion. Only one of the other young girls even thought to kneel beside her, shaking her, trying to revive her still, lifeless body. Her face was pure mix of panic through the tears.

O'Shea was already on the floor by the time Claudia had thrown her jumper on and reached the bottom of the stairs. He'd muscled his way through the mob which seemed more interested in the mad gripings and flatulent carrying on's of bilious old ladies. One of them was shouting in the face of a particularly scared shitless looking day tripper type.

Liam took quick stock of the situation, eased the crying girl aside, and laid the ghost of the Russian princess flat on her back, elevating her legs a bit, and trying his damndest to sort what manner of crisis they were dealing with.

Quiet as it's kept and unbeknown to most, O'Shea's personal paranoia messianic trip had always involved some manner of playing catcher to another lost in the rye. Be it farm animals, little old ladies, or pre-dawn trauma victims on the Riviera, he had fairly decent grasp of what to do when the shit went down.... This was however the first time such paranoid musings had actually come to fruition.

This strange, sudden bit of action sent a slight shock wave through the ranks of the Wookie and the small cadre of his crew, friends, or whoever the fuck they might have been. Having already deferred once to this ballsy little kafir stranger they were in no mood to have their finely honed caveman act sideswiped again. Patience was rapidly drawing to an end. They were working men after all with a job to do. But just the same, they were willing to let the stranger content himself with playing doctor while they sorted this mess out. Someone had overdosed in their employer's home; this was the most pressing problem of the moment.

"What the hell happened?" Claudia shouted at Brixton Remi; a sort of a small time-good time dealer acquaintance of hers from London.

"I don't know—they're in the back, someone screams and the next thing they're carrying her out here."

"Do you know what she took?" Liam asked.

He eyed the stranger, but said nothing.

Claudia turned to the jumpy Feminem boy who was last with the girl and repeated her question in French. His reply was unmistakably nervous.

"She's ok, she's ok, she's fine." This was what the face of nervous mumbling sounded like.

Liam felt for her pulse. "Bullshit she's fine—she's dying…. Is that the cocksucker who gave it to her? Ask him again what happened."

Claudia went back to the well, but all that returned was more rapid-fire French sounding like double talk.

"What the fuck's he babbling about?" Liam shot back moving in closer towards the girl, trying to get a look in her hazy eyes. Blood trailed down from a gash across the forehead. He wiped it away with the bottom of his shirt. The color was draining from her face, her lips the slightest shade of blue.

"He said they were in the bathroom having a few hits, and she was fine, but then she just passed out, she fainted."

"Yeah right, the famous killer weed. What *else* did he give her?"

The Berber-Russkies were suddenly attentive; quite interested in his answer. Apparently there were rules to Bob's hospitality. Anything beyond a bit of spliff or a rail of coke was in fact quite verboten in this scene.

"What happened to her head?"

"She fell against the sink." Claudia translated his words, "Now he's saying something about how she might have taken something *else*."

"What something else?" Liam's eyes locked on the man.

"She might have had a bump of something else—but

he's saying he didn't give it to her."

It was then O'Shea noticed the slow shifting of the bodies. Starting with the Feminem boy still mumbling some shit about this and that, the whole time slowly backing his way towards the blast doors.

"Wait—where the fuck is he going?"

Claudia called to him again, but he wasn't even fronting the pretense any longer. He turned towards the door and made like Ben Johnson when the gun goes bang.

"Motherfucker! Can you believe that?" Liam shouted to no in particular.

But Claudia knew it all too well. Her little friend seemed to open up the gates. Almost at once, as if by some alchemy turning spines to jelly—a mass, if not hardly discrete, exodus was in effect bottlenecking where it met the door. It was a fine culmination to the great suburban-hardo experiment reverting to the natural order of things.

And following hard on their heels, that heavier element who most certainly could have handled the scene, but had also most certainly already done the time. Criminal inquests and immigration checks were never their friends. Not wanting an encore, they too made for the door. Like moths flittering from the dying light, the last of the long tongued liars and shady midnight riders was soon gone.

Once the cards started to shift Claudia looked very quickly out of her depth. Almost at once the scene had revealed the deep levels of decay in the lifestyle, indifference as a way of living…. But several of the Berber-Russkie types remained. They were arguing among themselves now. They seemed to have their own problems to consider.

"*Christ*, do we even know her name?" Liam looked to Claudia.

"Zoë, I think her name's Zoë…at least that's what I remember."

"You know anything about her?"

"No."

Claudia was hovering around the periphery, somewhere between concerned and annoyed, if not somewhat equidistant to the door herself. She at least seemed to be weighing that certain something in her mind. Perhaps it was just the rude realization that judging the tests was somewhat easier than actually taking them.

He smiled, "You going somewhere on me chief?" His eyes flashed the best false sincerity they could conjure up, but options were limited and time even less.

She smiled back. "No."

"Find me a blanket or something to wrap her in, ok?"

"Right."

…. Liam kept at it, trying to revive her, but it was quickly dawning this was well beyond him. The basics looked badly fucked—all the blood seemed drained from her face, which was alarming as she was already a ghastly shade of pale. Her pulse kept its faint and erratic beat; her dark blue irises wouldn't focus to his snapping fingers, and most chillingly had taken on the still lifeless gaze of a doll's eyes.

This was moving dangerously past the point of cold water and a few slaps across the face—and his first aid resume fell well short of some duded up heroin overdose. It was apparent dallying about wasn't going to make the nut.

"Is it bad?" Claudia asked over his shoulder, returning with one of Bob's mulberry silk sheets. "Christ—it looks bad."

"It's not good."

"Do you even know what you're doing?"

He looked up calmly, as calm as she'd ever seen him, "Yeah, I do." He wrapped the sheet around her, "Unfortunately it's not going to be enough.... Call an ambulance."

"Here?" She looked around. "…. Are you fucking *mad*."

"Fine, I'll take her there myself."

He started gathering up her things, making some very obvious noise that they had to get her to a hospital as soon as possible. The Wookie-Greeter broke off from his particular bit of inner turmoil, seemingly understanding enough English to grasp this intention.

"Médecins—non!"

…. To be fair it must be said the old boy had his own problems. Bob—cordial is as cordial was—did not mind a low-key sampling of the wares in his spot, but he expected in return some manner of restraint. Heroin, and all the nasty entanglements and legalistic curiosities it entailed were indeed off limits.

It was a little something you could have called "rule number four" in Bob's finishing school manual of pre-dawn gangster etiquette—and it had been broken, and the Wookie was Bob's eyes when Bob had none. And since Bob was infallible in these matters, there would have to be some other culprit for such a shortcoming.

Compounding his troubles, rule number seven might have kicked around the edges of something like, "never bring underage prostitutes around the place". Old Bob functioned more or less on something like the DMV points system; and combined with rule number four, this made for an eleven on the "you're ever so fucked metric". Any additional points and something far worse than your driving privileges stood to be revoked.

But superseding *any* of the quaint house rules, bringing her to the emergency room would've been the ruby red, king hell cardinal sin of an endgame to this mess. For those with the prevailing ethics of Hammerhead sharks, the atavistic lifestyle mandate dictated that to buy the ticket was to take the ride….Whether or not you made the choice was immaterial to the gatekeepers down this dark alley.

The Wookie and his two remaining camerados were hovering closely behind them now. Liam hunched over Zoë getting ready to move her, as Claudia stepped into the fray once again coming between them—trying to exert some now clearly delusional measure of restraint on the proceedings.

The Wookie had grown quite agitated. Liam understood enough of their sidewalk patois gibberish-bullshit to get the point, but his mind had already moved the stone, the disconnect had been made. He glanced over his shoulder, not quite bothering to look. "I'm sick of listening to this shit—tell him to step the fuck back before he can't."

Life was suddenly tilling along at the good clip, but the thoughts flashing through his mind were strangely slow and easy—the coronation-culmination of scattered dust blown ideas. To freeze again would have meant an everlasting disrepair; there were no more inflections, no gradations, shades, or whatever else had trolled the bridge. So resolute was a mind past caring that he made nary the scant show of even acknowledging the head man's mad, venal strange-tongued crazy ramblings.

Rather, he made a move to lift her from the couch and then felt the burly hand of his greeter-friend violently spinning him around. The rest happened in that slow motion, half speed you hear so much about.... Strange days indeed, most peculiar momma.

The last thing the Berber-Wookie man might have seen was the pretty blue and silver gray lettering, the delicate avian swirling of the goose; he might have even glimpsed the 40% alcohol by volume, growing ever larger in his field of view, but he definitely caught the chaser of the point. O'Shea brought the bottle down on his head like Donnie Baseball finding the Rawlings sweet spot. It was the 1.75L "party bottle", 96 points of shattering skullduggery goodness finding the mark; as shards of glass fell to the ground, like so many tears in the sun.... A hit, a very palpable hit indeed.

And then there was the shattering of glass over the Persian rugs and the end tables, as one redwood of a Wookie came timbering earthbound. He was now off to the happy hunting ground behind the sun where he could rejoin with the faeries and the atavistic garden gnomes and retell their many foul deeds—Drinks were on O'Shea.

Liam dropped the bottle and made swift for the bruiser Russian, landing a quick roundhouse to the jaw of stunned disbelief—generally a low percentage swing, but nothing like the element of shock and awe in your repertoire on a drowsy Friday morning. The Russian went down in a half crouch, stunned and staggered, but still trying to regain his balance. O'Shea's heavy motorcycle boot, stained and scuffed with the soil of some 5,000 miles of detached indifference caught him flush in the face. He made a rather shrillish grunt and went over lights out.

The third one rushed over and went shoulder to shoulder with Liam. A clean hit knocking both of them back across the cheap glass table, Liam's back catching the brunt, and smashing it in the process. He even managed to catch a nice glancing shot across O'Shea's face in the tumble, opening a small gash just above his eye—some shit that was certainly going to hurt tomorrow, or rather today.

But the fates were in the Irishman's corner as he came to a stunned rest next to the shattered remains of the Grey Goose bottle. When they both stumbled back to their feet, one of them was holding a rather long, jagged, finely edged weapon dripping with hints of slumbering Wookie blood. The man not holding the shattered weapon dripping with hints of Wookie blood cursed some indecipherable shit, made a beeline for the door, and was gone.

And just like that the room was suddenly quiet. A bleeding O'Shea stood there with a wild eyed, barely in control of himself look. He dropped the remains of the bottle, took a deep breath and surveyed the scene. It was like an eerie trumpet call over a silent battlefield. This outburst was definitely in conflict with the house rules.

The Russian was lying beside the couch face down, brandishing a red welt on the side of his head that spelled *Timberland*. The Wookie on the other hand was lying peaceably under the other table by the speaker rack, curled up in a docile pacifist ball.

He would be unreachable for some time.... And suddenly, if just for a moment, all was as still, calm and quiet as that moment they'd shared together up in the studio.... With the exception of shattered glass, dripping blood, fallen hardos, and the sudden shrill bark which had replaced Claudia Sommerton's proper *Britishness*.

".... Liam—are you fucking insane!" She staggered over to study the downed Berber, his fallen minion, and the general study of the aftermath. Liam went back to wrapping the sheet around Zoë making ready to leave.

"I thought you were gonna kill him..."

"Bosh, I was just cultivating his ass a bit." He looked over at the sleeping slumping greeter-terrorist, his breaths still heavy, and gave him a gentle kick with the heel of his boot. "Isn't that right my little droog?"

Claudia was walking a quick lap around the room, closing the front door along the way, but not before stealing a quick peak out. Her calm sense of self from a few moments ago having dissolved into an exasperated sort of twitch as she quickly ran the scenarios through her head; the coming vignettes who machinations and devilsmoke were surely in the works even as they spoke.

But practically speaking all she could manage was a steady stream of Pentecostal snake charmer babble, "Jesus, Jesus—would you look at this...Jesus."

Liam was grinning rather inscrutably as he kept about his business. "Strange time to invocate *The Deity*—don't you think? See; deep down I had a *feeling* about you."

She cut him off in mid-humor, his twill attempts at it shocking her back to life.

"Oh shut up!" She thundered. Her posh voice gone, replaced by something along the lines of Sybil Fawlty. "Liam, do you not realize this bunch are insane!"

"Yeah." He sighed. "That's what they tell me."

She looked at him, a pure mix of revulsion dancing in her eyes. "Are you just not *registering* the moment? This is fucking *bad*—they will be coming *back*."

She was now standing over the fallen Berber, rubbing her eyes, trying to organize a thought.

"You need to learn to live a little." He said. "You're wearing it through the shoulders."

She was now ignoring him. More or less getting rhetorical with herself.

519

"I...I can't even begin to figure out which is going to be worse—suffering these wog maniacs, or dealing with the police."

"Cops?" He shot up. "Who said anything about cops?"

"Five a.m. OD victims in the emergency room tend to draw their attention Liam.... Or didn't you get that far in chivalry school?" She locked eyes with him, "Look, don't be fooled by the whole *effete* thing—the cops down here are one step above the Goddamn Mafia," she was pacing again. "Now once we get to the emergency room and they realize they have a little heroin case on their hands—someone is going to slink off and make the call.... Shit, if we're lucky they'll only be a few waiting in the Goddamn parking lot.... Of course if they're clever enough to figure out this girl was somehow *affiliated* with Bob we're in another level of hurt, but then again maybe it'll just be the cops who *work* for Bob! Either way, they'll be on us in a flash—and this *isn't* New York my good little samaritan, you can't just blend back in."

"Would you calm—"

"Oh yes, I almost forgot, then there's this poor bastard's crew. Where do you think that little bastard shill Remi ran off to? Yeah, the one who knows *exactly* where we're going with her....They're no doubt organizing some half-assed Casbah posse as we speak."

A rakish sort of mischief danced across his eyes, "Well then we haven't a moment to spare..." He looked at her, "And we *are* taking the elevator this time."

Liam knelt down beside the Wookie and started rummaging through his coat and pockets.

"What the hell are you doing?"

"Getting these—unless you've got a broomstick we can use?" He produced a set of car keys, ".... And this." He pulled out a large billfold wrapped around a silver snake clasp—and placed it in his jeans.

"Wonderful." She said. "You're robbing him."

"This is for *her*. I'll put it with her things."

".... Great. Not only are we humiliating Bob, we're

stealing from him as well."

He was still rooting around, "Wait a minute, oh, this is good." Out from his coat came a pack of Chesterfields. "These—I'm stealing."

O'Shea looked at the fallen, "You shouldn't smoke these. These are very bad for you." He placed them in his own pocket.

"Are you done?"

"No, not quite; he's like the bilko who keeps on giving." He produced a polished Glock 9mm from the old boy's waist. A strange *what-next* look passed between them.

"Shit…I thought these were hard to get in Europe?"

She shook her head, "Yeah right…"

He looked at her, "Need one?"

She smirked, "No thanks— already got one."

He tossed the gun into the nearby fish tank. "That was kind of fun," he slipped the bills into Zoë's shoe, reasonably safe from curious eyes. "I've always wanted to rob somebody."

He scooped Zoë in his arms, grabbed Bob's cricket bat with his free hand and made for the door. O'Shea swung it a few times in the dark hallway, making his intentions clear to any interlopers who might be lurking in the shadows. He quickly made for the elevator, Claudia trailing behind. It was quiet and still the whole way down.

The young girl's face was still a pale drawn color, but her breathing seemed slightly better. He brushed a bit of the hair away from her young face…Zoë? He wondered what her real name was, and her small patch of story he'd most likely never know. She was a petite thing, barely there, and wrapped in the blanket it almost felt like carrying a child. Zoë, the ghost of the Russian princess, he'd have to be content with that.

It was calm and quiet when the reached the street. The very first traces of sunlight were gathering weakly at the horizon, down the long slope of the hills leading to the sea. They hovered in the doorway for a moment; Claudia's eyes scanning the street, a bit of a wild expression to her as though any and all manner of retribution was waiting on the other side.... But nothing, just the calm warm air, the last gasps from a fine pleasant evening.

The plan was simple enough. Locate the car these keys were attached to and get a move on. His eyes scanned the length of the road—couldn't be too many possibilities parked down the ol' way this early morning hour...but nothing. With Zoë cradled in his arms he started down the road, moving quickly, randomly punching the key alarm till something clicked. They were about halfway down the block with no luck. But then he heard it, faint, just around the corner...sounded like...was it?

Freude, schöner Götterfunken Tochter aus Elysium! Ludwig Van's glorious Ninth blaring pixilated Muzak style from just behind an old livery truck; the flashing red from the brake lights leading them ever closer.... And then he saw it, the dark red and white racing strips—that same evil bastard from the Land of the Faeries; the Z4 turbo coupe, mocking him with all contemptible gusto...

"*Son of a bitch.*" He muttered. "—You again."

"What?"

"Nothing.... I'm just catching a bit of a pattern here. C'mon, let's go."

They climbed into the two seater; Liam gently setting Zoë on Claudia's lap before pulling a Bo Duke across the hood. Shit, at least the wheel was back on the right side of the car....*These* were the small comforts. The sound system was already engaged when he fired the keyless start, at once frightening shards of Enrique Iglesias filled the car at full blasting, Earth orbiting, migrating bird disorienting decibels that were surely tripping seismographs somewhere.

This was no way for humans to live, but time was short and he couldn't quite remember where the kill switch for the volume was, so he did what was righteous and gave the works a few short whacks with the cricket bat till it was mercifully silent.

"What are you doing?" She calmly asked.

"The world a favor." He gunned it out from the sidewalk and tore down towards the end of the street. They were speeding out towards the *Pont Anatole* near the junction of the main road back towards the center of town.

"Beautiful, he's left the friggin top off.... Shit-hell, could there be an *any* more conspicuous Goddamn thing we could be shuttling OD victims to the hospital at five in the fucking morning with?"

She laughed, "It's *your* show."

"Yeah right—which way to the hospital?"

"Just head down the hill towards the water, and try not to kill us all right?"

The car zipped around the corner and made a quick burn down the warren of old streets and cut up alleyways. There was no one else around, just the pleasant reaffirming whirl of the engine which let one know they were getting *somewhere*.

Liam spied around the dash at the cheesy collection of upscale toys: Bluetooth enabled with the DVD player, satellite navigation with custom interface, and then he noticed the Cyrillic keypad on the car phone.... Now, besides thinking—who the fuck *still* had a car phone, the oddity of it piqued his interest.

"Why's my Wookie have a Russian car phone?"

"I don't know, maybe because it's not his car, anymore than that was his place."

".... So what you're saying is."

"Righto Mensa."

She eased back in her seat, "Let's see—thievery, insult," looking at the destroyed sound system, "*injury*.... I think you've hit the trifecta with old Bob this evening?"

"Wonderful, then he won't mind this," and tossed the remainder of the extraneous shite out the window.

They tore out from the dense maze of streets near the entrance of the *Quarter l'Ariane* and made the long clover leafed turn past the Anatole Bridge, driving up a street marked down and ignoring all manner of red lights, signage, and prudent restraint before them.... She seemed a bit tense, which was somehow unbecoming for what was the essence of her devil-may-care act. But to watch a pro wavering in her convictions was a bit depressing. He thought to put her mind at ease.

"Look—I'm not insane."

The wind whipping through his hair, the ripped t-shirt, and the caked bits of blood and glass might have attested otherwise. "We're going to help this girl, make sure she's in good hands, and then get the hell out of there."

"And if there's a couple of Gendarmerie out front having a smoke?"

"Don't worry, there won't be."

He took the particularly tight corner near the *Rue Les Halles* at speed, the rear tires spinning out a bit before gripping down and cresting over a small rise in the hill. For a moment the ground-hugger was weightless having slipped the surly bonds of Earth before crashing down again on the cobblestone with a nasty scrapping sound.

"And what makes you so sure?"

The slightest smile crept across his face. "Cause as much as I'm digging this Bullitt moment, I've no desire to stick around for the Pappion remake…"

She studied him for a moment…yep he was *gone*. She was alone on this one. Transfixed by his delirious rumblings she nearly missed her next cue.

"Turn here!" She shouted. "Left! Left! Left!"

They burned off the main road back to the surface streets…. Rounding the donkey path corner at a stylish forty-five had been quite the trick, sliding out the slipstream to just miss a garbage truck making its morning rounds even more so. The engine revved high, the slip differential digging in like a pissed off badger on Methadrine, as the car corrected itself and continued down the back road. He'd forgotten what this nimble little beast held up its sleeve.

"Careful!" She shouted, "Jesus—you're going to kill us!"

There she went again he thought…another guilt-ridden worrier.

Tearing down the long expanse of the *Avenue de la République* Liam swung the car past the front gates of the Nice Museum. They weren't very far from the hospital now. Zoë looked worse for the wear but relatively unchanged—Claudia on the other hand looked shocked and awed.... He had a moment to reflect on the unfolding events of his evening thus far; a fine meal, horse meds, communion with the afterlife, oedipal rexes, post-pubescent drug dens, pre-coitus interruptus, overdoses, his first knock down drag out street brawl since college, and a mad flight to the ER.... Not to mention pissing on, pissing off an entire Corsican crime syndicate with its tentacles stretching back to the deepest, darkest parts of the Ukraine.

.... This certainly topped boat rustling and petty bladder-themed vandalisms. Once again, life moved in the most mysterious of ways, who knew what the next nineteen hours held in store? He could be hunched over a fire tomorrow with some Kalahari bushmen having a good laugh about all this.

The *Hopital Saint-Roche* loomed just up ahead.

He controlled his otherwise natural inclination to tear up to the front door in a full-on whip songed furor screeching to a peacock halt.... Rather, he crept up slowly, with little fanfare, looping around the circular drive and stopping alongside an idling linen truck. Good idea, he thought—leave the fucker running.

The old stone building and its faded yellow neoclassical façade looked rather gloomy in the faint morning light. The side entrance to the ER was quiet, nothing stirring, just a couple of orderlies favoring a pre-dawn smoke under the floppy canopy of banana trees in the courtyard.... The coast was clear.

"Now what?" She asked.

"*Now*, my little French speaker—you're on. Remember we're in and out—five minutes tops."

O'Shea came around the side and gathered Zoë up in his arms. Her breathing was better now, but her color was not—she was still far from out of the woods. Claudia was trailing behind him up to the door. "Any thoughts on how I'm supposed to explain this?"

"Shit, you're the Big Fish, think of something."

"Yeah, I'll just tell them we found her on our way to the predawn Mass."

"Whatever works."

Claudia flashed a nervous smile to the orderlies who were curiously observing this odd slice of life.

"Remember," O'Shea said, "try and keep your French ignorant tourist-conversational. This will be the most worthwhile wily bit of dumb American you'll ever play."

"Go to *hell.*"

"I guess that's a start..."

.... In his 27th year Big Terry McQuinn made the long journey over from Logan to Charles de Gaulle and took the primrose path down the Loire to the sunny shores of the Cote d' Azure. He was a hard as nails Boston Southie who probably saw *The French Connection* one too many times, and came down here with a suitcase of cash, the vigor of his youth, and instructions to make the proper introductions with the Marseilles natives who'd recently discovered the new Northwest Passage—a modern spice route from Persia to the New World.

He was handsome as a Lon Chaney werewolf; made a lot of friends along the coast, frequented the Baccarat tables of Monte Carlo and the whorehouses of Remy St. Pierre; not to mention gaining a certain carnal knowledge of a dusky, spoken for, Bardot soul-sister redux.... Well as fate would have it; them good ol' Gallic boys don't take too kindly to strangers 'round these here parts, particularly big galloping ten gallon American clichés, who pluck the wildlife out of turn, and drink from the metaphorical finger bowl as it were.

.... And, so it goes, the right kinds of introductions were made to the wrong kinds of people, precipitating the worst of cuts made to the best of men; and they wound up mailing pieces of Big Terry McQuinn back to the Humbolt Gentlemen's Club in Dorchester, COD, the last being affixed to his beloved Red Sox cap—a signed memento from The Yaz himself.... Someone hadn't missed the humor in the situation though and turned the hat around in true "rally cap" fashion.... No one from South

Boston thought Marseilles, or the Riviera, was worth the effort after that. At least the Columbians and Dominicans respected baseball.

The ER doors parted like the vaults of the Red Sea.

"Well, that wasn't so bad was it?" Liam had a chipper look on his face.

"Keep moving." She said, "They've already called the cops."

"How do you know?"

"You think this is my first time with this kind of thing?"

"Shit, I'd imagine you got it down by now?"

"Generally speaking yeah, but some asshole Yank sideswiped my *chi* waiting around for his Merit Badge."

They jumped into the still idling Beamer.

The coupe rolled down the drive in the low gear careful not to attract any unneeded attention, but as they rounded the circular entrance they could see several members of the Emergency staff coming out the main doors for a wee better look.... Well, no point with the subterfuge now he thought. He paused, revving the motor a bit and flipped them the English bird, or the American peace sign, whichever way they saw fit to take it.

He readjusted the mirror, watching as they congregated in the drive. "Well, they should just about crucify us with that one."

"Yeah, I thought the wave was a nice touch..." Her lilt sounded suspiciously sarcastic.

"Yeah, well, it's an American thing. I *doubt* you'd understand."

They rounded back onto the main strip heading north again, somewhat the reverse of the way they came. A bit more of the morning had arrived. A fine cast of light gradually chasing out the last sleepy shades of blue and purple. The sky was overcast, a cool breeze from the sea breaking through the warm muggy air.

Peaceful and still, just the low rumble of the engine.

With their most pressing concern addressed the situation had suddenly become quite…fluid. The hills rising around the upscale Cimiez neighborhood were approaching fast as the car moved along at a nice controlled pace towards the dénouement of nowhere in particular. They soon drifted off the main road into the winding tree lined neighborhood of old mansions and crumbling Roman ruins. It seemed as peaceful a place as any for a bit of a regroup.

"What's the plan?"

"Plan?" He shifted up to third, "I'm making this guff up as I go along."

She thought about it. "Well, we have Bob's car. Bob's car that you stole and took the liberty to redesign a bit…. Not to mention several of his associates—who you *also* took the liberty of redesigning a bit." There was something winsome in her voice, "*And* let's not forget the ER staff who probably just phoned in a very fine description of this Goddamn eyesore to the Gendarmerie."

"…. True, true."

But his mind was already elsewhere, racing and running through the options. No doubt this evil beast had some manner of GPS theft tracking system embedded in the works. Too bad the ghoulish thing didn't judge the moral equivalencies of the theft. But she was right; once Bob, or his flunkies, found the sand to actually turn the thing on it would only be a matter of time—they should be somewhere else when that happened.

"Maybe we should, you know, get rid of it?" She said.

"Maybe we should. Until then, let me just get my thoughts together, fair enough?"

He lit one for himself and began to regroup. Tooling through the tall manicured hedges and Beaux Arts landscape—the calm disconnect from the previous twenty minutes quite stunning on the balance. Once they'd passed the crumbling stone arches of the local Roman ruins he felt like he could take a breath. The fresh air of the gardens and the formidable permanence of his surroundings were somewhat reassuring. Just a nice controlled low speed drift back across the city and into the arms of some manner of blissful anonymity.

Liam was enjoying his smoke, just about ready to try what was left of the radio, when he first caught sight of it; a set of headlights trailing slowly behind them in the near distance....Which was *fairly* interesting he thought, being such a *lonely* road and all. He adjusted the mirror slightly, keeping his eyes fixed on those lights, waiting for some sort of tell.

But nothing, nothing seemed to be stirring, just the low beams drifting as lazily as he was. He kept his eyes sharp while trying to reel in a reflexive paranoid vibe. No need to throw the default switch on the caveman act just yet. The low rev of the engine was still reassuring.... Then another set of lights veered out a bit to the right, just behind the first, revealing themselves briefly in tandem.

That was a *bit* more interesting. Liam downshifted and hung a very innocent left down one of the small alleyways cutting across the multi-level gardens, not much of a going concern, and certainly not a thoroughfare of note.

Both sets of lights made the same slow left, keeping their distance.

"Son of a bitch..."

Claudia spun around in the seat; her shifty eyes peering just over the leather seats.

"Who is that?"

"This is *your* town Huckleberry—you tell me."

Suddenly car number one sped up a bit closing some of the gap.

"What are you waiting for?" She hissed. "Step on it!"

"They might be cops...you wanna bolt from a carload of French cops?"

She spun around forward. "I knew it." She said. "We're done."

He looked at her. Christ, she'd *just* about emptied the tank on what was left of the too cool for school vibe she'd been rocking.... Must have been a depressing thing to run the post-mortem on your own act, watching it unravel like some cheap sweater in the withering hail of some early morning fire.... He wasn't sure how much more of this babbling deadweight business he could tolerate. Her newest incarnation represented a potentially fatal millstone around both their necks.... Perhaps she needed to be *dealt* with?

"Jesus woman, get a grip." He whispered. "You're going to blow the whole deal."

But there seemed to be no reaching her at the moment. She had *the fear* in her eyes.

Liam glanced hard into the rearview.... Well, Fred Dewan knew many a good lawyer back in New York, one of them must have had some *pull* within the French judicial system.... Shit, if they hopped a plane tonight, they could be here in time for the arraignment.

Besides, time in a French jail would officially erase any lingering doubts about middling upper middle class street cred. He calmly hit the "sport" button on the center dash. Prudence and experience had told him so. A flip of the switch the telling the beast to gird its loins for the coming mischief.

He briefly caught sight of the Coupe's sleek, menacing silhouette passing in the shadows of a bank of shop windows. He *knew* they could pull this nonsense off one more time.... Just one *last* time he pleaded, and then wash your hands of it for good. But he could feel it though, *judgment* in the mix; it wasn't going to be the car or the driver who played any part in this, just the fates. The fates and a bit of the ganas to make amends for all the silly shit he had ever done...

A vibe of mild resignation lay thick in the air. Most certainly they had cashed their checks. One last trip to the well had rained down a world of hurt. Perhaps they would tell tales of the two foreigners who locked horns with a drug bund maw, having tried to make one wrong right. At least he could content himself with that.... Shit, maybe they could even sell the rights?

They seemed to hit a stalemate, a holding pattern which dragged on for several minutes. Like unfamiliar dogs doing the

Down All the Days

two-step before they decide what needed to be *done*.... Liam managed to keep about a hundred yards of road between them, until *something* must have been divined in the rear guard because the first set of lights started to pick up the pace.... Fine, well enough. O'Shea responded in kind, lunging ahead a bit, the whirl of the motor responding in a very reassuring if not somewhat elegant fashion.

But this queer dog-sniffing act was making him tense...they needed a game changer. Liam hung the first big right he could find, around the periphery of the gardens, fully intending to go Crazy Ivan on their asses with another quick reversal...a non sequitur of a route which should have ended any lingering debate. Hell, had he'd felt a bit cheekier he could have just pulled a flat out U-ie around the next bend and had a good look at them...perhaps even a wave?

However, he understood the vagaries of luck and knew he'd already scored more than his share. Until the perfect world arrived, he could settle for this; a clean shot switchback in the road up ahead that would reveal them nicely in the profile. He rounded the long turn and kept a fleetingly hopeful eye that he'd wound himself up for nothing. Shit, people *were* allowed to be out and about at this farmer's hour, playing out the codas to their own gimped up predawn dramas.... But both sets of lights slowly rounded the same corner. Once they were all in a straight line again, facing the south, the two trailers started to stretch it out a bit, closing the gap considerably. Finally, they were close enough for a decent view.

"Son of a bitch," he squinted. "What are they...plain clothes?"

Claudia spun around for another look. "Those aren't cops."

Before she'd even gotten the words out he'd mashed down the accelerator. The Coupe made a low, ominous grumbling snarl, announcing to all lesser sorts its looming intentions—and say what you will about *Ze Germans*; but in about 2.12 seconds Claudia Sommerton was pinned to the back of her seat like John Glenn riding the Atlas rocket.

The two trailers broke in kind. For a second he could

even get a look at car one.... Any lingering doubts could be laid to rest. It was the same Land Rover parked outside Bob's door. Small mercies at that.... But the big boxy oaf wasn't really suited for this type of limber work, rather finding its best expression in shuttling well-off Yuppies and their soccer broods.... But there was also plenty of room for indignant, insulted, and unscrupulous drug bund types; who in the silhouetted shadows were lined three abreast. He couldn't make out faces, only forms...the worst expression of a threat; faceless anonymity.

The second car looked like a Citroen of some sort. Much more nimble and light on its feet than the heavy rambling SUV...and strangely suited for the type of odd situation they'd found themselves in. No matter, they'd both be a patch of dust soon enough.

He had it up to about sixty down the postage stamp alleyway, heading back towards the lower ramparts of the gardens.

"Careful!" She screamed as they cut across the main road not far from where they'd first picked up the lights. He hit one of the safety rises at speed, suddenly testing the avionic capabilities of the car, and slamming down hard in a dust up of sparks and chipped Bob fender.

"Jesus, Liam—watch out!"

.... He had real backseat driver on his hands.

"Where are you going?"

"Out of here." He shouted back. "We need someplace straight."

O'Shea throttled up the engine, pointing down the hill again, zipping past the last section of gardens and the ruins of the amphitheater till they were burning down the long straight expanse of the Boulevard de Cimiez. The imperial regal elegance of the *Hotel Alexander* sailed past in a stylish yellow sandstone blur.

They were moving quickly under the heavy canopy of trees lining the boulevard. Barreling down a straight enough piece of road, but one lined with sanitation trucks, deliverymen, flower carts, and a fair share of alley cats and alley people, each requiring

Down All the Days

a rather deft bit of reflexes. *Avoidance* was of paramount importance.

He picked up some distance on his trailers along the straight stretch of road, but was quickly swallowed up again in the maze of small streets and sideways; backtracking east now, almost towards the hospital.... Speeding over the *Voie Rapide* overpass he caught sight of the first peace officer of the morning, oblivious to the mischief just above his head.

Alas, these narrow Nicoise streets were just not the proving grounds at Stuttgart, or the salt flats at White Sands....Lousy Romans could conquer the world, but those checkered boy-loving bastards hadn't the foresight for mornings like this when they laid the first stones for the city. At each bend of bay, just when he was ginning the beast up to power, O'Shea would have to downshift, slam on the brakes and deal with what new calamity had befallen them. This was no way to run a car chase. And each time the tortoise would trump the hare; just enough to be hanging uncomfortably close in the rearview.

Pure mind-blowing, speech-numbing speed was what was needed to offset a few carloads of agitated batty boys, who might have lacked the horsepower but more than compensated with a sure lay of the land. They soon reached the lower part of the broad hills forming the town.

The stone ramparts to *Vieux Nice* were approaching fast down the center road.... Perhaps seeking out the denser streets, the even *more* cramped quarters could be the way to go—even things up on the other perverse side of the scale?

She seemed to grasp this plan. "Are you mad, don't go in there!"

But it was too late. He cut across the back of one of the new tramcars trolling lazily along the Boulevard Jean Jaurès. He gunned it down the snug fitting road, his right side cresting up over the narrow sidewalk, pacing it just long enough to wave to the curious tram driver. Once ahead he cut across the front of the tram and down into the crooked maze of the Old City.

The Citroen followed right behind him, hugging close, the boxy Land Rover took the safer route to the side, having to

533

pick and choose its spots a bit more carefully once in ox cart country. The trio crashed down deeper into the heart of the quiet old neighborhood.

This was where the *real driving* was, all hand eye coordination and quick heel toe work to avoid the myriad of hazards as you navigated roads not much wider than a sidewalk. It was all gray hair, steely nerves, and a wee bit of chipped paint left in the dust.... But it must be said, those boys could drive a damn sight better than they could death match, Kung Fu street fight. O'Shea couldn't shake them; in fact they seemed to be *gaining*, the Citroen almost riding his bumper, moving with the surety of hounds to the hunters.

They crested over a broad stone staircase separating two slight levels of road, the slip differential adjusting nicely to the change in altitude, which set them zipping through a small square, breaking into the sunlight, before disappearing just as quickly down another shrouded side street. It hadn't been an especially *heavy* move, but something seemed to gin her works.

"Wonderful! Just wonderful. You've really done nicely for yourself!" She was almost hyperventilating the words—fear apparently had trumpeted fortune's bitter sarcasms.... But she had a point—they'd thoroughly bested him in this bold, but ill-advised bumper car strategy.

Strategies were running low and it wasn't readily apparent how much more of this abuse the mollycoddled sports car could take. What they needed was another piece of straight road to really open things up and sort this business once and for all.

"Heads towards the water!" She shouted in the windscream.

O'Shea did as told, the Coupe executing a nice handbrake turn around the next eye of the needle. The Citroen did the same, but the Rover did a sort of whale roll, sliding into a bay of café chairs stacked for the night, pulling away with a Kronenbourg umbrella impaled on its grill. In the rearview the boy spied one of Bob's crew leaning out on the hood trying to free it with what looked like a Marlin spike.... This little morning jaunt had had its redeeming moments.

But enough of this nonsense, O'Shea noticed a glimmer of the sea through the odd breaks in the buildings and hung the next big turn towards the Promenade. They blew by the elegant white stone façade of the old opera house and then screeched a smoked tire left through the signals onto the *Quai des États-Unis*.... Thankfully the lights were still green.

The Coupe and its entourage were now speeding east along the very edge of the waterfront, the peaceful beach at dawn just a few easy paces away, as the rows of palmetto palms in the median flashed by in a swift greenish blur. A few early morning joggers and late night walk of shame types who'd drunkenly humped it up on the smooth stone beach were all that was there to witness this, the inaugural Nizza Grand Prix.

O'Shea glimpsed in the mirror. Back on the straight grade he was able to put some road between them. But in life's rich pageant this presented another bit of a tradeoff. The prospect of a meet and greet with the police had just become more than a passing bit of circumstantial chance. They were, after all, down in the heart of things now—far removed from the backstreet jag that had brought them here.

On a *quiet day* this evil little red and white beast stuck out like late stage syphilis, but who knew what the maw held in store, especially in the wake of a trail of terrified call-ins about some epic drag race tearing through the heart of the city.

He glanced down at the dash, 88 mph past the courthouse and nary the sign of rude inconvenience.... But surely this was borrowed time. How far could one get in Bob's tricked out Peacock coupe when half the local prefecture was already somewhat indebted to the man. To the other half his head on a pike represented a sure promotion and quick rise in the Civil Service. Their best hope was to be quick about things before these foul brutes could align their stars and drop the hammer. Either way the margins were slim, foul the ball, and those *Pappion* visions of slow boats to South America and sad-fortune suppositories might well come to pass.

All this big-brained thinking nearly made the point moot when he took the unusual S shaped curve at the *Pointe Rauba Capeù* in something less than a graceful fashion. The rear tires drifted far out onto the promontory, skirting across the face of the smiling sundial, and close to the rocky ledge where the cliff divers liked to jump.

But the coupe was a forgiving creature, almost righting itself in the oversteer, and balancing nicely back down the center of the road along the seawall. The trailers having handled the mess with far less drama.

He glanced over. She had returned to her previous state of ashen. However, the adrenaline seemed to right his brain almost at once; the endgame looked clear. The massive Port of Nice loomed up around the next turn, the final bit of the Niçoise coast.

This would be it, their Austerlitz or their Waterloo.

O'Shea knew the path around the port well. He'd taken it many times on the bike over the last month and a half. Not necessarily the straightest shot into town, but he liked to circle around the horseshoe shaped square and admire the cruise ships and sub-orbital yachts drifting in and out of the harbor. But mostly he liked that it afforded him some hellacious *lean-in* jags with the nimble bike around the sharp fast ninety-degree turns. A fine Buddhist meditation before death if ever…

After rounding the turn at the war memorial he threw the Coupe into a steel trap, ground mauling third, and redlined the fucker out past the point where time travel might soon be possible. Immediately the car lunged forward, almost digging into the pavement with a strange sort of sickening *let it ride* sensation. The tachs briefly drifted into the red as the speedometer crept passed ninety. This was out past where the flat earther's feared to tread.

He'd watched a lot of ESPN so he knew what he was doing.… Take the trap hard, then ease off in the chute, maw it down, roll it though, find another piece of virginal straight road and repeat. Pick your line and take it hard, flow through the apex.

The execution of said, had been much easier on the nimbly quick, highly cooperative lightweight bike. In this equation the principal of less being more was truly the trump card between the stylishly executed and executed stylishly.

But where did that margin lie? Which also begged the question—he might have had Schumacher's colors but did the Sally-boy have the Red Baron's grit to match?

At about the same time this inner debate was raging the final bit of the stew, the saffron in the bouillabaisse, was added when the triumvirate blew past a half slumbering Gendarmerie parked quayside in his cruiser.

The siren's wail was easy to miss in the filthy frightening wind scream but his lights were not. Over his shoulder, Liam could see the Citroen keeping pace, the Rover wobbling lazily from side to side, and the cruiser's lights blazing indignant, bringing up the rear with all due self-righteous anger.

This had officially crossed the line from thought to expression, and therein lied the endgame. Claudia was speechless; her eyes half shut, one arm holding the seat strap, the other digging into the skin of his thigh.... Which on another jag might have been quite the kinky *git*, but here the pain strangely provided that wee extra margin for his concentration. The long row of chateau buildings paralleling the quays sailed past in a blur of stately facades and red tiled roofs. The first of the death-roll corners was looming up awfully fast.

.... The cop had been sitting at doughnut-rocking parade rest when they blew past. He peered up over his copy of Sartre's *Nausea,* the thin ciggie in his mouth falling into the machiato on his lap, balanced deftly on the hooker's head straddling his knees.... All right, fuck it—*all lies*, but neither could this Gallic flatfoot quite *believe* what just sailed past his eyes. This was a direct affront to his authority in the worst most bilious of senses. So he killed the Miles Davis, hit the blower, and tore out into the chase.

.... Which, it must be said, really made for an interesting morning because now Bob's Wookie crew were being tailed by a wailing police cruiser...certainly soon to be an army of hyper-amped wailing police cruisers. Bob might have had a little touch of *Keyser Söze* about him, but his flunkies did not. Negotiating a heavy police scene was not in their skills set.

It would seem *everyone* had a problem now. Which at least made most things relative.... Something even old Jean-Paul might have found cock-smiling amusing.

But the grimy, crafty shell of a lawyer lurking in O'Shea could see, more so than any chimp-wanking Speed Racer fantasies, the most opportune opening lay just ahead.

O'Shea drifted towards the outer lane, picking his line as it were, and giving the Bavarian beast one last kick to get right with things.

"What are you doing?" She gasped.

"Relax—I saw this on TV once."

The trick with high speed cornering was the proper follow through with the heel-toe downshift—that and being in possession of one very forgiving high performance sports car. The Coupe was running along the outer edge of the quay, trilling a nice sixty or so when lit the burner and steered hard into the chute.

The ball of his right foot tapped a nifty little Lindy across the brake and gas pedals in near unison, as the clutch momentarily popped into neutral. The engine revved as they slid through the apex of the turn, till the clutch found the sweet spot again and kicked back into gear. The blood pooling rush of the G-forces subsided and he gassed the bastard out of the line, the left bumper drifting a polar bear's whisker from the row of concrete dividers, till they were straight again, stomping Earth, looking for the next windmill in need of a *vigorous* tea bagging.

The whole affair was either the terrible affirmation of, or the Zen liberating meditation on, how three lousy seconds could decide your everlasting fortunes.... And for O'Shea, the second time today he'd been gamed by the vagaries of a few seconds fortune in the 2.5 billion of a lifetime.

The Citroen followed him through the turn, but it was a mudder racing in a Thoroughbred's league. The Coupe had a wicked amount of torque, far more screw in its jack than the Citroen, which was an honorable machine, but not built for this sort of terminal outlaw fringe work. He slid through the turn, the grip melting to a rip, and scraped up against the side of a Mercedes Quattro with some foreign flagged license plates, which was slightly amusing if anything else. He peeled off, badly shaken, but still moving.

Herd speed is a funny thing. We do it on the highway everyday—one minute you're trilling along under control like a good citizen, till you're swept up in a pack of cars, and the next thing you know you're tearing along at eighty with a set of flashing lights in your *own* rearview.... High speed chases in the South of France more or less ginned the same principal.

The Rover was the straggler of this herd, lagging enough to see the agitated cop gesturing wildly to pull over. Measuring the odds he too sped up. Racing along the same curve the Rover drifted badly in the lead turn, sailing wildly across the thin line between in-control and hopelessly fucked.

Its right rear tire abruptly called it a day, blowing out in spectacular fashion, large chunks of rubber raining down on the teak decks of the yachts moored below. The Rover veered left, wobbled right, and drifted into the other half of the already maligned Mercedes, who'd simply made the mistake of going cheap with the nearby garage service. It was a controlled crash, sort of stylish at that, but would still be a bitch to explain to the insurers, to Bob the bankroller, or the trailing Gendarmerie for that matter...

The latter, in his cop crazy overzealousness took the turn a bit wide himself, spinning out to avoid the Rover and sailing a nice 180° across the thoroughfare. He slammed his brakes, stalling just short of the row of parked cars, and coming to rest alongside the lazy line of oaks at the entrance to the Church of Notre Dame. In a flash he was out and over the hood of the cruiser, gun waving and anger blazing, instructing Bob's dazed minions to *eat* some pavement.

At that point the Citroen, watching this unfold real time style in the rearview, decided to more or less to call it a day—making the correct call that the boss, *wunderbar* as he was, didn't pay well enough for jail. Having lost the heart for the hunt he veered it left, quickly up a side street towards the *Rue Barla*—a confluence of streets which fan out in any direction along the coast, offering better than average prospects for simply melting away.

Liam made the second turn at a far more civilized speed

539

continuing straight down the reverse end of the harbor. As they zipped down the far side of the port's straightaway he could survey the mess back across the water. Several red and white cruisers, lights blazing, were rounding the turn at the war memorial speeding towards the scene.... Just one more bend round the locks at the southern quays separated them from the warm embrace of utter oblivion.

The luck of the fallen angels and the blessed Irish rang true at the most opportune of moments, as the Coupe slipped behind the massive shadow of Paul Allen's *Octopus*, moored at the southern dock. A yacht which quite easily could have blocked out the Aztec sun, setting off a seven year cycle of ritual sacrifice and appeasement, but at this moment providing all the background cover they would ever need.

"Do you think they saw us?" She asked.

"I don't know...hopefully all he saw a reddish blur disappearing around the corner and nothing more. But let's get the hell out of Nice before anyone gets their story straight."

They cleared the last bit of harbor and moved quickly along the slight rise of *Mont Alban*, rounding the curve which would lead them no time quick to Villefranche-sur-Mer. At its highest point they had a clear view back to the panorama of the port, where they could now see some manner of French coast guard patrol steaming past the lighthouse and into the harbor, blue lights flashing, low sirens wailing.

"Whoa...ain't comeuppance a bitch?" He smiled at her.

She smiled back and then smacked him across the chops. "Isn't it though."

They made it back through the village in about five minutes of restrained controlled drift with nary the rude interruption from the local cops; who in the tradition of fat cat, rich town ticket punchers probably *were* off somewhere knobbing hookers, swilling macchiato's and reading Sartre to pay much attention to this kind of action.

Once they reached the sleepy junction at the Pont St. Jean all was as quiet and still as it had ever been. Birds in their morning songs sang from the trees, a fresh breeze was blowing in towards the shore and there wasn't the least trace of the devils and dust they'd left just a few miles back.

He pulled over where a small side road met the underpass of the railroad trestle. There was nothing stirring in either direction, just one of the empty coastal trains slowly making its way back to the city from the yard in *Vance* for its first run of the day; its long shadow passing slowly along the elevated tracks above them. He killed the headlights and put it in neutral.

In a grand bit of strategy it was decided that Claudia would keep the Coupe and make quick for the French-Italian border. She could swing off in Menton and ditch the beast in a lot near the train station and then walk, cab, or broomstick her way across the border to the lovely start of the Ligurian Coast where the air was warm, the wedding tackle firm, and where Claudia Sommerton was always welcome. He had some reservations with this plan, but the options cupboard was a bit threadbare, and their wee union had proven a far too combustible mix for these parts.

Needless to say he would not be joining her. Unlike Claudia, the criminally transient lifestyle did not quite suit his mo'. O'Shea was now *technically* a multiple felon. Assault and battery, grand theft, reckless endangerment…about a ticket book's worth of traffic infractions and vandalism were just some of things they'd most likely want to chat about.

…. Shit, Louis Dega had only been in on some low-grade fraud-counterfeiting scheme and look what they did to him. Adventures in suppositorial banking were not a promising coda to this thing. This was quite a jacket for a sleepy Friday morning, and certainly not the type of handiwork he'd sooner stick around to admire.

Luckily he had some law school, so he could fairly grasp the gravitas of the situation. He and his cohort had burned every rule, mores, and bit of civility this small insular enclave lived by…. Prudence demanded they be hunted down, stoned, and or burned at the stake. She could keep the car; he was going to need something a wee spot faster.

"Mon chéri, it's been real."

He opened the door to jump around when his knee smacked the handle, his brain sending a searing pain telegram far out of line with the offense.

"Christ!"

Looking down it was revealed he was sporting several shards of Bob's heavy glass table embedded nicely in the side of his knee. The blood was already soaked through and caked.... He rocked back in the seat, looking over at her with a pained sort of grin.

"You gonna live?" She smiled.

It was then, for a moment, they shared a long stare, shifting slightly over to a smile, before finally melting to a laugh.

".... Yeah, just barely." He laid back in the seat, riding out the wave, letting the pain find a depth somewhere near manageable.

They'd run some queer gauntlet and walked away unscathed...relatively. The last twenty four hours a compendium, a checklist, righteously ticked off of a fair share of things you might only want to cover once in a lifetime.... At the end of the line you'd probably burned through all the fear, anger, elation, and adrenaline that a sane mind could muster. Running on a pure strain of vapor perhaps allowed that bit of perspective to appreciate you'd played something, *just slightly*, outside yourself.

She smiled. "Look at you, you're a mess."

He caught sight of himself in the rearview. Bloody face, bloody shirt, bloody jeans crusted with bits of vodka reeking glass and Wookie fur.... Shit, at least he still had his youth.

"Well naturally I'd invite you back to my place for a bit of breakfast, but that might be pushing it a bit too far."

"Probably so." She nodded.

"Too bad."

"Here, hold still." She said, rummaging around the back, finding a crisp white cricketer's jersey, and gently staunching the cut above his eye. She had a delicate way with it he wouldn't quite have expected.

"Well Liam James you certainly know how to show a lady a good time."

"I try."

"You better get out of here before that thing turns into a shiner—wouldn't want to stick out now would we?"

"What are you going to do?" She asked.

"Why swim out of here of course. How about you?"

"I don't know.... I've always wanted to try India."

"Lax extradition laws there?"

"Practically nonexistent."

"Sound like a plan, but let's get you to Italy first." His mind was racing, "You got your passport?"

"Don't need a passport silly. The continent's connected now.... Just a smile, a wink, and drift across into the crowd." But then her mind connected the dots, that mad dash out of Bob's had thrown her for a loop as well. "Got any cash though guv?"

He gave her the Amex Black and most of the money he had left. He kept about forty Euro for a cab as this would be a rather weird time to go looking for an ATM.

She was leaning over him, looking down. "Tell me something though?"

"Yes?"

"Why'd you do it?"

".... Wouldn't be much good if I didn't."

"I guess so." She smiled as he made ready to leave. "Well, it's not quite Paris, but we'll always have this."

"How about it Claudia, in the next life then?"

"I'll see you there Liam James." She leaned over and kissed him on the cheek.

He gingerly carried his aching bones out of the seat, allowing her to slide over. He slowly walked over towards the bridge. To the right was the dark sleepy road that led back to the house on the point.

"Liam," she called back.

"Yeah?"

"Careful—Bob's down that road somewhere."

"I'll keep that in mind."

"Just remember, if you get into trouble don't be too proud to call for help."

"Yeah, I think I heard some deranged type say that once. Probably great advice if you're a complete lunatic."

And with that she smiled and gunned the engine like a good libertine day tripper, and tore up the Chemin des Serres towards the Grande Corniche, the Italian coast, and the blissful embrace of righteous anonymity…

He stood along the edge of the bridge, the ultraviolet lights dimmed for the coming of the day.… There she went, one of God's own prototypes. A public menace, and a truly *dangerous* individual at that.… But then again, you needed a bit of dirt from time to time to remember what it felt like to be clean. He allowed himself a moment to watch as the car tore off down the road, its lights sliding off slowly into the distance, growing fainter and fainter till they were gone.

At the crest of the hill she'd find the motorway, the brightly lit Grande Corniche, which ran the skeleton tracks of what was once the Roman *Via Aurelia*. It was from here the legions raised a particularly frightening brand of hell up and down the Balearic coast.… Claudia Sommerton would be fine. Unfortunately her kind always were.

He turned and made for the dark jungle rising to greet him. His knee was barking, but hopefully a state of shock would soon be setting in. Just a warm numbness that could provide the pain-killing margin he needed as he coped with the next catastrophe of the morning.

…. Where the hell was he? All this time and the place was still confusing. The narrow road to the point was shrouded in an early morning gray-black light. He was soon in the canyon between the high walls of the grand estates, no light here, just an enveloping sense of darkness all around.… Shit, sort of frightening actually. He kept his pace on the quick side, moving through the narrow alleys bordering on both sides, between the imposing white elephants and vaulted sepulchers.... For the first time he felt like an interloper in a place he didn't quite belong. Maybe it was just the paranoia of the moment, but the swells might just have sussed this as well.

He reached in his pocket for his smokes, but was met by that rather stomach churning sensation of a set of keys not quite where they were supposed to be.... Despite the savage burn of the last hour his mind instantly raced through the miles, car chases, ravaged Wookies and opium dens, to Bob's stylish lair; a Corsican roulette wheel and a set of Mr. Henri le Fleur's *Properties of Distinction* keys resting on the orphelins of the wheel.

.... If that didn't complicate things slightly. Maybe he could just ring Bob up and have them work out some sort of fair trade exchange. But then again the only chip he had to offer was tearing up the Roman roads burning about eighty towards the Italian coast.

Well, at the least Bob now had another spiffy lair right down the street should the mood ever strike him. Chuckle Boy was letting that one warm the cockles of his heart when he realized the keys for the Ducati were on the chain as well.... This was not good. His motorcycle hotwiring skills, as many of his other urchin talents, had languished since he'd been kicked up the tax bracket food chain. Not to mention he wasn't quite up to any more random acts of larceny. A cab it would be.

He could learn to live with the loss of the bike, but he'd be fairly inconsolable for the loss of the *My Goodness, My Guinness* bottle opener he'd snagged back at the duty free in Dublin Airport.... But that was it, right? No other little "tells" about last night's mystery guest who'd sideswiped the delicately calibrated operation so egregiously? A couple of keys and a bottle opener, he laughed—let the fucker scour the Earth Serpico-style on that dime.

He could see the shadowy outline of the villa up ahead, sanctuary at last. But did he even deserve it? He knew the score, he was patently guilty, guilty as hell; he'd burned every bridge, trespassed every liberty, and flagrantly abused every law and

545

custom these people lived by…he was a *poor* guest at that.

He whipped out his phone and placed an emergency international call. The very reverent Fred Dewan answered at once.

"Fred, it's Liam. Yeah I know what time it is—look I need you to do me a favor and get on the computer and find me a seat on the first thing leaving Nice this morning. What? Lisbon? Dammit man that was weeks ago! No, I'm in a bit of a state here, anything with two wings pointing west would be great. What's that? Yeah, slight bit of trouble actually, but nothing I can't manage…. No listen, I'm not near a computer—I'm *on foot* at the moment, but you can reach me back on this line…. Sounds good, talk to you in thirty, right, thanks!"

He reached the front gates of the villa and started down along the far side of the ivy-covered wall trying his best not to take a header over the azaleas and palm fronds in the shadows. He glanced at his watch; time was the ultimate consideration now. No margin to be cheeky here. Those clowns would start piecing this mess together soon enough: the cops, the crooks, the tram drivers, the innocent bystanders…. No, a quick well coordinated dash out of this evil little tragical-comical, historical-pastoral mess was the only remedy.

He reached the lowest point of the stone wall and leapt up on the tall oak nearest the water's edge, ignoring the screaming protest from his knee, and gingerly made his way out along the sturdy branches to where they met the top of his wall. Despite the perils of his condition, he vaulted up on the balustrade and over the oriel spires before landing nicely on the lawn of his faded seaside home.

He hobbled up towards the house, slipping in through one of the open windows into the kitchen. He made it up to the bath and worked a quick triage on his various scrapes and bruises, before changing into another gray T-shirt and faded blue jeans…for some reason *consistency* felt important that morning. Fairly satisfied with this bit of tidying up he set about his exit strategy.

With a young man's bachelor grace he was fully packed in about four minutes flat, give or take a minute here and there.

A couple of Louie V knockoffs hit the bottom of the marble stairs with a thud as he followed, phone in hand, placing a call to the gypsy cab man back in Beaulieu. With that taken care of he moved out to the grounds to deal with some forgotten tasks.

He started down the stony path towards the pier at the water's edge, collecting his silver flask and indispensable iPod mega classic. The last bits of shadow had drifted away as the sun gathered strength out along the horizon. He kneeled beside the tall stone wall near the pier. He wanted to watch the sea for a moment. It was calm and still, a grayish blue glass hovering in the dawn. He ran his hand along the old crumbling rock ledge and understood in short order he would never pass this way again.

To be young and know that you were on the verge of some *reprieve*, still young enough to have life give you things rather than take them away.... He reached down gathering up a few loose stones and put them in his pocket. It seemed like the last thing which would connect him to France, and to this madness...and that was good, and that was bad.

There was the sound of a car horn from back up the hill, blasting rude-like out by the front gates. Local time had apparently just become borrowed time. He entered the kitchen by the back door and peered out through the narrow slats in the shutters...time to go. He grabbed a Red Bull from the fridge and his bags from the hallway and was gone.

Sun filled Friday morning; the phone rings in the back seat of a shady livery service carrying a young man to the airport. A confident, learned man on the other end assures the cocksure whip-songed whelp that he is good to go for the 7:30 a.m. British Airways freedom bird back to that parking lot known as Heathrow.

Congratulations, the man said, you're now the proud owner of a $2600 seat in Coach. Small comforts, the boy rejoined, as he would have flown in a garment bag with the feckin' luggage to flee this place.

Where are you heading, the man had asked?

I'll let you know when I get there was the reply.

Christopher M. Basso

Sun filled Friday morning, picture perfect day for flying. 6:49 a.m., weary traveler, defiled and degraded, hunkered down in the Napoleon café in the departures lounge of the Côte d'Azur International Airport. Having already made the muster at check-in, and assumed the position at security, he was free to slouch down behind his triple espresso and stray copy of *Der Spiegel*, which served as far better camouflage than reading material anyway. He felt rather secure in the knowledge that no enraged, duded up Russkie-Wookie confab was getting through the strong-arm act at security without the motherfucking ticket to ride.... Although the coterie of French soldiers standing nearby sporting shiny Armalites, and toting a seriously crazed looking Doberman were the shades of a mixed blessing at best.

7:04 a.m.

A voice in French on the loudspeaker, words he cannot understand. Tired...bone tired. That early morning sort of drained where your eyes itch and your feet burn, as the final reserves of mad energy are sent to their last.... Good man, that Fred Dewan—probably smart that he'd hired his uncle for the gig. Handsome Henry's half brother had been a far better Man of La Mancha than the old fellow anyway. Perhaps this was a bit of Providence from up on high...this was a declarative of respect more than a question. Fred Dewan, no less a vagabond, but far better a man.

7:07 a.m.

.... And all life's a circle, a riverrun of so vast a river. *Booming* voices crack the stillness, the scythe man one day closer; this is your life and it's ending one minute at a time—and Gibraltar is a girl so they say. *Booming* voices crack the stillness, proceed in procession, Gate J33, flight 1946, the London bound freedom bird boarding just down the way. He ditched his smokes, gathered up the wares, and patted the Doberman on the head as he made his way down the staircase to the tarmac. He was truly twisted by now, unhinged from the moorings in every physical sense; but in the greater sense, in the metaphysical sense, feeling quite right, better it must be said than in ages.... You've got to believe your own burning bush routine in the end, after all, who the hell else will?

A strong wind was blowing in from off the sea as he made his way towards the waiting jet. Nothing left now but a sun-kissed stroll across the apron. A bloom shot up through a crack in the stony ground beneath his feet. He was sure of it now, a bracing serendipity was in the air, and at his back, a fine welcoming sunlight trailed as he passed.

Côte d'Azur International Airport, shiny brand spanking new Airbus jet tears down the field, 7:35 a.m. wheels up—the long circular arc of the French coast below; mind the manners, mute the demons, close the eyes, drift out to sleep.... And Gibraltar as a girl where I was but a sad flower of the mountain. It was time to go see about such a girl.... How long is a flight to Africa anyway?

Christopher M. Basso

About the Author

When not hunting the corporate grizzlies of this world, the author can be found at his heavily fortified Appalachian compound, baking bread, casting candles, and engaging in a general end-of-days misanthropy.

Made in the USA
Lexington, KY
11 November 2012